THE DARK ONE: DARK KNIGHT

*An Epic Medieval Tale of
Adventure and Romance*

KATHRYN LE VEQUE

AUTHOR'S NOTE:

I never thought this book would actually make publication, but here it is!

The Dark One: Dark Knight was written twenty years ago, back when the author was still learning her craft and trying to find a writing style that best suited her. The novel is 'epic', meaning it is very long, very detailed, and it is truly an adventure from beginning to end.

Think "Ben-Hur".

It is also only the third novel the author ever wrote after "The Wolfe" and "The Defender".

Although the book has been edited for content, the author refrained from any intense re-writes or heavy editing, instead, choosing to present it to readers in its original form to preserve the integrity of Gaston's tale as it was meant to be told. Had she written it today, it would more than likely have been written in a much different style.

The original dedication to this novel was lost years ago, so suffice it to say that the author dedicates this work to her parents, Bill and Sylvia Bouse, who read this story twenty years ago and were perhaps a bit surprised that their daughter had written such an epic.

Also much thanks to Kris for painstakingly re-typing the novel from its original degraded hard copy, and finally to Linda, Steve, & Jennifer for their assistance in fleshing out amateur writing to help create finished product. I owe you such a great deal. You have my undying gratitude.

Enjoy The Dark One: Dark Knight.

CHAPTER ONE

Year of our Lord 1486 A.D.
Mt. Holyoak Castle, the month of July
Yorkshire, England

The mid-summer sun beat down on the earth with unmerciful force. Indeed, summers in the north central of England could be hot, but this heat was unseemly. If it was human or animal, it was sweating and complaining, and if it were anything else, it was wilting and dying.

But the heat of the summer was the last thing on Remington's mind. Crystal sea-colored eyes, so pale and clear they were nearly unnatural, gazed from the window of her second story bower, fixed on the road that led from the keep and disappeared on the horizon. Oleg had said a rider was approaching, and she waited with more patience than she felt for the rider to show himself. She prayed with a desperate fervor that it wasn't her husband.

Sir Guy Stoneley was captured at the conclusion of the battle of Stoke by none other than Henry Tudor himself. Loyalists to Richard III had made a valiant attempt to gain sway the country back into control of Yorkists, planning to set the Earl of Warwick upon the throne, but Henry and his army proved too powerful. The defeat had been overwhelming.

Her husband and other rebels were commandeered by the Tudor and hauled away to London. Last she heard, her husband was locked up in the White Tower. Remington prayed that he would never again see the light of day.

"They would not release him, would they?" came a faint feminine voice. "He is an enemy of the crown."

Remington tore her eyes away from the window long enough to glance at her sixteen-year-old sister. "Nay, Rory. He's not been released. The rider is someone else."

"But who, then?" Rory demanded, her wildly curly red hair shaking.

Remington shook her head, her eyes once again trailing to the window. "I do not know, sweetheart. We shall have to wait and see."

Rory let out an impatient sigh and stomped about the room nervously. When Sir Guy had left to fight, he had taken the majority of his men with him. The only men remaining behind at Mt. Holyoak were the old and the very young, and a skeleton troop of 20 men. Hardly enough against Henry and his army, but Sir Guy had been confident that the Yorkists would defeat the usurper Welsh bastard within weeks, months at most. He furthermore believed there was no possible way Henry would progress to the heart of Yorkshire, where his fortress was nestled in the Vale of York. Therefore, he took his entire complement of men and left Mt. Holyoak to the mercy of God.

The result was a massive fortress left virtually unable to defend itself, especially now that it was considered an enemy's holding.

Remington shook her head sadly; never in her life did she imagine that she would actually be considered an enemy of the crown, a traitor in her own country, and she had her bastard husband to thank for it.

A slight blond figure breezed into the bower, tiny and feminine. Remington's youngest sister, Skye, stood next to her oldest sister and gazed out of the window alongside.

"It's not him, is it?" she asked with as much courage as a thirteen-year-old girl could muster.

Remington's eyes blazed as she turned to her baby sister. "No Skye, it is not," she glanced at Rory, pacing the floor. "And even if it is, I swear to you that he will not touch you. I swear with God as my witness."

Rory stopped pacing. "You cannot stop him, Remi," she said. Rory had tried, God only knew she had. She was tough and strong for a girl, and could fight as well as some men. But when Sir Guy had forced himself upon her, again and again, she fought him every time but had ended up knocked silly while he assaulted her. And Remington...her sister, her attacker's wife, had borne worse treatment and wounds than

Rory cared to think of. Every time she thought of her sweet sister at the hands of her fiendish husband, it made her blood boil.

Remington swallowed hard, knowing that Rory had not said the words to seem cruel. It was simply a fact. Sir Guy did as he wished with his wife and her three younger sisters and there was naught anyone could do to stop him. Even his men had looked the other way when he raped eleven-year-old Skye.

"I.... I would wager to say that the rider could be Charles," Remington said hopefully after a moment. "He rode to gather news only a few days ago. Mayhap it is him."

"If it is, then he has returned quickly," Rory commented.

Remington silently agreed with her sister, bringing about the original question of the rider's identity. With a worried hand, she stroked Skye's silky blond hair and moved away from the window.

With everything her husband had done to her sisters, the younger girls had not lost their fighting spirit. They were a handful, the two of them, too much for their aged father. The man had died three years ago of an ailing heart and never once had the strength to deal with his high-spirited daughters. The destitute baron had married off his eldest to his neighbor in exchange for the man's protection, knowing the man was of questionable character but delivering him Remington, anyway. He knew his daughter suffered with the disgusting man, but he chose to ignore the fact. He had done what he had had to do, and moreover, there was naught he could do about the situation as it was. Remington was Sir Guy's wife, and no longer his daughter. Remington had always hated him for overlooking her plight.

When Jasmine, Rory and Skye had come to live with her after her father's death, Sir Guy had taken fiendish delight in raping the girls and treating them like chattel. Rory and Skye were tough and survived with their minds intact, as youngsters often do; yet Jasmine, now at the threshold age of twenty years, considered her life ruined. The younger two spent their days doing normal things young adults do, and playing evil tricks on Sir Guy's young cousin, Charles, whereas Jasmine was a generally sullen girl and spent a good deal of her time alone, terrified of the moments when the baron would come to call on her.

Charles Stoneley was Skye's age, a sweet and quiet boy. How on earth he was related to the deviant knight was a question for the gods, because he was nothing like Sir Guy. Too young to fight in the War of the Roses, he stayed behind, as laird of the keep and Remington loved the lad with all her heart.

"It's Charles, Mummy," the boy said, his eyes wide. "Why is he back so soon?"

Remington's heart softened at the sight of her seven-year-old son. His beautiful sandy-blond hair was tousled, as usual, and his eyes were alive with apprehension. Eyes the color of his mother's. "I do not know, Dane. But I intend to find out."

Jasmine did not say a word, looking at her eldest sister for decisions and comfort. At twenty-six years, Remington had seen more of life's heartaches than most women twice her age and was inordinately wise. But there was far more to Remington than her wisdom and intelligence; surely a lovelier woman had never existed, as her late husband had sworn just before he beat her within an inch of her life. Her hair was a chestnut-auburn color, but not just any plain shade; it was a miraculous myriad of golds and reds, intertwining and dancing in the light, playing off of her natural curls and falling to her buttocks. It could be an unruly mass but she never bothered to tie it back; she loved the feel of it on her neck. Her skin was as white as pure cream and her eyes, with her thick, dark lashes and peachy-colored lips, made her beauty truly striking.

As beautiful as Remington was, she was terribly vulnerable when it came to men. The only men she had ever been close to had ignored and abused her, and she was absolutely terrified of the opposite sex. All except for her beloved son, Dane. The lad was her assurance that there truly was a God.

They all made their way down to the massive double bailey of Mt. Holyoak. The fortress was intricately constructed thanks to her husband, for the man was a military fanatic and demanded the most secure and fortified fortress in all of England. Only a mile from the Irish Sea, he was paranoid as well, and was sure the Celts were planning on an eventual invasion and he was determined not to be caught off guard. The fortress was so fortified it could have held off Hadrian himself, even with a skeleton guard.

Mt. Holyoak sat on a natural hill, a hill whose sides had been planed down to create a fifty-foot drop all the way around the fortress that plunged into a man made moat below. The only way in, and out, of the fortress was a narrow road that led from the village up to the massive drawbridge.

Charles made his way up the road, thundering across the drawbridge and into the outer bailey, drawing his steed to a ragged halt. Old men and aged soldiers were there to greet him, taking hold of his horse and helping him dismount. Remington, clutching Dane's hand, was at his side.

"Charles!" she gasped. "What's wrong? Why have you returned so soon?"

Charles was exhausted; his young face was creased with dirt and fatigue as he met Remington's inquisitive gaze. "I bear news, Remi. Catastrophic news."

Remington felt bile rise in her throat and her palms began to sweat. She hoped she could open her mouth to speak without vomiting. "What news, Charles? I would hear it."

Charles was distraught. "Oh, Remi, 'tis terrible. I met up with several of Henry's men at an inn, not far from here, and they told me the news. I had to return," he put his hand on Remington's arm, his gaze painful. "He's coming, Remi. He's coming to Mt. Holyoak."

Remington was not only terrified, she was puzzled. "Who is coming?"

Charles swallowed hard, "The Dark One. The Dark Knight."

Remington gazed back at him a moment; hearing his words but not yet feeling the full impact. She was expecting to hear that her husband was returning home; instead, she was hearing something completely unexpected. Her mind went to mud and she was having difficulty understanding him.

"The Dark Knight?" she repeated. "Charles, what are you saying?"

Charles sighed with exasperation. He was terrified and distraught and couldn't understand why Remington wasn't feeling the same way.

"The Dark Knight," he insisted. "The man who single-handedly won the war for the House of Tudor. Henry calls him the Dark One. 'Tis said he is in league with the devil." He squeezed her arm. "You have heard of him, Remi. Guy mentioned him to you in his missives."

Remington gazed back at Charles apprehensively, her eyes widening as realization dawned. "De Russe?"

"Aye," Charles explained, relieved she was beginning to see the gravity of the situation. "Sir Gaston de Russe is coming to Mt. Holyoak."

Remington's mouth went agape with shock. "My God," she breathed. "Why on earth would the man come here?"

Charles shook his head, his exhaustion draining his energy now that his news was delivered. "I do not know. But he is coming. What are we going to do?"

Remington had no idea what to do. What could they possibly do? Women, children, and old men up against the Dark One? *The Dark Knight!* The man who betrayed Richard at the end and fought for Henry Tudor instead, turning the tables at the Battle of Bosworth, defeating the Duke of Gloucester.

Fear swept her. De Russe would tear them apart if they showed any resistance and well she knew it.

"Did you confirm this information, Charles?" she asked. "Did you seek out anyone of authority of ask?"

Charles shook his head. "Nay, I did not. The knights who gave me the information said they were in de Russe's personal guard. Do you know that de Russe has a personal knight corps of forty men?"

Remington did not care about the Dark Knight's personal corp. She was still focused on Charles' first answer. "Then you did not verify the information? What if they were lying, Charles? Mayhap he is not coming at all."

Charles looked deeply hurt that she would doubt his judgment. "They were powerful knights, Remi. I believed what they told me. Do you not trust me?"

She had not meant to offend him. "Of course, Charles - 'tis the knights I do not trust. They might have been trying to stimulate the young man's imagination. Is that not a possibility?"

He shook his head slowly. "Nay, Remi, 'twas no falsehood they told me. I would stake my life on it."

Remington stared at Charles a moment longer. "Did they say when?"

"They said that he is already riding from London." Charles wiped the back of his hand against his forehead. "Henry knows the strategic power of Holyoak and is sending de Russe to control it. Since we sit in the heart of Yorkshire, what better place to maintain peace in an enemy's land?"

Remington did not know what to feel. She was wild with relief that her husband was not returning, yet she was filled with terror on another matter altogether. The Dark Knight was coming to Mt. Holyoak.

She had to think this through. Mayhap there was something they could do, although she had no idea what it might be. There was no fighting a man with the devil on his side. Tearing herself away from her train of thought, she turned to the old maid beside her.

"Eudora, take Charles and feed him. He is exhausted," she said, pulling Charles to the old woman. "I shall speak with you later, Charles, after you have rested."

Charles barely nodded as Skye followed him and the serving woman inside. Jasmine and Rory took hold of Dane, retreating back into the castle, leaving Remington standing a bit bewildered in the middle of the inner bailey. Her gaze lingered on the innards of the massive structure, her mind working furiously. *What to do, what to do...?* The same answer filled her again and again - *there is nothing to do.*

"Lady Stoneley?" came an elderly voice. "What are we to do about the Dark One's arrival?"

Remington turned around and realized that a host of aged male faces were staring at her eagerly - men at arms twice, three times her age, and old Oleg, the steward. She knew they were expecting answers from her, answers she was unable to give.

"Prepare for it," she said evenly. "Prepare Mt. Holyoak as if my husband was returning. I fear we have no choice but to welcome Henry's Dark Knight."

The men looked at each other, grunting with agreement or disagreement, she could not be sure.

"But he is the Dark Knight," one of the older men-at-arms wailed. "Traitorous bastard, he will surely kill us all. I say we should flee for our lives before he arrives."

"Flee where, Henry?" Remington said softly, her gaze caressing Mt. Holyoak once more. "We have nowhere to go."

"Surely you have heard stories of this knight, my lady," another soldier said solemnly. "He's spawned from the very loins of Lucifer. He shows no mercy, no compassion, and no emotion. Some say Edward had a sorcerer conjure him up."

"If he shows no mercy, nor compassion, nor emotion, then it will be very much like my husband has returned," Remington said with bitterness. "We will simply have to show him great respect and obedience and pray he shows us some benevolence. I know of naught else to do, men; if any of you have suggestions, I am willing to listen."

The men looked to each other hesitantly, waiting for someone brave enough to speak. Yet it was painfully obvious that no one was willing. Remington sighed, feeling their fear.

"Be courageous, then, and prepare the keep for his arrival," she said. "I shall not have the Dark Knight entering a shabby keep."

Disgruntled and bewildered, the men disbanded to do as they were told. Remington took old Oleg's arm and together they walked for the castle.

"What are we to do, my lady?" Oleg asked. "Having the Dark One here will be far worse than Sir Guy."

Remington's mouth tightened into a thin line. "Somehow I doubt that. I have lived in hell for nine years, Oleg, and cannot imagine this man will make my life any worse."

"You seem too willing to be complacent," Oleg commented. "I know for a fact you have much more fight in you than you are showing."

Remington shrugged. "What good will it do? I could, conceivably, evacuate the castle. But to where? And for how long? Meanwhile, our people will starve and with winter approaching, they would most likely freeze to death. Nay, Oleg, I am convinced that there is no use to run and hide. We would escape right into our own deaths."

The old man bobbed his head in reluctant agreement. "So we do nothing but prepare the keep for the man like a god returned?"

Remington paused at the entrance to the keep, facing the frail old man who ran the castle so beautifully. "I am afraid so, Oleg," she sighed. "I would not want to tweak the nose of the most feared knight in all of England."

Oleg lifted his eyebrows in resignation. "I fear for our future, my lady. I have heard tales of this Dark One. Some say he is a stone statue come to night, only to be resurrected by the light of dawn."

"Unless the man flies into the bailey with the wings of a bat, I shall not give in to fear," Remington smiled, trying to alleviate the tension. "If he pulls a pitchfork from 'neath his cloak, or sprouts a speared tail, then I shall be a-feared. Otherwise, he is just a man like all others."

Oleg shook his head with apprehension. "God save us all."

Remington took his arm again. "We have much to accomplish, you and I. 'Tis best we get started."

"As you say, my lady," Oleg mumbled as they disappeared into the damp, cool innards of the castle. "Your will shall be done."

He did not sound as if he meant it.

CHAPTER TWO

He wasn't merely big; he was monstrous. He wasn't simply dark in color, but dark to the very bone. Descended from the Normans on his father's side granted him that inheritance, but his mother was Welsh and he bore the dark gray eyes of the Welsh. To look at him was to look into the darkness that was in every man.

It did not help matters that he dressed entirely in black. There was no other color as far as he was concerned. Men who wore colors were undeserving of male parts. He was disgusted with knights who were intent on gaily decorating themselves in brilliant hues; they might as well have turned in their spurs and donned a dress. Even his banner, a massive bird of prey clutching a lion in one claw and a mighty sword in the other, was entirely in black, gray, and white. But that's what Gaston's life was - it was either black, or it was white. There was no in between.

Which was why he betrayed his king. Oh, he knew well the implications of his actions. But he had gone with his inner senses and turned on a man who had killed his nephews to gain the throne, an unscrupulous monster of a man who would stop at nothing to rule England. Gaston had served his predecessor and brother, Edward IV, for many years. When Richard assumed the throne, by murder, Gaston had sworn fealty. He convinced himself that family politics were none of his business and that he was only a warrior.

Richard depended on the man tremendously, and was expecting victory at the battle of Bosworth until Gaston had had enough of the man and turned on him; he had convinced others to turn on him, too. When Richard had threatened Gaston and a very close friend of Gaston's, Matthew Wellesbourne, it had been the last nail in the coffin. Tides were turned and England was destined for a new king.

He had been labeled a traitor, the very worst of humankind to walk the earth. But Henry Tudor loved him and Gaston had had his reasons for doing what he had done. There was no one to answer to but himself, although his pride had taken a beating. Everyone knew of the Dark Knight, the premier Knight of the Garter who had defended Edward and then Richard. But when he brought about the fall of Richard, the term Dark Knight took on a whole different meaning.

The sky above was as dark as he was as he rode north-northwest toward the mighty fortress that was Mt. Holyoak. He had heard tale that Guy Stoneley had built it with the particular desire to have the most fortified, most impenetrable fortress in all of England and by many accounts, he had succeeded.

The fact of which pleased Gaston immensely. Aye, he had a fortress already - Clearwell Castle sat near the Welsh Marches north of Gloucester, nestled in the soft desolate hills. A hellish place, it could be, bleak and cold most of the time, which is why he left his wife there. He hoped that mayhap she would become so sick of the place that she would leave him forever so he would be free of the bitch. He did not care where she went, so long as she left their son. He'd kill her with his bare hands if she took Trenton away from him.

Henry had ordered Gaston to secure Mt. Holyoak, and secure he would. But he would also claim it as his own and make his own life there, far from his wife. He would send for Trenton and together they would live in peace and happiness. At thirty-seven years, he was coming to the point in his life where he was thinking on retiring from his profession. After all, he had been a knight for seventeen years now and had etched out an indelible reputation. There was no more need to put fear into the hearts of England at the mere sound of his name; he had accomplished all that he had set out to do.

Gaston looked forward to retaining Mt. Holyoak. If it even lived up to half of what he had heard, then it would indeed be a pleasure to assume command. With Henry on the throne and the country more or less calming, he would concentrate on training men for Henry's royal army and settling down to a life of relative non-violence, he hoped. Henry expected Gaston to maintain a tight hand in Yorkshire, and maintain he would. He sincerely hoped the Yorkists were intelligent enough not to try something stupid, for he was weary of fighting. A definite change for the Dark One.

"How much longer?" the knight by his side asked.

Gaston emerged from his train of thought. "Half a day," he replied. "We should be there come nightfall."

Sir Arik Helgeson, as blond and blue-eyed as Gaston was dark, nodded with satisfaction. "I am anxious to see this place. It promises to be as mighty as Camelot."

Gaston and Arik rode alone at the front of a six hundred-man column. They had sent three scouts ahead two days ago and were growing impatient, as the men were slow to return. They were hungry for news of the area, the climate of the people who were so recently defeated by the Tudor. Gaston had his soldiers marching with blades in hand and his knights were riding with their shields slung over their left knees, ready for any unexpected action. They were, after all, in enemy territory.

"Lord Stoneley modeled Mt. Holyoak after Roman defenses," Arik mumbled, fussing with the latch on his heavy helmet. Of the latest style, it was still new and uncomfortable. "The man was damn proud of the place, even if he was an idiot. He shall not be pleased to learn of your possession."

Gaston tightened the reins on his destrier, feeling the animal tensing beneath him. "Stoneley is one of the more repulsive men I have ever come across and is exactly where he belongs, in the tower. I wonder where those goddamn scouts are."

Arik shrugged. "Who knows? Probably having their fill of inns and wenches."

Gaston grunted dangerously. "If they are, then they will lose what is most dear to them and I can promise they will have no need for wenches anymore."

Arik laughed softly. Gaston did not. He was serious. Several feet behind them rode Gaston's knight corps; all thirty-five of them. Even though they were trusted, seasoned knights, they were not allowed to ride with their liege. Even Gaston's two cousins, one of whom had seen eight years of service with him, were not allowed to ride with him. Only Sir Arik, descended from Vikings, was allowed the privilege.

Gaston was very careful with the manner in which he treated his men. He would fight with them, counsel them, respect them, but he would not eat with them and rarely socialized. He believed that his distance and cool demeanor forced the men to continually strive for perfection; if he were to be too chummy or warm, they might become lazy or complacent in the knowledge that they had the Dark One's approval.

He was not beyond a word of encouragement and his men had his undivided attention in a war conference, but he was not their friend. He was their liege, and he was a firm believer in maintaining the distance. Through the entire campaign with Henry his philosophy had not failed him and his men were the best trained in all of England.

Arik rode alongside his liege, enjoying the countryside. He was as fine a warrior as had ever brandished a sword. He had the good fortune of having squired with the Dark Knight and the two had become fast friends at the very young age of eight. Gaston had one other friend, Matthew Wellesbourne, but Matthew and Arik were the only men he had ever allowed himself to get close to. Even his cousins, Patrick and Nicolas, were not truly his friends. They were his cousins and entitled as such to the privileges thereof, but he would not allow himself to become deeply involved with them. Only Patrick, his eldest cousin at twenty-nine, came remotely close to being a friend.

There was another young knight, a close friend of Patrick's that endeared himself to Gaston once by blocking an arrow meant for his liege. The young Italian reminded Gaston of the Roman statues in Bath, superbly muscled and leanly beautiful. The women went mad for Sir Antonius Flavius and Gaston could see why; he was probably the most beautiful man he had ever seen, in the masculine sense of the word, and had a heart like a lion. Gaston could hold intelligent conversations with Antonius, but he would never talk about himself to the young knight. To speak of himself would be entirely too personal.

The column of soldiers passed through the fertile lands of Yorkshire, through the towns of Sheffield and Leeds. The lands were softly rolling, extremely lush, and Gaston was quite fond of the landscape. Even when he had been fighting in it, he liked it.

"What is the name of the town to the west of Mt. Holyoak?" Arik cut into his thoughts.

"Boroughbridge," Gaston answered. "Mt. Holyoak is a mere four miles to the east in the Vale of York."

"Good," Arik grunted. "The sooner we establish our presence in Yorkshire, the better. Moving in the open makes me feel vulnerable."

Gaston glanced around, the gentle hills and clusters of trees. "This delightful topography makes you vulnerable? Arik, you twitter like a jittery old woman. There is nothing in those trees but birds."

Arik snorted in disagreement but said nothing. He would still be glad when they reached the protective structure of the fortress.

Eventually, the structure of Mt. Holyoke was sighted on the horizon. It was a massive fortress perched atop a rocky and slender hill, but it was different from the usual fortresses with miles of curtain walls and a keep somewhere in the middle of it. Mt. Holyoak was surrounded by the curtain wall, that was true, but the keep embraced within its innards was so large it looked as if it took up most of the interior space of the castle. More than that, the dark gray structure rose at least four stories, the turrets in the corners soaring at least six or more. Other than the White Tower, Gaston had never seen such a large keep. In fact, he was fairly awed by it. It was the biggest thing he had ever seen. He stared at the sight in disbelief before flipping up the visor of his helm so he could get a better look. Next to him, Arik let out a hissing sigh.

"My God," he breathed. "Have you ever seen such a sight?"

"Never," Gaston concurred. "Look at how the natural slope of the hill has been sheared off to make it impossible to scale. It must be a hundred foot drop from the top of the wall to the moat below."

Arik stared at it a moment longer, a slow smile spreading across his lips. "I like it," he declared. "By damn, I like it."

Since the column was halted, Patrick and Antonius dared to ride up next to their liege, both of them staring at the structure.

"I have never seen anything like it," Patrick said appreciatively. "A hell of a fortress, cousin. Congratulations."

Gaston put his visor down. "Congratulate me if, and only if, we are not put to spear as we approach the gate. With the drop-off on either side of the road, there would be nowhere to go but down."

"They must have been told of our arrival. Rumors abound in Yorkshire and there was no mistaking our army," Arik said, observing the unbelievably sheer walls. "Yet I see no outward defenses other than the raised drawbridge."

"If our scouts had returned in time, we would have known much more about this fortress," Gaston rumbled. "If, and when, those men return, I want them dispatched and scattered."

Arik nodded without a word. Such orders from the Dark Knight were not unusual.

"Aye, now," Gaston tightened his reins. "Let's see what type of warm welcome we are to receive."

Arik gave him a snorting chuckle as he lowered his own visor, telling Gaston that he was thinking the exact same thing. This fortress belonged to Yorkist loyalists and Gaston wondered if he were going to have to lay siege in order to claim what Henry had granted him.

Looking up at the sheer walls and gouged hillsides, he wondered if he could indeed lay a successful siege. It took him all of two seconds to realize he would have Mt. Holyoak. He *had* to have Mt. Holyoak. It was the only fortress in all of England worthy of him.

CHAPTER THREE

Mt. Holyoak was ready for their invaders. The army had been sighted a half-hour before, affording the occupants time to congregate in the outer bailey to greet their conquerors. A blanket of melancholy covered the old and young alike, each scared of his individual fate at the hands of the man they called the Dark One. Surely Satan himself was upon them, and it was not even an uncommon sight to see old women cross themselves.

The old men-at-arms gathered in semi-straight rows, awaiting their new liege and wondering if they would live to see the sun rise. All of the household servants were huddled together, whispering in urgent tones as they listened to the soldier on the wall give them a description of events as they unfolded.

Tensions were high, fears higher, and the sky above threatened rain of mighty proportions. Chill winds whipped through the bailey, blowing them all about and more than one person wondered if the Dark One himself had conjured the wind.

Remington was still in the castle, gazing from a high lancet window at the army below. It had only been two days since Charles had returned with word of the Dark Knight's approach and she felt grossly underprepared, but there was naught to do now but welcome the new lord of the keep.

Honestly, she had felt no fear or apprehension until this very moment when she looked out over her beloved landscape and saw a hoard of troops approaching, more soldiers than she had ever seen. When they reached the bottom of the hill, the army came to a halt and several men broke off from the group and started up the incline. As the men rose higher along the road, so did Remington's anxiety.

Over the years of living with daily fear, she had learned to bank her emotions well. Sweaty palms were the only outward indication of her inner turmoil and she turned for her mirror once more to make sure she looked presentable. As if the Dark Knight would care, but she wanted to look presentable nonetheless.

She had chosen a green silk surcoat that turned her eyes into glittering emeralds. The neckline was low across her white skin, skimming the very edges of her shoulders as it descended down each arm and hugged her slim torso. A belt of gold links hung at her waist and her luscious hair was pulled back from her face, secured at the crown of her head and creating the illusion of a fountain of hair cascading down upon her.

Remington never considered herself beautiful. She was not as hard on the eyes as some, she thought, but was truly ignorant of her radiance. Guy would tell her how lovely she was, but she never believed him. The man was a molester and an abuser; she was positive he was a liar, as well.

"Remi." Jasmine was standing in the doorway. "Hurry - they're almost here."

Remington continued to stare from the window at the approaching figures, the chill wind lifting tendrils of her hair.

"Go down and order the drawbridge lowered, Jasmine," she said softly. "I shall be down shortly."

Jasmine fled. Remington heard her sister's flighty footfalls and knew she should follow, but she was fascinated with the knights down below. The closer they came into view, the more intrigued she was with the knight riding in the lead.

Even from where she was, she could see he was twice the size of the other men around him. And the destrier he rode was the color of ink, as black as sin. She swore she could see the red eyes of the beast. He rode the animal with the arrogant confidence of a knight, implying untold power and strength with not so much as a word spoken. It radiated from him like a scent, yet it was far more heady. She knew without being told that the knight in the lead was the Dark Knight... the Dark One. It could be no one else.

Entranced, she watched the horses as they ascended the road. As they neared the very top where the road ended and dropped off into the moat, the ancient drawbridge began to lower laboriously. She could hear the wood popping and the hinges creaking as the wheels were turned, reversed to lower the bridge.

Remington snapped from her train of thought, knowing that the bridge lowering was her cue to attend to the bailey. With a deep breath to force her courage, she quit the chamber.

By the time she reached the bailey, the drawbridge was almost completely down. She stood, frozen, at the top of the steps just outside the keep entry as the bridge slammed to a halt and the rigging was secured. She could see straight through the opening, straight to the Dark Knight, who sat immobile atop his destrier at the edge of the drawbridge. She could see how absolutely massive the man truly was and the fear she was trying so desperately to fight down began to gain speed. Her breathing quickened and her heart began to race, but there was nothing more she could do other than face the fear that was fighting to overwhelm her.

The Dark One had come.

Gaston continued to sit at the edge of the drawbridge, like a statue. He was not about to enter the bailey of the massive structure and lay himself open to ambush. He would wait until someone from the fortress approached him and then he would state his business. The longer he sat, the more he wondered if the people inside were truly daft. Surely the lady of the keep would come out and express herself, be it to declare her intentions to fight to the death or simply hand over the fortress. His apprehension began to mount. He hoped he would not have to kill her in front of her people. He was trying to accomplish a peaceful take over and murder in the first few minutes of contact was not on his agenda.

Still standing on the steps, Remington watched and waited, waited and watched. The man outside on the huge armored destrier continued to remain stationary and the tension and confusion in the bailey rose. They were the victors and obviously they had met with no resistance - why did they not come in?

"What are they waiting for?" Jasmine whispered.

"I do not know," Remington shook her head, apprehensive as well as confused. "Mayhap they expect me to go to them."

"Do not go to them." Rory snapped. "Make the bastards come to you, Remi."

Jasmine shushed her younger sister harshly as Remington gathered her skirts. "I suppose there is only one way to find out. If they trample me with their chargers, bury me in my gold silk, will you please?"

Jasmine gave her sister a wry smirk, watching her closely as she crossed the outer bailey. Her strides were confident and proud, not at all timid as was her mood. The eyes of the young and old were on the straight, elegant back and the cascades of rich, colorful curls.

Remington's eyes were trained on the largest knight. She could only assume he was the leader and walked directly for him. She let go of her skirts because her palms were sweating so badly she was positive she would leave stains on her coat, but she held her head high and tried not to maintain any sort of an expression. She had grown very good at masking her emotions and she drew upon the practice. But, in faith, she was fairly terrified by the time she crossed the drawbridge with soft, dainty footfalls.

In the distance, thunder rolled like the devil laughing and a chill shot up Remington's spine. Icy wind whipped harsher about her, lifting her hair as if it had a mind of its own. The force of the gale met her head on, plastering her surcoat to her body and outlining every curve and flare blatantly, giving the knights full views of her round breasts and womanly hips.

Her green surcoat streamed out behind her like a wildly waving banner. She came to a halt several feet in front of the men, her heart pounding in her ears and fighting the urge to sway in terror, but she lifted her face expectantly. Patiently, she waited for the monstrous man to speak.

Gaston looked down at her. From the moment she had exited the castle in the brilliant green dress, his eyes had been drawn to her. When she crossed the bailey toward him, her body erect and proud, he had been riveted to her as he had never been riveted to anything in his life. Her hair was magnificent and her body, outlined by the wind, was beyond description. Pleasing was a grossly inadequate word. But it was her face, when it came into full focus that hit him hardest of all.

An angel, was his very first reaction. *I am looking into the face of an angel!*

The angel was waiting respectfully for him to speak, but in faith, he did not trust himself to. He forced himself to cool as unhappy confusion swept over him. Why did he react like that to her? By God's Bloody Rood, he'd never reacted to a woman in his life! They were nothing more than breeders of men, the inferior sex with minimal intelligence. True, some could be beauties, but they were a worthless lot for the most part. No woman warranted attention beyond a night of relief, and he was positive this woman in front of him was no exception.

… then why couldn't he catch his breath?

The woman continued to wait and he let her, allowing his eyes to rove over her delicious body under the veil of his visor. He shouldn't have, but he found himself so damn curious about his reaction to her that he couldn't stop himself. What was different about her other than her obvious beauty?

Nothing, he told himself sharply. *She is a simple woman, like all the rest.*

"Who are you?" he finally asked, his tone cold.

Remington felt herself jump at the sound of his voice. It was as deep as the thunder in the distance, echoing out of his mouth like the voice of God. Her breathing started to quicken but she forced herself to calm.

"I am Lady Remington Stoneley," she replied. "My husband is lord of Mt. Holyoak. I bid you good knights welcome."

Gaston looked at her. Hard. Her voice was seductive, sweet, and melodious. It matched her appearance. Welcome, did she say? "I have six hundred soldiers waiting not a quarter mile below," he rumbled. "I would enter the keep and secure it myself."

Her eyes, like crystal sea-green stars, gazed back at him. "Mt. Holyoak is yours now, is it not, my lord?" she asked, resignation in her voice. "You may do as you are so inclined."

"How many people are in the keep?" he asked.

"We have twenty-two men-at-arms, the same amount of servants, and my family, my lord," Remington replied.

"How many is in your family?"

A wild thought flashed through Remington's head at that moment. My God, did he intend to rape her sisters, too? And what of the other knights? They were entirely at their mercy, but she knew better than to lie to him.

"My three sisters, my husband's male cousin, and my son," she answered, her voice quiet.

"How old are the males?"

More panic shot through her. He wasn't planning on killing her son and Charles, was he? Utter terror swept her and to her dismay, she felt her eyes start to sting with tears. Dear God, she was trying so very hard to be brave.

"My husband's cousin is ten and four, my lord, and my son is seven years," she answered, her voice shaking.

He heard her quiver and imagined what she was thinking. As hard as he was, as completely professional, something buried deep inside him wanted to reassure her that he had not come to kill them, but it was far too soon. For all he knew, she was harboring a company of men just inside the gate to spear them all.

"Very well," he mumbled in reply. He motioned to the two knights to his right to move forward into the keep before addressing Remington again. "My name is Sir Gaston de Russe. I claim this fortress in the name of King Henry VII. You, your family, and your household are now my vassals. Is this clear?"

"Aye, my lord," she nodded, confirmation of what they had suspected. This man was indeed the feared Dark Knight.

And little wonder. He was dressed from head to toe in the most formidable plate armor she had ever seen, enlarging him even more than he already was. If it wasn't shining armor, it was black leather or mail. This man was a warrior the likes of which Remington had never seen.

Yet it was far more than merely the colors he wore; it was his *presence*. The simple act of living and breathing conveyed a world of foreboding and fear. Blind obedience was the only way to survive.

Gaston flicked his wrist and knights began to charge past her and on into the bailey, but Gaston remained still, absorbing the activity. The sky above was growing threatening and the wind was vicious, caressing her with icy fingers. Remington watched the strange, fear-some men riding into her ward, fighting the urge to hug herself against the wind. She would not allow the Dark Knight to see any weakness in her, or any show of her inner emotions. Over her shoulder, she could feel the weighty gaze of him and a chill ran up her spine. Involuntarily, she shivered from both the stare and the cold.

My God, what have I done? A strange sense of despair swept her and she felt the distinct taste of hopelessness. Should she have tried to hold him off, but for what purpose? She had not the men to maintain a strong defense and she knew everyone would have been killed trying to fight off Henry's knight. The lives of her people were worth more to her than maintaining the sovereignty of the keep that had shown her nothing but grief.

"Return to the keep, Lady Stoneley," came his voice from behind her, gravelly and deep so that it shook the very ground she stood upon. "I will speak with you at a later time."

Remington couldn't get away from him fast enough. It began to rain as she crossed the drawbridge, messing her surcoat and pelting her face with chilly droplets. Behind her, she could hear the unmistakable hollow sounds of hoof-falls as they crossed the bridge. It would seem that the Dark Knight was intending to follow her into the bailey.

Remington was bewildered and depressed by the activity in the bai-ley. The Dark One's knights had whipped the aged men-at-arms into a frenzy and they were climbing the ladders to the catwalks on the walls with an energy she had never seen before from them. Fear was a potent drug, indeed, and she felt so guilty. She had allowed the knights into the keep and she told everyone there was no use in resisting the inevita-ble. She could only pray that the old soldiers did not break their necks or have chest pains as a result of her philosophy. Already, they were suffering.

Her sisters, Charles, and Dane had disappeared into the castle, but Remington refused to go. She stood on the stone steps, watching de Russe and his men systematically clear the bailey and the towers. They moved like great cats stalking mice, leaving no door unopened, no crev-ice unchecked. De Russe himself checked the two great wall towers before descending the ladder, satisfied no one lay in wait for his army.

With a few barked words, two of his men remounted their chargers and tore from the bailey to signal the waiting troops.

Remington watched the Dark Knight intently. He never raised his voice, never made a sharp movement, but he did not have to. He had the fear and respect of his men without such devices. She found it difficult to comprehend that a person could radiate so much power and presence. It was as if de Russe was beyond a mere mortal and therefore entitled to the respect men reserved for gods.

Aye, she was frightened of him, but she was also fascinated. Curious, utter fascination. And all of this before she had even seen his face.

Before she realized it, he was standing in front of her and she startled, gazing up at him with genuine fear. He'd snuck up on her and she had never heard him coming.

"Go inside and wait for me," he said. "I have many questions."

She opened her mouth to speak but no words were forthcoming. Her breathing came in rapid gasps and she took an unsteady step back from him.

"How...how many men shall I prepare rooms for, my lord?" she stammered.

"I have thirty-five knights who will all be housed in the castle," he said. "Do what you must to make them comfortable."

"And you?" she asked, her voice soft.

He turned his helmed head to her. Remington's breath caught in her throat as a monstrous mailed hand came up and unlatched his visor. In a flash, it flipped up and she found herself staring into the most intense eyes she had ever seen. They were like precious stones, smoky-gray in color, masking all emotion and clouding his soul. Dark brows lifted, arched like the wing of a raven.

"You will put me in the master's chambers," he said. "That is where I will stay."

She nodded unsteadily, disoriented by the piercing eyes. She moved to turn when she heard his voice again. The tone was much quieter than it had been only a moment before.

"What is your name again?" he asked.

She met his eyes again, unnerved all over again by the power they conveyed. They seemed to reach out and touch her, everywhere.

"Remington," she replied in a choked whisper.

His eyes studied her a moment longer. Without a word, he slammed his visor down and marched off across the rapidly filling bailey.

In spite of her nerves, Remington did an outstanding job of setting out the evening meal. In truth, it was only late afternoon but she assumed correctly that the Dark One and his men would be famished from their journey.

A storm had rolled in from the east and was dumping copious amounts of water, unusual in summer, and the temperature had dropped. A fire roared in the massive hearth, warming the cavernous and smoky great hall, to dry out the men when they came in from the elements.

Remington ordered a varied fare. Mutton, boiled, roasted, and spiced, graced every table heavily. Bowls of boiled turnips and carrots, spiced apples, pomegranates, pears, and tiny grapes filled the tables to bursting. Bread, butter, and rich fruit preserves were also nicely displayed.

She also made sure that banks of expensive tallow candles lit the tables so that the men could plainly see what they were eating. She was afraid they might accuse her of trying to poison them if it were too dim to see the food. She did not want to give them any excuse to harm her people.

When everything was properly prepared and she was assured by Oleg that every one of the twelve empty bedchambers in the keep were provided with beds for the knights, she sent the servants back to the kitchens and bade them wait for her signal. Quickly, she changed into a clean surcoat of soft yellow that was magnificent with her hair color, and dashed back down into the hall to await the new lord of Mt. Holyoak.

And she waited. Jasmine, Rory and Skye waited with her. She had purposely told Charles and Dane to stay out of sight, terrified that the Dark One would somehow be threatened by their presence. With her sisters to keep her company, they paced the hall slowly, watching the food cool and speaking of trivial things.

They were all nervous. They had all seen the size of the man and felt his fearsomeness as if it were personally directed at them. Remington, as usual, bore the brunt of it, but also as usual, she had handled it well.

"What do you think of him, Remi?" Jasmine asked.

Remington shrugged. "There is nothing to judge him by, yet. He was neither cruel nor friendly."

"He is the devil," Rory said flatly. "That is why he would not let you see his face. You would know he was the devil for sure."

"I saw his eyes," Remington murmured. "They were not the devil's eyes."

"Oleg said he betrayed Richard," Rory said boldly. She was always bold and irreverent. "What kind of man would betray his king on the field of battle?"

"Quiet." Remington hissed. "If he hears you, he shall kill you."

"Ha," Rory snorted. "I am not afraid of him."

"Shut your mouth, Rory," Jasmine snapped. "You are afraid of him also. We all are."

"All of you shut your lips," Remington snapped. "I have enough to deal with without your jibing and snipes."

"The food is getting cold," Skye said softly, picking at the apples. "He will not want to eat cold food."

Remington looked over her shoulder at the mounds of food that had been prepared. She knew Oleg had gone outside to inform the knights of their waiting meal, but that had been a while ago. She signed; Skye was right, of course. She would have to return all of the food to the kitchens and have it reheated. She should have never brought it out as soon as she had.

Suddenly, they heard movement in the foyer of the castle, a great slamming and clanging and the unmistakable sound of armor. Voices, male voices, were loud and demanding and Remington shot to her feet, ordering the kitchen servant forward and her sisters away from the tables. The ladies took position against the wall by the hearth as Remington straightened her surcoat and moved towards the foyer.

She'd never seen so many knights before. They were everywhere, massive and powerful, shaking off the water and removing strategic pieces of armor so that they could sit more comfortably. She did not realize her eyes were bugging at the sight, but it was a truly remarkable vision.

After a few moments, several of the men noticed her and she cleared her throat. "Your meal awaits you, good knights. Be pleased to take a seat and be served."

They did not acknowledge her with so much as a word, although every man seemed to stare a great deal at her. She lowered her gaze, knowing her cheeks were flushing mightily and praying that someone would not make a grab for her. Thankfully, no one grabbed her as they filed past and on into the grand hall with its thirty foot ceiling and seven foot hearth.

There were so many of them that she stood back, eventually watching each face that passed her curiously. They took their seats loudly, clamoring for wine, and noisily helping themselves to all Mt. Holyoak had to offer.

Remington stood in the doorway, watching in awe. Her sisters had joined the serving maids, helping to keep the knights sated with their need for ale and food. God only knew how badly she wanted this evening to be pleasant and she silently thanked her sisters for doing their part, even the usually rebellious Rory.

The door to the keep opened again and several more knights poured in from the hellish weather. Remington recognized the Dark Knight.

His helmed head glanced about the place as he removed his soaked mail gloves and moved to unlatch his helm. Remington found herself biting her lip in anticipation of his face, wondering what he would look like. Wondering if the face would match the fearsome voice. She already knew his eyes were pleasant, beautiful even, but that said nothing for the rest of him. She did not stop to wonder why she was so curious.

The man next to him removed his helm, revealing white-blond hair, straight and flowing to his shoulders. His face was sharp and angled, but handsome. He said something to the Dark Knight and smiled at his own words, looking about the foyer as he spoke. The other three knights removed their helm, as well, and they were dark-haired. One man, young, had a particularly beautiful face and his skin was darker, while his companions looked somewhat alike with curly black hair and square jaws. Very attractive, she thought with surprise. She had no idea such handsome men would be accompanying the Dark Knight, but in the same breath knew that she could expect a whole crop of bastards come spring. It was inevitable.

The Dark Knight removed his helm. It took Remington a moment to realize she was looking at the feared face itself, and furthermore thought to herself that it was not so fearsome after all. His hair was as black as a moonless night, shorn up the back of his head and longer in the front so that it fell down over his eyes like a sweeping curtain. He ran his fingers through it a couple of times and slicked it back on his head to keep it out of his face.

The face. A granite jaw and prominent cheekbones met with her curious gaze, a straight nose and shadowy stubble. And the eyes found her, though not unkind, and she dipped into a quivering curtsey. He moved directly toward her.

"You and your knights may take a seat close to the hearth, my lord," she said in a weak voice. "The goblet with encrusted jewels is yours."

He glanced into the room but did not move, unaware of the hot stares of his men on Remington. The other knights moved ahead, but he remained.

"I would speak with you before I eat," he said. "Where may we go that is private?"

Shaken, Remington led him to the small room her husband used as his private solar. It was quiet, small, and cold. Gaston lit a bank of candles and turned to observe the room with quiet satisfaction. It was richly furnished with all manner of scrolls and documents stacked against the walls. Vellum had a certain smell, and this room smelled heavily of it.

"This is the solar?" he asked.

"Aye, my lord," she replied, deathly afraid to be alone with him. "My husband spent a good deal of time here."

His gaze lingered on the desk and the furnishings a moment, before he finally turned to face her. She kept her gaze lowered but she could nonetheless feel his eyes on her.

"How old are you?" he asked.

"Twenty and six, my lord," she replied.

He moved around a very large desk, inspecting it slowly. "And how long have you been married to Sir Guy?"

Remington's head snapped up. "You...you know of my husband?"

"Answer my question."

"Nine years, my lord," she said quickly, hoping she had not offended him.

His hands caressed the fine hide chair behind the desk. "How loyal are you to Richard?"

She blinked. "I...I do not understand, my lord. Henry is our king now."

"I am well aware of who is king, madam. Answer me. How loyal are you to Richard?"

Remington looked at him. Obviously this man was not loyal to Richard at all. Especially if the rumors she had heard were true. Of course he expected *her* to be loyal to the dead king because her husband had fought for him and because they were in the heart of Yorkshire. She wasn't sure how he wanted her to answer and decided to be completely honest.

"I am not loyal to Richard, my lord," she said. "I pledge my loyalty and my household to King Henry as my savior."

He actually looked surprised. It was the first emotion she had yet to see from him. "Savior?" he repeated. "Why would you say that?"

Her breathing quickened as her emotions coursed through her veins. The thought of her husband in prison stirred her up tremendously and she spoke words from her very heart.

"Because my husband is in jail and will be there for the rest of his natural life, God willing," she said, her voice shaking. "Henry has done this for me and I willingly turn over all that I have to him. You need not worry about loyalty to the crown here, my lord. Everyone in this keep will gladly give it."

His surprise was gone and he was back to his original cool demeanor. "You will forgive me if I do not take your word for it," he said coldly. "How many peasants populate the surrounding villages of Boroughbridge and Easlinghope?"

The rapid jump from one subject to the next left her momentarily confused. "Boroughbridge provides for three or four hundred people, while Easlinghope sustains close to a thousand. Baron Brimley of Crayke Castle is lord of Easlinghope."

Gaston nodded slowly. He knew most of this information already, simply from what Henry and his clerks had told him, but he wanted the information confirmed by someone close to the source. He would have preferred to hear it from the steward of the keep and had no idea why he had asked the lady to inform him. Much to his surprise, she seemed to have half-a-wit. Besides, she was most pleasing to look at and she smelled pleasant, too. He could smell her from where he stood.

"Tell me of Mt. Holyoak," he said. "What are her crops and sundry functions?"

"The vale is very fertile, my lord, and we are an extremely rich fortress in terms of crops and livestock," Remington replied, feeling less nervous with him now that they were on a subject she knew something about. "Sheep is our primary source of income. Half of the village of Boroughbridge is employed by our sheep works in one fashion or another. In addition to wool, mutton and lanolin, we grow wheat, millet and oats in great quantities and ship a good deal of it to London merchants. Harvest is approaching in August and we will be besieged with dealers come the time."

"Do you have a mill?" he inquired.

"Aye, milord, a large one," she said. "The peasants use it as well for their crops and we do not charge them a fee. Instead, they put a small portion of their harvest into a grain store which is then kept in reserves for years that are not so prosperous."

He absorbed the information, growing more impressed by the minute. It would seem that his mighty fortress had more to it than met the eye, although he was not surprised.

Satisfaction filled him. Not only was Mt. Holyoak strategically important, but she was rich as well. Guy Stoneley deserved none of this magnificence and he was not the least bit regretful that he had just confiscated another man's lands by order of the king.

"What do you plan to do with Mt. Holyoak, my lord?" Remington asked softly, breaking into his thoughts.

He looked to her. "Do with it? I plan to live here."

She tilted her head thoughtfully. "And you plan to keep my family here, as well? Or do you intend to send us away?"

"I do not know yet," he replied. "Have you somewhere else to go?"

"Nay, my lord," she answered. "My father died a few years ago and my sisters and I have no one else."

His eyes roved over her as if he were contemplating what in the hell to do with her. Remington felt like unwanted baggage.

"As long as you remain useful I will retain you," he said after a moment. "But you are not a primary concern for the moment."

Remington knew that; she was used to being forgotten and cast aside. Gaston gazed at the room a moment longer before rounding the desk toward her, his massive body filling the room like nothing she had ever experienced before. He was a few feet away, yet she could feel the heat from his body like a roaring blaze and her face began to feel warm.

"I would eat now," he told her, his voice quiet yet amazingly low and powerful.

She took a deep breath to steady herself. "I have ordered mutton prepared a variety of ways my lord. I hope they are to your liking."

He did not answer as she opened the door and preceded him from the room. She did not wait for him, nor did she pause to allow him to pass before her. She continued into the great hall, her head lowered, feeling far more despondent than she had earlier. She had even lost her appetite, her eyes seeking out her sisters to make sure all had gone well in her absence. All she wanted to do now was make sure the knights were taken care of and retire for the evening. Her head was beginning to ache.

Gaston was behind her, watching the delicious sway of her hips underneath the yellow surcoat. She was obviously intelligent and well spoken, which piqued his interest, but he had more important things on his mind than this woman. He took the seat she indicated at the head of the table between Arik and Patrick.

"The food is delicious," Patrick remarked.

Nicolas, his younger brother by four years, had a mouthful of mutton. "This place is full of food and pretty wenches. A delightful castle."

Gaston ignored them both and dug into a trencher full of roast mutton and carrots. The gravy was rich and the food well prepared and he found he was far hungrier than he had thought. Behind him, along the wall, the four sisters hovered out of sight, making sure all was flowing smoothly.

Remington's apprehension was fading but her stomach was still in knots. She was terribly uncertain about her future, the future of her family, but too terrified to press the Dark Knight for any more information. She would simply have to wait, remain useful and obedient, and pray he allowed them all to stay.

Nicolas put his goblet to his mouth, drinking deeply of his ale. When he pulled the goblet away, his face was ringed with a huge black outline the shape of the edge of the goblet. It looked like a silly, painted-on smile and he was completely oblivious as he dug into his turnips.

Antonius was the first to see it. The wine he had been preparing to swallow went flying across the table, spraying Patrick in the face. Patrick cursed loudly and demanded an explanation when Antonius pointed to his brother, too weak with laughter to explain himself. Patrick took one look at Nicolas' face and burst into hysteria.

"What?" Nicolas asked, food hanging from his mouth. "What's so funny?"

The other knights saw it and chuckled, pointing and snorting at Nicolas' expense. Only Gaston and Arik were not laughing. Arik cocked an eyebrow at Nicolas while Gaston simply went back to his food.

"What is the matter?" Nicolas demanded hotly.

Patrick, snickering, rubbed at the black line and pulled his finger away to show his brother the charcoal. Instantly, Nicolas was incensed and he shot to his feet.

"What is this?" he demanded. "Who did this?"

Rory couldn't stand it. She started to laugh, stamping her feet. "My God, you pompous fool. Can you not take a joke?"

Remington felt a bolt of shock go through her. "Rory!"

Rory was laughing, thinking her joke to be most funny. Skye, her mouth open, pressed herself against the wall as if to fade into it while Jasmine, in total denial, fainted dead away to the floor. Remington was beside herself.

"He looks like an idiot, do not you think?" Rory said to her sister.

Remington clamped her agape mouth shut and rushed to her sister, grabbing her by the arm. "Damn you, Rory, you are going to get us all killed." she hissed. "Get out of here!"

"Nay!" Nicolas boomed, cutting off Rory and Remington's escape route. "I shall teach the wench a lesson she shall never forget."

"Please, my lord, I beg not." Remington pleaded. "I promise you this will never happen again."

"You shall teach me no lesson, you saddle-brained oaf," Rory announced. "I would like to see you try!"

Nicolas reached for Rory, but the redhead was too fast for him. She yanked away from her sister and the knight, moving out of arm's distance and bumping Patrick in the process. Wine sloshed out of his cup and onto Gaston, who reached out and grasped Rory by the scruff of the neck.

The room went silent. The knights froze, as did Remington. Jasmine, being helped up by Skye, saw what was happening and slid to the floor once more. Remington did not know what to do; she was seized with panic. God only knew it never helped to plead with her husband when he was assaulting her sisters, but this man wasn't her husband. He was the Dark Knight. God help them all.

She could only try to plead her sister's case. If she did not, then Rory was certainly doomed. She thought mayhap to prostrate herself at the Dark Knight's feet but her legs were shaking so she couldn't seem to move correctly. Instinctively, she reached out and covered the massive hand that held her sister with her own soft, warm hand.

"Please, my lord, do not be harsh with her," she begged softly. "She is young and spirited and unused to the grand presence of knights. I fear her warped sense of humor overrides her judgment at times."

Gaston looked into the crystal-clear eyes, the sweet face, and realized that he was actually listening to her. He'd never listened to a woman in his life. And her hand... by God, he could feel the warmth of it all the way up to his shoulder. And the softness, like the finest silk, caressed him although she had not so much as moved her hand in that manner. Her touch was beseeching, imploring.

He was going to throw the little redheaded vixen in the vault and throw away the key. How he dealt with troublemakers would reflect greatly on how he was perceived, especially with this first offense. But with the lady's soft pleading, he reconsidered and was shocked at himself for doing so.

"Nicolas," he said, his eyes moving to his cousin. "Do what you will with her. Yet I would see no blood, bruises, or broken bones on her person. Do you comprehend me?"

Nicolas was unhappy with the command but had better sense than to voice it. He closed his outraged mouth and grabbed Rory by the hair. She began to screech and kick, swinging her fists and making contact with his abdomen. Nicolas grunted, grabbing one of her arms and twisting it behind her back to control her, but not before Rory bit him and almost took off his finger.

"You bloody little witch!" Nicolas roared. "That damn well hurt!"

"Let go of me, you brute," Rory spat. "Let go of me and I shall give you a fair fight."

The entire population of the hall was greatly entertained by the spectacle, laughing and encouraging Nicolas with bawdy comments. They lifted their tankards in respect of a good battle and turned back to their food as the shouting faded from the room.

Remington was horrified. She was still focused on the archway hearing the faint yells of her sister and sickened to the bone. It occurred to her that the practical joke on Nicolas might not have been random. Terrified of what her sister was capable of, she raced to the end of the long table where Gaston and his knights were sitting and thrust herself forward in the space that Nicolas had occupied.

"Forgive me, my lords," she said quickly, checking under bowls, shaking out napkins and generally disrupting their meal. Yet instead of being perturbed, they watched her curiously. Especially Gaston.

"What are you doing?" he asked over the rim of the goblet.

She paused, suddenly aware of a host of faces looking at her. Her cheeks flushed pink.

"I...Rory is fond of practical jokes, as you can see," she offered apologetically. "I was making sure that no more of you good men fell victim to her havoc."

Arik snorted and wiped his mouth with a crimson napkin. There was a huge red streak across his face and Patrick and Antonius erupted into fits of laughter. Arik knew something humiliating had happened and looked at Gaston.

"What now?" he asked.

Gaston wasn't smiling, although he wanted to. "Someone has put red color in your napkin, I believe. The liquid you just mopped from your mouth activated it."

Arik closed his eyes a moment, silently beseeching the gods for strength and patience. "Am I to assume I look as if I am wearing rouge on my lips?"

"Aye," Gaston took a healthy sip from his cup.

Remington was looking at the knight as if she expected him to draw his sword at any moment and run her through. Anger at her sister and complete terror were running neck and neck.

"My lord," she croaked. "I am so terribly sorry. I shall punish Rory severely for her transgressions. Pray forgive, my lord."

Arik looked at her, picking up his napkin to wipe his mouth and then suddenly remembering the dye in it. He tossed it to the floor and ripped Antonius' napkin from his hand, daintily dabbing at his lips.

"Nay, madam, I am sure that will not be necessary," he said steadily. "If I know Nicolas, and I do, your sister will have punishment enough."

Remington's eyes widened with fright but she said nothing. Her gaze shifted once again to the archway her sister had disappeared through, wondering what was transpiring. Was he raping her, or worse? She tore her gaze away, moving to Jasmine and Skye plastered against the wall by the hearth. Quickly, she moved to them.

"Get out of here," she whispered. "Go find out where that knight has taken Rory."

"And then what?" Jasmine whined. "We can do nothing against him."

"Shush," Remington hissed sharply, glancing over her shoulder towards the Dark Knight to make sure he had not overheard. "Just do as I say. Go find Rory."

Like blond wispy fairies, Jasmine and Skye slipped from the room, leaving Remington and the servants to deal with the hoard of men rapidly drinking themselves happy. Remington was glad to be rid of them for that latter fact, as well. She did not want her sisters to fall victim to drunken soldiers.

The meal progressed to empty trenchers and a good deal of loud, wet belching. Remington continued to stand in the corner and direct servants, making sure goblets were kept full. Oleg emerged from the kitchens and stood silent watch with her, fully aware of what had happened with Rory. He, too, was concerned for the spirited sister but did not voice his concerns. It would only upset Remington.

As the evening rolled toward midnight and the knights had taken to singing and games to entertain themselves, Remington decided it was time for her to retire. She'd had enough of men in armor and merriment in their fashion. She was weary to the bone and worried for her sister, and only wished to vacate the hall to see to her own needs. Leaving Oleg in charge, she moved quietly to the Dark Knight's table.

As she came closer she was aware of her twisting stomach, anxiety for the mountainous man. She was positive that after this evening he would banish them all with good riddance, and she furthermore did not blame him. But she prayed, just the same, that he would be merciful.

"My lord," she curtsied by his chair. "I would ask your permission to retire for the eve."

He glanced disinterestedly at her. "The night is young, madam. Are you not planning on eating?"

"Nay, my lord," she said. "This meal was meant for you and your knights to enjoy, without intrusion of the people of Mt. Holyoak. If I may bid you good-night, then."

He studied her manner, extremely careful and respectful. She had the look about her like a frightened doe, which most people did when confronted with the Dark Knight. He was used to it, immune to it, but for some reason, he did not want her to look at him like that... look at him as if he were going to tear her arms from her sockets.

"Very well," he flicked his wrist. "Retire, lady of Mt. Holyoak."

The knights watched her back out, far more respectful than most women. It was subservient to the point of over-reactive.

"She is a beauty," Antonius observed when she was gone. "I know Sir Guy Stoneley. He is an evil bastard on the best of days and I certainly did not expect that he would have such a beautiful creature for a wife."

Arik stared at the empty doorway a moment longer, before looking back to his goblet of water. "See how she acts, Antonius? That woman has known nothing but fear her entire life."

Antonius shook his head and returned to his drink. "Were she mine, she would know nothing but pleasure and happiness. Ah, what a damn pity."

"Nay, the pity is that she must deal with that wild sister," Patrick said. "We shall have to watch that redhead. If she is bold enough to play tricks on our first night here, there is no telling what more she is capable of."

"Sleep lightly, lads," Gaston rumbled, watching the dance of the fire over the rim of his cup. "She shall not be sated until she has humiliated every one of us."

"Damnable Yorkist," Patrick said lowly. "I shall have her head if she tries anything with me."

"She's not a Yorkist, she's a pretty young girl," Arik said, his lips and face still red. "I would bet money that she would not care if this house was loyal to the prince of Persia. Nay, what she does, she does for revenge on the male sex."

Patrick looked at him and smiled broadly. "I cannot take you seriously, man, when your lips are as red as a court whore's."

Arik lifted an eyebrow and put his drink to his lips. "Beware, lad, or I shall kiss you fully."

Antonius sat back in his chair with a sigh, mesmerized by the flames and feeling his fatigue. "I wonder what it would be like to kiss Lady Stoneley," he said. "After all, with her husband in the White Tower, she must be fairly lonely."

"Stay away from Lady Stoneley," Gaston said, his voice quiet but unmistakable. "She is not for you. Keep your mind on your profession, Antonius, for I will not hear that you have been making a fool of yourself after a married woman."

Antonius nodded in resignation, but there was a good-natured smile playing on his lips. Turning the conversation back to another subject, he and Patrick became animatedly engaged and forgot all about Lady Stoneley and her sisters. Even Arik joined in, leaving Gaston brooding silently over his wine.

He had not forgotten Lady Stoneley.

Rory was not in her room, nor was she in any of her other usual places. Remington skirted the perimeter of the entire castle looking for her sister but had yet to see a sign of her. She spied Sir Nicolas entering the castle from the inner bailey alone and her anxiety soared; had he left Rory for dead somewhere, beaten and mauled? Knowing Rory, she would have not made it easy for the knight to punish her and Remington was terrified for her sister.

Quickly, she descended from the southern tower where she had been searching and made way to the inner bailey in search of Rory.

The flame-haired sister wasn't hard to find. She was sniffling and sobbing, carrying on angrily. Remington heard her cursing and banging about in a small room in the inner wall turret, talking to herself furiously. Oblivious to the light rain that was falling and the mud on her skirt, Remington entered the dark, dank room.

"Rory?" she asked softly. "What on earth are you doing?"

Rory's head snapped up, her sea-crystal eyes like flames from hell. "You!" she yelled. "This is *your* fault. You let them in."

Remington was gripped with terror. "What did he do to you?"

"*Do* to me? How can you ask me that question?" Rory cried.

Remington's fear was now fed by annoyance. "Tell me, dammit. What did he do to you?"

Rory sobbed in frustration, smacking her fists against the wall. "It was…terrible. He was so heartless, cruel…."

Remington had had her fill of emotions for the day; she grabbed Rory roughly by the sleeve and shook her. "Tell me what he did to you, Rory, or so help me I will kill you myself."

Rory yanked herself away from her sister in a fit of sniffles and grunts. She pressed her back against the cold stone of the wall and eyed her sister. "He…spanked me."

Remington wasn't sure she heard a-right. She blinked and straightened, tilting her head curiously. "He *spanked* you?"

"Aye," Rory cried. "And it is your fault. If you had not lowered the bridge then they would have never come in."

Remington calmed dramatically to the point where she almost smiled. The knight actually spanked her sister; not beat, nor thrashed, but merely spanked. Enough to sting, yet not enough to hurt her. She was soundly surprised.

"Get hold of yourself and go to bed," she told her sister after a moment. "We will have much to do on the morrow, I fear."

She turned away from Rory, but her sister was not about to be ignored.

"You do not care that he put his hand to my backside," she accused loudly, racing across the room and blocking Remington's exit.

Remington met her sister's gaze steadily. "Rory, if there is any justice in this country, then you have received it. 'Twas *you* who were terrible and reckless when you put charcoal on his cup. And dye on the other knight's napkin. What I cannot truly determine is when you did it; I was in the hall most of the time and never saw you."

Rory's eyes cooled to smoldering embers. "Skye put the dye on the napkin, not me."

Remington shook her head helplessly. "You two are a pair. 'Tis a wonder Guy did not kill you both for the trouble you caused him."

Rory's jaw ticked. "I would say, in fact, the transgressions were far greater on his part. At least Skye and I never physically hurt him."

Remington was stung by her sister's words, although she was only too aware of how very true they were. Still, to hear them voiced in an accusing manner struck her. Bitterly, she turned for the door.

"Go to bed," she mumbled, feeling the soft mist caress her face.

Rory eyed her sister a moment. "Are you going to service the Dark Knight as you serviced Guy?"

Remington paused, slowly turning to her sister. "What do you mean?"

"As his whore," Rory said, her bitterness and humiliation affecting her common sense. "Guy always said you were his whore. I was wondering if you would be the new lord's whore, too."

Remington slapped her sister across the face faster than either one of them thought possible. Rory reeled with the blow, sorry she had said something so entirely uncalled for. She did not know why she had said it; mayhap because Remington was blaming her for her spanking. She had expected her sister to stand up for her. Rory hated taking responsibility for anything.

Remington's control was gone; she was so brittle and unbalanced that she continued to fly after Rory even as her sister tried to recover from the blow. She picked up a small stool and hurled it at her sister as Rory screeched and ducked just in time to avoid the projectile. It smashed harmlessly against the wall behind her.

"Stop it, Remi," Rory cried. "I am sorry. I did not mean it."

Remington wasn't finished raging. She knew what Guy had called her, among other things, and she was raging at him as well. Rory was, at the moment, a convenient whipping post, the catalyst to a much larger problem.

Yet even with her anger, she was not irrational. There were tears of frustration in her eyes as she threw the second stool at her sister, badly aimed.

"Go to hell, Rory." she whispered hoarsely.

Leaving her sister thankful for her hide, she staggered back across the inner bailey toward the door to the castle, wiping hastily at the tears and droplets that pelted her face. She hated herself when she flew out of control, which was extremely rare, for it allowed the pain and anger she felt to somehow seep deeper inside her. Instead of a release, it was like opening the stopper just a little bit more, allowing emotions to creep that much further. The dimly lit interior of the castle beckoned her, and she answered gratefully.

High above in the southern tower, Gaston watched her cross the bailey like a drunkard and wondered what the matter was. Not that he had been looking for her intentionally; he had personally taken the night watch to better acquaint himself with Mt. Holyoak and just happened to see her moving in the darkness.

She disappeared into the castle and his eyes lingered on the open doorway a moment longer. He was puzzled by his reaction to her, yet he did not dwell on it. He had a keep to explore.

CHAPTER FOUR

Days passed and Gaston immersed himself into Mt. Holyoak. He rode the perimeter of the lands, studying the landscape and becoming acquainted with the farms and encampments within the territory. He went into Boroughbridge and became familiar with the layout of the town and took a feel for the peasants, a hearty lot more loyal to each other than to the Yorkists or the Lancastrians.

The people of the village were respectful of him, over-reactively so. They acted as anyone else did when they came face to face with the Dark Knight; they looked at him as if they were fighting the urge to run for their very lives. Gaston was pleased, of course, for he wanted them to fear him. Fear bred a healthy respect, he thought, especially with the less intelligent.

Satisfied with Boroughbridge, Gaston continued his reconnoiter and passed through the great corrals where the sheep of Mt. Holyoak were kept. His first sight of the corrals was astonishing; from the crest of the hill, there was nothing but a sea of white for miles. In the distance was the great stone barn where the sheep were shorn come spring. Bleating ewes and the strong smell of dung assaulted his nostrils, but it did not dampen his enthusiasm.

This is mine, he thought. *All of this is mine.*

He did not return to the keep at night, instead preferring to camp on his land to become still better in tune with it. He traveled with Arik and Antonius, leaving Patrick and Nicolas in charge of his castle.

After five days of becoming familiar with his new lands, Gaston finally returned to the massive fortress with a new respect for his castle he was now in possession of. He reminded himself to thank Henry for his generosity. Even if Henry had sent him to Mt. Holyoak for the sole purpose of controlling Yorkshire, he was still vastly pleased with his reward.

He and his knights were passing very close to the fortress when he suddenly caught sight of a figure in the distant trees. It was a slight female figure and something told him it was Remington. He did not know how he knew, he just did.

"Continue on," he told his men.

Arik caught sight of the figure as well. "Who is that?"

Gaston gathered his reins. "Lady Stoneley, I suspect."

"How do you know that?" Arik wanted to know. "I can barely make out the figure from here."

Gaston ignored him, spurring his charger in the direction of the trees.

Remington heard him coming. She straightened from her task and shielded her eyes from the bright sun, watching with surprise as the great dark destrier roared towards her. The sheer power and size of man and beast entranced her and she was frozen to the spot, watching with curiosity as her bore down on her.

Aye, she knew who it was. There was no mistaking the Dark Knight, yet she found she was not as fearful as she had been days earlier when he had ridden into her keep. She had five days to become accustomed to the idea that he was now her lord and it was easier to control her apprehension. Besides, he had not been cruel to her in any way and she reasoned she had nothing to fear.

The destrier came to an unsteady halt a few feet away, kicking up dirt and rocks. Gaston gazed down on Remington, his eyes drinking in the sight of her. It took him less than a second to realize that he was pleased to see her. By God, he had barely been around the woman and already he was missing her. He should have been angry with himself, but instead, he was actually curious.

"Good day to you, my lady," he said.

She bobbed a quick curtsey for him. "Good day to you, my lord. Did you enjoy your journey?"

He nodded his helmed head. "Aye," he replied. "Mt. Holyoak is the jewel of Yorkshire. I am verily pleased with my acquisition."

She nodded, lowering her gaze. "I bid you welcome home, my lord."

He glanced around, hearing the birds and studying the undergrowth. But his eyes came back to her lowered head. "What are you doing out here?"

She held up her basket. "Gathering flowers, my lord. For pomades and perfumes."

"Pomades and perfumes?" he repeated. "Of what sort?"

"Honeysuckle," she showed him the blossoms from her basket. "Violets, too. And in the garden in the kitchen yard, we have massive bushes of lavender."

To her surprise, he dismounted his warhorse and lumbered over to her. He was so massive that she was positive the ground quaked when he walked. But she held her ground against the giant, the Dark Knight, as he approached.

He reached up and removed his helm in one clean stroke, his smoky gray eyes meeting her intensely. His hair, like an unruly child's, hung down over one eye.

"What scent do you prefer?" he asked.

"I favor honeysuckle and the lavender, my lord," she held up a blossom. "My sister, Jasmine, favors the violet as does my youngest sister, Skye."

He nodded faintly. "And the redhead?"

"Rory?" Remington put the basket down. "She hates all of it. She would smell like a skunk if we did not force her to bathe once in a while."

The corner of his lip tugged briefly. "I would meet your sisters today. I have not yet had the chance."

Suddenly the underbrush behind her began to rustle and a young boy burst through, his hands clutching bunches of flowers.

"Mummy! See what I...," Dane stopped when he was confronted with the Dark Knight and his young face went pale with fright. "I...I...."

Remington saw how terrified her son was and went to him, putting her hands protectively on his shoulders. "My lord, this is my son, Dane Stoneley. Dane, this is Sir Gaston de Russe."

Dane was scared, but not too terrified to remember his manners and bow respectfully. Gaston planted his huge feet apart and crossed his arms, his imposing presence filling the air like the scent of her flowers.

"How old are you, lad?" he asked.

"S-seven years," Dane replied.

Gaston studied him a moment. A year younger than his own son, Trenton, and a sight smaller. But he was a well-formed boy with his mother's eyes and an inquisitive face.

"Where do you foster?" he inquired.

"Foster?" Dane repeated, glancing at Remington for support. "I... I do not know, my lord."

"You are of the age when such matters should be decided," Gaston said, looking to Remington. "Did your husband not make arrangements for him?"

Remington shook her head. "Nay, my lord, he had more important matters on his mind with Richard's wars."

Gaston pursed his lips thoughtfully. "Then I see I shall have to do the man's duty."

Remington and Dane looked at each other curiously. "You are going to send me away?" Dane asked confused.

"All well-bred young men foster by the time they are eight years," Gaston explained, puzzled that the boy was so uninformed. "Do not you want to be a knight?"

"Like you?" Dane asked. "Can't I stay here and learn from you?"

Gaston smiled faintly and Remington was astonished; she did not believe him capable of such a soft action. But he was not only smiling, he was demonstrating a good deal of understanding with her young son and she was doubly surprised. She did not believe the Dark Knight capable of anything other than fear and death.

"'Tis right that you should want to learn from me, of course," he said, eyeing the boy thoughtfully. "Very well, then, Dane Stoneley. I shall consider allowing you to stay at Mt. Holyoak."

Dane beamed, displaying his missing front teeth. "I want to fight with a sword and a battle-axe," he said eagerly, and then his smile faded. "But what of my father? What will he say when he returns?"

Gaston looked long at the boy. "He shall not be returning as far as I know, lad. I am lord of Mt. Holyoak now."

Dane looked puzzled, not at all sorry that his father would not be coming home. "Are you my mother's husband, then?"

"Nay, lad, I am not," he answered.

Dane was sinking further into confusion. "But...you are lord, and my mother is lady. You will not marry her?"

Gaston shook his head. "Truth is, Master Dane, I already have a wife. She and my son live at my keep far to the south. A man can only have one wife, and your mother is already married to your father. Now that I am lord, your mother is no longer lady of Mt. Holyoak."

Remington felt as if she had been hit in the pit of the stomach, although she had no idea why. Was it because he mentioned that she was no longer lady of Mt. Holyoak? Was it the realization of that finally setting in? She did not stop to think that it was possibly because he had said he was married. Why should the fact that he was married bother her? She cared not what his marital status was.

Dane absorbed the information, though he was still terribly confused. "Then you are to protect us?"

Gaston nodded once, firmly. Dane tilted his head thoughtfully. "Will you protect my mother if my father returns?"

Gaston's smoky eyes glittered curiously. "Protect her from what?"

"From my father," Dane insisted.

"That is enough, Dane," Remington added quietly.

"Why must I protect her from your father?" Gaston ignored Remington. He wanted to hear what the boy had to say.

"Because he hurts her," Dane said hesitantly. "I can't protect her, although I have tried. He just hits me, too."

Remington turned away, her body shaking with embarrassment and shame. Gaston saw her quivering hand move to her head and he received confirmation of what Arik had suggested on the day they had arrived. The woman was abused.

He wasn't surprised. He knew Stoneley, as he knew all of Richard's barons. The man was vile and low, and he felt a tremendous urge of protectiveness towards Remington and Dane. The fool baron had a beautiful family and he abused them. By God, what he would not have given for a wife and son like Remington and Dane. A wife with unearthly beauty and a son with his mother's features, intelligent and curious. Why was Stoneley blessed with such a beautiful family when he himself had been cursed with a hellish mistress? It wasn't fair.

"He shall not hurt you again, Dane," Gaston said quietly. "I promise you that."

Remington whirled around, her eyes boring into Gaston. "You cannot promise him that, my lord. 'Tis not fair to him."

"I can and I will," Gaston said evenly. "He shall not touch you again. Either of you."

Remington let out a small cry of disbelief, wiping at her eyes. "Dane, take my flowers back to the castle," she told her son. "I shall come later. Go now."

Dane, still thinking mightily on the Dark Knight's words, did as he was told and disappeared through the bramble. When Remington heard the last of his footfalls, she turned to Gaston.

"How dare you make promises like that," she hissed. "I forbid you to give my son false hope."

"'Tis no false hope I give, madam," he replied. "I never make promises I cannot keep."

Remington's face flushed. "So you intend to always be at my son's beck and call to protect him from his father? It is simply not possible. Sir Guy is my husband and has every right to do with us as he pleases. The contract of marriage forbids you to interfere."

Gaston let out a heavy sigh and leaned against the tree. "Mt. Holyoak is my property now. If I keep you on, you are technically my property, too."

"That is ridiculous," she snapped softly. "I am Guy's wife, to do with as he pleases. And Dane is his son. You cannot own us."

"Mayhap not," Gaston said, meeting her incredible sea-crystal eyes. "But I can protect you."

Remington shook her head and turned away from him, embittered and confused. Gaston studied her miraculous hair and the myriad of colors within, wondering if it were as soft as it looked.

"Has he always beat you?" he asked quietly.

Remington thought a moment. She couldn't remember when he had not; there had never been a time during her married life that she had not lived in daily fear. She found the question ludicrous.

"If you only knew," she whispered.

"I want to know," he said. "Tell me."

She simply couldn't talk about it. This man was a stranger, a feared stranger at that, and she couldn't bring herself to tell him her most terrible secrets.

She took a deep breath and faced him. "I would return to the keep now, my lord," she said with forced bravery. "I have gathered enough flowers for the day."

He looked back at her, seeing the terrible vulnerability underneath the beauty. How could Stoneley abuse something as tremendously fragile as this woman? He couldn't fathom the reasoning and that, in turn, angered him.

And then the strangest feeling swept him, a sort of pity for Lady Remington, yet it was deeper than mere pity. It was broader, softer and by far more unsettling. He did not realize that for the first time in his life, he was feeling compassion.

"If that is your wish, angel, we shall return," he said. "I am anxious, for God only knows what my cousins have done to my keep in my absence."

Remington blinked. Had she heard right? Had he called her angel? She was so stunned she couldn't answer him and he caught her stare.

"What is wrong?" he asked, pushing himself off the tree.

She managed to shake her head unsteadily. "Nothing, my lord."

She moved past him and onto the path, acutely aware of his massive presence behind her. Much to her surprise, he did not mount his destrier but instead chose to walk beside her. She fell silent as they passed through the thickness of the trees and emerged onto a wider path used by the peasants.

Gaston's booted steps were heavy beside her, like great stones crashing to earth in rhythm. She stole a glance from the corner of her eye and watched his powerful gait, thinking the size of his hands to be bigger than her head. A heady sense of pleasure filled her to think this man had pledged to protect her against her husband, although she did not believe it for a minute.

She was so intently studying the size of his hands that she failed to realize the destrier was plodding along behind them without benefit of a lead, following Gaston like an obedient dog. When she finally did become aware of the fact, she was impressed.

"Your horse is well trained, my lord," she said softly.

He grunted. "Taran is my other self. We have been together for many years."

"Taran? I like that name." She turned to look at the destrier, whose head was as long as her torso. "He seems docile enough now."

Gaston glanced back at the horse. "Taran is Welsh for 'thunder.' And I assure you, my lady, his mood is temporary. He seems to be quite interested in you."

She looked at the horse more fully, his rich charcoal-gray color and black, intelligent eyes. "He is beautiful." Before Gaston could stop her, she reached out to stroke the animal's muzzle.

Gaston tried to shout for her to halt her actions, but the words did not come fast enough. As soon as she stroked the silky fur, he had visions of Taran biting off her hand and he reached out to pull her away. But, to his amazement, the horse did not make a move against her. In fact, he seemed to enjoy it.

Astonished, Gaston watched her as she fell back a pace to walk beside the horse, speaking in a sweet, soft voice and stroking his face. Taran's lids half-closed with blissful attention.

"By God's Bloody Rood," Gaston muttered. Then, he actually snorted in amusement and Remington looked up.

"He is a sweet animal, my lord," she said. "Is he always this calm?"

Gaston shook his head. "Nay, madam, that horse had been the scourge of many an enemy. In fact, I would say he has killed almost as many men as I have."

They came to a halt. Remington put her hands on the horse's head and lay her cheek against his nose, laughing when Taran's big tongue licked at her. Gaston was so astonished he put his hand to his face in disbelief.

"He is as gentle as a lamb," Remington declared. "I choose to disbelieve your slanderous statements against this animal, my lord. He is not a killer."

A shadow of a smile creased Gaston's lips. Taran had never even been that affectionate with him at the best of times and he was, frankly, flabbergasted.

"I assure you, madam, he is indeed formidable," he said helplessly.

Remington smiled at him, a smile that hit him like a bolt of lightning. His reaction was so sharp that it was almost painful, but in the same breath he couldn't ever remember seeing a more beautiful smile. His knees actually felt shaky and he cursed himself for his foolishness. Women were a nuisance, a bother, self-centered bitches with no purpose on earth other than to give a man pleasure and breed more males. Mari-Elle was living proof that a female was a useless, vile creature and he stuck firmly by his beliefs.

… Then why did he feel like a giddy squire?

He cleared his throat quietly and resumed walking. Remington continued beside him, a few feet away, and it took him a moment to realize that Taran was walking behind her. Not him, his master and keeper, but *her*. A stranger.

He mounted Taran at the bottom of the hill and cuffed the horse when he struggled against him. Remington continued to walk and he reined his dancing horse slightly behind her, following her up the hill. Irritated with his horse's behavior, he did not even see Remington enter the castle as he halted his snorting beast to an unsteady halt.

There were several men there to greet him, his squire rushing to take hold of the animal and almost getting his hand nipped off in the process. Gaston dismounted and snapped harshly at the horse as Patrick and Nicolas strode up.

"Well?" he demanded of his cousins. "Give me a report."

"All is well, my lord," Patrick replied. "Nothing unusual to report."

Gaston removed his mail gloves, letting his gaze rove the walls of the inner bailey. "The men looked well-positioned and the keep appears in order."

"We have been working since you left," Nicolas said.

Gaston nodded. "Very well, then. As for the moment, I intend to take a bath and a hot meal and I shall send for you when I am finished. There is much to discuss."

A woman with bright red hair suddenly emerged into the bailey and began to march purposely across the compound, away from Gaston and his men.

"Hey! You there!" Nicolas shouted at her. "I told you to stay to the castle!"

Rory continued to walk away from him, intent on going to the stables. She had a leggy gelding she was fond of riding and planned for a long ride this day. She heard the knight yelling at her, but she ignored him soundly.

Nicolas ran after her. Patrick and Gaston watched him jog across the courtyard.

"How have the women behaved in my absence?" Gaston asked, a twinkle in his eye.

"Well, for the most part," Patrick replied. "But that redhead is a banshee. Nicolas thought there was a truce between them after he spanked her our first night and was pleased when she graciously drew him a bath last eve. Fact was, she put some kind of coloring into the water and he did not realize it until he got out of the tub and was dyed a lovely shade of yellow. She is supposed to stay to her room, but obviously, she is not."

Gaston took a slow, deep breath as he watched his youngest cousin grab Rory by the arms and begin his verbal assault.

"Unremarkable. I would have expected no less from a witless young girl," he removed his helm. "Confine her to the vault until I decide what to do with her. I shall not have her disrupting my knights, and especially Nicolas. He is too hot-tempered to deal with her and I am afraid he might hurt her."

Patrick nodded, leaving Gaston to go to his brother and the redhead. Gaston did not give them a second glance, even as he entered the castle and heard the young girl cursing a blue streak as the knights physically carried her to the vault.

He took a flight of smaller stairs to the second floor, looking forward to soaking in hot water. Yet he paused here and there, glancing in rooms and checking alcoves. He had only taken a brief tour of the castle and set about reacquainting himself as he made his way to his room.

The keep of Mt. Holyoak reminded him of the White Tower, a massive place with a myriad of rooms and passages. As he rounded the second floor landing, he suddenly plowed head-on into a small, female body and sent her crashing to the floor.

Jasmine looked up at Gaston with shock and terror, sitting quite squarely on her behind.

"My apologies," he said, reaching down and pulling her to her feet, studying her curiously. She was a delicate, lovely girl with blue eyes and straight blond hair, but not nearly as beautiful as her eldest sister. "You are Lady Jasmine, are you not?"

She nodded, rubbing her backside. "Aye, my lord."

He acknowledged her with a slight nod. "Then, if you are not injured, I shall be on my way."

Jasmine stepped aside and gave him a wide berth, turning to watch him as he marched down the hall. Had she not been so frightened of him, she would have thought him to be a ruggedly handsome devil. He was so tremendously masculine that there was no other way to describe him. But she did not think of men in terms of handsome or desirous; men were terrible, vile creatures and she generally hated the sex. Rubbing her bottom once more, she continued on her way.

Gaston reached out to open his door and was cautious when he saw the door slightly ajar. Inside his room, he could hear banging about and his sword drew forth from its sheath in a clean, swift movement. Carefully, he inched the door open.

He had hardly taken a step into the room when he was suddenly flooded with the scent of lavender. He heard a good deal of splashing now, pouring water, and deduced that no one lay in wait for him. Unmistakably, someone was taking a bath in his room and he had vague suspicions as to who the culprit was. The lavender gave it away.

Remington sat in a huge tub in the center of the chamber, her head wet and her hands vigorously lathering a white cake of soap. The clothes she had been wearing to gather flowers in lay in a pile by the hearth, while still other garments were carefully laid out on the bed. He was amazed that it had taken her so little time to prepare a bath and plunge into it; he had seen her not ten minutes before.

He pushed into the room; his eyes riveted to her back the color of fresh cream. Never had he seen such pure, flawless skin and it amused him that Remington had yet to notice him.

"What are you doing in my room?" he asked.

Remington shrieked, immersing herself in the water up to her chin. Her eyes were so huge they threatened to leap from their sockets as she turned to him.

"My lord!" she gasped. "I thought.... I had no idea that ...oh!"

A corner of his lips turned up. "You thought *what?*"

Her cheeks were a delightful shade of pink; she was deeply mortified. "I was dirty after gathering flowers this morn and...I thought you were too busy in the bailey for some time. I had hoped to take my bath and be gone in plenty of time."

"Why did not you simply take the tub to your room?" he asked.

"Because it is too heavy for the female servants to carry it, my lord, and the men are too old," she explained. "We must do all of our bathing in this room."

"I see," he said. Much to her horror, he was moving closer. "I could have moved it for you."

"I did not want to be a bother, my lord," she said, eyeing him warily. "As I said, I had hoped to be done well before you returned."

"Yet I have returned and you are not finished," he said.

Remington was starting to shake; she was not only embarrassed, she was terrified. He had the same look Guy had right before he....

"I am finished now," she said, her voice rising with fright. "If you will but allow me a moment to dry myself, I shall be gone."

Her sudden terror caught him by surprise; what had he said? Yet he realized that his mere presence frightened her and, for once, he was sorry. He did not want to frighten this woman, although he knew not why.

"Nay, madam, take your time," he said, backing away. "I have duties that can use my attention. I am in no hurry."

But Remington was ignoring his words, hell-bent on leaving the room as hastily as she could. She did not like the look in his eye. She knew what he was thinking and she wanted no part of the horrible, unspeakable deed. Stripping her naked, putting his hands roughly on her, and...

"If you will turn around, please," she asked, her voice cracking. Much to her shame, she was beginning to cry. She simply wanted to be out of the tub and away from him.

"Truly, Lady Remington, you may finish your bath," he insisted, his voice growing gentler. "I will antagonize you no further."

She did not even wait for him to turn around; she shot out of the tub and grabbed the huge piece of drying linen, her sobs evident now and her body shaking. Puzzled and concerned, he watched her jerky movements, wondering what he had done to upset her so. But even as her mental state concerned him, it did nothing to dampen his appreciation of her nude body. From the brief glimpse he had stolen, he could see that she was absolutely perfect.

She was sniffling and coughing as she wrapped the linen about her. Snatching the dress, she wrapped that around her haphazardly as well, trying desperately to cover herself from him. Gaston could see how terribly upset she was and he felt the least bit guilty.

"My lady," he moved to the door. "Please finish your bath. I shall bother you not and I am sorry to have upset you in the first place."

"You did not upset me," she insisted loudly, wiping at her nose. "I am leaving now."

Holding all of her garments to her recklessly, she started to dash past him, desperate to leave his presence. But he reached out to stop her, his massive hands grasping her upper arms and covering them completely.

"What have I said to upset you so?" he asked, not unkindly.

"No," she shrieked, trying to pull away from him. She was shaking so badly that her knees gave way and she fell backward, smacking into a chair and landing on her behind. She looked up at him as if he were planning on eating her alive and her arms wound themselves around her body protectively. "Oh, please...do not...."

He was stunned. She was like a panicked animal, desperately trying to escape whatever terror was hounding her. He'd never seen such a violent reaction to his presence, but he furthermore wasn't so sure it was entirely him. How could it be? He'd done nothing to warrant this behavior.

Armor and all, he slowly crouched where he stood, several feet away from her. His smoky gray eyes were wide with concern.

"Do not *what?*" he asked gently.

Remington blinked at him, aware that she had let her fear get the better of her. Where Guy was concerned, she was always irrational with terror and she was suddenly deeply ashamed of her actions. She couldn't stop herself from slipping into hot tears of embarrassment and fright.

"Why are you crying, angel?" he asked again, his deep voice more soothing than anything she had ever heard in her life.

But she couldn't speak, instead, burying her face in her hands. She wished he would simply go away and leave her to compose herself.

He watched her sob for a moment, feeling a strange tugging at his heart. Then, very slowly as not to provoke her further, he stood and removed his plate armor. It dropped with little noise against the wall by the door, piece by piece. He shirked his mail hauberk and trews and his heavy black boots. When he was free of the equipment, he took several careful steps towards Remington, being mindful not to get too close. She continued to sob softly, absolutely drained emotionally.

"You are going to make yourself ill," he said softly. "Get up off the floor, my lady, and sit by the fire."

His voice jolted her a bit and she wiped her eyes and face, clutching the garments awkwardly.

"I do apologize, my lord, for my display," she said hoarsely, trying to rise. "I would return to my room now and leave you in peace."

He wanted to help her to her feet but he wasn't sure how she would react to him. Clumsily, she stood and picked her way across the cold floor to the door. Her drying hair was a mass of dark spiral curls, dampening her back but infinitely charming. He watched her with gentle eyes, something completely out of character for him.

She closed the door softly and left him standing there, puzzled to the core. He somehow knew that Guy Stoneley was responsible for the outburst and he was truly curious as to what she had meant by "do not". Do not hit me? Do not hurt me? Do not...? His head came up sharply and he stared at the closed door.

Do not rape me?

He wondered.

CHAPTER FIVE

Remington avoided him for the rest of the day. She was polite and respectful as always, but she had difficulty looking him in the eye and he was sorry. But he had other things on his mind, more pressing matters that were occupying his attention. After the evening meal on that night, he met with Arik, Antonius, Patrick, and Nicolas in the solar to discuss a few points.

"I want every feudal baron and earl in Yorkshire to meet here with me to discuss their role in Henry's reign," Gaston said. "I want them to understand that I am Henry's arm of strength in Yorkshire and will brook no disobedience."

"They will not swear their fealty," Arik said.

"They will if they expect to survive," Gaston said in a low voice. "They will be loyal to me and I, in turn, will not destroy them. A most agreeable arrangement."

Arik shook his head. "Mayhap you should wait, Gaston. They already know you are here. Mayhap fear alone will keep them reined."

"I do not want them simply to behave, I want their oath," Gaston replied. "Not only am I to control greater Yorkshire, but I find myself in the position to control West Yorkshire, South Yorkshire and Humberside. Henry has powerful knights stationed in all three of these shires, but those men will answer to me."

Arik look surprised, as did the other knights. "You never mentioned this detail," he said dryly. "So, in essence, Henry has sent you here to keep a firm hand on most of this enemy land."

Gaston nodded once, leaning back in his chair. "'Tis the most volatile part of England right now. He would have the Dark One in the heart of it, ready to quell whatever problems might arise."

The other knights fell silent a moment, listening to the crackling of the fire in the hearth. "By all means, then, call for the barons and earls loyal to Richard and inform them of your mission," Arik said, studying his wine. "'Tis best to let them know where they stand from the onset."

"To be honest, I expect no uprisings," Gaston said thoughtfully. "Henry's demonstration of power at the battle of Stoke announced that he is the rightful king of England. I believe even the Yorkists have resigned themselves to the fact, considering there is nothing to fight for with Richard dead. 'Twould be futile to resist Henry."

The fire spit and the men enjoyed their wine.

"So what now?" Antonius asked in his rich Italian accent.

"I do not think I shall know what to do with myself with no battles to look forward to."

The statement brought smiles to the lips of Patrick and Nicolas, but Gaston raised an eyebrow. "We face an even greater challenge. Henry would have us train troops, legions to be deployed in other parts of England. We should be receiving the first batch of recruits within the month."

'Twas an honor and they all knew it, yet it was nothing new. Arik helped train nearly half of the crown troops and was considered one of the finest troop masters in the civilized world. And, of course, every man wanted to train under the Dark Knight. He had been considered the very best trainer of men before the call of war tore him away from his duty.

With the battles over for the moment, he could return to what he enjoyed. If he could not be fighting, then he wanted to train men on the arts of fighting.

"Mt. Holyoak is certainly big enough to house hundreds of men," Patrick remarked. "There are sublevels below the outer wall that are unused."

Each man sat alone with his thoughts, feeling the wine and the good food. The warmth from the hearth pushed away the chill of the room, leaving them with sleep in their mind.

"I will send missives on the morrow, then," Gaston said. "What's the steward's name – Oleg? Find him before the morning meal and he will assist me."

They were dismissed without another word. All except Arik. He continued to sit with Gaston, drowning more of the wine.

"Has Lady Stoneley said anything about her sister's captivity?" he asked.

"Not a word," Gaston replied.

"Hmpf," Arik shrugged. "I expected more from her. Her sister has been in the vault all afternoon and screaming like a banshee."

Gaston did not reply, thinking on the incident earlier in the day. He refrained from mentioning it, probably because he couldn't make any sense of it and was in no mood for Arik's insightful philosophy.

Arik, feeling the wine in his veins, rose to depart when there was a young knight in the doorway.

"Begging your pardon, my lord, but we have a bit of a problem," he said respectfully.

"What kind of problem?" Arik asked.

"Lady Stoneley was caught attempting to break her sister out of the vault," the knight replied. "When we tried to stop her, she fought and… well, she fell and hit her head."

"What?" Gaston rose to his feet, focusing on the knight. "Is she dead?"

"Nay, my lord, she is quite alive, but unconscious," the knight answered. "We took her back to her room."

Gaston was already moving past the knight. "How did she fall? Did someone push her?"

"Sir Ottis hit her because she struggled with him when he tried to stop her," he answered.

Gaston gazed down on the young knight, his eyes glittering like the deadly steel of his broadsword. He flicked his gaze up to Arik and, without a word, quit the room. Arik followed, as did the young knight.

Jasmine was attending her sister when Gaston entered the room. Skye stood vigilant by her side, helping her sister apply a compress. Old Eudora was chattering softly, trying to ease Jasmine's tears.

Gaston moved to the edge of the bed, his eyes lingering on Remington. She was pale and her breathing was labored.

"How is she?" he asked.

Jasmine jumped as if she had been gored. Terrorized blue eyes riveting to him; the feared one himself.

"This is all your fault," she spat, forgetting to whom she was speaking.

"Jasmine," Skye hissed.

But Jasmine paid no heed. "Men are all alike. Brutal, self-centered bastards who care nothing for the well-being of women. Look at what your soldier did to her."

Gaston looked at her impassively. "Had she not been trying to release your sister from her cell, then this would not have happened. I asked you a question; how is she?"

Jasmine shuddered, sniffled. "I do not know."

Young Dane raced into the room as fast as his legs would carry him. One look at his mother and his eyes flew to Gaston accusingly. "You said you would protect her."

Gaston gazed down at the boy. "I would have had I been there, Dane."

Hurt and confused, Dane moved to his mother and gently touched her arm. "Just like father all over again."

Arik and Gaston exchanged glances. Arik moved away from the bed, leaving Gaston standing alone.

Jasmine put her hand over Dane's mouth, silencing him against any further slips. The boy struggled against his aunt a moment, pulling away and moving to the other side of the bed where he could touch his mother unimpeded. The sadness on the young face spoke volumes.

He already knew Guy had abused them both, but he had no idea to what extent the abuse went. He should not have cared in the least; this was another man's wife and son. Yet he found himself caring a great deal.

"Get out. All of you," he growled. "Except you, Dane. You may stay."

Jasmine opened her mouth in outrage but Skye grabbed hold of her, pleading with her sister to be silent. Arik made sure they left the room, eyeing old Eudora menacingly until she complied. When the women had vacated, he closed the door softly behind them.

"Gaston..." he began.

"You, too," Gaston said, his voice as low as the rumble of thunder. "Get out."

Arik did without a word, leaving Gaston alone with the mother and son.

Slowly, he moved around the side of the bed and picked up the compress Eudora had been preparing. As gentle as a mother, he placed it on Remington's head, observing her delicate features in the glow of the firelight. He was unaware Dane was watching him.

"Why did not you protect her? You said you would," Dane said softly. He was growing sleepy.

Gaston looked up at the innocent face. "I told you that I was not present when this happened. Had I been there, your mother would not have been injured," he said. "I am not a magician, Dane. I cannot be everywhere at the same time."

Dane looked at his mother with longing. "Why does she not wake up?"

"I am awake," Remington mumbled.

Gaston removed the compress. Slowly, the sea-crystal eyes opened and blinked lethargically. She focused on him for a moment before closing her eyes again.

"Be swift with your punishment, my lord," she whispered. "I am ready to accept your judgment."

"There will be no punishment, my lady," he replied softly, sitting on the edge of the bed. The entire side of the bed sank under his considerable weight and Remington rolled right into him. She moaned at the swift motion, grasping her head as he reached out to steady her against him. Her torso was pressed against his left thigh.

"No punishment?" she repeated, wincing.

A crease of a smile appeared. "I consider what happened to you punishment enough. But tell me one thing; why did you do it?"

Remington opened her eyes, looking up at him. His expression was actually gentle. "Because she has done nothing to warrant imprisonment. Aye, she's a spitfire and a handful, but she is not malicious. Her jokes are innocent, my lord. Rory is not evil."

He cocked an eyebrow. "You mean to say that you do not consider saffron dye in a knight's bath to be malicious? What of the charcoal on Nicolas' cup?"

"Harmless," she whispered. Her head was killing her. "Were she to have taken a dagger to him, then I would deem the punishment to fit the crime. But she has done nothing other than a few harmless pranks."

He considered her explanation a moment. "Then why did you not simply come to me and ask me to release her?"

"Would you have done it?" she asked softly. "I doubt it."

"You reason well enough, madam. After I heard your argument, I most likely would have reconsidered," he said. "I will always listen to you."

Her eyes opened again and she looked strangely at him. "Why?"

He actually smiled and her insides jiggled enough to make her nauseous. "As I said, you reason well. Your intelligence is worth listening to."

"Then you will let Rory go?" she asked hopefully.

"Not unless we come to an agreement," he said firmly. "I will not have her disrupting my household by playing childish jokes on my knights. The next man she plays a trick on may not be as tolerant as Nicolas."

"Tolerant?" she raised an eyebrow. "He's hardly the calm type, my lord. He and Rory have been going at each other like two tomcats. They yell and screech until I have had enough."

"So that is what has been going on since I left?" he murmured, more to himself. Then he focused on Remington again. "We will discuss your sister further on the morrow. I suspect that tonight you wish to sleep."

Her hands were pressed against his thigh, preventing them from being any more intimately positioned than they already were. Her hands felt as if they were touching solid rock, yet the heat coming forth from his skin was making her warm, as well. She could feel her cheeks heating.

"My head *is* hurting," she admitted quietly. "Talking only makes it worse."

He rose slowly, steadying her so that she did not roll off the bed. His hands were incredibly large and warm and, to her amazement, tender. Yet she was instinctively afraid of his touch and she pulled back indiscreetly. Gaston pretended not to notice.

Dane was sitting on the other side of the bed, his hand protectively on his mother as she adjusted her pillows feebly. He alternately eyed Gaston and helped his mother and Gaston couldn't help but feel that this young boy had been forced to grow up far sooner than he should have. There was a sort of wisdom to his face that was difficult to fathom.

"Dane, you will leave your mother to sleep," he said firmly, moving around the side of the bed. "I will do you the honor of escorting you to your room."

Dane looked hesitantly at his mother. "But...but what if she needs my help?"

Gaston put his hand on the boy's shoulder, turning him for the door. "I shall send her maid in to take care of her," he said. "Bid her a good sleep."

Dane looked over his shoulder, his eyes still full of longing. He was afraid to leave her alone, afraid the knight would come back and... "Good night, Mummy."

Remington smiled weakly, watching as the Dark Knight escorted her son from the room. Strangely, she knew she could trust the knight with her son's life. He was a stranger, a trained warrior and technically, her enemy. Yet she had seen the way he had dealt with her son and he had been entirely tolerant and even kind. Not like Guy.

As for Rory, she would be better equipped to deal with that problem after she slept off this terrible headache. She knew she shouldn't have tried to free her sister and, in truth, she had not been attempting to release her. She simply wanted to talk to Rory to see what had happened, when the guards had come upon them and out of fear, she had defended herself.

Defending herself was a habit. She knew better than to go against the lord's wishes, for she had learned several harsh lessons from Guy. But he somehow found something wrong with whatever she did anyway and her sense of self-defense was better than most. Her sense of fear, of self-preservation, of panic was highly developed thanks to her husband. A perfect example was just a few minutes ago when the Dark Knight touched her; his touch was as gentle as a woman's, yet she instinctively flinched. There was nothing good in a man's touch.

The faint crackle of the hearth lulled her into a deep, dreamless sleep.

Gaston and Dane wandered down the hall to a heavy carved door with the Stoneley crest on it. Dane paused and faced Gaston, his young expression still veiled.

"Thank you for...thank you, my lord," he said, reaching up to unlatch the heavy bolt.

Gaston gave the door a shove for assistance, watching the stiff little body moving through the opening. He reached out to close the door behind him when something made him pause.

"Dane," he said hesitantly, not sure of what he was even thinking. "Your mother....did your father hurt her often?"

He nodded solemnly. "All the time. My aunts too."

His brow furrowed. "He hurt them as well?"

"Sometimes he hit them, but sometimes he did other things to make them cry," the boy said, not at all concerned that he should not be telling this stranger these things. "I do not know exactly what he did, but I heard Aunt Jasmine say one time that he defiled her."

Gaston leaned against the doorframe, crossing his arms. He knew what the boy meant and he was moved to a new level of disgust. "Just her? Or your other aunts, too?"

"All of them, I think. When my mother tried to stop him, he would make her bleed," the boy said. "They would cry all the time and at night, sometimes, I could hear my mother scream."

Gaston closed his eyes a brief moment, resting his head against the doorframe. So that was what went on in this place, he thought grimly. Those women were condemned to a living hell within the walls of the keep. And none were more humiliated and abused than Remington.

Anger such as he had never known seized him. An odd sense of such protectiveness that his whole body tensed. No wonder she jumped when he innocently touched her. And 'twas no wonder she had become completely irrational when he had come across her in her bath. By God, the woman had known nothing but pain from the touch of a man, and she was reacting accordingly.

Aye, young Dane had opened his eyes to a good many things about Mt. Holyoak.

"Dane, you mustn't tell your mother that you told me these things," he said softly, straightening. "Do you understand? She might not appreciate the fact that I know your father was cruel. This must be a secret amongst knights."

He nodded, although he did not completely understand. Yet he and the Dark Knight now shared a secret and he would not betray the trust. He somehow felt special, a part of something, a belonging.

"I won't tell her, I promise," he said.

"Good lad," Gaston gave him a brief smile. "Now get into bed and not another word from you until morn."

"Aye, my lord," Dane dashed to his bed and sat down to remove his shoes, eager to obey.

Gaston closed the door softly, his mind lingering on the little boy and his beauteous mother. The lad's confession only served to reinforce his earlier declaration.

He would protect them from their nightmare.

CHAPTER SIX

The next day dawned warm and humid, and the men were sweating buckets underneath their plate armor and mail. Gaston's hair was completely wet with perspiration, slicked back on his head to keep it out of his face.

He was supervising the cleanup of the sublevels of the outer wall in preparation of the arrival of the new recruits from London. The tanner and the blacksmith had to be relocated, adding to the task, and Gaston set the masons to work on an additional shelter to house more knights. The shelter, located where the tanner and the blacksmith had been housed, used the outer wall as one wall and was planned to house up to forty knights.

It was dirty, smelly, hot work and tempers were ripe. Arik snapped at Patrick, Patrick would snap at everyone, and Antonius was soundly reprimanded by Gaston when he removed every strip of clothing from the waist up. Antonius had the body of a Roman statue, muscular and lean and completely beautiful and he was not ashamed to display his flesh. It tanned quickly underneath the hot sun, but Gaston put an end to it and angrily sent the man to the sublevels to supervise the cleanup.

But not before Jasmine had seen him half nude from her bedchamber window. At first she was embarrassed, but she quickly discovered he was the most beautiful sight she had ever seen and was greatly disappointed when Gaston put an end to her fun. Yet she came away from the window with her opinion of the male sex slightly swayed, a very large step indeed. Mayhap not all men were vile, horrid creatures. There was apparently one that was quite easy to look at.

The castle provided minimum relief from the heat. Remington had seen to her morning duties dressed in a gauzy linen surcoat that swept the floor behind her when she walked, the v-shaped neckline draping beautifully between the swells of her breasts. Her curly mane was swept back into a gold net to keep it off her neck, but rogue tendrils escaped and curled against her face and shoulders.

By late morning it was far too hot to do anything more than sit and embroider and she found her sisters doing exactly that in the solar.

Jasmine and Skye were working on Skye's loom. The youngest sister was not particularly talented on the frame and Jasmine was doing her best to repair the damage.

"What are you making, Skye?" Remington asked curiously. She couldn't for the life of her tell what the figures were.

"I am trying to weave an Ariadne and a spider web," Skye said insistently. "If Jasmine would leave me be, it would work out."

Jasmine rolled her eyes, pulling at a piece of thread. "This is no spider web, Skye, unless it was woven by a drunk spider. And Ariadne looks as if her body has melted."

Remington giggled at Skye's embarrassment, opening her thin golden fan and waving it at herself swiftly. "Keep trying, sweetheart. You shall catch on."

"What about Rory?" Jasmine asked, biting her tongue between her teeth in concentration.

Remington glanced through the narrow window that looked out over the bailey. "I intend to go and see her now, to make sure she isn't melting herself."

"Is the Dark Knight going to let her out?" Skye asked. She missed her closest sister.

Remington moved away from the window, fanning herself. "I do not know. He said he would consider it, I think."

"Even after you tried to break her out?" Skye asked, wondering if the Dark Knight had punished Remington last night but was afraid to ask.

"I was not trying to free her, I was merely attempting to speak with her," Remington insisted. "I was opening the door to go in, not let her out."

"Did you tell de Russe that?" Jasmine had stopped her movements and was looking up at her.

"Nay," Remington avoided her sister's gaze. "I saw no point in it. He would not believe me, anyway.

"Well, I say there is no harm in trying," Jasmine said. "He does not seem so quick to judge as Guy did."

Remington almost cringed at the sound of her husband's name. The more time passed, the more afraid she was that he would eventually return. They had been so happy in his absence and she couldn't bear to think that life would again turn bitter when he came home. If he ever came home.

"Yesterday, de Russe told Dane that he would protect us from Guy," she said softly, the hair on her face lifting gently from the fan as she gazed at the window pensively.

Jasmine and Skye looked shocked. "He did?" Jasmine said incredulously. "How can he say that?"

"I do not know," Remington glanced at her sisters. "But he said it, and I believe him. I am not sure why I do, but I do."

"He cannot protect us from Guy," Jasmine went back to the loom, mayhap a bit angrily. "No one short of God can protect us."

Remington watched her sisters a moment, wanting them to feel the same faith she did. "He is the Dark Knight, is he not? 'Tis said he is in league with the devil. Mayhap if God will not help us, the devil will."

She turned and left the room, leaving her sisters pondering the future.

The inner bailey was full of men assisting the stonemasons. Sand and mortar was being distributed from a huge wagon and great stones for the building were being carefully carved and carted off.

Remington was surprised; she had no idea that there was so much going on in the double baileys and wondered if it would even be wise to bother the Dark Knight about something as trivial as her sister's imprisonment. Yet, for Rory's sake, she went to seek the man out anyway and prayed his mood was forgiving this day.

She had never seen so many soldiers, all working like the innards of a great beehive. She knew from Oleg that he had brought nearly 600 men to Mt. Holyoak, but it seemed that every one of them was working at this very moment. And there was not one man who did not pass her a suggestive or leering glance, making her most uncomfortable.

Remington swallowed hard, pushing her way through the men and into the outer bailey in search of Gaston. One soldier almost dropped a great stone on her and she yelped in surprise, jumping out of the way just in time to avoid being smashed. Fanning herself furiously over her fright, she stood a moment and scoped out the bailey for possible signs of the Dark Knight when her eyes came to rest on the very tall blond knight he always kept with him.

Bolstering her courage, she picked her way towards him.

Arik was surprised to find himself looking down at the entirely delectable and completely angelic Lady Stoneley. Flushed from the heat, she looked radiant and he gave her a non-committal smile.

"My lady, to what do I owe the honor?" he asked, pulling her toward him to allow a burdened soldier to pass by.

Remington waited until the soldier had moved by before stepping back a pace. "I am looking for Sir Gaston. Can you tell me where he is?"

"In the sublevels, my lady," Arik answered. "Is there something I can help you with?"

"Not unless you can release my sister," Remington answered.

Arik shook his head regretfully. "I surely cannot, my lady. Might I inform Gaston of your request to speak with him when he is finished?"

Remington looked disappointed, but she did not press. Pressing with Guy only got her slapped. "I would be grateful, my lord. But do not trouble yourself overly to deliver the message. I can wait."

"My name is Arik," he said. "And it would be no trouble at all."

She smiled shyly, displaying her delightful dimples. "My thanks, Sir Arik. You have been most kind."

"Not at all," he returned her smile. God, she was a lovely creature. And he knew that every man that saw her had the exact same thoughts, men with less self-control than himself. "As a matter of fact," he continued. "I was just about to return to the inner bailey. Might I escort you back to the castle?"

"Thank you, my lord," Remington said demurely.

He extended his elbow and with great reluctance, she accepted. Together, they started back to the inner bailey.

"This weather is unusually hot," Arik commented.

"Aye, but not the stickiness," Remington replied. "Here in the vale, we are always prone to a great deal of moisture and insects."

"I noticed," Arik said, eyeing a swarm of gnats a few feet away. "Tell me, my lady, where is your family from?"

"Halsey Manor," Remington replied. "When my father died four years ago, there was no one to inherit the place. It fell into my husband's control but it sits empty now."

"Is it close by?" he asked, looking down at her with interest.

"Mayhap seven or eight miles to the northeast," she replied. "Not far."

"Were you born there?"

"Aye, I was, as was my father," she answered. "My mother was Irish from County Cork. Skye was born in Ireland.

"Ah," Arik nodded. "So you are half Irish and half English. A lovely combination."

Her reaction was to blush pleasingly, but his compliment instantly reminded her of Guy's flattery and she hated it. Instead, she cleared her throat and changed the subject. "Where are you from?"

"My parents are Norse, settled in Kent just before I was born. I was their only son and they were adamant that I be an English knight. A noble profession."

Remington thought of Dane, and of Charles. They, too, thought knighthood to be noble. She thought it was professional bloodlust.

They crossed into the inner bailey and Remington was nearly run over by a reckless wagon driver. Arik snatched her against him to prevent her from being crushed, but she suddenly turned into a fighting cat and roughly yanked herself away from him. She couldn't stand to be held by a man, any man for that reason.

The wagon passed and Arik looked shocked. "I apologize, my lady, if I offended you. It was just that...."

Remington shook her head, backing away from him. "It was not your fault, truly. I just...I must return."

She spun on her heel and raced back into the castle, leaving Arik confused. There was suddenly someone beside him.

"What happened?" Gaston asked, watching Remington disappear into the innards of the castle.

Arik lifted his shoulders. "Nothing at all...I think. Oh, hell, I do not know. She had come to speak with you about her sister and I happened to pull her out of the way of a speeding cart. She acted as if I tried to take advantage of her."

Gaston sighed slowly, long and deep. "Her son told me yesterday that Sir Guy used to beat her, quite severely I gather. She fears men in general, I think, so it would be best to tread lightly around her until she realizes we are not a threat. That goes for the sisters, too."

Arik crossed his arms. "Then I was right with my first observations. That woman has been terribly abused. The boy, too? And the sisters?"

"From what I understand, all of them to some extent," Gaston answered unemotionally, though that was far from the truth. He found that he was quite emotional about it, although he had no right to be.

"This bothers you," Arik stated.

Gaston looked at him, seeing that Arik was studying him curiously. "'Tis no concern of mine."

Arik did not believe him for a moment but he let it slide. "The fact remains; what do you intend to do with the lady and her sisters? With Stoneley locked away in prison for the rest of his natural life, his wife and her family are in question."

"There is no question. She will stay here and remain chatelaine," Gaston said flatly. "And her family stays with her."

"The old man runs the castle, Gaston, not Lady Stoneley," Arik pointed out. "You could keep him on and get rid of the rest. They are of no use."

"Why are you so eager for me to order them away?" Gaston asked curiously. "In the first place, where in the hell would I send them? Lady Remington told me that they have no family and nowhere to go."

"Untrue," Arik countered. "She told me that the manor house, occupied by her father until his death, stands empty not eight miles from here. You can send them there and they would be away from the fortress."

Gaston crossed his arms and faced Arik. "Why are you so intent for them to leave Mt. Holyoak? In faith, I have not given it much thought, but I see no reason why they cannot remain."

"I am only thinking of them, Gaston, truly," Arik said. "Think on it, man – within the month you will have nearly double the soldiers you already have, trainees and recruits. This place will be turned into one massive training ground literally crawling with men. Now tell me, how safe do you think four women will be against over one thousand men? And I have grave doubts that we should retain any serving wenches, as well."

The thought had indeed occurred to Gaston and he saw the truth of Arik's words. He could leave orders for the women to be left alone, threat and intimidate all he could, but it would not prevent a truly lustful man from obtaining his ends. He would die for his actions, of course, but the fact would remain that the actions occurred nonetheless. And he couldn't allow that to happen to Remington or to any of them.

"I have a few weeks yet to make my decision," he said, looking away from Arik. "As for now, I will seek out my lady and see what she wished to speak with me about."

Arik snorted, amused. "Since when do you seek a woman out?"

Gaston was not amused in the least. He eyed Arik, his jaw ticking, and his knight received the silent message loud and clear. Clearing his throat, he turned and disappeared into the crowd of laboring men.

⚔

Nicolas had charge of the castle as the others toiled in the sun outside. It was his duty to coordinate the watches and keep an eye on the keep in general, and he went about his duty with the usual eagerness. He was an extremely intelligent boy, if not a bit rash, and was most competent in his duties.

He kept wandering by the solar where Jasmine and Skye were holed up. He would pace, eye the women, and continue on his way. This routine had been going on for most of the morning until Jasmine and Skye had grown quite irritated at his attention. Twice, Jasmine told him to go away, but he had ignored her soundly. Angered, she and Skye set forth a plan of action.

And it was for revenge, too. After all, he was the reason Rory was holed up in the vault like a common prisoner and they sought to make amends for their sister. They reasoned that the action coming from them would be forgivable; were Rory to exact her own revenge, the Dark Knight would most likely banish her from the keep forever.

It was an easy plan; the next time Nicholas wandered by the door, they would douse him with a bucket of water for his troubles. Skye stole a bucket from the kitchens and filled it full with water from the cistern, escaping back to the solar undetected.

Giggling and snorting, they waited in the shadows by the open door for Nicolas to make his appearance.

He did, like clockwork. As soon as he appeared Jasmine let the water sail at him with all of her might, completely soaking his head as if he had dunked it completely under water. Her aim was perfect and they squealed in triumph as he sputtered and gasped.

"What was that for?" he roared.

"For being a nuisance," Jasmine answered saucily.

"And for sending Rory to the vault," Skye sneered, sticking her tongue out at him for good measure.

Nicolas pursed his lips together angrily. "Is that so? Well, it would seem that the two of you could use the same discipline your sister sampled."

He took one step and they scattered, screaming and shrieking and dodging around him in their haste to exit. He grabbed for each girl in turn, missing the both of them, and rapidly whirled on his heels to give chase.

They would feel the flat side of his palm against their backsides, too.

They made a crazy trio, Jasmine and Skye screaming in terror, or mayhap delight, their skirts hiked up around their thighs as a knight in heavy armor chased after them.

The ladies took him up two flights of stairs, racing madly down corridors and then plunging downstairs again. Nicolas lost some ground, but he never gave up. He was intent on catching the two misfits and he would have them.

Nicolas was descending another flight of stairs when his eye caught a bucket with a ladle in it, perched on a ledge. He snatched the bucket and tossed the ladle aside, the devious little boy in him planning to give the women a taste of their own medicine. They had run a circle and were back in the same corridor that they had started in; sooner or later they would make the mistake of passing him, thinking he had given up chase.

With a sinister chuckle, he ducked into the solar.

Remington entered the corridor, her mind still on her reaction to Arik when he had literally saved her life. He had put his hands on her and she had jumped like a boar in a snare. She was deeply embarrassed at her reaction; she had not even thanked him for saving her from the wagon. But the more she walked, the calmer she became, and she vowed to make it up to Sir Arik at supper. Mayhap she could make up for her lack of manners by playing her flute for him. She hoped he would forget about the incident.

The corridor was warm and she fanned herself furiously as she made her way to the solar. She was an avid fan of Greek and Roman writers, as was Guy, and his solar was filled with mythology. Not only Greek and Roman, but Gaul and Celt as well. She loved to lose herself in the stories, and a hot day was an outstanding opportunity.

She suspected nothing as she turned to enter the solar and was flabbergasted when she was hit in the face with a great gush of water. Instinctively, she let out a whoop of surprise.

"My lady." Nicolas was horrified; the bucket in his hand clattered to the floor. "My God. I thought you were...oh, my sweet Lord. I thought you were your sisters."

Remington opened her eyes and looked down at herself; she was completely soaked. Her face, her hair, the entire front of her dress was soaked to the skin. She looked up at Nicolas, her mouth agape, when she was struck by the horror on his face. The man was literally white with shock.

She couldn't help it; laughter began to bubble up and before she could stop herself, she was screaming with laughter. Nicolas looked at her as if she was quite mad, but her laughter was infectious. Relieved she wasn't angry, he joined in her laughter. In fact, they both looked rather comical; soaked through.

Jasmine and Skye appeared in the hall several doors down, their faces a mask of surprise.

"Remi. He got you," Jasmine declared.

Remington looked at her sisters, her laughter fading and a twinkle of mischief coming to her eye. "Aye, he did. And for revenge, I will get *you.*"

Jasmine and Skye screamed and tore off as if the devil were chasing them. Remington snatched the bucket from the floor and raced off after them, wet surcoat and all.

At the end of the hall was a stone cylinder filled with water. She dipped the bucket in and continued after her sisters, albeit more slowly than before. But she was determined to catch them.

Dane and Charles found her in the upper hall and joined her on her quest when she told them of recent events. Each armed with a bucket of water, they went in search of Jasmine and Skye.

Gaston entered the castle seeking Lady Stoneley. He was barely into the structure when he met up with Jasmine and Skye, their faces flushed from running.

They stumbled to a halt in front of him, curtseying clumsily. He eyed them as they staggered and bobbed, looking over their shoulder as if any moment they expected Satan to appear.

"Where is Lady Stoneley?" he asked, wondering at their strange state.

Jasmine blinked. "Uh...behind us, my lord," she said. "Up the stairs."

Skye looked mortified but supported her sisters' explanation. "Aye, she is. Up the stairs."

He nodded curtly and they scattered like chickens. Raising his eyebrow at their curious behavior, he took the narrow flight of stairs to his immediate right.

Remington saw the shadow on the wall and pressed herself flat against the opposite wall, shushing her giddy companions harshly. Poised with their buckets, they waited for the shadow to grow closer. They were so caught up in their joke that they failed to notice the distinct sounds of armor approaching until it was too late.

Remington caught site of the armored boot in time to halt her own assault, but she was too late to stop Dane and Charles. They let the water fly and Gaston walked right into a downpour.

For a moment, no one moved. Remington's bucket clattered to the floor in absolute horror as Gaston shook his head in one quick movement, splattering water on the stone walls. His eyes rolled open slowly and he focused on Remington.

"May I ask what I did to deserve that attack?" he asked, his voice like rolling thunder.

Remington began to shake, from her wet dress and from fear. "My lord, pray forgive. We thought you were my sisters."

"I see," he said evenly, running his fingers through his hair to slick it back. "No wonder they directed me up the stairs."

"They did?" Remington asked, her heart sinking. "Oh, my lord, I am so sorry. Had we but known it was you...."

He wiped his eyes, noticing she was soaked and the wet dress left very little to the imagination. "What are you doing?"

Remington was miserable. She waved her son and cousin back up the stairs, hoping they would escape the Dark Knight's wrath. "Seeking revenge," she said hopelessly. It sounded silly, even to her.

"Revenge on your sisters for getting you wet?" he motioned to her dress.

"Nay, Sir Nicolas did this," she said, noticing that his eyebrows shot up with surprise. She continued quickly. "But they had thrown water on him first. He was seeking retribution and thought I was them."

Dane and Charles were almost to the top of the stairs and Gaston let them go; he was not interested in the boys. He was focused entirely on Remington for several reasons, one being that she looked entirely delicious in the clinging dress.

"And he threw water on you?" he clarified.

"Aye," she answered, defeated.

He nodded slowly, eyeing her a moment before turning as if he were going to descend the steps. Instead, he opened his mouth.

"Nicolas." he bellowed, so loud it echoed off the walls and nearly scared the wits from Remington.

"Please, my lord, do not punish him," she pleaded, moving timidly towards him. "It was a mistake."

He looked over his shoulder at her. "Go change your surcoat. I understand you wish to speak with me, and you shall. After I deal with my knight."

"Sir Gaston," she said. "Sir Nicolas did nothing wrong. He was simply attempting to dispense justice with my sisters. An eye for an eye, as it were."

A chill shot up his spine when she said his name. Her voice had a soothing, sensual quality, anyway, but when she spoke his name, it was like an open caress. He turned his full attention to her.

"I understand your explanation, but it does not excuse his behavior," he said, trying not to stare at the pert breasts almost directly in his face. "If you will excuse me, then."

She looked so sad that he almost gave into her and it shocked him. He gave in to no one, man or woman, King or challenger. Her huge eyes were staring back at him and he found his attention drawn to her lips; shaped like a budding flower and nearly the color of a peach. Surely they tasted as well, too. He found himself fighting an overwhelming urge to kiss her.

But she lowered her gaze and turned away, making it much easier for him to fight off his urge. He watched her ascend the remainder of the stairs, watching the sway of her bottom as it tantalized him. By God, there was nothing about that woman that did not taunt and tantalize him into insanity. Unused to dealing with such a temptation, he found himself distracted and moody, unfortunately for Nicolas.

❧

Remington changed into a cotton surcoat of shell pink and let her hair from its net, running her fingers through the rapidly drying locks. In the heat, she was dry in no time and waited nervously for Gaston to come calling.

Aye, he made her nervous, but it wasn't so much because she feared him anymore. It was more the way he made her feel when he looked at her, a strange shakiness that she did not understand. Her heart thumped wildly and her knees quaked when he trained those smoky gray eyes on her, mysterious and veiled, yet inquisitive at the same time. It was difficult to describe and even more difficult for her to understand.

It never occurred to her that he was handsome. He was just a man and she had never looked at a man in those terms. The fact that his raw masculinity reached out and embraced her like a glove never occurred to her either. She was far too fearful to allow any of those ideas into her head. Too well trained to ignore the obvious in light of self-preservation.

It wasn't long before there was a knock at her door. She opened it to old Eudora, bustling in with an armful of linens. Remington let out a sigh and sank into a chair.

"Heard what happened, Missy," Eudora said, busying herself. "Jasmine and Skye are still missing."

Remington made a wry face. "As well they should after what they did."

"Mayhap so," Eudora replaced the covers on the down pillows. "I also heard that the Dark Knight punished one of his knights for watering you. Sent him to the vault, to Lady Rory's cell."

"What?" Remington shot off the chair. "He put Sir Nicolas in the same cell with my sister?"

"Aye, he did," Eudora said. "Told him that they had both better come out of the vault smiling come morn or he would do something drastic."

Remington was outraged. "Better both be...now what in the hell did he mean by that?"

"Exactly that," Gaston entered the room, eyeing the old woman. "Be gone."

Eudora dropped the rest of her linens and scampered out. Remington faced him, almost hysterical. "Please explain yourself, my lord."

He slanted her a glance and moved to the wine decanter against the wall. Pouring himself a full cup of wine, he turned to face her calmly.

"I did not send Nicolas to the vault to assault your sister or do her harm," he said evenly. "My philosophy is simple; the conflicts originally started between Rory and Nicolas, and they will end with Rory and

Nicolas. I expect them to make peace with each other before the night is through or I will take matters into my own hands."

"There are no conflicts," Remington insisted. "Since when are practical jokes conflicts?"

"They are not – yet," he said. "Throwing water and sabotaging bathtubs are one thing, but they could quickly escalate into something more sinister. I do not want people of this keep taking sides if someone 'innocently' gets hurt."

She put her hands on her hips irritably. "My sisters have always been like this. 'Tis simply the way they are. I do not think you can change their nature."

"I am not trying to change their nature, my lady, simply curb it a bit," he said steadily.

"Are you against fun, then?" she demanded respectfully.

"There is a place for everything," he answered her, yet gave her no answer at the same time. "Now tell me, what was it you wished to speak to me about?"

Remington studied him a moment before answering. "Rory. I wanted to ask you to release her this day, but I can see that I would be wasting my breath to do so."

"You will see her tomorrow," he said. "Was that all?"

"Aye," she replied. "I am so sorry to have bothered you. And I am so sorry that you had water thrown on you, since you have no sense of humor."

He looked at her, hearing her taunt. No one taunted him except Arik. "I have a sense of humor, properly placed."

She raised her eyebrows as if she did not believe him. "As you say, my lord."

"I do," he insisted. "But I do not make a fool of myself."

Her gaze softened somewhat. "I could never imagine the Dark Knight a fool. Any man who would think so is dead now, I am sure."

"How true," he dipped his head gallantly to thank her for her confidence. "You are wise as well as beautiful."

Her smile vanished. His smile vanished, too, as he watched her turn away from him abruptly.

"I will make sure Jasmine and Skye are well aware that you have forbidden them any further pranks," she said, her manner clipped. "I am sure you have other duties to attend to, my lord, and I will take no more of your time."

He crossed his arms, observing the stiff back. "What have I said?"

She looked at him, puzzled, but guarded. "I know not what you mean, my lord."

He studied her intensely. "Aye, you do. You were smiling not a moment ago and now you are angry. What did I say to offend you?"

"Nothing, my lord," she turned away softly.

He wanted to grab her and turn her to him but he was acutely aware that she would probably turn into a hysterical creature.

"You do not like being told of your beauty," he said after a moment. "Why not?"

He saw her body twitch convulsively and her hand flew to her mouth. 'Tis...tis not true, I tell you. I am not angry."

Her voice sounded strangely tight. "Aye, you are. Do not you know how beautiful you are?"

She whirled recklessly to face him, her hand over her mouth and her eyes were brimming with tears. "Do not...would you please leave me alone."

He went to sit on the bed. He wasn't leaving until he knew what was upsetting her so, if for nothing more than the simple fact that he would never do it again.

"Tell me, Remington," he said gently. "Why do not you like to hear of your beauty?"

He used her Christian name with no title, rolling off his tongue as if it were the richest, finest wine. His voice could be incredibly soothing when he wanted it to be, but she was almost immune to it. She had made herself immune to men for so many years she did not know how to act any other way.

Something deep inside of her was curious, wanting to know what it was like to have a man be kind to her. That same element wanted to respond to him, open up to him. But the overwhelming majority of her was terrified.

Her tears spilled over and she started to sob softly. She heard him rise from the bed, relieved he was leaving her alone as requested. But, to her surprise, she felt huge arms wrap themselves around her shaking body. Instinctively, she bolted like a wild animal.

Gaston did not let go. He held on to her for dear life.

"Nay, angel, do not fight me," he said gently. "Relax, Remington, relax. Do not fight anymore."

She shrieked and pushed at him, terrified, but he held firm, speaking to her in even, comforting tones. He never even knew he had it in him. In fact, this woman had succeeded in teaching him things about himself he never realized before. And he thought he knew everything.

He swept her into his arms, struggling and all, and carried her to sit on his lap as he deposited himself on the edge of the bed. Her strength waning, her struggles were lessening, but she was still crying pitifully.

"Don't," she kept saying. "Please don't."

He held her tightly, soothingly, hoping she would calm. He was afraid if he let her go she would forever be terrified of him. It was like breaking a horse; he had to ride out the storm to the very end. He could not give up if he were going to accomplish anything.

The fact was, he wasn't even sure just what he was trying to accomplish.

"Do not *what*, angel?" he whispered urgently.

Her fighting dwindled, reducing her to almost hysterical sobs. Her stiff body was relaxing in defeat. He grasped her chin and forced her to look at him.

"Do not **what?**"

Her eyes, wild with fright, gazed back at him helplessly. She did not want to say anything and reveal her shame, but he was so insistent, so genuine in his desire to know, that she felt her barrier crumbling. Dear God, she had too much pride to reveal herself to this stranger but she was so confused and frightened she couldn't think anymore.

"Do not hurt me," she choked out in a whisper.

He did not ask her anymore. He pulled her close to him, feeling her body relaxing imperceptibly, but she was still shaking terribly and crying. His hands, of their own accord, caressed her softly. He did not even realize he was doing it.

In faith, he felt wonderful and in spite of her terror and life-long convictions, she wanted to respond. She wanted to enjoy what she had never experienced because his arms, his touch, promised comfort unimaginable. It was disorienting and vaguely thrilling just the same.

Her shaking lessened and her sniffles diminished. He sat and held her to him, smelling the sweetness of lavender in her hair and thinking her to be a soft, warm, wonderful creature. But how could a mere woman be all of those things? How could a mere woman affect him this way?

It was impossible, he told himself. The Dark Knight was omnipotent, unaffected by the whims of mortal man. And especially not weakened by the feel of a woman… *right?*

Mari-Elle burst into his mind. Thin, dark, coldly handsome. Betrothed at six years of age and married at twenty. He spent thirteen years of his life in a despised marriage, hating the sight of the woman he had married. Hating her because she was an icy, calculating bitch that gave herself to every man who caught her eye. Gaston would have killed them all except there were too many to count. She had no respect for him other than his reputation and station. It was simply her nature.

He assumed most women were like his wife; he even hated the word wife. If they were not cold and ruthless, they were brainless and silly. There was no in-between; there was only black and white to him, as always.

Except for Remington. He did not know quite what to think of her yet, but he knew one thing; she frightened him. And he had never been frightened of anything in his life.

He gradually became aware that she had gone limp against him, her breathing soft and regular. He smiled faintly to realize she had fallen asleep in his arms. Her soft body molded against him like the missing piece of a puzzle and he could feel her sweet warmth radiating against him.

Slowly, he slid back on the bed so that he was leaning against the headboard. Remington sighed ragged in her sleep and snuggled closer to him and he instinctively pulled her tighter. With a long sigh of his own accord, Gaston lounged away the afternoon with the lady of Mt. Holyoak sleeping in his arms.

And he wasn't the least bit distressed about it.

Remington awoke to a gentle shaking. She tried to ignore it, burrowing deeper into the bed, but the shaking was persistent. Dear God, but her bed was warm and comfortable. And it smelled nice, too. Like leather and sandalwood.

… Leather and sandalwood?

Her eyes opened and she found herself staring into white linen. Tanned skin peeked out from beneath the folds of a shirt. She blinked, remembering what had happened and embarrassed to the hilt. Slowly, she sat up and found herself face-to-face with smoky eyes.

He smiled gently. "I am sorry to wake you, madam, but supper will be served soon."

"Supper?" she blinked, smoothing away an errant lock of hair. "How long have I been asleep?"

"A few hours," he said. "You were exhausted."

She put a hand to her face, feeling groggy and her head hurt. She was aware he was looking at her and she fought down a blush.

"I…I do not know what to say, my lord," she said sheepishly. "I feel most foolish for my outburst."

She felt his hand on her hair, stroking it. "No need, angel. I rather enjoyed watching you sleep."

Her eyes snapped to him. "Why do you call me that?"

"Call you what?" He looked confused, and then suddenly realized what she meant. "Angel? Because you remind me of one."

Her brow furrowed faintly. "I remind you of an angel? How do you know? Have you ever seen one?"

"I have," he said firmly. "The moment I saw you crossing the draw-bridge nearly a week ago. I knew that I was gazing into the face of an angel."

He was smiling slightly and she was unsure if he were jesting or not. Perplexed, she slid from his thighs and stood on unsteady feet. Reluctantly, he let her go.

"I apologize again for falling asleep on you," she said quietly. "I have kept you from your duties overlong."

"Look at me," he said quietly.

Hesitantly, her eyes came up and locked with his, and her entire body washed with a warm, languorous feeling. Was he indeed in league with the devil to have this effect on her?

"Do you not believe me when I tell you that you are beautiful?" he asked, his voice like warm honey.

She stared back at him; he obviously wasn't going to let the subject rest without an explanation. Dear God, she had never truly allowed herself to voice her feelings. She wasn't even sure how to start.

"Nay," she whispered.

He blinked, puzzled. "Do you think I would lie to you?"

She shook her head, the look of hurt filling her face again. "Nay, I do not," she gestured lamely, turning away from him. "I…I just do not like hearing it."

"Why in the hell not?" he demanded, raising his voice.

She jumped, spinning around to face him. He put up his hands soothingly. "I am sorry, I did not mean to yell. But why, angel? I would like to tell you what I am thinking, but not if you do not want to hear it."

She looked at him for a moment, long and hard. Then she licked her lips, thinking. "My husband told me I was beautiful all of the time," her voice was barely a whisper, sickened at revealing her innermost terrors. "Especially…especially when he…would couple with me. He used to tell me how beautiful I was as he slapped me senseless."

Gaston was stunned. He stared at her a moment before letting out a long, hissing sigh. "My God, Remington," his voice was hoarse. "I had no idea."

She sat slowly on the silk chair, staring at the cracks in the floor. She curled her legs underneath her bottom, somehow feeling strangely relieved that she had confessed to him. Her courage grew.

"He made love to me hours after Dane's birth," she murmured. "I almost hemorrhaged to death, but no one could stop him. Eudora tried and he almost killed her. That is why she walks with a limp, you know. When my sisters came to live with us, he took fiendish delight in deflowering them one by one. Jasmine was the first, then Rory. Rory gave him a good fight, but she succumbed in the end. Even Skye; he took her when she was eleven."

Gaston closed his eyes tightly to the horrors her disclosure brought to his mind. Dane's small tale did nothing to encompass this disgrace.

Remington rested her chin in her hand. "If he wasn't beating us, he was taking us to bed. Sometimes he would bed three of us in a night. Yet to make up for his cruelty, he would buy us clothes and finery and perfumes. He always thought that made up for the worst of times."

Gaston couldn't imagine the shame she had suffered, all of them had suffered. His gaze was incredibly compassionate as he watched emotions play on her lovely face. After a moment of thought, her eyes came up to him.

"You wanted to know about us, my lord. Now you know."

He shook his head faintly. "I know your husband, Remington. He's an unscrupulous bastard, but I had no idea just how foul the man was."

She shrugged, unwinding her legs and rising. "He's in the Tower now and hopefully he shall rot there. I'd sooner kill myself than allow him back into my life. Back into Dane's life."

"Dane seems remarkably unaffected by all of this," Gaston murmured.

Remington nodded firmly. "He's been spared the brunt of it, thank God. Guy never actually went after him, but Dane had to witness what his father did to us. He is most protective of me, as you have seen."

"He's a good boy," Gaston agreed. "He shall make a fine knight."

Remington hugged herself, rubbing her arms against the chill of the room now that the sun had set. "What about your boy, my lord? How old is he?"

Gaston rose from the bed with a grunt. "Trenton is eight years old, tall and well-built. And smart."

"Like his father, I am sure," Remington said. "And your wife? What is her name?"

His warm exterior deteriorated rapidly. "Mari-Elle. And I do not speak of her."

Remington was shocked at the reprimand. She instantly lowered her gaze uncertainly. "Then I apologize, my lord. I meant no harm."

He wiped his hand across his face, letting out a harsh sigh to regain his composure. "Of course you did not. It's just that…well; do not speak of my wife. I prefer to imagine that she does not exist."

Remington was deeply curious but banked herself. She did not want to provoke the man on an obviously sore subject. "As I prefer to imagine that my husband does not exist. Mayhap they can slip into non-existence together and we can be rid of them."

She was smiling faintly, an innocent remark and nothing more. But he was acutely aware of how true he would like that to be, not simply to be rid of Mari-Elle, but so that he and Remington could become… friends. He wanted Remington for a friend.

"Too bad they did not marry each other," he grinned back.

Remington laughed softly and he was enchanted by the white, straight teeth and bow-shaped mouth. She was absolutely stunning when she smiled.

He had a tremendous amount of work to attend to, but he was reluctant to leave. He liked talking to Remington; he liked the way she made him feel. And he liked the way she smiled.

"I suppose I must go now," he said, but he was not moving for the door. Instead, he was moving for Remington and she was watching him openly. The fear was gone.

"I have ordered roast mutton and venison for supper," she said. "I hope it is to your liking."

"You eat a lot of mutton, do not you?" he asked, jesting with her. "Can I expect a fleece pie for dessert?"

She smiled broadly, her dimples deep. "Sheep is the primary crop of Yorkshire and we eat everything but the coat, my lord. But I will order you up a fleece piece if that is your wish."

He studied her a moment, his gaze softening. "My wish is for you to call me Gaston in private," he said.

She looked surprised, but recovered. "I would be honored, my lo…. Gaston."

He gave her a lop-sided grin. "It will become easier with practice. I shall see you in the dining hall, then."

He moved for the door, leaving her feeling breathless and warm. She had no idea why.

"Can't I call you the Dark Knight?" she asked, still jesting with the light mood.

"No," he said flatly as he reached the door. "I do not like that title."

"You do not?" she was genuinely surprised. "But everyone calls you that."

"Edward started it, and I hated it even then," Gaston said, his hand on the latch. "But there is naught I could do against our king."

She cocked her head at him. "Can I call you the Devil, then? Or Satan's Spawn? Or Fruit of Lucifer's Loins?"

He raised a black eyebrow. "Call me those things and I shall take you over my knee. I am none of them."

"But I am an angel?" she was smirking playfully at him and he found himself swept up by her light, jesting manner.

"Aye, you are that," he said with a vague tug of the corner of his lips. "A saucy wench, but an angel just the same."

He quit the room, leaving Remington feeling as if the weight of the entire realm was lifting from her shoulders.

⬥

"You told him, Remi?" Jasmine asked with disbelief. "Everything?"

Remington, Jasmine, Skye, Charles and Dane were gathered at the small lake near Mt. Holyoak. Charles and Dane were swimming and frolicking in the cool water to stave off the heat while the ladies were lounging underneath the trees several feet away.

Remington fanned herself slowly, her lightweight blue surcoat hiked up around her knees. "I did not tell him everything," she said. "I did not tell him about your babe, Jasmine. He does not need to know that."

"But why did you tell him anything at all?" Jasmine lamented. "He's a stranger."

"He's lord of Mt. Holyoak now and our master," Remington replied, sighing. "But to answer you, I do not know why I told him all that I did. He made me feel comfortable and safe, and I told him. He had promised to protect us, and I suppose I wanted him to know what he was protecting us against."

Jasmine lay back on the grass, her arm resting on her forehead as she gazed up into the old oak tree.

"He was certainly staring at you last night during supper," Jasmine said softly. "Do you suppose he likes you?"

Remington shrugged. "He told me I looked like an angel," she said. "He's not as fearsome as I once thought him to be."

Jasmine sat up. "You did not answer me. Do you think he likes you?"

"It does not matter if he does or not," Remington said firmly. "He has a wife and I have a husband. Besides, I do not want a man. I do not even want the one I have."

Skye looked up from the flower wreath she was weaving. "Speak of the devil and he shall appear."

Her sisters looked over their shoulders in the direction of Mt. Holyoak and were not surprised to see four destriers crossing the field towards them, most recognizably the Dark Knight's charcoal-gray charger.

"Now, I wonder what they are doing here?" Remington said, shading her eyes from the sun. "I thought they were busy building a team house."

Jasmine's eyes riveted to Antonius. "Mayhap it was too hot for them."

The chargers were halted several feet from the ladies and the knights dismounted. The women were surprised to see they wore no armor, merely shirts, breeches and heavy boots. They seemed to shun the tunics and hose so favored by the court men, preferring more sturdy clothing instead. Except for Antonius; he looked like a god in hose and a loose-fitting shirt. Jasmine felt her heart flutter wildly at the sight of him.

Gaston was so large he nearly blotted out the sun as he came upon them. "Good day, ladies."

Remington smiled at him, fanning herself more forcefully. He always seemed to make her hot. "Good day, Sir Gaston. How is your building coming along?"

"Too damn hot," he said, moving underneath the shade. "The men are seeking shelter for the afternoon. May I?"

Remington indicated for him to sit beside her and he did, his big body lowering itself gracefully. Nicolas and Arik crouched near Skye, while Antonius smiled at Jasmine. Remington was amused to see her sister flush madly, yet wary at the same time of the knight's attention.

"I had two men faint on me this morning with this cursed weather, so we decided to call a halt," Gaston said, his gaze moving out to Charles and Dane in the water. "By God, I have not been swimming since I was a lad."

"The water is wonderfully cool," Remington said. "You should refresh yourselves."

Gaston leaned back on his elbow, lying on his side. "I think not for me. But my men are welcome to."

"You are too kind," Arik said drolly. "I am allergic to water."

"How is that possible since your ancestors were Vikings?" Antonius wanted to know. "You should be a natural to water."

"What about you? You come from Rome, for God's sake," Arik returned. "Yet you so much as look at water and you become seasick. You are a pathetic excuse for a Roman."

Antonius smiled. "I would have done fine as a centurion or legionnaire. Just not as a sailor."

"Or a galley slave," Nicolas snorted, drawing soft laughter.

"Centurion," Arik scoffed. "Good Christ, you have lofty dreams. You are nothing more than a commoner."

Antonius thrust his chin up. "I would have married well, then."

Remington was playing with a piece of grass, chuckling at Antonius' expense. Arik focused on her.

"And what of our Celt beauty? Do you swim?" he asked.

Gaston looked at her, noticing she was flushing with the attention. "You are Celt?"

"My mother was born in Ireland," she told him softly. "She claimed to be descended from the Tuatha de Danann."

"The fairy race?" Gaston remarked. "Aye, you could pass for a fairy princess."

Remington was still uncomfortable with his references to her looks. She gazed up at Arik. "I am afraid I must embarrass you gentleman, Sir Arik. I can swim like a fish and I love the water."

"Celt, eh?" Nicolas repeated. "That must be where the wild woman gets her red hair."

Remington smiled at his remark, fiddling with the grass. Silence filled the air for a few moments, though not uncomfortable. Skye held up her flower wreath, pleased with her handiwork, and put it on her head.

"Lovely," Nicolas said. "You look like a wood nymph."

Skye blushed sweetly, displaying dimples like her older sister. "Thank you, my lord."

Nicolas lay back on the grass, lazily, smiling at the young girl. "How old are you, Lady Skye?"

"Fourteen, my lord," she replied, blushing redder by the moment. "I shall be fifteen come Christmas."

Remington put the grass down and leaned back against the tree. "Where is Sir Patrick?"

"Trying to convince your sister to join us," Gaston replied. "She is a stubborn wench."

"She shall not come," Remington said. "The more he pleads, the more resistant she shall be."

Skye stood up and brushed herself off, passing Nicolas a coy glance as she walked away toward the water. Remington was concerned when the young knight rose to follow. Jasmine, too, stood up, followed closely by Antonius. Together, they wandered aimlessly in the general direction of the lake.

With a loud sigh of satisfaction, Arik stretched out on the vacated blanket and closed his eyes with contentment. "Thank God they've gone. Now I can get some sleep."

Gaston eyed his second, his gaze moving to Remington. He was puzzled to see her face awash with distress as she anxiously followed her sister's movements.

"What's wrong?" he asked softly.

Remington tore her gaze away and glanced down at him. "Nothing, my lord," she looked back to Jasmine and Skye.

Gaston accepted her answer and dug into the basket next to her, drawing forth a large green apple. He bit into it with gusto, chewing loudly as his gaze drifted out over the green countryside. He was about to comment on it when he looked up at Remington and saw that she was in the same stiff position as she had been moments earlier. He took another large bite of the apple and tossed it aside, rising to his feet.

"Walk with me," he said to Remington.

She jerked her head up to him. "I...uh, where?"

He reached down and pulled her to her feet. When she tried to disengage her hands from his, he firmly took one and tucked it into the crook of his arm. Silently, he began to walk the edges of the lake, away from the others.

"Why are you looking at my men like that?" he asked.

"Like what?" she asked innocently, though she was looking back over her shoulder.

"Like they are going to ravish your sisters," he said. "Honestly, Remi, they're perfectly safe with my knights."

"It's just that...you called me Remi?"

He blinked at the total change of subject, seeing that she was looking up at him with wide eyes. "That's your name, isn't it?"

"Aye, it is," she nodded slowly. "But you have never used it."

He shrugged. "I have heard your sisters call you by it," he said. "I won't use the name if it offends you."

"Nay, it does not," she said quickly, offering him a small smile. "You may call me Remi if you want to."

"I want to," he looked down his nose at her, but there was a faint smile on his lips. "Now answer my question. Why are you so worried?"

He was so tall she had to crane her neck sharply to look him in the face. "I would be honest with you, then," she said quietly. "As I told you last night, my sisters are...compromised, thanks to my husband. I do not want them being hurt."

"Hurt by what?" he wanted to know.

"Hurt by men who are looking for virgins to wed," she snapped softly. "They are not maidens."

He understood, sort of. "I am sure Antonius and Nicolas can deal with that fact."

She stopped, facing off against him. "Gaston, purity of a bride is very important to a prospective husband. I will not allow your men to hurt my sisters because they fell victim to something beyond their control. But more importantly, if they are not looking for a wife, I do not want them taking advantage of my sisters. Being a whore to one man is quite enough."

He crossed his massive arms in front of his broad chest, arms as thick around as she was. "So what would you have me do? Find out their intentions before I allow them to pursue your sisters? That is a little overbearing, do not you think?"

"Nay, I do not," Remington said hotly. "You just do not understand."

She spun away from him but he grabbed her, pulling her back against him. For a brief second she couldn't breathe as his eyes bore down into her and her body went even hotter than it already was. Pressed against his chest, she wondered why her limbs tingled painfully and she tried to pull away, but he would not let her.

"I understand you are overprotective of your sisters," he said, his voice a growl. "You must allow them to live their own lives, Remi. They'll not always have you around to champion them."

"I must protect them," she insisted, a look of desperation filling her eyes. "I have always tried to protect them but I am not always successful. Gaston, I must do what I can."

He fully understood her fears now. She was entirely helpless against her husband and she hated herself for it. His grip on her wrists loosened and he stroked the backs of her silky hands.

"Very well, angel," he said softly. "I shall talk to my knights and find out what their intentions might be."

"Thank you," she was electrified by his gentle caressing. She'd never experienced anything so sweet, as small a gesture as it might be.

He gazed into her sea-crystal eyes, his expression soft. "Anything for you. Anything at all."

Her cheeks flushed and he laughed softly, releasing her hands but again tucking one into his elbow.

A destrier burst through the undergrowth on the other side of the lake and Patrick rode into view. It took Remington a moment to realize Rory was astride behind him.

"Well...would you look at that?" she said with surprise. "He brought her."

Gaston watched the chestnut destrier round the lake. "Patrick is quite convincing when he puts his mind to it. Lady Rory did not stand a chance."

"Is that so?" Remington slanted an arrogant gaze at him. "Rory is fairly persuasive when she wants to be, as well. If she did not want to come, nothing he could have said would have convinced her."

"Ah, but Rory relies on brute strength to accomplish her goals," Gaston said. "Patrick relies on his wits."

Remington's mouth opened in outrage. "Are you saying my sister is stupid?"

"Not at all," Gaston said steadily, passing her an amused glance from the corner of his eye. "The fact that she had agreed to come with Patrick proves that she has some intelligence."

Remington put her hands on her hips. "You border on slander, Dark Knight."

He looked at her fully. "I told you not to call me that."

She lifted her chin defiantly, but there was a good deal of humor to it. "My apologies, oh Devil's Spawn."

He put his hands on his hips, raising a disapproving eyebrow at her. "You saucy bit of baggage. I ought to blister your backside this instant."

Her defiant stance brown down in an instant and she actually laughed at him, loudly. He raised both eyebrows, although his lips were twitching. "You think it funny, do you?"

Her eyes were bright at him. "I think you are funny, my lord."

"I am not," he mumbled, feigning irritation.

"Aye, you are and you are not even aware of it," she let her gaze linger a moment longer before focusing back on her sister. "I would greet Rory, with your permission."

"By all means," he let her go.

He made his way back to Arik, still lying underneath the tree. He picked another apple from the basket and leaned back against the trunk of the ancient oak to enjoy it, his gaze never leaving Remington as she spoke animatedly to her sister.

"You are interested in Lady Stoneley," Arik mumbled, his eyes closed.

"She is pleasant enough conversation," Gaston replied.

Arik snorted, brushing a fly on his face. "Gaston, you have smiled more in the past few days than I have ever known you to smile in your life. And you are smiling at her. And the fact that we are here, resting under a tree when there is much work to be done, only reinforces my suspicions."

Gaston munched on the apple, ignoring his only friend. Arik opened one eye. "I do not blame you, though. She's incredible."

Gaston continued to ignore him soundly, chewing on the last of the core and throwing it away. "Are we prepared for Lord Brimley on the morrow?"

"Aye," Arik replied. "Being the closest baron, we received an answer from him the same day we sent the missive. He should be arriving by noon tomorrow."

"Good," Gaston said. "Hopefully the meeting with Brimley will establish a favorable climate for the rest of our talks. I want these meetings to be a mutual exchange of information, not a list of threats."

Arik shrugged and rolled over onto his side. "'Twill be interesting to see what transpires, my lord."

On the other side of the small lake, Remington screamed with laughter as Charles and Dane splashed at her. He could see Rory shaking her fists at the young men. It took him a moment to realize that Antonius and Jasmine were missing.

"Damn," he muttered, pushing himself off the tree. "Where's Antonius?"

Arik looked about weakly. "I do not know," he replied. "But look; Nicolas and Rory are standing within a few feet of each other and have yet to raise their voices. Amazing."

"Not really when you consider they spent the night together." Gaston was concerned regarding the whereabouts of his knight and the lady. "I guessed they would either kill each other or emerge on pleasant terms. I am pleased it was the latter."

Gaston wandered out from underneath the tree, his trained eyes roving the little dell they were in. Much to his relief, he saw Antonius and Jasmine sitting under a tree on the crest of a small rise not too far away and he scratched his head, irritated with himself for jumping to conclusions.

But truth was, he did not care what his men did on their own time. He was not a meddler; the fact of the matter was he did not want Remington to be angry with him should something unfavorable happen to her sister.

With a disgusted shake of his head, he turned back for Arik and the tree, wondering what other food was in the basket.

Remington suddenly let out a loud scream and he whirled, his body instinctively preparing for battle when he saw that she had gotten too close to the edge of the lake and Charles had pulled her in. He relaxed, smiling faintly as he watched her sputter and attempt to climb out of the lake. With every step she took, her young cousin would pull her further out into the water. Dane yelled happily in his cousin's favor.

Remington was up to her waist when she grabbed hold of Charles' fair head and dunked him under the water. He came up, sputtering and grabbed her before she could escape. Remington found herself completely submerged by her cousin and son, but not before Rory and Skye jumped in to the rescue. Within seconds, the water was churning with a good-natured family brawl.

"You are smiling again," Arik stood next to Gaston, watching the goings-on.

Gaston made sure his smile vanished; truthfully, he had not realized he was grinning. He disregarded Arik's presence and walked to the edge of the lake, watching Remington and Rory obliterate Charles. He was a strong young lad but no match against the two of them. Skye was hauling Dane from the water just as Charles conceded defeat.

"Mercy, Mercy, I beg you," he pleaded.

Rory dunked his head under once more and quickly pulled him back up. "Swear on the Bible that Remington and I are the most powerful and cleverest women in the realm. Swear it."

"I do," Charles declared in mock fear. "You are the most powerful, brutal wenches in all of England."

"And because we are so powerful, we are also infinitely merciful and we shall spare you any further drowning," Remington said, sloshing into the shallow water. Her dress was clinging to her like the skin of a grape; drawing looks of distinct interest from Patrick and Arik.

Gaston saw the looks and was seized with a tremendous sense of possessiveness. The woman wasn't his in the least but he was swept with the urge to cover her from lustful eyes, including his own. He absolutely agreed with his knights' silent opinions.

He went back to the tree and snatched up the blanket that lay upon the ground. Remington had emerged from the lake like Venus, pulling at her wet surcoat and laughing with her sisters when he came up upon her and threw the blanket around her body.

"What...what are you doing?" she asked as he wrapped her tighter than a babe in swaddling.

"You shall catch a chill," he mumbled.

"In this heat?" she shook her head.

He wasn't listening to her. He turned to his men. "Mount up. We return."

The gaiety of the mood was quickly dulled by his abrupt manner and sharp orders. Remington watched, puzzled, as his knights did as they were told. Patrick even took Rory with him, mounting her wet body behind his and smiling at her when she mumbled something in his ear.

Skye, Charles and Dane were already trekking up the small incline away from the lake, turning to the path that led back to Mt. Holyoak. Nicolas, on his huge charger, rode several paces behind them. Antonius did not mount his destrier as ordered; instead, he and Jasmine began to walk back to the keep at a leisurely pace. It would seem the party was over.

Remington was irritated. Why did he disband their picnic so abruptly? His manner was curt and harsh and she received a sharp impression that the Dark Knight had somehow returned, but she had no idea why.

He was fumbling with his destrier several feet away and she tossed the blanket off, folding it carefully. He did not acknowledge her in any way as she put the blanket over her arm and waited politely for him. After a minute or so, she began to feel distinctly ignored and she was shocked to realize she was actually hurt. What had she done to make his attitude change so quickly? Moreover, why should she care about his attitude toward her? Had the man lulled her into a false sense of security by being kind to her, kind enough so that she would reveal her darkest secrets, and now he was bored with her?

Hot humiliation shot through her. Damn him. Well, she would not be treated like the day's entertainment, forgotten after the newness had passed. Quickly, she turned and began to walk back toward Mt. Holyoak alone.

She had just entered the trees when he rode up beside her.

"Do not you want to ride? It's terribly hot to walk," he commented.

"No, thank you, my lord," she said stiffly, wishing he would go away.

The dress was drying but it still clung to her skin, and his eyes roved over the delicious curve of her delicate shoulders. With the horse still moving, he dismounted with the ease of a gymnast and resumed walking beside her. He felt her irritation but had no idea why she was annoyed.

They walked in silence the entire way back. Remington refused to look at him or even acknowledge his presence. They trekked up the road to the keep and were about to cross the bridge when he stopped her.

"Nay," he said quietly. "Wait a moment."

She looked up at him, annoyed all over again, when she saw he was looking into the outer bailey. The soldiers were lined up, waiting for the next wet woman to run the gauntlet. Between Rory and Skye, they had quite a show and they waited with anticipation for the grandest lady of all to see if she, too, was wet. It was the best entertainment they had seen in a long while.

Gaston's jaw ticked as he took the blanket from Remington's arm and wrapped her gently in it, his eyes never leaving the soldiers.

"Wait here a moment," he said, his voice low.

Curious, Remington did as she was asked and watched him cross the drawbridge with loud, deliberate steps. By the time he was over the bridge and passing under the portcullis, the men saw him coming and were scrambling to disband.

Gaston stopped as soon as he passed under the archway, his hands on his great hips. Remington couldn't see his face, but she could see the soldiers scattering as if the devil had just appeared and demanded their souls.

It was truly astonishing; he had not said a word yet hundreds of soldiers had leapt to do his bidding in a panicked rush. Remington was stunned at what had happened, watching him with wide-open eyes as he returned to her.

"What...what happened?" she asked.

"Nothing," he replied, taking her arm underneath the blanket.

Perplexed, she allowed him to lead her across the drawbridge and into a now-vacated bailey.

Dinner was a festive occasion that night. A band of traveling minstrels had sought shelter for the night and began providing music and dancing at an early hour. The knights entered the hall listening to the music, pleased with the welcome addition to their meal.

Remington and her sisters did not eat with the men, as had become custom ever since their arrival. Instead they stood back in the shadows and made sure no man wanted for anything. The servants were very busy with the room full of knights and the roast pork was a huge success. Remington had specifically ordered two fat pigs killed because she thought Gaston might be sick of mutton.

She watched him from her perch in the corner, studying his profile. If she were forced to admit it, she would have confessed the man to be incredibly handsome. There was a tremendous sensuality to him, as well, something that made her go weak every time he looked at her, but she had no idea that it was his sex appeal that made her limp. She thought it was her healthy fear of the man and his reputation.

But she did not think of men in terms of handsome. They were simply men, a necessary evil.

The minstrels were a lively group of six older men, very accomplished at their art. They were traveling to Raby Castle, just east of Durham, for the Earl of Hamsterley's birthday celebration at the earl's request. As the meal progressed, they sang and performed several bawdy skits, much to the delight of the knights.

Remington ignored the ribald jokes as she perused the room, making sure all was running smoothly. At one point, however, she drew the attention of the loudest minstrel of all and he made a dash for her.

"Ah," he exclaimed loudly. "The most beautiful serving wench in all the land."

Remington saw him coming and tried to escape him, but he happily captured her arm and pulled her towards the center of the room.

"Look what I have captured," he crowed with delight. "The goddess Aphrodite in the flesh."

The knights were well into their wine and began chanting "flesh, flesh," and banging their tankards against the table.

The minstrel wasn't trying to be deliberately cruel or embarrassing, merely lively. But Remington was mortified at the attention.

"She is lovely, is she not?" he asked gaily and was greeted by a roar of approval. He then turned to Remington. "Can you dance, lass? Dance with me."

Remington was having a terrible attack of nerves. She shook her head firmly and tried to pull away from him, but he held her tight. Yet her mortification was of a good-humored sort; she wasn't truly panicked. But she wished terribly that the man would let her go.

"Aye, you can," the minstrel encouraged her loudly, supported by the cheers from the knights. "Dance with me."

She was a bright shade of red, even more so when the minstrel handed his mandolin to his comrade and took her in his arms. She stiffened; her panic was quickly becoming real at the closeness of his body.

"I do not want to dance," she begged in a whisper. "Please let me go."

Again, the man was not trying to be cruel. He smiled encouragingly at her. "Just once around the floor, lass, and I shall leave you be. I promise."

She did not want to do it; she did not want to be held close to him. Visions of drunken Guy popped into her head, demanding the same thing of her. *Dance with me,* he would slur. *But take your surcoat off first so that I might feel your nakedness.*

She was on the verge of panic, the verge of tears as the minstrel tried to pull her stiff body into a comfortable position. But suddenly there was a massive body next to them, as tall as he was wide, and the minstrel's arms were removed.

Gaston was between them, facing the musician. "Lady Stoneley does not wish to dance, artisan. Choose another."

The minstrel shrugged good-naturedly and spied another woman who would do just as well. Gaston took Remington by the arm and quickly escorted her to the edges of the room.

He could feel her shaking terribly in his grip as he leaned her against the wall. His eyes were gentle.

"He meant no harm," he said quietly. "Are you very well?"

She nodded, trying desperately to get a grip on herself. "Fine, my lord. Thank you for intervening."

"My pleasure," he said softly.

He moved back to his men, resuming his seat and leaving Remington alone to calm her breathing. She was so embarrassed and shaken that all she wanted to do was throw up and cry, in that order. But she would not allow her emotions to grip her so completely, and she forced herself to re-focus on her duties in the hall.

The rest of the evening was pleasant and uneventful. She knew how badly Dane and Charles wanted to attend the meal with the knights, but she would not allow them to mingle with the warriors. She was terrified that the young boys would be in danger around the drinking, hardened men and she had no desire to see them hurt. As much as they hated it, she confined them to their rooms but she was convinced it was for the best. Besides, as male relatives to a prisoner of the crown, she felt them to be particularly vulnerable in the presence of the Dark Knight and his men.

She was fully aware of Gaston's vows to protect her and her son, yet she did not trust him. It wasn't him personally, but simply more her nature. She did not trust any man's word, no matter who it was. Besides; the Dark Knight had betrayed his king to fight with the usurper. Mayhap the man's word was as rotten as a corpse.

He confused her tremendously. His reputation was sinister, yet the man she had grown to know over the past few days was anything but. True, he could strike fear into the heart of men with a mere look, but he had been nothing but gentle and chivalrous to her. The paradox was enough to keep her awake nights.

CHAPTER SEVEN

The next day dawned bright and hot as expected. The stonemasons were at work early on the troop house and Remington awoke to sounds of labor in the bailey.

She lay in bed a moment, slowly awakening, realizing that she had slept well and her mood was already light. It had been a long time since she had woken up thinking forward to the day ahead with pleasure.

She took a quick bath with scented water, drying herself vigorously and brushing her hair until it crackled. Donning a fresh surcoat of pale green satin, short sleeved and with a square neck embroidered in gold, she moved to Dane's room to awaken her son.

But Dane was already awake. In fact, he was gone and Remington was pleased that her son was so industrious this day as to rise before her and see to his small chores. With that in mind, Remington bustled on her way with a whistle on her lips.

The day was looking brighter already.

Dane was up, very well. He had been up before the sun rose and had proceeded to the lake to catch fish. He loved to catch fish, for no other reason than he felt a sense of accomplishment. Armed with a small pole Oleg had helped him fashion, he had already caught two fish when he was joined by another prospective fisherman.

Gaston crouched down next to him, silently watching the surface of the water. The bugs were rampant in the humidity, swarming atop the water. He peered into Dane's bucket.

"Two fish already," he remarked. "Excellent. By noon you should have caught enough fish to feed my entire army."

Dane grinned. "There aren't that many fish in this lake."

Gaston lifted his eyebrows. "Oh, I would not say that. 'Tis a big lake."

Dane glanced at him shyly before returning to his task. Gaston watched the boy a moment, thinking of his own son whom he had not seen in a year.

He had seen Dane leaving the fortress at sunrise, heading for the lake. Curious, he had watched the boy for some time from the top of the tower, the little dot next to a pool of blue. His own heart ached for the simple things in life, the things he had never enjoyed because of his profession. True, he had fished as a boy, but his life was dedicated to his training. Always his training.

His whole life had been dedicated to kings and battles. He'd never longed for anything else because he enjoyed his work. Yet ever since he arrived at Mt. Holyoak, he had experienced a strange sense of emptiness, as if there were more to life than war and politics. Being a soldier most of his life, he had no idea what "more" might be.

Seeing Dane retreating to the peace of the lake under the rising sun gave him his very first inkling that, mayhap, he was not as content as he had originally thought.

"Do you come here often?" he asked the boy.

Dane nodded. "Almost every day in the summer. In the winter it is too cold, and the fish do not bite."

Gaston nodded in understanding. "By God, I cannot remember the last time I fished. I must have been a lad, just a bit older than you."

"Did you fish with your father?" Dane asked.

Gaston drew in a thoughtful breath. "Nay, I cannot remember ever fishing with my father. He was a very busy man."

"My father never fished with me, either," Dane said, playing with his line. "He said it wasn't a man's sport."

Gaston sat down on the grass, resting his arm on his bent knee. "I would not agree with that."

Dane was pleased to hear that. He sat silently for a few moments, a thousand thoughts running about his busy head. "How did you get to be so big?"

Gaston grinned in a rare gesture. "I was born tall, I suppose. But I built my strength through years of practice and training."

Dane turned to look at him with wide-eyed innocence. "You are as wide as a door. Do you eat a lot, too?"

He shrugged. "I eat enough."

Dane was still watching him intently, gazing at legs bigger than he was. "Why do they call you the Dark Knight?"

Gaston's smile faded as he plucked a piece of grass. "Because I always dress in black, I would guess. Mayhap I remind them of death. People will call you what they will and there is naught you can do about their whims."

"I heard some of our men-at-arms say that you were the devil's friend," Dane said. "Are you?"

Gaston's brow furrowed. "Hardly, Dane. Do not believe everything you hear. Make your own judgments, lad."

Dane absorbed his words, turning back to his fishing. His thoughts were coming faster than his mouth could express them, typical for a seven-year-old boy.

"I am glad you are staying here," he said after a moment.

"Will you leave when my father returns?"

Gaston thought on his careful reply. "Your father is a prisoner, Dane. Do you know what that means?"

Dane nodded solemnly. "He's in jail."

"Correct, he is," Gaston said. "And as long as Henry is our king, I do not believe that your father will ever return. Does this distress you?"

Dane pursed his lips in thought. "My father wasn't very nice. I like you better. Will you stay here forever, then?"

Gaston gazed at the impish face, at Remington's eyes. "I would like to, yes."

"But what about me and my mother? Will you let us stay here with you?" he asked.

"If you would like to, I would be happy to have you stay," Gaston said evenly. *I would like you to be mine.*

Dane's brows drew together distressfully as he watched his line bob over the water. The more he stared, the more disturbed he became. Gaston tossed aside the blade of grass he was toying with and sat up.

"What's the matter? Why do you look like that?" he asked.

Dane eyed Gaston hesitantly. "I…I wish you were my father. Am I bad for thinking that?"

Gaston's heart went out to the little boy. He reached out a hand and put it on the sandy head, covering it completely. "Nay, lad, you are not bad. And I am flattered."

"But you already have a son," Dane said sadly.

Gaston tousled his hair. "A man can never have too many sons. I shall tell you what; we can pretend, can't we? You can pretend that I am your father, and I shall pretend that you are my son. It will be our secret. Very well?"

"A knight's secret," Dane said eagerly.

"Exactly," Gaston replied, standing up. "A secret between men."

Dane grinned openly at him. "I won't even tell my mother."

"Good," Gaston said with a sharp nod, his ache for Trenton somehow eased. "Now, I must be going. Do not stay out here too much longer; it is already growing grossly hot."

"I won't," Dane promised.

Gaston gave the lad a wink and trudged off across the grass, back toward the keep. Dane watched him go, complete adoration shining in his young eyes.

The fatherless boy and the boyless father had a secret.

⁂

Remington met Gaston in the outer bailey. His heart jumped at the sight of her in the pale green surcoat, showing off her marvelous figure. By God, if she wasn't a lovely sight. But her beautiful face was creased with distress.

"Have you seen Dane?" she asked. "No one seems to know where he is and…."

He put up a hand. "He is down at the lake, fishing. I have just come from him."

She visibly relaxed. "Thank God. I was about to launch a search party."

"No need, madam," he took her arm gently and began to walk with her back toward the castle. "He likes to fish, does not he?"

"And why not?" she craned her neck to look at him. "It's peaceful and serene, away from the chaos and horrors of Mt. Holyoak. It is his escape and I encourage it."

Gaston was acutely aware of the stares from his soldiers around them and he felt himself bristle, but maintained his outward calm. "I will have Arik make him a better pole. The man is a master craftsman."

She smiled. "That would be sweet. His birthday is coming in August, you know. It would be a wonderful present."

"Done, then," Gaston said, wanting to get her inside and away from lustful stares. Arik's words suddenly rang true; what would happen to her if there were indeed a thousand soldiers lusting after her every move? Gaston could see a bloodbath coming, for he knew he would protect her at all costs. But the thought of sending her away tore at him.

"Did you enjoy the pork last night?" Remington broke into his thoughts. "I thought you might enjoy the change."

He glanced at her with a half-smile. "I did indeed. You are highly perceptive."

"I am glad," she said, and then chuckled. "Because the cook informed me this morning that we have nearly three hundred pounds of pork left that must be eaten within the next day or it will go bad. I hope you like pork a great deal."

He snorted, amused. "Look around you, Remi. I have six hundred soldiers that will guarantee the pork will be eaten."

"You should see the kitchen," Remington explained softly, smiling. "There is so much pork it looks as if a pig exploded."

His grip on her elbow tightened as he chuckled. "As long as it does not smell like a sty, I will tolerate a pig explosion. But next time, let's only slaughter one pig, shall we?"

She shrugged. "I thought your men would eat more than they did. Their appetites were disappointing."

"'Tis not unusual in this heat," he remarked, casting her a glance. "I did not see you eat. In fact, you have yet to dine with my knights and me. Why is that?"

She met his gaze. "Because I thought you would prefer the company of your men, my lord. I am content to make sure your meals run smoothly."

They paused at the doorway to the castle, looking at each other. Gaston scratched his chin thoughtfully.

"You will dine with us tonight, Lady Remington," he said. "You and your son. Let the servants take care of the running of the meal."

Remington smiled slowly. "Is that an order or a request?"

He cocked an imperious eyebrow. "Take it as you wish. Only I expect to see you by my side tonight."

Her smile broadened, her dimples deepening and his heart fluttered against his ribs. "'Twould be an honor, my lord."

He held her eyes a moment, his smoky eyes openly caressing her. She was so unlike any woman he had ever met, but he hastened to change the subject. The mood was growing far too warm and making him vastly uncomfortable. Uncomfortable because he had never before had feelings of this magnitude.

"Where is your husband's cousin?" he asked. "I have hardly seen the boy."

Remington pointed to the only tower on the castle of Mt. Holyoak, a massive cylinder six stories high. "He keeps a room in the tower, my lord, where he likes to experiment. He spends most of his days up there."

"Experiment? With what?" Gaston strained his eyes against the bright sun.

"As you have seen, my husband is an avid reader and has collected quite a bit of material, including Arabic treatises that delve into alchemy and other sciences," she folded her white hands in front of her, gazing into his face with a look that made him sweat. "Charles is highly intelligent and he likes to experiment with the recipes in the books."

He wondered if she knew how much her eyes affected him. "Has he discovered anything useful?"

She smiled and shook her head. "Not yet. But he will, I am sure."

Nicolas suddenly burst out of the castle door, his eyes wide. He was dressed in most of his armor, his helm on his head. But the strangest phenomenon was occurring; it was as if his helm were raining on his head, for his entire face was wet, dripping onto his chest armor. He looked right at Remington.

"Where is your sister?" he demanded.

Gaston spoke before she could answer. "You will not use that tone with her. Ever."

Nicolas passed a glance at his cousin, his cheeks flushing. "My apologies. Might you know where Lady Rory is, my lady?"

Remington was looking at him with morbid curiosity; the water running from his helmet glistened suspiciously. "I have not seen her this morn. What is the matter with your helm, Sir Nicolas?"

His eyes widened as if he had just been challenged. Then the helm came off and Remington was astounded to see great clumps of white pieces on his head, intermingled with yellow slime.

"She put eggs in my helm, my lady, and I failed to see them until it was too late," he said with controlled anger. "Might you have any idea where to find her?"

Remington should have been mortified to the bone. But, instead, laughter was the first thing that popped into her mouth. She tried to control her giggles, but she couldn't. Within seconds she was laughing hysterically.

Gaston eyed his knight critically. "Go wash that stuff off."

Remington screamed louder when Nicolas plopped his helmet back on his head, smashing the eggs further. "It is not funny," Nicolas shot back, then eyed Gaston quickly, adding: "My lady."

She opened her mouth to apologize but was seized with hysterical giggles again and weakly grasped Gaston for support. Nicolas looked absolutely ridiculous.

"I am sorry, Sir Nicolas, truly," she sputtered. "How do you know Rory did it?"

"Who else?" Nicolas asked loudly. "She is sorely tempting fate, my lady, for one of these days I shall do more than welt her bottom."

Remington's laughter diminished. "Like what? She can fight as well as you can, my lord. I would not want to challenge her in a fight."

Gaston interrupted his cousin's anger. "Go clean yourself up, I said. Get out of here," his manner was curt and Nicolas obeyed grudgingly. He watched his cousin move out across the inner bailey a moment before turning to Remington. "Do you know where your sister might be?"

Remington's laughter was gone at his expression. "I…nay, I do not. Surely you are not going to punish her?"

His eyes turned back to her, like hard steel. "She obviously did not listen to you when you told her no more pranks. Mayhap she will listen to me."

Remington's eyes widened. "What are you going to do to her?"

"That is not of your affair, madam. Kindly tell me where to find Lady Rory," he was cold and professional.

A creeping fear filled her. "I told you I do not know where she is. But if I did, I would not tell you."

His gaze flickered at the defiance. "I shall find her myself, then. Return inside, Lady Stoneley."

She met his hard gaze with a cold look of her own, turning on her heel and marching into the coolness of the structure.

Gaston did not move a moment, listening to her boot falls fade. He suspected she would turn the castle inside out until she found her sister and he slowly eased himself after her, taking refuge in the solar for the time being.

He would not have to lift a finger to find Lady Rory. Her sister would do the work for him.

The noon hour approached and Remington had not done what she was supposed to do. Irritated, Gaston donned all of his armor and went back out into the heat of the day to involve himself in the final aspects of the team house and sub-level repairs. Moreover, he was expecting Lord Brimley of Crayke Castle and he wanted to be alerted to the man's approach.

Arik and Antonius had the soldiers working like slaves, knowing that Gaston wanted the improvements completed before the week was out. Nicolas and Patrick were supervising below ground level with a few other senior knights, while the rest of his knight corps had prepared the castle for Lord Brimley's arrival. It was a chaotic organization at its very best.

As expected, Lord Brimley and a force of about one hundred men were sighted on the horizon in the early afternoon. Shouts abounded on the wall as Gaston and Arik moved to secure a view for themselves. High on the wall, they could indeed see the approach. In fact, Mt. Holyoak was so strategically placed that nearly every spot on the wall had an unimpeded 300-degree view; the only portion blocked being the point where the castle itself stood. On a clear day, Gaston mused that one could see all the way to Flanders.

With Arik, Antonius and Patrick by his side, Gaston moved to greet the baron.

Lord Brimley was an older man with white hair and a well-manicured white moustache. His sons, Walter and Clive, were average-looking men of good intelligence who fought for Richard. Gaston knew of the men vaguely but little beyond that.

Lord Brimley and his sons left their small army encamped at the foot of the rise and rode alone to the drawbridge. Gaston stood in the middle of the outer bailey, his arms folded across his chest, as they rode into the keep. He was the first man to speak.

"Lord Brimley, I presume?" he asked in a deep baritone.

Brimley wore armor but no helmet; his hair was perfectly combed. His sons, too, wore no helms and eyed the Dark Knight with veiled contempt.

"You are correct, sir," Brimley replied, his manner stiff but not hostile.

"I am Sir Gaston de Russe," Gaston said formally. "'Twas I who requested your presence on behalf of our illustrious king, Henry. We have much to discuss, my lord, if you would kindly dismount."

Squires were hovering in the shadows waiting to take the horses as the three men warily dismounted. Lord Brimley's eyes scanned the interior of the keep.

"Might I ask what has been done with Lord Guy's family?" he asked.

"They are here, my lord, safe," Gaston replied. He was an excellent judge of character and sensed no hostility from the man, merely caution. He seemed to have a noble face and carried himself well.

Brimley cleared his throat, removing his leather gloves. "Are they part of the bargain, sir?"

Gaston looked at him a moment. "I do not understand, my lord. What bargain?"

Lord Brimley studied Gaston a moment. "The castle. Do they come with the castle as fixtures or are they prisoners of the crown as well?"

"They are not prisoners, my lord," Gaston replied evenly. "I have made them welcome."

Brimley walked towards Gaston, slow, deliberate steps, yet not provocative. He looked extremely concerned in a fatherly sort of way, his brow furrowed. He glanced at his sons a moment before turning back to Gaston.

"Before we go any further, my lord, I would ask you one thing," he said respectfully. "If Sir Guy's family are not prisoners as you say they are not, then I should like to take them with me when I leave. I would offer them safe haven in my fortress rather than leave them here with Henry's guard dog."

Had the man delivered the message in anything other than an even, polite tone, Gaston would have taken tremendous offense. Yet he could see that the man was genuinely concerned for Remington and her brood. He was surprised.

"They are quite safe here, my lord, I assure you," he replied. "I see no reason to displace them."

Brimley let out a sharp sigh, the only outward sign of irritation. His leather gloves slapped at his thigh. "Do not misunderstand me, Sir Gaston. I harbor no love for Sir Guy, but Lady Remington's father was a friend of mine. I must be frank with you and tell you that I am vastly uncomfortable with four young women in a nest of soldiers. They have suff... that is to say; my wife and daughter would take good care of them. And they would be away from this tremendous war machine."

Gaston observed the man intently. "You are correct when you say they have suffered. But they are safe now and I swear to you on my oath as a knight that no harm has, or will come, to them. They are perfectly safe remaining here at Mt. Holyoak."

Brimley peered at Gaston curiously, surprised the man knew of Sir Guy's cruelty. Or was it possible that they were not speaking of the same thing? He was confused a moment, trying to sort out his train of thought. He very much wanted to take Lady Remington and her sisters away from Mt. Holyoak now that it was occupied, but the Dark One did not seem eager to be rid of them.

Was he, perchance, as deviant as their predecessor?

Gaston watched the man's neck flush red and anticipated the man's thoughts. In faith, he was greatly surprised to see such concern for women. And obviously, Lord Brimley knew of the atrocities that had been committed. Was Remington's secret not such a secret, after all?

Lord Brimley looked up to try another approach when his eye caught something over Gaston's shoulder. In fact, his sons turned their attention for the castle door and Gaston's head snapped around. He knew before he even looked that Remington had made an appearance.

Her expression was most welcoming as she crossed the courtyard towards them. He was livid that she was interfering in his business, yet with the same thought he knew he had not told her that she was to stay away.

"Lord Brimley. What a surprise," she said graciously, offering her hand to the old man. "I did not know you were coming."

The baron took her hand and kissed it sweetly. "My lady, you grow more beautiful by the hour. Surely the angels are jealous."

She blushed prettily; Remington was very polished in her feminine skills, in spite of everything. Her gaze moved beyond the aged baron to his sons.

"Greetings Walter, Clive," she said pleasantly. "I am glad to see you looking well and whole."

Gaston carefully analyzed his reaction when the men responded openly to Remington's charm; jealousy filled him like a black tide, washing into every fiber of his body. Had he not been paying attention to it, he most likely would have run amuck and speared them all with his great broadsword in a fit of rage. As it was, he was somewhat prepared for his reaction, for he had had a similar experience once before. It was an amazing, frightening thing and he found himself swallowing hard, trying to fight it down like St. George battling the fearsome dragon.

Walter had Remington by the hand, speaking pleasantly to her as his brother stood by like an eager dog. Gaston's stomach tightened into knots.

"We have business to attend to," he mumbled to Lord Brimley, then raised his voice to Remington. "My lady, if you will excuse us, please?"

It had taken tremendous control to utter that sentence without rushing to her and snatching her hand from that of the knights'.

Remington removed her own hand, thankfully, and smiled at Gaston. "Of course, my lord. My apologies for detaining you."

His gaze lingered on her for a moment. She looked sweet and radiant, not at all like the defiant woman he had parted ways with earlier. He wondered if the show was for his benefit alone; mayhap she was planning sneaking Rory out of the castle while he was occupied.

He suddenly did not care if she was or not. For the first time in his life, he felt the urge to take a woman in his arms. Jolted by the urge, he tore himself away from her and preceded his guests into the castle.

Remington followed with Clive, going so far as to make sure the men were settled comfortably in the large solar and ordering refreshments. She was the consummate chatelaine, poised and perfect and beautiful.

She passed by him, laughing pleasantly at a comment from Clive when he reached out and grabbed her arm gently. He was seated in a great high-back chair and Remington bumped up against his massive arm, smiling expectantly at him. They were nearly on the same level.

"Lord Brimley expressed concern for your welfare," he said. "He seems to feel that you are threatened here at Mt. Holyoak surrounded by my soldiers. Do you feel threatened?"

Remington looked surprised. She looked to Lord Brimley. "Surely not, my lord. Sir Gaston and his men have been most chivalrous."

Brimley looked flustered and cleared his throat. "Truly I have only been thinking of your welfare, my lady. I proposed to take you and your sisters back with me to Crayke simply to keep you from underfoot with so many soldiers about. I meant no offense."

Remington did not realize she was holding Gaston's hand, although he had never been more acutely aware of anything in his life. "As much as I appreciate your concern, I am quite content to remain here at Mt. Holyoak," she said. "However, Rory is another matter. She is most distressed with recent events and has been difficult to deal with. Mayhap you could take Rory back to Crayke Castle for a time, at least until she gathers her wits."

Gaston groaned inwardly; the sweet, innocent expression was indeed a façade. She had succeeded in throwing him off his guard and now was publicly saving Rory from his wrath. By sending her off with Brimley, she would escape his punishment. God damn, if she wasn't a clever opportunist.

"Just Rory? How are Jasmine and Skye faring?" Brimley wanted to know.

"Well, my lord, well," Remington said. In other words, they were not in trouble with the Dark Knight. "I believe Rory is the only one in need of change."

Gaston's fingers drummed on the table as he listened to her, sly little wench. He realized she was caressing his hand with her fingers and he was torn between relishing the feel of her and wanting to take her over his knee.

Brimley looked somewhat pleased. "Very well, then. If it's very well with Sir Gaston, we will be taking Rory when we leave."

Remington gave Gaston her most radiant smile, pressing her other hand into his large palm. "My lord?"

He rolled his eyes to her in a knowing gesture. He *knew* exactly what she was up to and he wanted her to know it, too. A black eyebrow lifted slowly like a great raven's wing.

"If she chooses to, she may go," he said with veiled irritation.

Remington squeezed his great hand quickly and let it go. "Thank you, my Lord. I shall find her to deliver the news."

Gaston passed a glance at Arik as Remington bounded from the room. Arik gave him such a knowing gaze that he tore his eyes away. If Arik was unaware of Gaston's tender feelings toward Remington, he was fully alerted now and Gaston cursed himself for being so careless.

For the fact that Gaston was showing human emotion had Arik beyond surprise. Overwhelmed was an apt term. The man allowed himself no feelings at all except for those beneficial to his cause, emotions of anger and determination and triumph. Never, ever had he seen the man *gentle*. The Dark Knight was not a title synonymous with gentleness.

Disoriented, he tried to focus on the meeting at hand.

Gaston did not mince words. He told them of his mission, to keep the peace in a land filled with Yorkist sympathizers and to maintain his seat. It was no longer Guy Stoneley's fortress. It now belonged to the Dark Knight, and he fully intended to use its power should the need arise.

Brimley absorbed the information, not surprised. The afternoon passed as Gaston had hoped, calm and informative. But Brimley was frank; every baron and feudal knight in Yorkshire and the surrounding shires were loyal to Richard and Anne. It was not a boast, merely a statement of fact, and Lord Brimley furthermore ventured that Gaston was going to have his hands full of rebels for some time to come. And then the key question came.

"To whom do you swear your loyalty, my lord?" Gaston asked. He appreciated the baron's frankness, without anger.

Brimley fixed him in the eye and Gaston knew what he was going to say before the words came out. "I am a Yorkist, sir. I shall always be a Yorkist."

"A Yorkist is no longer king," Gaston said evenly. "It would be a waste of effort to be loyal to a dead man."

"We cannot change loyalties as easily as you, my lord," Walter said. It was the first time the man had spoken.

Gaston met his gaze steadily. Walter leaned forward, setting his goblet down. "I have been sitting here for the better part of the day listening to you act as if you have been loyal to Henry your entire life when, in fact, you have been serving Yorkists for twelve years or better. Your cowardice doth disgust me, my lord, turning coat and betraying your king."

Gaston had been grappling with this type of attitude for some time now. He knew what he had done, and he knew his reasoning, and they were his reasons alone.

"Suffice it to say that I do not regret what I did," he said. "I am confident that Henry will be a most competent king, something England has sorely lacked for the past three years."

Walter's jaw ticked but he held his temper. "You are the Dark Knight. You were Edward's shining star, and Richard's most prized warrior. All of England cowers at your feet, my lord. I do not understand how you could have betrayed those who made you what you are."

"They did not make me, my lord, and I am not required to explain my actions to you," Gaston replied, irritated that the focus was shifting to him. "The fact remains that I would like to have your promise of fealty to Henry, and I would furthermore like your assurance that there will be no more trouble from Crayke. Might I have that oath on those matters?"

"Why should we swear loyalty to a traitor?" Walter slammed his fist on the heavy table. "You have betrayed your king, de Russe. How can you sit there and demand our fealty to a bastard with a tenuous claim to the throne, at best?"

Gaston's gaze was exceedingly calm, his eyes glittering like cold steel. When he spoke, his voice was so low it was almost seductive. "I am the Dark One, am I not?"

It was a direct question. Walter faltered a moment, puzzled. "Aye, you are."

"And I furthermore did not achieve my reputation by being a fool. Does that stand to reason?"

Again, Walter looked confused but nodded just the same. "Aye."

Brimley and Clive passed glances as Gaston folded his hands deliberately, focused on Walter. The air crackled with uncertainty.

"Would you trust me with your life?" Gaston asked again.

Walter blinked. He had no idea where this conversation was leading and wondered if the Dark Knight had lost his mind. Yet as much he hated to admit it, he did indeed trust the man with his impeccable reputation.

"Aye," Walter blinked slowly, with resignation. "I would trust you with my life."

Gaston sat forward, resting his folded hands on the table. When he met Walter's gaze again, it was if he had reached out and grabbed the man without actually touching him.

"Then trust me when I tell you that Henry is worthy to be our king," he said quietly. "I do not give my loyalty easily nor lightly. I do not act upon whim. Know this to be true."

Walter swallowed, visibly impacted by his words. He met Gaston's gaze for a moment longer before relaxing back into his chair. Contemplatively, he turned his gaze to his father.

Brimley was looking back at Gaston. The silent moment ticked away as each man pondered his own thoughts until Brimley stirred.

"I can promise you no trouble from Crayke, sir, but at this point I can promise you nothing more," he said. "We must have time to sort our priorities on this matter. You have given us much to think on."

"I can ask for nothing more," Gaston replied. "I would hope that you would speak with your allied barons on this meeting and assure them of our intentions. Peace will be met with peace, and loyalty with sworn allegiance from the crown. And the support of the Dark Knight."

"And if there are those who would not know peace?" Brimley asked, his white eyebrows rising.

Gaston slanted the man a gaze that he was famous for; it was likened by men who had seen it to Judgment Day.

"Then they shall die."

Brimley showed no fear. He nodded faintly and looked to his sons. "It would seem our visit is ended."

Clive and Walter rose, as did Gaston and Arik. Brimley faced Henry's knight with a new respect.

"In truth, Sir Gaston, I had no idea what to expect this day," he said. "Your reputation paints you to be a mythical beast of sorts. I am surprised to see that you are a man of intelligence, not simply a man of war. We will speak again."

"I look forward to that time, my lord," Gaston answered.

Brimley nodded curtly, knowing the meeting was ended and anxious to return home. He felt better exiting the meeting than he had going in, and that was a positive factor in his mind. He motioned to his sons and they quit the solar in a small group.

"Why did not you ask him to stay the night?" Arik asked after the men had left.

"It would have been too much, too soon," Gaston replied. "They are terribly uncomfortable as it is and I am sure would prefer the company of the stars to mine. They already have camp set up in the woods east of Mt. Holyoak."

"What about Rory?" Arik asked, his sly tone unmistakable.

Gaston gazed coolly at him. "What about her? We shall be rid of her if she goes to Crayke and thereby the problem will be eliminated."

Arik shook his head. "But you were going to punish her. Since when do you go back on your word?"

He was pushing and Gaston knew it. "You are not a clever man, Arik. Do not try to probe me innocently, for you shall fail. Now I must make sure our guests get off safely."

Arik shut his mouth, although he was thinking a great many things. But he knew better than anyone not to voice his opinions.

Trouble was, Rory did not want to go. Remington found her with Charles as they experimented with secret potions and powder and Rory balked at the suggestion. She insisted staunchly that she had not put the eggs in Nicolas' helmet and refused to take the blame.

Remington pleaded, yelled and threatened her sister in an attempt to convince her to leave with Lord Brimley. Rory ranted and threatened to return. She had not done the dastardly deed and she would not leave simply to escape the wrath of the Dark Knight.

Remington was flustered and angry at her sisters' stubborn nature. She was trying to save the willful girl's hide. It never occurred to her that Rory did not want to leave for an entirely different reason, and its name was Patrick.

Dane joined them later, chewing on a hunk of warm bread and excited about the fish he had caught. But one look at the experiments Charles and Rory were performing made him forget about his insignificant fish and he begged to help.

Remington was forgotten, as was Lord Brimley. With a resigned sigh, she perched herself on a stool and watched the mysterious research without enthusiasm.

She fully expected Gaston to ream her for her shrewd actions. She saw an opportunity and chose to make the best of it, pleased with her cleverness, yet Rory was refusing to cooperate. She was afraid, but not completely terrified. Anything Gaston did to her could not be as bad as what Guy planned for her daily.

The sun had set by the time Lord Brimley took his leave of Mt. Holyoak and Oleg ordered up the evening meal of, what else, pork. The cook spiced it up with cloves and nutmeg and baked apples to accompany it.

Smells of cooking drifted on the warm evening air, filling Gaston's nose. He was hungry for he had missed the nooning meal and he found his attention focused on the fare ahead. And he fully remembered he had requested Remington's company at dinner, wondering if she would be conspicuously absent to avoid his anger. Yet somehow, cowardice did not suit her. He could only imagine that she would face his wrath head-on.

He was not disappointed. The meal was already well in hand when Remington appeared, clutching her son's hand. Gaston couldn't help but straighten in his seat at the sight of her; she was dressed in a surcoat of wine satin, catching the light and making her rich hair appear richer. Dane was well groomed, as befitting a proper young man, his eyes alive at the sight of so many knights. It was the first time he had attended a formal meal and he was enraptured.

She headed directly for him, her head held high. He rose as she approached, greeting her with a courteous bow.

"My lady," he said, and then looked at Dane. "Master Stoneley, a pleasure."

"My mother said I could eat with you tonight," he said eagerly.

"Indeed you shall," Gaston indicated a chair for Remington. "Arik, seat our young friend."

Arik moved down a seat, allowing Dane to sit next to him. He smiled at the lad's enthusiasm.

Gaston helped Remington into her chair, smelling the floral scent until he was dizzy with it. Every time she moved, every time she tossed her hair, he was assaulted anew and thought it a most wonderful smell.

He seated himself and resumed eating. Remington was served by a wench, politely digging into her food under the intense gazes of her sisters. Even Rory had entered the room behind her and stood in the corner with the other two, whispering and staring.

Nicolas had not noticed Rory yet; his back was to her and he was buried in his meal. Remington wished Rory would go away until the storm blew over, but true to her nature, she would not hide. She was still angry at her sister for disobeying her wishes to go with Lord Brimley.

She was entirely silent; so was he. They ate in silence, neither one looking at the other for the duration. Dane, however, kept up a running conversation. He grilled Arik on the arts of war, the skill of the bow, anything he could think of, but he was so refreshing that the knight did not mind. He answered the young man's questions politely.

Somehow the conversation turned to entertainment, singing and other skills well-bred nobles were supposed to be well versed in. Dane looked proudly at his mother.

"My mother can play the flute. Did you know that?" he announced.

Remington froze in mid-chew, choking down a large bite as attention turned to her. Dane smiled happily. "She plays like an angel. Do you want to hear her?"

Remington coughed. "I do not think so, Dane. Not tonight."

"I think I would like to hear you," Gaston said quietly.

Her eyes snapped to him. "I...I really do not want to, my lord. I have not played in some time."

He studied her a moment. "Later, then. I will insist upon it."

Her gaze was guarded, wary. The minstrels that had played the evening before were entertaining again, having stayed one additional night by request of some of the knights. They struck up their instruments again, much to the delight of the men.

Remington had eaten her fill and waved for her trencher to be taken away. Dane, next to her, continued to eat as much as the men and was being a delightful conversationalist. She thought it surprising that he was actually enjoying himself; usually he was fairly reserved. But these giant men brought an excitement out in him and she could see that he held absolutely no fear of them. His admiration won out over all.

Guy did not like conversation at meals, which explained Dane's usual quietness. It was too easy to provoke his father and he ate his meals in fear of being slapped. But these knights, these men among men, wanted to hear what he had to say and he was in boy-heaven. He did so want to be like them, like Sir Gaston. Not his father.

The minstrels sang and told jokes like they did the night before and Remington sat back in her chair, listening to them yet acutely aware of Gaston next to her. She could see his massive hand out of the corner of her eyes, gripping his cup.

She stared at the back of his hand, remembering that it had grasped her this afternoon with such gentleness for all of its size. And lord, was it big. She was positive if he splayed his hand, it would outstretch the perimeter of a trencher. Gaston was by far the largest man that had ever lived, in her opinion. He was as wide as the doorframe and just as tall. It was difficult to comprehend such size, but for all of his mass, his face was entirely handsome.

Remington blinked; aye, he was handsome and it was about time she realized it. She had always known it, but she was not ready to admit it to herself. To think of him as handsome would open the gate for other emotions she had never experienced yet was terrified to know. She had spent so many years masking her emotions that she was unwilling to allow them to surface.

She turned her head slightly and found herself staring at his profile. He was far more than handsome; he was sensual, virile, and masculine. Beautiful. Could a man be beautiful? She wondered.

The minstrels struck up a slow ballad, traditional and lovely. A few of the more drunken knights grabbed the nearest serving wench and drug them out into the center of the floor, breaking into an elegant dance.

Antonius rose, smiling at Remington as he moved away from the table. She thought to herself that he looked much like a Roman god, sculpted and elegant. It took her a moment to see that he had gone directly to her sister and instantly the two of them were gliding across the floor.

Before Remington could react, Nicolas and Patrick had the same idea and soon Rory and Skye were traipsing the stone as well, swung giddy by their knights.

"Mummy." Dane tugged on her arm. "Mummy."

She tore her eyes away from the scene and looked at her son. "What is it?"

"Arik has a sword he says I can have." Dane was twitching with excitement. "Can I see it? Please?"

She was torn. He looked completely delighted and she found it difficult to refuse him. God only knew the boy had had so little excitement out of life.

Jasmine's blue dress swung by and caught her attention, for a second, until Dane tugged on her again.

"Very well, very well," she agreed, looking to Arik. "Take good care of him, my lord. He's just a boy."

"Mummy," Dane protested weakly.

Arik smiled and put his hand on Dane's shoulder. "Beg your pardon, my lady, but he is nearly a man grown. However, for your peace of mind, I shall watch him like a hawk."

Remington watched the two of them retreat from the hall, leaving her alone with Gaston. They had yet to say one word to each other.

The dance suddenly livened and the delighted shrieks of the women filled the hall as they were swung about by their partners. Remington could see Jasmine laughing happily into Antonius' arms and she felt her protectiveness turning into confusion. Was Gaston right? Was she too overprotective?

Nay. She told herself sharply. She had to protect her sisters from those who would do them harm, supposedly chivalrous knights included.

And Jasmine, somehow, most of all. She was the most vulnerable; the most bitter. And she was the only sister to bear a bastard from her sister's husband. The child was nearly two years old now and living with a family in Boroughbridge. It had almost killed her sister to give up the blond-haired girl and Remington was sick every time she thought of little Mary.

She had to protect Jasmine.

She suddenly stood up. "'Tis time we retire for the night, my lord. Thank you for permitting my son and I to dine with you."

He reached out and put a hand on her arm. "Sit down, Remi."

She turned to him sharply. "I...we have had a full day, my lord. My sisters are tired."

"Nay, they are not," he tugged on her arm and she plopped back into the chair. "They are enjoying themselves as you should be."

She stumbled a bit, glancing nervously at the dancers. He sat forward in his chair, his great head by her shoulders. "You do not know how to enjoy yourself, do you?"

She peered at him over her shoulder. "You are the one without a sense of humor, my lord. Not I."

"Eggs in a knight's helm is not humorous," he said flatly.

Her lips twitched. "I disagree."

His gaze raked over her. "You were most calculating this afternoon, madam. I had no idea you were so sly."

She turned her attention back to the dancers. "I know not what you mean."

"Yes, you do," he studied her profile, her flawless skin. "I should punish you as well as your sister for going against me."

She raised an eyebrow and looked at him impatiently. "Lock us both in the tower?"

It was a saucy statement and he raised his eyebrows in response. "I was thinking more of locking you both in the vault for thirty days."

"What?" she gasped, turning her full attention to him. Gone was her flippant attitude.

"Unless," he held up a finger quickly. "Unless you are prepared to do penitence of my choosing."

"Penitence of your choosing?" she repeated, puzzled. "What in the world would that be?"

His eyes twinkled and she was greatly confused. "A dance, my lady," he said softly. "One dance will spare you and your sister my wrath."

Her mouth opened, dumbfounded. Then she was frightened. "A *dance*?" she repeated. It wasn't that she did not like to dance, but that meant that he would have to...hold her.

Arms around her only meant pain and humiliation. She hated to be touched as a result of her husband's abuse and as Gaston had learned, she quickly turned into a hurricane of terror when cornered. But thoughts of Gaston's arms flooded her mind, arms so strong and beautiful that they made her feel faint. She had slept in his arms, better than she had slept in years.

He stood up, holding his hand out to her just as another slow ballad began. She gazed up at him and he could read the terror and hesitation and smiled gently.

"Dance with me, angel," he said softly. "I promise I shall be gentle."

She did not want to be held by anyone...but the thought of his arms around her brought unfamiliar feelings of warmth and comfort. Reluctantly, she placed her hand in his and allowed him to pull her to her feet. The next time she looked at him, her eyes were welling with confused tears and he stopped.

"Oh, Remi, forgive me," he whispered. "I will not make you do something you are uncomfortable with."

To his surprise, she stood firm. "Nay, I will dance with you," she sniffed, dashing away the tears. But he wasn't moving, instead, he was pulling her chair out again. "Gaston, truly. I shall dance with you. I think...I think I need to dance with you."

His eyes studied her closely to see what exactly she meant. Weakly, she smiled. "I have not danced in years. I think I need to dance this night. If not with you, then with someone else."

"Like hell," he stood his full height. "You will dance with me and me alone. I forbid another man to touch you."

He led her out onto the dance floor and took her in his arms with infinite tenderness. She stiffened instinctively, but forced herself to calm, giving in to his warm arms. With great skill, he swung her into the group of revelers.

They danced three dances together. Color flushed Remington's cheeks and she found it hard to believe that she was actually enjoying herself, but she was and it was all of Gaston's doing. He was a wonderful dancer and she was growing more enchanted with him by the minute. He could make her laugh; make her feel as if she were the most beautiful woman on earth.

The same minstrel who tried to dance with her the night before tried to cut in on Gaston, who sent the man cowering with an icy glare. Remington laughed, cradled in his arms, thinking that someday she might even like being held by a man. It was certainly easy to tolerate Gaston.

Arik found Gaston on the outer wall late that evening, well after the castle had retired for the evening. The world around them was still but for the crickets chirping in the trees and the soft whistle of the wind over the landscape. Above, the nearly full moon bathed the land in a silver glow.

"What are you doing?" Arik came upon him where he was leaning over the ledge of the wall, inspecting the grounds below.

Gaston flicked his hand in the direction of Brimley's camp, a half mile in the distance. "Watching."

"Any activity?" Arik could see the faint glow from the pyre.

"None," Gaston replied. "Seems they are all sleeping like babes. They *must* trust us."

Arik smirked. "Fools," he turned his back on the wall, leaning back and looking up to the sky. "I heard you convinced Lady Stoneley to dance tonight."

"After much pleading and coaxing," Gaston confirmed. "She not only looks like an angel, she dances like one. In fact, there is not one thing about the woman that is imperfect and at times she makes me feel most inferior."

Arik looked at him, gushing like a smitten boy. He had never seen him so...open. He should have been thrilled for him, but he found he was skeptical instead.

"You are quite taken with Lady Stoneley, aren't you?" he asked carefully.

Gaston shrugged. "I enjoy her company if that's what you mean."

"It is not what I mean and you know it," Arik said. "What was it you told Antonius? Keep your mind on your business, not on Lady Stoneley?"

Gaston's jaw flexed. "Your point being?"

Arik looked at him a moment. "She is married, Gaston. And so are you."

Gaston stood up, angrily. "I do not need you to remind me of that fact, my friend, for I am only too aware of it," he snapped. "I enjoy Lady

Stoneley on a conversational level and that is the extent of it. I have no time for mistresses."

Arik was fully aware of the thin ice he tread upon. He was acquainted with the Dark Knight's temper, and fists, and took several steps back, crossing his arms thoughtfully. "If you ask my opinion, my lord, there is more to it than that. I would say you were quite taken with the woman, as I have indicated before. And she's scared to death of you."

"Why do you say that?" Gaston demanded.

Arik shook his head in a helpless gesture. "Guy has scarred her terribly, Gaston," he said. "You have probably seen more examples of that than I, and it's obvious that you frighten her. Not in the physical sense, but more on the emotional level. She is attracted to you, I think, and afraid of her feelings."

Gaston looked at his friend a moment, his great body relaxing. He turned back to the wall. "I enjoy her company. That is all"

Something on the wall caught his attention; Gaston looked over Arik's shoulder to see Remington on the far end of the western wall, making her way toward him. Arik swung around and caught sight of her.

"I must be going," he said quickly.

"Good," Gaston grumbled. "I am weary of your company."

Arik grinned and, with a final glance at Remington, moved for the stairs. But she called out to him and he paused at the top, his expression politely inquisitive.

She was dressed in a flowing robe of icy blue, layers of silk that swathed her in luxury. She looked glorious, but her lovely face was tense.

"Have you seen Dane?" she asked Arik. "He is not in his room."

Arik looked puzzled. "I took him there myself, my lady, several hours ago. If he is not there, then I have no idea where he might be."

Remington's brow furrowed with worry and her eyes sought out Gaston. He could see in the bright moon glow that her eyes had taken on the blue of the robe and he was amazed at the chameleon-quality of her eyes. "Have you seen him?" she pleaded.

He shook his head. "He is around here somewhere, Remi. No one has left the gates since this afternoon."

Arik raised his eyebrows. "Remi?" he mouthed to Gaston.

Gaston ignored him and went to Remington, who was in obvious distress. "Go back to bed. I shall look for him.

Her angelic face was tense. "But he never strays after dark. He is afraid of the dark."

Gaston put his hands on her shoulders and steered her toward Arik. "I have the watch tonight, all night, and nothing to do. I shall search for him right now. Arik, please escort Lady Remington back to her room."

Her soft eyes were pleading as she covered his massive hand with her own. "He is afraid of the dark," she repeated softly.

He patted her hand reassuringly. "I promise I will not rest until I find him. Go with Arik, now, and rest assured."

With a sigh of reluctance, she allowed Arik to take her down the narrow stairs, the only such flight on the wall. Every other method of access was a ladder. Gaston hovered at the top of the stairs, watching Arik carefully assist her. When she crossed into the inner bailey on Arik's arm, he finally turned away and tried to determine the best place to look for a seven-year-old boy.

Unfortunately, Dane was not to be found. Gaston searched for two hours on his own and then commandeered a company of soldiers to assist him.

Every inch of the walls and bailey were searched. Even the half-finished troop house and the sublevels were covered, but still no Dane, and Gaston began to feel distinctively uneasy. What if the boy had indeed run off? Or worse, taken away? His thoughts turned to Lord Brimley's encampment and he pondered the possibility that Dane was somehow within the perimeter, be it of his own choosing or against his will. Brimley had been, after all, eager to take Stoneley's family back with him to Crayke Castle.

The night went on and still no Dane, and Gaston began to seriously consider raiding Brimley's camp in search of the lad. But the castle of Mt. Holyoak had yet to be searched, and he would complete his sweep before moving forward with such a provocative action. He had been preaching peace all afternoon; to go charging into Lord Brimley's camp with swords drawn would brand him a hypocrite and he was positive that it would ruin any chances for an alliance.

Silently, his soldiers moved through Mt. Holyoak in search of the boy. Gaston took the most active role in the search, trying to think like a seven-year-old boy would. He had been lively at dinner with no outward signs of distress. So where in the hell would he go?

Five hours into the search, Gaston was mystified and upset. Dane was nowhere within the castle walls, of that he was sure, and he felt a sense of panic. He knew without a doubt that Brimley's camp was verily close to a strip-search, but he reined his emotions and wisely ordered two of his trusted knights to assemble a raiding party. Were he to do it, he would assemble an overload of men and probably crush Brimley into the earth. He ordered the men to form and wait for him.

There was one place he had not checked, and that was the family wing. Aye, he had checked Dane's room when they first began the search in the castle, but he had not checked the other bedchambers. It was entirely possible that he was sleeping with someone else.

The corridor was dim as he walked silently to the first door. Rory was asleep, spread out over the sheet and was looking most angelic in spite of her devilish nature. She was a faintly pretty girl, more so when she was sleeping. Quietly, he closed the door.

Skye and Charles were asleep in their respective rooms with no company. Somewhat disheartened that Dane wasn't with Charles, he moved to Remington's door.

She was asleep on her side, facing him. The faint glow from the hearth illuminated her features gently, making her appear almost surreal. By God, if she wasn't the most beautiful woman he had ever laid eyes on. He felt his heart soften as he gazed at her, fighting off a roaring river of emotions that threatened him.

She was lying atop the coverlet, still in the turquoise robe and he guessed she had fallen asleep waiting for her son to return. Even with the fire, there was a definite chill in the room and she twitched in her sleep, curling up her legs to stay warm.

He moved into the room silently, folding the great coverlet up from the ends and wrapping it around her, tucking her in firmly. He was bent over her, covering her shoulders and smiled when she sighed contentedly, like a child. His hand, with a mind of its own, smoothed the hair on her head, feeling the silken strands between his fingers. His nostrils, not to be left out of the experience, demanded to smell her hair and he lifted the curls to his face, inhaling deeply.

He stood there a moment and gazed upon her, memorizing every line of her face and feeling the most marvelous, peculiar emotions he had ever sampled. By God's Bloody Rood, she was only a woman. Why on earth did he react to her as if she were something more incredible than life itself?

Because she was different. He had only to look at her and know that. He had only to look at her and realize he was in the mighty grip of something far more powerful than he was.

He ran his index finger down her silky cheek and stood up, moving for the door. As much as he would have liked to have stayed and gaze upon her all night, he had more immediate duties pressing. Dane was still missing and he had to find him.

He closed the door softly and paused a moment, defining his thoughts. It suddenly occurred to him that there was one bedchamber he had not checked - his. He almost decided not to, knowing it to be a waste of time. Yet, something told him to check for his own peace of mind. After all, he wanted to be able to say he had looked everywhere for Dane when he cut into Brimley's camp bent on destruction.

His room was dark; even the coals in the hearth were black. A quick glance about the room told him there was nothing there except emptiness and he was in the process of closing the door when his eyes came to rest on a foot.

A small foot, which in turn was attached to a small body, lying in the folds of his coverlet. Sighing with relief, he moved back into the room and peered down at Dane, sound asleep, clutching the small sword Arik had given him.

Gaston's mouth twitched with a smile at the small boy snoring so contentedly, having no idea of the uproar he nearly caused. Gaston realized he was a good deal more relieved than he thought possible at the sight of the lad, gratified that he had not come to any harm. He rather liked the little fellow.

He debated about waking him but thought against it. He would, however, return him to his own bed. Carefully, he leaned over and gathered the child against his mighty chest and Dane stirred.

"What...what...?" he sputtered.

"Hush, Dane," Gaston's voice was low. "I am taking you back to your bed, lad."

Dane blinked, suddenly remembering where he was. His wide eyes focused on Gaston. "I was waiting for you."

"Waiting for me? Why?" Gaston asked.

"To show you the sword Sir Arik gave me," he said, hugging the sword to his body. "He said I could have it."

Gaston pretended to study the sword intensely. "Aye, a fine weapon indeed. Perfect for a young man to begin his training with."

Dane yawned, holding the sword as if he were in possession of the Holy Grail. He mumbled something sleepily as Gaston carried him out into the hall and back to his room.

Remington heard a faint sound in her son's room and was instantly awake. She tossed the coverlet off, not even stopping to think how she became wrapped in it, and dashed across the bedchamber through the adjoining door to Dane's room.

Gaston was laying him down upon the sheets when she burst in and he shushed her sternly.

"He's just gone back to sleep," he whispered, pulling the covers over the boy.

She gazed down at his sandy head a moment, blinking sleep from her eyes. Gaston stepped back, watching the boy snuggle down into the thick mattress. Groggily, Remington also moved away from the bed and stumbled over her own feet.

Gaston caught her as she tripped, holding her against his hard body to steady her. She grabbed onto him, although she did not realize what she was doing. Holding her to him felt to be the most natural, pleasant thing in the world and his arm went around her shoulders of its own choosing.

"Where was he?" she whispered. "What is he holding?"

"I found him in my bed," Gaston said quietly. "He was waiting for me to return so he could show me the sword Arik gave him and fell asleep."

"Arik gave him a sword?" Remington looked doubtfully at her son.

His arm squeezed her lightly. "Do not worry so. It is quite dull, as it was Arik's when he was a lad. 'Twill be perfect when he begins his training."

She looked up at him, startled. "You would still send him away from me to foster?" she asked, her voice growing louder. "You told him that you would consider allowing him to remain here."

He shushed her again and moved her into her own room, quietly closing the door. When he turned around to face her, she was sitting on the edge of her bed surrounded by the voluminous skirt of her robe. The picture was breathtaking and he did, indeed, take a breath.

"And I am considering it," he said patiently. "But all young men are sent away to foster when they reach seven or eight years of age. You are aware of this Remi. You want your son to grow up to be a strong, fine man, do not you?"

"He must be sent away to foster in order to attain those qualities?" she shot back softly. "Gaston...he is all I have. I do not want him to be sent away."

He put his hand on his hips, not answering her for a moment. "We shall talk about it later. Go back to sleep now."

She continued to sit there and look at him, sadness in her face. He gave her a brief flash of a smile and moved for the door. He had a company of men waiting for him in the bailey that he was anxious to attend to.

"Gaston?" she said softly.

He paused, his hand on the latch. She offered him a timid smile. "Thank you for finding him, truly. You did not have to go through so much trouble."

"He is my vassal and his welfare concerns me," he replied. "Goodnight."

She stood to show him from her chamber as a proper lady would, assuming he would move out of her way when he saw her approach. But he did not, however, and she nearly walked into him. Startled, she craned her neck back sharply to look at him and was met by eyes of molten steel, shrouded in smoke.

"I would thank you for dancing with me this eve," he said quietly. "You are a delightful dancer."

She smiled and his heart thumped loudly in his chest; he was sure she could hear it. "I rather enjoyed it, too. And it should be I who thanks you for putting up with my foolish behavior when you first suggested the dance. Sometimes I.... well, I never much liked to dance with Guy."

"Do you like to dance with me?"

She did. But she was afraid to admit it. Yet he was looking at her with such warmth that she couldn't help herself. "Aye, I did."

Gaston couldn't help himself. He knew he should not touch her in any way, but he simply could not stop his hand from moving to hers. The moment he touched the pure, warm silkiness of it, he knew he had to taste it. Gazing into Remington's wide eyes, he brought her hand to his lips and kissed it.

"And I like to dance with you," he said hoarsely. He had such a deep voice that it all came out in a rumble.

She couldn't speak. No one had ever kissed her hand so sweetly, so tenderly. In fact, no man had ever shown her such consideration and gentleness. The fire in her cheeks spread to her belly and made her shake. As new and wonderful as her emotions were, she was still filled with a deeply ingrained terror of being touched. Until this moment, she had never been touched kindly by a man in her life.

She wanted to take her hand away. His lips were still on her palm and she could feel the stubble of his face. But she was so electrified by his touch that she couldn't manage to move her hand. Uncertainty and utter fascination were all she could seem to feel.

He was immensely pleased when she did not yank her hand away; he had fully expected her to bolt. He could see that she was staring at the bottom half of his face with an astonished expression and he kissed her palm again just to see how she would react.

Her eyes flew to his in surprise and he smiled broadly, his mouth half-covered by her hand.

"Have you never experienced something so gentle, angel," he asked softly.

She shook her head honestly. "N-never."

His smile faded to an ironic gesture. "Nor have I."

She stared at him a moment and suddenly tore her hand away, stumbling back from him. Her expression was open and accusing.

"You are married, my lord." she said. "Master or no of Mt. Holyoak, you have no right to toy with me as such. I am not part of the castle as a servant or the land, or the sheep of the field. You may not use me as your...whore. I will not allow it."

"Whore?" his brow furrowed deeply. "Remi, I never said...."

"Is that what you have been planning all along?" she accused. "You show kindness to my son, to me, simply so my guard will go down and you shall be able to do as you please? I know this to be your intention. You are all alike, you are all...."

She was getting quite loud and he had heard enough. He moved toward her, faster than she had ever seen anyone move, and before she realized what had happened she was plastered to the bed, covered by a massive body.

She instantly assumed the worst and opened her mouth to scream, but he slapped a huge hand over her lips and covered half her face and neck.

My God, this can't be happening. She was more terrified than she had ever been in her life, terrified because he was easily three times her size and weight, and she could do naught to fight against him. She was so badly frightened and startled that tears began to flow.

No. Her mind screamed to the heavens. *Please no.*

Gaston knew her fear and regretted his actions deeply, but he felt them to be entirely necessary. He would rather run himself through than frighten her like this, but he knew it was the only way she was going to listen to him. Her ranting had grown out of control so quickly that the only way to douse it was equally as fast.

When her tears came, falling hot on his hand, his heart nearly broke. "Remington, listen to me and listen well," he said in a husky whisper. "You shall not be my whore, nor anyone's whore. Nor shall your sisters. Those days are long over. 'Twas never my intention to deceive you or your son and I have done nothing that was not completely sincere. I would never hurt you, Remi. I swear to God I would never hurt you."

Her body was relaxing underneath him and he looked down into the sea-crystal eyes that were so capable of changing color.

"Do you believe me?" After a long pause, her head dipped again. He removed his hand. "I am sorry I frightened you, but you were growing quite loud and I was afraid you would awaken Dane." He eyed her. "Do you truly believe me or are you just agreeing with me because you are frightened?"

She was shaking; he could feel her. "I...I believe you. I do not know why I should, but I do. You have not lied to me yet."

"And I never will," he replied. Their bodies were molded into one another and he could feel a fire beginning in his loins; he shifted so she could not feel his rapid arousal.

"But you kissed me," she whispered, obviously still overcome.

He made a wry face, trying to alleviate her apprehension. "I kissed your palm, Remi. You let those idiots Walter and Clive do that as well. I did nothing scandalous."

He was correct; he had not, and she was growing embarrassed. It was only right that she apologize profusely and hope he wasn't offended by her words.

"Oh, Gaston, I am so sorry," she said earnestly. "It's just that...I have never trusted men. I have never trusted anyone but my sisters. My husband was beyond vile and I suppose I have learned to judge all men by his actions. I know of no other way."

He knew that. His weight was shifted off of her, yet he was still lying intimately close with Remington on her back, gazing up at him. The desire to kiss her on her pink lips was, once again, overwhelming. He raised an eyebrow thoughtfully.

"The man should thank God he is in prison, for if I ever see him, I will kill him," he said frankly. "What he has done to you is more than contemptuous; it's inhuman. In fact, I think I shall ride to London this night and run him through."

Her eyes widened but she saw he was jesting. A slow smile crept to her lips. "Would you?"

He pretended to take her request very seriously. "Say the word, madam, and I am bound for the Tower."

She appreciated his chivalry, his understanding. Before she could stop herself, her hand went up and stroked his cheek. "Thank you, my Dark Knight."

He froze when he felt her touch, delicate and soft. He resisted the urge to stroke her back. "Do not call me that," he mumbled, but there was a smile playing on his lips. *Damn, but if she wasn't too close.*

Remington stroked his cheek again, liking the feel of it. Liking the feel of *him*. Unbeknownst to her, the voyage of discovery had begun.

Gaston felt her caresses and he lost all of his hard-fought control. His great head descended on her, slowly, so that she would not be alarmed. Ever so delicately, his lips hovered over hers and he reverently breathed in her hot breath of life. He continued to hold for a brief moment, giving her ample time to state her displeasure, but he had no such protests.

With the most infinite tenderness, his lips claimed her own.

Remington froze. She could not form a coherent thought as his lips suckled hers with the incredible gentleness. He clung to her top lip, to her bottom lip, brushing her face with his scratchy stubble. As paralyzed as she was with fear and uncertainty, she was not beyond experiencing the sensations. Soft warmth, giddy tingling filling her body like a thousand pins pricking her, her breath coming faster and faster. Guy had never been so considerate, so sensitive.

She wasn't frightened until she felt herself respond to him. When she began to kiss him back, timidly, and her soft hands found the back of his neck, he answered by fiercely winding his arms around her slim body and pulling her against him hungrily. His rush of strength scared the wits out of her, and she whimpered.

He felt her stiffen and stopped his passionate assault. His eyes were wide with concern.

"What's wrong, angel? Did I hurt you?" he asked in a strange, tight voice.

She shook her head, her eyes huge with confusion. "Nay, Gaston, you did not...we should not be doing this."

"And why not?" he asked huskily.

She looked long at him. "Because you are married, my lord. And so am I. This is wrong."

He loosened his grip but he did not let her go. Instead, one of his huge hands came up to stroke her face, her hair tenderly.

"I am married in name only," he told her. "The woman I married holds no place in my heart, Remi. It was an arranged marriage and I had no choice in the matter. Honestly, I have never truly felt married all of these thirteen years because I have tried my best to stay as far away from Mari-Elle as possible."

She gazed back at him, feeling his sincerity. She wanted so desperately to believe him, to have complete trust in his word, but she had learned many hard lessons on trusting men and it was difficult. Her hand came up to his face again, curiously touching the strong line of his jaw.

"I simply do not know what to think anymore," she whispered. "I am afraid."

"Of what?" he demanded softly.

"Of you," she breathed. "Of your touch, of your words. Guy taught me great distrust of the male species, Gaston. I know of no other way, yet when I listen to you speak and experience your actions, I am confused and afraid because I want to have faith in you. You are the only man I have ever known to be kind to me."

His hand was still caressing her, the smoky gray orbs glittering dully in the faint firelight. "Guy has all but ruined you, Remi. I hold nothing but contempt and hatred for him and I swear to you that all men are not like he. There are those of us who do not hit women and are true to their word. If it takes me the rest of my life, I will convince you of that fact."

She sighed. "I want to believe you, truly. But I am still frightened."

"There is nothing to be afraid of," he whispered, brushing his lips to hers.

She believed him. For the moment, she truly believed him. Her arms went around his great neck, responding to the sweet kisses. She was so terribly inexperienced because Guy had rarely kissed her, yet her natural impulses took over and she matched Gaston's passion. When his tongue ran itself over her lips invitingly, she responded by opening her mouth to him.

She went stiff again as his tongue plunged into her delicious depths, but her reaction was one of desire rather than fear. He licked and plundered and suckled her until she was gasping for breath, completely dazed with the newness of his touch. Her mind was a black, curious void of passion, anticipating each new sensation with the glee of a new bride. Never in her life had she been so fortunate as to have experienced this bit of heaven.

His great hand was moving along her body, skimming the curve of her hip and trailing up her torso with tremendous reverence. She could feel his fingers dancing delicately across her stomach, moving for the ties of her robe. He gently tugged at the knot until it loosened, and she startled as his hand snaked underneath the folds of the garment, his hot palm on the flat of her naked belly.

Uncertainty shot through her at the intimate touch, but his wonderful mouth moved to her neck and earlobes and she forgot about his hand for the moment. His steamy tongue licked the circle of her ear and she quivered violently. She vaguely remembered hearing a moan, not realizing it was her own.

"God, Remi, you are so sweet," he breathed against her neck.

She was a quivering shell of desire, completely lacking her own will or the power to speak. Gaston and his marvelous touch had made her feel more wonderful in this moment than Guy had managed in nine years of marriage. Had she stopped to think of it, she would have been astonished.

His hand was on the move again, drifting up to the swell of her breast. Her first instinct was to bolt away from him, but when his fingers delicately traced the underside of her breast, she trembled again and held her breath in anticipation of the next step.

She did indeed consciously moan when his fingers pinched her nipple, rolling it into a hard pellet. Her breathing came fast and furious as his hand closed over her entire breast, massaging it expertly. Hands that were causing her to melt right into the mattress.

The robe was opened wide and he descended on her breast with a great sigh of pleasure. She cried out softly, her hands entwined in his thick black hair, completely consumed with the feelings he was causing within her. Surely there was nothing on this earth sweeter than Gaston and his sure touch.

"Mummy?" a soft voice floated into the dim room.

Gaston's head came up, as did Remington's. They looked at each other a moment before Gaston discreetly pulled the ends of her robe together and pushed himself off of her.

Remington sat up quickly; too quickly, but Dane did not notice. He also did not notice her flushed cheeks and guilty expression.

"What's wrong, sweetheart?" she asked him.

He moved into the room, eyeing Gaston. "I heard you cry. What's the matter?"

Remington was thankful of two things at the moment; that her son was too young to realize what was going on, and that the room was too dark to see the scarlet color of her cheeks.

"Nothing, Dane," she swallowed. "Go back to bed, now. 'Tis almost dawn."

Dane was looking at Gaston. "What were you doing to my mother? You were squashing her."

Gaston was remarkably composed. He stood from the bed, adjusting his breeches inconspicuously. "Where is your sword? A good knight never leaves his sword behind, Dane."

Dane's eyes widened. "I shall go get it right now."

Gaston grabbed hold of the lad as he tried to dash off. "Nay, lad, do not worry about it now, but remember for future reference. As it is, you should do as you mother says and return to bed."

He directed the boy toward the connecting door and on into the bedchamber. She could hear him speaking steadily to her son, coaxing him back to bed. It occurred to her that Guy had never once tucked his son into bed, never once used a soothing tone with him. Over all of her raging emotions, her heart warmed as Gaston put her son to bed with his new sword.

He returned to her bedchamber after a moment, closing the adjoining door softly.

"He's in bed but I doubt he shall go back to sleep," he said with a faint grin. "He seems convinced that, somehow, I was intent on harming you."

"'Tis all he has ever known, Gaston," she said softly. "He is nearly as skittish as I am at times."

His features hardened. "No longer."

She gazed up at him remembering his mouth on her flesh. A warm, fluid sensation filled her until she thought she would slither to the floor. It was overwhelming, wonderful and confusing.

He met her eyes intensely, knowing what she was feeling because he was feeling it, too. He cleared his throat. "I have a few items that need tending, my lady. I will see you after sunrise."

She nodded, too dazed to answer him. Her mind was swirling with emotions and feelings until she was dizzy with it all. Yet when she heard the latch unbolt, she snapped out of her trance.

"Rory asked me when you first arrived if I was to be your whore," she mumbled. "I slapped her. But she was right, wasn't she?"

"I think we just covered that particular area," he said, although his tone was not unkind. "You shall not be my whore."

"Then what?" she looked at him searchingly. "What will I be?"

He lowered his gaze. He couldn't answer her, at least not at this moment. Silently, he quit the room.

CHAPTER EIGHT

Thankfully, Dane had indeed fallen back to sleep and had forgotten all about walking in on his mother and the Dark Knight. Moreover, this was a special day for him; his mother had promised him that on Wednesday he could go to the Mid-Summer Faire in the neighboring town of Ripon. Remington had forgotten all about it until he had burst into the middle of her bath, telling her of all the marvelous things he was going to purchase with his coinage.

Remington had promised him before Gaston had ever arrived and she went to seek his permission.

The inner and outer baileys were absolutely abuzz with activity. She picked her way through the obstacles, weaving a path toward the main hovel of business, the nearly completed troop house. More than the previous days, she was acutely aware of the soldiers' stares upon her and she was nervous. Gaston's soldiers were probably the heartiest, earthiest troops in all of England. Men used to the harsh realities of life and the bitterness it had to offer. She was scared to even look them in the eye.

She rounded the wall and proceeded into the outer bailey. The closer she drew, the busier it became and she paused, trying to discern the best possible path. She could see a few knights here and there and quickly decided to ask them where she could find Gaston.

She was nervous to see him after what had transpired last night. He had left so abruptly that she did not know what to think. Was he as confused as she was? Did he, upon reflection, decide that kissing her had been a colossal mistake? Her stomach was twitching so that she had not been able to break her fast when she rose.

Remington gathered her skirts higher as she dodged a pile of stone in the middle of her path. Coming to the dusty bailey dressed in a rose-colored silk was not the wisest choice, for the hem of her surcoat was already coated with a thin film of dirt and she tried to shake it off as she walked.

Suddenly a strong hand was biting into her upper arm and she flinched, instinctively trying to pull away.

"Yer a pretty little goat," an older, filthy soldier leered. "What's yer name, lass?"

Angry, she tried to yank free. "Let go of me, you brute."

His grip tightened. "That's not very friendly. I just asked ye yer name."

Other soldiers had started to gather, grinning lewdly and Remington was on the verge of panic. These were not the well-trained knights that graced her grand hall every eve; these were the lowers, men with no manners and even less intelligence.

"You do not need to know my name," she succeeded in tearing her arm away from him, but his dirty hand left an imprint on her fine silk and she clucked at it miserably." Get away from me, all of you. *Get.*"

She scrambled back from the soldier as he made another swipe at her, much to the amusement of his comrades. But he let her go on and she practically ran until she found one of Gaston's knights.

The knight was an older man, completely bald, but with an intelligent face. He knew her on sight.

"Greetings this day, Lady Stoneley," he said. "How may I serve you?"

"Sir Gaston," she asked, panting from fright and exertion. "Where is he?"

"In the troop house, I believe," the knight strained his eyes to the structure. "Aye, I believe I see him. Shall I fetch him for you?"

"Nay," Remington did not want to be left waiting, alone. "Take me to him, please."

Without hesitation, the knight took her elbow courteously and led her to the edges of the troop house. Masoners and soldiers were covered with dust from the stone, moving busily as they neared completion of the walls. The knight let her go a moment to seek out Arik.

She could see Arik whirl around when the knight whispered in his ear. His face rippled with concern and he sent a man in search of Gaston. As it was, he and the other knight returned hastily to her side.

"Good morn to you, Lady Remington," Arik said pleasantly.

"And to you, Sir Arik," she smiled at him. "I must thank you for the sword you gave Dane. He is tremendously proud of it; he even slept with it last night."

He returned her smile. "I am pleased, then," he replied. "He will prove to be a bright, eager pupil."

Her smile faded a bit. "I suppose. But is it necessary to teach boys to be men at such a young age? I wonder at the intelligence of such a concept."

"'Tis best to start them young, before they grow older and less impressionable," he assured her. "Have no fear, my lady. I will take good care of your son."

She blinked and her brow furrowed slightly. "You? What do mean? Are you leaving, too?"

"Leaving? Hell no. I mean, no," he quickly corrected himself. "I shall be here, training Henry's troops and a passel of young knaves like your son."

She tilted her head slightly. "Dane is staying here to train?"

Arik smiled and crossed his arms. "Aye, he is. Word came down from the master this morn. Young Dane starts his training come August."

Remington was surprised; more than surprised - *pleasantly* surprised. Thank God Gaston had taken mercy on her and had decided not to send her son away. Relief and gratitude filled her; she must remember to thank him most properly for his compassionate decision.

Gaston suddenly appeared at her side, his entire body covered in a fine white powder. She giggled at the sight of him.

"You look as if you have been rolling in the dirt," she said.

He lifted an eyebrow. "Is that why you are here? To laugh at me?"

"Nay, my lord, assuredly not," she said, fighting off her grin. "I have come to ask you something. Might I have a moment of your time?"

Anything for you. "Of course," he said shortly. "Arik, Roald, excuse us please."

The two knights retreated and Gaston fought himself to keep his gaze, his manner, from turning soft on her. It was extremely difficult when she was smiling so openly at him.

"I know you are busy, so I will be brief," she said. "I promised Dane several weeks ago that he could attend the Mid-Summer Faire in Ripon. The faire is today, my lord, and I would like to keep my promise. Will you give us your permission to go?"

"Just you and Dane?" he asked.

"All of us," she clarified. "My sisters have been looking forward to it, as well."

He signed, brushing at the dust in his hair. "I see no reason why not," he said. "How far is Ripon?"

"Eight miles to the north east, not far," she said. "It is a lovely ride."

He looked thoughtful. "I will assign a few knights to accompany you. When will you want to leave?"

"As soon as possible," she said. "Dane is bouncing off the walls and I do not know how much longer I can contain him."

He smiled for the first time. "Ah, the excitement of a faire," he agreed. "I remember it well. Very well, then, gather your things and I shall send someone for you when the escort has been assembled."

She smiled broadly. "Thank you, my lord. Dane thanks you."

He allowed himself the luxury of softening, his eyes roving over her curvy form. Then he noticed the grimy handprint and he reached out to touch it.

"What is this?" he demanded, his tone sweet one moment and deadly the next.

She had completely forgotten about her encounter and glanced down at the stain. "A soldier grabbed me," she said, unconcerned. "I escaped him, though."

He looked at the dark smudge a moment. "Which soldier?"

"Over there, at the corner of the inner wall," she pointed in the general direction, not comprehending his tone. She should have listened well; it was by far the most deep, threatening tone he had yet to use. Instead, she turned back to him. "Do you think you will be able to come to the faire? Dane would love to have you with him. Charles thinks faires are a silly bunch of nonsense and refuses to go, so there will be just womenfolk to accompany my son."

"Show me which soldier," he ignored her prattle.

As if she were slapped in the face, she caught on to the inflection in his voice and she was wary. "Gaston, no harm was done," she said quietly. "There is no need to punish the man."

He took her by the arm, gently yet firmly. "You will show me who lay his hand upon you."

She was beginning to grow frightened as she allowed him to take her back across the courtyard. His massive body was tense; she could feel it. When they drew close to the group of men she had indicated, he came to a halt.

"Which man?" he asked steadily.

She was extremely hesitant to tell him, but she had no choice. "That one."

Gaston let her go and went up to the soldier. "You, man," his voice was like the low rumble of thunder. "Come here."

The soldier straightened, his eyes wide at the sight of the Dark Knight. His comrades ceased their movement, all watching Gaston with a good deal of apprehension and a healthy fear. And there was no mistaking the lady standing several feet away; they all knew what was about to happen and why. Foreboding filled the air.

"Aye, my lord?" the man stammered.

Gaston gazed at the dirty, aged face. "Did you touch Lady Stoneley?"

The soldier peered around Gaston to Remington, standing tensely by the inner wall. "That's the lady of the keep? I dinna know, my lord, I swear it. I would hae never touched her had I known she was the Lady."

"Then you did indeed grab her," Gaston wanted to make sure he understood correctly before he dispensed justice.

The soldier swallowed. "Aye, but it was a mistake."

Gaston did not reply. In fact, before anyone could blink, he reached out and threw his huge arm around the back of the man's neck as if he was about to hug him. Then, with the bent elbow of his other arm, he shoved hard against the soldier's head, bending his neck unnaturally over his other arm. As a twig snaps when bent in half, so did the soldier's neck. He was dead before he hit the ground.

Gaston gazed down at the dead man impassively. "And to make sure the mistake does not happen again, you will serve as an example to all of those who might think of touching Lady Stoneley or her sisters."

Everyone around the soldier seemed to be paralyzed for a moment, no one moving or speaking or even daring to blink. Arik and Antonius moved up behind Gaston and glanced down at the dead soldier, then turned to walk away without so much as a grunt or a word. Arik went to Remington.

"Come, my lady," he said gently.

Remington was like a stone statue; her eyes were wide as the sky and her hand was frozen over her mouth. She stared at the dead man in deep shock and Arik put his hand on her arm.

"Lady Remington?" he urged delicately. "Let us return to the castle."

Ever so slowly her hand came away from her mouth and she turned to focus on Arik. She opened her mouth to speak but nothing came forth. He knew she was lost when he saw the sea-crystal eyes glaze over and roll back into her head.

Gaston turned around to see Remington passed out cold in Arik's arms. Still lingering on the man he had just killed, he motioned for the soldier's comrades to take his body away. Only then did he move to Arik.

"Give her to me," he rumbled.

Obediently, Arik handed her over and Gaston clutched her against his massive chest tenderly; even Arik could see the softness in his lord's touch.

"I want the troop house finished before I return," Gaston said quietly.

"Where are you going?" Arik inquired.

"To a faire," Gaston replied, carrying Remington off across the outer bailey, towards the castle.

Remington was extremely subdued as they plodded along the road to Ripon. It was of no matter to Dane, for he chattered endlessly to Gaston, Antonius and Patrick, curious about every aspect of the equipment they carried. They were patient with the boy and answered him accordingly, but each man's mind was detached from the conversation at hand.

Antonius kept eyeing Jasmine from where she sat on her small gray palfrey, and she would blush prettily and smile at him. Patrick was intent on passing gazes at Rory, who would actually act coy, as Skye, sitting next to her sister on the wagon, would stick her tongue out at him. It was a crazy, charming game that went on mile after mile.

Only Remington avoided Gaston's searching gaze. He rode slightly ahead of her wearing his full battle armor, which frankly intimidated her. But she was also confused and bewildered at the events in the bailey and she spent this quiet time trying to discover for herself if she did something terribly wrong to have caused a man's death. Was her mistake in not stopping Gaston, or was it going to the bailey in the first place? She simply did not know and her stomach cramped endlessly from her nerves.

Gaston rode calmly at the head of the column, alone as usual since Arik was not present. He brought six knights and an equal number of men-at-arms along, very seasoned fighting men, for he was unsure of the conditions in Ripon. In the heart of the Yorkist community, he was most certain to be viewed as a traitor and an enemy and he had no desire to be caught defenseless, especially with women and children present.

He would have liked to have ridden with Remington, to have eased her mind about what happened, for he knew she was brooding about it. But it had been completely necessary for her safety and for the safety of her sisters; when rumor got around as to the severity of the punishment, no man would so much as look at her.

Ripon sat in the Greenland at the foot of the Pennine Mountains. Even as they drew close to the town, they were greeted by gay peasants and merchants traveling in and out of the city. The faire had started yesterday eve and was in full swing.

Gaston grew cautious when he realized there were soldiers everywhere, knights of different houses whom he had fought with and finally, against. And there was no mistaking that they knew the Dark Knight on sight. He could see it in their eyes as he studied the men beneath his lowered visor; he could see their bodies tense and their faces grow taut.

He was not sorry he had come, indeed; he was pleased to make a show of force, yet he was concerned for Remington and her sisters. Should any fighting start, he did not want them in the way.

"Look." Dane cried out gleefully as they entered the outskirts. "A puppet show. Can I go see, Mummy? Can I?"

Remington looked to the source of his excitement; a makeshift puppet stage and a dozen children hovering about it. She could hear the children laughing.

"Very well," she slid from her bay palfrey and helped her son from the wagon. A soldier appeared to take the horse from her and she jumped at his swift action, terrified he was going to grab her and terrified Gaston would commit murder again. But he led the horse away and she calmed her racing heart, taking Dane by the hand and leading him towards the puppeteers.

"We are going on further," Rory called to her. "We shall meet you inside."

Remington waved to her and the wagon moved forward once again, driven by Rory. Gaston lingered behind, retaining Sir Roald with him and three soldiers.

Dane loved the puppet show, especially when the witch-puppet began throwing out candy to the audience. Remington stood back, a faint smile on her lips as her son scrambled about on the dirt in search of the sweets. Gaston stood slightly behind her.

"We can buy him sweets elsewhere," he mentioned to Remington. "He does not need to eat them off the ground."

She turned to look at him. "It is of no fun to eat sweets that have not been thrown at you, my lord. Surely you know that."

His helmet was on, his visor down, and she couldn't see his face. "Indeed I do. But the larger children are getting all of the goods. See?"

Dane stood up, two pieces of candy in his hands and a frown on his face. The puppet show was ended when the treats were thrown and the crowd of children disbanded.

"I only got two pieces of candy," he wailed when he came upon his mother. "Those bigger boys took the rest."

"We can buy you more," Remington made amends. "Come now, let's go inside and see what else there is."

They made their way inside the small gates that opened up onto a wide street. Ripon was a bustling city and the faire was a large one. Remington felt her tension leave her as her eyes grazed the hustle and bustle; she liked crowds and people. There would be much to see and do here.

"Where to, my lady?" Gaston asked behind her. Taran followed like a trained dog once again, his great head butting against Gaston as he tried to move closer to Remington.

She glanced about. "I am not sure. Let's just start walking and see where we end up."

They proceeded onward. Roald walked casually beside Gaston, leaning toward his lord.

"There is a jousting exhibit and competition, my lord," he murmured.

"How do you know that?" Gaston asked.

"There is a sign posted at the gate," Roald replied.

Gaston snorted. "I wonder what idiots we will see here today, then. An open competition will bring them from all over."

"Idiots that hate us," Roald mumbled. "They might make a competition to see who can kill us first."

Gaston grinned. Roald was always the doomsayer of his corps and he was amused by him. "Bring them on. It has been a while since I have competed for sport."

Remington was several paces ahead and stopped at a booth boasting fine leather purses and shoes. While Dane danced impatiently beside her, she carefully inspected a lovely pair of white doeskin boots. The merchant was intent on showing her a purse to match and she studied the pouch with equal care.

Gaston watched Dane wriggle and complain and finally took pity on him. He walked up and took the boy by the shoulder.

"Look over there, Dane," he pointed with his huge mailed hand. "There is a man with trained dogs."

Dane's eyes lit up. Gaston walked him across the avenue and together they watched five trained dogs jump through hoops and dance on their hind legs. Dane was enthralled, clapping loudly with every accomplishment and Gaston had to smile at the boy's enthusiasm.

He was growing quite attached to the lad in lieu of his own absent son, and watching Dane made him long for his own boy.

He had not seen Trenton in almost a year. He had spent so much of his time fighting for Henry and avoiding Mari-Elle that Trenton had suffered in the process. He so desperately wanted to have his son with him, but he could not offer the boy a proper life. At least at Clearwater, he was in a stable environment. Even if he had grown up thinking his father wanted nothing to do with him.

Yet Gaston saw his chance for knowing his son was nearly passed, for the boy was soon to foster at Northwood Castle in Northumberland. He had made arrangements with Lord Longley, an old soldier and friend of Gaston's father, after Trenton was born.

But as he watched Dane, he realized that there was no reason for Trenton to go to Kent. After all, Dane was staying at Mt. Holyoak to foster; why shouldn't Trenton come as well? Gaston planned to make Mt. Holyoak his seat, his haven for the rest of his life, and he wanted his son with him. Who better to train the boy than he and Arik?

He crossed his arms with a grunt of satisfaction at his conclusion. Aye, his son would come to live with him and he himself would oversee the boy's development. He only hoped he could undo everything Mari-Elle had undoubtedly instilled into the lad.

The little dog show was over and Dane took great delight in petting one of the friendly animals, a wiry little mutt with short white hair. The dog waged his tail furiously and licked Dane's hand.

"He likes me," Dane said proudly, beaming at Gaston.

"Aye, he does," Gaston agreed. "A smart animal."

Dane continued to pet the dog and Gaston turned his head in the direction of approaching horses; destriers, no doubt, from the sound of the thunder. He briefly wondered what fools would be riding chargers in the midst of civilians.

Remington picked that moment to cross the street toward them. He caught her out of the corner of his eye and whirled around, preparing to yell at her to halt. His heart went racing into his throat, visions of her plastered all over the dirt filling his mind. Gaston had never come close to panic in his life; the distinct taste of it on his tongue brought him to a new level of awareness.

But the chargers were already coming to a stop, and so did Remington. She took a few steps back as the great warhorses danced in front of her, four of them in all. Astride them sat four well-seasoned, over-dressed knights.

Gaston went from the verge of panic to the brink of extreme protectiveness. He could see Roald taking hold of Remington's arm and pulling her back, away from the men, but Remington did not appear the least bit concerned. One of the knights threw up his visor.

"By damn. Remington Stoneley, in the flesh." he crowed. "I have not seen you in over a year, girl. Where are you man-eating sisters?"

Remington smiled broadly at the man and Gaston had to clench his fists to keep from raging out of control. Already, he was making his way toward them, fighting to keep a casual pace.

"What are you doing here, Derek? I heard you were in Manchester," she said gaily.

The knight was a young, fair, generally dashing man. He waved a careless hand at her. "I was, but I came back here to catch a glimpse of you. You look ravishing, love, as usual."

She blushed prettily and Gaston nearly exploded. But he kept his calm demeanor, rounding the chargers to stand next to Roald, several feet back, scrutinizing the knights, arms crossed to make their arms bigger and even more imposing.

Dane scooted to his mother and Remington took his hand affectionately. "Dane, do you remember Sir Derek Botmore of Rainton?"

Dane shook his head, suddenly shy, and Sir Derek laughed. "Thank God he looks like you and not his father," he said, leaning forward in his saddle. "Say, I heard a nasty rumor that Guy was thrown in the White Tower after Bosworth and that Mt. Holyoak is occupied by Henry's arm. What about that?"

Remington's smile faded. "Sir Gaston de Russe is our lord now," she said evenly.

Sir Derek sat back in the saddle, his brow furrowed in deep thought. "De Russe? De Russe? Christ, Calvin, where have I heard that name?"

"The Dark Knight," the knight on his flank said assuredly. "You have heard of him, Derek. The bastard that betrayed Richard and turned the tides at Bosworth, among other things. He and Matt Wellesbourne go hand in hand when speaking of traitors."

Derek waved him off. "The White Lord cannot be grouped with de Russe," he told him. "There is a reason why they call the man the Dark Knight. He is pure evil."

Remington's light mood was gone. She hated to hear these men speak so callously of Gaston, even though they spoke the truth. She had never asked him about Bosworth because she honestly did not care; she knew him to be a fine, noble man and knew he must have had his reasons for what he did. Whatever the reason, though, it did not matter to her.

"He is an excellent lord, Calvin, and I will not hear you say such horrible things about him," she said firmly, motioning to the two knights behind Derek and Calvin, as well. "Surely you are no angel yourself, any of you. George, Robert, do not try to hide behind your visors for I know it to be you. Cowards who chose to pursue the tournament circuit rather than fight for your king."

Sir Derek put up a hand to silence her. "To each his own, Remington. Calvin meant no harm," he said. "As to your accusation of cowardice, I beg to differ. It takes a good deal of bravery to fight in tournament after tournament against men who are trying to skin you alive."

"The same as with on the battlefield, only we get paid for taking risks," Calvin cut in with a grin. "If I am going to risk life and limb, I want to be well-compensated."

She shook her head, the mood entirely broken. "You are nothing but little boys. Get out of my sight before I take you all over my knee."

Derek's face brightened lewdly. "Me, first."

Gaston had all he could take from the young idiots. He stepped forward but was caught off guard when Dane latched onto his leg as if afraid of the men who were speaking to his mother. Astonished, he put his hand on the boy to reassure him but continued forward.

"Be gone with you," he growled. "You have taken enough of the lady's time."

The four men were startled by the deep voice and pure size of the man; Gaston found it hard to believe that they had failed to notice him until this moment.

Remington turned to look at him, visions of him snapping the soldier's neck on her behalf filling her mind. She was suddenly fearful that Derek's life was in jeopardy, as well.

"Sir Gaston, this is Sir Derek Botmore," she said quickly. "His father is Lord Botmore, one of the more powerful barons in Yorkshire. They have a large fortress just south of Rainton."

"Sir Gaston?" Sir Derek repeated in a whisper. "*The* Sir Gaston?"

"Your father is expected to meet with me soon. I do not want to see you with him when he comes to my keep," Gaston said.

Derek's mouth opened in outrage, and then quickly shut it again. "If that is your wish, my lord, then I will oblige you."

Gaston did not reply. Derek eyed him for a moment longer before looking to Remington.

"Remington, always a pleasure," he said with a forced smile; he was truly frightened of the massive man with the legendary reputation.

"That is Lady Remington to you, pup," Gaston took another step forward. "You will show no disrespect to the lady of Mt. Holyoak."

Derek cleared his throat and slammed his visor down. Reining the chargers a wide berth around Gaston, he and his companions lost themselves in the crowd as they headed for the tournament arena. Gaston turned to watch them go, patting Dane again after a moment.

"Arrogant whelps," he mumbled.

Remington was watching him. He turned to look at her, seeing an expression he had never seen before; her eyes were smiling and her face was almost seductive. There was nothing particular about her expression for she wasn't truly smiling; it was simply the *way* she was looking at him. His visor went up for the first time since their arrival.

"What is it?" he asked quietly.

"Not a thing, my lord," she replied, a smile creeping onto her lips.

He was jolted by the entire action, his body tingling with excitement. Before he could press her further, she coyly lowered her lashes and turned away.

Dane let go of his leg but slipped his hand into the great mailed glove. Gaston held his hand tightly as they followed Remington along the line of merchants. Roald, the men-at-arms, and the horses brought up the rear.

Woodcarvers tried to sell them items both useless and common. A merchant dealing in weapons tried to convince Remington that she needed an exquisite bejeweled dagger, but she giggled and politely waved the man off. There were jugglers and acrobats parading up and down the avenue to a long pole. One of them sat Dane in a chair and proceeded to balance the chair atop the pole on his chin as Dane clung to the chair for dear life. Gaston firmly indicated for the man to put the lad down, and he did so. But then Dane begged to be put aloft again and Gaston rolled his eyes, moving the child along before he demanded to join the circus.

Remington watched her son and Gaston together, the affection was evident between them. Dane acted as if Gaston were the most important person in his life and she completely understood; he had never had a true father, nor a real male figure to look up to. He was completely in love with Gaston as only a little boy could be.

Her heart warmed at the interaction, at Gaston's uncanny ability with the boy. She could see what a wonderful father he was and it softened her and hurt at the same time. She greatly envied Mari-Elle de Russe her husband, for it was something Remington would never have the pleasure of knowing. A man to love her son, and to love her. Once she never even thought of such unattainable things, but seeing Gaston with Dane not only made her think of it, it made her *want* it. The thought was enough to bring tears to her eyes.

A perfume merchant made her forget her tears as he tried to sell her on everything he had. She sniffed at a couple of bottles, but nothing caught her attention. Gaston pushed his way forward and picked up one of the bottles, inhaling deeply. Dane maneuvered between his mother and the knight, watching them both eagerly.

"You do not smell perfume like that," Remington admonished softly. "You sniff it delicately, two or three times to better digest the scent."

He looked at her seriously and took her advice with the next bottle. His eyebrows lifted with mild approval and he held it out to her for her opinion.

"Ah, lady, your husband knows a fine scent when he smells it," the merchant gushed. "See if you do not approve of his taste."

Remington looked at the man in shock; she could barely smell the vial Gaston was offering to her. Strangely, her breathing grew rapid and her insides twisted painfully at the one word the merchant had used; *husband.* He called Gaston her husband.

It suddenly hit her that she wished for it to be true. Somehow, in the two weeks she had known him, something completely wonderful and utterly devastating had happened. He had endeared himself to her completely as her savior, her hero, her friend, and her son's idol.

She was in love with him.

She did not want to love him.

"Ah, I see your son has his father's features," the merchant continued recklessly. "See if he holds his father's good taste, as well. See if he likes the perfume, too."

Remington felt a painful shock go through her and suddenly she was reeling away from the table, rushing away blindly with no destination in mind, simply to get away. She couldn't control the tears that were gushing freely now, not even knowing why she was crying, but that she was. Every emotion she had ever felt was magnified ten-fold by the merchant's words, the slap of realization painful to her soul.

Gaston tried to catch her as she whirled away but Dane stood in the way. Quickly, he set the vials down and passed the boy off to Roald.

"Stay here," he told them.

She had dashed behind the vendor's shacks and he followed, walking quickly but not running because just one of his strides equaled three of hers. She was several yards ahead of him, dashing into a heavily tree-lined park that was surrounded by peasant huts.

She ducked behind a thick oak. He could still see the rose of her surcoat and saw that she had come to a halt, and he slowed his steps accordingly. Quietly, he came up on the tree and made sure he was in plain view as not to startle her.

She was sobbing against the trunk, her face pressed into her crooked arm.

"Remi, what on earth is the matter?" he asked gently.

She had heard him approach, knowing that he would come for her, but she truly wanted to be alone. She could not comprehend the myriad of emotions taking their toll on her spirits.

"Go away," she cried softly. "Please, Gaston, just go away."

"Not until you tell me why you are crying," he said. "Was the perfume really that bad?"

She choked out a laugh among the sobs, but it was short-lived. He waited patiently while she cried, wanting earnestly to know why her heart was broken. In the back of his mind he suspected a reason, but he was reluctant to pursue it. He was fearful to know if she was crying because the merchant had called him her husband and she loathed the idea. But something inside him needed to know.

"Are you upset because he called me your husband?" he said softly, moving closer to her. "It was an innocent mistake. He saw us together, and Dane, and naturally assumed we were a family. Is it so terrible?"

"No," she burst out, turning her face to him and stumbling back against the tree trunk. Her beautiful face was red with tears and intense feelings. "It's not terrible at all. That is the problem, Gaston. I...."

She stopped dead in her tracks and all sobbing ceased, her eyes wide at him. Shocked as she was that she had almost spilled out the contents of her mind, she sniffled and stepped away from him quickly, wiping at her face. "I...just do not like being reminded that I have a husband," she whispered, although that was not what she was thinking. *I want my husband to be you.*

His brows drew together in faint concern and he removed his helmet, tossing it to the ground. Slowly, he pulled off one of his gauntlets. "Is that all? There is nothing else?"

"Aye," she said, her voice squeaking and her lip quivering.

His gaze devoured her for a moment and she was positive he could read everything she was thinking. They were hidden behind the oak tree, surrounded by undergrowth from prying eyes, and his huge head came up to her cheek. "I do not believe you."

She burst into tears right then and there. He pulled her up against him, sorry for the very first time in his life that he was wearing armor. He did so want to feel her against him.

He cradled her as she bawled like a baby. "Tell me, angel. What is so terrible that you cry as if your heart is broken?"

Her hand was partially covering her face, her cheek against his cold armor. Her sobs were open, painful, and she felt him kiss her forehead and lay his cheek against the top of her head. It undid her even more until she could hardly breathe through the force of her sobs.

"Slow down, angel," he whispered against her forehead. "You are going to make yourself ill. Slow down and breathe and tell me what the matter is."

How could she tell him? She had never been able to verbalize her feelings because she had so deeply suppressed them. She had no idea where to begin, or how to lie to him, because she was terrified to tell him the truth. But she had no control over her mouth for a moment.

"I want to die," she squeaked.

"You want to die? Why in the hell do you want to die?" his eyebrows drew together.

She coughed and sobbed and he held her tighter. "Because my life is ruined."

"It is? Why?" he asked gently.

"Because…because it is," she stammered, feeling light-headed with all of her crying.

"You are not making any sense," he kissed her forehead again. "Stop your tears, now. Dane will not wait patiently for us much longer."

She sobbed anew at the sound of her own son's name and he frowned gently. "Now what? What did I say?"

"Dane," she cried softly. "He loves you."

"I am very fond of him, as well," he was beginning to smile at the comical nature of the situation; she was absolutely silly but he was enjoying it in a peculiar sense. "Come now, Remi. Stop crying or Dane is going to go on without us."

She almost couldn't cry anymore. Her head hurt dreadfully and she had the hiccups to boot. Biting her lip, she wiped and wiped at her wet face until the tears had evaporated. He held her the entire time, stroking her hair with his uncovered hand.

"That's better," he held her back, gazing down into her angelic face. "Would you like to get something to eat now?"

She nodded, sniffling. He reached down and collected his helmet, plopping it back on his head and pulling his gauntlet back on. She watched him absently, feeling depressed.

His head came up from adjusting his gloves and he smiled at her, a rare bright smile. "What do you want to eat?"

She shrugged as he took her arm. "Ask Dane."

Dane was eager for a meat pie. Gaston found a vendor that made a wonderful cheese and meat concoction and the young boy devoured two of the dishes. Remington picked at hers, keeping an eye out for her sisters, as Dane delved into a raspberry custard. They ate together under the shade of a tree while Gaston and his men stood watch several feet away.

There were streets and streets of merchants come to Ripon for the Mid-Summer Faire. Dane had no shortage of interests as he went from booth to booth, scanning the wares until he came across something that interested him. Remington and Gaston followed him, not speaking to each other, pretending to be interested in other things. In faith, Remington had no idea what to say to him and turned her attention to whatever the faire had to offer. To think of Gaston and her outburst threatened to bring on the tears again.

They met up with her sisters at a cloth merchant's store and the four women began pouring over the winter fabrics. Excellent wool from Leeds and as far north as Scotland graced his tables and Remington bargained heavily for several different materials. With winter coming, they wanted to stock up on their heavy garments.

Gaston watched Remington barter with the merchant, noticing how cleverly she wheedled the man down from his original price. Whereas most women could be very aggressive, Remington used her natural charm and pleasant manner to achieve her goal. In fact, in the end, the merchant was barely making a profit on the substantial sale and lamented loudly on it.

Rory and Jasmine nodded confidently to one another as Remington counted out the money; they would each have three new winter surcoats with the fabric secured and Gaston's men began loading the bolts into the wagon.

"That woman barters like a barrister," Antonius murmured to Gaston. "I personally would not want to go against her."

"She is intelligent," Gaston said simply, proudly in fact.

Antonius made a sort of a longing sigh and Gaston banked the urge to shoot him a hard glance. Instead, he broke rank with his knights and moved forward to take a bolt of material that Remington was trying to handle. He put it in the wagon and turned around, his hands on his hips.

"Anything else?" he asked with a touch of sarcasm.

She raised a stubborn eyebrow. "Could be, my lord. I shall know when I see it."

He wanted to swat her on the backside playfully but dared not touch her. Instead, they progressed down the street again, mayhap a bit more comfortable with each other. The more time passed, the easier it was to forget about her crying jag.

At mid-afternoon a parade passed down the street, loud women and even louder men dressed in wild costumes and brightly painted. They were singing and dancing and Dane thought it all great fun as they passed by and threw bits of ribbon to the crowd. He caught a ribbon to go with his dirty candy, mightily pleased.

The parade passed and the crowd disbanded, moving along their way. Remington had Dane by the hand and was walking forward with her sisters as the men paced leisurely behind them, followed by the wagon. From the rear, they heard the weighty fall of hoof beats and the jingle of armor.

"I thought it was you," came a voice, very low and unfriendly. "You have a lot of courage to show your face in Yorkshire, de Russe."

Gaston turned around calmly. Four massive knights astride huge, scarred chargers stood beside the wagon. Several men-at-arms were following the knights, all as ruthless-looking and hardened as the knight sounded.

Gaston recognized the man and felt his adrenalin flow. He wanted Remington and her sisters the hell away from them, for he was more than certain that contact with this knight would result in no good.

"The battles are over and we have a new king and a united England," Gaston replied steadily. "I can go anywhere I damn well please, as can you, le Tourneaux."

The knight sat haughtily atop his charger, his gaze moving to the wagon full of fabric. He unsheathed his broadsword and stabbed a bolt, tearing it as he tried to hold it aloft to get a look at it.

"What are you doing? Shopping?" he asked distastefully.

Gaston moved closer to the wagon. Remington, fearful of the unfriendly knight, was hardly aware that Patrick had discreetly herded the women into a group and had placed his big body between them and the unsavory soldiers. Gaston's men-at-arms had taken up defensive stances as well, and Antonius and Roald stood calmly by the horses hitched to the wagon, their gazes never leaving Gaston.

Gaston pulled the material off of the sword and tucked it secure around the bolt. "My lady is," he said. "Is there something you wanted in particular, le Tourneaux, or are you simply trying to make a nuisance of yourself? If it is the latter, you have achieved your goal and may be on your way."

"What do you mean 'your' lady?" The knight raised his visor, his face leathered and hard. "Your wife is in Chepstow, as I recall."

Gaston's jaw ticked. "I was referring to the woman whose keep I now occupy."

The knight leaned forward, resting on the pommel of his saddle. "I had heard wind that Henry sent you north to keep rein on Yorkshire. A proper reward for betraying Richard, eh? Every man has his price, I suppose; even you."

Gaston's expression was controlled. "Be gone with you, Eugene. I have no time for your nonsense today."

"'Tis no nonsense I give you," le Tourneaux retorted. "Yet what I would truly like to give you is my broadsword through your gut, you traitorous bastard."

A twinkle came to Gaston's eyes. "You may try, of course, but be forewarned I will not be an easy target for you."

"To hell with you," le Tourneaux hissed through yellow teeth. "You who betrayed all that Richard stood for, you filthy whoreson."

"Do not call him that!" Dane charged forward, his little face red with anger. Remington gasped as Patrick tried to catch him, but the knight was too slow. Gaston, however, was fast enough and wound his thick arm around the boy as he raced by.

Le Tourneaux snorted with amusement. "And who is this? One of your knights?"

Dane kicked against Gaston. "I shall kill you," he yelled at the knight. "You can't talk to Sir Gaston like that! He is the greatest knight who has ever lived!"

Le Tourneaux guffawed loudly, as did his men. Gaston did nothing more than whisper in Dane's ear. Angrily, the little boy turned and went obediently back to his mother. Le Tourneaux's eyes fell on Remington as she clutched Dane to her.

"Ah, a fine woman, de Russe," he said, drinking his fill of Remington. "A reward from Henry, no doubt. Aye, I shall wager you were well rewarded for being akin to Judas."

Gaston shifted on his big legs and Remington saw Roald and Antonius flinch, waiting for the signal that would unleash them. But Gaston made no provocative action.

"Out of my sight, le Tourneaux," he rumbled. "If you linger you risk my wrath."

Le Tourneaux may have hated Gaston, but he was no fool; he knew the Dark Knight meant what he said and he had already provoked him to the limit. But he couldn't leave without one last leer at Remington.

"If you get bored of the Dark One, seek me out," he said, already spurring his charger into a walk. "I shall show you what a real man can do."

Remington heard a sword unsheathe before the knight had even finished his sentence. In a blinding flash, she saw Gaston's sword come forth and catch le Tourneaux on the back of the neck and she grabbed Dane to her, screaming. From that moment on, it was pure chaos.

Le Tourneaux was dead as he hit the ground, his head half-cut off. The other three knights went into immediate action, battle-hardened men not afraid of a good fight and harboring a good deal of resentment toward Gaston. Swords reflected the sunlight in blinding sequence as they came forth and there was suddenly no more division between le Tourneaux's men and Gaston's troops; it was a huge brawl in the middle of the avenue and people everywhere were screaming, running for cover.

Remington pulled Dane and her sisters with her, running for their lives. Dane was hollering that he must help Gaston, but Remington ignored him. They dashed clear of the fight, bumping into panicked peasants as they went and hearing the crash of goods as tables went over in the rush. The sounds of metal on metal followed them.

Remington suddenly stopped when they were a safe distance away, turning to see if she could catch a glimpse of Gaston. Rory and Jasmine almost crashed into her in their haste to leave the scene.

'Why are you stopping?" Rory demanded.

Remington stood on her toes, peering into the swarm. "We're safe here," she said. "Moreover, I am not leaving the men alone. We must wait here until it is over."

Rory and Jasmine turned to watch, too, as Skye clung to Dane fearfully. The three elder sisters stood side by side, their eyes riveted to the fight in progress.

"Do you see Patrick?" Rory asked after a moment.

Remington shook her head. "You like him, do not you?"

Rory's cheeks flushed. "He is the only knight who had been kind to me."

"He is the only one you have not played jokes on," Jasmine said, her voice edgy. "Do you see Antonius?"

"Your Roman god? Nay, I do not see him," Remington said with a faint smirk. "But the fight is still going on, so they must be whole...."

Her voice trailed off as she caught sight of Gaston. He was a good head taller than the other participants, his black hair glistening in the sun. He was locked in combat with a knight and a soldier, both men trying to do the Dark Knight serious harm, yet Gaston fended them off as if he were doing nothing more than practicing. The soldier took a blade to the abdomen while the knight was the unfortunate recipient of an armored elbow to the neck, followed by a mortal blow to the head.

Remington had never seen a fight before, and was astonished at the speed and fury. Roald and Antonius managed to kill three soldiers while Patrick took out another knight all within the first minute or so. Seeing their comrades dead, the rest of le Tourneaux's men decided there was nothing left worth fighting for and turned tail, making exit post haste. There was no chance of victory against the Dark Knight.

As quickly as it started, the fight was over. Merchants and shoppers alike slowly peered out of the hiding places, shaken but quick to recover. Fights were not unusual between soldiers of opposing houses and rapidly the street began to resume normal activities.

Gaston picked his helmet up from the ground where it had tumbled from the wagon seat and put it on his head, ironically, he thought, after the fact. Glancing at his men to make sure no one had been injured, his eyes sought out Remington.

She wasn't hard to find; the most beautiful, heavenly woman he had ever seen was walking toward him in the company of her sisters and son. He was relieved to see she was unharmed, and even more relieved to see she was smiling at him. His heart melted, his body went limp, and he wanted nothing more at that moment than to take her into his arms. Dane broke away from the women and ran toward him at break-neck speed.

"I saw you. I saw you!" he yelled enthusiastically. "You fought off all those men by yourself."

Dane almost bashed into him but he reached down and caught the excited lad with gentle hands. "Well, I did have some help," he said, looking up from the boy to find Remington standing in front of him.

Dane was babbling about the battle but all Gaston could do was gaze back at the boy's mother. Her sea-crystal eyes were liquid as she stared back into his smoky gray orbs, her face completely soft and utterly captivating. He read no fear, no terror, only trust and admiration. And pride. He definitely read pride.

No one had ever been proud of him. Mari-Elle was only interested in the benefits of his reputation, his kings had only been interested in what his strength could accomplish. No one had ever taken *pride* in his work, his skill. Except Remington; he could read her face.

Still gazing at Remington's face, he passed Dane off to the nearest sister. "Take him a moment and remain here. We shall return shortly."

He reached out and took Remington by the hand, pulling her with him as he took long strides down the avenue. She nearly had to run to keep up with him.

"Where are we going?" she asked.

He glanced down at her and smiled, and her heart did flips in her ribcage. He did not answer her but continued to lead her to the end of the street and took a sharp turn to the left. He slowed his pace a bit for her as they wound their way around carts and people, and Remington was thrilled out of her mind that he was holding her hand. She wanted everyone to look at them and think that they were together; a pair. In love. *I want you to be my husband.*

She recognized the perfume merchant's shop and Gaston pulled her inside, pulling her against his chest as they waited patiently for the merchant to finish with another customer. When the shopkeeper saw them, his face brightened.

"Ah, good knight, I see you have returned with your wife," he said happily. "How may I serve you?"

"I was sampling a scent earlier," Gaston said in his rich baritone voice. "I would purchase it for my...wife."

He felt Remington stiffen, turning to look at him questioningly. He gazed back at her emotionlessly.

"Ah, yes." the man was already moving for the pretty pewter vial, inlaid with common stones. "A fine scent. I have soap and oils that are the same...."

Gaston did not let him finish. "Wrap them up, then, all of them," his gaze moved back to Remington. "I would have my wife smelling wonderful."

"As wonderful as she looks, no doubt," the merchant said, busily wrapping the goods in pretty cloth. "May I say that she is the most beautiful woman I have seen today. You are a very lucky man, indeed, my lord."

Gaston should not have allowed it; he was actually permitting himself to live a lie, for the briefest of moments. He would have given his soul to the devil for the lie to have been truth. His arms went tighter around Remington, her back to his chest, and he felt her cave into him.

"She is the most beautiful woman you have ever seen," he told the merchant pointedly. "Not just this day, but any day."

The merchant and Gaston began to bargain over the price, but Remington was living in a world of frozen time. He continued to hold onto her and she continued to let him, drawing strength from his massive size and potency. She fully realized that he was beginning to treat her like a whore, a kept woman, but she did not care. It was no worse than being an abuser's wife. At least Gaston made her feel safe, honored, respected. Her inner self, the neglected, beaten wife, demanded to be allowed the fantasy of being the Dark Knight's wife, if only for a moment.

They left the merchant's shop, Gaston clutching one hand and her purchased bundle in the other. She watched him as they proceeded down the street, studying his strong profile. He completely overshadowed her naïve senses.

He caught her stare, knowing she expected answers. Honestly, he did not know what to say. Only that he wished his lies had been truth.

"Thank you for the perfume," she said softly. "It was terribly expensive."

"You are worth every pence, madam," he replied, avoiding her eyes.

She was quiet a moment. "Why did you say what you did?"

He felt cornered, uncomfortable. He cleared his throat. "Why did I tell the man that you were my wife? Because it would have been far more complicated to explain our true relationship to him, and furthermore, it was none of his business. Suffice it to say I made up a convenient story."

His tone was steady, almost callous, and Remington felt a tremendous letdown. Convenient, did he say? As convenient as she was to him, aching and vulnerable and hurt? She yanked her hand free of his grip and came to an abrupt halt, thrusting the cloth bundle at him.

"Here," she said shortly.

"Here what?" he looked at her outstretched hand.

"I cannot accept this expensive gift," she said stiffly.

He put his hands on his hips. "And why not? I bought it for you."

Hurt was joined by anger and she began to twitch. Her stormy eyes met him. "I cannot be bought, my lord. If you will kindly take your perfume back."

"Bought?" he repeated, growing annoyed. "Remi, what are you talking about?"

She almost threw the perfume at him but controlled herself. A look of great pain crossed her face. "Why do you toy with me, Gaston? You kiss me, hold me tenderly, buy my lovely gifts, call me your wife when you know perfectly well our relationship will never end in matrimony," she said softly, stepping closer to him, her eyes imploring. "What is it you want from me? I do not think I understand your attentions."

He was unbalanced by her words. By God, he wasn't sure of his own feelings; how could he explain them to her?

"I...I am not sure I understand, either," he said quietly. "All I know is that I want to be with you, I want to see you smile and hear your laughter. For the first time in my life I have found a woman I can care for and I shall be damned if I am going to lose you."

"*Lose* me?" she repeated incredulously. "Gaston, I am not yours to lose."

He gripped her shoulders, his mailed gloves biting into the soft flesh of her arm. "Listen to me well, madam. I shall never let you go. You and I and Dane will live at Mt. Holyoak for the rest of our days and I will love you both as if you were mine in the eyes of God and our king." His hand reached down and raised the cloth package she held. "This was not meant to buy your favors as one would a whore, Remi. It was meant as a token of my affection for you."

Her eyes were wide. Slowly, she shook her head. "Oh Gaston...I simply do not know. I am so confused."

He raised her hand and kissed it softly. "So am I."

They proceeded to the next street and met up with the rest of their party. Jasmine and Skye took great delight in the perfume as Dane latched on to Gaston again. Gaston took the boy's hand as they went on their way.

The rest of the afternoon passed peacefully enough. Dane purchased a puppet modeled like a jester and a wooden cart and horse. Skye purchased ribbon for her hair and Jasmine bought a lovely quartz crystal bowl. Only Rory could not be persuaded to purchase frivolous things, instead admiring beautiful swords with Patrick and Antonius. Remington and Gaston hung together, yet few words were spoken between them.

As the sun was lowering in the sky, herald trumpets were heard from the direction of the arena and Dane's curiosity was piqued.

"What's that?" he demanded of Gaston.

"I believe the start of the tournament is being announced," Gaston replied.

"Tournament?" he turned to his mother eagerly. "Can we go watch the tournament, Mummy? Can we?"

"I do not think so," she said. "It has already been a full day and we must get started back home."

Dane's face fell. "But I have never seen a tournament. Can we just stay a little longer?"

Remington glanced at Gaston. "My lord?"

He shrugged. "I suppose we can watch a few minutes of it. As it is already, we shall be riding for an hour in the dark."

Leaving two soldiers to guard the goods in the wagon, Gaston took Dane and the rest of the group to the tournament field. Already, the knights were taking the field to the loud cheer of the crowd and Dane peppered Gaston with hundreds of questions, all before they even sat down. Dane sat between his mother and the knight, his eyes wide as saucers as he watched the gaily colored knights ride by on their massive chargers.

There was a good deal of pomp and ceremony to the beginning of the competition. Eight knights of local Yorkists houses paraded in fine armor and bright banners and the crowd in the lists roared with approval. Remington recognized a few of the houses, including Sir Derek, and she caught on to the excitement of the crowd.

"Have you ever competed in tournaments, my lord?" she asked.

"More than I can count," Gaston replied, scrutinizing a particular knight as he blew by.

"Did you win?" Dane asked.

Gaston smiled at the boy. "More than I lost."

One of the knights seemed particularly interested in Remington. He ran his charger by three or four times, finally reining the snorting animal in front of their group.

"Are you promised, my lady?" he pointed his gloved finger in Remington's direction. "I am in need of a favor."

She did not know he was speaking to her. She looked around, at her sisters, and they all shrugged at each other. But Gaston knew exactly who the knight was speaking to and rose to his feet.

"She is," he boomed. "Be on your way."

The knight continued to pause in front of them. "My lord de Russe?"

Gaston had enough encounters for one day. He crossed his arms threateningly. "Who asks?"

The knight drew up his visor. "Sir Hubert Doyle, my lord. I served with you...."

"Under Edward," Gaston finished for him; he recognized the knight.

"Aye," the knight smiled. "'Tis good to see you again, my lord. I heard what happened at Bosworth and I would like you to know that my support is with you."

Gaston eyed him coolly. "You did not serve Richard, did you?" It was more a statement.

The knight shook his head. "In good conscience, I could not, my lord. I pray that you are not offended by this."

Gaston sat back down, waving the man off with a faint flick of his hand. "Good day to you, Doyle."

Sir Hubert closed his visor. "I apologize for my rash statement to your lady wife. I did not recognize you; in truth, I was looking only at her."

Gaston looked at Remington; her eyes widened slightly. Lying to the merchant was one thing, by fibbing in front of her sisters and Gaston's knights was quite another.

"I fault you not, man," Gaston said. "She is the only woman in the world worth looking at."

The knight gave him a smart salute and charged off, leaving Remington flushed; she did not care to look at her sisters. Dane stood up, watching the knights congregate at the end of the field.

"Are they going to fight now?" he asked Gaston.

"In a moment," Gaston replied, looking past Dane to his mother; her cheeks were still flushed.

The tournament got off to a fast start. The first three rounds ended quickly, with the losers being unseated in the joust quickly. Rory and Skye turned into rowdy saloon wenches, cheering and yelling their lungs out for the knights whose colors they liked best. Gaston tolerated their screaming, knowing how the cheers from the crowd always supported him, but Patrick was having jealous fits over Rory's attentions. Behind them, Jasmine and Antonius sat conspicuously close and snickered.

The sun began to hang low in the sky and Gaston sent a couple of soldiers to retain supper for the ladies. The men returned with roast chicken and sweetened carrots that were quickly devoured by Dane and his aunts. Remington did not have an appetite and politely watched the jousting bouts in front of her.

"I am afraid we must be going," Gaston finally said, hating to spoil Dane's fun. "But we shall be riding in the dark and I would like to get on our way."

Remington agreed silently, pulling Dane along behind her. The boy did everything but kick and scream; he begged, pleaded, and drug his feet as his mother led him out of the lists.

"Dane," Gaston said sternly. "Knights do not act like spoiled children. They do what they are told without question. You do not want me to think that you cannot follow orders, do you?"

Dane stood straight. "Nay, my lord."

Gaston nodded curtly, pleased that the child was reasonable. The group left the tournament arena and met with the wagon where they had left it. Rory, Dane and Skye piled into the front of the wagon while Antonius helped Jasmine mount her little palfrey. Remington was moving for her own bay mare when she noticed the animal favoring its right foreleg. Concerned, she called to Gaston.

"See here," she pointed to the leg. "I think she's lame."

Gaston ran a trained hand up the horses' fetlock, feeling the telltale bump in the tendon. He checked the hoof for any other outward sign before straightening.

"Indeed she is," he said. "You will have to ride in the wagon."

The wagon bench was already full with her son and her sisters, and the small bed was filled with bolts of material. Gaston and Patrick shifted the bolts around but there was barely enough room for her to perch her bottom on the end of the wagon bed. It would be uncomfortable at best.

Remington hopped up on the end of the wagon and tried to get comfortable when Gaston reached out and pulled her off.

"You shall ride with me," he said.

A bit reluctantly, she allowed him to lead her over to Taran and she stood next to the horse while he adjusted the saddle. Taran, smelling

Remington, nudged her with his great nose. She put her hands on the huge head.

"Hello, Taran," she crooned. "I have missed you, too."

Gaston watched the two out of the corner of his eye. "You are going to spoil my horse if you keep on and he shall be no good to me."

"Keep on what?" she asked. "I am doing nothing but showing him affection."

"He is a warhorse, not a kitten," Gaston put his hands around her waist; they completely encircled her and then some. Gently, he lifted her onto his saddle. Putting his foot firmly in the stirrup, he mounted heavily behind her. Settling Remington into a comfortable position, he made sure everyone was ready to leave and spurred the horse forward.

Darkness fell quickly and so did the chill. Dressed in rose silk, Remington was quickly cold and Gaston retrieved her cloak from the wagon. Wrapped in the thick woolen garment, she was soon warmed by the hard iciness of his chest armor biting into her. Making the best of it, she settled back against him for the long ride home.

Gaston rode broodingly, feeling Remington's softness before him and it made him miserable. What in the hell was he thinking? How could he tell Remington those things? True nonetheless, but he couldn't believe he had told her his innermost feelings. Yet she had responded in kind and he knew she felt the same way, no matter how confused they both were. He was elated and forlorn at the same time.

They had been on the road a couple of hours when Dane began to wail. Concerned, Gaston reined in Taran to a halt.

"I can't sleep when the wagon is moving," he cried. "My stomach hurts."

"He is prone to motion sickness," Remington told Gaston softly. "Especially when he is tired."

"Can he make it to Mt. Holyoak?" Gaston asked. "We have another two hours at the most."

She shrugged. "I doubt it. He shall be vomiting the rest of the way if we continue. Unless he walks, of course."

"It will take all night if he walks," Gaston said flatly. "I suppose we had better stop for the night, then."

Remington nodded quickly. "We can use the bed of the wagon to sleep in, and the material for shelter."

Gaston was already in motion, ordering the soldiers to take the wagon from the road and set up a makeshift camp. Dane and his aunts were delighted with the prospective adventure.

Patrick and Jasmine gathered pieces of wood and soon there was a roaring fire illuminating the campsite. Gaston's men had succeeded in turning the bed of the wagon into a delightful cozy hovel, using a few other bolts of material for shelters. Breaking out the bread and wine they brought with them, the hastily erected camp was a happy little place.

Dane was dancing around and being generally loud, not at all like the young boy who had declared his illness not an hour before. Gaston eyed him suspiciously; not at all sure that this wasn't part of a greater scheme to prolong his trip to the faire. As he set up a hasty perimeter for the night, the ladies and Dane warmed themselves by the fire and threw bits of bread at each other. It was a fun sense of adventure that they all felt, spending the night under the stars. To the men, it was nothing special nor unusual.

Fortunately, Dane wore himself down after his busy day and passed out cold in the back of the wagon. One by one his aunts joined him until the wagon bed was full. Remington did not think much of it until she made her way to the wagon to go to sleep and discovered there was no room left.

Gaston came up behind her as she tried to figure out what she was going to do about sleeping arrangements. "It appears that you are left out," he said softly. "But my men have made a couple of shelters that should prove satisfactory."

In truth, she wasn't at all concerned. She knew Gaston would look out for her. In fact, she wasn't at all tired, either. The moon above was bright and she did not feel like sleeping. She felt like staying up all night next to Gaston, even if they did nothing more than sit in silence.

"Are you going to sleep or are you going to stand guard," she asked him.

"I shall stand guard for a while," he said. "That is why Patrick and Antonius are trying to get some rest, so that they can relieve me in a few hours."

She glanced over at the two knights, lying down on the earth not far from the fire. "Where are Sir Roald and the other soldiers?"

"Around," Gaston's eyes grazed the dark forest. "Probably resting, too. Why do not you get some sleep as well?"

"I am not tired," she moved away from the wagon and back to the fire. He followed.

"You have had a busy day," he said, standing next to her as she warmed her hands.

"So have you," she looked at him pointedly. "You killed two men."

She had not said anything about those events all day and he wondered if it was because she was trying to forget the horror of it. He could see plainly that she had not forgotten.

"I had to," he replied simply.

"For me?" she asked.

"In a sense. 'Twas your honor I was defending both times," he crossed his arms, staring into the fire.

"I have never had anyone defend my honor," she said faintly.

He did not know what to say. Silently, she went back over to the wagon and fumbled about. He continued to remain by the fire, staring at the flames as he listened acutely to everything around him. He had learned a long time ago that his sense of hearing was nearly as valuable as his sense of sight when it came to guard duty

Remington appeared beside him, her cloak open. "Can you smell it?"

He sniffed the air. "Smell what?"

"The perfume." she insisted, opening her cloak wide and lifting her chin to reveal her neck. "Can you smell it now?"

He eyed her a moment before slowly lowering his head. He buried his face in the soft white crook of her neck and inhaled deeply. Roses, lavender, and lily of the valley filled his nostrils. And the scent of Remington.

"Aye, Remi," he whispered against her skin. "I smell it."

She closed her eyes at the feel of his face against her; this is what she wanted, what she had planned. It was as close as she could come to seducing him, for she knew nothing of the art of seduction. She could only go with her natural instincts, and her instincts told her to put on the perfume he had bought her.

She was suddenly shameless. She was confused, aye, but she knew how badly she wanted to feel his touch. Her fear of men, of being close, was evaporating by the second. She had never in her life wanted to be held until this very moment.

Her arms went around his neck and she threw her head back, pressing his face into her skin. All armor and cold steel, he responded with a fierce passion and clutched her tightly enough to crush her.

"Remi, Remi, my angel," he whispered. "By God, I want you."

She felt his lips roving over her neck, the swell of her breasts, and hot shivers rippled down her spine, kindling a fire in her loins the likes of which she had never felt before. Coupling, however, still frightened her a great deal and she suddenly pulled back from him as their heat intensified.

His gaze was inquisitive, lusty. "What's the matter?"

She was hesitant to answer him, not sure of where to begin. He saw her reluctance and read something else into it.

"I am sorry, angel," he said softly. "I shouldn't have done that here in the open, for anyone to see," he glanced over his shoulder and took her hand. "Come with me."

She opened her mouth to protest but the words refused to come forth. She wanted to tell him of her fear, her reserve, as he led her into a darkened thicket, but she choked out of pure bewilderment. Where on earth to begin?

They were well secluded from the rest of the camp when Gaston suddenly went down on his knees, running his hands down her thighs. Already, his attentions had her hot but she fought to maintain her calm.

"Gaston...," she murmured.

"What is it?" his hands were on her ankles, snaking under her dress.

Her breathing was coming fast and her stomach quivered as if she were ill. She found it difficult to hold a coherent thought. "Please...."

"Please what?" His hands were gripping her knees, running down the length of her calves.

She couldn't answer him for a moment as his hands whipped her into a panting frenzy. His touch was golden and she closed her eyes to better enjoy it when suddenly they drifted up her thighs and cupped her rounded bottom. At that precise moment, she snapped out of her passion-hazed trance.

"Gaston!" she gasped, jumping away.

His brow furrowed and he could see he had startled her with his bold touch. He dropped his hands from her bottom. "I am sorry, angel," he whispered. "I did not mean to frighten you."

Relieved that he understood her hesitation, she found it easier to speak to him of her reasons. Her hands moved to cup his great face.

"When Guy took me, it was with brutality and force. Never a kind word or a gentle touch, and I grew to hate it." Her voice was quivering. "I still...hate it."

He caressed her calves gently, groping for words. "Then you and I have something in common. I have never made love to anyone I have remotely cared for. I have always looked at it as a necessary service," he swallowed hard; words came difficult to him. "I do not do it now because I need to. I do it because I *want* to."

She looked hard at him, her fingers tracing the strong lines of his face. He saw her eyes beginning to well. "I am afraid."

"So am I."

"And I am married," she choked in a whisper.

"So am I."

"What about your wife?" She was starting to cry softly.

"She means as much to me as Guy means to you," he said gently. "'Tis only you I care for, Remi. Only you."

"Forever?" she breathed, tears falling from her eyes onto his face.

"Until I die," he answered without a doubt.

Black and white. He had always seen everything in black and white; black was Mari-Elle and their farce of a marriage. White was his growing feelings for Remington, overwhelming his senses.

She fell against him, kissing his forehead, the bridge of his nose. Hot tears from her frightened eyes fell on his face, bathing him and drilling deep into his heart.

"I shall be your mistress, Gaston," she whispered, her lips on his forehead. "Just promise me that you will never leave me and I swear I shall be your whore."

He knew how painful it was for her to say those words, and it was equally painful for him to hear them. She did not deserve the title, the connotation, and his heart was nearly bursting with anger and regret and happiness, everything he could possibly feel was a swirling mass in his chest.

His hands came out from under her surcoat and he clasped her face between his huge hands, still on his knees.

"I shall never leave you, angel, and you will not be my whore," he murmured. "'Tis a title for a cheap woman with no meaning to a man other than to relieve his needs. You are my lover, my life that will never be, and the fantasy of my heart. I never want to hear the word 'whore' again."

She sobbed louder and he kissed her to quiet her fears and her pain. All they knew was that they needed each other in the most powerful way possible.

He remained on his knees, unlatching his armor and casting it aside. Remington tried to calm her tears, releasing him long enough to allow him to remove his breastplate and short hauberk. She knew what was coming, having never experienced it on an affectionate level before, and she was torn between terror and eager anticipation.

He removed his shirt and Remington studied him; his chest was splendid, broad and beautifully muscled with a fine matting of crisp black hair. Never had she seen anything so exquisitely magnificent. Timidly, she reached out and brushed her fingers across his skin and he responded by kissing her fingers fervently. She was so curious about his chest that she had not realized that he had removed her cloak and spread it on the damp grass.

He grasped her arms and lay back on the cloak with incredible gentleness, his mouth kissing her passionately. Forgetting about his chest, she wound her arms around his neck and responded to his kisses with all of the nervous energy she was feeling. She could do nothing but trust him, and trust him she did.

He pushed her skirts up and undid the stays of her surcoat, pulling the bodice of it down far enough to allow his hands access to her rounded breasts. As she had remembered, his hot mouth on her taut nipple was the most wonderful of sensations, and she bit off her moans on her hand as he suckled her to the brink of delightful pain.

Their passion was gaining momentum by the moment. The more he suckled and probed her breasts, the more she writhed beneath him and the more aroused he became. Neither one of them had ever known such an abandoned response and it only served to excite them even more.

They were lost in each other; nothing else in the world mattered at the moment. Remington's fear was gone, her instinctive inbred response to being touched. She arched shamelessly into his mouth, his hand, her body aching for everything he had to offer, everything that had been denied her for all of these years. She had no idea that a touch could be so sweet, a kiss so tender. She did not even realize her tears were still falling; now they were for her newfound joy.

Gaston wanted her so badly he couldn't think straight. The more she responded, the more forceful he became. Somewhere in the recesses of his mind he knew he must be careful with her and go slowly, but that thought was blocked out by blind passion overloading his brain. Never in his life had he wanted a woman, much less wanted a woman as badly as his lungs needed air, or his stomach needed food. This was what he had wanted all of his life and had not even known it.

He pushed his knees between her legs, pulling her knees up with his free hands. His mouth never left her. Somehow, he managed to undo the stays on his breeches and free his massive organ, demanding to be sated. His fingers trailed to her inner thighs and he heard her moan softly, although his own mouth swallowed all of her sounds. Slowly, his hands moved up to the dark curls between her legs and delicately roved over the outer flesh.

Remington startled when she felt his fingers caressing her. He did not probe her, merely touch her, and it gave her a chance to fight down her natural fear. Guy had raped her so many times she had lost count, and he had never taken the time with her that Gaston was. A touch she had learned to hate was quickly turning into the most powerful experience of her life.

His fingers finally probed her, gently at first, for he felt her body stiffen beneath him. He kept on with his forceful kisses, trying to relax her again, for he was so massively hung that she would have to be completely relaxed in order for him to enter her. The last thing in the world he wanted to do was hurt her. He inserted his finger into her carefully, hearing her gasp softly.

"Did I hurt you?" he whispered raggedly.

She shook her head. "Nay, Gaston....'tis just that...."

He kissed her fears, her explanations, away. Nothing mattered anymore except the two of them, right now.

He pushed two fingers into her, mimicking the thrusting rhythm that would soon be taking place. She was unbelievably tight, but slick as rain. Her muscles throbbed and pulled at him and he was near insane with his desire. Quickly, for he was in danger of spilling himself on her cloak, he removed his fingers and placed his manhood against her.

Remington's eyes flew open, meeting his cloudy orbs. "Gaston, I am scared."

He kissed her fiercely. "I swear to you that you will like this, angel. I know you consider this so much hell but I promise you that you will not after this night."

She gazed into his eyes, trusting him implicitly. He had not lied to her yet. Slowly, her slim thighs wound around his thick legs and her hands caressed the back of his neck. "Show me, then."

He made sure he was meeting her eye when he thrust slowly into her; he wanted to see her face, measure her reaction. She was so tight that it took three full thrusts to move into her, and even then he wasn't seated to the hilt. Remington's eyes widened, but she did not utter a word.

He couldn't help himself; he was a hairsbreadth away from spilling into her and refused to do it before he had taken any pleasure with it. Withdrawing completely, he thrust hard into her and she gasped with shock. He thrust again and again, feeling himself peaking and absolutely astonished that he was climaxing so quickly. Beneath him, he could feel her pelvis moving against him. It was his undoing; he blasted his scalding seed into her with a growl of utter satisfaction.

Remington felt him throbbing within her and knew exactly what it meant; she only remembered Guy's releases too well. She had actually been enjoying his movements and was disappointed to realize it was over so quickly. Yet even after he climaxed, he continued to move within her, still full and hard.

He wanted her to enjoy this as much as he had and moved his hands under her hips, holding her to him as he thrust into her. Remington felt her body responding, the heat in her loins like liquid fire, growing in intensity. Every time their bodies came together it was as if the sparks were flying at the point where they touched; she swore she could feel them.

He was measured and firm and she was completely lost. If this was what being a mistress meant, such pleasure and comfort, then she would gladly be his mistress for the rest of their lives. Marriage was a horrible, cold thing; being illicit lovers was something beyond wonderful.

He heard her swift panting and knew she was close to her release. He shifted himself slightly and put his hand where their bodies were joined, probing her taut little bud of pleasure. Pinching the nub between his fingers, he squeezed gently and Remington peeled off a loud scream. His mouth descended swiftly on hers to block out the remainder of the cry as he felt her honeyed walls throb and suck at him as she found her release. From the intensity of the scream, he knew she had never before experienced her pleasure and he was surprised and pleased; it was almost as if she were a virgin, in a sense.

Remington wasn't sure what had happened. All that she knew was that she had felt such rapturous pleasure as she had never had before sampled and she was dazed. What black magic had he done to make her feel like a boneless, warm lump of flesh? The man had brought her loins to a roaring blaze and then doused the fire with the most amazing sorcery.

He cradled her tightly and she clung to him, trying to slow her breathing. Her body was relaxed, warm, and comforted; she had never felt so wonderful in her entire life. If there was any doubt, any reserve about loving this man, they were gone. She wanted to talk to him, demand to know what he did to her, but her eyes closed against his amazing warmth and before she realized it, she was dead asleep. And so was he.

She rode in the wagon on the trip back to Mt. Holyoak. Dane rode with Antonius, clearing a space for her on the wagon between Skye and Rory. Gaston rode up ahead of them astride Taran, quite alone, as his knights and soldiers lingered behind.

It was a warm July morning. The sky was bluer than Remington had ever seen it and the birds somehow more musical. Her heart was light, her mood gay, and she couldn't ever remember being happier. It was the most glorious morning ever. Even though Gaston had barely spoken to her since dawn, she did not care. He had kissed her awake and that had been enough.

"You are quiet," Rory nudged her. "What's on your mind?"

Remington shrugged. "Not a thing," she said casually. "I am simply concerned about the material we used for tents last night; one of the bolts has a large grass stain on it."

"We shall wash them out," Rory said, her eyes falling on Patrick's back.

Remington saw her sister's look and couldn't resist teasing her. "So you think him magnificent, do you? I must say, I agree."

Rory made a face at her and clucked to the horses. "No one asked you."

Remington and Skye giggled. "Do not be so defensive, Rory," Skye said. "We like him, too."

"Men are a bother," Rory said lamely. "He's…. he's too old, anyhow."

"He's twenty-nine years," Remington said. "And you are sixteen. The ages are perfect."

Rory thrust her chin up and looked away, to Remington and Skye's delight. They goaded and teased her the entire way back to Mt. Holyoak.

The drawbridge was already down as the fortress came into sight. Inside, the outer bailey was a far sight cleaner than it had been the day they left, due to the fact that the troop house was nearly complete. All of the stones and sand were gone, the clutter vanished. The small party rode into the lower inner bailey and dozens of soldiers were swarming about, taking care of the horses and charge of the wagon.

Gaston dismounted and went to the wagon, lifting Skye down and then turning to Remington. She smiled faintly at him as his hands closed around her waist and he had never wanted to kiss anyone so badly in his whole life. He settled for a wink.

Arik was at Gaston's side, his fair face grave and Gaston was instantly on his guard. He knew Arik as well as he knew himself and was well aware that Arik did not get worked up for no reason.

"What's wrong?" he asked. Remington was still standing next to him, her beautiful face upturned to the knights.

Arik did not even look at her. "In private, my lord."

Gaston snapped orders to Antonius and Patrick to see the women safely inside and followed Arik into the castle.

The solar was cool and dim, a refreshing change from the heat of the summer day. Gaston tore off his sweaty gauntlets.

"What's so damn impor...?" he started, but Arik cut him off.

"Mari-Elle is here," he said lowly.

Gaston looked at him, thinking he had not heard right. He froze in mid-motion as he prepared to remove his helmet, thinking he misunderstood him. By God's Bloody Rood, he *had* to have misunderstood him.

"What?" was all he could manage to say.

"She and Trenton arrived yesterday, late," Arik went on. "It would seem that she has missed you terribly in the year you have been gone and wrote Henry as to your whereabouts. Henry was obliged to tell her, of course, and as nearly as I can guess, she was on the road even before we arrived here."

His chest felt as if it were in a vise, squeezing and squeezing until he could hardly breathe. He stared back at Arik until the knight was uncomfortable under the disbelieving stare. Mari-Elle was here? At Mt. Holyoak? He could barely comprehend what he was hearing.

"By all that is holy," he mumbled, in a hoarse whisper. "That bitch is here? Within these walls?"

"I have put her and Trenton in the northern wing, away from you and away from the rest of Stoneley's family," Arik replied, eyeing his lord. "Gaston, I know how badly you hate her and I know she is not welcome here, but I thought you should be the one to tell her. There is naught I could do but make her comfortable and wait for your return."

Gaston stared back at him, his mind spinning with shock. "Remington," he murmured, and then spoke louder. "By God, I have got to find her!"

"By all means," Arik agreed whole-heartedly, having no idea the true meaning of Gaston's words. "Tell her to lock herself in her room and stay the hell away from your wife. Mari-Elle knows the former chatelaine resides within these walls and is already sharpening her fangs. She plans to act the conquering hero's wife to the hilt."

"To the Devil with her," Gaston snapped, his helmet sailing into the wall. "I shall kill her before I allow her to shame Remington." He swung around unsteadily, moving for the door. "That goddamn bitch isn't going to invade my sanctuary and ruin my life any more than she already has. I shall kill her first."

"Gaston," Arik grabbed his liege. "Get hold of yourself, man. Remember Trenton."

Gaston stopped suddenly, his mind working furiously. "My son," he murmured. "She brought the boy and I will thank her for that, but she leaves this day. I do not want her here any longer than necessary."

He charged out of the solar and ran headlong into Remington and her sisters as they directed the soldiers carrying the material in from the wagon. His heart lurched painfully at the sight of her but he reined himself sharply; his first instinct had been to reach out and grab her. Instead, he called to her politely.

"My lady," he said steadily. "Might I have a word, please?"

Remington eagerly went to him and he swept his arm in the direction of the solar. Following her into the room, he closed the door softly behind him.

Remington turned expectantly to him, her angelic face alive with happiness. He couldn't help but smile back and took her in his arms.

She never thought she would like to be held, but she craved his arms around her. It was as if a whole new world had been opened for her, a world where Gaston was the center of her life.

He continued to hold her for several long moments, smelling the perfume he had given her and remembering last night as the most powerful emotional event of his life. He was greatly shaken by the news of his wife's arrival and simply needed to hold Remington to orient himself. Strange, he found he could think with incredible clearness embracing her softness.

"I have received some news, angel," he said softly, relaxing his grip enough to look in her face.

She was concerned. "What news? Has something terrible happened?"

His jaw ticked. "Terrible to you and I, indeed," he said. "Arik has informed me that my wife and son arrived here at Mt. Holyoak yesterday while we were at the faire."

Remington's jaw dropped. She stared back at him with utter disbelief for a moment before trying to pull away from him. He held her tightly, pulling her into a crushing embrace once more.

"Nay, my angel, do not leave me now," he whispered urgently. "I need you more than ever. We must be strong together and I will greatly depend upon your strength."

He felt her relax, her arms going fearfully around his neck. "Oh, Gaston. Why is she here?"

"I do not know," he kissed her hair and released her, moving away to compose himself. "But I intend to send her home. She is not welcome here. This is your home; and mine."

Remington was deeply shaken. She watched Gaston tick angrily, running his fingers through his hair to slick it back, his face taut. She could see how terribly upset he was and realized that she did indeed need to be strong through this; he would have enough to deal with without her whining and crying. She knew what she was getting into from the very beginning; he was a married man. But she never imagined she would have to deal with his wife so soon.

"What would you have me do then, my love?" she asked quietly. "How can I help you?"

He looked at her in the midst of his pacing and thinking. "What did you call me?"

She looked puzzled for a moment. "I called you 'my love.'"

He leaned forward on his arms, bracing his hands on the desk. His eyes were intense. "Am I?"

She smiled at him, shyly, and lowered her gaze. "I suppose you are, Dark One."

He actually chuckled in the midst of his catastrophe. "You walk a fine line, madam. Granting me with the greatest gifts in one breadth and insulting me the next."

She raised her glance coyly. "I granted you a gift? I do not understand."

He raised an eyebrow. "Did you mean what you said? Am I your love?"

She nodded without hesitation. "Aye, Gaston, you are."

"Then that, madam, is the greatest gift of all the world," he said softly. "Nothing in my life will ever mean more to me than that."

She was tremendously touched by his words and felt her cheeks flushing. He watched her through tender eyes, a wonderful moment in the middle of his living hell. He would remember it always. They gazed at each other a moment, absorbing the intensity of their feelings for one another.

"Now," he continued quietly. "As for what you can do, you will take to your rooms and stay there. Keep Dane with you; I do not want him leaving the family wing. Nor your sisters and cousin, either. They are not to leave that second floor corridor until I say otherwise. Do you understand me?"

"Aye, Gaston," she nodded, although already she was thinking on disobeying him. She was tremendously curious to see this woman, his wife.

He nodded shortly. "That's my angel," he came around the desk and put his hand on her arm. "I shall have Patrick escort you and your sisters upstairs and you will stay there. I shall come and see you later, after I have talked with Mari-Elle."

She nodded obediently and moved for the door, thinking their talk was over. His hand, however, tightened around her arm and he pulled her back into his consuming embrace.

Remington found herself gazing into his smoke-hazed eyes, devouring her, and she wrapped her arms around his thick neck. His lips nibbled her ear, her cheek, her nose, before finally encompassing her soft lips. His kiss brought back memories from the night to her mind and quickly, her passion was aroused. She opened her mouth wide to him, eagerly plunging her tongue into his mouth as he had done to her, tasting his essence.

He wanted to take her again right then, but he knew he could not. Reluctantly, he pulled back and spanked her affectionately on the behind. She grinned and straightened her surcoat and, without another spoken word between them, they exited the solar. Somehow she knew he would make everything very well again.

Patrick took Remington up to the family wing. The rest of the family, including Dane, was already there and the knight made sure everyone was situated comfortably. His next destination was the tower room where Charles was holed up with his experiments; he wanted to make sure the young boy stayed to his rooms as well. Patrick knew Mari-Elle, and he knew what the witch was capable of. Keeping Remington and her small family away from the woman was of utmost importance.

Gaston, for his part, retreated to the outer bailey to check the progress of his troop house. He knew Mari-Elle was aware he had returned and he furthermore knew she expected him to come calling. As an obvious sign of his displeasure, he would keep her waiting until it was convenient for him to see her. Additionally, the time spent would help to calm his raging anger. He was still quite shocked at her sudden appearance; it was the very last thing he expected; yet he knew precisely how to deal with her.

With his mind focused on his immediate future, he went about his regular duties.

CHAPTER NINE

Remington and her sisters sat in her spacious bedchamber as they began sewing on their new material they had purchased at the faire. Confined to their rooms, it was the perfect time to work on the tedious task.

Skye set out the patterns and did the cutting; she was very precise and careful. Jasmine would do the basic basting while Remington and Rory did the more difficult stitching. In spite of her tomboy nature, Rory was an excellent seamstress. Bored, Dane played by the hearth with his new cart and horse toy.

"Why does not he want his wife here?" Jasmine asked her eldest sister.

Remington shrugged, trying not to appear too involved. "He does not speak of her, and I did not press him. I have no idea why he hates his wife."

Rory watched her sister a moment. "Are you upset with this? I mean, the woman suddenly showing up?"

Remington focused on the material in front of her. "It matters not to me."

Rory snorted. "Remi, we know you and the Dark Knight have eyes for each other. It's no secret."

Remington's head came up and she looked at her sisters in surprise. "What...what are you talking about? He's married, and so am I."

"Aye, you are both married – so what?" Rory said. "You hate Guy, and he hates his wife, too. Isn't it natural for you two to come together since each finds the other attractive?"

Remington did not know what to say. She lowered her head to her sewing. To her surprise, Rory reached out and gently touched her hand. "We do not blame you, Remi, nor do we think you are wrong. God knows you deserve some happiness."

Remington kept her head lowered and tears sprang to her eyes. Her emotions were running so wild that she was having difficulty controlling them of late. Rarely, if ever, had she cried in front of her sisters simply because she always forced herself to be the strong one. If the entire world was coming down around them, she wanted her sisters to look up to her and see just how unaffected she was by everything.

Skye crept forward on her knees and put her hands on her sister's legs. "You are crying," she accused softly. "Why, Remi? What's wrong?"

Remington's sewing plopped into her lap. "Nothing is wrong. It's just that....oh, nothing is wrong. Go back to work."

"It's that bitch, isn't it?" Rory bristled. "She's upsetting you simply by being here."

"It's not her," Remington retorted, sniffing loudly. "It's everything."

"*What* everything?" Jasmine asked softly. "Do you love him, Remi?"

Remington looked stumped. She gazed back at her blue-eyed sister a moment, thinking of a thousand denials but not one would come forth. "Aye."

She could hear the collective sighs. Even Dane sat up from where he was playing on the stone hearth, his eyes wide at his mother.

"Truly? You love him?" Skye gasped.

Remington almost contradicted her statement simply to protect herself. She did not know why she had even confessed, but she had. Her shoulders slumped in resignation of what she had done, of what was yet to come.

"He's the most wonderful, caring, sensitive man I have ever known and I cannot help but love him," she said softly. "He's the man dreams are made of."

"But...he's so big. And frightening," Skye protested. "God, Remi, he's the Dark Knight. All of England fears the man."

"Not me," she said simply. "He calls me his angel."

They were all silent a moment, realizing Remington's admission began to open the way for a whole new world. If she wasn't afraid to allow herself feelings after what she had been through, then mayhap they should not be afraid, either. Each one of the sisters had her eye on a prospective knight, but they had been hesitant to move beyond simple looks and casual words.

"But what of his wife?" Rory wanted to know.

"He promised me he would send her away," Remington said, picking up her sewing. "I am not worried."

The sisters looked at each other doubtfully, but Remington seemed confident enough. Since the subject was apparently closed for the moment, they resumed their sewing.

Dane approached his mother solicitously, leaning against her arm. "Is Sir Gaston going to be my new father?"

Remington gazed into her son's eyes. "Nay, Dane, I am afraid not. I realize it is difficult for you to understand, but he will never be your father. Yet he will always care for you a great deal."

Dane looked puzzled and thoughtful. He turned away from Remington and went back to his toys.

Remington sighed heavily and picked up her sewing again. She was glad he had not asked any more questions because, truthfully, she wasn't sure how to answer him. How could she explain it to him when she herself did not understand it?

Someone rapped heavily on the door and Skye opened it to find Oleg standing in the archway. His old face was lined and haggard as he eyed the four women.

"The Mistress of Mt. Holyoak requests your presence at the nooning meal, ladies," he said.

Remington felt as if she had been slapped. Her calm nerves and confident posture were rapidly fading in lieu of darker, angrier emotions.

"You mean Lady Mari-Elle?" she asked evenly. "Oleg, inform the lady that we are not allowed from our rooms under direct orders from Sir Gaston. If she wants us to attend the meal, then she will have to speak to the master."

Oleg nodded wearily. "Aye, my lady."

Remington sat her sewing down, again, and stood up. "What's the matter with you?"

Oleg threw up his hands. "What isn't the matter? The Lady Mari-Elle has brought her entire household with her, including her own stewards, a cook, and a physician. They are taking over Mt. Holyoak and I have been reduced to a common house servant."

Remington was outraged. She clenched her jaw angrily, pacing the length of the floor to the elderly servant. "Oleg, I want you to gather all of our servants and tell them to take to their rooms until this situation with Lady Mari-Elle can be solved. I do not want them serving her, or her household. Do you understand?"

"Aye, my lady," Oleg said briskly, somewhat relieved.

"Sir Gaston has promised to send his wife home this day and I fully intend that the residents of Mt. Holyoak stay out of her way until such time as she leaves," Remington continued. "We have had one abusive master and I shall now allow my vassals to be further abused by a spoiled, imperious woman."

Oleg crinkled a smile. "As you say, my lady."

He turned to leave but Remington grasped him gently to stay him a moment. "And if the Lady Mari-Elle has a problem with my orders, you tell her to come and speak to me directly. I shall tell her exactly what has happened and why."

Oleg was vastly relieved, yet he expected no less from Lady Remington. The woman had the courage of ten men. He quit the room, full of his message for Lady Mari-Elle.

Remington turned to her sister, her face glazed with a cunning, sinister look. "That's right, Oleg; send the bitch to me. I shall give her an earful."

Rory's face lit up like the high-noon sun. "Can I help you?"

Remington lifted an eyebrow, pursing her lips thoughtfully. There was no mistaking the devious aura about her. "Gaston wants her gone and so do I. Mayhap…mayhap we could make her miserable enough to leave," she looked pointedly at Rory. "You, my lady, are a master of pranks. Any ideas?"

Rory was in her heaven. She rose from her chair, clasping her hands behind her back with mock thoughtfulness. "Quite a few, actually. I think we could make her life quite hellish."

Remington smiled wickedly, knowing she shouldn't be encouraging this action, but feeling her desperation. True, she trusted Gaston, but she wasn't beyond giving him a little help. Their relationship was so new, promising such wonder and magnificence that she wanted this woman out of the way in order to pursue her happiness. Selfish on her part; absolutely. But for once in her life she felt like being selfish.

Lady Mari-Elle de Russe paced leisurely across the floor of the large foyer, her expert eyes studying every inch of the décor and wealth. Wealth that now belonged to her husband and, to her. She could see that Mt. Holyoak was wealthy indeed, not extravagant, but certainly self-supporting and then some. She was terribly pleased that King Henry had seen fit to grant her husband such a prime holding.

Money, station, and reputation; everything Gaston had that was hers. In spite of the fact that he had betrayed Richard, it mattered not since he was in good standing with Henry Tudor. And why not? His mother was a Tudor cousin and therefore, Mari-Elle found herself in the prestigious position of being related to the King of England.

Moreover, Gaston was her partner but she held no love for him; she never had. He gave her what she most wanted and stayed away to allow her to enjoy it; wealth. Money that kept her supplied with men, jewels, and clothes. Her life had been perfect until a few short weeks ago.

Her current lover, Count Luc-Pietre de Moulors, had been amusing enough to keep her occupied. He was suave, handsome, thinly built and witty. Exactly her type and she considered keeping him for an infinite amount of time until she discovered her pregnancy. Panicked, she banished him from Clearwell and set out to make rapid plans. She had not seen Gaston in nearly a year and everyone would know the child was not his. To bear him a bastard would give him reason to send her away, cut off her allowance, or mayhap even kill her.

Mari-Elle was clear. She wrote to Henry and discovered that Gaston had recently been sent north to Yorkshire, to a keep called Mt. Holyoak. Mari-Elle packed up her entire household and set out for Yorkshire, desperate to be with her husband. She had to convince him that she had missed him terribly and to beg his forgiveness, to lie with him and conceive another child.

Her plan would work perfectly if everything went according to her schedule. Much had happened between her and Gaston and she knew he hated her, and frankly she had not cared in the least until a few weeks ago. Now, she could only hope she was convincing when she pledged her undying love to the man. He knew her well; *too* well, and she knew he would take a great deal of convincing.

Trenton walked beside her, his dark gray eyes observing his surroundings solemnly. He was extremely tall for his age, almost as tall as his mother, with his father's dark features.

"Father returned hours ago," the boy said. "Why hasn't he come to see us?"

"Do not feel badly, dear," Mari-Elle said. "You know your father has never liked children, and he certainly never wanted a son. But he will grow accustomed to you, I promise. That's why I brought you here, isn't it? For you to get to know your father."

Trenton shrugged in the same gesture Gaston used sometimes. He knew his father did not like him, but he was proud of his father nonetheless. There was a great deal of prestige being the Dark Knight's son. He was torn between hating his father terribly and loving him desperately, wondering what he had ever done to make his father stay away all the time.

He was a good boy, with a good heart, fortunately not damaged too badly by his mother's devilish ways. More than anything, he was simply confused. His mother did not have time for him, his father was non-existent, and there was truly no one for him. He spent his days at Clearwell playing with his dogs or exploring in the neighboring woods when it wasn't too cold, a lonely life for a lonely boy.

"I believe this keep will do quite nicely," Mari-Elle said with approval. "Far different from Clearwell, is it not?"

"It is bigger," Trenton said. "But not as well decorated."

"That will change," Mari-Elle said confidently, already imagining the possibilities. Then, her eyes fell on her son. "Let us go and find your father, shall we? He must be outside somewhere.

Controlling his nervousness and excitement, Trenton followed her.

They stood on the steps overlooking the inner bailey for quite a while. Soldiers and knights whirled past them, but no one stopped, even when Mari-Elle tried to gain their attention. Finally, she spied a familiar head and sent Trenton across the courtyard to Arik.

"Sir Arik," Trenton called.

The knight turned around, smiling at the lad. "What is it, young de Russe?"

"My father, Sir Arik. Where is he? My mother wishes to speak with him," Trenton said.

Arik's eyes rose over the boy's head and he stared straight on into Mari-Elle several yards away. Tall, elegant Mari-Elle. She was lovely in a high-bred sort of way, but her face was too thin for his taste. Her dark hair was pulled back sharply and arranged with all sorts of jewels, and her brown eyes gazed haughtily over the courtyard. He sighed, feeling his sincere dislike for the woman.

He looked back at Trenton, forcing his face to brighten. "Would you like to come with me as we search for him?"

Trenton nodded. "Aye, I would."

Gaston wasn't hard to find. He was inside the troop house, watching the final touches being put into the ceiling.

"My lord," Arik called to him. "You have a visitor."

Gaston turned sharply, his eyes falling on his son, a younger version of himself. He was suddenly sorry he had not sought out Mari-Elle earlier, if for no other reason than to see Trenton.

"Greetings, Trenton," he said, coming closer. "I am pleased to see how much you have grown since I last saw you."

"It was a year ago, my lord," Trenton said, trying to control his quivering. He couldn't believe he was actually facing his father. "I was only seven years old."

"And now you are practically a grown man," Gaston said with satisfaction. He looked at Arik. "What do you think of my son?"

"He shall be a great knight as you," Arik replied. "Look at the size of his hands already."

Trenton looked at his hands, turning them over. "I...I am set to foster soon, mother says."

"She is correct," Gaston replied. "You will be fostering here with me. You and I have been apart far too long, Trenton. I would keep you here with me and oversee your training."

Trenton's jaw hung slack. "I will train here? With you?"

"Indeed," Gaston replied, wondering of the boy's shock was from displeasure or happiness.

Trenton was stunned. His gray eyes widened at his father a moment, but he said nothing. Truth was, he was speechless. Arik slapped the boy affectionately on the back.

"Say what you had in mind, lad," he said. "Your father is a busy man."

He was always busy, always moving, always fighting. Trenton cleared his throat, for he was terribly nervous in his father's presence. "Mother seeks you, my lord. She wishes to speak with you."

Gaston's face darkened. "Tell your mother that I am indisposed at the moment and will join her when I am able," he said evenly, then paused thoughtfully. "I have changed my mind. I shall send a soldier to your mother. You may stay here with me and help me oversee the finish of my troop house. What do you think so far?"

Trenton was in a daze; his father actually wanted his opinion? After everything his mother had told him, after everything he had been led to believe, he was confused and delighted beyond his young mind's grasp. All he could do was nod as his father took him along, explaining the purpose of the addition.

Arik watched them slowly walk away, knowing how terribly Gaston had missed his son and pleased to see them together and away from the influence of the bitch.

Turning on his heel, he would deliver the master's message personally.

The nooning meal was served with a good deal of flourish and style. Mari-Elle's cook was from Normandy, a talented artisan that had turned a simple meal into a sumptuous affair.

Gaston entered the hall last, as was usual, passing a skeptical eye over the room. Strange smells from exotic dishes assaulted his nose and he found himself wishing for the simple smell of mutton. Trenton, beside him, caught sight of Mari-Elle first.

"There's mother," he pointed eagerly. "She's waving to you."

Gaston clenched his jaw as he focused on his wife. Tall, thin, and cold, exactly as he had remembered, except...except she was smiling. Instantly he went even more on his guard than he usually was. Trenton ran on ahead and Arik approached casually.

"Ah, the spider calling to the fly," he mumbled in the direction of his lord's ear.

Gaston's jaw flexed dangerously. "Except this fly is about to quash the spider. Have you checked on Remington and the rest of the family?"

"I sent a couple of knights upstairs to make sure they were taken care of," Arik replied. "I did not want to miss the entertainment."

Patrick and Nicolas joined the small group, suddenly very conspicuous in the archway to the great hall.

"She's turned this meal into a goddamn courtly affair," Patrick murmured. He had always been the most mild-tempered of Gaston's knights, but even he had little love for Mari-Elle.

"Get in there," Gaston snapped softly. "Eat and be done. We shall not turn this into a social occasion."

They wandered into the hall to their usual places. Mari-Elle had taken the extreme liberty of setting herself next to her husband and greeted Patrick with overbearing affection. She began to seat the men around her, her thin face flushed with pleasure. Gaston stood a few feet away, his hands on his massive hips as he watched his wife with great disapproval.

Mari-Elle's eyes met with his and her expression grew very soft, loving even. "My lord husband," she said in a husky voice. "I am so glad to finally see you."

He did not reply for a moment. His displeasure was obvious, like a slap in the face. "And I am surprised to see you. We have much to discuss, wife."

She smiled prettily and lowered her lashes. "As my lord pleases. I am at your disposal. Would you take your seat now, my lord, and be served?"

He moved past her briskly, ignoring her soundly as he took his seat. Mari-Elle sat next to him, making sure to brush his leg with her knee. He did not react, instead, drinking deeply from his tankard. He always drank too much when he was around her.

Servants began flowing from the kitchens, bringing out trenchers for the men. There were suddenly several serving wenches at the head of the table where Gaston sat, all setting food in front of the knights. The wench serving Gaston set his plate down carefully and fully brushed her breasts against his arm as she pulled back. Annoyed, he shot her an icy look and was shocked to see Remington wink back at him.

His eyes rapidly went to every serving wench at the table; Skye and Jasmine, dressed as servants, were assisting the knights. Rory smiled boldly at him. It took him a second to realize his mouth had popped open and he quickly shut it.

Arik met his eyes questioningly but he ignored the look; he was try-ing to figure out what the devil the women of Mt. Holyoak were doing dressed in coarse linen serving clothes, wooden clogs and leather girdles.

He was so stunned he almost forgot about his food. Mechanically, he dug into his plate, eyeing Remington and her sisters as they served his men.

"Where is my food?" Mari-Elle demanded imperiously; she was the only one that had not been served. "You – wench!"

Rory was closest. She swung around so fast she hit Mari-Elle on the side of the head with the pitcher of wine she was holding. The woman teetered, her wimple knocked askew.

"You stupid…!" She suddenly remembered Gaston sitting next to her. If she were going to convince the man that she was a changed woman, then she would have to start acting like it. She calmed herself and straightened her wimple. "You seem to have forgotten my food."

Rory lifted her eyebrows in feigned horror. "My heavens! Sorry, chicklet, I shall get it right away."

She skittered away and Gaston found himself biting off huge guf-faws that promised to fill the room. Across the table, Patrick's red face was staring into his lap and Nicolas had his napkin over his mouth, chewing slowly but laughing silently like a fool. Antonius coughed heavily and pretended to drop his knife to the floor.

Gaston was shocked at what was apparently going on. Shocked and angered that Remington and her sisters had disobeyed him, but mightily amused at what promised to take place. He knew he should stop it, but he was frankly curious at Mari-Elle's reaction to Rory's brassiness. He decided to allow Remington and her sisters to continue their charade, if for nothing more than to be fortunate enough to gaze at Remington. He missed her already.

Gaston's knights recognized her but no one said a word. Whatever she was doing was her own business, yet a few wondered if Lady de Russe had ordered her to serve as a common servant. Obviously Sir Gaston wasn't upset in the least, so wise men that they were, they made no comment.

Remington came up on Gaston's arm. "More wine, my lord?"

He gazed up at her, trying desperately not to show any emotion. "Aye."

He raised his goblet and she lowered the pitcher and they bumped. The collision wasn't hard, but suddenly the pitcher was flying backwards and nearly the entire contents spilled itself on Mari-Elle's lap.

Mari-Elle jumped to her feet with shock and Remington let the pitcher fall.

"Oh, my lady, I am so sorry," she gasped with a good deal of overacting. "I am ever so clumsy, my lady, please forgive me."

Gaston watched, baffled, as Remington grabbed the rag on her dress and began wiping the wine off his wife's fine surcoat. He could see that every swipe of the rag left a black streak and Mari-Elle looked down at herself, horrified.

"Look at what you are doing," she screeched. "Stop this instant!"

Remington dropped the rag in mock horror at what she had done. "My lady, a thousand apologies. Please."

Mari-Elle was fully preparing to swat the unfortunate serving girl but she caught Gaston's critical look over the top of the wench's head and reconsidered. Though it was far more difficult this time around, she forced down her anger.

"I am sure it will wash," she said through clenched teeth.

Remington bowed and scraped herself away from the table, backing up several feet until she was well clear of them. Then, as Gaston watched, she straightened regally and smiled the most devious smile he could ever remember seeing. He was torn between wanting to take her over his knee and wanting to applaud her bravado. In spite of his conflict, he was growing increasingly curious about Mari-Elle's behavior.

The woman he had married would have been whipping the hide from the servants by now.

As he was dwelling on Mari-Elle's change of character, Rory barged forward, a full trencher in her hands. Carefully, she sat it down in front of Mari-Elle.

"There you are, chicklet," she said happily. "Enjoy!"

Gaston looked at the food on the trencher and just knew there was something wrong with it. He passed a glance at Arik and the two of them quickly looked back to their food. Whatever the woman got, she deserved worse and they were not about to put a stop to it. Yet. The show was far too amusing.

Mari-Elle began to eat and they held their breath. But nothing happened and she continued eating, smiling at Gaston now and again. He ignored her, acutely aware of Remington replenishing wine at the next table and stealing a glance at her here and there. At the far end of the table, Rory was laughing loudly with several of the knights and then suddenly cuffed one on the side of the head.

"That wench is....unusual," Mari-Elle commented. "Are all of the servants here as cheeky as she is?"

Gaston did not answer; Arik replied when he saw that he wasn't going to. "For the most part, they are a loyal lot, my lady."

Mari-Elle turned her nose up and resumed her meal. "Thank God I brought my own people with me. We shall soon have Mt. Holyoak running smoothly."

Gaston looked at her, then. "Your conclusion is based upon the assumption that I will allow you to remain at Holyoak and is, therefore, faulty. As it is, the fortress and its house run quite sufficiently for my taste and your interference is neither needed nor wanted."

Remington was at the next table and listening to the conversation closely. A knight held up his tankard and she obliged with her pitcher of wine.

Mari-Elle blanched. "I am not welcome in my husband's fortress?"

Gaston had sincerely hoped to avoid this until later when they were in private, but he had spoken rashly in reaction to her suggestion that Mt. Holyoak was *their* fortress. It was his, and Remington's.

"We will discuss this later, madam," he said coldly.

Trenton bowed his head over his food, his appetite gone. So his father was a cold bastard just like his mother said, only...today they had spent over an hour together and his father had been very kind to him. He wanted his father's love so much, but he was deeply confused. Why did his father hate his mother so?

Stung, Mari-Elle returned to her food, knowing her task ahead would not be an easy one. She would have to be more clever than Gaston, a monumental chore.

Remington moved to Gaston's table once more, topping Arik's and Patrick's cups. She moved around to Mari-Elle.

"More wine, my lady?" she asked pleasantly.

Mari-Elle nodded shortly and watched the wine fill her cup. Then, much to Gaston's concern, she turned to Remington and scrutinized her closely.

"You are rather pretty for a common serving wench," she said cattily. "Are you, mayhap of a higher station?"

Remington blinked at the question, the statement. "Nay, my lady. I am what you see."

Mari-Elle raised an eyebrow. "I am sure you have not gone unnoticed by the knights," she said. "Tell me then, girl. You served the former lord, did you not?"

"Aye, my lady," she had in more ways than one.

'And is the climate of the household still attuned to Richard?"

Remington actually found that her dander was rising with the woman's haughty tone. She had been quite docile until this moment. "We are loyal to Sir Gaston, my lady."

Mari-Elle gave Remington one last arrogant look and returned to her wine. "We shall see. Where is your mistress, then? I ordered her to attend this meal."

Gaston raised a black brow. "You do not give orders here, madam. You receive them. I specifically ordered Lady Remington to remain in her rooms until your departure. You will not, nor do you need to, see her."

"Lady Remington?" Mari-Elle repeated. "What kind of name is that?"

"French, I believe, my lady," Remington was starting to flush around her cheeks.

Mari-Elle glared at Remington. "I did not ask your opinion, girl. Leave us."

Remington swept away, her jaw clenching and her face red. She brushed past Skye and Rory near the kitchen door.

"Bitch," she hissed. "No wonder Gaston hates her."

"Look at the boy, Remi," Skye whispered. "He looks terribly uncomfortable."

Remington gazed at Trenton, a smaller version of his mighty father. "Poor thing," she murmured, and then looked pointedly at Rory. "Whatever you put in her food, I hope it makes her so miserable she wants to die."

Rory grinned. "Oh, I can guarantee that she will be feeling quite awful in an hour or so. Charles gave me a root that will make her food run right through her. She shall be in the privy all night."

Jasmine joined the little group, setting her wine pitcher down. "Charles and Dane have surely finished sabotaging her room by now," she whispered. "Just wait until Lady Mari-Elle retires for the night. God help her."

Remington had a delightful mental picture of what lay in store for Lady de Russe. It never occurred to her that Gaston might become angry over what they had done; she thought she was helping him.

"Remember; we deny all knowledge," she whispered urgently. "Unless Gaston plans to put us to the whip, we continue to deny everything. And you, Rory; the suspicion will be on you and you must not give in. We know how you like to confess your sins."

"What if Lady Mari-Elle puts us to the whip?" Skye asked, fear shadowing her face.

"Gaston won't let her," Remington said confidently. "See how he ignores her? I promise you, the woman is as good as gone."

"Is it time for our song yet?" Jasmine asked eagerly, picking up her lyre from its perch on the wall.

Remington passed a sly glance at Mari-Elle, studying the woman's sharp profile. "Oh, yes."

Remington couldn't sing a note. In fact, the only sister who could remotely sing was Jasmine, and she couldn't sing if she were playing her lyre because she lacked the coordination. But they had a special song in mind for Lady Mari-Elle, composed by Rory no less, and they would sing it or die trying. Anything to welcome the new mistress of Mt. Holyoak.

Quietly, they took their places by the huge hearth and Remington stood forward, clearing her throat loudly until the room eventually quieted. Gaston saw her standing bravely in front of the room, wondering what in the hell she was doing. He slanted a concerned glance at Arik, who merely lifted his eyebrows. The meal was growing more interesting, and more puzzling, by the moment. Something told him to put a stop to it, but morbid inquisitiveness won over.

"Good knights and honored guest," Remington began; she had a most delightful speaking voice. "In honor of our arrived mistress, we have commissioned a special song. With your permission, my lord Gaston?"

Gaston nodded slightly, his eyes glittering at her. A roomful of people was watching them and he carefully banked his reaction.

Remington resumed her spot between Rory and Skye. Jasmine began stroking the lyre beautifully, the rich chords filling the hall. The men relaxed, settled back, and waited for what was sure to be a most delightful song. They were positive nothing else could come from such a lovely woman.

They were wrong.

Which was why they were startled when the chords suddenly stopped and all four women dug into the song with the fragility of waves crashing onto jagged rocks. The first word, a roaring "Oh" sounded like four drunken tavern wenches lifting their tankards in tribute to a fine man gone by.

It certainly made them sit up and take notice. Patrick sprayed his wine all over the floor at the boom, his eyes widening in surprise. Antonius, who had been balancing his chair on two legs, almost fell over had Nicolas not reached out and grabbed him. The loudness, the rowdy manner coming from the sisters was beyond believing.

They were not even singing; they were yelling at the top of their lungs.

Oh! We serve the lord, his keep, his hold
We love to eat, to piss, to scold
They call us bawdy. Hiyo! 'Tis an art.
In honor of our new mistress, a ceremonial fart.

They put their tongues between their lips and let out the most obnoxious sound ever heard. The entire room burst into screaming laughter, tankards banging so loud on the tables that it was difficult to hear. The room was full of rabble-rousing men, demanding more of the song.

Gaston could only stare at the four women near the hearth, barely comprehending what he had just heard. Absently, his hand went to his head in utter disbelief and beside him, Trenton erupted into giggles. Mari-Elle, however, was not amused.

"My lord," she hissed. "Are you going to allow them to continue to insult me?"

Gaston did not answer as they started in with another one of their roaring "Oh's." The "Oh's" seemed to get louder and he could hear Rory at the head of it.

Oh! Welcome to our humble fortress and keep
Do not let the shit in the bailey stick to your feet
Enjoy your visit, my lady, we pray
Do not let the door hit you in the arse should you
Decide not to stay.

The room went wild with screaming, riotous men voicing their approbation. The four sisters smiled and curtsied swiftly before dashing off the floor and into the kitchens. Gaston watched them go, laughter such as he had never known threatening to spill forth. When he looked at Mari-Elle's reddened face, he wanted to laugh all the more.

Patrick and Antonius had to excuse themselves; they were too far gone to control their laughter and risked being rude by abruptly leaving. Nicolas had his napkin up in front of his face, shielding him from everyone's eyes. The mood of the room was still one of hysteria.

"Do not you feel honored, Mother?" Trenton asked, still giggling. "They sang a song to you."

Mari-Elle's thin face was taut. "Some song," she put her napkin down stiffly. "My lord, if you will excuse me, I would like to rest. I find I am not feeling well."

Gaston gazed impassively at her. "Rest while you will. I will seek you out shortly."

Angrily, she rose and quit the room. Gaston was thankful that Remington and her sisters were nowhere in sight. He, however, was most interested in seeking out Remington and discovering her reasons for disobeying him, even if she and her sisters had performed brilliantly.

"Arik, take my son in hand," he rose from his chair. "I have something to attend to."

"No doubt," Arik lifted an eyebrow.

Gaston ignored the remark and disappeared into the kitchens.

The nervous servants pointed him in the direction the sisters had taken and he followed swiftly. He wound his way out of the kitchens and came upon a small staircase. Realizing they had retreated to their chambers, he went after them.

Remington was in her room stripping off the coarse garment and girdle, giggling to herself. Dane and Charles were in Charles' room after quickly informing Remington that Lady Mari-Elle's room was a minefield. Feeling wicked, but gratified, Remington set about removing the scratchy servant's garb.

She did not stop to think of consequences because she did not think there would be any. She so terribly feared Guy's wrath, but somehow, she did not fear Gaston's. It was difficult to explain, but she knew he would never hurt her, or shame her in any way, no matter what she had done. With him, she felt…. free. Free to be herself. Free of fear. Even if she had been sly and naughty!

The door to her chamber swung open and banged loudly against the wall. Startled, she whirled around to see Gaston looming in the doorjamb. And he did not look pleased.

She suddenly wondered at the wisdom of her actions, but she did not back down. "My lord?" she greeted innocently.

His gaze was hard. He waited a moment before stalking into the room, kicking the door shut behind him. "Would you mind telling me what that was all about?"

She was clad in a peasant's blouse that hung to the middle of her thighs and nothing else. Her lovely legs, exposed, drew Gaston's hot gaze. She took a step back as he moved in closer and took a deep breath to bolster her courage.

"We...I wanted to catch a glimpse of your wife, my lord," she said evenly. "Since she did not know who I was, I saw no harm in serving the nooning meal to satisfy my curiosity." She looked into his hard face and felt a chill of fear shoot up her spine, and her bravery waned. "Are you terribly angry?"

"Angry that you disobeyed me when I ordered you to stay in your rooms, aye," he put his hands on his hips. "Angry with your performance downstairs? I should be. It was certainly bold and insolent enough."

She turned away from him, her head lowered. "And I do apologize for provoking your fury, my lord, but when Oleg told me of the things your wife had done with my...your house, I was quite incensed."

"Ah, then you lied to me," he said. "You did not simply want to sate your curiosity, you wanted to exact vengeance."

She turned to him, half-pouting and half-defiant. "Aye, I did. She does not belong here."

He looked at her a moment before pacing to the bed, sitting lightly on the edge. He extended his hand to her and pulled her between his thighs. Relieved he wasn't going to spank her, she ran splayed fingers through his hair, remembering the passion from the night before with great happiness.

"I understand your feelings, Remi, but she is my wife and I alone will deal with her," he said softly.

Rebuked, she refused to meet his eye but continued to stroke his hair. He watched her angelic face, remembering how tremendously drawn he was to her as she acted the serving wench. She was far too beautiful and sweet for a common servant; even Mari-Elle had known it.

"'We love to eat, to piss, to scold?'" he suddenly repeated, and she burst into giggles.

"Rory wrote the song," she insisted.

"'A ceremonial fart?'" he recounted with disapproval, though he was smiling. "Really, Remi, how vulgar."

"I never said she was a poet," she snickered. "But it was effective, was it not?"

He shook his head. "Effective in making everyone hysterical and provoking Mari-Elle," he agreed. "I should not be surprised with anything you four do."

Her expression suddenly went sly as she ran her hand down the sides of his face. "Nay, you should not. With any luck, we shall have your wife gone by morning."

His eyes narrowed. "What does that mean? What else have you done?"

"Me? Nothing, my lord," she said innocently. "And how is Trenton faring? He's truly a beautiful boy, just like his father."

"My son is well," he said shortly. "Remi, what else have you done? Why is Mari-Elle likely to leave of her own free will by morn?"

She looked annoyed. "I told you, I have done nothing," she insisted. "May I get dressed now, my lord?"

His hands moved up the backs of her legs, almost to her rounded bottom. "Nay, you may not."

"And why not?" she asked, smiling, feeling the wicked warmth of lust already flowing through her veins.

He responded by sinking his teeth into the soft flesh of her neck, drawing the most pleasurable of moans. He answered with a low groan of his own accord and the peasant blouse came off.

He flipped her onto her back on the mattress, covering her body with his massive frame. She clung to him, already parting her thighs and wrapped her legs around him. His mouth was on hers, his tongue thrusting into her mercilessly, licking the honeyed orifice. Passion that was merely building one moment was instantly full-blown and fierce.

He left her a brief moment to strip off his shirt and peel off his breeches and then he was on her again, urged on by her soft pleading. His mouth fastened to a rosy nipple, sucking it into a hard pebble and slipping his hands underneath her back, pulling her up to his lips, trapping her.

She was desperate to get him inside her, to feel the same sensations that rocked her the previous night. He obliged her, slipping his huge manhood at her threshold and thrusting slowly and firmly until he slid his entire hard length into her.

Remington was incoherent with her need. She wrapped her small body around him, her face against his neck, rising to meet him as he thrust into her. He was hard and firm, rhythmic, and driving her to the brink of madness. The familiar fire in her loins from last night was raging once again and she begged him to put a sweet end to her torment as he had once before. It had been the mightiest of experiences, one she wished to repeat again and again.

Yet, even as he moved within her, full and rock-solid, it was more than the act itself. It was the simple action of being held by him, touching his flesh, being touched. It was *him*, like no one else. He cared for her, was kind to her, respected her. That, as well as the physical touching, was a most powerful aphrodisiac.

He growled, his hands under her hips, lifting her to meet him with tender savagery. She could do naught but clutch him tightly, his body so huge and powerful that she felt overwhelmed by his sheer maleness. She moved with him, meeting his rhythm, feeling the fire within her building to a roaring blaze.

Without his obvious manipulation as he had done last night, she felt the tremors of release begin and begged him to drive harder, harder. He obeyed, bringing her to such a raging climax that she cried aloud with relief and pleasure, feeling the moment of time where all else seemed to stop for a brief second, where only her exquisite pleasure mattered, before beginning the inevitable downslide to complete contentment. She wished she could stay there forever, feeling him moving within her like a great battering ram.

He felt her convulsions, milking him, demanding his own release, and he relented, joining in her pleasure. He swore he had never climaxed so hard as he continued to move, slowing his actions, winding down. Their sweaty bodies lowered to the bed, enveloped by the softness, and he held her tightly against him in a protective embrace.

Remington dozed lightly, utterly exhausted and satisfied. The feelings were entirely new to her, more wonderful than she had ever suspected. His huge hands caressed her back and stroked her hair as they cuddled contentedly, realizing their relationship was deepening by the moment.

"Can we stay here forever?" she whispered.

"Would that I could, angel," he kissed her head, his mind turning briefly to Mari-Elle. Sex with her had never, ever come close to this. It had been a duty.

She kissed his chest softly, running her hands lightly over his skin. "You are so gentle for your massive size," she said. "I would not have thought it possible."

"Were I not gentle, I'd most likely flatten you like a pancake," he teased.

She giggled. "'Twould be a most pleasurable form of death, my lord."

He propped himself up on an elbow, gazing down on her lovely face. "You will listen to me now, Remi, or I will take a stick to you. I want you to stay in your rooms until I tell you otherwise. There will be no disobedience from you on this, madam, in any way. Am I making myself clear?"

She nipped playfully at his lower lip. "Aye, Gaston. I swear to you that I will not leave my rooms. I shall simply wait here in bed for you to return to me."

He lifted an arched black eyebrow, the same way he had lifted it the first time she had ever gazed into his eyes. This time, however, she reached up and touched his brow. "If you choose to wait in bed, then that will suit me. But know I mean what I say, Remi. I do not jest with you."

She was gazing at him dreamily, a faint smile on her face. "Tell me, Gaston, when you first saw me did you know that we would be lovers?"

He signed in annoyance. She wasn't listening to him. "Nay, I did not. I do not take lovers."

"But you took me," she traced her finger along his lower lip.

"Believe me when I tell you it was simply by chance," he said. "I never planned it, at least not at first."

She perked up. "Not at first? When, then? When did you know?"

He looked at her a moment. "After your sister put charcoal on Nicolas' cup and you were terrified that she had booby-trapped the entire table. You practically tore the table apart looking for tricks with this wild look on your face," his hand moved over her shoulder tenderly. "I knew then that I would have you."

She smiled. "I thought you were going to crucify Rory. We were terrified of you; my sisters still are."

"And you are not?" he asked with feigned outrage.

Her smile faded. "I fear Guy more than you. The man knows no mercy, no compassion, no gentleness. He strikes for no reason, without warning. He is an animal."

Gaston's face hardened. "And the animal fears me more than God. He shall never touch you nor see you again, Remi, I swear it. If I have to get down on my knees before Henry to plead for his unending imprisonment, I will. I shall kill him if he sets foot outside of the Tower."

She believed him.

CHAPTER TEN

Gaston sought out Arik to find out where exactly his wife had been housed. Arik personally led his liege to the northern wing, a seldom-used portion of Mt. Holyoak. All of Mari-Elle's household had been roomed here and Gaston passed by several people he recognized from Clearwell. He ignored them here, as he ignored them there.

He had not even reached his wife's room and he could hear her shrieking. His veins ran cold; this was the same woman he knew and despised. His resolve to get rid of her strengthened ten-fold as he quickened his pace down the hall. He would not listen to that irritating voice any longer than he had to.

The door to her chamber was open partially and he shoved it open the rest of the way as he barged in. Mari-Elle was in the process of reaming one of her servants, a poor girl getting her ears boxed, when she caught sight of her husband.

From what he had seen of her at the nooning meal, he half expected her to turn instantly sweet and subservient in a desperate ploy to throw him off his guard. But he was not surprised when she turned to him like a wild animal, her eyes bulging.

"At last!" she cried. "You have arrived, my lord."

He raised his eyebrow and gave her an intolerant look. "You will not be so glad when you hear what I have to say. Dismiss your women."

Mari-Elle let out a desperate gasp, dramatic to say the least. "My lord, they are trying to *kill* me," she began to weep exaggeratedly. "You have an assassin within your midst."

He scowled; he had no time for her ridiculous stalling tactics. "Dismiss your women, Mari-Elle."

Suddenly she doubled over and grabbed her gut, moaning in pain. He watched her curiously as she disappeared into a small alcove and he could hear her snapping at a servant and grunting. He passed a glance at Arik, still behind him.

"This is going to take all day if she keeps this up," he grumbled. "Be on your way, man. I can handle her myself."

"Are you sure?" Arik quipped seriously.

Gaston twisted his mouth drolly and Arik snorted in response, exiting the chamber.

Mari-Elle was grunting and cursing like a barmaid and Gaston's patience was nearly at an end, but he reined himself. Drawing in a deep breath for strength, he crossed his arms and planted his feet apart, waiting.

It took several minutes, but Mari-Elle re-emerged from the alcove looking the least bit pale. She swallowed hard, holding a handkerchief to her lips as she weaved across the room to the wine decanter.

"Someone is trying to kill me," she gasped, pouring herself a dose of wine. "I have been poisoned."

He frowned intolerantly. "What are you talking about?"

She took a deep drink before answering, distraught. "Someone has poisoned me. My stomach is in knots and…. and everything is coming out of me as quickly as it went in. I am slowly dying, I tell you."

He did not believe her for a moment and raised his eyebrow to let her know just that. She caught his look.

"To make matters worse, my room has been sabotaged." She rushed to her bed as fast as her shaky legs would take her and threw back the covers. Seeing nothing, Gaston peered closer and noticed a fine sheen on the covers and pillow.

"Honey." Mari-Elle informed him. "I ruined my best dressing coat with it. And this," she bent down and picked up a pair of slippers next to the bed, turning them over; honey poured out. "I put my feet in this slime."

Gaston watched the honey dribble to the floor and knew exactly who was responsible. He put his hand over his mouth casually so Mari-Elle would not see his twitching lips.

"But that's not the worst of it," Mari-Elle went on dramatically. "The assassins saved the best for last." She suddenly threw open her bed robe and from the neck down she was a lovely shade of yellow, saffron yellow.

"The tub was filled with steaming water when I retired this afternoon from the nooning meal and like a fool, I got in it. Now look at me."

Gaston closed his eyes; he had to or he would giggle like an idiot. He quickly turned away from his wife so she would not see that he was struggling for composure. "Cover yourself, madam, so that we might talk."

Angry and upset, Mari-Elle did as her husband ordered, and moved for the nearest chair. "You have evil within your midst, Gaston. A killer who has sworn me to death."

As soon as her bottom hit the chair, it collapsed as if it were made from rotted wood. Gaston spun around when he heard the crack to see Mari-Elle sitting on a pile of wood and silk. Out of obligation, he moved forward to help her up, but not before she grabbed a piece of broken wood and hurled it at the wall in her fury.

"I swear if I will not have someone's head for this!" she yelled, tossing another piece of wood. "They shall not get away with any of this! I swear vengeance; vengeance, I say!"

Gaston grasped her by the arm and pulled her to her feet, greatly annoyed when she pressed against him. "Oh, my lord Gaston, how comforted I am to know you are here to protect me. Thank you, my lord, for being here."

He held her away from him quickly and pointed her to another chair. "Sit, madam, and shut your mouth. I will speak now."

Mari-Elle eyed the chair, kicking its legs and shaking the arm to make sure it was not on the verge of collapse. Looking it over and satisfied I was not going to spill her onto the floor, she turned and settled herself there. But the moment her backside touched the cushion, she shot up with a wild screech of pain and grabbed her buttocks. Whirling, she identified the sharp nail sticking out of the cushion.

"By God!" she roared. "A knife with which to gore me!"

Gaston was on the brink of hysteria. He eyed the cushion and worked the long nail out, examining it. Then he tossed it to the floor carelessly, eyeing his wife. "You are lucky you did not sit down with force. That nail would have pierced you soundly."

Mari-Elle looked at him with disbelief; how could he be so callous? She opened her mouth to tell him so when she was suddenly seized with a fit of cramps and had to make a mad dash for the chamber pot lest she embarrass herself in front of her husband.

Gaston shook his head, a smile toying on his lips. "I will return later when you have control of yourself, madam." he called to her sternly. "I expect to have your complete attention."

He left his wife grunting and cursing harsh enough to raise the roof.

Mari-Elle did not leave by the morning. In fact, she was so ill with diarrhea and nausea that she could not get out of bed. Remington was a bit disheartened that her plan had not gone exactly as planned, but she consoled herself in the knowledge that Gaston's wife would be gone as soon as she was able to stand. Dane and Charles had gleefully told her of the tricks and gags they had planted in her room and she laughed herself silly. Surely no woman could stand all that had been done to her and not want to leave.

Gaston had not come to her that night and she was terribly disappointed, yet she knew he must have had a good reason for his absence. 'Twas ironic that a woman who used to start with terror at the sound of men's boot falls approaching her room was suddenly eager to hear them, but her life had changed so much since he had arrived that it was almost as if she were living out a dream.

Forgetting her discouragement that he had not come, she dressed in a pretty surcoat and pulled her hair away from her face, planting herself in a comfortable chair to embroider the hours away. Remington did lovely embroidery and was currently working on a piece depicting a hummingbird and a wild assortment of flowers.

She worked on it alone in her room, sitting in the bright sunshine that streamed in through her window. The morning was tapering into the afternoon and the day was warm, and she felt a tremendous sense of peace. Never in her life had she felt this sort of settled existence; she lived day-to-day fearing her husband, terrorized by his mere voice or presence. It had been no way to live, but live it she had. With a young son and sisters depending on her, she had had no choice.

To be able to sit and not fear what the day held was truly an answer to prayer.

In the room adjoining hers, she could hear Dane and Charles playing some sort of chess game. Charles was trying to explain the rules to Dane, who wanted to play it his own way. She smiled; they felt the peace, too.

There was a knock on her door and she bade the caller to enter. Gaston swung open the door, drinking in the sight of her. She always took his breath away.

"Greetings this day, madam," he said evenly. "I am pleased to find you in your room, not frolicking about like a serving wench."

She lay her embroidery in her lap, her entire face brightening. "Me? Frolic? I should say not."

He twisted his mouth wryly and closed the door. "From what I saw yesterday, you frolic with the best of them. Rory could take lessons from you." He moved across the room. "Speaking of which, she has been very busy, hasn't she? Writing blasphemous songs. Sabotaging bedchambers."

Remington lifted her eyebrows innocently. "I know not what you mean, my lord. Rory was with me all of yesterday, as you know."

He leaned on the wall next to the window, his gaze alternately on her seated directly next to him and roving over the countryside beyond the opening.

"I see," he said. "Then you know nothing of the destruction of Mari-Elle's room?"

She continued to play the innocent, lowering her gaze to her needlework. "I heard from Patrick this morning that Lady Mari-Elle has had a most difficult time of it. Ill, I believe he said. So ill she is yellow."

His eyes narrowed. "How would you know she is yellow, considering I did not tell Patrick?"

Remington's mouth twitched. "Isn't it true an ill person usually turns sallow? Yellow, as it were?"

He eyed her a moment, turning his eyes out of the window again. "What did you put in her food that is making her so ill?"

"I did not put anything in her food, my lord," she said. "I was never near her trencher."

He pursed his lips irritably. "Fine, then, what did Rory put in her food? Or Jasmine? Or Skye?"

She fixed a delicate stitch before answering. "I do not know, my lord."

"Remi," he shifted on his huge legs. "I am growing weary of this game. Simply answer my questions, if you would."

Her eyes came up, wide and guiltless. He felt as if they were sucking him in. "I am answering your questions. What am I not answering?"

He raised a slow eyebrow and she could read that he was serious. "You are answering, indeed, but you are giving me no answers at all. I want to know who has done this to my wife."

She felt as if she had been slammed in the chest by his massive fists, for suddenly she couldn't breathe. Her head went down sharply and her hands fumbled with the material shakily. She had no idea why she reacted so sharply to his words; what had he said? There was nothing to upset her other than the fact that he called another woman his wife.

His wife.

She would never be his wife. *I want for you to be my husband!*

She suddenly wanted him away, out of her sight, so she could compose herself. Her resolve to keep everything a secret fled and she would tell him everything if he would only go away.

"Rory put crushed apricot seeds into your *wife's* food," she said shortly. "'Twas Dane and Charles who vandalized your *wife's* room. The apricot seeds will make her wish as if she could die, but she will recover fully, I assure you." She emphasized the word "wife" every time, using the term as he had. She couldn't help the bitterness that filled her, although she had no right to feel anything.

He eyed her, the abrupt manner. "Thank you for telling me the truth."

He did not leave as she had hoped, but continued to watch her and she rose swiftly, turning away so he couldn't see her face. The needlework was put aside and she threw open the doors of her wardrobe, anything to occupy her hands, anything not to look at him. She was embarrassed for her outburst, but hurt all the same.

She heard his boot falls behind her and she moved to get out of his way, but he caught her to him fiercely.

"Nay, madam, you are not going anywhere," he whispered, his face not an inch from her own. He had lifted her off the ground entirely. "You do not like the word wife, do you?"

She pushed against him, succeeding in freeing her arms. She was actually angry; she was usually quite good at controlling her temper.

"I do not like it when you refer to…her," she admitted.

"She is my wife, Remi, as much as I abhor the fact. I merely use the term to describe her relationship to me and I certainly do not use the term to make you uncomfortable," his grip relaxed a bit and he lowered her to the ground. "You reacted the same way when the merchant at the faire called me your husband. You loathe the titles of husband and wife, do not you? They mean nothing but heartache to you."

She stopped struggling and her brow furrowed. "Is that what you think? That I hate the titles?"

"What else am I to think?" he said softly. "You hate the term wife because of what it means to you."

She shook her head vehemently. "Nay, Gaston, not at all. 'Tis true I hate being Guy's wife, but I certainly would not hate being yours."

He looked at her long and hard. Slowly an eyebrow rose. "Is *that* what this is about, then? You are jealous of a woman I hate because she bears the title and you do not?"

Remington suddenly felt like a fool, a selfish, petty fool. She closed her eyes against his stare, lowering her head. "I am sorry, Gaston. I did not mean to sound like a spoiled child. Please do not be angry with me."

He took her face between his great hands, forcing her to look at him. Frankly, he was a little stunned; he believed she hated marriage so much that she would never have considered such a thing to anyone else. Obviously, he was wrong. And he was never wrong.

"Angel, I am not angry," he said gently. "But I had no idea you felt that way. I thought you hated marriage."

"I hate my husband," she whispered, drinking in her fill of his sensual face. "But I love you. I always will love you, wife or no."

God, if it could only be. His lips descended on hers, sweetly, achingly, hungrily. He had to taste this woman until all he could taste was her. He'd never known he was capable of such powerful emotion as he clutched her to him, feeling her warmth in his hands and her fragrance in his nostrils.

He had not realized he was pushing her backward with the forcefulness of his actions until she bumped into the wall and he trapped her, ravishing her lips, her neck, the swell of her white breasts. Remington gasped, her hands bracing themselves against his wide shoulders, her heart pounding a thousand beats a minute. What the man couldn't do to her!

"Mummy?" came a distinct yell on the other side of the adjoining door. "Mum-*MY*?"

Gaston's head came up and he stepped away from her, adjusting his swollen groin. Dane burst into the room a split second later.

"Charles isn't playing fair," he accused. "He says knights always lead a siege, but it's the men-at-arms. Isn't it, Sir Gaston?"

Gaston gazed over the boy's head into the room beyond; he could see small wooden figurines all over the floor and knew a battle when he saw it.

"That depends, Dane," Gaston put his hand on the boy's shoulder and walked with him through the adjoining door. The ever-elusive Charles stood nervously, his arms crossed, as Gaston entered.

"Depends on what?" Dane wanted to know.

"On who is leading the siege," Gaston said, looking at the placement of the soldiers. The "castle," a wooden box in the middle of the floor, was surrounded by rushes that acted as the moat. "Now see here; you have your troops placed incorrectly. If you are going to lay siege, then by all means lay one. Surround them, boy; do not simply walk up to the door and knock."

Charles crouched down, observing the layout. "But is it not correct, my lord, to approach the weakest point in the fortress? The drawbridge?"

Remington stood in the doorway, leaning against the jamb, listening to the realm's mightiest soldier discuss tactics with two young boys.

"Not always," Gaston put his hands on his hips as if he were deep in a war conference. "Each situation is different and you must evaluate it accordingly. Tell me; how deep is the moat?"

"Deep?" Dane and Charles looked at each other. "Eight feet, my lord," Charles replied with a shrug.

"Good," Gaston said firmly. "Not much of a moat, the fools. How tall are the walls?"

"Uh...twenty feet?" Dane said timidly, sitting cross-legged on the floor.

"An easy breech," Gaston said confidently. "See here, you must surround this castle and delegate at least thirty men to build ladders, and begin commencement of flame arrows on the drawbridge. You will seize the fortress from all sides."

Remington smiled, as Dane and Charles were terribly engrossed in his instructions, acting as if they were the real things. Gaston stood over them, issuing orders without being the least bit threatening and they ate it up. She watched as troops were repositioned and Charles broke up kindling for "ladders" to top the "walls".

Gaston crouched down as he directed the boys. When everything was placed, Dane suggested that Gaston be the lord of the castle and defend the keep. Gaston grinned and sat on his bottom, picking up a wooden man and placing him on top of the box.

"Make your move, good knights," he said.

It was vicious battle. Blood spurting, limbs hacked off, all incredibly graphic as Remington watched and listened with great amusement. Absently, she wandered up behind Gaston and put her hand on his shoulder. He put his huge hand over it.

"Not now, Remi," he said, his eyes on the movements in front of him. "I am trying to defend my fortress."

"Die. Die," Dane cried, launching an effective projectile at Gaston's lord.

She smiled at all three of them; scarcely believing he was actually playing their games. This man, the Dark Knight, who never played games but played to win; was by far, the mightiest knight in the realm.

She was deeply touched and warmed by the sight and decided to leave them to their battle. But not before she planted a kiss on Gaston's head and tousled her son's sandy hair. They both ignored her, as did Charles. Gaston did not even think to scold her for being indiscreet in front of the boys.

Wandering back to her chamber, she left the door wide open so she could hear them as she sewed. Not strangely, she did not get much further on her needlework; her eyes were glued to the massive man with the soul of an angel.

＊

By the time the nooning meal had come around, it was unbearably sticky. Remington and her sisters ate in their room as ordered, fanning themselves in an attempt to seek some relief from the humidity.

Patrick joined them for the meal, sharing a chunk of bread with Rory. The tomboy sister was unused to feminine games and blushed furiously when he complimented her in the least. Remington watched the two of them, wondering where Gaston had gone. She did not want to ask his cousin, fearing that she would appear too attached to the master. She knew theirs was not a public game.

Jasmine made the suggestion that a swim was quite in order and everyone agreed except Remington. She looked to Patrick, knowing Gaston's orders had been quite firm, but Rory began to pester him until he relented and promised to ask. He quit the room in search of Gaston, but not before depositing a kiss on Rory's hand. Rory tried to slap him but he was too quick for her.

Gaston was in the outer bailey; one hundred new recruits had arrived two weeks early from London and he was highly irritated. Could no one do as they were supposed to? Mari-Elle was *supposed* to stay at Clearwell, and these raw soldiers were not *supposed* to be here for another ten to twelve days. His mood darkened as Arik, perturbed as his lord, directed the settling loudly.

Patrick came upon them, giving the new men the once-over before turning to his cousin. "Gaston, I come with a request?"

Gaston's face was taut with irritation. "From who? If it is Mari-Elle, tell her to go to the Devil."

"Nay, not from your wife," Patrick replied with a smirk. "I come from the masses. They want to go swimming, with your permission."

"Swimming?" he tore his attention away from the problem at hand and looked down at his cousin. "The ladies?"

Patrick crossed his arms, smiling. "It is terribly hot. Besides, there is no danger of them running into your wife outside of the keep."

Gaston rubbed his chin. "You have a point," he let out a sigh of pure exasperation, his mood irritable. "Assign a few knights to go with them; I want you here with me right now." He slugged Arik in the arm, suddenly, pointing to something that had just caught his attention in the ranks. Arik was off and shouting at the novice soldiers.

Sir Roald and two other knights appeared at Remington's door not a half hour later. "I have come to take the fish to the pond, ladies," he announced with a wide grin.

Amid all shrieks and sighs of thanks, the sisters practically crashed into one another as they hastened to gather linen towels and other supplies. Two large wicker baskets were thrust at Sir Roald and another older knight as the ladies, along with Dane and Charles, preceded them from the room.

They had to pass the baileys on their way to the lake, baileys filled with fresh recruits. One look at the four women and the whistles and wolf-calls abounded. As much as the knights tried to shield them and they tried to hurry through, it wasn't quite fast enough to avoid their attention.

Gaston heard the whistles and hoots and knew what had happened. Taking the ladder to the inner wall two rungs at a time, he mounted the wall in time to catch a glimpse of Remington scurrying from the outer bailey with Sir Roald's arm grasping her protectively. He did not blame the men; they were only human and knew a beautiful woman when they saw one. But he would have to explain things to them rapidly or there would be more than one dead soldier.

The heavy trees were thick with moisture and everyone was sweating rivers, including the knights in armor. Rory and Jasmine broke through the trees first and took off on a dead run for the relief of the lake, while Skye and Dane bounded after them. Charles stayed with Remington and the three knights as they made their way to the huge oak tree, their usual spot.

Sir Roald spread a large woolen blanket to protect the ladies from the ground and sent one knight into the trees to patrol. He smiled at

Remington chivalrously, backing away to a discreet distance to keep watch.

Remington noticed Charles seemed to be infatuated with the knights. The lad had never shown any interest in warring arts and for him to show interest was unusual. Remington suspected it had something to do with Gaston's mock battle that morning.

"Did you enjoy your time with Sir Gaston this morning?" she asked.

Charles nodded. "Aye. He's an intelligent man. For a knight."

"Then you are not afraid of him anymore?" she said, arranging her skirts.

"Nay," Charles insisted. "He's not like I expected after all."

"What did you expect?"

"To be honest, I do not know," Charles toyed with a piece of grass. "I was scared of his reputation, I suppose. The knights that told me of his coming told horrible stories about his fierceness and ruthlessness. When I heard about the soldier he killed in the bailey, and the fight at the faire, I was all the more frightened of him."

"And that is why you have been holed up in the tower?" she asked gently.

He nodded, embarrassed. "When he came into Dane's room this morn, I thought I was going to throw up from fright. But he's...different. He's...."

"He's a mortal man with intelligence and compassion," Remington finished, giving him a little shove in the arm. "He's not your hated Dark One; Devil's Spawn, or whatever else he is called."

"He's not, Remi, I will admit it," Charles said. "He seems to like you an awful lot, though. Aren't you afraid his wife will be jealous of you and send you away?"

"Nay," she replied simply, looking out to the lake. "I am not afraid of her."

Charles let it go, turning his attention to the lake, too. "I think I shall go in, too. Can't let them have all the fun."

Remington was left alone under the oak tree. With a sigh of contentment, she settled back against the trunk and watched the faint breeze trickle through the leaves. Sunlight danced on the woolen blanket and she found her thoughts turning toward Gaston again. It seemed that all she ever did now was think of him.

Somewhere in the midst of her daydreaming she dozed off. Drifting in and out, she heard screams of delight and Rory's loud voice. In her dreams she saw Gaston, his incredible sensual face, the curtain of hair that fell down over his eyes. She dreamt something about the faire, although she couldn't quite grasp the thought. Peace was finally hers on this lazy, muggy day.

Somebody was shaking her gently, calling her name. She rolled her eyes open to find Sir Roald looking back at her.

"My lady, we must return now," he said. He sounded tense.

She blinked the sleep from her eyes and sat up, glancing down to the lake. Like waterfowl, her family was still romping about and throwing water on each other.

"Why, Sir Roald? What's the matter?" she asked.

His jaw was rigid as he glanced about uneasily. "If you do not mind, my lady, I will collect the baskets and we will be gone. If you would kindly retrieve your family from the water."

He was awfully tight and almost forceful. She rose unsteadily, wondering what had the man so spooked. She glanced around as he quickly gathered their things but saw nothing unusual. Puzzled, she began to walk to the lake to do as she had been asked.

And then it struck her. Sir Roald was the only knight present. There had been three. What had happened to the other two? Uneasy, although she knew not why, she hastened to the water's edge.

Sir Roald had gathered everything into a pile at his feet, although he had not picked anything up. His hand rested on the hilt of his broadsword as he scanned the trees. Something was terribly wrong, although he did not know just what. His knights were missing, not responding to his calls, and he was eager to return to the safety of Mt. Holyoak. Sir Gaston would have his head if anything happened to the lady.

Remington was hustling her son out of the lake when they all heard a high-pitched whine. It was brief, going from barely audible to a loud scream within a mere second, and suddenly Sir Roald went hurtling to the ground in a crash of mail and flesh.

Everyone started violently; Skye and Jasmine screamed loudly. All eyes were riveted to Sir Roald, lying on the ground with an arrow sticking out of his chest and Remington bolted into action.

"Run!" she yelled. "Run for the fortress!"

They tore off as if the devil himself had just burst through the trees. But the moment they started to run, charges broke through the underbrush and hurtled themselves across the green grass, on a direct course for the fleeing family. Remington was terrified; she knew they couldn't outrun them. But they could lose them in the bramble, if only to slow them down.

"The bushes. Head for the bushes," she urged everyone, especially Dane. She was panicked for her son's safety.

They were almost to the dense foliage when the destriers were upon them. Jasmine was grabbed first, followed by Skye. Remington tried to duck away from a large roan horse but she wasn't swift enough; a huge mailed hand had her by the dress and she was hooked.

She twisted and thrashed as she was hoisted up onto the saddle, punching and kicking with every bit of strength. She lost sight of Dane and Rory; she had not even seen where Charles had gone. Mayhap he was a prisoner, too. She could hear Jasmine screaming and she increased her efforts to free herself.

"Remington!" A voice hissed in her ear. "Stop it. Remington, do you hear me? *Stop!*"

She recognized the voice but it did not ease her terror. For the moment, she stopped fighting and turned to the helmeted knight.

"Who...who is it?" she gasped.

"Derek," the knight said. "I came to rescue you."

She was puzzled now as well as terrified. "Rescue me from *what?*"

"From de Russe," he insisted, trying to help her sit straight on the destrier. "Remington, I know you said all those things at the faire because you had to. I told my father what happened and he ordered us to rescue you from Mt. Holyoak. We have been waiting here for a day, waiting for you to come to the lake. I remember how much you loved the lake."

Her mouth fell open. Her fear was rapidly subsiding, replaced by a vague understanding and full-blown exasperation. "Nay, Derek, you misunderstand. I did not say those things because I had to; I said them because it was the truth. Sir Gaston has been exceedingly generous and kind to us."

Two knights exploded through the undergrowth, reining their excited animals next to Derek. "Rory and young Dane made it to the castle, Derek. We couldn't risk being seen when they escaped onto the open road."

"Calvin," Remington said accusingly.

"Do not fret, Remi," Derek assured her calmly. "We shall get them."

"I do not want you to *get* them, I want you to let me go. Let us all go," she insisted angrily. "Derek, you are crazy. Gaston will kill you when he finds out what you have done."

"Do not worry," he repeated to her, then looking at his men. "The escapees will surely alert de Russe. Come now, we ride."

Remington opened her mouth to protest but Derek took off with such speed she nearly fell off. She clung to the destrier's saddle, terrified of what was to come.

Knaresborough was nearly ten miles to the southwest. Derek's father maintained a fair-sized fortress, certainly nothing the size of Mt. Holyoak, and Remington knew instinctively that Gaston would obliterate it in his quest to retrieve her. Derek did not seem to want to listen to her, convinced she was a prisoner of the Dark Knight. He had to listen.

"Derek," she screamed. "Stop, please."

He held on to her tightly, ignoring her pleas. She tried repeatedly to convince him to stop, but he did not answer. Instead, he urged his horse harder.

They ran and ran. Remington wasn't even sure how many men Derek had with him, but she could see that every man was positive they were doing something chivalrous and good. Rescuing damsels in distress from a ruthless overlord. If they would only listen to the truth!

They cut south to the River Ure. Once across the wooden bridge that spanned the waters, there was nothing between them and Knaresborough. Remington saw this as her only opportunity to stall, to talk sense into the man as he slowed his destrier to a halt.

"Derek, I feel ill," she gasped, although it was a lie. "Can I please rest for a moment? Please?"

His helm looked at her a moment before she saw it dip in approval. Gently, he lowered her to the ground and she ran for Jasmine. Hysterical, her sister fell into her arms and the two clutched each other tightly. Skye was not to be left out, wriggling from her captor and throwing herself against her sisters. They were terrified.

Remington turned angry eyes to Derek. "I told you we did not want to leave. Why do you not listen? What will it take for you to believe me?"

He flipped up his visor, his soft blue eyes and blond lashes focused on her. "Remington, he's the enemy, for God's sake. What sort of magic has he performed on you to make you loyal to him?"

If he only knew! "Derek, I demand you return us to Mt. Holyoak. Return us now and I promise Gaston will go easy on you."

"Hmpf. I think not," he said firmly. "You are an ungrateful little chick. Come now, mount up."

Jasmine suddenly went into a screaming fit of hysterics and collapsed on the ground. Remington and Skye went down on their knees beside her, trying to revive her.

"See what you have done?" Remington accused hotly. "Derek Botmore, you are a lout and an idiot!"

Derek sighed and dismounted heavily. This rescue was not going at all well. His former captives were most unappreciative of his efforts.

"Remington, come here," he motioned with his finger.

Thinking mayhap he was willing to see reason, Remington left her sister's side. "What is it?"

"You do not understand, love," he said carefully. "I am saving you."

"From what?" she demanded. "I told you that we are not in any danger. Sir Gaston has been entirely accommodating. Derek, Mt. Holyoak is our home and we wish to return."

He looked at her a moment before shaking his head in disbelief. "You are ill, love. You are not thinking clearly."

"Do not turn this around on me," she said angrily. "I know exactly what I am saying. 'Tis you who are not thinking clearly. I never exactly asked for your help."

He put his hands on his hips. "Listen to me, Remi. With Guy locked away, you do not have to stay at Mt. Holyoak any longer," his hands grasped her arms suddenly, firmly. "Come to Knaresborough with me, love. I shall take good care of you."

She saw his ploy, his open invitation and she was infuriated. Roughly, she yanked away from him. "I do not want you. Take me home. Now."

His face hardened. "Do not make me force you, Remington. I am doing you a favor. What is the matter with you?"

She took a step back from him, shaking with anger. "Take me home or I shall walk every step of the way. I mean it, Derek!"

He did not answer and she turned away from him, moving back to her crumpled sister.

"I must do what I feel is best for you, Remington," he said loudly. "You must trust me."

"You are not my husband," she snapped back. "You have no say in my life or the lives of my family members."

He slapped his thigh, maddened. "You are unreasonable!"

"And you are out of line, sir," she said hotly.

"Remi, what's going on?" Skye's voice was shaking.

Remington turned back to Jasmine. "He thinks he is saving us from Gaston."

"Saving us?" Skye repeated. "From what?"

Remington fixed her sister with a pointed look. "Exactly my question, sweetheart."

Jasmine suddenly moaned and twitched, clutching at her stomach. "Oh, God. I am going to be sick."

She continued to cry and carry on, but that was the extent of it. Remington tried to comfort her, bending low so she would be heard over the moaning. "Jasmine, what's the matter? Where do you hurt?"

Jasmine moaned and groaned and one eye opened, peering at her sister. "Nowhere," she whispered, then moaned again. "I am stalling for time."

Remington almost collapsed with relief atop her sister, but refrained from showing her alleviation. Quickly, her mind set in motion to add to Jasmine's stalling tactic. They must give Gaston time to catch up to them.

"See what you have done!" she whirled to Derek furiously. "You have aggravated her stomach ailment. If we travel anymore she will become violently ill."

Derek hissed a curse and slapped at his thigh; this was not going at all well. He marched up on the women, gazing critically on Jasmine.

"Well, what's wrong with her?" he demanded.

"I just told you, it's her stomach," Remington snapped. "We must rest here."

They couldn't afford to stay there any longer. Already he was granting the pursuing Dark Knight ample time to catch up to them. He began to wonder about the wisdom of this caper; never had he met such stubborn victims. But he had no desire to kill one of his rescues, if in fact she was ill as her sister made her out to be.

In pure agitation, he tossed his helm to the ground and ordered his men to take a rest.

Small dots representing Rory, Dane and Charles were racing up the hill toward Mt. Holyoak under the hot afternoon sun. The sentries on the wall saw them and set forth the warning cry. There would be no reason to run in the sun unless something terrible had happened; the fact that there were only three of them returning being reason enough to worry, and the sergeant made the decision to give the alerted call.

Gaston, in the sublevels with Arik, heard the cry and knew in his gut that Remington was in danger. Some sixth sense told him something had happened and he fought off his panic as he made his way to the fortified drawbridge.

Rory, Dane and Charles were pounding across the bridge about the time Gaston arrived. Rory, exhausted, tripped and plowed into Arik. Dane went straight for Gaston, sobbing as the huge man picked him up gently.

"Rory, what the hell is going on? Where are Remi and the rest of them?" he demanded harshly.

Rory was gasping for air, trying to answer. Charles, on his knees, raised his flushed face. "Knights, Sir Gaston. Lots of them."

A bolt of terror shot through him. "Were they wearing colors? Did you recognize them?"

Rory and Charles shook their head. "The armor was very fine, hardly damaged," Charles breathed. "And one of the destriers was red. Very red."

Charles described no one Gaston knew. Dane was clinging to him, his little arms wrapped around his neck and his legs wound around his narrow waist, sobbing. Gaston clutched Remington's son, patting his back as he talked.

"The knight at the faire had a horse like that," Dane whispered against Gaston's neck.

It took Gaston a second to comprehend the boy's words. Then, he pulled back to look the lad in the face. "What knight, Dane?"

Dane sniffled, wiping his eyes. "The knight that talked to my mother. You called him a whip."

Gaston looked at him a moment, trying to figure out what in the hell he was talking about. Then, suddenly, it dawned on him. "Sir Derek? The knight I called a whelp?"

Dane nodded fearfully. "It looked like him because they had the same horse."

Gaston slanted a glance at Arik, who understood the silent command. He fled. Charles and Rory clung to each other, finally catching their breath but still very, very frightened.

"Rory, do you know Sir Derek?" Gaston asked. "Did you recognize him?"

"I wasn't looking, to be truthful," she said weakly. "Remington said to run, and I did."

Remington. The sound of her name brought the reality of the crisis slamming into him like a ton of bricks and he felt a sense of urgency shoot through him such as he had never known. He sat Dane gently to the ground.

"Charles, I have an important task for you," he said sternly. The young man instantly straightened. "Aye, my lord?"

"You will take Lady Rory and young Dane and escort them to their rooms. I will depend on you to make sure they do not stray," he said.

"I will trust their safety to you while I retrieve Lady Remington and her sisters. Will you do this?"

"Aye, my lord," Charles nodded, his eyes suddenly turning wistful. "I may not ride with you?"

"Nay, lad," Gaston said. "I need you here, at the fortress."

Gaston had put his words nicely and Charles was not disheartened. The fact that he had the Dark Knight's trust actually made him feel quite important. Taking Dane's hand, he led the boy and Rory away.

Gaston was on the move, a man with a mission. Knaresborough was not far and he wanted to intercept the party before they made it to the fortress. His two squires followed him, latching on pieces of armor and strapping on his sword. Gaston paused a moment, still coordinating orders and troops, lifting his arms as the boys locked on the rest of his plate armor. When one squire secured the last latch on his grieve and positioned the plate over his boot, Gaston was completely protected and therefore, impatient to get going.

He put Patrick in charge of the fortress with explicit instructions regarding Mari-Elle and Remington's family. He did not want any unexpected confrontations while he was away, especially not between Rory and Mari-Elle. With the temper of the two women, they would most likely kill each other and he did not want any surprises upon his return.

A groom brought Taran forward, still fumbling with his tack. Gaston mounted the animal as the groom secured the last strap and adjusted his reins as Arik moved the last mounted soldier into formation.

This was a light company, well-seasoned warriors that were worth their weight in a fight. They were mayhap the most elite of the men-at-arms, a step above, yet not on par with the knights. They were tough and Gaston roved an approving eye over them as they settled in and waited for his final command.

He would catch the fools before they had a chance to make it to Knaresborough, and he would take great pleasure in gutting every one of them personally. If Remington were unharmed, he would be merciful. If they had been unfortunate to touch her, then he would make sure they were so miserable that they would beg for death. Every time he thought of her in the clutches of her kidnappers, his heart beat so fast that his palms sweated and the tightening of his chest was unbearable.

He set out with unmovable determination, the likes of which he had never known. No battle ever held as high a stake, including Bosworth. He would retrieve what was his and he would make those responsible pay in the worst way.

"What is our elapsed time?" he asked Arik as they went charging under the portcullis.

"Since Rory and Charles informed us? Around ten minutes," Arik replied over the thunder of the hooves.

"And we assume that the abductors have at least a ten minute start on us," Gaston thought aloud and he tightened his grip on the reins. "We have got twenty damn minutes to make up for."

The army rumbled into the lake clearing and Gaston's eyes fell on Roald. He drew Taran close to the knight and dismounted, kneeling beside the body. He was sickened by the senseless loss of a long-devoted knight.

But Roald wasn't dead. Yet. He gave a little twitch and tried to move somehow, but Gaston and Arik held him still.

"Roald," Gaston said urgently. "Did you see which way they went?"

Roald opened one eye, seeing Gaston and knowing if the arrow did not end his life, his liege would. He had failed miserably in the fulfillment of his duties.

"I...I do not know, my lord," he rasped. "I remember being struck and then nothing more. They were taken and not killed outright?"

"It would seem so," Gaston said.

Roald felt a bit of relief, but he knew he would still answer for allowing such a thing to happen. "I apologize for failing you, my lord. 'Tis inexcusable and I ask that you be merciful with my punishment."

Gaston waved a couple of soldiers over. "I believe the arrow in your chest is punishment enough, Roald," he turned to the soldiers behind him. "Return him to the fortress and then comb the woods for the bodies of the other two knights. I want them found."

He was met with a sharp response and he rose, his eyes gazing over the landscape.

"They went south," Arik said. "The quickest way would be to avoid the towns and cross the river where it is least used."

Gaston nodded faintly. "Send the scouts to pick up the trail. We ride."

Arik let out a piercing whistle and two soldiers broke off from the troops, racing in the direction Arik indicated on Saracen stallions. They were the fastest beasts Gaston had ever seen and an invaluable intelligence asset.

He and Arik were mounted and waited when one of the soldiers came racing back.

"We have found obvious evidence, my lord," the man said, pointing. "Almost due south."

Gaston nodded sharply. "Ride ahead, then, and mark my trail. Waste no time."

The soldier was gone and the army followed close behind, trampling over the soft green grass and tearing up the growth with their mighty warhorses.

Jasmine, through a good deal of expert acting, managed to delay their departure for nearly an hour. Every time someone would raise their voice or move in to pick her up, she would scream and grab her gut as if she were going to explode. Intimidated, the knights and soldiers accompanying them were reluctant to force her.

Every man, whether he would admit it or not, is intimidated by a female simply for virtue of her mysterious sex. Women breed and have strange, private afflictions that serve to scare the hell out of any man. They were positive Jasmine was suffering from a strange, female affliction and none wanted to be cursed by touching her.

Remington and Skye sat vigilantly beside their sister, fighting off smiles and praying Gaston was not far behind. The afternoon was waning away as the sun moved lower in the sky and Remington knew they could not fight Derek off much longer. He and Calvin stood in a huddle several feet away, whispering to each other and glaring at the women.

Finally, Derek broke off from Calvin and marched to Remington. "A word, if you will," he said.

Remington rose reluctantly and faced him. "Well? Are you going to take us home?"

His jaw ticked. "You do not seem to understand. Mt. Holyoak is no longer your home, which is why I am taking you to Knaresborough. Is Jasmine well enough to travel?"

She crossed her arms stubbornly. "No."

Derek put his hands on his hips. "Then that is her misfortune. We are leaving now, ill or no."

"You cannot," Remington cried. "She shall…. she shall retch violently the entire way. She shall faint and take to convulsions."

Derek snatched her arm. "Let's go."

She dug her heels in. "Let me go, Derek. I told you we do not want to go with you. Why can you not understand that?"

He stopped suddenly and she almost fell down. "Because you do not mean it. I do not know what de Russe has done to you, but you are not acting yourself. You are coming home with me."

She fought and twisted. "No, Derek. I do not want you, and I do not want to go to Knaresborough."

His grip tightened and his eyes narrowed as he studied her. He did not say anything for a moment, but she could tell by the way he was looking at her that he was not thinking pleasant thoughts.

"You are his whore, aren't you?" he said in a low voice as if the thought just occurred to him. "That is why you do not want to leave. He showers you with meaningless gifts and lies and you have fallen for his ploy." He yanked her hard when she tried to turn away from him. "Remington, how could you be so blind?"

"You do not know what you are saying," she said through clenched teeth. "Let go of me."

Instead he grabbed her face, forcing her to look at him and she struggled to free herself. "He has brainwashed you. Can't you see that?"

She kicked out and succeeded in breaking his grip. She stumbled a few feet away, still feeling his harsh grip on her face. "All I see is a spoiled young man who is being told no for the first time in his life," she spat. "You cannot understand why I do not want you and you are therefore trying to plant lies in my head to force me to bend to your will."

He looked at her, pleading. "He is not for you, Remington. He is your captor, for God's sake. He shall use you a little while and then when he tires of you, he shall move on. They all do."

She was starting to lose her composure. Derek was voicing her very own negative thoughts that she had fought so hard to suppress, thoughts she was even afraid to admit she had. Dark, shapeless phantoms in the corner of her mind; how could he know exactly what she had been thinking?

"You are wrong, Derek," she said hoarsely. "Take me home. Now."

Derek took a timid step toward her; smart enough to know she was wavering. "He tells you that you are the most beautiful woman he has ever seen, and he tells you that he is mad for you. He likes to hold your hand and he is very kind to your son, anything to gain entrance into your heart and into your bed. Tell me if I am wrong."

How did he know? Her breath began coming in short pants and her knees began to shake. Tears, hot and confused, sprang to her eyes. It wasn't true. Derek was trying to unbalance her; anything to convince her that going to Knaresborough was in her best interest. He was being spiteful simply because she had said she did not want him.

"You are wrong," she whispered.

"I am not," he countered softly. "You know I have always had a weakness for you, love. I shall make you happy, I promise."

She took a deep breath, fighting for control. A thin smile played on her lips. "So that I may be your whore? Really, Derek, how hypocritical! You accuse me of being another man's lover, yet you would have me do the same thing with you."

Derek's face went tight. "You need me."

She looked surprised. A guffaw of laughter bubbled from her throat. "Need you? Why on earth do I need you?"

"Because I am the only one who would care for you, treat you as you should be treated. I'd take care of your sisters, too, so that they would never know want or need." He was truly sincere and approached her with open hands. "Why can you not understand, Remington? I am saving you from hell so that your life may be happy."

"With you," she supplied drolly.

"Aye," his eyes glittered. "With *me*."

She found the entire conversation difficult to believe. She had known Derek since they had been small for they had been distant neighbors. He was a few years older than she, always an irresponsible lad, but he had been very friendly to her. She never imagined he had been harboring feelings for her because he had always been absorbed in himself.

She put up her hands as if to shoo him away. "This is ridiculous. Please take me home."

"I will not," he said sharply. "You are coming with me."

"I do not want to come with you!" she yelled at him.

He watched her as she marched back to her sisters, her back rigid and her fists clenched. God, why was this so difficult? When he had set out two days ago, it had been to rescue damsels in distress. Of course, one of the damsels was meant for him. But now he found himself holding unwilling females who did not want or need his help.

It was madness, and certainly not worth his life.

"I am trying to save you, you silly wench!" he held out his arms in exasperation.

"I do not want to be saved!" she shouted.

He had had enough of Lady Remington and her frail sister. His jaw clenching in determination, he took a step toward her menacingly. They were all going whether they wanted to or not.

A thin wail pierced the air and suddenly there was an arrow in front of Derek, planted in the ground not six inches in front of him. Derek blanched and took a step back, but suddenly another arrow sailed in behind him and plowed into the earth. Paralyzed by the obvious message, Derek began screaming orders for his men to prepare for battle.

Remington turned her attention in the direction the arrows had come from and was astonished to see soldiers and knights bursting through the trees, riding side by side as they thundered toward them. Derek's knights were running to the mounts, the soldiers were fumbling with their weapons, and Derek seemed frozen to the spot.

Riding alone ahead of the line of men was the unmistakable form of the Dark Knight.

Remington yanked her sisters to their feet and they plastered themselves against the trunk of the huge oak, standing back as Gaston's men
engaged Derek's sadly outnumbered force. Cries and the clash of metal
resounded through the thick air.

Gaston was riding straight for Derek, a wicked-looking crossbow
in his left hand. Taran thundered over the earth like an unnatural
being, snorting and kicking up great clumps of dirt. But Gaston never
wavered in the saddle, never flinched, and Remington could see that he
wasn't even gripping the reins. He was reloading the crossbow as the
horse crossed the clearing.

Derek bolted, straight for Remington. She caught him out of the
corner of her eye and tried to escape him, but he grabbed her savagely
and hauled her up against his body. Gaston knew a shield when he saw
one and slowed Taran to a dancing halt several feet away.

"Call off your attack, de Russe," Derek yelled.

"Let her go," Gaston replied calmly.

Derek put his hand to her throat and Remington struggled furiously. "Call it off, I say."

Gaston's helmed head gazed down a moment before turning slightly
in the direction of the fighting. A loud, shrill whistle suddenly penetrated the air sharply and all of Gaston's men, if they were able, suddenly ceased their onslaught. Every de Russe soldier looked to their lord
expectantly. It was the most amazing thing Remington had ever seen.

Even Derek was impressed, briefly thrown off balance at the display
of solidarity. But he rapidly regained himself. "That's better," he said.
"Now, de Russe, since I seem to have the advantage, I will make the
rules. Firstly, you will allow me and my men safe passage across the
Ure and all the way to Knaresborough. The women will go with us.
Secondly, if there is any interruption from you, the ladies will not fair
favorably. Do you understand?"

Gaston popped the butt-end of the crossbow on his thigh. "I
understand."

Another faint wail filled the air and suddenly Derek lurched as if he
had been hit with Thor's hammer. His hands dropped from Remington
and she shrieked, scooting away from him as he fell onto the ground,
dead from an arrow to the back of his neck.

Stunned, she stared at the body a moment before lifting her gaze questioningly, seeing Arik emerge from behind a neighboring oak, a Welsh crossbow in his grip. He smiled at Remington and she suddenly felt ill.

"You did not have to kill him," she said to Gaston, starting to shake violently.

He did not reply, but lifted a hand to his men. It seemed to be the sign for retreat, because suddenly his men were disengaging themselves from Derek's soldiers and moving across the grass to find their mounts. Only then did he spur Taran forward, reining the animal next to her.

"Are you very well?" he asked.

She let out a ragged sigh, dropping her gaze and moving to her sisters, who were still flattened against the tree. She grabbed hold of both of them, hugging them tightly. Gaston dismounted, securing the crossbow to his saddle before walking over to the women.

"We need to return, ladies, for it will be dark soon," he said gently.

They continued to cling to each other a moment until Jasmine caught sight of Antonius. In a burst of tears, she broke from her sisters and threw herself in his arms. Nicolas, too, waited patiently for Skye to be free of her eldest sister before tenderly ushering her to his steed.

Remington stood by the tree, shaking and ill. She refused to meet Gaston's eye, too many of Derek's words ringing about in her head. She should have been happy to see him, grateful in the very least that he had rescued her, but she found that all she could feel was uncertainty and bitterness.

"Come on, Remi," he said softly. "Let's go home."

She looked at him, her body literally hurting with all of the emotions she was feeling. "I do not want to ride with you."

He looked at her a moment. "Why not?"

"I just do not," she whispered. "I would rather ride with Arik."

He did not move. "Are you angry because the knight is dead?"

It was extremely difficult to control herself. "He came to save us. From you. He thought that all of the things I said at the faire were forced, and that you were actually holding all of us prisoner. He thought he was doing us a favor." Her emotions, her anger, her hurt were gaining momentum and her lip began to quiver. "He wanted us to go live with him in Knaresborough and he wanted me to be his woman. He knew you were my lover and out of his mouth I heard all of the things you have said to me, sweet lies and cunning plans to make me want you. He said you would tire of me and move on to the next whore."

Her voice rose to a shrill, shaking tone and he moved forward quickly, grabbing her arms and forcing her to walk with him. She cried and struggled, trying to pull away from him, but his grip was like iron.

"Calm down, angel," he whispered. The helm came off and went thudding to the ground as he walked. "Walk with me and calm yourself."

"Let go of me!" She twisted until her arms hurt, but he would not budge. She finally took to crying pitifully and he stopped near the river's edge, far away from his men, and faced her.

"Do not you know he would say anything to make you believe that he was right in what he did?" he said softly.

She jerked back from him but she did not run away. "I never thought he was right in what he did and I begged him to return us home, but the things he said...they made so much sense. It was as if he could read my mind."

"What else did he say?" he demanded carefully.

She sniffled loudly and the sobs started fresh. "He told me you were only kind to Dane to gain access to my bed. He said that the gifts, the sweet words, the touching, it was all a lie. He said that I was a whore. And that's true, I am."

He shook his head. "I told you I never wanted to hear that word again."

"It's true!" she snapped savagely. "I shall never be your wife, Gaston, so what else am I but a whore?"

His eyes glazed with pain, her pain and his. "I will not hear this. You know very well that you mean the world to me."

She turned away from him, her pain cutting like a knife through her soul. "That may be, but it will never be an honorable relationship. It will be secret and clandestine," she whirled to him. "I cannot live with the fact that I will never be more than your mistress. I am selfish, I know, but I want everything, Gaston. I want to be your wife; I want to bear heirs to honor you. Do not you realize that if I conceive a child, it will be a bastard? Do you truly want your children to bear that title? It's as bad as being labeled a whore." She suddenly sank to her knees, her face in her hands. "I cannot do this to myself, or to you."

He stood there a long time, staring down at her head. His chest was twisting in agony, painful because all of her words made sense. She was right, and he had been so wrong and so entirely selfish. In the distance, his men were mounted and ready to go and he raised his head from her long enough to give them the hand-signal to retreat. He would catch up with them later; for now, he had a much larger problem on his mind.

When his army was trudging across the field toward the road, he sat heavily opposite her. Pieces of armor came off to better allow him to sit comfortably.

"What would you have me do?" he rasped. "Tell me and I shall do it. Tell me to move heaven and earth for you and I shall do it."

She shook her head. "There is nothing you can do. I was stupid to have allowed myself to respond to you in the first place. I knew the risks, I knew that two marriages stood in our way, but I allowed myself to love you anyway and that was my gravest mistake."

"And my greatest triumph," he responded in a hoarse whisper. "You have allowed me to taste so much in this life that I never knew existed, Remi. I will not let you go."

She removed her hands from her face and wiped her eyes. "I want you to."

He was stung by the simple words, feeling pain such as he had never experienced slice through him. He couldn't let her go. He would sooner kill himself than live without her. He reached out and grabbed her, pulling her roughly against his chest and she let out a yelp of surprise, her eyes meeting his smoky orbs.

"You are mine, Lady Remington. I cannot believe you listened to the foolish words of an idiot and allowed yourself to think for one moment that I was deceiving you, that I would not be faithful to you until I die," he growled gently, his hands leaving her arms and grasping her face reverently. "Do not you know of my love for you? How can you possibly doubt my sincerity when I have done naught but show you and tell you how much you mean to me?"

Her mouth hung open at the passion of his statement and, as always, she instantly believed him. She could see the naked pain in his eyes and she knew his words to be true. Slowly, her fingers crept onto his armored shoulders.

"I do not want to be your mistress, and I do not want our children to be bastards," she whispered. "I want us to be a family, to love each other, and I want to bear you ten sons as strong and fine as you are. But I know it cannot be and it must stop."

"I won't let you stop," he put his lips to her forehead, closing his eyes as her scent filled his nose.

She let out a harsh gasp as his lips caressed her, the sudden fire of need filling her. He had the power to render her absolutely senseless and even she knew, in spite of her words, that she could not stay away from him.

"Tell me you were not lying to me," she whispered desperately.

"I have never nor will I ever lie to you," he breathed against her.

"Tell me you shall never tire of me and take another lover," she begged softly.

"There is not a woman in this world that could compete with you, my angel," he whispered. "I will never tire of you. Ever. I swear to you on my very soul."

She put her arms around his thick neck and he tumbled forward into the grass, pulling her atop of him, but all the while his mind was working furiously. She wanted to marry him, to bear his children, to be his for eternity, and he wanted the same thing. But there were two obvious problems that had to be solved before that could happen. He found he was willing to do anything at all.

Her cheek was nuzzled against his scratchy face. "I am sorry, Gaston. I shouldn't have been so angry or accusing."

He stroked her hair. "You have had a most trying day, madam. I am not sure how rational I would be after having been abducted."

She rose up to look at him, brushing her lips against his cheek. "But I am terribly crazy. Did not I warn you of that?"

"You did not, but it's too late to do anything about it now," he was pleased with her attempted humor, relieved that her tears were fading.

She smiled weakly and his heart thumped against his chest as he arched up his neck and pecked her on the nose. "Do you really want to be my wife, Remi?"

Her smiled faded. "More than anything on this earth."

He studied her a moment, brushing a stray lock from her face. "The problem would not be Mari-Elle," he said thoughtfully. "The problem would be Guy."

"Problem?" she repeated. "What are you talking about?"

He raised an eyebrow and sat up, pulling her onto his thighs. "I could give Mari-Elle Clearwell and the majority of my wealth for her cooperation."

She wasn't following his reasoning. "Cooperation for what?"

"A divorce," he said. "I am sure with enough money, she would grant one willingly."

Remington looked at him as if he had just voiced his desire to walk on water. "A divorce? Gaston, it's impossible. The church will not allow it."

He raised an eyebrow. "You forget, angel, I have Henry on my side. With enough petitions and donations, anything is possible."

For the first time, a light of hope rang in her eyes. She couldn't even bring herself to believe it was possible. "Truly, Gaston? Do you think so?"

He nodded his head. "As I said, anything is possible. But it is not just Mari-Elle, it is Guy. I sincerely doubt he would consider divorcing you."

Remington bit her lip in thought. She knew Guy better than anyone and she knew that a divorce was simply out of the question. Unless.... "Mayhap he will grant me a divorce in exchange for being released from prison."

Gaston looked sharply at her. She searched his eyes hopefully, seeing that he was indeed considering that possibility. "If I wished it, then I am sure Henry would grant it. After everything I have done for the man, he owes me."

She dared a timid smile. "Oh, Gaston, do you think it might be possible? Truly?"

He looked set. "There is only one way to find out. I will speak to Mari-Elle, and then I will go to London to speak with Henry. And I can assure you that I will not take no for an answer."

She put her hand to his face and he kissed her palm. "You would do this for me?"

He smiled faintly. "Anything for you. And I would also do it for my purely selfish reasons, of course. You promised me ten sons, and mayhap a few daughters who favor their beautiful mother, and I would have every man in England to know me for my gorgeous wife instead of my dark reputation."

She blushed at his words and he kissed her sweetly, listening to her soft giggles as opposed to her soft sobs. She was so terribly easy to please and he loved to make her smile.

"Come now, we must be going," he said after a moment, although he could have kissed her for the remainder of the night. "Dark will be upon us soon and I'd like to catch up to my troops."

She stood up and he rose beside her, so tall and strong and proud that her heart swelled with happiness and she caved into him. Gathering bits of armor, he put his arm around her and led her over to where Taran was grazing against a line of trees.

Her gaze lingered on Derek's dead form a moment as Gaston paused to retrieve his helm; the young knight's men had cleared out long ago and had failed to take his body with them.

"He really believed he was saving us from you," she said softly. "I wish you had not killed him."

He glanced impassively at the dead man. "His fate was sealed the moment he touched you. But I will send a few of my soldiers back to retrieve his body and return it home, if you wish."

They reached Taran and the horse nickered softly at Remington. She put her hands on the silk muzzle and Gaston fussed with his saddle. "His father will be devastated," she said regretfully. "Derek was his only son."

"It is not as if the man will be my only enemy in Yorkshire," Gaston replied lightly, reaching out to take her around the waist. "By God, if you aren't a tiny thing. My fingers overlap one another when I encircle your waist."

"I am not small, you are just large," she said as he lifted her onto the saddle. "Massive. Monstrous. Huge."

He gave her a wry smile. "Very well, I get the point. And you do not have to be nasty about it."

"Nasty? Me?" she said innocently as he mounted behind her. "Perish the thought."

He grinned, slapping his helm on but not locking it closed. "You are not like your sisters or your wicked cousin who puts nails in chairs, are you? And who was it that referred to your sisters as man-eating?"

Remington's smile faded. "Derek. He always called them that."

Gaston gathered Taran's reins. "Are they really? Should I warn my cousins?"

She felt her humor return with his question and giggled softly, her only answer.

CHAPTER ELEVEN

Mari-Elle was waiting for him on the steps to the castle as the army entered the outer bailey. He could see her through the inner gate and he let out a silent curse. Patrick suddenly appeared.

"I tried to discourage her, Gaston, but she would not listen to me," he said. "In fact, she is most enraged that you personally rode out to rescue Lady Remington and her sisters."

Gaston handed Remington down to Patrick and dismounted, keeping his eyes averted from his wife. "Damn," he muttered. "Well, I suppose I'd better get this over with."

"Wait, Gaston," Remington said softly. "Are you planning to throw her out? Mayhap that is not so wise."

He raised an eyebrow at her; they were a couple of feet apart, an entirely proper distance, but he felt her heat like a roaring fire. The entire way home his loins had been painfully engorged for want of her. But with Mari-Elle watching, he was thankful for the span between him and Remington.

"Explain," he ordered softly, loosening his gauntlets.

Remington glanced discreetly, making sure no one was within ear's length. "You said you wanted her to be cooperative...I do not believe she will be so cooperative if you throw her out, household and all, and tell her she is unwelcome. Were you to show her a bit of tolerance before you ask for her agreement on a most serious matter, her mood might be more receptive."

He let out a long sigh, showing his great reluctance at her suggestion. "Remi..." he scratched underneath his hauberk. "You simply do not know what you are asking, angel. There is too much between Mari-Elle and I for me to *tolerate* her. She would be suspicious."

"I think she is suspicious already," Remington looked to the tall woman without turning her head. "Mayhap you had better introduce us and we shall continue this conversation later."

He looked over his shoulder and saw that Mari-Elle was crossing the inner bailey toward them. He straightened as she drew close, feeling the familiar hatred filling his veins.

Mari-Elle was looking quite closely at Remington and Gaston stepped forward, almost between them.

"I am pleased to see you safely returned, my lord," Mari-Elle said, her gaze intense on Remington. "So I see I was correct with my first observation of this young lady; she was not a serving wench after all. Lady Remington, I presume?"

Remington curtsied quite respectfully. "Lady de Russe, 'tis an honor. You will please forgive me for my deception last night, but I usually serve meals to the men of Mt. Holyoak and I had no idea how you would react to such knowledge. It gives me a better opportunity to see to their satisfaction, if you will, by serving the meal myself. I thought it would be easier if I dressed inconspicuously in servant's garb so that you would not feel uncomfortable."

Well said, Mari-Elle thought, although she did not believe her for a moment. "I see," she said coolly. "And what about the song?"

Remington hoped her cheeks did not flush bright red. "I apologize if you were offended, but when you live with men whose sense of humor can be bawdy at best, unfortunately you respond in kind. We are unused to fine ladies in our midst at Mt. Holyoak."

Gaston was immensely pleased at her explanations and manners towards his wife, and it only served to deepen his feelings for her. He struggled to keep the prideful look from his face.

Mari-Elle still did not believe her, although the excuses were entirely plausible and respectful. She raised an eyebrow at her imperiously. "You had better become quite used to me, Lady Remington. I am the lady of the keep now and there are certain rules of decorum we adhere to," she turned to her husband. "Might I have a word with you, my lord husband?"

Remington was sure she had used the word 'husband' simply to prick her. Yet her motive seemed not to be pushed by jealousy; jealousy was an extremely readable emotion and Remington could sense none. But she did sense possessiveness.

Gaston looked at his wife with veiled contempt. "Lady Remington is still chatelaine, madam, until I say otherwise," he jabbed his wife back in Remington's defense. "And I will join you in the solar in a few moments, after I have seen to the settling of my men."

Mari-Elle dipped her head courteously. "As you say, my lord," she passed a glance at Remington. "I see that you have suffered no ill effects from your kidnapping. Was it, in fact, a kidnapping? Or were you simply trying to escape my husband?"

Remington could sense nothing but hatred from the woman, cold and black and it made her skin crawl. Patrick, Jasmine, Nicolas and Skye walked past them at the moment and Mari-Elle turned her attention to them as Remington was forming a reply.

"Patrick, Nicolas, I am pleased to see you returned safely," she said. "Lady Margaret and Lady Theodora will be pleased that you are maintaining your health so that you may return to them whole."

It was a blatant, vicious statement. Jasmine, surprisingly, did not react, but Skye's eyes widened.

"Aren't your cousins married yet, my lady?" Patrick said, his jaw tensed. "Surely they are old maids by now."

Gaston hid a smile of pleasure at Patrick's response, but Mari-Elle merely laughed. "You silly boy. How can they be married if they are promised to you?"

Patrick maintained his composure, praying Jasmine would do the same. "I do not recall any promise to Lady Margaret, my lady. She was mildly amusing and occasionally interesting, but beyond that I have no use for her. If you will excuse us."

He pushed his brother and Jasmine and Skye onward, out of Mari-Elle's range. Mari-Elle smiled and shook her head.

"Men never do keep their promises, do they?" she said more to herself than to anyone else.

Gaston's patience with the woman was at an end. "Inside, wife. I will speak with you later."

"Of course, husband," Mari-Elle replied, properly obedient.

She started to back away, eyeing Remington. "Surely you are exhausted after your ordeal mistress, and wish to retire. I would ask that you accompany me inside, as I am still unfamiliar with these surroundings."

Gaston was not about to let Mari-Elle alone with Remington and shook his head sternly. "Nay, madam, I still have several questions for Lady Remington before she retires."

Mari-Elle's almost pleasant expression tensed. "Of course."

She turned and was gone in a billow of purple satin, marching off across the inner bailey with angry steps. Gaston turned away but Remington watched her for a moment.

"She knows, Gaston," she whispered.

"She does not know anything, but I would wager that she suspects," he said, watching the groom lead Taran away. "She is naturally suspicious. 'Tis perfectly very well for her to keep lovers, but she is insanely distrustful of any woman I speak with."

"She keeps lovers?" Remington turned to him, surprised.

His eyebrow twitched ironically. "Since before we were married."

"Oh, Gaston. How...." she almost said "terrible" until she realized how it sounded. Embarrassed, she turned her head from him. "Do you truly have any questions or was that simply to be rid of her?"

He moved a step closer to her. "To Mari-Elle, a lover is simply a pet to amuse her for a while and then she moves on to another. I use the term loosely. I could refer to the men as sex-slaves, or the Fancy of the Day," his voice lowered. "You are, in every sense of the word, my lover. When I refer to you with the expression, I mean it from the bottom of my heart. There is nothing to be ashamed or embarrassed of, angel."

She shrugged, offering him a small smile. "I was about to accuse her of outrageous infidelity until I realized what a hypocrite I was. But I do not feel that way, Gaston. I know what we are doing is wrong, but I love you so that somehow it must be right."

"It is right," he said huskily. "Love is never wrong, angel."

She looked at him a moment, suddenly wrapping her arms about her in the cool night. "Have you ever loved anyone?"

"Aye, verily," he said shortly.

She blinked; suddenly regretful she had even asked the question. He had answered so quickly, with such certainty, that she suddenly felt second best and strangely belittled.

Arik shouted at him and he waved his second off a moment before turning back to Remington. "Well?"

"Well what?" she answered stiffly. "I am cold, my lord, if you will excuse me."

"Remi," he said in a husky growl. "Aren't you going to ask me who?"

"Nay, my lord, for it is none of my affair," she said coolly. "I will bid you good night, then."

She started to walk away but she heard him laughing low behind her. Puzzled, she turned to look at him; she had never truly heard him laugh and her heart jumped crazily at his smile. He had the most beautiful smile she had ever seen and she suddenly realized she wasn't the only one who thought so. That is, if the woman he had loved previously loved him in return.

Irritation and uncertainty swept her. "Why are you laughing at me?" she demanded.

He continued to snicker, closing the distance between them. "Because you are jealous and I find it amusing. No one had ever been jealous on my behalf and I am flattered."

"Do not be," she turned swiftly and marched into the castle.

He watched her go with a smile still playing on his lips. "Oh, Remi, do not you know who it is I love?"

Mari-Elle was waiting dutifully in the solar when her husband joined her nearly an hour later. Truthfully, she was fuming that he had kept her waiting so long, but acted nothing but the proper wife.

"My lord, how kind of you to break off from your duties for me," she said. "Would you care for some bread and cheese? You missed the evening meal and...."

He put up a sharp hand to cut her off as he moved into the room. "Stop prattling, madam. I have no desire to eat," he stopped in front of her and braced his legs apart, crossing his massive arms. "We have several serious matters to discuss and I would begin. Firstly, why are you even here?"

Slammed, Mari-Elle sat quickly in the nearest chair and folded her thin hands. "I...I missed you, my lord. We have been apart for so long that I longed to see you."

His brow furrowed. "You *missed* me? Please, Mari-Elle, if you are going to make excuses, then try to think of believable ones. I want the truth, madam. Why are you here?"

"I told you the truth," she insisted. "My lord, I have had ample time to think on my life and I realize how I have grievously wronged you," she looked down at her hands pathetically. "I have been a terrible wife, I know, and I have prayed seriously on the fact. I wish to make amends, Gaston. I want to be a true wife to you."

He had known her far too long to believe anything she said. "'Tis too late for that," he said coldly. "You ruined your chances thirteen years ago."

He went instantly wary when tears appeared in her eyes. "Can you not forgive me, my lord? I was young and foolish and knew naught the treasure I had in you. I am so proud of you and your reputation, my lord. As is Trenton."

He found himself angry that she had pulled his son into this. "Trenton is naught to do with you, madam. You birthed the lad and for that I shall always be grateful, but you are no more a mother to him than I am a father. Yet to my son, I will make amends. But not with you."

Her hand flew to her face and the tears started. "Why must you be so cruel when I am trying to apologize for my sins?"

"Confess your sins to God, madam, for he is the only one who cares. I do not. Furthermore, you will gather your household together and leave Mt. Holyoak no later than the day after tomorrow," he raised a stern eyebrow at her. "Is that clear? You are not welcome here at my keep."

"But I am your wife," she suddenly shot back, much more like the Mari-Elle he knew. "How can you disregard me like rubbish?"

"Easily," he responded. "Since you treat me the same way. You will return to Clearwell and you will stay there, for I am giving it to you."

She was preparing to hotly respond when his last words suddenly caught her attention. "Give it to me? What are you saying?"

"Just that," he said. "I will give you the title to Clearwell and three-quarters of my wealth."

She stared at him, wondering what in the world was going on with the man. Had he suddenly lost his mind? Clearwell was worth an enormous amount, and with the added gift of wealth, the numbers were staggering. She swallowed, her tears vanishing.

"Why would you do this?" she asked in a hoarse whisper. "I do not understand."

For the first time, he uncrossed his arms and moved to the chair opposite her, feeling the heat from near the hearth. He watched the flames for a moment.

"Mari-Elle, we have never had a marriage. It has been a contractual obligation," his voice was quiet. "My father and your father betrothed us when we were six years old and we had met only three times before a priest joined us in matrimony. The only thing of value that has resulted from this union is Trenton. The rest I have tried sorely to ignore."

She watched his face, thinking him terribly handsome but far too large for her taste. He met her gaze. "Are you happy?" he asked.

"Happy?" she repeated as if the concept had never occurred to her. "I…I suppose so."

"Then that is another way in where you and I are different," he said. "I am tired of living this life, Mari-Elle, and I am tired of hating and resenting you. I want out."

"Out? What do you mean?" she asked in alarm.

"I want to end our marriage," he answered calmly. "I will leave you well supported and you will want for nothing, and all I ask is that you agree to an annulment. I will walk away with Trenton and one-quarter of my wealth. You will get everything else."

Her eyes widened as his words sank in. Annulment. My God, if he had asked her three months ago, she would have agreed without hesitation. She would have been free and very, very wealthy to pursue her loves and interests. She was suddenly angry with him for not having suggested this sooner. True, the church frowned upon divorce, but an annulment was different. There were all sorts of excuses that could be used, and with Gaston's connection to the crown, anything was possible.

But she thought of the babe growing within her, the child that had made her menses cease and even now cramped and fatigued her greatly. She was terrified of physicians, which made an abortion out of the question, and she certainly did not want to face life with a bastard child. Nay, as much as it pained her, she would have to refuse his offer solely on the basis of her honor. She did not want gossips spreading rumors of her infidelity, bearing a child out of wedlock.

She lowered her gaze. "As generous as you are being, my lord, I must refuse. I would remain married to you."

"Why?" he asked, his voice louder. "I do not want to be married to you."

She swallowed hard, a pained look on her face. "And I do not blame you for all of the grief I have caused you, but.."

"Grief?" he shot out of his chair, clenching his big fists as he swung away from her. "My God, Mari-Elle, you have caused me more than grief. You have given yourself to every pretty peacock that catches your eye, and I ignored you because I cared not for you in the least. As long as you were discreet, I looked the other way. I cannot count the men you have whored with; shaming and disrespecting our marriage you are suddenly so intent on maintaining. I cared not for your liaisons until you bedded with Richard and threw it in my face with every chance that arose," he turned to her, his jaw flexing. "I could live with your gigolos, and I could live with your lavish spending. But you humiliated me to the core when you slept with our king."

Her eyes were wide, uncertain. "Is that why you betrayed him at Bosworth and fought for Henry Tudor?"

"Among other reasons," he mumbled, running his fingers through his thick hair to slick it back. It had been a long time since he had allowed himself to get worked up over Mari-Elle's indiscretions with Richard. He took a deep breath, forcing himself to calm. "I want to end this marriage, Mari-Elle. I know we would both be a far sight happier."

She looked at her hands, mulling over her thoughts. "I cannot," she whispered after a moment. "For Trenton's sake, I cannot. I want to be your wife, your lover, and your friend. I promise I shall work hard, Gaston, I won't fail."

"There is nothing to fail at; it is already dissolved. I do not want you, Mari-Elle. I have had enough of you in my life and I simply wish to be rid of you. I believe my offer is most generous."

"It is, my lord, but I am not interested," she said, raising her face to him. "I shall not agree to the annulment."

He gazed down at her. "Do not force me, Mari-Elle. The consequences will be severe."

Her head came up sharply. "Is that a threat? You would murder me to obtain your freedom?"

"I did not mention murder," he said evenly. "I simply suggested that you not force my hand. I am more powerful than you could possibly comprehend."

She was shaken and unbalanced. She remembered her vow when she had first come to Mt. Holyoak; she must be smarter than her husband. *Think, think!*

"Then you force me to make another confession, Gaston, although I was fully intent on sparing you," she said softly, trying to appear sorrowful. "I do not want your pity, but I can see that I must be truthful."

He was fully annoyed; another lie. "What?"

She sat back in the chair, her gaze on the hearth. "I…I am dying, Gaston. I have an ailment that strikes down so many women, a most private ailment. I do not know how much longer I have to live; neither does my physician. I am simply trying to make good of my life with the time I have left, with you and with Trenton. You would not deny me a last request, would you?"

He cocked his head. "Really, Mari-Elle. Do not think to play on my sympathies, for I have none. Dying, lying and all, I want you out of my keep within two days. And I will have my annulment."

Her first reaction was to screech at him but she held her temper; she thought her dying excuse to be quite clever, however, quickly thought of. And she intended to use it to her full advantage.

"I beg you, my lord, show some compassion. Would you traumatize Trenton further by a divorce and then my death?" her voice was shaking. "He would be devastated."

Again she brought Trenton into the conversation and he was angry. "Leave him out of this. This is not about him; it is about our sham of a marriage. You will grant me an annulment, or anything else I ask for, or I shall get it anyway and leave you destitute. The choice is yours."

Clever tears sprang to her eyes and she put her hand to her mouth to seal off her sobs. "Please do not be so cruel!"

"I am not."

"You are," she let out a sob. "You are as black as your namesake, Gaston. How can you show so little pity for your dying wife?"

He rolled his eyes in exasperation and turned away from her. He was tired of her, of arguing. He wasn't used to being denied his wants or desires.

Mari-Elle rose, extending a hand to him beseechingly. "You said yourself that you will ever be grateful to me for bearing Trenton. If you truly mean that, my lord, then show me the consideration due the mother of your son."

He glared at her. "What consideration?"

She sniffled delicately. "Allow me to stay until my strength returns, allow me to try and redeem myself in your eyes."

He shook his head. "I do not want you here."

"I know," she said quickly. "And I understand your reservations. But after being poisoned upon my arrival in addition to my ailment, I am truly too weak to travel home. Mayhap you will be gracious and allow me to stay for a short period of time. And, also, mayhap I can prove to you in that time that I am sincere in my desire to strengthen our marriage. Please, Gaston?"

He was furious and frustrated, and thoroughly tired of her lying and pleading. He suddenly swung to face her, his face dark. "I will allow you one week to recover and after that you are gone. I will hear nothing of reconciliation, and I will have my annulment. Do you comprehend me, madam?"

"You cannot mean that," she whispered.

"Aye, I can, and I do," he returned snappishly. "I want your acknowledgement that you understand what I am telling you."

She closed her eyes against his loathing stare. "I understand, my lord."

"Excellent," he stood back from her. "Return to your room, now. And if you are so weak, I do not expect to see you out and about until the day of your departure."

She fully understood the order and indicated such with an obedient nod. Silently, she quit the room, yet she knew the battle was not over. She had only just begun.

Remington couldn't sleep that night to save her life. She tossed and turned and twisted, angry with Gaston for having loved someone else. He had never told her that he loved her, so she had no reason to think he was anything more than extremely fond of her. Sure, he wanted to marry her, but he mentioned two specific reasons why; children and wanting a lovely woman to come home to. He never said anything about love.

She sat up in bed, beating at the pillows before throwing herself down on them again. They still did not feel right and she jumped out of bed altogether, pacing to the window.

The night was cool and the moon was bright, casting silver light on the scene below. She could see the sentries on the walls, torches moving about as they went on their rounds. Somewhere, a night bird gave song.

There were suddenly very heavy boot falls in the corridor outside and she knew it was Gaston returning to his chamber. Her first reaction was to run to her door and open it, but she reined herself. She was too angry with him, too confused for her own good. Certainly she had no right to be angry that he had loved another woman, but she was hurt and enraged just the same.

The boot falls passed her room and went down the hall. She heard a door slam and knew he had retired for the night.

Remington sank onto her silk chair, hot tears springing to her eyes. Irate or no, she had hoped he would at least say good night to her, but apparently he had forgotten about her. Damn him. She sat back in the chair and wiped her tears away angrily, having no idea why she was feeling so confused. At least with Guy, she had known what to expect. With Gaston, she felt as if her brain was mush.

She heard a distant door creak open and again there were boot falls in the corridor. Her heart jumped into her throat as she realized it was Gaston once more, hoping he would knock on her door but knowing he was most likely going about his business. Even in the middle of the night the man seemed to have duties. She wondered if he ever slept.

She startled sharply when she heard soft raps at her door. Fighting the urge to run and throw it open, she took her leisure crossing the room, purely to make him wait. Slowly, she undid the latch, hoping it would show him that she was not at all eager to see him. The door creaked open and she peered up at him.

"What is it, my lord?" she asked calmly.

His face lacked any humor whatsoever. "Let me in."

Silently, she complied. He entered her room dressed in snug leather breeches and a black linen shirt, the sleeves rolled above the elbow. Remington had to draw in a sharp breath; he looked absolutely magnificent.

He went directly to her wine decanter and poured himself a full cup of wine. Draining it, he poured himself another. Remington began to forget about her own insecurities when she saw how upset he was.

"What's the matter?" she asked softly.

He drained the cup and still poured himself more. Turning, he let his eyes rove over her from her feet to the top of her chestnut-auburn hair. "Come here."

She obeyed, wrapping her arms around his narrow waist and hugging him tightly. He held her with one arm, the cup in his other hand. They stood there for several long moments, simply content with the feel of each other. He drank only half of his third goblet of wine before setting it down, sweeping her into his arms and carrying her aimlessly toward the window.

She clung to his neck, feeling his warmth and strength course through her. So what if he did not love her; she could live with his great affection and attentions. Mayhap in time she could make him love her a little.

"Mari-Elle is being most uncooperative," he said after a moment, cradling her in his arms and rocking her softly like a babe. "She says she wants to reconcile our marriage."

"What?" she pulled her face from the crook of his neck, a shocked expression.

"Exactly my reaction," he said drily. Even shocked, she was the most beautiful woman he had ever seen. "She claims she is dying, if you can believe that, and she seems to be intent on patching the ruins of our marriage before she passes on."

Remington scowled in outrage. "That's ridiculous. She does not look as if she is dying, Gaston. She's as healthy as I am."

"I agree and I told her so, but she claims that Rory's little gag with the crushed apricot seeds has left her quite weak and has only served to aggravate her life-threatening condition," he sighed, resting his forehead against hers. "I told her she had one week to recover and get the hell out of my keep. I shall seek an annulment with or without her consent."

"Oh, my love, I am so sorry," she whispered.

"As am I," he said. "But 'tis no matter. She shall not stand in our way, I promise you."

She kissed his cheek softly, burying her face in his neck once again. She did not know what to say to him. An annulment was along the lines of an act of God, and she did not believe in miracles. In fact, she seriously doubted there was a God who could create men as terrible as her husband.

Yet; Gaston believed it possible, and she clung to his belief. He was her god now.

He held her, caressed her, his mind moving ahead to London and Henry. The king was already creating quite a bit of trouble within the church for his demands that ecclesiastical immunities be dissolved, that priests and clergy be held accountable to the laws of government as normal men were. For Henry to go to the papal legate on Gaston's behalf and demand an annulment might add more fuel to the strained fire.

He was well aware of the problems of Henry's relationship with the church, but he would do what he had to do to achieve his ends. It was either that or murder both Mari-Elle and Guy Stoneley.

He shook his head at the thought, disgusted that he had even considered it. Mayhap he had learned lessons in politics from Richard after all.

Remington lifted her head to smile at him and he brushed his lips on hers, suddenly very fatigued. He had her back and all he wanted to do was wrap her in his arms the rest of the night, to forget about the most eventful day for a while.

The adjoining door suddenly creaked open and Dane was in the archway, sobbing softly. Both Remington and Gaston looked to the little boy.

"What's wrong, sweetheart?" she asked her son, sliding from Gaston's arms.

"I....had a....dream," he sobbed, rubbing his eyes.

She took her son in her arms and brought him to sit with her on the bed. Gaston sank down beside them.

"What dream? What was so awful?" she cooed gently.

"Father," he blurted. "I saw father, and I saw you, and he was trying to kill you."

Remington kissed the top of his crying head. "Battles and lords and sieges," she admonished Gaston softly. "Now he's having nightmares of death."

He raised his eyebrows and put his hand out to the boy. To his surprise, Dane left his mother and cuddled up in Gaston's arms.

"You shall protect her, won't you?" Dane sniffled.

"Of course," Gaston said gently. "But it was only a dream, Dane. Dreams can't hurt us."

"But sometimes my dreams come true," he insisted. "This one will, too, and you have to save my mother."

Gaston gave Remington a disbelieving look and was puzzled to see that she looked entirely calm and agreeable, even. She met Gaston's stare and gave a reluctant shrug.

"He has on occasion, dreamt of things that have come to pass," she said softly. "Ever since he was old enough to tell us of his dreams."

Gaston lifted an eyebrow to tell her exactly what he thought of that nonsense. She looked away.

"Dane, your father is not going to kill your mother, I promise," he said. "Do you think you can go back to sleep now?"

The little boy shook his head. "I want to sleep in here with you."

Gaston and Remington looked at each other. "This is my bedchamber, Dane, not Sir Gaston's."

"I know that, but he sleeps in here with you, and I want to sleep with the both of you," he squirmed from Gaston's arms and dove under the coverlet of the bed, tossing about.

Gaston and Remington watched him with astonishment for a moment. So the boy was intuitive as well as having prophetic dreams, Gaston thought wryly. He reached down and tugged off a huge boot, and Remington looked at him with surprise.

"What are you doing?" she asked.

He yanked off another boot. "I am going to sleep in here with you and Dane," he stood up, bare-footed, and swept his arm in the direction of the dozing boy. "After you, my lady."

Hesitantly, she stood up and removed her robe, revealing a thin white nightshift, as fine as a spider's web. She heard Gaston groan. "By God's Bloody Rood, madam, how am I expected to sleep with you wearing such a provocative garment?"

She looked down at her shift. "It covers everything, my lord."

"Covers, aye, but you can see right through the damn thing," he pointed out.

She looked up at him, a sly smile playing on her lips. "Shall I put the robe back on?"

"Hell no," he moved around her and pulled back a corner of the coverlets. "Now get in there before I do something drastic."

"Pray what?" she teased innocently.

He gave her a stern look and bent close to her ear. "I will show you later after Dane has been placed in his own bed."

With a smile, she climbed into the bed next to her son. Half asleep, Dane snuggled close to her as Gaston eased himself onto the mattress on the boy's other side. Remington held Dane, and Gaston held them both.

Morning announced itself sharp and clean.

The next few days were strange at best. Mari-Elle kept to her rooms, as she had been ordered, but her servants were all over the keep, drilling soldiers for gossip and planting rumors of their own. In no time, the quiet solitude of Mt. Holyoak was darkly tinged with enough idle talk and hearsay to fill a moat.

The rumors centered around Remington and her sisters, of course, harmless tales that were more bothersome than anything else. It was obvious Mari-Elle was trying to turn the tide of favor against the Yorkist wife in hopes that she would vacate the keep. Mari-Elle wasn't truly suspicious or jealous of Remington, but she was threatened by her presence. It never occurred to her that she was her husband's mistress; Gaston did not have that sort of reputation.

Her husband, however, would have nothing to do with her. She would send for him, seek him out, and when she did manage to find him he was barely civil. It was frustrating, especially since the child in her womb was growing larger and her time at Mt. Holyoak was drawing to a close. The time was coming for more drastic measures.

July was a brutal, humid month and more and more time was being spent at the lake. After the morning meal, Remington packed up Dane and made her way to the inner bailey to seek Gaston out; she no longer asked permission to swim, only to let him know where she was going. More often than not he accompanied her.

She found him in the outer bailey reviewing the new recruits. She and Dane stood patiently by the gates as Arik drilled and Gaston observed carefully. Four hundred more men were expected within a few days and he wanted to have the first class out of basic training.

She watched him underneath the rapidly warming sky; his glossy hair slicked back as usual, giving him a hawk-like appearance. Rarely, if ever, did he give orders directly to the troops, but when he spoke it was as if God himself had issued commandments. They tripped over one another in their haste to carry out his commands.

It was impressive and overwhelming, and Dane soaked it up like a sponge. He couldn't wait to start his training, but Gaston had already warned Remington that contact between them would be severely limited, and the boy would be housed with the other squires near the stables. As his mother, she was not so anxious for him to begin his fostering.

A boy sat several feet away on the edge of a hay cart, watching the proceedings intently. Remington studied the boy for a moment until she realized it was Trenton. It was not a difficult discovery, for he looked exactly like his father. He sat as still as stone, never wavering his gaze and Remington could see the hero worship in his eyes, just as in Dane's.

Dane, however, was growing tired of simply waiting and dug his inflated pig's bladder ball out of the basket. He began to toss it about as Remington admonished him to be still. He would obey for a moment or two, then start tossing the ball all over again. Inevitably, he lost control and it went rolling over to the hay cart.

He dashed over to the wagon just as Trenton picked the ball up. He extended it to the owner.

"Here," he said.

Dane took the ball, studying the lad. He was a good deal taller than himself, but his face was still babyish. "Thank you," he said. "I have not seen you around here before."

"'Tis my father's keep," Trenton said. "I will be staying here now."

Dane blinked, puzzled. "Your father?"

Trenton pointed to Gaston. "That's my father. He's lord of the keep. Are you a servant?"

Dane shook his head. "My mother is lady of Mt. Holyoak."

Trenton frowned. "*My* mother is lady of Mt. Holyoak."

Dane scowled fiercely. "Is not. My mother is Lady Remington Stoneley."

Trenton scowled back. "And my mother is Sir Gaston's wife. That makes her the lady of Mt. Holyoak."

Dane threw down the ball at the challenge. In spite of the fact that Trenton was a good head taller than he was, he shoved him anyway. "Sir Gaston loves my mother and she is still lady of Mt. Holyoak."

Trenton was back in his face and shoved him so hard he fell to his bottom. "You are a liar."

"Am not!" Dane scrambled to his knees and took Trenton down by the legs.

Remington rushed over to the two scuffling boys, yelling at them to cease their fighting. Gaston heard the beginnings of the dispute and was already on his way over. He reached down and pulled the boys apart by the neck, holding each of them at arm's length.

They were still shouting at each other and Trenton had a cut on his lip. Gaston gave him a good shake.

"Good men, you will cease this fighting," he said severely.

The boys listened somewhat, but they were still huffing and glaring at one another. When their struggles slowed, Gaston let them go and crossed his arms critically.

"May I ask, then, what that display was all about?" he asked reprovingly.

"He started it," Dane yelled.

"Did not," Trenton responded.

"Dane. Trenton," Gaston snapped. "If you cannot tell me what has caused this argument, then you will both retreat to your rooms for the remainder of the day. Is that understood?"

Dane opened his mouth but thought better of it. Gaston eyed his son, silently ordering him quiet. Trenton obeyed, reluctantly.

"Now," Gaston started again. "Dane, why do not you tell me why you were scuffling with my son?"

Dane tore his eyes away from Trenton and stared at Gaston as if he had just announced he was Jesus Christ. "He's…. he's your son?"

"Aye, he is," Gaston answered. "Did not your mother tell you he was here?"

"Well….no," Dane admitted, feeling terribly hurt for some reason. It wasn't the fact that his mother had not directly told him; he knew something was up by the way they had been kept to their rooms, and he knew Lady de Russe had arrived. But he had not known Gaston's son had arrived, too. He was quite enjoying being Gaston's sole son.

"Then allow me to introduce you to my son, Trenton de Russe," Gaston indicated the larger boy. "Trenton, this is Lady Stoneley's son, Dane. You two will be fostering together."

The boys looked at each other in a new light; however, it only added to the hostilities. Dane finally lowered his gaze, kicking at the ground.

"Dane, aren't you going to tell me what happened?" Gaston prodded gently.

Dane looked at Trenton and looked at the dirt again, fidgeting. "It was nothing, my lord. We were just fighting, that's all"

"I know you were fighting, I saw you," Gaston said, and then turned to his son. "Trenton? What happened?"

Trenton looked a bit sheepish and shrugged. "He said his mother was lady of the keep, and I said my mother was lady of the keep. And we fought."

"I see," Gaston stroked his stubbly chin. "Trenton, Lady Stoneley is chatelaine here. Do you understand that?"

Trenton nodded. "But what about mother? She is your wife."

"And she is chatelaine at Clearwell," Gaston replied evenly. "It would be far too much work for her to be chatelaine of two keeps."

Trenton looked at Dane doubtfully. "He said you loved his mother. How can you if you are married to my mother?"

Gaston felt as if he had been struck. He did not dare look at Remington; if he had, he would have seen she had gone completely white. He found himself swallowing hard.

"Lady Remington is a valuable asset to Mt. Holyoak, Trenton," he said, hoping he could bombard the boy with a lot of clever words and avoid the real question. "I appreciate the work she does for me here at the fortress."

"But you sleep in her bedchamber," Dane insisted, trying desperately to prove his point to his new enemy. "And I have seen you...."

"Dane." Remington reached out and grabbed her unruly son, embarrassed and horrified. "We will be at the lake, my lord. Good day to you. Good day to you, Trenton."

He watched her scuffle off, holding Dane by the ear. The boy's whimpers and grunts faded as they crossed the outer bailey. Gaston motioned to one of the knights on the outer wall and two soldiers were following Lady Remington from the keep.

He turned to his son, wondering how in the hell he was going to control the damage. Trenton was looking at him, quite confused, and he could see that this was going to take some time. He put his hand on his son and steered him over to the hay wagon, and bade the lad to sit. He lowered himself next to him, eyeing his son and groping for the correct words.

"Trenton," he began softly. "You know that your mother and I do not exactly get along at times."

"She hates you," Trenton said with quiet bluntness. "I have heard her tell her friends that."

Gaston clasped his hands in front of him. "I am sorry you have heard such things, but whatever she thinks of me, please know that we both love you a great deal."

Trenton pondered his father's words. "She says that you never wanted me, and that you hate children."

Gaston felt anger surge through him. "That's a lie, Trenton. I love you very much. You are my only son."

"Then why are you always gone?" the boy turned his face to his father, pleadingly.

Gaston could read the pain and he was doubly pained by it. He knew how his absences reflected on his son, because they reflected on him the same way. "I am a soldier, Trenton, and I serve the crown," he said. "You know that there has been quite a bit of upheaval within the past few years and I have been in the middle of it, fighting for our king. If I could have taken you with me, I would have gladly, but life on the move is no place for a boy. You were much better off with your mother at Clearwell."

Trenton lowered his head. Gaston looked at the dark hair, the color of his own and wondered what the lad was thinking. "Then do you have friends like mother does?" Trenton asked softly.

Gaston wasn't quite sure what he meant. "Arik is my friend."

"Nay, I mean friends like mother," the boy repeated. "Friends from France, and Spain, men who talk strange."

Gaston grasped his thoughts and took a deep breath to steady himself. "Nay, Trenton, I do not. What your mother does is her own business."

"But...but you sleep in Lady Remington's bedchamber?" Trenton asked timidly. "Mother sleeps with her friends, too."

Damn, what that bitch had exposed her son to. Gaston felt himself tensing. "I have my own bedchamber, Trenton."

Trenton sat a moment, mulling over the conversation, and thinking on everything he had ever heard about his father. He truly loved his father and over the past few days saw that his father was a kind and patient man, nothing as his mother had told him. He was a man who took time with him and made him feel wanted. Not even his mother had ever made him feel wanted.

The discussion lagged a bit and Trenton looked at his hands, embarrassed at the entire confrontation. Gaston rose from the edge of the wagon.

"Would you like to go swimming?" he asked.

Trenton's head shot up, his eyes wide. "Swimming? Aye, I would!"

Gaston's heart squeezed at his son's eagerness for something as simple as swimming. The lad was just like Dane; so tremendously easy to please, as those who have been abused usually are. Though he knew Mari-Elle had never laid a hand on the lad, the emotional damage she had done was apparent.

He smiled at his son. "Come on, then," he put his hand on the boy's shoulder as they crossed the bailey, pausing only long enough to exchange a few words with Arik.

Just as they were passing under the portcullis, they came face to face with Oleg and old Eudora, lugging two heavy baskets between them. Gaston pointed his finger at the burdens they held.

"Where are you going with those?" he asked.

Oleg was extremely intimidated by the Dark Knight. Being somewhat superstitious, he half-expected the man to speak with a serpent's forked tongue. "We are taking food to Lady Remington and Master Dane, my lord. The lady's sisters will be joining them shortly."

Gaston peered into the baskets. "By God, there's enough to feed my army," he took the wicker burdens to himself; the combined weight was barely mentionable. "My son and I were heading that way as it was. We shall make sure the feast is delivered."

Oleg nodded hesitantly, clutching Eudora's arm and backing away. Gaston eyed the old man a moment, not puzzled at the terror he read but annoyed somewhat; he would have hoped that over the weeks he had occupied Mt. Holyoak that the populace would come to fear him less and respect him more.

Oleg and Eudora watched the man and his son walk down the narrow road that led to the wooded fields below.

"If I was twenty years younger, I'd have that man," Eudora quipped softly.

Oleg shook his head, letting out a loud sigh. "He's the devil, woman. Can you not see that?"

Eudora snorted. "Lady Remington does not think so. In fact, I'd say they are rather fond of each other."

Oleg rolled his eyes. "God help us all. Adultery."

Eudora looked at him disapprovingly. "I'd hardly call the marriage between Guy and Remington a marriage at all. It's a license permitting the master to beat her senseless, it is. Allow the woman some happiness, you old spittlecock."

Oleg shook his head. "Call you it what you will, but it's still adultery."

Eudora shook her head. "I call it wonderful if they truly have feelings for each other," she shoved the old man in the arm. "Come on now, we have got work to do."

Oleg took one final glance at the figure of the father and son as they reached the bottom of the hill and disappeared into the trees. He wasn't sure about the new master at all; nay, he was still quite frightened of him. At least he could anticipate Sir Guy and know his moods, but this Dark Knight was too mysterious and dark to fathom. The fear of the unknown was great.

Remington and Dane were in the lake when Gaston and Trenton arrived. Dane was nearly naked, splashing about as Remington stood in the water up to her knees, her dress hiked up around her thighs. Gaston set the baskets down, his eyes drawn to her shapely legs, familiar desire filling his veins.

Trenton just stood by his father, eyeing the lake and its occupants wearily. Gaston undid a couple of stays on his shirt. "Well, take your clothes off and get in there."

"In there with him?" Trenton asked reluctantly. "What if he tries to drown me?"

"Trenton, I can guarantee you that Dane will not try to drown you," Gaston said, waving at Remington as she caught sight of them.

"He's a very reasonable lad and I am sure you two can patch up your differences."

Trenton wasn't at all sure, but he obediently removed his shoes and pulled off his tunic and undershirt. Remington approached the two of them, holding her wet skirt off the ground.

"How nice of you to come and join us," she said with a timid smile, looking at Trenton. "Dane will be happy for another boy to play with."

Trenton eyed her until Gaston cleared his throat. "Thank you, my lady," he sputtered.

The boy moved past her and toward the water. Remington's eyes followed him. "He hates me, does not he?"

"Nay, he does not hate you," Gaston took a few steps, standing very close to her. "Actually, I think he is a little afraid of Dane. The boy is a scrapper."

She watched Trenton circle the lake, he and Dane eyeing each other like a couple of dominant cocks. Remington sighed.

"Dane is jealous of him," she said quietly. "Because he is your son. He was quite enjoying having you all to himself."

"He better get used to him," Gaston said. "The boys will be fostering together and I will not be pulling them apart at every turn. They must learn to get along."

Remington clucked regretfully. "And that is why you brought Trenton down here, of course. They did not get off to a good start," she said. "Mayhap I should speak with Dane again and...."

He put his hands on her shoulders and turned her around for the tree. "Nay, madam, you will leave them to work out their own problems. Unless they are going to kill each other, I say leave them be."

She let him sit her down and he sat down next to her, stretching out his thick legs with a sigh of satisfaction. "I cannot stay long, but I wanted to be here while the boys got used to one another," his gaze left the lake and trailed up her bare feet and naked shins. "You are indecent, madam."

She wiggled her toes and smiled. "And it feels wonderful. Besides, you have seen me a sight more indecent than this," her smile faded a bit. "How did you explain Dane's remarks to Trenton?"

"Carefully," he replied. "Because of Mari-Elle's indiscretions, he is not entirely shocked, but I downplayed it as much as possible. I do not want him repeating anything to his mother."

"Why not?" Remington wanted to know.

"Because I do not want you labeled an adulteress," his eyes lingered on her face. "I care not for myself, of course, but I do not want you gaining an unsavory reputation. Mari-Elle gossips with the best of them, including the fine ladies at court. Were she to find out I was in love with you, then it would spread like wildfire and I would not have you branded a mistress."

She swallowed hard, her head beginning to spin with the impact of his words. She heard little else after that "in love with you". *I want you for my husband.* "Tell me again, Gaston," she breathed.

He looked puzzled, but from the expression on her face, he could see that something had impacted her greatly. "Say what?"

She was flushed with surprise and excitement. My God, had he really said it? "What you said...tell me again."

He shook his head. "Honestly, Remi, I do not know what you mean. All I said was that Mari-Elle would brand you a mistress to her courtly friends if she found out I was in love with you."

She closed her eyes with the thrill of hearing it again, falling back to the grass with a smile as wide as the world. Her arms laid themselves over her forehead and she began to giggle giddily. He looked down at her, grinning.

"What in the world is the matter with you?" he asked.

She peered at him from underneath her crossed arms and giggled again. "Oh, Gaston, you *said* it. I never thought I would hear you say it."

"You had better tell me what it is I said or I will tickle you until you beg for mercy," he growled seductively.

She put her arms behind her head, smiling up at him as he looked down at her. "You said you were in love with me."

"Well, of *course* I am," he said as if it were the simplest thing in the world. "Surely it is of no surprise to you. True, I have not exactly told you, but ...."

"It is a surprise," she insisted. "I knew you were fond of me, but I did not believe that you loved me. Love is a silly, feminine emotion, Gaston. I have never known a knight to succumb to it."

"Madam, I have not only succumbed, I have been mortally marked," he said. "What do you think all of this talk of annulment had been about? I would not do that for anyone, but for you, I would do anything. Anything at all."

Her smile faded and her face fairly glowed with love and admiration. "I love you, Gaston. I have never loved anyone in my life."

"Nor have I," his voice was soft. "Until I met you."

They gazed at each other, wanting to hold and caress one another until they were both senseless. It was a tremendous act of willpower for Gaston not to even touch her cheek, but he had to be careful with his son about. Yet as he gazed down into the sea-crystal eyes, he found his desire burning holes in his determination and he tore his gaze away before he broke completely.

"Kiss me, Gaston," she whispered.

He closed his eyes briefly, fighting for strength. "Nay, angel, not here in front of the boys."

"Then take me into the trees and ravish me until I faint." Her breath was a seductive whisper.

He stood up rapidly and strode away from her, toward the lake, and she sat up with a smile. It was a pleasure to know he had such a difficult time resisting her and she was happier than she had ever been in her life to know he loved her. The Dark Knight was in love with the daughter of a simple baron.

She watched him as he stood next to Trenton, saying something to Dane she couldn't quite hear. Dane splashed stubbornly at the water, listening to Gaston but obviously not liking what he was hearing. Finally, Trenton ventured timidly into the water and picked up the bladder ball that was floating on the surface. Gaston turned and left them.

He approached her with a raised eyebrow. "I will turn on my heel and return to the castle if you mention anything more about ravishing you. Do you understand?"

She smiled coyly, lowering her lashes. "As you say, my lord. Heaven only knows I would not want to tempt you."

"You tempt me simply by living," he said, kneeling next to the basket and rummaging inside.

Remington looked over with interest. "Is there any cheese? I am starved."

He drew forth a large wedge of white cheese and handed it to her. She chewed slowly, watching every move he made with nothing but lust on her mind. He put a large slab of mutton between two huge pieces of bread and ate with a good deal of satisfaction.

"I am expecting more troops from Henry in the next few days," he said, looking out at the lake where Trenton and Dane were playing dutifully with the ball. "When they arrive I want you to make sure that you do not travel outside the castle without an escort."

"I travel with an escort now," she glanced over at the two soldiers on the rise overlooking the lake.

"Aye, but it will be far more important in the future that you are never without protection," Gaston looked down at her. "And that goes for your sisters, as well. I shall have nearly a thousand soldiers walking the grounds, men with little discipline or self-control."

She nodded, returning to her cheese with a bit of rising apprehension. It also sounded as if she and her family were to be made prisoners upon the arrival of Henry's troops.

"Your intention is to turn Mt. Holyoak into a training ground?" she asked.

"The largest training ground outside of London," he said. "And it shall be, too."

She finished the cheese thoughtfully. "Mayhap, then, it would not be wise for my sisters and I to stay here," she said after a moment. "Halsey Manor is not far from here and sitting vacant. Mayhap we would be safer there."

He looked at her, hearing Arik's own words and wondering if she and Arik had been talking. He did not want her away from him, not even for a moment.

"I do not believe that will be necessary," he said steadily. "You will be safe enough here, as long as you adhere to the rules."

She did not reply, turning to the wine bladder and taking a dainty sip. Secretly, she was glad he had not agreed with her. She did not want to leave him, soldiers or no soldiers.

Her sisters appeared on the crest of the hill opposite the lake, descending noisily into the little valley. Gaston finished the last of his meal, eyeing the trio.

"Here come the gaggle," he mumbled.

Remington smiled at him. "Be of good cheer, my love. They are not so bad."

He snorted and dug into the basket once more, this time for a large green apple. "I will be related to them one day, so I suppose I had better become accustomed to them," he said. "Hopefully my knights will marry them soon and I will not be burdened with the baggage."

"My sisters are not baggage," she insisted with feigned outrage, slanting him a taunting look. "I hope that they never leave me and that we live together forever. All four of us, 'Twould be wonderful...."

"Stop right there, madam," he pointed the apple at her. "I refuse to support three old maids. If they are not married off, then I will sell them to the highest bidder. I hear men are most desperate for English brides in Turkey."

"Turkey?" Remington repeated loudly. She wasn't even sure where Turkey was, but she knew it was far away. "My sisters will marry Englishmen, I shall have you know. They'll not marry barbarians."

The corners of his lips twitched and he chewed loudly on the apple. She watched him a moment. "Aren't you going to sit with me?"

He took the last large bite and tossed the core. "Nay, madam, not with the horde approaching. Besides, I must return to my duties. I have left Arik and Antonius overlong with the new recruits."

She was disappointed. "Do you have to?"

"Aye, angel, I do," he wiped his hands on his thighs, facing her fully. "I shall see you tonight, however. All night, most likely."

She smiled seductively, leaning back against the tree. "I look forward to it, my lord Gaston."

He grinned faintly and opened his mouth to reply when two yelling boys suddenly cut him off. Trenton and Dane were sloshing out of the water, yelling at each other as they marched toward their respective parents.

"Mother," Dane hollered. "Tell him that we are descended from the Tuatha de Danann."

"They're fairies," Trenton yelled at Dane. "You aren't a fairy."

Gaston glanced down at Remington, but she was smiling softly at the boys. "Sit down," she told them.

Wet and angry, they obeyed, but they sat several feet apart from each other. Remington's manner was most calm and patient, delaying Gaston's natural urge to demand they behave. Since they were addressing her, he decided to let her deal with them.

Her sisters finally reached the little group, looking curiously at Trenton.

"Who's this?" Rory pointed at him.

"This is Trenton de Russe," Remington looked at her sisters deliberately. "Sir Gaston's son."

She saw the eyebrows go up on all three of them, turning to look at Gaston at the same time. He gazed impassively in return and Remington motioned her sisters to sit. "Sit, sit. I am about to tell Trenton and Dane of our roots."

She turned back to the boys as her sisters got themselves comfortable.

"Now," she said, her eyes lighting up. "Trenton, do you know of the Tuatha de Danann?"

Trenton looked uncomfortable, and bright little splotches appeared on his cheeks. "A...a little, my lady. They are Ireland's fairy race."

Remington nodded. "That's right. They existed many centuries ago when the world was a dark, magical place, a place of dragons and fairies and great wizards. But they were not originally from Ireland; nay, folklore tells us that they were from an island even further north than Ireland. Before they came to Ireland as conquerors, they made an alliance with a fearsome race called the Fomoiri. The Fomoiri were half-man and half-monster, terrible beings from across the sea, and it was wise to seal an alliance with them. The chief of the Fomoiri, a beast named Balar of the Evil Eye, gave his daughter Ethne in marriage to the son of the chief physician of the Tuatha de Danann, and a great relationship was forged. Or so the Tuatha de Danann thought."

Trenton and Dane stopped all of their quarreling and were listening quite intently. She smiled, pleased at their interest. Even Gaston was listening.

"When the Tuatha de Danann first came to Ireland, they encountered a race of farmers called the Fir Bolg, whom they went on to defeat in the battle of Mag Tuired. Unfortunately the king, a man named Nuada, lost his arm in the battle and thereby had to forfeit the throne."

"Why?" Dane demanded, interrupting her.

"Because only a whole man can be king," Trenton snapped at him as if he were an idiot.

Dane opened his mouth to retaliate but Remington continued quickly.

"That's true, Trenton," she said. "Therefore, the throne was offered to a man by the name of Bres, whose mother was a Fomoiri. Bres, unfortunately, was a terrible king. He taxed his people heavily, throwing the entire country into poverty. Even the greatest Tuatha de Danann warriors were reduced to farming to maintain their lives, chopping wood and tilling the earth. It was a truly awful sight to behold."

"Warriors like my father?" Trenton asked.

Remington glanced at Gaston; he was leaning against the tree trunk, his arms crossed casually. He smiled at her and she felt her cheeks flush. "Aye, like your father. Can you see Sir Gaston tending the earth like a peasant?"

The boys shook their head solemnly. "Why did not they fight the king?" Dane wanted to know.

Remington held up a finger. "Ah, they would eventually. But first, they waited while the elders of the Tuatha de Danann protested and petitioned the king, trying their best to resolve the problems by peaceful means. When their pleas did not work, a poet by the name of Coirpre wrote a song about the king, a song so insulting and slanderous that the entire population of Ireland began to doubt their king's wisdom. As dissension spread, Bres turned to his fearsome Fomoiri brethrens to help him keep his throne by force. Meanwhile, the chief physician of the Tuatha de Danann had made an arm for Nuada from pure silver, and as a whole man, he could now make his bid to regain his throne."

"A silver arm," Trenton scoffed. "It would not work like a normal arm."

Remington smiled at the boy and held up a finger. "But remember, Trenton, the Tuatha de Danann are a fairy race. With a little magic, anything is possible. As I was saying, Nuada prepared to regain his throne. However, he needed help. The help of the most powerful warrior in the kingdom." Her eyes widened as she embellished her story with a great deal of animation. "A great feast was held at Tara, the palace of the kings, and the very greatest warriors in the land were present; Ogma, In Dagda, men who had conquered Ireland long ago. But the mightiest warrior of all had yet to arrive; Lug."

"Lug?" Trenton repeated. "Who is he?"

"The best warrior in the whole world!" Dane told him eagerly; he loved this story with a passion and knew every twist and turn.

His mother smiled at him as Trenton piped up. "My father is the best warrior in the whole world."

Gaston pushed himself off the tree trunk and sat behind Remington, leaning back on an elbow. "But this was hundreds of years ago, Trenton. For their time, they were the greatest."

Remington feeling him, turned to look into his gentle face. Discreetly, she snuggled back against him. His hand inconspicuously rested on her thigh, under the folds of her surcoat.

"Lug was the son of Ethne and the chief physician's son, Cian. He was perfect in every way, handsome and strong, brave and powerful," she glanced at Gaston with a grin. "Just like Sir Gaston! Nuada demanded that Lug lead the battle against the Fomoiri and Lug agreed with a specific plan; everyone had duties that would, together, bring down the terrible Fomoiri. Goinbniu, the smith, made all of the fearsome weapons; Coirpre, the poet would humiliate the enemy through his songs, and Ogma, the champion of the gods, would supply the armies. In Dagda, the all-mighty protector of the Tuatha de Danann, would strike down hundreds with his massive war club, and the chief physician Dian Cecht would bring the slain Tuatha warriors back to life by casting them into a magic well. Lug himself stayed out of the battle until he caught sight of his grandfather, Balar of the Evil Eye."

The boys let out a collective groan at the mention of the hated enemy. Rory made a terrible fuss and pretended to swoon, to which

Jasmine swatted her on the behind. Remington shook her head at her sisters' theatrics, preparing to finish her story with great flourish.

"Balar obtained his nickname because those who were unfortunate enough to look upon it were guaranteed destruction. Lug could see that Balar's soldiers were preparing to open their lord's eye by use of a great handle attached to the lid and he knew he must act swiftly or all was lost." She paused and snickered when the boys made a terrible fuss over an eyelid with a handle, making terrible faces. "Quickly, Lug took his slingshot and sailed a stone into Balar's eye, driving it clear through his skull so that it came out the other side and gazed upon his own troops. With the defeat of the enemy guaranteed, the Tuatha de Danann warriors beat the Fomoiri back into the sea and never saw them again. From that day on, the Tuatha de Danann ruled Ireland."

Trenton and Dane were still caught up in the great tale, their innocent eyes wide with excitement. "Is that all?" Trenton asked, waiting for still more.

"I am afraid so," Remington replied, feeling Gaston's hand caressing her leg. "My mother said that she was a direct descendent of Nuada, the Tuatha de Danann king."

Dane actually took a deep breath; he had been holding it nearly the entire time. "I like that story. Tell us some more. Tell us about Perseus."

Remington begged off. "Mayhap later. I think you boys have heard enough glory for one day."

"You can never hear enough glory," Gaston murmured behind her.

"You are not helping," she whispered back.

He smiled broadly and sat up, tossing away the piece of grass he had been fiddling with. "Do not bother Lady Remington anymore, lads. She has been gracious enough to tell you one magnificent story this day and you should be grateful for it," he pointed to the lake. "If you intend to swim anymore, you had better do it now before the sun sets further."

Trenton and Dane jumped up, their quarrel completely forgotten as they hustled themselves back to the water.

"My father is greater than Lug," Trenton ran saying.

Remington smiled and turned to Gaston as her sisters moved away noisily, pulling off their slippers and heading for the water.

"I think his father is greater than Lug, too," she said softly.

"And I think Lady Remington is a gifted storyteller," he responded softly, his gaze licking over her. "How is it that you know that story so well?"

"My mother used to tell us that story all of the time," she said. "She told us a great many stories that I will pass down to Dane."

He rose on his massive legs. "Now that you have their attention, I have a feeling they are going to make you tell them every story you know until they bleed you dry," he pulled at his simple mail tunic, the only piece of armor he wore this day. "As much as I have enjoyed this, I must return before they send out a search party. And do not you be out here overlong, either."

"I won't," she promised, smiling at him as he started to walk away.

"I mean it, Remi," he pointed a finger at her. "I shall keep watch from the battlements. If I do not see you returning within the hour, I shall come looking for you."

"No need, my lord," she said softly, her eyes twinkling. "'Tis my sworn duty to obey your orders, large or small."

"I give no small orders," he rumbled, but his eyes were smiling.

The evening meal had been ordered by Oleg and prepared by Remington's regular cook. Mari-Elle's servants had been cleared out of the house and were confined to the second floor wing with their mistress. Mari-Elle was distraught and outraged that her husband's soldiers were treating her as if she were in prison, but there was naught she could do at the moment. That would come later, tonight. She may have been struck down, but she was certainly not out.

The smells of seasoned mutton filled the air of the grand hall and Remington resumed her customary place making sure Gaston and his knights were served and kept happy. Even Dane and Trenton were eating at the head of the table with Gaston, seated across the table from one another, but at least there had been no more fighting. Remington tried to pay special attention to both boys, hoping to ease the hostilities.

She brushed past Gaston on her way to topping Trenton's goblet with a berry-punch concoction. He reached out and grabbed her arm gently, pulling her against his chair. Their eyes met and bolts of lightning flew between them, sharp and thrilling.

"You are paying more attention to these young men than to the master of the keep," he said softly. "I am quite outraged."

She smiled sweetly. "I shall make it up to you tonight, my lord. I promise."

He released her arm slowly. "I will hold you to that promise," his eyes suddenly moved beyond her to the doorway and she saw his face tighten. "Damn."

She turned to see Lady Mari-Elle de Russe strolling into the dining hall, her thin face eyeing Gaston and Remington quite hostilely. Remington took a step away from Gaston and curtsied as Mari-Elle marched up.

"My lady," she said. "We did not know to expect you for dinner."

"Yet I am here," she said coolly. "You may seat me. By my husband, preferably. Who is this little urchin?"

Dane looked up at the mean-looking lady, his eyes wide. He was sitting on Gaston's right hand and did not want to relinquish his seat.

Remington's hackles instantly went up but she forced herself to calm. "This is my son, Master Dane Stoneley. He and your son were enjoying their meal together."

Mari-Elle looked at Gaston. "Since when do prisoners share the same table with the conqueror, my lord?"

"He was invited," Gaston replied, his voice low. "You have not been. Return to your rooms and take your meal there."

Trenton's little face went pale; he could feel the tension and he hated it. It frightened him when his parents fought.

"I...I thought I might be able to enjoy my meal in the hall, since I have been confined to my rooms all day," she put her hand protectively on Trenton. "And I have not seen my son at all."

Gaston glanced at Trenton and saw the worry on his face. Not wanting to upset his son further, he waved at Mari-Elle. "Very well, then, be seated next to your son."

Arik moved down to allow Mari-Elle to sit. Remington moved away from the table and returned moments later with a trencher of mutton, gravy and bread. She sat it heavily in front of Mari-Elle, testimony to her irritation.

Mari-Elle eyed the food. "What is this meat, madam?"

"Mutton," Remington answered shortly. The woman had piqued her temper calling her son an urchin.

Mari-Elle turned her nose up. "Mutton. Have you no beef or fowl?"

Remington's pretty jaw clenched and Gaston watched her reaction. "Nay, my lady, only mutton. If you want beef, then you will have to kill the cow yourself."

Mari-Elle's eyes narrowed at her. "Do not get flippant with me, mistress."

Remington lifted an eyebrow, remarkably cool, but there was no mistaking the challenging air of her stance. "I was not attempting to be rude, my lady, merely stating a fact. If you will only taste the meat, I am sure you will find it most delicious."

Mari-Elle glared at her a moment before lowering her eyes to her plate. Gingerly, she took a taste and pushed it away. "Awgh. I cannot stomach mutton," she declared. "You will serve me something else, mistress, and no more of your backtalk."

"But it's good," Dane insisted, across the table. "Do not you like it?"

Mari-Elle looked imperiously at the boy. "You were not invited to speak and I would demand you to hurry and be gone."

Remington couldn't stop herself. She walked around to Dane and put her hands protectively on her son. "He is more welcome at this table than you are, my lady. Or had not you noticed?"

Gaston looked sharply at her, but Mari-Elle was faster to the draw. The Mari-Elle of old suddenly burst forth in all of her sinister glory and the trencher of mutton and gravy went flying, missing Remington and Dane by mere inches. Gone was the woman trying to impress her husband.

"How dare you speak to me like that," she snapped savagely.

Dane scrambled off the bench; he did not want to be between his mother and the angry lady. Across the table, Trenton lowered his head and started to cry softly. As Gaston rose to his feet, Dane did the only thing he could think of; he ran around the table and grabbed Trenton by the arm.

"Come on," he hissed.

Trenton yanked back from him, but Dane grabbed him again. "Come on unless you want to get hit."

Trenton saw his mother and father on their feet, and after a split second of indecision, allowed himself to be pulled along by the younger boy.

The boys were forgotten by the adults at the table. Gaston's face was severe.

"Mari-Elle, I want you out of my sight," he said in a low, controlled voice. "You were not invited into my dining hall and I do not wish to see you here."

"I did not start this and refuse to be punished," Mari-Elle snapped back, although her voice was not raised. "Your Lady Remington is quite insubordinate."

"And you my lady, are insulting and arrogant," Remington shot back. "How dare you tell my son he is not welcome at his own table."

Mari-Elle opened her mouth but Gaston cut her off. "Out, Mari-Elle, or I will remove you myself. Lady Remington, you will retreat as well. I will hear no hollering to spoil my appetite."

Mari-Elle spun on her heel, already moving to do his bidding, but Remington stared at him in shocked silence. He took his seat and refused to look at her.

"I meant it, Remi," he said softly. "I will seek you later."

Humiliated and stunned, she took several calming breaths before replying. "Do not bother, my lord."

He drained half his goblet of wine, his eyes moving up to her as she turned away from him. He watched the straight back, the luscious hair, knowing she did not understand his reasons for punishing her, but he had to show who was in control. Additionally, it would not do at all to show favorites in front of everyone.

Mari-Elle was halfway across the room when she suddenly stopped and swayed. Clutching at her stomach, she let out a piercing cry and sank gracefully to the floor in a dead faint.

The entire company of knights were on their feet, looking curiously at the crumpled woman as Arik and Patrick went over to her. Gaston, knowing this to be more of his wife's melodramatics, drained his cup before rising. Damn woman was a bloody pain in the ass!

Remington paused at the entrance to the kitchen, watching as Gaston crossed the floor to his wife. He stood a moment over her, his hands on his hips impatiently as he listened to Arik's assessment. Then, reluctantly, he swooped down and took her in his arms.

The last glimpse Remington caught of Gaston was as he left the hall with Mari-Elle in his arms, her rich ruby dress flowing about him. Jealousy shot through her like a spear and she clenched her jaw painfully to keep the tears from coming. No one would see how hurt she was, especially Rory and Jasmine when they passed her an inquisitive glance. Without a word, she disappeared from the hall.

Mari-Elle had regained consciousness by the time he reached her rooms. Her physician, a thin man with sparse gray hair, was summoned and took special care with his examination while Gaston waited with little tolerance. It made him all the more peevish that his wife's ladies were tittering in the corner, paying more attention to him than to their mistress.

"Well?" Gaston demanded.

The physician straightened, digging into his bag. "It is her stomach, my lord. Ever since her arrival, she has been most sensitive."

In other words, the crushed apricot seeds had upset her system more than intended. Gaston sighed. "And?"

"And I believe I must tend your wife in private, my lord," the man said. "There are certain things I must do to her and...."

Gaston put up a silencing hand, "I understand."

The physician kicked the ladies out, too, and when the room was vacant, he lifted his eyebrows at Mari-Elle. "There is something you are not telling me. Have you been bleeding?"

Mari-Elle, looking pale, shook her head. "Nay, I have not. This child is making me exceedingly ill."

The physician shook his head. "My lady, I have taken care of a good many pregnant women, and your womb does not feel as if there is life within."

"And I have actually borne a child and know exactly what pregnancy feels like," she snapped back. "Do not tell me that I am not with child, physician. I have all of the symptoms."

He crossed his arms. "Do your breasts ache?"

"Aye."

"And your menses have stopped?"

"Aye, nearly three months now,"

"And do you feel weak and ill?" '

"All of the time," Mari-Elle insisted. "Why are we repeating what we already know?"

He sighed and moved toward her again, poising his hands over her belly. "May I?"

She grunted with annoyance. "Very well. But be quick about it."

He prodded and probed, pushed and jabbed until Mari-Elle was near to exploding. Finally, he straightened again.

"It does not feel right to me," he said. "Your womb should be hard, but it is soft for the most part except in one area. Only there is it firm, and the firmness is too high."

"Too high? What do you mean?" Mari-Elle felt her own stomach.

He shook his head. "I am not sure, my lady, but I believe something is wrong. Very wrong. Was your fainting spell tonight for real or simply for your husband's benefit?"

She looked puzzled, perhaps a bit cornered. "It was real enough at first, but I felt fine by the time Gaston brought me back to my room."

The physician scrambled about in his bag. "I shall give you something to help you sleep this night."

"Fine," Mari-Elle said irritably. "And you will send Gaston to me."

"And if he asks me what is wrong?" the physician wanted to know.

"Tell him it is a private female ailment," she snipped. "We have been over this before."

He did not answer as he stirred a bit of white powder into a cup of wine. "Drink this."

She did and made a face at the bitterness. Settling herself back on the pillows, she nodded to her surgeon. "Now, Dooley, you will send my husband to me."

The old man rose, bag in hand, and opened the door. His gaze lingered on his mistress a moment, a sense of doom filling him. There were a couple of possibilities for her condition, both fatal, but he would not tell her that. She was a demanding, spoiled bitch and he had little like for her, but she paid him well for his services and he enjoyed the money. Besides, if it were either of the two possibilities he suspected, there was nothing he could do and he did not want to alarm her needlessly.

The first potentiality for her condition was indeed a pregnancy that had planted itself too high in her womb. If that were the case, she would rupture and bleed to death within a few weeks at most. The second was a cancerous tumor growing within her, and her life expectancy might not be much longer than with the first possibility.

Dooley knew for certain he would be searching for a new mistress before too long.

Gaston went to seek out Remington. Her family was still down in the dining hall, save Charles, and the lad was probably up in his tower room. He was glad that the wing was deserted as he rapped softly on her door.

Remington heard him, but she was angry and jealous and refused to answer. He knew she was in the room.

"Remi, open the door," he said softly.

Still she did not answer, lying on her bed in a heated rage. How dare he punish her, send her away like a naughty child, and then presume to act as if nothing had happened. And carrying Mari-Elle from the hall had simply added fuel to her fire; if he hated his wife as he said he did, then why did not he let someone else take her to her room?

He rapped again. "I know you are in there. Open the damn door or I shall break it down."

She rolled over on her side stubbornly. She would not answer him. In fact, he would be lucky if she ever spoke to him again.

There was a loud slam that shook the very walls of the castle and her door popped and snapped and then exploded into kindling. Splinters of wood shot across the room and sprayed her where she lay upon the bed. Remington cringed but she did not move; she knew Gaston had been true to his word and had destroyed the door. And she trusted him enough to know that the door was the only thing he would tear apart.

He stood just inside the archway, his hands on his hips as he glowered at her. He had not even raised a sweat busting the old door. Frustrated, he kicked a large piece of wood away and went directly to her wine decanter.

"You are drinking too much," she said, hearing his movements.

"I will be the sole judge of that," he rumbled.

She still lay on her side, her arms wrapped protectively around her body. "You always drink too much after you have had contact with your wife."

He paused, the goblet mid-way to his lips. After an eternal pause, she heard him sigh and then the sound of the cup as it met with the table.

"Can we dispense with the animosity tonight?" he finally said. "I am in great need of your comfort."

She felt her anger abate with his words; they were soft, almost pleading. She had never heard him beg before. Slowly, she rolled onto her back and looked at him.

"What's wrong?" she asked.

He shrugged irritably. "Everything. But the last thing I want to be wrong is you and I. Get up and come to my chamber."

She sat up and raised an eyebrow at the door. "Heaven only knows there will be no privacy here. Did you truly have to break it down? A little more pleading and I would have opened it."

"I did plead but you ignored me," he held out his hand and pulled her from the bed. "I shall have it repaired tomorrow."

She picked her way over the broken frame, a remembrance drifting over her as she viewed the carnage. It was horribly disturbing and she felt her stomach twist as she recalled the event, but somehow with Gaston beside her, she was able to face it quite rationally. His strength had become hers.

"I tried to lock Guy out one time," she said softly. "He took an axe and chopped the door down. Then he took the butt and beat me with it. My eyes were swollen shut for three days."

His grip tightened on her arm as he led her into the corridor. The dim hall was cool as he took her down to the master chamber, a vast, room furnished with heavy, dark furniture. She took a second glance at it as he closed the door behind them, seeing that he had brought his own items with him and had nearly redecorated the entire room. Heavy furs lay in front of the hearth and on both sides of the bed, filling the already-musty room with a more animalistic scent. There were weapons strewn about, boots, clothing, and it suddenly occurred to her that the room looked like him. She could see him, and smell him, everywhere.

"It looks a bit different since you were last here," he commented, removing the mail tunic he wore and casting it over a chair.

"I like it," she said, sinking down on the end of the bed. "It feels like you."

He sat down to remove his boots. "I should hope so, considering it is my room."

She smiled faintly at him. "I just meant that the room no longer reminds me of Guy," she said softly. "The more time passes, the more you become a part of our lives and it is easier to forget about my husband."

He looked at her a moment. "Do not use that term to describe him anymore. When next I hear it, you will be referring to me. Only I am worthy of that title, madam, when it pertains to you."

He wasn't angry, merely stating a fact. She nodded once, slowly. "Of course, Gaston."

He stood up and removed his shirt, leaving him clad in only snug leather breeches. Remington felt her chest tightening and her limbs go warm at the sight of his magnificent chest, surely the most beautiful piece of flesh in the entire world. Antonius, as sculpted as he was, couldn't come close. Gaston was built like a god.

He ran his fingers through his hair, scratching his scalp with satisfaction as he moved to the huge hearth and stoked it to a roaring blaze. She could only sit there and watch him; the most glorious male God had ever created. She still found it hard to believe he was hers. Sometimes she wondered if she would awaken from this dream only to find Guy looming over her, demanding service. If it were a dream, she would stay asleep forever.

When the fire was blazing, he held out a hand to her. "Come over here, angel. The room is cold."

She had not noticed; she had been so involved in watching him and he always made her blood boil. Obediently, she went to him and sat on the huge rug next to him. He took her in his arms and leaned back against the huge leather-covered chair behind him.

Content as a fat baby, she snuggled against him and gazed dreamily into the flames, feeling the thick fur against her legs.

"What kind of fur is this?" she asked.

"Bear," he replied. "Killed the animal myself when I was seventeen. It damn near ate me for supper."

She ran her fingers over the soft rug. "I have a sheepskin coverlet for winter."

"Tell me," he said thoughtfully. "Have the sheep already been shorn?"

"Aye, they were shorn in April of their winter coats," she said. "They will be shorn again come September. And then we will have to deal with the merchants from London as they barter for the wool."

"Yorkshire wool is the finest," he said. "Honestly, I have been focusing so much on the arrival of my new troops that I have scarce had time to learn in detail the workings of Mt. Holyoak.

But I suppose I will have to leave that to you, my lady. Unless, of course, you would rather switch duties with me."

She giggled softly, "Can you see me in front of five hundred men, trying to teach them to hold a sword? The sword is as big as I am."

He smiled, stroking her arms as he held her. The fire spit and crackled, the comfortable smell of smoke lingering in the air.

"Is Mari-Elle all right?" she asked, not particularly caring, but curious all the same.

"Who knows?" he replied. "If I am lucky, she shall die before fall and then I will only have Guy to deal with."

"Gaston, it is not nice to wish someone dead, no matter who they are," she admonished gently. "Heaven only knows I have been tempted to wish it for Guy, but I am afraid that fate will punish me by taking away someone dear to me. 'Tis bad luck to wish another dead."

His arms held her tighter. "Nevertheless, I wish it anyway. Besides, Fate is a friend of mine and would never betray me."

Pressed against him, feeling his heat, was the most satisfying feeling she had ever experienced. Never had she simply sat with her husband, enjoying his company. Guy was the terror of her life and there had been nothing to enjoy; there had been no friendship in their marriage, no respect, no joy. It existed of fear and intimidation, of pain and humiliation.

Sitting with Gaston, it was as if she were reborn. She never knew this sort of life existed.

She was warm, deliciously so with his massive body and the heat from the fire. As much as she tried to fight it, her lids grew heavy.

"Did Trenton and Dane behave themselves after I left?" he asked.

She jolted from her dozing state. "Aye, they actually played together. A sea battle, I believe, for they were using lily pads as boats. "

"'Twas your battle story that inspired them," he said, shifting a little and pulling her closer against him. "I am glad to know that there was no more quarreling."

"Not to worry," she said sleepily. "Rory was watching them and they were too frightened of her to get out of hand."

He raised his eyebrows in agreement. "I would not be hesitant to take that woman into battle with me. She would be most formidable."

"She knocked out three of Guy's teeth once," she said with a bit of pride. "But he broke her arm for her troubles."

Gaston sighed heavily, low and deep in his chest. His disgust for the man grew with every new fact that he learned. He was silent for several moments.

"I have decided something, Remi," he said finally.

"What is that, my love?" her eyes were closed and she was fading fast.

"I am going to kill Guy," he said it so casually that she did not grasp it for a moment. "I am going to break every bone in his body and mention you or your sisters with each snap. The man will wish he had never been born."

Her eyes opened and she blinked at the fire a moment. Then, she sat up and looked at him. "You are going to murder him?"

"I prefer to call it justice," he said evenly. "I will make him pay for everything he has done to you and your family."

Her eyes widened. "Gaston...why must you do this? He is away from us, locked up for the rest of his life. Why must you kill him? "

"To avenge you," he said simply.

She looked gravely concerned and thoughtful and he watched her furrowed brow, knowing how distasteful murder was to a lady. Her puzzled eyes met his. "Did I somehow ask this of you? I never meant to ask that you commit murder on my behalf."

"You did not," he said. "But I would punish this man who has been punishing you for simply being his wife. I must right what he had wronged."

She wasn't at all comfortable with his declaration. "As much as I love your devotion and chivalry, I would wish you to stay the hell away from London and from Guy. I want you to stay here, with me, forever. Let God punish him for his sins, Gaston. To be rid of the man is enough for me."

"Well said," he said, running his fingers lightly over her hair. "But I must go to London to see Henry if we are to obtain an annulment, and while I am there I must see Guy for the same reasons. So you see, either way I will see the man."

She looked at him a moment. "I do not want you to kill him."

His face hardened. "Why not?"

She swallowed. "I...I have a difficult time believing in God, Gaston, but I believe that we will be held accountable for our sins. I do not want you to burn in hell for murder, and I do not want to burn in hell for allowing you to carry out your plans. Guy is not worth losing our eternal souls."

He gazed at her a moment before relaxing and pulling her back against him. He could see that she was frightened and sincere and, truthfully, he had never given much thought to the afterlife. He did not voice his thoughts, but with all of the men he had killed, he was already guaranteed a prime spot in Purgatory. One more would not make or break him.

Obviously, she wasn't thinking about the soldier he had killed in front of her, or Eugene le Tourneaux. Mayhap because they were more spur of the moment, not given to plan. The fact that he was planning a murder seemed to greatly disturb her, but he looked at it in a different light.

Guy Stoneley was a vile bastard who had humiliated and beaten his wife, a woman whom Gaston just happened to love madly. He would do anything for her, including kill, to insure her happiness. *Anything for you.*

"We shall not speak of it, then," he said softly.

She did not believe for a minute that he had rethought his statement. Gaston de Russe did not say anything he did not mean, and she was greatly troubled. It wasn't one reason in particular, but the entire concept. She knew the Dark Knight and his reputation, and knew that killing for him was a natural function of his profession, but she couldn't bring herself to condone the killing of her legal husband. Murder, for whatever reason, was wrong.

She turned into Gaston, pressing her body as close as she could, her face in the smooth skin of his chest. He enfolded her tighter, his huge arms almost completely obscuring her torso.

The fire crackled and hissed, filling the silent room, as they were lost to their own thoughts. In spite of their individual opinions about the future of Guy Stoneley, to be together as they were was the most natural, heavenly thing in the world. Gaston felt as if, somehow, he was whole when he was with her. She fit against him as if she had somehow been carved from the spot and the void had never healed, instead, waiting for her to fill it once again. It was beyond anything he had ever experienced.

He thought she had fallen asleep but her head came up, her half-lidded eyes gazing up at him.

"Make love to me," she whispered.

His lips came down, brushing hers gently. "Are you sure you are not going to fall asleep in the middle of it?"

She stiffened and tried to push him away, though it was in good humor. "If you do not want to, then say so. I will return to my own bedchamber."

He grinned. "That day will never come."

She closed her eyes as he grazed her neck with his gentle lips, his stubble scratching her. His kisses grew hotter and she clung to his neck, half-laying on his reclined body. His hands roved over her promising curves, delighting in her form, eager to remove her of her garments so that he could touch the silky skin. She had the most remarkable skin.

With a groan, he rolled her onto the bearskin, his fingers working the stays of her surcoat. His mouth was probing hers, tongues clashing and tasting. After a moment, she realized he was having difficulty with the stays and she pulled back.

"Might I help you with that?" she teased, already bending her arm behind her and unhooking the seam.

He looked sheepish. "I am not as adept as some," he mumbled. "I have had little practice removing a woman's surcoat in the heat of passion."

"I am glad," she said, pulling the surcoat off from her shoulders. "That means you have not felt desire such as this very often."

"If at all," his mouth plunged to the milky-white of her shoulder, tasting her sweet flesh.

She gave herself over to him, acutely aware of every sensation, every touch. His huge arousal brushed against her thigh and she opened her eyes long enough to see that he still retained his breeches.

In a flash, her hand moved down and yanked the fastener, releasing his waistband. He came back up to her hungry mouth, grinning in between kisses.

"My lady is bold this eve," he growled. "Might I help you with that?"

He was so large that her arm was too short to effectively remove his breeches. She smiled as he raised himself from her long enough to pull them down. "I have had little practice removing men's trousers."

"I am glad," his entire body, sculpted and superbly muscled and taut covered her, his arms winding about her body fiercely. She instinctively wound herself around him, her arms around his neck and her legs wrapping his rock-hard thighs. His erection rubbed her inner thigh, the cleft between her buttocks, driving her insane with need.

"Take me now, Gaston," she breathed.

His lips tore themselves away from her neck. "Not yet."

"Gaston!" she pleaded.

His mouth moved down her body, to her delicious breasts. "Not yet."

"Why the hell not?" she panted, crying out softly when his lips engulfed a swollen nipple.

His hands massaged her, pulling at her breasts and pinching her nipples until she was absolutely writhing with passion. His massive hands still splayed on her breasts, his mouth blazed a trail down the center of her torso, losing himself in her scent and texture. Every curve was explored with his tongue, every inch touched or caressed somehow. He had to experience *all* of her.

His mouth moved to her tender groin area, tasting and kissing. His hands left her breasts and he moved between her thighs, bringing up both of her legs and spreading them wide.

Remington's head came up, puzzlement in her passion. "What are you doing?"

He lowered his head to her throbbing core, a wolfish grin on his sensual face. Obviously, she would not have asked such a question if she had experienced what he was about to do. There was no mistaking his intentions. His gentle fingers delicately traced the dark curls, tenderly spreading the thick folds and Remington's eyes widened.

"Gaston," she breathed. "What are you...?"

She was cut off when his hot mouth descended on her very private, very sensitive core. A moan spilled forth from her moist lips and she arched her back with the force of her passion, the top of her head nearly flush with the rug. Frozen in that position, she could do naught but feel every lap of his tongue, every suckle, as if nothing else in her world existed, only Gaston and his amazing touch.

His hands held her buttocks, trapping her against him as he continued his onslaught. Her sharp pants of passion excited him beyond belief, driving him nearly insane for want of her. As new as she was to the art of love, he knew her peak was seconds away, and he did not want to miss it. Releasing her buttocks, he arched over her and drove himself into her hot, slippery flesh in one great thrust.

Remington was already climaxing as he came into her, only enhanced by his massive organ filling her as she had never been filled. His thrusts were firm and complete, prolonging her pleasure until tears of pure joy ran down her temples. The harder he pushed, the more potent her contractions until she began the inevitable downslide toward relaxed bliss.

His arms were braced on either side of her head, his body aloft from hers as he rammed into her again and again. She was so damn tight and slick that he could imagine no greater pleasure, for any man, ever. There was indeed a heaven and her name was Remington.

When his release came shortly, it was with the most violent of blasts. Her name gushed forth from his lips as he spilled himself, still moving, feeling her juices and his combine and making her unbelievably wet. He continued to move, still wanting to feel her around him, still wanting to be within her until out of sheer fatigue, he slowed his pace and finally ceased.

With a great sigh, he lowered himself on the rug and pulled her with him as he went. She moved to unwind her legs but he would only allow her to remove one, so he would not lie upon it. The other leg he kept wrapped over his hip.

"Nay, madam, remain where you are," he rasped. "I would still feel myself in you."

Even semi-flaccid, he was absolutely enormous and she could feel his manhood throb and twitch as it diminished further. But it was the most wonderful, intimate feeling ever and she absorbed every move. Her lips, against his chest, moved over him softly.

They lay together, listening to the fire, for a countless amount of time. Nothing mattered at that very moment more than them, together.

"Shall we move to the bed?" she whispered.

He grunted; he had been dozing off. "I suppose. Are you cold?"

She snuggled up against him. "Never. How could I be? You are as hot as any fire."

His hand was gently touching her hair, caressing it against her back. "But the bed would be more comfortable than the hard floor."

He moved a little but she stopped him. "I am comfortable wherever you are, my love. Stay, stay."

He did, tightening his arms about her. They were both dozing off when there was a soft rap at the door.

Gaston lifted his head, wary. "Who comes?"

"Me," it was Arik.

He looked at Remington apologetically, mayhap a bit guiltily. Still embedded in her, he withdrew his member and put a huge hand over her mouth to stifle the soft groan. She grinned at him and sat up as he went in search of his breeches.

"My lord?" Arik called through the door.

"I am coming," Gaston said, his words turning to a mumble as he secured his breeches.

Meanwhile, Remington had moved to the great bed and had hid herself behind the great silk curtains that hung from the canopy frame. In front of her on the bed was a lightweight cotton coverlet; she snatched it and wrapped it about her body as added protection.

Gaston gave her a final glance to make sure she was settled before opening the door.

Arik's face was grim. "You are not going to be happy to hear this."

Gaston's mouth twitched with irritation. "What, then?"

"Your wife is demanding that you attend her," he said. "Her physician tried to find his way up here to inform you personally, but was effectively halted by Nicolas. He insists your wife is greatly in need of your comfort."

Gaston snorted. "Hmpf. A pity. Was that all?"

"Nay," Arik raised an eyebrow in silent request for his lord to brace himself. "The soldiers you sent to return young Botmore home have returned. All but one of them is dead, and he was spared simply to relay a message to you from Lord Botmore."

Gaston's face went tense. He moved back into the room and pulled on his shirt. Arik followed him and Remington found herself pressing further into the folds of the curtains to keep out of sight.

"Apparently Lord Botmore is completely devastated over the death of his son and is vowing revenge on you," Arik said, leaning against the canopy post as Gaston pulled his boots on. "He not only killed five of your soldiers, but he damn near hacked them to death."

Gaston stood, donning his mail tunic and sliding into a heavy leather vest. "Too bad his son was stupid enough to cause all of this, but of course, his father will not admit it. The lad brought it down on himself when he kidnapped the women."

Arik watched Gaston secure the vest. "You mean when he captured Lady Stoneley. You would not have killed him had he only abducted the sisters."

Gaston moved to strap on his scabbard. "Since when do you read my mind and know my motives? 'Tis a dangerous sport, Arik, even for you."

Arik grinned wryly. "I have made my life out of dangerous sport, my lord. There is nothing else where you are involved."

Gaston slid his massive broadsword into the crafted leather and metal scabbard. "Where is my soldier?"

"In the new troop house," Arik replied.

Gaston preceded him from the room, his boot falls filled with purpose. Arik secured the door behind them and together they marched down the hall.

"I rather like the smell of roses and lavender," Arik remarked.

Gaston did not respond for a moment. Then he paused at the top of the stairwell and looked at his friend. "What does that mean?"

Arik shrugged evasively. "Just that. It mingles well with the leather and metal in your room."

Gaston's eyes glittered dangerously. "Not another word, Arik."

Arik smiled; he found it amusing to see Gaston cornered. He had smelled Lady Remington from the moment he entered the room. "My lord, I would sooner cut out my own tongue than gossip. Surely you know that. "

Gaston did not say any more, descending the stairs and trying to ignore his second in command. He was positive Arik knew what he was thinking, and he did not want anyone to know.

CHAPTER TWELVE

M ari-Elle waited and waited for Gaston to come to her. Midnight came and still he did not, and she waited and fumed.

What more could she do? She had begged, lied, wheedled and cajoled, and still he had been unresponsive. She had tried to play upon his sympathies for his son, but he had merely become angry.

Frustrated, she sat up in bed and pondered her future darkly. There was not much time left to lie with him and then convince him that this child was his, and she was nearly out of ideas. The fainting spell, convenient as it was, did nothing to sway him. Mayhap ... mayhap something more drastic would.

A light ignited in her devious mind and she bound from the bed, wincing when her lower abdomen pulled sharply at the sudden motion. She made her way unsteadily to her wardrobe and began to rummage again, tossing things aside in her quest. After a few minutes of cursing and grunting, she finally had what she was searching for.

A lovely bejeweled dagger filled her palm, the blade about three inches in length. She smiled as she turned it over, examining it. What if she were to present herself to Gaston as a woman desperate to take her life if he did not give in to her needs? She was quite good and ranting and hysterics, and surely he would forget his stubbornness when he saw how very sincere she was.

She clutched the dagger to her chest, feeling more hope than she had since her arrival. She closed her eyes, a picture forming in her mind, her hysterical threats, pleas, Gaston's soft voice, as he coaxed the blade from her hand. Defeated and crushed, she would throw herself in his arms and he would comfort her. From that point on, she knew she could seduce him. Once his guard was down, the rest would be easy.

Donning her best dressing surcoat, she went in search of her husband's bedchamber.

Remington was asleep in the great bed, the soft crackle from the fire the only sound in a soundless world. She had been planning on returning to her own room, door or no door, when she had inadvertently smelled the cotton coverlet that she had clutched to cloak herself. Inhaling the pillow and the mattress, she was delighted to learn that they smelled of him, leather and male musk. Happy and warm, she had collapsed onto his bed and drifted off to sleep.

Mari-Elle, being an intelligent woman, had little trouble locating Gaston's room. She simply asked the nearest soldier and he directed her gladly, for there was no standing orders to restrict Mari-Elle to her room. All orders had been given to her directly and she had been expected to obey.

She entered the dim wing, following the directions the soldier had given her, and made her way silently down the hall. All of the doors were closed save one, which looked as if it had been torn off its hinges. She looked at it a moment, puzzled, and actually stuck her head inside the room. It was a ladies room, vacant, and through the open adjoining door, she could see another empty bed.

She clung to the stone wall as she made her way toward the great double doors at the end of the hall, knowing upon sight it was her husband's room. Her stomach twisted with nerves as she approached, silently beseeching God for help with what she must do in order to preserve her honor and livelihood.

The torches on either side of the doors burned low and sooty as she tried the latch quietly; amazingly it wasn't locked, and she quietly shoved the right door open, carefully inspecting the room as it was revealed to her, trying to grow accustomed to the dim light.

The fire was low in the hearth and the room was dark, but she could make out the massive bed directly to her left. Huge, swathed in yards and yards of dark fabric that hung from the canopy frame, she could also see a figure bunched up in the center of it.

She dashed the faint smile away from her lips as she approached with the stealth of a cat. She would wake him gently, aye, before launching into her tirade, and she was verily pleased that the element of surprise was on her side.

Slowly she approached, her eyes growing used to the dark and she could see that the figure was almost buried in the coverlets. She rounded the bed on the far side of the figure, not wanting to be too close to him lest he lash out and strike at her for surprising him. But even as her pleasure filled her, it suddenly occurred to her that the figure on the bed was far too small to be her husband.

Cold, complete fury flushed her veins even as her brain tried to deny what she was seeing and suddenly she ceased to think as a rational being. All she knew was that this wench in her husband's bed had most likely received the seed of life she so desperately wanted. No wonder Gaston had been uninterested in her if he had a bitch to bed. This small body sleeping peacefully after sucking her husband's seed dry was beyond contempt and Mari-Elle was filled with the fury of hell. She would show no mercy.

She suddenly remembered the dagger in her hand. With a small, hysterical cry issued from behind, clenched teeth, she brought the dagger high and jumped onto the bed, descending on her prey like a carnivorous hunter. Her revenge would be mindless and swift.

Remington heard the cry, for it had awakened her. Suddenly the bed was being jostled and she instinctively threw the covers down from her face to see what in the hell was going on. The last thing in the world she expected to see was Mari-Elle descending on her like an avenging demon, the dirk in her right hand glittering evilly.

Terror shot through her and she let out a scream of her own, trying to roll away, but the weight of the crazed woman on the coverlets severely hampered her free movement. From the corner of her eye she could see the blade coming down and instantaneously she felt the searing pain of penetration in her upper right chest, the heat of agony flooding through her like the fires of Hades.

Both women screamed loudly as contact was made and Mari-Elle let go of the dirk, leaving it imbedded near Remington's collarbone. Gasping with fury and the panic of what she had done she flopped wildly off the bed and made a mad scramble to the door.

The room was full of shrieking, horrible gasping noises and
Remington fell off the bed and Mari-Elle tripped to the floor in her
haste to leave. She staggered to her feet, glancing behind her at the
woman struggling beside the bed, the only thing filling her mind was
to escape. She could scarce believe what she had done, yet she did not
regret it. With any luck, the whore would bleed to death before Gaston
returned and take the secret of who stabbed her to the grave.

Remington's right arm was useless but she tried to rise, afraid
that Mari-Elle was going for a more deadly weapon. Bleeding all over
Gaston's sheets, she pulled herself to her knees long enough to see that
Mari-Elle was bolting for the door. Struggling to her feet, she clutched
at the canopy frame as she attempted to pursue, knowing there was no
possible way she could stop her but making the try all the same. Her
loss of blood was making her desperately weak and her head swam with
shock, but she had to break free of the room and find help.

Help was already coming in the form of Rory. Having heard the
screams, she shot out of bed and was barreling down the hall when
she saw Mari-Elle stagger out of Gaston's bedchamber. Shocked at the
apparent state of the woman, she rapidly closed the distance to see if
she could be of assistance when Mari-Elle suddenly grabbed hold of a
spear that was in a crafted iron display stand and thrust it at her.

"Get back!" she hissed.

Rory was truly surprised, wanting to assure the woman that she only
wanted to help, when Remington suddenly stumbled through the doorway. Covered in blood, there was no mistaking the hilt that protruded
from her shoulder and the flame of understanding shot through Rory
like a bolt.

"You bitch!" she snarled, torn between wanting to rush to
Remington's side and wanting to charge Mari-Elle. "I shall kill you for
this!"

Mari-Elle thrust the spear at Rory again and the redhead took
advantage of the weak attempt. Grabbing the spear, she yanked as hard
as she could and disarmed the woman.

Mari-Elle yelled and ran with Rory in hot pursuit. Remington,
struggling to push herself off the cold floor, watched her sister run
after the woman and tried to stop her, but she could no longer speak.

All of her energy was sapped, draining away even as she tried to stand. She did not know why she was trying to stand, for she had no idea where to go. It wasn't as if she could go in search of Gaston with a knife sticking out of her.

She heard more cries, recognizing Jasmine and Skye. The last thing she remembered before sweet darkness claimed her was collapsing into her sisters' arms.

Rory chased Mari-Elle to the bottom floor of the castle, gaining ground rapidly. Mari-Elle had long legs and was quick, but Rory was determined as hell to catch her and kill her. Black murder was the only thing on her mind as she ran down Mari-Elle like a hunter on a kill. She would take great delight in driving the spear through the woman's gullet like a harpooned fish.

Nicolas was making his rounds when he caught sight of Mari-Elle racing toward him like a madwoman. Deeply confused, he put out his hands to stop her, but she cried out and veered away from him.

"My lady!" he called out in concern, trying to stop her.

Just as quickly his eyes caught sight of Rory in chase, wielding a heavy spear with obvious intent. Shocked, Nicolas tackled her and tried to disarm her, but she struggled ferociously.

"Let me go!" she hollered, kicking and fighting. "She killed Remington! Let me go!"

Nicolas blanched, ceasing his struggles with her but he continued to grip the spear. "She....what? Killed Remington?"

Rory yanked the spear free from his grasp. "Stabbed her!"

She started to run but he stopped her harshly. "Where is she?"

"Upstairs in the hallway." Rory ripped free of his grip. "Let me go, you bastard."

Nicolas took hold of her and the spear; Lady Mari-Elle was long gone, disappeared into one of the labyrinth of halls that made up this place. He knew he had to find Gaston.

"Go back upstairs," he ordered tightly. "Go to your sister. I shall find Gaston."

Anger flooding over, the severity of the situation was beginning to settle and hot tears spilled onto her cheeks. She wanted to argue, for she herself wanted to kill Mari-Elle, but the overwhelming need to be with Remington took hold and she let the spear go. Nicolas seeing her pain and terror patted her on the cheek. "Go, Rory. I shall find Gaston."

Obediently, she turned and walked unsteadily down the hall, finally running. He waited until she mounted the stairs before throwing the spear to the ground in a fit of emotion. As he jogged to the outer bailey, he could only pray Gaston did not run him through as the bearer of bad tidings.

Gaston had had enough of death for one night. Out of the six soldiers sent to return Sir Derek Botmore, five of them were dismembered so thoroughly it was as if they were parts to a grisly puzzle. The sixth soldier, exhausted from bringing his five companions home, told a horrible tale of blood and torture and madness. Gaston heard the man out but did not ask any questions; the soldier was almost to the point of madness himself and Gaston would let him rest a bit before grilling him.

He would not avenge the deaths, for they came as a direct result of his actions. Granted, he was doing what he must to rescue Remington and her sisters, but the constant seeking of revenge had to stop somewhere. Unless Botmore attacked Mt. Holyoak, he would make no provocative action.

He and Arik were engaged in a leisure conversation when Nicolas came running up, his armor clanging loudly.

"Gaston!" he called.

The two men turned toward the younger knight, wondering what the rush was about, Nicolas did not give them a chance to ask.

"Trouble, my lord," Nicolas came to an unsteady halt. "Your wife has stabbed Lady Remington and...."

Gaston did not even realize he had reached out and grabbed his cousin. "*What?*"

Nicolas met his eyes steadily, although he was quaking out of fear. "You'd better go, Gaston. Rory says she's dead. I have not seen for myself yet."

Gaston's mind went blank. He was aware he was running, passing through the darkened baileys with Arik beside him, but little else. Even the innards of the castle passed by him in a flash, his mind neither thinking nor feeling nor hearing anything else but Remington.

He took the stairs like a man possessed. With each fall of his boot he could hear the death chant... *Dead. Dead. Dead.* When he finally burst into the upper floor hallway, he was running faster than he ever had in his life.

He heard the crying, the moaning, and he burst into the room from which it emitted. Rory and Skye were standing around the bed while Jasmine and old Eudora were tending the body on the mattress.

He rushed up on the bed so fast he almost lost his balance and pitched forward. Yet, he could see that his fear had been for naught as she twitched and cried, testimony to the life still flowing within her.

Slammed with indescribable relief to see that Remington was not dead, it was rapidly dampened by the sight of a knife hilt protruding from her shoulder. Blood was everywhere.

"She won't let us remove it." Jasmine was crying softly, not turning to look at him. She had felt him behind her, hearing his panic.

Remington's eyes opened, a sea of color in a pasty face. She focused directly on Gaston.

"No!" she screamed at him. "Do not hurt me!"

His heart broke into a millions pieces and he took Jasmine by the arms to move her aside so that he could be close to Remington.

"Remi, angel, it has to come out," he said tenderly, motioning Arik to the other side of the bed.

"No," she breathed, a cry of panic, of pain. Her eyes rolled closed. "Leave me alone."

Arik moved the women back and gave them all quiet, concise orders before moving to the other side of Remington.

"She's not thinking straight," he whispered to his second. "Hold her while I remove it."

"Nay," Arik returned quickly. "You hold her. She shall want you to hold her."

Gaston looked at him a moment before nodding curtly. Arik was astonished at the pain he read in his lord's eyes. It was as if this Gaston was someone entirely different from the Dark Knight he knew. The Dark One knew no pain.

Gaston felt ill at all of the blood he was seeing on her slim body as he braced himself against the side of the bed. Gently, his huge hands came down on her arms and her eyes opened again, looking at him with panic.

"Gaston?" she whispered urgently, looking for some sort of reassurance that he wasn't going to hurt her anymore.

"It's all right, angel, I am here," he said softly, smiling at her encouragingly. "I shall not leave you."

Arik moved toward the hilt of the blade as Gaston kept her attention. "It was Mari-Elle," she told him weakly. "She came into your room and stabbed me. Gaston, she was insane. Her eyes were wild."

His jaw clenched but he maintained his outward calm. "Do not worry yourself over her, angel."

Remington swallowed hard and he felt her relaxing under his grip. Her eyes closed lethargically. "I am... tired. I want to go to sleep."

"Then sleep, my sweet angel," he whispered, touching his cheek to hers. "Go to sleep and forget about this for a while."

Arik suddenly gripped the blade and yanked it free in one clean stroke. Remington went stiff with the shock and the agony, spewing forth an anguished scream, but Gaston continued to hold her tightly.

"It's all over, Remi, I promise," he said hoarsely.

"It hurts," she cried softly.

He smiled sadly, kissing her cheek tenderly, wishing to God he could take the pain upon himself. "I know, sweetness, I know. Believe me, I know. But it's all over now."

She cried softly from pain and fatigue as Arik quickly examined the wound and then proceeded to bind the shoulder tightly. Jasmine, Rory and Skye stood in a terrified huddle at the base of the bed while Eudora assisted Arik with the bandages.

When she was expertly tended, Gaston pulled her carefully over to her left side to relieve any pressure on her right shoulder. Shaking and sobbing, she gripped his hand with a death-grip and refused to let go.

"Arik, find Rastus and send him up here with something for her pain," Gaston ordered softly. "And I want him to check the wound when the bleeding has stopped."

Arik nodded, wiping his hands with a rag Eudora had handed him. "It looks fairly deep, but clean," he commented. "Barring any great unforeseen damaged, it should heal completely."

Gaston nodded, gazing down at her huddled body. "Nevertheless, I would have my surgeon take a look," he motioned Arik closer so that he would not have to raise his voice. "I want you to find Mari-Elle and confine her to the vault. I will deal with her alone."

Arik looked at his lord, knowing he fully intended to murder his wife and thinking it was high time the woman got what was coming to her. "Aye, my lord."

Gaston nodded faintly, turning to look at the women gathered just into the shadows. "I shall remain with her. You may return to your rooms."

"But this... this is my room," Jasmine hiccupped, her face pale.

"Then take Remington's bed," Gaston told her. "And check on Dane to make sure he is well."

Obediently, the sisters filed out behind Arik, but Eudora lagged behind a moment.

"You look exhausted, my lord," she said to Gaston. "Might I bring you a warm drink?"

He glanced at the old woman a moment, nearly dismissing her, but suddenly the thought of warm wine appealed to him. "Thank you, madam. That would be appreciated."

Eudora smiled a motherly smile. "I shall be right back, lamb...I mean, my lord."

Embarrassed at her slip, for she was very used to addressing her charges affectionately, she quickly left the room and closed the door softly behind her. Gaston smiled faintly as the footfalls faded, lingering on the pet name. He had been called a lot of things before, but never a lamb.

"Lamb?" Remington murmured.

He looked down at her. "That's enough from you," he said with feigned severity, crouching down beside the bed. "Are you going to let go of my hand long enough to allow me to remove my sword and mail?"

She shook her head every so faintly, her eyes still closed. He gazed at her bloody hair, stained neck, thinking he had never been more relieved over anything in his life. The panic, the fear he had felt during those bleak moments when he thought she might have been killed were the very worst moments of his life and he was grateful to whatever God watching over them that she was alive.

Had the knife found its mark a couple of inches lower, or mayhap a bit more to the center of her chest, he would have lost her for sure. His stomach twisted painfully at the thought and he wearily chased the horrifying ideals away. He could not lose her, not when she was becoming his all for living.

Mari-Elle would pay dearly for her transgression. He already hated her so much he was beyond hating her any more.

Eudora returned a half hour later to find him sitting on the floor next to the bed, Remington clutching his right hand to her breast. She entered silently with a tray, gazing down upon Remington's sleeping head.

"Can you remove your hand to eat?" she whispered to Gaston as she set the tray down.

He was desperately tired. He let out a long sigh as he glanced at Remington's sleeping face. "I tried once and she started to cry." Carefully, slowly, he dislodged his hand and was glad when she continued to sleep. Rising stiffly, he looked over at the food and drink on the tray. "Thank you, Eudora. I am rather famished now that I think on it."

The old woman flushed at the use of her name by the mighty and powerful Dark Knight. "My pleasure, my lord. Would you like me to return later to sit with her so that you can get some sleep?"

Gaston took a sip of the hot, spicy wine. "Nay, madam, I will remain with her. Dane will need you, as will her sisters. I can take care of Lady Remington."

Eudora nodded and moved for the door. Suddenly, she paused, her gaze falling on Remington once more. "Lord Stoneley..., he did not

care for her as a husband should," she looked embarrassed to be voicing her thoughts. "I am glad that you are kind to her, my lord. She's
had so little kindness."

He looked at the old woman a moment before gazing to Remington.
He took another satisfying sip of his warmed wine. "Your concern is
appreciated."

Eudora lowered her gaze and slipped from the room. Gaston stood
there and drank his wine, watching Remington sleep with an overwhelming sense of possessiveness. Never again would she be unprotected, out of his sight or no. He wondered what had transpired, how
Mari-Elle had found her and how the fight began. All questions she
would answer later, for he intended to ask only one question of Mari-
Elle before he cut her heart out.

What in the world possessed you, madam?

He was half-finished with his meat pie when there was a knock on
the door. Annoyed at being disturbed, he answered it with a less than
pleasant expression.

Jasmine stood hesitantly in the corridor and he raised his eyebrows
expectantly at her.

"My lord, Dane is not in his room, and he is not with Charles in the
tower," she said reluctantly. "Might you know where he would be?"

Gaston leaned heavily on the door, having difficultly believing the
course this night was taking. It was hard to keep the annoyance out of
his tone. "Nay, I do not. Call to the soldier at the base of the stairs and
tell him to send Patrick and Antonius to me, please."

Jasmine scooted away and Gaston closed the door, moving to put
his sword back on. Between Remington, Dane and Mari-Elle, it would
appear that he would get no rest this night; yet, truly, he was far too
worked up to sleep.

With Eudora and Patrick inside the chamber and four soldiers
guarding the door, Gaston felt confident enough to leave Remington
and go in search of Dane. As much as he hated to leave her, he felt a
distinct sense of foreboding at the boy's absence; if Mari-Elle was capable of stabbing the mother, there was no telling what she might do to
a defenseless boy. He did not even know if Mari-Elle had been located

yet, for Arik had yet to return to him. All he knew was that he had to find the boy and see for himself that he was all right.

Sending Jasmine off to bed, he took Antonius with him in search of Dane.

The first place he went to was Charles' tower room. The lad was up, even in the middle of the night, hunched over a table reading a leather-worn book. Gaston and Antonius entered the open door, casting an interested eye over the mysterious room.

"My lord Gaston," Charles hopped off his stool. "Jasmine told me of Remi's misfortune. How can I serve you?"

Gaston cocked an eyebrow at the symbol of a pentagram. "Mayhap you have a sorcerer's cauldron to tell me where to find Dane?"

Charles grinned. "Nay, my lord, no magic. Only experiments and such. Pray, did you check the stables?"

"Not yet," Gaston replied. "But I shall. I only came here to make sure he wasn't turned into a table or vanished into the walls."

"I swear to you, I know no magic," Charles reiterated. "But I shall help you search for him if you wish."

Gaston waved the boy with him and Charles leapt at the chance to work side by side with the Dark Knight, however small the task.

CHAPTER THIRTEEN

Dane had always liked the smell of hay. There was something comforting about it, and when he and Trenton fled the dining hall, there was no doubt as to their destination, in the hay, far away from the fighting and yelling. Sweet, consoling, and shielding were the lofts of Mt. Holyoak's stable.

There were soldiers milling about but none paid much attention to the boys as they tore into the stable area, taking the ladder to the loft high above the stalls. All that mattered to Dane was getting as far away as he possibly could, and Trenton was following blindly.

They scrambled far back into the loft against the stone supporting wall, huffing and puffing. No one spoke for a minute as they caught their breath, frightened that somehow they had been followed, that someone would appear at any moment to drag them back into the heated argument.

"Why ... why did we come here?" Trenton found his voice, observing his surroundings.

"Because it's safe," Dane insisted. "I always come here when there is fighting and it is safe."

Trenton looked at the younger boy a moment, studying him. "Do your parents fight a lot, too?"

Dane avoided his gaze, settling back on the straw. "All the time."

Trenton thought a moment. Sometimes he felt as if he were the only child on earth whose parents fought constantly. When they were together, that is. He felt himself warming just a bit more to his new friend.

"My mother and father fight every time my father comes home," he said quietly. "Finally, he just started staying away more and more. I had not seen him in a year until we came to Mt. Holyoak."

"Does he beat her?" Dane asked.

Trenton shook his head. "Nay, but I have heard him tell her he would like to throttle her. He's never hit her."

"Never?" Dane looked surprised. "My father hits my mother every day almost. Why does not he hit her if she is disobedient?"

Trenton shrugged. "I do not know, he just does not. But they do not like each other; in fact, my mother hates him."

"Why?" Dane simply couldn't imagine anyone hating Gaston.

Trenton settled back on a pile of straw and grabbed a stalk. "I do not know. Maybe because he's never home."

"Have not you asked her why she hates him?" Dane pushed.

Trenton shook his head. "Nay."

Dane pondered this point of view for a moment. "Do you hate your father?"

"Nay," Trenton shook his head. "I wish... I wish I could be just like him. I want to be as great a knight as he is."

Dane looked at him sharply; that was his dream, as well. Jealousy spread over him but he fought it down as best he could. "We're going to be fostering together, you know."

"I know," Trenton said.

Dane shoved his thumb to his chest. "I am going to be the best. I am going to work harder than anyone."

Trenton's brow furrowed. "Not harder than me. I am going to be just like my father."

Dane prepared to retort sharply but bit it back, sulking back against the hay. Eyeing Trenton hostilely, he shoved a piece of hay in his mouth and worked it thoughtfully. "We are a lot alike, you know. We both have parents who hate each other and fight a lot."

Trenton lay down, too, feeling very tired from the day's events. "I am not going to fight with my wife. I am going to marry someone I like, mayhap the prettiest girl in the realm. I'd never fight with her."

Dane lifted his eyebrow critically. "I am never going to get married."

"Why not? Do not you want sons to carry on your name?" Trenton demanded.

Dane shook his head stubbornly. "Wenches are no good."

Trenton looked at him a moment, crossing his arms behind his head and chewing on hay in an exact imitation of his younger, wiser friend. Dane seemed to know it all, whereas Trenton was more apt to follow than lead.

"All right, mayhap I won't get married," Trenton said begrudgingly. "But I shall keep a pretty woman just the same."

Dane shrugged carelessly, staring at the ceiling. "Me, too. But no wife."

"No wife," Trenton agreed.

Exhausted and left to their own thoughts, Dane fell asleep first. Trenton followed shortly.

Safe from the hell of the castle in the bosom of the stable, they slept dreamlessly.

Arik met up with Gaston in the middle of the outer bailey. "Mari-Elle is nowhere to be found, Gaston. We have combed nearly the entire keep."

"She's around here somewhere and you will find her," Gaston said shortly. "Take every man I have if you have to and find her. She's off running loose and I cannot find Dane."

"God, you do not think she might have done something to the boy?" Arik asked, horrified.

"I do not know, which is why we must find them both," Gaston was already veering away from him, toward the stables, and Arik went on his way.

Charles walked beside Antonius, feeling as important as any knight. Additionally, he was fairly confident he knew his young cousin well and had little doubt they would find him in the stables. Even with the terrible things Gaston was saying about his wife, Dane was smart and quick and knew how to avoid danger, thanks to his inbred response to his father. If Mari-Elle was in search to kill him, Dane could hide and never be found. That is, if he knew the danger existed at all.

A bit of foreboding filled the young man as they entered into the stable area. What if he was wrong?

"Where would he be?" Gaston turned his attention to Charles.

Snapped out of his depressing thoughts, Charles pointed to the nearest hayloft. "Up there, somewhere. If he is here at all."

Gaston hoisted himself up to the first loft; he did not even use the ladder. He merely gripped the edge of the platform and pulled himself up to look. Charles swallowed hard at the display of pure strength; for as huge as Gaston was, to have pulled himself up without any effort was testimony to the man's raw power.

Antonius took a look at the second loft, descending empty-handed. Gaston then moved to a smaller loft and hoisted himself up, peering at the contents. He held himself in place for several long moments before releasing his massive body to the ground.

"Both he and Trenton are up there fast asleep," he said with obvious relief. "Antonius, return to the castle and bring them some blankets, and then stand guard. Until we are able to locate Mari-Elle, I do not want either boy unprotected."

"You do not think she would hurt her own son?" Antonius asked with disbelief.

Gaston shook his head. "Until I meet up with the woman and determine her mental state myself, I will take no chances," he waved Antonius on. "Go now. They are safe for the moment."

The knight rushed off and Gaston faced Charles, "And you, young master, will return to your fortress of solitude, I thank you for your assistance."

"Would you like me to stay here and watch over them until your knight has returned?" Charles asked helpfully.

Gaston almost denied him, but he could read the eagerness in the boy's face. He so wanted to be useful and important, as they all did. Gaston wasn't sure what sort of relationship Charles had had with his elder cousin, but it was most likely not a good one. Guy Stoneley managed to belittle and intimidate everyone around him and he took pity on the young man.

"Very well, then, perch yourself on this ladder and do not move until Antonius returns," he ordered.

As obedient as the most perfect knight, Charles dutifully went to the ladder as Gaston's mind turned to Mari-Elle. He knew she was lurking about somewhere, but he would leave it to Arik and the others to find her. He himself would return to Remington now that he knew the boys were safe and wait until his fugitive wife had been located. He knew she would be found and did not want to bother himself with the search. Returning to his injured love was far more important.

Half way through the inner bailey he caught a shadow out of the corner of his eye, over by some storage bushels that held long-range arrows. Instinctively tensing, he stopped and turned to the source of movement, finding it difficult to make any assessment in the moonlight.

Suddenly a body was flying out at him and he recognized it to be Mari-Elle.

"Save me, my lord!" she cried.   He instantly viewed her hands, making sure she was harboring no weapons. "Halt where you are, madam."

She slowed unsteadily, disheveled and shaken and completely unlike the wife he knew. "Gaston, you must save me from…. from that madwoman."

His jaw ground as he moved forward and grabbed her severely. It was all he could do to keep from ripping her arms from the sockets. "With me, madam."

"But Gaston," she shrieked. "Your Lady Remington tried to kill me. Thank God I was able to turn the knife against her, otherwise she would have surely gutted me."

He slapped his hand over her mouth so hard that she let out a muffled cry. "Not another word," he growled.

He took her to the small portcullis that led to the vault of Mt. Holyoak. She twisted and tried to talk, but he held her firmly. Nicolas and two other lesser knights, in their search for

Mari-Elle caught sight of the struggles and raced to his side.

"You found her!" Nicolas exclaimed.

Gaston's face was as dark as his reputation. "'Twas her misfortune to find me. Away with you now, I will deal with my wife alone."

Nicolas bowed swiftly away, wondering if indeed Gaston would kill her after what had happened. Surely he would never see Lady de Russe alive again.

He drug her down into the bowels of the vault, a vacant place at the moment, but equipped with a good deal of torturous instruments and the like. It was a hellish place that stank of blood and sweat and urine and he led her directly into the very first cell.

It was black as tar until he lit a stale torch, propping on the wall sconce as the room came to light. Mari-Elle, free of his vise-like grip, cowered several feet away.

"She attacked me, Gaston," she pleaded softly, seeing his face and knowing her death was imminent. "I went to your room, my lord, to seek your forgiveness for my gross display of manners at the evening meal. She met me at the door and attacked me with a dagger. Gaston, I was terrified for my life. I managed to turn the knife on her and then I just ran, ran as fast as I could. Her sister must have heard the screaming and ran to finish the job that was never completed, and I was terrorized as I found myself fleeing from yet another assassin. I ran and ran until...."

She began weeping hysterically into her hands and he watched impassively.

"She would have never attacked you," he said quietly. "I would suspect that it 'twas you who came to my room with the intent to stab me and when Lady Remington answered the door, you went mad with rage and attempted to kill her instead."

"Nay, Gaston. 'Tis not true," Mari-Elle pleaded, sobbing and weeping like a fool. "She raised the knife on me. I was defending myself."

A shadow of a doubt crossed his mind. He knew Remington would have never maliciously stabbed Mari-Elle, but she might have tried if she thought she was defending herself. His doubt gave way to great frustration, deeply annoyed at himself that he was thinking on postponing his wife's execution until he could speak with Remington and find out what had truly happened.

Mari-Elle would pay, but whatever he did, it would be with full understanding of what had occurred.

"I do not believe you," he said.

"You must!" she cried, her anger surfacing through her tears. "I was defending myself from your jealous mistress."

He put his hands on his hips in a slow, deliberate move. "Surely you do not intend to cast the first stone."

It was confirmation of what she knew to be true. Fury ran neck in neck with her terror. "No wonder you want an annulment. How could you shame your family that way, Gaston? How can you shame Trenton?"

His jaw twitched menacingly. "You, of all people, have no right to accuse me of shame. Where in the hell was this misplaced pride when you were bedding every man who crossed your path?" he was suddenly upon her, his huge body causing her to shrink away. "You have no god-damn right to accuse me of infidelity, Mari-Elle, you who serviced our king like the whore that you are. You, madam, have shamed our family beyond repair and an annulment will add little more. I'd say given the circumstances, the church will gladly grant me what I ask for."

"Not when they hear my side of the story," she shot back. "What was a poor wife to do when her husband was gone month after month, fighting for the king and whoring to no end? Of course I sought comfort elsewhere."

"You were not looking for comfort," he snapped forcefully. "You were looking for pets to entertain you, men you could spend my money on, and as for whoring I should think you would know better than anyone that I do not take lovers. I have little time or desire."

"Then how do you explain that little chit in your bed?" she raged. "Do not tell me you two were occupied with mere pillow talk to pass the hours."

He had to move away from her or he would strangle her with his bare hands. "What Lady Remington and I do is of no concern to you," he rumbled, twitching with anger. "She is more of a woman than you could ever hope to be. Now, madam, make yourself comfortable for this will be your home for the rest of your miserable life. I shall return shortly."

She went pale, her thin face sweaty from exertion. She looked stunned and he had difficulty believing her shock was real. "You would kill me for defending myself?"

He paused at the door. "Nay. I would kill you for harming Lady Remington. You will be a thorn in my side no longer."

Her mouth opened in panic. "But what about Trenton? You would deprive my son of..."

"You birthed the lad, Mari-Elle, and that is all. You were never his mother; you never loved him nor cared for him," he said with quiet bitterness. "He shall hardly miss you."

She shrieked weakly and collapsed to her knees. Quitting the cell, he bolted the heavy door and locked it with the giant lock that was hanging from the hook-and-eye. He did not even know where the key was to open the lock and he did not care.

Remington was still asleep when he returned. Patrick informed him briefly that Rastus the surgeon had already seen her, but little more. Rushed, Gaston chased both Eudora and Patrick out for the moment, his eyes riveted to her face as he knelt beside the bed. She had rolled onto her back somewhat, her angelic face reflecting the soft glow from the hearth. He regretted deeply that he must wake her, but he must know what happened in order to deal better with Mari-Elle.

She did not respond to his gentle voice at first, and he took to kissing her softly, hoping that she would respond to his touch. As he hoped, she stirred slightly and her eyes fluttered open. The first thing she did was try to raise her right arm to touch him and she cried out from the stab of pain.

He soothed her tenderly. "It's all right, angel, just lie still. I am sorry to have awoken you, but I must speak with you."

Her left hand covered her shoulder as if she could massage the pain away. Her breathing was shallow and rapid. "What... what's wrong?"

"Nothing at all," he said softly. "But I need to know what happened this eve with Mari-Elle. Can you remember very much?"

She blinked, her pupils dilated with pain. "She came into your room while I was asleep. I remember seeing her hovering over me with a terrible look to her eye, and I saw the dagger before she stabbed me. She ran away and I think I tried to follow her," her breathing was faint; Rastus had given her a powerful sleeping potion that was trying to reclaim her. "I do not remember much after that. I am sorry."

He kissed her cheek gently. "No need, angel. Go back to sleep now." He had all he had come for.

"Where are you going?" she asked, her voice no more than a whisper.

"Nowhere to concern yourself over," he said. "I shall return as quickly as I can."

"Have you found her? She hasn't hurt anyone else, has she?" she moved a bit and winced.

He put his huge hand against her cheek, feeling that she did indeed have a bit of a fever. "Nay, my sweet angel, she has not. Everything is fine," he pulled back the coverlet over her naked shoulder. "Go back to sleep."

She sighed and closed her eyes, sleep claiming her almost immediately. He kissed her tenderly once more before ushering Eudora back into the room, leaving Patrick standing in the hall as he closed the door behind the older woman.

"There is no longer any need for you to stand guard in the room," he told his cousin. "You may return to your regular duties."

"Did you find Mari-Elle?" Patrick asked.

Gaston ran his fingers through his hair. "Aye."

"Where is she?" his cousin asked.

"In the vault," Gaston said ominously, nodding his head in the direction of the door he had smashed earlier. "Get some men on that door come sunrise, but I do not want them disturbing Remi. She needs to sleep."

"Aye," Patrick nodded, glancing at the door. "God's Toes, Gaston, what in the hell went on here tonight?"

Gaston rolled his eyes in frustration. "What in the hell *hasn't* gone on?"

He left his cousin shaking his head, wondering what sort of chaos was overtaking them. Everything seemed normal until Mari-Elle arrived, but Patrick suspected she would not be a problem after tonight. Gaston was a merciful man with those who deserved it; Mari-Elle, in his opinion, did not.

Gaston met with Arik on his way to the vault.

"I hear you found her," Arik said gravely. "Did you dispose of her yet?"

"I am on my way," Gaston replied, grim.

Arik started to walk with him but Gaston stopped him. "Nay, man, I will do this alone."

Arik paused. "Gaston... mayhap I should do this," he said. "After all, 'tis Trenton's mother we speak of and I do not believe your son will be comfortable with the fact that his father killed his mother."

Gaston pondered his statement a moment. "Yet I cannot ask anyone else to do what must be done. The woman has been a thorn in my side for thirteen years, Arik. The shame and cruelty she has brought into the house of de Russe is mine to bear. Tonight she tried to kill someone... she must be punished, and I alone must do it. "

Arik looked at him, trying to read his thoughts. "Are you using the attempt on Remington's life as an excuse to rid yourself of your hated wife? Or are your motives more true than that?"

Gaston's jaw ticked. "What are you saying? That I am being completely selfish in my motives? With Mari-Elle out of the way, I will be free to pursue my desires? Arik, I should hope that you would know me better than that."

"I thought I did," Arik said quietly, though not accusingly. "But then I have never known you to be in love before."

Gaston's gaze lingered on his tall; pale friend. He thought to deny the allegation, but reconsidered. He was not a graceful liar.

"She must be punished," he said simply. "Who is to say that if I set her free, that she will not try to kill again? I cannot risk a murderess running amongst us, no matter who she is. You have always known my wrath to be swift and severe."

Arik nodded, fairly convinced that Gaston's motives were sincere. Of course, he heartily agreed with him, but his lord of late had puzzled him greatly. For his own peace of mind, he felt the need to pry a bit.

Gaston continued to the stairwell that led to the vault. Arik had followed, anyway, although neither one knew why or tried to stop him. The sharp, acrid odor assaulted their nostrils as they moved to the first locked cell.

"The bolt is locked," Arik pointed out.

Gaston looked at it a moment. "No matter," wrapping his hands around the thick wooden bolt, he pulled and worked at it until it weakened. Grunting with effort, he continued to tug and twist until the old wooden bolt popped free of the door with a great snap of rotted splinters.

The bolt hung loose, swinging on the wall as it was still attached to the lock, and Gaston opened the door. Arik shook his head at the display of strength; the man was beyond believing.

The cell was dark except for the dim flicker of the torch. Gaston could see the figure of his wife huddled against the wall and put out his hand to stop Arik from following any further.

Arik understood and stepped back into the hall as Gaston proceeded in, looming over his wife. He called her name once, twice, and then finally knelt down beside the slumped form.

"Mari-Elle," he said firmly, putting out his hand to yank her to her feet.

He gave a tug but she was dead weight. Angered, he grasped both her arms and hauled her to her feet and was astonished to see a great pool of blood on the floor underneath her.

"Arik," he snapped.

Arik rushed to his side, his blue eyes widening at the blood. It was everywhere, soaking her skirt, the dirty straw. Gaston tried to rouse her as Arik searched for the wound.

"Where is this coming from?" Gaston demanded.

Arik was fumbling with the folds of the surcoat. "I do not see a weapon, or a tear in the surcoat, nothing," he looked around the floor. "Lay her down, Gaston. Mayhap we can discover where she has injured herself."

Gaston laid Mari-Elle on her back. Her pulse was extremely weak and the two men scrutinized her closely for damage. The blood was saturating her from the waist down, it seemed, and finally Gaston tossed up her skirts to get a better look. He was shocked to see that she was bleeding from her privates, gushing bright red and black clots.

"My God," he hissed. "What in the hell happened?"

Arik, having seen his share of blood and gore throughout his career, was nearly sickened by the sight. A distasteful expression creased his face.

"Mayhap you should send for her physician," he suggested. He certainly did not want to deal with it.

"There is nothing he can do," Gaston replied. "She's already dead."

Gaston had blood on his hands as he checked her pulse again. It was virtually non-existent, but it was still there. He shook his head. "Send for her physician.."

Arik left the dank, dark cell. Gaston crouched beside Mari-Elle, watching her life's blood drain away, knowing there was nothing he could do and not particularly sorry. In a sense, he was relieved; as cruel as the thought was, he was glad that some strange ailment had claimed her life. It had saved him the trouble.

Furthermore, when he told Trenton that his mother had passed on, he wanted to be able to tell him that it was of natural causes. Not because his father had wrung the life from her.

She died as he sat and watched. When the physician arrived twenty minutes later, the man did not look at all surprised. In fact, when he saw the state of his mistress, he slowed his movements considerably and seemed to take his time drawing forth his instruments and potions.

Gaston watched the thin healer, rising as the man ducked beside the body and examined her quite thoroughly. Arik and Nicolas had accompanied the physician and stood crowded in the doorway as the careful investigation was completed.

The moments passed slowly and the smell of urine was sharp to the nose as the knights waited for the healer to complete his task. Finally, the aged man stood up and began to replace his instruments.

"Well?" Gaston asked. "What killed her?"

The physician looked at the Dark Knight, the man of whom stories had been told and retold. He was incredibly massive and fierce-looking, and the physician did not blame his wife for taking smaller, less-threatening lovers. Surely a man this size had a voracious, violent appetite.

Dooley was also very aware that the child that had killed Lady de Russe was not her husband's. However, the woman had paid for her sins and there was naught her betrayed husband could do to her now.

"A rupture in her womb, I believe," Dooley said evenly. "Your wife was pregnant, my lord, and sometimes when the child roots itself too high in the womb, it will rupture the organ and bring almost immediate death."

Gaston was astonished but held his even expression. "She was pregnant?" he repeated slowly. "How far along was she?"

"Two, possibly three months," the physician replied. He could see the shock in the knight's eyes and suddenly had no desire to take the blame for the woman's indiscretions. "My lord, she swore me to secrecy. I was ordered to keep my mouth shut, and I did."

Gaston stared at the man a moment longer. "You are sure this is what killed her?"

The healer nodded. "As positive as I can be," he replied. "I have seen mishaps such as this before, and bleeding to death is always inevitable. I tried to forewarn your wife when I realized this pregnancy was not normal, but she would not listen. When I indicated something was wrong, she ignored me."

Gaston was stunned, angered, relieved. Yet he expected no less from Mari-Elle. True to the woman's character, the sport that she had so loved eventually killed her and he was not sorry in the least. In fact he felt as if a weight had been lifted from his shoulders. After 13 years of shame and humiliation, it was finally over.

Without a hind glance, he marched from the cell.

CHAPTER FOURTEEN

Trenton did not take the passing of his mother very well. Even though she had been a less than desirable parent, she had been the only parent he had ever known and he felt the loss terribly. Gaston tried to comfort his son as best he could, but the boy seemed not to want him around, and that fact saddened him greatly.

Yet, he was not surprised. He was still a virtual stranger to his son and he knew Trenton felt very much alone. He tried to explain that his mother had died suddenly, of natural causes, but he could tell Trenton doubted his word. After everything that had happened between Mari-Elle and himself, he could understand the boy's reluctance to believe that his father had not killed his mother.

As he stood facing his son, he realized he was greatly relieved to be able to tell the lad the truth that he had had nothing to do with the woman's death. Even if he had, it would have been justified, but he was relieved all the same. An eight-year-old boy might not understand adult "justice". Reluctantly, he did as was asked of him and left his son to grieve alone.

Remington slept until nearly noon the next day, running a moderate fever and then feeling lousy when she awoke. Her stomach hurt, her entire body ached, and Gaston sat with her while she twitched listlessly and snapped at Rastus when he changed her dressing.

Gaston relayed Mari-Elle's death, watching her lovely face go even paler. She said nothing after his explanation, not a question nor a comment, and he could see that she was shocked. He wondered if it was because she doubted his story as to the circumstances regarding his wife's death. She knew he was very capable of killing her himself and he thought he could read a new sort of fear in her eyes.

In truth, Remington did not know what to think. He had never lied to her before, but she thought the fact that Mari-Elle happened to bleed to death of a female ailment just when she happened to be locked in the vault very peculiar. She did not want to doubt his word, but the nagging suspicion remained.

She loved him so much that she believed him in spite of her reserve. She did not want to believe him capable of killing a woman, any woman. God only knew he had been nothing but tender and gentle with her.

The two of them went on to decide it would be best not to let Dane or Trenton know how she had received her wound, and Remington explained her condition to her son by saying she had accidentally fallen and hurt herself on the corner of an iron-and-glass table. If Dane did not believe her, he did not let on. There had been countless times where she had lied about a bruise or a scrape simply to spare him, and she wondered if he thought mayhap Gaston had injured her somehow. As much as he loved the Dark Knight, he was very used to male cruelty and somewhat took it in stride.

The afternoon progressed on, the heat and humidity of July miserable. It added tremendously to Remington's discomfort, especially with the fever, and Gaston felt truly sorry for her. Even though she wriggled endlessly in her attempt to find the impossible cool and comfortable position, she never uttered a word of complaint.

Finally, he had had enough watching her roll about and sent Eudora for cool water and a sponge. He chased the old woman away on the pretense he was going to further clean her wound, when in fact, he was going to strip her down and bathe her all over. He wanted to, and she needed something to make her more comfortable.

She was lying on her back, propped up slightly on some pillows as he sat the basin of cool water down beside her. Pale and sweaty, she eyed him suspiciously.

"What are you going to do with that?" she demanded. He unlaced the front of her shift, but was thwarted from removing it completely because it only loosened to her abdomen. She frowned.

"Surely you cannot be thinking to..." she was cut off as he grabbed hold of the shift and tore it straight down the middle, opening it completely. She gasped with surprise and he grinned at her.

"Do not worry," he told her. "I am merely going to bathe you, not ravish you. Although on second thought, the latter is not a half-bad idea."

"Gaston!" she admonished, though she was pleased with the attention. She'd never been bathed by a man before.

He gave her a wink and gingerly removed her right arm from the sleeve. She lifted her left arm and he pulled the other sleeve off, his gaze raking her seductively. She raised an eyebrow at him in disapproval, knowing his thoughts before he even voiced them.

Clearing his throat loudly and forcing himself to focus on the task at hand, he wrung out the sponge and began to bathe her as tenderly as a mother.

Remington simply lay there and let him, never having experienced something so completely caring in her whole life. He wanted nothing from her for his service; he was doing it entirely because of his feelings for her. They were his sole motivation and she was deeply touched.

He thoroughly and gently removed the dried blood from her skin. She intently watched his face, smiling at him when their eyes would meet and then amused to see how terribly hard he was trying to keep his attention on his task. She could read the desire in his eyes.

"Do not you have duties to attend to?" she asked him softly. "You have been with me all morning."

"You are my duty for the moment," he said, running the sponge along her flat belly. "I have nothing urgent, nothing that Arik and my knights cannot attend to."

She kept watching his face as he concentrated on his task. "What about Mari-Elle's funeral?"

He did not respond for a moment. "Arik is seeing to the details. I am sending her back to Clearwell for burial. I do not want her buried here."

"But what of Trenton?" she asked, concerned. "Surely he will want to attend his mother's funeral? Will you send him back to Clearwell, too?"

"Trenton stays with me," he said, unemotionally. "He understands."

She looked away as he bathed her legs, her toes. His attitude was insensitive at best and she found that surprising where Trenton was concerned.

"But...Gaston, she was his mother," she said after a moment. "How can you be so cold-hearted? Good or bad, she was still his mother. She had raised him from infancy and you, my lord, are practically a stranger to him. I think he should be allowed to see to his mother's burial."

He looked at her, a long look. Without replying, he lowered his head again to continue his task and she grew irritated. How could he be so cruel to his son? She drew up her legs, away from him, and yanked the thin sheet over her body to cover her naked flesh.

"I would sleep now," she said quietly, trying to roll to her left side.

He watched her a moment before tossing the sponge back into the basin. "Do not do this."

"Do what?" she grunted as she fought for a comfortable position. "I am not doing anything, except trying to find one spot on my body that does not ache like the devil. Why do not you go and seek Trenton? I am sure he could use his father right now."

She closed her eyes, hoping he would get the hint and leave her alone with her annoyance. But he continued to stand there for the longest time and she fought the urge to peer at him from behind her lashes.

"Do you think that I killed her?" he finally asked.

She opened her eyes. "Did you?"

"Nay."

"Then I do not think you killed her," she replied. "But I think you are being very hard on Trenton because of your hatred for his mother."

She saw his jaw tick and he came over to sit beside her on the bed. His huge hand gently grasped one of hers and she could read a flicker of dull emotion in his eyes.

"Mari-Elle died because she was pregnant," he said softly. "Her physician said the child had planted itself too high in the womb and she bled to death. It was coincidental that it happened in the vault, I assure you. I never laid a hand on her."

Remington's mouth fell open. "Oh, Gaston. Is that why she wanted to make a marriage with you suddenly? Because she was pregnant with someone else's child?"

He shrugged. "Most likely. She wanted me to bed her so she could tell me the child was mine."

Remington was filled with a hatred of her own for the woman. Reaching up, she pulled his great head down to her bosom to comfort him, to chase away the humiliation he was surely feeling. If the woman had not already been dead, she would have killed her herself.

"My love, I am so sorry for what she has done to you," she whispered. "But she has been duly punished for her sins, I believe. Yet I do not think you should punish Trenton for her sins as well. Let him see to her funeral."

"If you think it best, then I will," he said, his eyes closed against her warmth. "But I should go with him, as his father."

"Of course you should," she agreed. "But I do not want to leave you alone. The remainder of Henry's troops should be here with in a day at the most and I will not leave you with a keep full of soldiers."

She smiled. "So leave Arik and your cousins to protect my sisters and I. They are quite capable."

"Of course they are, but that is not the issue," his head came up, his eyes locking with her own. "I do not want to leave you, not even for a few days."

She was missing his point. "But... you said I would be well protected."

"You will. I just ...," frustrated because he could not find the proper words, he shook his head and reburied it in her bosom.

Remington tried to force him to look at her. "Just what? What were you going to say?"

He mumbled something into her skin but she couldn't hear him. "Gaston, speak to me. What did you say?"

He raised his head, looking like a little boy who had just been called upon by his instructor to recite. "I said I do not want you to forget about me."

She raised her eyebrows in surprise. "You do not wa...you would put so little faith in me?"

"No," he said quickly. "I mean, I have the greatest faith in you. 'Tis just that...oh, hell, I do not know what I mean. Just let me hold you for a time."

He pressed his head to her one more time and her good arm lay across his broad, broad shoulders. "You are terribly insecure, my lord."

"And why not? I have never had anything that truly belonged to me, at least nothing I was afraid of losing," he said softly.

"God, Remi, we have only known each other for a few short weeks and already I feel as if I can't take a breath without you by my side. It frightens me."

Her arm tightened. "You shall never be without me. I swear it."

He continued to hold her, to smell her and feel her warmth. Eventually her breathing became deep and regular and he lifted his head, studying her sleeping face. Carefully, he raised himself and made sure the linen sheet was tucked in about her shoulders. He was reluctant to leave, but he did indeed have duties to attend to and while she slept was a perfect opportunity.

Eudora was waiting in the hall like a vigilant dog and he ushered her in quietly, telling her explicitly where he would be and when should she need to find him. He wanted to make sure he could be found should Remington need him.

The bailey was bustling. Henry's troops had been sighted not an hour away and Arik was busy making preparations for their arrival. Gaston found his second on the inner wall, yelling down at some men who were clearing the last of the building debris.

"Well?" Arik asked before Gaston even came to a halt. "How is she?"

"Running a mild temperature and in a generally irritable mood, but well considering," he replied, his eyes roving over the newly finished team house. "Tell them to move the timbers from the side. I want that field clear."

Arik bellowed to the men again. "Mari-Elle's body is in the chapel. Her servants have already prepared the body and even now her ladies and household are holding vigilant prayer. You would have thought the bloody queen died the way they are carrying on."

"Is my son with them?" Gaston asked, watching the activity below him.

"Nay, I have not seen the lad," Arik glanced at him for the first time. "How did he handle the news?"

Gaston shrugged vaguely. "Quietly. 'Tis difficult to say," he leaned forward on the wall. "I have decided to accompany my son back to Clearwell to see to his mother's funeral. I will leave you here, in charge, until I return. I shall most likely take Patrick and Antonius with me to ride as escort, plus a few other lesser knights. I expect to be gone no more than four days."

"Four days?" Arik repeated. "Gaston, it will take you two days to reach Clearwell, especially with a funeral procession. How will you accomplish this?"

Gaston did not like to be questioned, not even by Arik. "I shall leave when the funeral is over and ride hard. It will not take more than a day and night to return home. Satisfied?"

"But you shall be carrying Trenton," Arik reminded him. "You must consider that. He is not used to riding as a soldier, Gaston. 'Twill be hard on him."

"He shall recover," Gaston replied shortly. "He's a sturdy young man, Arik, not a weakling child. Furthermore, with Henry's troops settling in, I do not want Remington or her sisters anywhere near the baileys. And they are never, ever to be alone. I want knights guarding them at all times."

Arik wasn't really surprised by the command, but he was against the entire idea of the women being at Mt. Holyoak altogether. "As you say, but I still think they would be much better off at Halsey Manor. I am extremely uncomfortable with them here, Gaston."

"I realize that," Gaston had the same concerns. "But as long as they are properly protected, we will have no trouble. And when word spreads that...well, suffice it to say we shall have no trouble when the men realize they take their life in their hands simply to gaze at the women."

Arik did not reply as he watched men-at-arms haul away large pieces of wood. "What are you going to do about Guy?"

"What do you mean?"

"Just that. With Mari-Elle gone, you have one problem solved," Arik went on casually. "But what are you going to do about Remington's husband?"

Gaston did not say anything for a moment. He stood unemotional, massive arms folded, watching his outer bailey being cleared. "Petition the church for an annulment. I have the power to obtain one, Arik. Do not doubt it."

Arik looked at him, surprise written on his face. "An annulment? My God, you mean to marry her? Honestly?"

"I do," Gaston replied, meeting Arik's gaze. "For the first time in my life, I know what I want. All of this time I have always felt...oh, hell, incomplete, I suppose. It's as if there was a void inside me I was constantly trying to fill by fighting and soldiering. That's why I am the best at what I do, Arik; I have been striving to satisfy myself since I was young, always trying to be better than I was the day before." He let out a heavy sigh, showing emotion for the first time as he leaned against the parapet. His gaze wandered up to the second floor of the castle above him. "I always thought I would be content when I was the best warrior in the realm, but even that failed to satisfy this gap in my soul. But now I have found what I was looking for, and I intend to have her."

Arik looked at him, astonished. "I have known you since we were both seven years old, Gaston, and I have never seen you this impassioned about anything. God be with you if that is what you truly desire, then. Most men fail to achieve even a part of that within their lives."

Gaston looked down over the bailey, watching the great gates opening and watching Patrick and Nicolas directing an entire company of men in the preparation efforts. "I'd give this all up, Arik. All of it just to be able to call her wife."

Arik found it difficult to believe what he was hearing; yet he was pleased all the same. In fact, he was more than pleased; mayhap the cold, stiff man he had known all of these years had finally found the key of happiness.

From experience, he knew Gaston was emotionally attached to no one, save his distant son. He had no friends, only loyal vassals, and Arik had never seen him respond to a woman in any way. Except this woman. It was astounding to say the very least.

He smiled at his lord. "Hopefully that will not be necessary. If anyone can procure an annulment, you can."

Gaston did not respond, lingering on his confession and his future. He felt strangely vulnerable; yet, his heart was lighter than he could ever remember. In fact, he had never felt this good about anything in his life.

"Not a word to anyone," he finally said. "This will not become public knowledge until I myself inform my vassals."

"Of course," Arik replied, deciding to see to the preparations below first-hand. But before he left, he slapped Gaston on the shoulder. "But I have a feeling your mightiest battle yet lies ahead."

Gaston raised an eyebrow in resignation. "And Pope Innocent will prove to be a powerful adversary should he not see things as he should."

Arik snorted a chuckle and moved for the ladder. Gaston paused only a moment longer before following, his mind moving from Remington to the tasks at hand, still amazed at the course his life was taking. The unexpected twist of the past few weeks left him wondering if he might wake up at any moment and discover it all to have been a dream.

Henry's new recruits arrived in droves. Gaston stood back, scrutinizing every man as Arik, Antonius, Patrick and Nicolas directed and sectioned off groups of men, settling some, lecturing others. Mass, organized chaos at its very best and Gaston watched with satisfaction at all he was master over. Aye, he would train them well, as Henry expected him to, reinforcing the north so that there would never again be any threat of rebellion from Yorkist loyalists.

The noise level was incredible. One thousand men filled the double baileys of Mt. Holyoak like water filling a lake, covering the grounds completely as Gaston's knights worked with feverish, precise organization to place them.

Divided up into companies, each of Gaston's thirty-five knights was in charge of a company of 30 men, more or less. These new soldiers had a company leader, a comrade of their choosing with whom they were allowed to communicate with regarding commands or questions. This company leader would then in turn act as liaison between the knights and the troops. Never were the soldiers allowed to speak directly to the knights unless permission was given, and under no circumstances were they to speak to Gaston. He was their liege, their trainer, and their god.

It was a very exacting hierarchy that they were sworn to adhere to under penalty of severe punishment.

It had always been thus in Gaston's theatre of training. That was why his men were considered the very best in the realm. As with everything else in Gaston's life, it was either black or white. You obeyed or you were punished; there was no in between, no excuses, and no failures.

The afternoon drug on in the oppressive heat as the new recruits were settled and given food. Gaston would not work them this day because they had been traveling since the night before, but he would demand them to an early sleep. He would order them up well before dawn to begin their regimens.

He immersed himself in his duties, although he had not forgotten about Remington. He would like to be there when she awoke, but item upon item pressed itself until he lost track of time. Well, mayhap if he could not be there when she awoke, then he would absolutely see her for before supper.

Remington slept a good deal of the afternoon, especially in the heat. Dane was in the company of his aunts, leaving Eudora free to tend to Remington exclusively. Even after she awoke, not a word was said about the night's events, nor Mari-Elle's sudden death. Eudora had heard all of the rumors, of course, but she would not repeat them to her mistress. The lady had had enough sorrow and woes in her short life, and if she had indeed found a man that cared for her enough to kill for her, then Eudora was happy for her.

Jasmine wandered in toward the waning hours of the afternoon and dismissed the old servant. She seemed pensive and distant and Remington lay on her side, watching her sister's wispy form as she gazed out over the bailey.

"They say he killed his wife because of what she did to you," Jasmine finally said.

"She died without his help, Jassy," Remington replied softly. "It was purely coincidental."

Jasmine shook her head. "He's so big, Remi. Does not he scare you?"

Remington smiled faintly. "Nay. He's as gentle as a kitten. You mustn't fear him, either."

Jasmine shrugged, her blue eyes watching the activity below. "I have never seen so many soldiers in my life. There must be thousands, at least."

Remington shifted slightly, wincing with the pain. "What's wrong, Jasmine?"

"Wrong? What do you mean?" Jasmine said. "I mean that you are not usually this solicitous," Remington said plainly. "What are you thinking, sweetheart? Are you afraid because you heard that Gaston killed his wife?"

"Nay," Jasmine insisted. "If he did, she deserved it for what she did to you and I applaud him. Antonius said he should have killed her long ago for the shame she brought him."

Remington realized then that Gaston's secrets were not merely between them. His knights knew of Mari-Elle's indiscretions and she was not surprised that Jasmine had been told.

"Do not….do not repeat to anyone what you have been told, Jassy," she said softly. "Gaston is a proud man and what his wife did humiliated him terribly. He hated her a great deal."

"So did the knights," Jasmine sniffed. "Just as our household hates Guy. Why couldn't the hand of God snuff out Guy's life the way Mari-Elle's life was taken?"

Remington almost blurted the physical reasons as to why Guy could not have died in the same manner, but she held her tongue. "He's out of our lives forever, Jassy. That should be sufficient."

"I know," Jasmine turned slowly to face her sister, her expression veiled. "Which is why…are you sure he shall never return?"

"We have Gaston's word," she said softly, and then added hesitantly. "And do you want to know why? He's going to London to petition the church for an annulment to my marriage. He wants to marry me, Jasmine."

Jasmine's eyes widened. "Truly? Oh, Remi, is it possible? Can he do it?"

"He says he can, and I believe him," Remington said, pleased at her sister's happiness.

Jasmine smiled hopefully. "Then I do, too. Rory and Skye will be so happy."

"Do not tell them, not just yet," Remington admonished softly. "The less people who know, the better."

Jasmine nodded, mulling over the revelation. Then it made what she was about to ask that much easier.

"Remi....since Guy will never again harm us, I...." She struggled with her words, finally deciding to come straight to the point. "I want Mary back. I want to go get her today."

Now Remington was shocked. "Mary? Well....I see no reason why not, Jassy. But why today? Can you not wait until I am feeling better so that I may go with you? I should, you know."

Jasmine's face washed with great emotion and Remington was sorry she had dampened her enthusiasm. "I can't wait another day, Remi. I want my baby back. It has been nearly two long years and I have never even seen her."

Remington was not about to deny her, for she wanted the same thing. Mary's second birthday was drawing close next month and she knew a day did not pass when Jasmine was not thinking of her baby. The baby Guy had sired and then forced her to relinquish. Remington only knew she would die if Dane were taken away from her.

"Very well," she said softly, gazing at her sister a moment. "Does Antonius know?"

Jasmine shook her head shamefully. "Nay. I have not told him. I have not had the nerve. I thought it would be better to let him see the baby and then explain."

Remington smiled faintly. "So he has declared his intentions for you?"

Jasmine shrugged, flushing. "He tells me he cares for me."

"Does he know about Guy?"

"Aye," Jasmine whispered. "I told him... I had to."

"Had to?" Remington repeated, and then suddenly understood. "He bedded you?"

Jasmine nodded. "I cried the whole time. I have never....I never knew it could be so tender, so loving. Remi, I have been raped on a daily basis since I was seventeen. I never knew the act was meant to be wonderful."

Tears sprang to Remington's eyes, tears of guilt and pain at what her sisters had been subjected to. She couldn't stop what had happened and she was forever cursing her helplessness. To hear Jasmine's confession was both wonderful and agonizing.

"Then get me up," she said, struggling to sit. "I am going with you."

"You cannot," Jasmine rushed to her sister, wanting to stop her but not wanting to touch her for fear of causing her further pain. "You were almost killed last night and..."

"I was not," Remington snapped gently, fighting to a sitting position as the world around her reeled. "I shall be fine, truly. Just....let me sit here a moment and rest. Get my wine-colored silk from the wardrobe, please."

Jasmine held onto her sister's good arm, watching her fearfully. She was far too weak to risk a ride into town, yet she was well aware of Remington's determination. If she said she was going, then she was going.

"Oh, Remi, I do not think...." she sputtered.

"My wine-colored silk," Remington repeated patiently, the world rocking a little less. With all the pain that her sister had been through, she could have been on her deathbed and would have still insisted to ride into town with her to pick up the child. She had to do this.

Jasmine let out a little sigh of fear and released her sister, moving obediently to the wardrobe and drawing forth a beautiful silk with gold leafing.

"Good," Remington said, feeling terribly weak. "Now, send one of the soldiers guarding the hall down to the stables and see that two palfreys are saddled. Tell him to have the animals brought around to the side gate, by the kitchens."

Jasmine stood by indecisively a moment while Remington struggled gingerly from her torn shift. She glanced up at her sister. "Go. Hurry, for we want to return before dark."

"You do not have to do this," Jasmine said softly.

"Aye, I do," Remington grunted as she reached for her surcoat. "'Twas my husband who caused you this pain, sweetheart, and I must do what I can to make it up to you."

"You do not," Jasmine insisted gently.

"I do," Remington fixed her with a hard look. "Hurry up, now, and do as you are told."

With great reluctance, Jasmine went into the hall and sent the nearest soldier on the errand. Pausing for a few minutes to retrieve her own cloak and heavy shoes, she returned to her sister's room.

Remington was already half dressed but could not manage the stays. She stood weakly, gripping the canopy post for support as Jasmine silently did her stays.

"You are too weak," Jasmine hissed when the last stay was fastened.

"Go find my hose and shoes," Remington ignored her statement, although she indeed felt terrible. She honestly did not know how in the hell she was going to ride into Boroughbridge and back.

Jasmine had to put her hose and her shoes on for her, as her right arm was nearly useless. Rastus had actually bandaged it tight against her torso, but she had complained so much about the bindings that he had removed them. Swinging loose, she wished the arm were still bandaged tight because the pain was excruciating every time she moved it.

Her pain and weakness was making her shake and sweat, and Jasmine was terribly reluctant to let her go.

"How are you going to ride a horse with that arm?" she demanded.

"With my left hand," Remington said firmly. "'Twill be no problem. Get my cloak, please."

Jasmine let out a sigh of pure frustration and retrieved the matching cloak. Remington winced visibly when the material was laid across her shoulders.

"Remi," Jasmine protested at the pained expression.

"Quiet," Remington snapped. "Let us be gone. The horses should be ready by now and...."

"Nay, they are not," Gaston stood in the doorway. Both women swung around, startled at the sound of his deep baritone. He did not look pleased.

"Gaston," Remington exclaimed weakly. "I thought you were with your new troops."

He entered the room deliberately, eyeing her. "I was until a loyal soldier told me that your sister had ordered palfreys readied. Your palfrey."

Remington looked exceedingly guilty as Jasmine leaned close to her sister, raging quietly. "That damn soldier ran right to him."

"Well that he did, madam," Gaston said sharply, pointing to the door. "I will speak with your sister alone."

Jasmine bolted, slamming the door in her wake. Remington eased herself onto the bed as Gaston approached her.

"Do not yell at me," she said softly, avoiding his hard gaze. "'Tis not as it appears."

"Just where in the hell were you going?" he demanded. "Look at you, Remi. You can hardly stand. How were you going to stay mounted on a horse?"

She hung her head as he loomed over her. "Well? I am waiting for an answer."

She was reluctant to tell him anything, but decided to inform him of the whole, sordid affair. He already knew the majority of Guy's atrocities; surely one more would not shock him. For Jasmine's sake, she must tell.

"Sit down," she begged softly, raising her face to meet his when he did not move. "Please?"

He did, but he sat in a chair opposite her, not next to her on the bed as she had hoped. "I am waiting, madam."

She met his gaze. "Jasmine has a secret. Not even Antonius knows this."

"What?" he demanded. Remington took a deep breath to bolster her strength and her courage. He was most intimidating when he was angry. "Two and a half years ago, she became pregnant. Guy, of course, was the father and the moment the child was born, he gave her away to a peasant family to raise as their own. Jasmine has mourned for two years in want of her baby and now that Guy is never to return, she intends to have her back. I was going to go with her because she did not want Antonius, or any of the other knights, to know."

His tensed expression instantly softened, as she had hoped. He stared at her a long moment before rising from the chair. "By God's Bloody Rood," he muttered, raking his fingers through his hair to slick it back. He chewed on her statement a moment before finally turning to her. "Why must she go now? Why today?"

"When you were separated from Trenton, was there not a day that passed that you did not wish to hold him?" she returned softly. "She cannot wait any longer, Gaston. She wants her baby and I must take her."

"But why you?" he demanded softly, moving to the bed. "Why can't Rory or Skye go with her?"

To his dismay, Remington suddenly burst into soft sobs. Tears coursed down her cheeks and he knelt swiftly to wipe them away. "I am sorry, angel. Do not cry. Please."

"I have to go because... because I was the one who took the baby to them at the first," she whispered miserably. "Guy made me hand the infant over, alone. I must go because the family will not recognize Jasmine. But they will recognize me and know that I have returned for her."

He let out a hissing curse, wiping at the tears and kissing her left hand. "God, Remi," he whispered. He was so torn with indecision that it was making him insane, and his hatred of Guy Stoneley was growing by leaps and bounds. He would not deny her, but he certainly did not want her going this day. She was far too weak. "But do you have to go today? Can this not wait for a day or so, love?"

She wiped at her nose. "You shall have to ask my sister."

He kissed her hand again. "I will, then. You should not be out and about."

He rose, his gaze lingering on her dark head a moment and the rage of the devil filling him. To think of her at the mercy of her deviant husband made him crazed, but he calmed himself with the knowledge that her trials were over.

With everything Mari-Elle had done to him, it had been nothing compared to her humiliation. When he thought of Jasmine bearing a bastard from her sister's husband, it infuriated him to the point where he literally tore the door off its hinges as he attempted to open it.

Remington gasped, her eyes wide as he sheepishly propped the door against the jamb so it would not fall. She knew he wasn't angry with her, but his display of strength awed her just the same. Recovering her shock, she cocked an eyebrow.

"We will have no more doors left in this corridor if you continue with your uncontrolled outbursts," she teased gently.

He twisted his mouth wryly in agreement, making sure the door was not about to fall over before stepping into the hall in search of Jasmine.

The blond sister was not difficult to find; she was walking toward him, eyeing the door with apprehension. "Where's Remi?"

"On the bed where she should be," he replied, looking at the woman through new eyes. No wonder she was the more emotional of the group with everything that had happened. "I would speak with you, Jasmine."

Jasmine looked at him and knew instantly that Remington had told him everything. Her eyes widened. "She told you."

He could see the fury of betrayal and he sought to calm her. "Aye, she did," he said quietly. "I have but two questions for you; must you go this day, and if you must, do you believe the family will turn the child over to you with my assurance that you are the true parent? Remington is fearful they will not release the child to anyone but her, and I do not want her out of bed much less traveling."

Jasmine was gearing up for a rage, but Gaston's calm words doused her fire. He was speaking casually, as if the fact that she bore a bastard meant nothing in the world. He did not speak to her as if she were a lower life form, or a charity case. He spoke to her as one would speak to a lady of noble breeding. But the concern in his voice was evident and it disarmed her.

Her guard went down. "I…. I want my babe."

He could read the torment in her eyes, torment of separation from a child that he knew very well. "Will they release the child on my word?"

Jasmine's eyes began to well but she fought them back. "I do not know, my lord. If they do not?"

He looked at her a moment. "Gather your cloak and a blanket for the child. Let me tell your sister our plans and we shall be on our way."

Jasmine blinked bewilderedly; amazed that he would actually take an active interest in her problem. She'd never had a man take her side in anything, and she found the support to be overwhelming.

Nodding unsteadily, she moved past him to gather her things.

Gaston went back into the bedchamber where Remington was to find her lying back on the bed with her eyes closed. Her angelic face was pale and drawn and he felt a pang of concern for her fatigue.

"Sit up, angel, and let me get this cloak off," he said gently, pulling her up carefully.

"Did you speak with Jasmine?" she asked wearily.

"Aye," he tossed the cloak aside and gently lifted her, placing her on the pillows and pulling the coverlet over her. "You rest now and I shall return later."

"Where are you going?" she asked, closing her eyes as he tucked her in.

He braced his arms on either side of her, gazing down at her sweet face. "To retrieve a relative. I shall send Eudora in with your supper, and I want you to eat something. Do you understand?"

She smiled softly at him, her left hand reaching up to stroke his stubbled face. "I love you, Dark Knight."

He kissed the palm of her hand and touched her forehead quickly to make sure her fever was moderate. "Rest. I shall be back."

CHAPTER FIFTEEN

Remington cried the first time she saw Mary. Nearly two years old with silken blond hair, she was the most beautiful child she had ever seen. For the first day Jasmine could not go five minutes without weeping, setting off Rory and Skye every time. Gaston merely shook his head at the women; they were comical as well as touching and he was pleased he had been able to assist.

It had not been overly difficult; the peasant family already had six children to feed and was not reluctant to return Mary to her rightful mother. But the child had been clean and well fed, and Gaston had paid the family well enough to support them easily for years to come.

When he saw Jasmine cuddle her daughter for the first time, the great expense had been worth every pence. He had chuckled at himself for becoming soft in his old age, smiling at the mother and daughter and wondering fleetingly if he and Remington would be so blessed one day.

Antonius had not been difficult, either. Gaston explained the situation because Jasmine had been too choked up to speak a complete sentence. Confession ended, without another word said, Antonius had put his arms around the two ladies and had kissed them both tenderly. Gaston had been impressed with his knight's compassion.

It was late when he checked in on Trenton. The lad was sound asleep in his big room, his face unlined with the terrible events he had suffered through. Gaston was deeply saddened at his son's grief and he wished he could comfort the boy, but Trenton seemed to be mightily confused and distant. Gaston could only hope the morrow dawned a bit brighter for his son.

He slept with Remington that night in the small lady's bed, much smaller than his massive one. She ran a fever most of the night, sleeping listlessly, but by the time morning broke so had the fever. When

Eudora brought the morning meal, Remington sat up and ate nearly an entire bowl of porridge and honey and he was pleased to see that she was recovering well.

After the dishes were cleared away and Remington and Gaston were talking between themselves, Dane wandered into the room aimlessly. Both adults focused on the young lad.

"What's the matter, sweetheart?" Remington asked. "Why the long face?"

He frowned and toyed with the coverlet. "Nothing."

Gaston was sitting in the big chair next to the bed. "Did you see your new cousin?"

His scowl was evident. "Aye."

Remington raised her eyebrows expectantly. "And?"

He turned away from his mother irritably. "And it's just a girl. Another girl."

"Girls aren't so bad, Dane," Gaston said with a faint smile. "You shall come to realize that one day."

Dane made such a face that Gaston almost laughed. "I do not want any more girls."

"Then go find Trenton. Surely you two can find something to do," Remington suggested.

"He does not want to play," Dane said forlornly. "I knocked at his door but he told me to go away. I told him I was sorry about his mother, but he yelled at me and told me it was your fault."

He was looking at Remington, who in turn glanced at Gaston. He scratched his chin leisurely and rose on his massive legs. "Mayhap we should go see Trenton together, Dane."

He did not give the lad a chance to protest as he grabbed him by the shoulders and urged him through the door. He paused a moment before following him, long enough to kiss Remington sweetly. "I have got other duties to see to this morn."

She smiled. "Aye, a whole keep full of new soldiers to keep you busy."

He returned her smile. "Rest this morn, angel. You need to regain your strength."

Her face fell with mock disappointment. "But I was so looking forward to playing with Mary."

"Leave the child to become used to her mother," he said sternly. "You shall have plenty of time to play with her later."

She stuck her tongue out at him and he scowled severely, but the mood was light. With a shake of his finger, he moved past the unhinged door.

Dane was silent the entire walk to Trenton's room.

"My mother did not have anything to do with your wife's death, did she?" he finally asked as they approached Trenton's door.

"Nay," Gaston replied firmly. "Nor did I. Her death was of natural causes, Dane. Do not worry yourself."

Dane still looked doubtful as Gaston knocked on his son's door.

"Go away," Trenton hollered.

Gaston unlatched the door. "By what right do you use that tone, Master de Russe?"

Trenton looked surprised to see his father, but visibly frowned at Dane. Gaston could sense the hostility, the jealousy, and the pain. Rapidly, he came to a decision.

"Gather your most important items, Trenton," he said briskly. "Clothes, shoes, anything of sentimental value. You will no longer be occupying this room after today."

Trenton looked uncertain. "Wh... why, father? What's wrong?"

He would not allow his son to wallow in grief. The sooner he moved on with his young life, the better, and Gaston had plans for him.

"Nothing, but there is much to do as you lie about here in self-pity," Gaston said, moving into the room. "Tomorrow, we leave for Clearwell to bury your mother. When we return, you will begin your training alongside Master Stoneley. We will move your items into the troop house this day."

Trenton moved mechanically off the bed simply because his father seemed so determined that he do so. Blindly, he dug out his traveling satchel and began to gather his things, not even stopping to think what he was packing. He was so terribly confused and hurt that he was simply doing as ordered with no feeling about it whatsoever.

He did not even know why he hurt so much. He knew his mother had not really cared for him, but she had been there when his father wasn't. She was the only parent he had even known. Now she was gone and he was in the company of strangers, including his father.

His mother had told him that his father did not like children. It was hard to believe when his father was so nice to him, but his mother would not lie... would she? He was afraid and disoriented.

"Am I to start training, too?" Dane piped up eagerly. "Can I move my things into the troop house?"

Gaston thought of Remington's reaction when he informed her that Dane would no longer be living within the walls of the castle. He furthermore dreaded telling her that he would allow no contact with her son for the first three months, and then limited contact thereafter. If Dane were to be a strong, independent man, then he would have to cut his mother's apron strings.

Unfortunately, Gaston did not think that Remington was emotionally up to the separation at the moment.

"We shall move your things when Trenton and I return from Clearwell," he said, putting his huge hand on Dane's shoulder. "Meanwhile, not a word to your mother. 'Twill upset her to know her son is growing to be a man sooner than she had hoped."

Dane nodded, a bit disappointed that he could not move into the troop house right away, but encouraged just the same. He so desperately wanted to learn to be a knight.

Trenton had jammed nearly everything he could grab into his traveling satchel. Dane bent over and picked up a pair of leather shoes from the floor.

"Here," he put them on the bed next to the bag.

Trenton's face darkened as he picked up the shoes and packed them, avoided Dane's gaze. Dane frowned; he did not like being ignored.

"Why are you mad at me?" he demanded. "I did not do anything."

Trenton's brow furrowed sharply. "I am not mad....I just do not feel like playing with you today."

"Why not?" Dane scowled. "I want to go fishing."

"I do not want to fish," Trenton returned hostilely.

"Then let's go search the woods for fox pups. I know where there is a fox burrow," Dane suggested.

Trenton actually looked interested, but his face rapidly darkened again. "I do not wanna."

Dane was not going to take no for an answer. "Come on! After you get back from Clearwell, we shall be training all day and won't have time to explore the woods or go fishing."

Trenton was slowly being swayed, but Gaston could see his reluctance. "Go on, Trenton. This will be the last free day you have for some time."

Trenton looked at his father, finally shrugging as he latched his bag. "Mayhap for a little while."

Gaston smiled. "Good lad."

Dane was up and running for the door. "Come on, Trenton. Hurry up. You are too slow."

"Am not," Trenton snapped, following.

Dane was already rushing down the corridor, but Trenton paused in the doorway. His brown eyes were wide on his father.

"You are going with me to bury mother?" he asked softly.

"Aye," Gaston replied. "As your father, 'tis my place. Never again will you and I be separated, Trenton. I promise you."

That simple statement greatly bolstered Trenton's sagging spirit. He wanted to believe it to be true, but after everything his mother had told him, it was difficult.

Not knowing what to say, he lowered his gaze and disappeared after his friend.

Arik had the new recruits up and moving. Even though it was hours before noon, the men had already been up since before daybreak. The smell of sweat and dirt was heavy in the outer bailey as 15 companies of men went through the basic motions of hand-to-hand combat, repetition of movements that were supervised by their company commanders as well as Arik, Patrick and Antonius. Nicolas ran up and down the ranks yelling like a fiend, demanding the men to go above and beyond their limits.

Gaston stood atop the inner wall, observing his troops like Zeus from Olympus. Arik kept turning to look at him, silent messages passing between them making sure all was progressing with Gaston's approval. 'Twas Gaston who detailed the regimes, the schedules, and his men who carried them out.

Gaston only remained an observer for less than an hour before he went down into the mass of men and began coaching them himself. He enjoyed being an active participant, instructing and encouraging and seeing the results.

The morning progressed, the humidity soared, and Gaston had his knights remove their armor. Since they were not practicing with weapons, he saw no harm in allowing his men to be more comfortable. Even he removed his armor, and his shirt, parading about the ground like a mythical beast, Hercules from old as his magnificent torso glistened under the warm sun.

Just before noon, the sentries high on the outer wall announced riders approaching with the burst of a horn. Gaston, Arik and Patrick met the incoming soldiers at the portcullis, studying the three soldiers on well-kept warhorses. Even though there was no outward sign of a threat, Gaston kept the portcullis down, feeling rather naked that he was armorless.

The horses were sweating rivers and the soldiers appeared exhausted as they drew the horses to a weaving halt.

"My lord de Russe," one of the knights saluted sharply. "I bring news from Sir James de Wolfe of Templehurst."

Gaston knew de Wolfe well. He was young, but extremely talented and skilled. Henry had put the knight in charge of Humberside, just as he himself was in charge of order in Yorkshire.

He ordered the portcullis raised.

"What's amiss?" he demanded.

One of the men dismounted. "Trouble, my lord. Three feudal barons, loyal to Richard, have launched a siege to Templehurst in hopes of driving de Wolfe out. He sent us to request reinforcements from Mt. Holyoak."

"What is the strength of the opposition force?" Gaston asked.

"Mayhap five to six hundred men," the soldier replied. "De Wolfe has a force of four hundred, but we are holding Templehurst without a problem at the moment. 'Twould seem the barons are less interested in killing us as they are interested in simply chasing us out."

Gaston raised an eyebrow, glancing at Arik. "De Wolfe is hated about as much as I am. He fought for Northumberland, you know. Pledged loyalty to Henry when the earl was killed at Bosworth."

"De Wolfe's family goes back to the days of Richard and the quest," Arik commented. "He comes from a long line of distinguished, powerful knights. He should have no trouble holding Templehurst until we arrive."

Gaston jerked his head in a silent command and Arik was moving. He could read his lord's mind when it came to battles. Gaston ushered the soldiers in to Patrick's care and moved for the castle, focusing on what lay ahead. Allowing time to assemble his troops and necessary preparations, they could be on the road to Templehurst within two hours.

His squires raced after him as he made his way to the master chamber. He passed by Remington's room without stopping, preferring to don his armor before saying his good-byes.

As he reached his room and his squires began helping him dress, it occurred to him that this battle would be a new experience; he was actually concerned with his own mortality. What if something happened and he did not return to Remington? Horrible, bitter fantasies filled his mind and he angrily chased them off. He had never even been seriously injured in battle in all of his thirteen years as a knight; surely a simple skirmish would not destroy him.   Even before he left, he was eager to return to Remington.

He leaned over while one of the boys pulled a padded woolen shirt over his head. He already wore leather breeches and boots, and another squire helped him into a leather vest and pulled it snug to protect against the chafing of the armor.

His shortened hauberk went on next, followed by his breastplate, plate armor for his arms, and his leg armor. The squires worked quickly, silently, as they had done this for their lord many a time and were quite adept at it. Gaston simply stood still with his arms outstretched as they worked, his mind focusing on the battle ahead.

This was what he had been sent to Yorkshire for, to keep the peace. He had been hopeful from the first that he would not have to forcibly crush the resistance, but the Yorkists were a die-hard lot and this war had been going on for many, many years. It would take many more years to ease the tensions.

In little time he was in full battle armor, all gleaming steel and black leather. The squires left him quickly, racing from the room with his various weapons gripped in their hands, taking them to the bailey where they would be secured to Taran. Gaston preferred to keep all of his war implements with him in his chamber so that he knew exactly where they were should they be needed. Weapons that were kept close were less easily sabotaged or stolen.

His huge boots echoed loudly in the hall as he made his way to Remington's room, mulling over in his mind what he was going to say to her. Good-bye did not seem quite sufficient, yet he was embarrassed to make a huge emotional display. He hoped the words would simply come to him as he crossed through the threshold with the destroyed door.

Remington was sitting up in bed in a clean robe. Her hair was still damp, evidence that someone had washed it clean for her, and she faced him expectantly, her eyes instantly widening.

"I heard you come down the hall," she said, eyeing his armor. "What's the matter?"

He would have liked nothing better than to take her in his arms, but the bulky armor and her wound made that feat difficult. He moved to the end of the bed, extending his massive gauntlet to her and she instantly grasped it with her good hand.

"Nothing to worry about," he said. "One of Henry's vassals has requested assistance with a few unruly barons."

Her face fell. "A war?"

He smiled faintly. "Nothing of the sort, angel. A skirmish. A fist-fight, most likely. Mayhap if I yell loud enough I can force them to behave without a sword drawn; who knows? I doubt I shall be gone long enough for you to miss me."

"I miss you already," she said sadly, pulling gently on his hand. "I wish you did not have to go, my love. I am afraid for you."

His smile broadened. "Fear not for me, my lady. Fear for those fools who have dared provoke my wrath. All of the north knows that the Dark Knight is constable, and anyone who knowingly inflames my anger is stupid."

Her gaze lingered on him. She knew it was silly for her to make a fuss, for the man had been fighting wars for years and had survived whole. Yet her heart ached to know that he was leaving her, even for a little while.

"What of Mari-Elle?" she asked softly. "She must be buried in this heat."

He sighed. "I know that. If I do not return by the morning of the second day of my departure, then you have my permission to bury her."

She nodded somberly. He tapped her gently under the chin. "How are you feeling? Better?"

"I was until you told me of your imminent departure," she said, depressed.

He bent over, armor and all, and raised her hand to his lips. His mouth was warm and soft and wild chills shot up her arm as he kissed first the back, and then the palm of her hand tenderly.

"Be of good cheer, my lady," he said softly. "Know that I will return to you as soon as I am able."

His manner was relaxed and confident, helping her to feel more confident, too. Timidly, she brushed the breastplate of his armor with the tips of her fingers. "You look as you did the very first time I saw you. You were the most terrifying sight I had ever beheld."

"And now?"

She smiled, brightening her pale face. "You are the most wonderful, powerful, and magnificent sight I have ever beheld."

He straightened, latching his helm to the lip of his breastplate. "Compliments for me? Am I not still terrifying?"

"Not to me, my love," she whispered.

He could feel the emotions raging from her, mingling with his own and making his chest tighten. Gently, he touched her cheek with a gloved finger, wishing he could do much, much more.

"I shall return," he said, his voice hoarse. By God, if he did not miss her already.

Remington heard his footsteps fade down the hall. Even though he had been unconcerned about the entire situation, fear still clutched her. The fact that she had just smiled at him not moments before did not prevent hot tears from filling her eyes as she stared into the space of her chamber.

CHAPTER SIXTEEN

M ari-Elle had to be buried at Mt. Holyoak. The heat at early August was oppressive and the body had begun to deteriorate terribly. Just after sunrise on the second day after Gaston's departure, Lady de Russe was buried in the small grove of oaks where generations of Guy's family had been buried. Located on the edges near a large oak, it was a peaceful enough spot.

Remington, although still weak, attended the funeral. Dane, Trenton, Rory, Jasmine, Skye, and Charles stood silently as the priest from Boroughbridge performed the mass and lay to rest the woman's evil soul.

Remington kept glancing at Trenton as he stood beside the casket, wondering if he still blamed her for his mother's death. She hoped not; she would certainly like to befriend the boy and did not want his hatred preventing it. Moreover, she was to be his stepmother someday and she did not want to spend the rest of her life dealing with her bitter stepson.

Dane stood next to his friend as the priest threw symbolic dirt over the grave and intoned the words concluding the ceremony. Sir Roald was one of the four knights Gaston had left behind in charge of Mt. Holyoak, and he moved forward out of the shadows with a few others to lower the casket into the grave.

Remington watched the knight who almost died protecting her. His chest wound was recovering slowly, sapping his strength, and he moved sluggishly these days. He smiled pleasantly at Remington as he moved about his duties, yet she couldn't help but feel guilty that she had caused his pain.

The funeral disbanded, two of the knights already barking orders to Mari-Elle's household to prepare to depart. Their wagons were packed and waiting for them in the outer bailey and Remington knew Gaston had left explicit orders to rid Mt. Holyoak of his dead wife's staff as soon as the funeral was concluded. She watched the sobbing ladies and servants make their way back toward the keep under the watchful eye of Gaston's knights.

Trenton was still standing over the grave, watching Sir Roald and the other men bury his mother. Dane was trying to lead his friend away, but the boy wasn't listening. Taking a deep breath for courage, Remington stepped forward.

"Trenton," she said gently. "The cook has made some wonderful berry tarts, just for you. Would you like to go inside and have one?"

He blinked at the grave before turning to look at her. Gaston's eyes gazed back. "I am... I am not hungry. Mayhap later."

She was greatly relieved that he did not lash out at her from the first. "I understand. But it is terribly warm already. Why do not you and Dane go swimming? You can play sea battles."

Trenton was still looking at her and she could see the inner workings of his young mind. "Are you going to marry my father now?"

She choked on her tongue. Out of the corner of her eye, she could see Sir Roald paying attention to the conversation.

"Nay, Trenton, not now," she said; it was, after all, the truth. She wasn't going to marry him this very second. Quickly, she looked to her son. "Dane, take Trenton and have the cook pack you some food before you go swimming. Charles, why do not you go as well?"

Charles was lingering a few feet away. He moved forward, standing behind his young cousin. "I'd like that. It's too hot in the tower anyway."

Trenton turned to look at the young man. He'd seen him only twice and observed him openly. "Why do you stay in the tower? Are you being punished?"

Charles smiled. "Nay. 'Tis my laboratory where I perform experiments and feats of learning."

Trenton's eyes widened slightly; it was the first emotion he had shown. "What kind of experiments?"

"Great stuff," Dane exclaimed. "We can make things explode."

Life came back into Trenton's face. "Really? Can I see?"

Charles glanced at Remington, who nodded thankfully. Motioning the boys with him, they headed back toward the keep.

Her sisters joined Remington on the walk back. Oleg and Eudora were several paces behind, walking Mary between them and Jasmine kept turning around to smile at her daughter.

"She's so beautiful," she gushed quietly.

Remington glanced at Mary, then to her mother. She had never seen Jasmine so happy or radiant. They all knew of Antonius' unconditional acceptance of the child and his intent to marry Jasmine. It was only rumor, though, for he had yet to formally ask for her hand. That was most likely because he would have to ask Gaston, and Gaston had already promised to be hard on his knight. He was jesting, of course, but Antonius still had yet to work up the nerve.

The same went for the other two knights who had formed a fondness for the remaining Halsey sisters. Patrick and Rory were inseparable, and Skye worshipped Nicolas. Gaston felt the talk of marriage between the younger sisters and his knights was premature, but Remington disagreed.

"When do you think they'll return?" Skye asked as they mounted the hill.

"Gaston seemed to think it would not be long," Remington said. "Mayhap today or tomorrow."

"I hope so," Skye said wistfully.

Remington and Jasmine smiled at each other, hearing the longing in their sister's voice. Only Rory kept her mouth shut.

"What about you, Rory?" Remington asked with a teasing smile. "Do not you miss Patrick?"

Rory turned her face away. "No."

The other three sisters burst out giggling. "There is no harm in admitting you miss him," Jasmine insisted. "He's a fine, gentle knight. Not to mention that he is most beautiful with black hair and green eyes."

Rory's head snapped around to her giggling sisters, her green eyes narrowing. "He is certainly the most handsome of all of the knights. Gaston is far too big, Antonius is too small, and Nicolas is... well, I'd better not say what he is."

A quarrel naturally ensued, though not particularly hostile. Each lady was trying to prove to the other that her knight was the strongest, the bravest, and the most handsome. Remington thought she had the best argument by far and actually had Jasmine agreeing with her as they crossed the drawbridge and under the raised portcullis.

As they were enveloped by the shadowed coolness passing through the archway and into the outer bailey, they heard the sentries on the wall announcing incoming riders. There were soldiers moving to protect them as they passed through the bailey, still other soldiers rushing to the open portcullis.

The iron grate lowered with a resounding bang and shouts on the wall initiated the raising of the drawbridge. The ladies paused at the entrance to the inner bailey, curious to see if the approaching men were indeed the army returning. Sir Roald was up on the wall, conversing with the sentries and other soldiers and straining to look for himself.

"Do you think it's them?" Skye asked hopefully. Remington shook her head, watching Sir Roald descend a wooden ladder and head directly for her. "We shall soon find out."

He came to an abrupt halt in front of them. "We have riders approaching, my lady. They are flying the banners of the holy church."

Remington looked puzzled. "The church? Will you let them in?"

"I have little choice if they are flying the papal cloak," he said, but she could tell he was not pleased. "I would ask that you and your sisters retreat to the safety of the castle."

Remington glanced at her sisters. "I agree that my sisters should return, but I would like to remain if I may. After all, I am lady of Mt. Holyoak and would know their business."

Roald wasn't pleased with her statement, either, but he agreed. He escorted Remington to the top of the inner wall where she could watch the scene unfurl, yet remain in relative safety.

Leaving her in the company of several seasoned soldiers, he resumed his post on the outer wall.

Remington waited with the soldiers, slightly uncomfortable with them but trusting they would not accost her in any way. Ever since Gaston had killed the soldier who had grabbed her, the men had kept a respectful distance.

It seemed like an eternity before she heard the distant shouts of the riders outside the wall. Sir Roald called down to them, waited for a reply, and then responded. The conversation was most one-sided, but from what Remington could gather, the party had come to see her.

Her.

She was surprised to say the least. What would the church want with her? She watched with anticipation as Sir Roald reluctantly ordered the bridge lowered and the portcullis raised. He turned to look at her then and she could see even at a distance that he was not pleased in the least.

She descended the wall without being told to do so. Passing through the inner gate, she nearly collided with Sir Roald.

"What do they want with me?" she asked urgently.

His jaw ticked as he watched the portcullis go up. "They say they carry a message from the king," he looked at her then. "And your husband."

Remington's eyes widened. She swayed back from the knight, almost falling backward had she not quickly caught herself. Her shock, her fear, her natural terror of the man called her husband suddenly swallowed her up and she took a step away from Sir Roald, shaking her head slowly.

"Nay," she rasped. "I shall not read it. I shall not read it."

Sir Roald was no fool; he knew that the lady and his liege were lovers. But he also knew it was more than a purely physical relationship, for he could tell by the way Gaston gazed upon her. The man was in love.

He had furthermore heard the rumors of Lord Stoneley's cruelty and could read the horror in her face. Quickly, he sought to protect her, at least until Gaston could return.

"You do not have to, my lady," he assured her. "Retreat to the castle and I will deal with the church as best I can."

Remington was shaking so badly she could hardly walk. She did not want to read any missive from Guy; she wanted to forget him completely. Oh, where was Gaston?

Quaking, she turned away from Sir Roald and hastened back into the safe innards of Mt. Holyoak. Her rapid footsteps soon turned into running pats as she raced up the stairs and tore the length of the corridor until she reached the confines of her bedchamber. But even then, as she looked about the empty room, she was not comforted. She must find safety, someplace where no one could harm her. Panic, fear-borne, was welling in her chest.

Gaston made her feel safe. She wanted him here, dear God, but he was off fighting another man's battle. She wanted him; *nay*, needed him. Her breathing came in harsh rasps and her body was near collapse due to her injury and her mental state, but she felt uncomfortable staying in her own bedchamber. But there was one place she did feel safe, because it reminded her so much of Gaston.

The door to Gaston's bedchamber flew open and was slammed shut with equal force. Remington threw herself upon the bed, smelling of leather and Gaston, and buried herself under the covers. Here, she would hide until he returned. She would not leave it for a minute. She wanted nothing to do with the church or their missives.

Come home to me, my love. I need you.

Templehurst was a bloodbath from the moment Gaston had arrived. Three rebellious barons had attacked the fortress with the sole purpose of razing the structure to send a message to Henry. They were Yorkist loyalists to the core and wanted nothing to do with the Welsh bastard king, even one year after the decisive battle at Stoke, and had decided to make an example out of Sir James de Wolfe.

The battle was worse than the soldiers had led him to believe. The fortress was badly compromised even though de Wolfe had done an outstanding job of holding off the onslaught. Wasting no time, Gaston had ordered an immediate assembly of block-style ranks and, just after dawn, they began to lay siege to the attackers.

Gaston's men were magnificent, as always. They mercilessly pummeled the opposing barons with sheer skill until the ranks started to weaken and headway was gained toward the fortress. De Wolfe, inside Templehurst, could do naught else but watch from his vantage point as the Dark One came to his aid. He did, however, give every man who was able a crossbow and from the walls, they weakened the baron's forces as best they could.

Gaston was in the middle of the fight as he always was. Astride Taran, he was an invincible force, immune to the paltry attempts of enemy soldiers to fall him. There was no one who could even come close to the Dark Knight before they were cut down by the massive broadsword he wielded. Nearly a half-length longer than a standard broadsword, it was also several pounds heavier and quite capable of cutting a man cleanly in half.

Gaston, Arik and Patrick were working in a cozy group, fighting off enemy soldiers and engaging a host of knights who had fought for Richard and Edward in days past. Gaston recognized a few of them, but that fact did not render exception. They took their lives in their hands, literally, as they engaged the Dark Knight. Gaston personally struck down three mighty knights before the rest retreated, leaving the fighting to the overwhelming number of men-at-arms.

He was tireless in the field, effortless as if he were doing nothing more than strolling along the river. Every blow was calculated, every thrust meaningful. There was no waste of effort in Gaston's tactics. As large as he was, as purely powerful, no man could survive for long against him.

The first day of fighting saw the barons' forces breaking rank and dispersing. There were groups of holdouts, but nothing of major concern to Gaston, who personally rode to the moat of Templehurst and ordered the bridge lowered. Without question, he was obeyed.

Sir James met him at the gate, a devilishly handsome man with dark hair and wide green eyes. He was extremely large, nearly as large as Gaston, and the two made quite a pair when they shook hands for the first time.

Pockets of fighting went on around Templehurst into the night and Gaston worked his way to every group, fighting fiercely until the rebels disbanded and scattered. Baron Tivton of Crigglestone Castle was the final resister, engaging Gaston near the northwest wall of Templehurst with a hundred or so men. It was a few hours before dawn as the armies clashed in the second wave of violent fighting.

The skirmish was short lived. Weary and defeated, Baron Tivton was captured and slapped in irons, displayed in the bailey of Templehurst until Gaston and James could decide what to do with him.

Gaston stood in the large solar of Templehurst, a cup of wine in his hand as James and Arik discussed punishment. Usually he was an integral part of such discussions, but not today. He was tired, ready to return home and into Remington's arms. Campaigns such as this usually satisfied him, but all he could think of was Remington's soft body against his and his impatience to return was growing by the minute.

"My lord is quiet," James said in his deep, husky voice.

Gaston broke from his train of thought, smiling weakly. Arik eyed him, knowing exactly what his problem was but keeping his mouth shut.

"'Tis nothing, merely my own fatigue catching up with me," he replied vaguely. "Tell me what has been decided so that we may carry out the sentence."

"I believe the baron should be drawn and quartered," James said, glancing at Arik. "But your second believes he should be sent to London for Henry to deal with. What are your thoughts, my lord?"

Gaston scratched at his itchy face, sporting heavy stubble. He thoughtfully drained the last of his wine. "Spare him. Send him home with a warning for all other warlords who might consider action against the crown. My mercy is not infinite; it is applicable only one time. The next foolish incursion will bring my full wrath and there will be no lives spared."

James nodded, satisfied with the judgment. "My lord is wise."

Gaston put the cup down, twisting his big body to loosen his tightening muscles. "These people we have fought this day are English such as we are; they are not Scot nor Welsh raiding the land. We must learn to get along amongst ourselves no matter what king we support. For the good of England, we must do this and we must start somewhere. Mayhap a show of mercy will convince them that Henry is truly intent on a peaceful reign."

James rose, moving to Gaston. "I appreciate your reinforcements and your prudence, my lord. Both have been invaluable to Templehurst this day."

Gaston began pulled his gauntlets tight, retrieving his helm from a nearby table. "Your presence here at Templehurst is equally invaluable to Henry and myself, de Wolfe. I could ask for no finer vassal."

James bowed to his liege, following he and Arik from the room and into the bailey.

The sultry day was miserable already. Patrick, Antonius and Nicolas were waiting for them as they exited the castle and Gaston knew they were as eager to return to Mt. Holyoak as he was. He almost laughed; since when did his knights have anything on their mind other than soldiering? Since when did he? Being a victorious campaign, they should be celebrating loudly with ale and any food they could find. Instead, they were subdued and impatient.

James thanked Gaston again, watching as the Dark Knight rode from his destroyed bailey. Confident that his situation was contained, he spun around to his own knights and began demanding motivation for clean up.

The men probably could have used a rest, but Gaston was eager to return. He set a slow pace for their benefit, however, even though he could have easily raced the entire way home. Taran danced nervously, unused to the easy pace.

"At this rate, we shall be home next week," Nicolas muttered to his brother.

Gaston, riding alone several feet ahead, heard him. "We shall be home this eve, Nicolas. Your Lady Skye will not be lonely tonight."

Patrick snorted in amusement as Nicolas looked sheepish. Arik simply shook his head. "Women. I cannot recall speaking of women after a battle. Since when did the female sex become acceptable war conversation?"

"If you had a woman you would know," Patrick shot back tauntingly, then turned to Nicolas and Antonius. "We must make it our mission in this life to find Arik a woman who will have him."

The two knights chuckled in agreement but Arik put up his hand. "God, no. Knowing you three, you shall saddle me with Medusa. I shall find my own woman, if you please."

Gaston listened to the banter silently, thinking of Remington. His heart ached to be away from her, even for a day or two. He was glad his days of warring were drawing to a close so he would not have to be separated from her any more than necessary. He decided right then that when he traveled to London to seek Henry, Remington would accompany him. He couldn't stand the thought of leaving her behind.

It seemed he could only think of her. Distraction could be deadly in his profession, but he wasn't concerned. He could fight battles in his sleep and Remington was a welcome subject to his mind. My God, he couldn't wait to hold her again.

The army did not even stop for the nooning meal; it was eaten as they marched. Gaston, however, never ate on a battle march. He would wait and sup this eve with Remington, in between making love to her.

The army by-passed Boroughbridge and Gaston could literally smell his keep. His anticipation grew as he strained to catch a glimpse of the massive structure on the horizon, and he was not disappointed. Like a massive gray sentinel, the stone edifice rose out of the northeast sky and Gaston's body washed with satisfaction. *My keep*, he thought with contentment he had never known. *Remi's and mine.*

He would be holding her in no time.

Mt. Holyoak greeted its conquering son with open arms. The gates were flung wide and an honor guard lined the drawbridge as Gaston brought the army back to the fold. He couldn't remember ever feeling more welcome, or more at home, even though the honor guard had been standard fare at Clearwell. Mayhap it was because he felt more comfortable at Mt. Holyoak than he ever had at the home he had shared with Mari-Elle. Mt. Holyoak was already in his blood.

Sir Roald met him in the outer bailey, smartly saluting his lord as he dismounted Taran. Gaston's eyes were scanning the grounds for Remington.

"Where is Lady Stoneley?" he asked his knight casually.

Sir Roald looked even paler than usual. "We have a bit of a situation, my lord. A papal envoy arrived while you were away with a message from our king, and another message from Lord Stoneley for his wife. Lady Stoneley has taken to, uh, your room and will not come out."

Gaston tried to control his shock. "What did the missive say?"

Roald shook his head. "I know not, my lord. I have not read either one of them, since they were not directed at me. Lady Stoneley refuses to read the missive from her husband."

Gaston's nostrils flared slightly, an overwhelming indication of his level of emotion. Arik had heard the majority of the conversation and stepped forward.

"Where is the envoy?" he asked.

"I have made him comfortable but little more," Roald said. "He's a pushy bastard and I have kept him restricted to the lower floor. He demands to be shown Lady Stoneley; he believes her to be a prisoner."

Gaston fought to maintain his control. "You said Lady Stoneley is in my room?"

"Aye, my lord," Roald replied.

Without another word, he left his knights and disappeared into the innards of the castle.

The familiar dank smell comforted him as he made his way to his bower. By the time he hit the second level he was nearly running. He had to get to Remington, to speak with her and comfort her before he dealt with the envoy. If he went to the envoy now he would most likely explode and commit murder. Only if he saw Remington first could he gain a handle on his rocketing emotions.

The family wing was softly lit, the heat of the day seeping away. The doors were open, as they usually were during the day, and he passed by Rory and Jasmine on his way to see Remington. The sisters did not utter a word to him; with expressions of glee, they raced from their rooms and off to find their returned knights.

He was focused on the great double doors of his bower straight ahead, but as he passed by Remington's room, he suddenly heard her voice and jerked to a halt. Fully prepared to charge into the room and pull her into his arms, he came to a skidding stop at the open door, his eyes drinking in the atmosphere of the room.

Remington lay upon her bed, her back propped up with several pillows. Dane lay with his head upon her lap and Trenton sat with his legs folded right next to her, his handsome young face alive. From the tone of her voice and the looks on the boy's faces, he knew that she was telling them another glory tale.

"But if the lion of Nemea was invulnerable to injury, then how did Hercules kill it?" Trenton was asking.

"Hercules was very clever, Trenton," Remington replied. She sounded tired. "First, he whacked the lion over the head with a club, and then he strangled it with his bare hands. Quite a feat, I would say."

"Who else did he kill?" Dane demanded.

Remington ran her fingers through her son's hair. "It wasn't so much as who he killed, but why. Hercules was not a vicious murderer; in fact, he was a very wise and great man. If he did kill, it was because he had to. And he mostly killed ferocious animals with a taste for flesh."

"Then what else did he kill?" Dane rephrased his question.

Remington looked thoughtful. "He killed the man-eating birds of Arkadia, and he killed the three-headed monster Geryon, whose home was near the sunset. But he did a lot of good things, as well."

"What?" Trenton asked.

Remington put her hand lightly on Trenton's knee. "He captured the bull that was destroying the island of Crete; a huge, terrible bull that was tearing up the palace and the land. Hercules caught it and ate it. He also caught the huge wild boar of Mount Erymanthos and brought it back to his older brother as a prize. He was the strongest, bravest man in all the world."

"Like my father," Trenton said eagerly.

Remington smiled. "Aye, like your father."

"But I doubt that even I could wrestle a wild bull and kill it," Gaston stepped into the room casually, his face riveted to Remington. He smiled at the boys. "More glory tales, I see."

"Father." Trenton shot up, standing on the bed. "You have returned."

"Did you kill a lot of knights?" Dane sat up with dizzying speed and bound to the floor. "How many did you kill? Did you cut their heads off?"

Gaston gave Dane a horrified look and patted him on the head affectionately. "By God's Bloody Rood, Dane, 'tis much more merciful to kill a man in a quicker fashion. Besides, I went to keep the peace, not put men to their graves."

"What happened, then?" Trenton jumped in. "Was it a fierce fight?"

"Fierce enough, lad," Gaston found Remington's eyes again. "But I am returned, whole and sound."

The boys practically plowed him over in their eagerness to hear of his battle but he waved them off politely. He was desperate to be alone with Remington. "Why do not you go into the bailey and watch Arik disassemble the troops. Afterward, ask him to tell you of the battle. He is a much better storyteller than I."

Yelling in agreement, they tore off, each trying to be the first through the door and squabbling when they were unable to fit through the jamb side-by-side. Gaston shook his head with mirth, pulling off his gauntlets.

"Gentlemen!" he roared lightly. "Control your eagerness, if you would. Do not run down the stairs lest you fall and break your necks, and remain on the inner wall until the troops are disbanded. Am I clear?"

They responded affirmatively, still shoving and shouting as they walked very quickly down the hall. Gaston, snickering, turned to Remington.

"What in the world am I going to do when they get large enough to take me on?" he wondered aloud. "Will every day be a battle?"

Her smiled faded, the fact that they were finally alone settling heavily on her. "They worship you, my lord. As do I."

The gauntlets hit the bed and he was beside her, his great hands on her face, pulling her to his lips for a kiss. Their lips, soft and warm and eager, pulled and suckled on one another until demanding tongues insisted on being sated. Mingling and mixing, they tasted one another until Gaston had to stop or he would explode. His heavy member was already painfully engorged.

"God, Remi," he whispered against her cheek. "I missed you so. Roald told me what happened."

She looked at him fearfully. "I have not been downstairs yet. He brought a missive from Guy."

"I know, angel," he patted her cheek. "And I intend to find out what the messages say, but I had to see you first."

She forced a tremulous smile and kissed him again. He responded, with far more sweetness and less force. "I missed you terribly, too. We had to bury Mari-Elle this morning."

"I suspected as much. How is Trenton handling it?"

She shrugged. "He spent the day with Charles and Dane up in Charles' tower room, blowing up things. He is actually doing remarkably well, considering."

He fingered a strand of silken hair. "Roald said you were holed up in my room and refused to come out, yet I find you here with the boys as your audience."

She lay back, pulling him down beside her. With all of the armor, it was tremendously awkward, but neither one of them cared. "I was planning on staying in your bower until you returned, but Dane and Trenton found me about an hour ago and demanded I tell them more stories. I could not disappoint them."

He stroked her face. "My sweet angel, always thinking of others before yourself."

He kissed her cheek, his mouth drifting lazily over her shoulders and the swell of her breast exposed by her surcoat. Remington soaked up every moment, feeling his strength boost her own. She needed him as badly as her body needed blood to survive.

"I should tend to the envoy," he said after a few moments, his voice husky. "I will send for you when I have read the contents of the missives."

"You do not want me to come with you now?"

He pushed himself up heavily, nearly four hundred pounds of flesh and steel. "Nay, not now. I would see this papal liaison alone and determine his intent before I summon you. I do not want this man upsetting you and fully intend to tell him so. Roald says he's a pushy bastard."

She sat up, watching him replace his gloves. "What do you suppose the missives say?"

He shook his head. "Honestly, I do not know. Mayhap it is not as bad as we both think; mayhap Henry and Guy are merely sending their respective greetings." He did not believe that for a moment, but he said it to ease her mind somewhat. She was terribly frightened and he did not blame her.

CHAPTER SEVENTEEN

Gaston was right. It was bad. The envoy, a fat little man with a nasty attitude irritated him from the word go, and he delivered the king's message with great flourish. Gaston knew he had gone pale after he read it.

"So you see, my lord, the king supports Sir Guy's wishes that his wife join him in his captivity. Of course, the church supports the rights of a man to have his wife returned to him. Sir Guy is terribly concerned for Lady Remington's safety now that you occupy his keep."

Gaston struggled to maintain his composure. He would have liked nothing better than to wrap his hands around the man's throat, dump him on the road somewhere, and say he never received the missive. But it would only delay the inevitable a bit longer, until another envoy was sent.

"Sir Guy only mentions his wife joining him. What about his son? What about the rest of the family? Are they to be left in my charge? "

"Sir Guy feels that the only true danger is to his wife, as the spouse of an enemy. He does not believe you will harm the young boy," the fat man sat heavily in a silk chair. "The missive I carry for the lady is her husband's explanation of his request. May I, then, deliver the message in person?"

Gaston's face was impassive as he stood by the hearth, his thick arms crossed in front of his broad chest. "Sir Guy's reasoning about his son makes no sense. Surely I would harm a male heir over his wife. Why does not he want the boy?"

The priest blinked. "You have harmed the lad?"

"Of course not," Gaston returned smoothly. "But Sir Guy's request is illogical. Why would he ask that his wife join him in jail? The Tower is no place for a lady."

"On the contrary, my lord, Sir Guy's accommodations are quite adequate," the man eyed Gaston a moment. "Why are you reluctant in this matter, my lord? Have you, in fact, already harmed the lady and her son and you are therefore reluctant to admit it, lest you provoke your king's anger?"

Gaston snorted. "Henry would rather slit his own wrists that become angry with me, as you well know. And I will refuse Guy's request that his wife join him. Lady Remington is serving as my chatelaine and I depend on her greatly. She is of far more use to me here than locked away with her husband."

The priest's eyes narrowed slightly. "You cannot refuse the request. As papal liaison, I hold the authority of the church to return Lady Stoneley to her husband. As you well know."

Gaston did not react to the challenge, but his eyes darkened into stormy, swirling orbs. "And I hold the supreme authority in Henry's military circle, not to say Mt. Holyoak. You are foolish, priest, to imply that your power exceeds mine. If I wish Lady Stoneley to remain, then remain she will until Henry himself wrests her from these walls."

The priest swallowed, the first waver he had shown in the confrontation. "You would go against the church?"

The words suddenly echoed in Gaston's head. If he wanted the cooperation of the church in Remington's annulment, then it would not be wise to dig his heels in like a stubborn mule. He would have to comply, but it would be on his terms.

He turned away from the priest, his mind working calculatedly. The only logical thing he could do was to obey the missive and allow Remington to go to London. But; he would escort her and he would seek audience with Henry to make sure she was kept away from Guy until the annulment could take place. He would tell Henry everything and hope the man was grateful enough for Gaston's loyalty to grant him his heart's desires.

He turned back to the envoy, watching beads of sweat appear on the man's forehead. Aye, he would comply. But he would kill Guy Stoneley before he would allow Remington to be confined with him in the Tower.

"Nay, I would not go against the church," he replied finally. "I shall summon Lady Stoneley so that you may deliver her husband's message."

He would summon her personally so that he could tell her beforehand what the missives contained. Fact was, he was still reeling with shock and disbelief as he made his way up to her rooms. Not that the request itself was unbelievable. On the contrary, there was nothing strange about a man requesting his wife and certainly nothing unusual that the king supported the request. Henry had no idea of the situation and thought he was doing the merciful thing. The church was merely along as a neutral party, to make sure the request of a prisoner was enforced. No one in his or her right mind would deny the church.

He hit the family's wing with purposeful boot falls, his heart constricting with pain. Things were certainly not working out as he had planned, but no matter; he could work with it. After all, everything would work out in the end the way he had planned, so it did not matter what road he took to get there.

Remington was standing by her wardrobe, inspecting one of her surcoats closely. A few others were thrown on the bed. She was clad in a luscious pale topaz silk that brought out the magnificent color of her eyes and hair. A pretty gold headband held her hair off her face, showing off the sweet oval shape. He softened visibly at the sight of her, so terribly sorry for what she was going to have to go through.

Her head came up and she smiled as he entered the room. He returned her smile.

"What are you doing?"

"Inspecting these surcoats for wearability come the winter," she said, suddenly looking irritated. "It all started when I changed my surcoat not a few minutes ago. Suddenly, it looked as if all of my surcoats were wearing poorly and then I realized I had seen a few of them on Rory. Do you know she has been wearing my dresses to impress Patrick?"

He shrugged lazily. "That may be so, but she cannot do them justice as you can."

"What a terrible thing to say, Gaston. Rory is a lovely girl with a splendid figure."

"True enough, but she still cannot compare to you."

She smiled shyly, hanging a dress back in the cabinet. "You say that because you love me."

"I say it because it is true," he said frankly. "What do you think attracted me to you in the first place? 'Twas your beautiful face and magnificent figure. You were wearing this surcoat." He reached onto the bed and fingered the emerald satin.

She fingered the dress. "You remembered?"

"I will never forget as long as I live," he said quietly, eyeing her a moment. "Angel, I have come from my meeting with the envoy. I am afraid the news is not very favorable."

She took a deep breath, lowering her gaze. "What is it? Henry is releasing Guy, isn't he?"

"Nay, not that. Apparently, Guy has convinced Henry that Mt. Holyoak under my occupation is a dangerous place for you. Pleading for the king's grace, he asked that you be brought to him in the Tower and the king has agreed. The church is here as a liaison between Guy and myself to insure that the request is carried out."

She looked at him a moment, shock written all over her face. "Guy wants me... with him in the Tower?"

"Aye," Gaston replied gently. "I have no choice but to comply, angel, but believe me when I tell you that you shall never see Guy. I plan to escort you to London and furthermore intend to delegate you to the wardship of the church until this matter is taken care of."

Her brow furrowed as his words settled in. She was absolutely spinning with the news and found it difficult to grasp his calm statement. "Guy wants me with him?"

Gaston sighed; she had not heard much, if any, of what he had just said. He took her in his arms, but she was stiff with shock.

"You are not going to be with him, Remi, but I have to bow to the church," he said against the top of her head. "Especially if we want their cooperation with your annulment. I shall take you to London as requested, but I will forbid any contact between you and Guy. Do you comprehend me, love?"

She nodded jerkily and he held her back so he could look in her face. "Do you really?"

Her wide, frightened eyes gazed back at him. "I will not have to see him?"

"Not if I have anything to say about it," he said softly, his heart aching for her. "But even if you do have to speak with him, I will be by your side. I promise you that. Tell me you shall be brave, angel. For me."

She swallowed hard, her face twisting with pain and fright. "I shall....I shall try. But why does he want me with him? Why can he not leave me here?"

"Who knows, angel," he sighed, holding her tightly. "Why the man should suddenly decide after a year that he cannot live without you is beyond me, but I do not know the facts for certain. All I know is that he has expressed fear for your safety now that I occupy his keep."

"What about Dane? What about my sisters?" she pulled back sharply, searching his face.

"He only requested you. Thankfully, the rest of your family can remain safely here."

She fell back against him, gaining some control over her shock. "Oh, Gaston, I am going to be ill."

He rubbed her back gently. "Not just yet. The papal envoy demands to see you to make sure you are whole and sound and I told him I would bring you to him. After you meet with him, we can both become ill together."

Honestly, she was handling the news much better than he thought she would. He had expected hysterics and was pleasantly surprised that she was able to control herself. Now that he had delivered his message, he almost felt more out of control than she did.

"You won't leave me?" she begged softly.

"Not ever," he said. "I am so sorry this had to happen, Remi. It never occurred to me that Guy would do this."

"I did not even know such a thing was allowed. I thought once he was a prisoner, that all of his rights and privileges were taken away," she said with a hint of regret.

"'Tis not unusual for special prisoners to be given special consideration," Gaston answered. After a moment, he released her. "Come on, angel. Let's get this over with."

He took her hand gently and led her from the room.

The envoy scrutinized Remington closely. Sitting rigid in a chair, she answered his questions with thinly veiled annoyance while Gaston loomed a few feet away. She did not like the look of the priest, and she certainly did not like the messages he bore, which afforded her little patience during his interrogation.

Finally, after several minutes of inquiry, he handed Remington the missive from Guy. Gaston could see her hands shaking as she broke the seal and he cursed silently. To see her upset was the surest way to provoke his temper, and at this moment it was directed at the priest. He was having a difficult time controlling himself as she steadied the parchment enough so she could read it.

"Lady Stoneley is recovering from a severe wound, priest," he growled. "I do not appreciate having my chatelaine upset so."

The priest gave him a strange look. "How can a message from her dear husband upset her?"

Gaston's jaw ticked but Remington glanced up at him. "It's all right, my lord."

The men went quiet as she read the vellum once and rolled it up again. Amazingly, her eyes were clear and her hands calm as she laid it upon the table with disinterest.

"And what if I do not wish to go?" she asked pointedly.

The priest was surprised. "You... you do not wish to go and live with your husband? My lady, I find that astonishing. Why not, may I ask?"

"Because I have no desire to live as a prisoner, as he is," she said in a clipped tone. "I am quite enjoying my freedom at Mt. Holyoak, where I can be with my sisters and son. I have no desire to go to London."

Gaston did not react, but he was damn curious to see how the envoy was going to handle her refusal. Truth was, he was feeling foolish that he had not thought of the idea himself. If she refused to go, he wasn't at all sure if the priest would force her. However, since Gaston was ordered to comply with Stoneley's wishes by decree of Henry, technically, Gaston could physically force her to go should the church demand it and that thought unnerved him.

The envoy adjusted the collar of his heavy robe, his fat face coated with perspiration and an unholy odor emanating from him. Carefully, he sat in a chair several feet away from Remington, his brow creased with thought.

"My lady, it has been over a year since you have seen your husband," he said quietly. "I spoke with him before coming here and he confessed to me that he has missed you terribly and he is fearful for your welfare now that Mt. Holyoak is occupied. Are you not the least bit anxious to see him?"

"No," Remington said flatly, meeting his eye unwaveringly. "He's a filthy bastard and I hope he rots in jail. I am happy to be rid of him."

The priest was taken aback by the bluntness of her statement. Then, suddenly, as if a thought had just occurred to him, his gaze moved between Gaston and Remington.

"My lady, you do not have to say those things because the Dark One listens. You are perfectly safe with me," he leaned forward and Remington was greeted with a foul stench when his robes shifted. "You need not fear him with God as your protector."

Remington's face washed with an uncharacteristically hostile expression. "If God is my protector, then why was I forced to endure nine years of hell with a man who beat and humiliated me as part of his daily routine? If God is merciful, then why did He allow my husband to abuse my sisters?" She rose slowly, her rage gaining steam and her eyes riveted to the priest. "If God is my protector, then why does He sanction my husband's request that I join him in jail? Speak to me not of God, priest, for He has ignored me my entire life and I am not about to give faith in Him now."

The envoy swallowed, shaken at her venomous tone. He opened his mouth to interrupt but she cut him off savagely. "No! You will not defend Him in my presence, for as far as I am concerned, God does not exist." She was standing in front of him, her beautiful face full of anger and hatred. "Return to London, Man of God, and tell my husband that I am glad he is moldering in Henry's Tower. Tell him that I hope he dies a slow, painful, lingering death, as was the one he sentenced me to nine years ago when he married me. And by the way, I told you I had no use for God, and I do not. But I do believe in Satan. I am married to him!"

The priest could only stare back at her with astonishment. Gaston, too, was overwhelmed with this side of Remington he had not yet seen. She was absolutely magnificent; strong, proud, distinct with her words. She had actually succeeded in subduing the arrogant priest, something Gaston himself had been unable to do.

"My lady," the priest said hoarsely, "I find your hatred of God unreasonable. He is with you always, no matter that you feel He has abandoned you."

"Shut up!" Remington snapped brusquely, turning away from him. She was completely in control of the conversation and both men knew it. "I will hear no more of God. You will return to London and inform my husband that I have no intention of joining him. I will discuss this no further."

The priest looked at her, agape, and then glanced at Gaston. He met the man's eyes with a look of stone. "I believe you have your answer, priest."

The priest blinked with confusion, trying desperately to regain control of the situation. What had happened that he had lost his edge, his divine jurisdiction? When did this woman grasp the reins of power and wrap them around his neck? Suddenly irritated, he stood up.

"I brought no polite request for you, Lady Stoneley, but a command from your husband. You are given no choice but to return with me to London."

Remington turned to him, slowly and stealthily. After a moment, she raised a well-shaped eyebrow. "And if I refuse? Do you intend to wrest me all the way back to London yourself?"

"I do not have to," the envoy looked to Gaston. "My lord de Russe has orders from Henry to comply with the demand. If you refuse, 'tis he who will wrest you back to London."

The priest did indeed know the extent of his power, and he apparently knew Gaston's role as well. Gaston felt himself waver inwardly, not daring to look at Remington. He could feel her eyes on him questioningly.

"Is this so?" she asked him.

He still did not look at her, his eyes fixed to the priest. He almost refuted, but he could not in good conscience. The priest was right and both men knew it.

"Aye," he said after a moment. "He has that power to order me to comply, my lady."

"Then you will have to tie me up, for I shall run away if given the chance," she said, losing her controlled facade. "Do it now, de Russe, or I shall run from this room and you will never catch me."

He looked at her when she called him "de Russe". So coldly, so uncivilly and by God, he hated the tone in her voice!

"Is that what you truly want?" he asked her. "I will do it if your threats are sincere."

She sat in a chair, putting her hands in front of her as if she were preparing to be bound. Gaston watched her, his heart breaking.

"Can't you see she does not want to go?" he turned to the priest, his voice gritty. "How can you, a man of the cloth, in good conscience force her to do something she obviously does not want to do? Were not her reasons good enough to warrant reconsideration on your part?"

The priest met Gaston's gaze as rivulets of sweat ran down his flushed face. "What she wishes is of no concern to me, my lord. She will do as she is told, and so will you."

Gaston hardened like granite. His face remained unreadable, but when he spoke, there was thunder in his voice. "Be gone from my sight. I will send for you when the lady is ready to leave."

The envoy's face twitched at the tone, as low and threatening as he had ever heard. His haughty demeanor slackened briefly.

"As soon as possible, if you will," he moved for the door, avoiding looking at either of them. "I have already been a week long on this journey and we will be expected before the month is out."

He shut the door behind him heavily. Gaston's eyes were fixed to Remington. She was staring straight ahead, her wrists still pressed together as if awaiting the rope.

"Remi," his voice was a whisper. "You tried, angel, but 'twas in vain. Your efforts were, however, magnificent. I had no idea you could rouse that level of anger within your sweet little body."

"Bind me," she said through clenched teeth.

His breathing began to quicken as he gazed upon her. "Do not do this to me. I love you, Remi. Everything will be all right, I swear it."

As when a cork pops from a bottle of fermented wine due to unrelenting pressure, so did Remington's nerves. All of the careful control she had exerted since Gaston had informed her of the envoy's message suddenly exploded and all of the fear she had ever felt toward Guy came slamming into her like the hard crash of a waterfall. Fear consumed her, ate at her, and she threw herself up from the chair and propelled her body against the wall stacked with books.

Screaming and ranting like a woman gone mad, she ripped the books from their shelves and threw them every which way. Gaston ducked as books came sailing at him, his split second of indecision to let her go ended. He had to stop her before she hurt herself.

He grabbed her tightly, but she fought against him with more strength than he thought possible for a woman. It was anger, hatred, and total terror expressing themselves and within the confines of his massive arms, he let her rant. She pounded him, slapped him.

"It will not work! The church will not listen to you and it will not work!" she screamed. "They will force me to be with Guy and I will not allow it. I shall kill myself; do you hear me? I shall kill myself!"

"I shall kill Guy first!" he shot back, receiving a sharp blow to his cheekbone as she flailed wildly. "Remington!" Receiving no coherent response, he shook her hard. "Remi!"

He shook her so hard that her neck snapped and she gasped from the shock. Her wildly constricted pupils suddenly dilated with recognition, as if suddenly realizing that for a brief moment she had been truly insane. He saw her start to quiver violently and the tears finally bubbled forth. He saw a terrifying panic in her eyes.

"Kill him, Gaston!" she hissed.

He did not hesitate. "I shall do it."

She squeezed her eyes shut, fighting off the sobs. "No, no, do not. I did not mean it."

"I did," he was gripping her arms tightly, feeling her pain and terror seeping into his veins. He couldn't stand seeing her so terrified; his natural instincts to protect her were running rampant. "No, Gaston," she breathed heavily. "I do not want to you murder for me. Let him rot away in the Tower; let him become fodder for rats. I could never live with the guilt if you killed him for me."

He felt her shaking violently in his grasp until he realized it was he who was shaking, too. Fiercely, he gathered her against his chest, breathing in the faint scent of the perfume he had purchased for her.

"It's all right, angel," he whispered against her hair. He had her gripped tightly in his arms, her feet dangling a good distance off the floor. "The church will listen to me, and we shall be married by this time next year. I vow it on my oath as Henry's Dark One. Nothing will stand in my way, not God, nor king, nor your bastard husband."

She was sobbing softly in his arms, frightened and tired. "I hate him!"

"I know," he crooned. "So do I."

They spent a good deal of the evening in the solar. Remington had a death-grip on his neck and refused to let go, and he ended up sitting on the desk and holding her across his lap like a child. But he was content to stay there the rest of his life, holding her, keeping her safe from those who would seek to harm her.

He found as of late that he was only content with her in his arms, as if she were the other half of him. Alone, he felt as if a great piece of him was missing.

The evening meal came and went and they continued to hold each other in the dim room, listening to the crackles of the banked fire. Remington had long since fallen into a deep sleep, a catch in her breathing every so often to remind him of the emotional upheaval she had suffered. He caressed her gently, staring into the fire and considering exactly what he would need to do upon his arrival to London.

He would take Remington with him and seek out Henry. After a private audience, wherein he fully intended to explain everything to his king, he would settle her in a secured portion of the castle under the protection of his own elite guard, and then he would seek an audience with the papal legate, Bishop John of Imola. Unfamiliar as he was regarding the procedures of annulment, he would seek the bishop's advice and proceed, with or without the man's blessing.

Gaston did not know much about Pope Innocent IX, only that Henry had a love/hate relationship with the church, mostly hate. But Gaston knew one thing; with enough money and royal interference, he would have his annulment. Even if it meant liquidating everything he had of value as a donation to the church. He might very well lose Clearwell and Mt. Holyoak, but he would have Remington and that was all that mattered. The rest was insignificant.

He would beg if he had to.

And he would have Dane and Trenton, two of the finest sons a man could have. Even if Dane was not of his blood, he was of Remington's and therefore, a part of him. Ever since he met the boy he had considered him his own flesh. It was never his intention to steal another man's son; it merely became the way of things.

There was a soft knock on the solar door and Arik entered quietly, eyeing the both of them questioningly. He took a couple of halting steps into the room, his eyes on Remington.

"Is she all right?" he asked softly. "What happened?"

Gaston was weary, so damn weary he could barely speak. "Guy has requested that Remington join him in his captivity, and Henry has graciously granted his prisoner's request."

Arik's eyes widened briefly. "My God, Gaston. What are you going to do?"

He shrugged slightly, Remington dead weight against his arms and chest. "Take her to London as I am ordered to and start annulment proceedings the moment I arrive. I shall make her a ward of the church until the matter is settled."

Arik stroked his scratchy face thoughtfully, moving to sit on the desk beside his liege. He snorted softly after a moment. "Hell of a problem, I'd say. Guy was smart to send the church as an envoy."

"I do not know he did that for certain, but it was certainly a shrewd move," Gaston raised his eyebrows in a resigned gesture. "Who would deny the church?"

Arik nodded in agreement. "Guy is an intelligent man, Gaston. I was mildly acquainted with him some time ago and know him to be cunning and sharp. I have no doubt that having the church bear his message was a planned move."

"But why?" Gaston asked and Remington shifted at the sound of his raised voice. He put his huge hand on her head, covering her ear until she stilled. "Why would he do this now, one year after the defeat of Stoke? In all that time, he had no contact with her and suddenly he decides he cannot live without her? I do not understand his logic."

"Mayhap that is not his logic," Arik replied softly. "Mayhap he is angry because another man has his possessions and he simply wishes to regain a portion of what is his."

"But why Remi?" Gaston gazed at the top of her dark head. "Why not send for...oh, hell, I do not know. Why not demand his plate or coinage, or his personal possessions to surround him?"

Arik looked at Remington, at Gaston. His blue eyes were grim. "Think, Gaston. He can pump Remington for information. Having been living in the same keep with Henry's Dark One, she would be privy to privileged information, knowingly or not. Guy wants to find out what she knows."

Gaston's eyes darkened. "And being the intelligent, sly man he is, he is almost certainly linked with a network of Yorkist spies. In prison or not, he has most likely not been isolated from his peers and comrades. He would be passing them any information for their resistance."

"Exactly."

Gaston held Arik's gaze a moment longer before turning away, a weary sigh escaping his lips. "Once again, she is a pawn. I will not allow this, Arik. I will not allow this man to harm her any more than he already has, no matter what Henry says."

"One would hope that Henry has already thought of the possible reasons behind Guy's request, outside of unrequited love," Arik said with muted sarcasm. "He must not believe her to be a threat, knowing that you would not have become personally involved with her or divulged any crown secrets."

They both looked at each other as the enormity of the statement hung between them. "Have I changed overmuch since I met her, Arik? Am I not the same man you rode into Mt. Holyoak with those weeks ago?"

"You have changed, but it is a positive one," Arik replied. "I thought you quite incapable of feelings until you met lovely Lady Remington."

"I thought I was immune," Gaston mumbled, burying the lower part of his face in the top of Remington's hair. "I was wrong."

Arik smiled faintly. Watching how tenderly Gaston was holding Remington made him reconsider life in general; he would not have believed it had he not seen it with his own eyes.

"Do you remember once, years ago, when I asked you why you did not make friends?" he said quietly. "Do you remember your reaction? You knocked out two of my teeth."

Gaston nodded vaguely, the light of the dim fire reflecting on his face. "Remington is not merely my friend, Arik. She is quickly becoming my life and that scares me."

"Why did you hit me those years back?" Arik pressed quietly. "What was so terrible in that question?"

Gaston shifted a bit, mulling over the question. "My father was a mighty warrior, a younger son of the Duke of Exeter. He married my mother when she was thirteen. I was their only child, born a scant year later, and I remember my mother and father well. Mother was more like a sister to me and she always called me her very best friend. My father was also my best friend, taking me everywhere with him." His look grew distant. "I was sent away to foster when I was seven and I missed them more than I could stand. When I had been away six months, I received word that my mother had died as a result of a bad pregnancy. My father followed her in death three months later, succumbing in a battle. I swore then and there that I would never have another friend, Arik. I did not even like to hear the word because it reminded me of my parents. Emotions like friendship hurt too much."

Arik was somber, his expression gentle. "But you *do* have friends," he said quietly. "Matthew Wellesbourne is your closest friend."

Gaston shrugged. "He is an exception. We are alike, Matt and I. He understands me."

Arik thought on Matthew Wellesbourne, the White Lord, as he was known throughout England. He was a good man, a decent man, having saved Gaston's life at Bosworth. Matthew had lost a hand but Gaston had retained his head. It was the essence of friendship, something few men ever experienced. Gaston's fear of emotional attachment did not seem to include Wellesbourne.

"I remember when you lost your parents, although I did not know you well," Arik murmured. "I remember a little boy crying all night long into his straw pillow and suddenly emerging the next day looking like the devil's apprentice. I have never seen such... hardness on one so young."

Gaston stared into the fire a moment before turning his attention to Remington. "I thought I was holding to my vow quite well until I met Lady Stoneley. Now it is as if all of the emotions I spent my life fighting off are suddenly manifesting themselves. I could not deny my feelings for her if I wanted to."

"Aye, you could, but you do not want to," Arik teased lightly. "And I do not blame you. I am very pleased, Gaston, to see that you are allowing yourself to love."

He did not know what to say; he was already embarrassed with his emotional blubbering. "Which is why I cannot let her go."

Arik's smile faded. "You have to face the very real possibility that the church will not grant her an annulment, Gaston. What will you do then?"

He drew in a long breath through his nose as if contemplating the realism of it. "I will kill Stoneley and marry her anyway."

"I asked you not to," Remington whispered, raising her head. She turned slightly to look at Arik. "Greetings this eve, Arik."

"Greetings, my lady," Arik responded, clearing his throat and standing from the table.

"How long have you been awake?" Gaston chided her gently.

"Long enough. How could I sleep with you two making so much commotion?" she unwound her arms from his neck and winced. "Ouch. I have no feeling left in them."

He gently helped her to stand and took to rubbing the circulation back into her arms. He rubbed her so vigorously that her whole body began to shimmy from side to side and they both laughed. He gathered her against him, both of them facing Arik.

"Well? Why are you still standing there?" Gaston demanded lightly.

Arik fought off a smirk. "Awaiting orders, my lord."

"Get out. That is my order," Gaston watched his second move obediently toward the door and called out after him. "Prepare a guard of one hundred and fifty of my elite warriors. I would also take eight knights with me, including Patrick and Antonius. You and Nicolas will have command of the fortress."

"Aye, my lord," Arik swept from the room with a lingering glance to Remington.

"I shall kill him for looking at you like that," Gaston said into her neck.

She was still tired, leaning against him. "Take me to bed, my lord. I am exceedingly weary."

He rose behind her. "I shall escort you to my bedchamber, my lady, but you shall be doing very little sleeping."

She grinned. "You would take advantage of a weakened, crazy woman?"

He pursed his lips thoughtfully. "Aye, I would."

True to his word, he did take advantage of her. From the moment he lay her upon his bed until the sun rose, they never stopped making love. Remington could do very little with her weakened right arm, and Gaston was perfectly content to do all of the work himself. He caressed, teased, touched, and penetrated, feeding off of the sounds of pleasure emanating from Remington's lips.

She wanted to touch him as he was touching her, but his attentions soon rendered her quite powerless to do anything other than lie back and enjoy it. At one point, she dozed off as he was planting soft kisses on her back and awoke to find that he was still kissing her, only he had moved to her feet. With a stretch and a smile, she parted her thighs and welcomed him deep inside her.

She still found it hard to believe that this massive, powerful man was hers, body and soul. Every time she touched his perfect body, she was filled with wonder and awe anew. To see him looming over her with his beauty and grace boggled her mind.

They climaxed together no less than five times that night, mayhap more that she did not remember, because Remington was so exhausted by the time the sun rose that she drifted off into a deep sleep still cradled in Gaston's arms. She was so tired she barely recalled, other than the feeling of complete happiness, the exact details. They lay in a tight clinch, her thighs still wrapped around him and his shaft still buried within her.

Gaston slept, too. He knew there was much to do this day, but he couldn't bear to part with her. That was why he had generals, was it not to carry on in his stead? Let Arik and his cousins handle the men; right now, he only wanted to think and feel Remington.

It was noon before he awoke. Remington was pressed up against him, sound asleep, and he found himself warming to her once again. His great organ, heavy and flaccid, suddenly sprang to life as his hands drifted down her back.

Remington stirred at his touch, feeling his arousal brushing up against her buttocks. Her legs were still wrapped around his hips and when she tried to move, she moaned softly in agony.

He smiled, shifted as she lowered her stiff legs. "Why do you move? You will only be in the same position in but a moment."

She grinned, a delightful sleepy, grin. "How bold you are, my lord. Wasn't last night enough for you? I would think you were bled dry by now."

He snorted. "Was it enough for you?"

Her eyes opened, the sea-crystal color as pure as the air. "I will never have enough of you."

He stroked her face tenderly, his lips nibbling on the sweet line of her chin. She was hot for him, her body already highly attuned to his. Taking his hand, she placed it on her wet heat and he groaned low in his throat.

He grew rougher, more demanding, and she came alive. The wound and her fatigue were forgotten as she responded to him with rekindled intensity. Mouths open, tongues entwined, they tasted and teased and clashed, hands kneading and caressing. Gaston rolled onto his back, taking her with him, and she was on fire with the feel of his throbbing organ against her thigh.

Her mouth left his, sucking and kissing his magnificent chest as his huge hands wound themselves in her silken curls. She bit at his nipples just as he bit at hers and he laughed softly. She paused but to raise a wicked eyebrow at him before her hot hands were on his massive shaft, stroking his organ firmly and cupping his egg-sized testicles.

She knew what she was doing and he did not stop to think how she had become so adept; his eyes rolled back into his head and when her hot, wet mouth came down on him, he growled like a tiger. It was Remington's turn to laugh.

He could take naught but a few seconds of her touch before he was pulling her up by the hair, his mouth fusing to hers. They tumbled, rolled, grasped and touched until they rolled their way off the bed and onto the floor. Remington was so aroused she was panting loudly with each breath, her body on fire like she had never known. She knew they were on the floor and did not particularly care, but as she stood to climb back on the bed, Gaston bent her over the mattress and drove into her from behind.

She cried out loudly from his sudden, act of control and domination. Her face was pressed into the bed, her taut nipples brushing against the covers as Gaston's strength plowed into her repeatedly. She was begging for a release, pleading with him to relieve her pain when he suddenly withdrew completely. Remington's head came up to question him, but no sooner did she raise her head than he was placing firm pressure against her second maidenhead, her anus, and her question was cut off by a loud, rattling moan from deep in her throat.

He relieved her, all right. No sooner did he enter her than she climaxed violently and collapsed in a heap. He completely supported her hips with his hands, driving himself into her with more satisfaction than he had ever thought possible. He erupted turbulently, spilling himself with unbelievable force.

Shaken and breathing as if he had just run the entire distance from London to Mt. Holyoak, he pulled Remington up against his sweaty body and then collapsed with her onto the bed.

Neither one of them spoke for some time. Gaston was actually speechless and Remington was basking in the most wonderful, intimate act they had shared yet. She was in heaven.

"I never knew," she murmured against his chest.

"Nor did I, angel," he agreed fervently. He meant it.

She raised her head. "Guy tried to force me to have sex with him as we just did, but he hurt me terribly. With you....Good Lord, I have difficultly believing the sweetness."

He kissed her, not knowing what to say. Words had never been too terribly easy for him and he wasn't sure he could accurately convey his feelings to her. He was afraid his voice would crack with emotion.

She was smiling at him, listening to the faint sounds of the bailey below. "You have duties that await, my lord?"

He heard the sounds, too, and passed a disinterested look toward the slit window. "Aye, I suppose so."

She looked regretful. "A pity we cannot stay here all day. And all night. And all day."

He snorted. "We'd kill each other, I fear. I'd die a young, but very happy, man. Not a bad suggestion at that."

She laughed, and then cuddled back against him with a happy sigh. "As it is, I fear our passion may have come to bear."

He knew exactly what she was saying and she felt him stiffen beneath her. "Remi...?" he asked hesitantly.

"I am not completely sure," she said truthfully. "But my menses are usually quite regular and... well, it's past my time by a few days."

He sat up so fast she yelped with surprise. His smoky eyes were wide. "You are carrying my son?"

"I do not know," she repeated, unsure of his reaction. "But it is possible. I wanted to tell you so that you would not be surprised if... if I have news for you in the future."

He stared at her, dumbfounded. She pursed her lips, half in irritation, half in uncertainty. "Surely the thought had crossed your mind, Gaston. After all, we have had several encounters and after last night, quite possibly your seed has found its mark. What did you think would happen if you kept me abed as you have? Nothing?"

He read her annoyance at his silence and put up his hand to ease her. "Nay, angel, it's not that. It's just that...I never thought we would be so blessed. Not this soon, at any rate."

She was puzzled, some of her anger abating. "And why not?" He shrugged, looking away. "I do not know. I just did not. It took Mari-Elle several years to become pregnant with Trenton and she always accused me of having impotent seed. I did not believe her, of course, but somehow the thought always stuck with me."

She still could not tell if he was pleased or not. "If what I suspect is true, then your seed is anything but impotent. To have planted it within my womb within a matter of weeks is a testimony to your virility, my love," she eyed him hesitantly. "Are you not pleased, then?"

His gaze snapped to her and he cupped her lovely face between his great hands. When he spoke, his voice quivered. "Remi, if it is true, then you have made me the happiest man on the face of the earth. If I loved you before, madam, a child would only add to this impossible dream."

She broke into a wide, beautiful smile, kissing him eagerly. He responded with fierce tenderness, pulling her against him and tasting her sweetness.

"I must confess something, Gaston," she said after a moment. "I, too, thought I was somewhat infertile. In the entire time Guy and I have been married, I only conceived once. Guy blamed the lack of heirs on me, of course, and when Jasmine conceived, it only reinforced his accusations. If this is true....if I truly bear your child, then I am as amazed as you are."

He looked at her thoughtfully. "Mayhap it wasn't us after all. Mayhap it was them all along, looking to cast the blame elsewhere for their shortcomings."

She nodded hopefully, wildly happy in his arms. It had only been a few days since her menses had failed to appear, and in truth, she had been a bit apprehensive. But no more. If there was a God, she prayed to him awkwardly that she was indeed pregnant with the Dark One's child.

CHAPTER EIGHTEEN

Gaston put off their departure for an entire week. He had troops to train, a keep to run, and had little if any time for the papal envoy. The fat little man was outraged at the delays, and since Gaston refused to see him, he managed to corner Remington one day in the downstairs corridor and lay into her like an enraged father.

Remington, deeply upset by the man's words, ran straight to Gaston and found him outside with his new soldiers. It was early afternoon and the hot August sun beat down upon the suffering males as they went through their paces.

The knights were out of armor, stripped naked to the waist as they paced among the columns of men as they practiced quick placement of shields. The troops were in mail, sweating rivers, and already they had lost half a dozen men to heat exhaustion.

Remington stood by the inner bailey gates, her misty eyes searching for Gaston. He was not difficult to locate; the largest man by far in the middle of a collection of men, his bronzed skin and red-kissed shoulders standing a head and a half above the rest.

Arik caught sight of her before Gaston did and greeted her pleasantly. The two had developed a genuine like for each other within the past week.

"What brings you out here on this hellish day, madam?" he asked.

"I must speak with Gaston," she said, wiping daintily at her nose. "That damnable envoy just gave me an earful in the hall. I would tell Gaston."

Arik frowned. "Was he deliberately rude? Was he harsh?"

She was verging on a pout. "He's an arrogant little bastard. Is Gaston too busy to speak with me now, Arik?"

"Never," Arik bade her to stay where she was as he sought Gaston on her behalf.

Watching him walk toward her across the hot, dusty bailey brought a rush of warmth to her cheeks. He moved so gracefully and with such presence that she felt her knees go weak at the mere sight of him. *I want for you to be my husband.* The familiar chant filled her, only this time he echoed the sentiment. He was hers.

"What's amiss, angel?" he asked with concern. "Arik said you were upset?"

She nodded. "The envoy cornered me not a few minutes ago and demanded that I be ready to leave by the morning. He says he will not wait any longer; if I am not ready to leave on the morrow, he will return to London alone and tell Henry that you deliberately disobeyed the king. I think he means what he says, Gaston."

Gaston's face hardened. She could see him thinking, for his eyes took on a distant look even though he was focused on her. "Where is he now?"

"Inside," she flipped her hand carelessly in the general direction of the castle. "Somewhere. I hope he trips on his ecclesiastical robes and breaks his neck."

He grunted, a half grin on his lips. "I shall speak with him. Go inside now, love. 'Tis too hot outside for you."

She sighed, glancing up at the brilliant blue sky. "I cannot remember such heat. Rory wants to go swimming; will that be very well?"

Gaston glanced over his shoulder at his men, nodding faintly. "I suppose I could spare Nicolas to take you."

"Thank you," she said, dragging her hand over her forehead. She had not taken three steps away from him when she suddenly stopped and faced him.

His eyebrows drew together at the faint smile suddenly playing on her lips. "What?"

She gave him a sly look, one of her very best.

"Congratulations, father."

He forgot all about his men, the bailey, the keep, the envoy, and the king. He was on her in one stride. "Are you sure?"

She smiled and nodded her head slowly. "Oh, yes!"

He stared at her. Then, the smallest of twitches tugged at the corner of his mouth. He had not allowed himself to think on the prospect since they had last spoke of it because he did not want to be disappointed. Listening to her confirmation was almost more than he could take. "Honestly?"

"Come early April, I will bear you a son," she said confidently.

He could show no outward signs of his joy, he knew that distinctly. But, God help him, he wanted to shout and jump and hug everyone he could get his hands on. Including and fore mostly Remington. He was struggling so to contain himself that he started to shake and Remington noticed.

"What's the matter?" she asked, suddenly concerned.

"Nothing, Remi," he cleared his throat and stood back from her; he was dangerously close to displaying his joy in front of a thousand men. "Go inside now. I shall send Nicolas to you."

She blinked. No thanks? No words of joy? "Aren't you happy?"

He let out a choked gasp, taking another step away from her and raking his fingers through his hair to keep it back. A nervous smile burst forth as he gazed at her. "Remi, I am closer now than I ever have been in my life to breaking protocol and taking you into my arms. Too close! Go inside before I lose all control and ravish you in front of my men."

She grinned in return. "Then you are happy."

He could only manage an unsteady nod. "Aye, happy. Happier than you will ever know, angel. In fact, I shall show you just how happy I am later in private."

She understood and proceeded to head back toward the castle, turning every so often to glance back at him. He still stood where she left him, staring at her as if she were the Virgin Mary.

"You are pregnant?" Jasmine gasped loudly.

Remington shushed her harshly as Mary played at their feet. "Not a word, Jassy. Promise me. No one knows but Gaston and I."

Jasmine, her eyes wide as the sky, nodded with disbelief. "Oh, Remi... I am so happy for you. But...."

"But what?" Remington demanded.

Jasmine looked as if her eyes were going to pop from her skull. "I am pregnant, too."

"What?" Remington exploded.

"And so is Skye."

"What?" Remington found herself screaming.

"Remi!" Jasmine yelled back, pleadingly.

Remington collapsed on the bed behind her, her face glazed with shock, "You? Skye? My baby sisters?"

Jasmine nodded unsteadily, measuring her sister's reaction. Remington was as shocked as she had ever seen her, her beautiful face pale and her eyes wide. Then, suddenly, she bubbled out a choke of laughter. "And I was worried about the serving wenches," she said lamely. "I was worried about all of the bastards we would have come spring, and look at us. 'Tis us I should have worried over."

Jasmine smiled timidly, watching her sister as she shook her head in disbelief. "Antonius has been praying for a son ever since he found out. What about Gaston?"

Remington shook her head, still dazed. "I do not know. When he spoke of the baby, he referred to it as his son. Of course he wants a son."

"Skye is frightened, which is why she did not tell you," Jasmine said. "Not even Nicolas knows."

Remington looked sharply at her sister. "He does not? She must tell him."

"She will," Jasmine said quietly. "But I promised her that I would break the news to you."

Remington stood up. The supper hour was growing near and soon they would be required in the grand hall. She went to her wardrobe and drew forth a beautiful surcoat of scarlet silk as her little niece toddled after her. When she laid the surcoat on the bed, the baby pulled it down on the floor and rolled around in it.

"Mary." Jasmine extracted her daughter from the surcoat as Remington undid the stays of her dress.

"Leave her be, Jassy," she said with a faint smile. "We must become used to young ones around here again. By summer, there will be three more to add."

Jasmine smiled as Mary began to tug on the coverlet, trying to pull it down on the floor as well. "I am so happy, Remi. Happier than I have ever been in my whole life."

"I can tell," Remington gazed fondly at her sister as she lifted the scarlet dress over her head. "It shows on your face."

Jasmine helped her with the surcoat. "When are you leaving for London?"

Remington lost her smile and her mood. She had told her sisters everything, of course, and the women were devastated. No one had mentioned the subject in almost a week.

"The envoy wants to leave tomorrow," she said softly. "Gaston said he would speak with him."

Her eyes met with her sister's, fear and terror and apprehension passing between them. "I am scared for you, Remi," Jasmine whispered. "What if Gaston is unable to keep you from Guy?"

"He won't let Guy near me, I promise you," Remington said with more confidence than she felt. "He is the Dark Knight, is he not? The king will grant him anything he asks."

Mary began to fuss and Jasmine swept her daughter into her arms. "She's hungry. I must take her to her nurse," she moved for the door, pausing in the archway. "Remi... you shall come home soon, won't you? You won't stay in London long?"

"Long enough to obtain an annulment," Remington replied. "Do not worry, Jassy. You shall see your nephew before he grows old enough to foster."

Jasmine smiled and quit the room, a sense of foreboding filling her like nothing she had ever sensed.

Dinner was a lively occasion. As Remington and her sisters helped serve the knights, there seemed to be a special aura filling the air that had not been there before. Warmth, affection, comfort...'twas difficult to describe, but it existed nonetheless. Nicolas watched Skye, Patrick watched Rory, Antonius watched Jasmine, and Gaston could not take his eyes from Remington. In the clear scarlet, she was positively the most beautiful woman he had ever gazed upon and he felt extremely fortunate.

Dane and Trenton were official pages now and not allowed to join the diners. Instead, they lingered in the recesses of the hall with a half dozen other pledges and hovered to do the biddings of the knights. Remington tried hard not to focus on her son, but it was exceedingly difficult since they were both serving the knights. Gaston had asked her not to speak to him at all, which she thought was ridiculous, but she did as she was asked, even when they bumped into one another.

Dane did not say a word. He rushed away as if he had bumped into nothing more than a chair and Remington's heart broke in two. Biting back tears, she grabbed a pitcher of watered ale and moved to Gaston's table to replenish the drinks.

Gaston had seen the exchange and was pleased that both Remington and Dane were doing as they were told. But he could tell the moment he looked at her face that she was close to crying and he felt for her. When she moved to top his drink, he gently took the pitcher from her and sat her down on the bench next to him.

"You did well, angel," he said for her ears only. "'Twill become easier with time."

Her lips twitched and she blinked, fat tears splattering onto her cheeks that he quickly wiped away. Within the privacy of the head table, he was not uncomfortable touching her harmlessly.

"He will think I have forgotten him," she sobbed quietly.

He smiled sympathetically. "Nay, he will not. He knows that he is a trainee, and therefore no longer entitled to the courtesy once enjoyed as the young master of the keep. He realizes his place, love. Do not worry that he will resent you for treating him as you should."

She put her hand to her face and sobbed softly. He chuckled and pulled her head into the crook of his neck. Arik, on the other side of her, gazed back with sympathetic amusement.

"'Tis difficult to cut the cord at seven years of age," he remarked. "Dane is a fine student, my lady. You will be very proud of him one day."

She sobbed softly. "I hate you both."

Both men laughed heartily. Gaston kept her cradled against him as he finished what was left in his cup. Jasmine, placing a fresh plate of bread on the table, looked stricken when she saw Remington crying in Gaston's arms.

"What's wrong with her?" she demanded.

"Motherhood," Arik commented.

Jasmine's eyes widened. Gaston caught the look and knew that she was in on their secret. His dark expression instantly quelled any further words from Jasmine and the sister quickly vacated the table.

Remington, meanwhile, stopped her tears and discovered she had a terrible headache. She pulled away from Gaston and composed herself.

"With your permission, my lord, I shall retire for the night," she sniffed.

He peered closely at her. "Are you feeling well?"

"My head aches," she said truthfully, and then fixed him in the eye. "A lack of sleep."

He cleared his throat in a startled, reflexive gesture. "As you wish, my lady. I shall see you later."

She rose from the bench, murmuring something to Rory before continuing the length of the room. Gaston turned casually to watch her retreat, aware that every man in the room was watching her glorious form. Once, the realization would have made him insane with jealously. But he was so secure with their relationship that he found himself bristling with pride.

She's mine, lads!

Remington was almost clear of the room when a figure rose from one of the tables and blocked her exit. Gaston was up and moving when he realized the envoy was attempting to detain her again, and he would not allow the man to deal her another tongue-lashing. Everything that needed to be said had been said not an hour before, between himself and the priest. He had yet to inform Remington of the outcome of that meeting.

"De Tormo, the lady was retiring for the night," he said as he came upon them. "You will not detain her."

The priest turned and looked at him, his eyes narrowed. "Retiring alone? A rare occurrence, I am told."

Remington swallowed hard, looking at Gaston. His face was like stone, impassive and unreadable as always. After several uncomfortable moments, he advanced another step on the priest. He smiled, but it was a dangerous gesture.

"I am not in the habit of murdering priests, even fat obnoxious ones, but I can readily change my practice," he said, his voice a low rumble. "If I were to kill you now, are you assured of spending eternity in heaven? You see, I have nothing to lose, for my soul is already damned. Is your afterlife as guaranteed?"

The priest blanched. "You would not dare and risk the wrath of the church!"

Gaston cocked a lazy, confident eyebrow. "And I, priest, know a few things about you. 'Tis most hypocritical for an ordained priest to take a serving wench to his bed, a serving wench that can be easily bought with a few coins. I wonder how the diocese would look upon that?"

The priest stiffened and his eyes widened. "I have done no such thing."

Gaston crossed his arms. "And I say that I can find at least a half dozen women that will swear on the bible that you have. Mayhap more. Women that will accompany Lady Stoneley to London, ready to testify if called upon by the papal counsel."

The veins in de Tormo's neck bulged. "How...how dare you threaten a man of God! And you, a knight, sworn to uphold the church? You should be cowering at my feet, de Russe, not threatening blackmail!"

Gaston moved closer, his eyes glittering like deadly precious stones. "'Tis no threat, de Tormo. I never threaten. But I do promise. You will go down in flames, I swear it!"

De Tormo was having difficulty catching his breath. Remington, her eyes wide, alternately watched the priest and Gaston. She was having difficulty grasping what Gaston was saying, but the priest had no trouble at all. He knew.

De Tormo was no fool. He could read his death in the knight's eyes and it scared the hell out of him. De Russe wanted something, and he wanted it badly enough to threaten to kill a man of the cloth. This threat went beyond that fact that de Tormo had heard of his relationship with Lady Stoneley; nay, this went deeper. He was intelligent enough to know that and savvy enough to respond.

"Then what is it you would have of me?" the priest choked out. "My oath of silence? What?"

Gaston backed off slightly. "In the solar. I do not conduct business in the open."

The priest bowed away, flicking an uncertain glance in Remington's direction. She watched him slink away, and Gaston put his hand on her arm in a reassuring gesture as he attempted to follow.

"Wait," Remington put her hand on him. "May I come?"

He looked hesitant. "This is business, angel. Go on to bed and I shall seek you later."

"I would like to come," she said, a request and not a demand. "I assume that what will be said will directly affect me?"

He gazed back at her, swallowed by her intelligent eyes. Aye, she was smart with a head for business. He had seen it. This was no empty-headed chit, but a magnificent, brilliant woman, the mother of his future child, his future wife. He respected her astute mind more than he had ever respected almost anyone, including Henry.

"Very well," he relented softly. "But I will do the talking, madam. Understood?"

"Of course, Gaston," she looked surprised that he would even say such a thing. "Did the priest really take a serving wench to his bed?"

Gaston pulled her into the dim foyer as they headed for the solar. "No. But it is amazing what money can buy."

Her eyes widened. "But why do you do this? Why are you worried that he knows of us?"

He sighed. "Listen when I speak to him, angel, and you will understand then."

He opened the door and ushered her into the solar. De Tormo was sitting in the hide-covered chair next to the hearth, looking distinctly apprehensive. He did not look up when Gaston and Remington entered the room.

Gaston closed the door and went right to the point. "I have a proposition for you, priest."

The man turned, then. "I suspected as much. What is it? How am I to perjure myself, my lord?"

Gaston actually sat opposite the priest, unusual that he would sit in the presence of anyone. He never sat when conducting business, but he did this time. He wanted to be, somehow, less threatening. He wanted information, and he wanted help, and he did not want to beat the man into agreement.

"Undoubtedly you have heard the rumors regarding Lady Stoneley and myself," he began quietly. "To deny them would be futile, I fear. It is because of this that I must seek your counsel."

The priest still looked apprehensive, but a sort of weariness had set in as well. "Speak, then."

Gaston was truly annoyed by the man's haughty attitude, but he admired it as well. If this man could stand up to him this well, imagine how he could stand up to his superiors. Gaston, in spite of the fact that he did not like this priest, wanted him on his side. Any way he could have him.

"I will come to the point," Gaston said. "I wish to marry Lady Stoneley. What is involved in obtaining an annulment?"

The priest looked shocked. His eyes widened and he looked to Remington a moment before turning back to Gaston. "An annulment? On what grounds?"

"Cruelty," Gaston said shortly. "Guy Stoneley has beat and raped his wife and her sisters for nine years."

The priest shook his head slowly. "Not sufficient. A man's wife is his chattel, as you know. He can do as he wishes without interference from the church."

Gaston pursed his lips into a hard, flat line. "But he still must adhere to the moral code of the church, in which he took his vows."

De Tormo considered the argument. Then, he shook his head again. "Too vague, de Russe. Now, were he to worship the devil and force her to participate, it would be another matter. But you cannot base an annulment on simple discipline."

"Discipline," Gaston repeated with outrage. "He beat them, priest. There is nothing in the world a woman could do to warrant that kind of severe discipline."

De Tormo was quite calm and neutral, not at all staunch and opposed to what was being suggested. Remington found it surprising that he would not lecture then endlessly for breaking God's commandment.

"Discipline can be interpreted many ways, de Russe. What is your interpretation might not be another's," he replied evenly. "Nay, an annulment must be based on something much more severe, as I said. If Guy were proven a traitor to England, or...."

"But he is in jail as a prisoner of the crown," Remington suddenly said, forgetting her promise to remain silent. "Isn't that considered a traitor?"

"Not unless he swears he is a traitor, which he will not," the priest replied. "If I were to ask him if he were a traitor to England, you know he would refute it. Nay, a man is only a traitor to his country if he is in league with another government or country. Guy is not guilty of betraying England herself, only his king."

Remington looked at Gaston in confusion. He understood the priest perfectly and put out a hand to her. Hesitantly, she placed her hand in his huge palm. "What he is saying is that Guy did not betray his country with the purpose of placing a foreign ruler on the throne. Guy fought against England for England. He's not a true traitor in the sense of the word."

She hung her head in understanding; aware that Gaston had pulled her against the chair he sat in. He still held her hand. She listened to Gaston and the priest converse, mildly surprised that the tone was civil. In fact, De Tormo seemed to have lost his arrogant disposition and was speaking quite politely.

Then, something occurred to her. Devil worship, did the priest say? A thought struck her like lightening, so much so that she actually jumped. Gaston turned to look up at her, but she was focused on the priest.

"What if I could prove to you that Guy worshipped the devil?" she asked, her eyes glittering.

The priest blinked. So did Gaston. "You can prove this?" De Tormo asked hesitantly.

She nodded eagerly. "Aye, I can. Come with me and I shall show you."

She flew to the door, opening it eagerly. The men were still sitting. "Get up!"

They followed her to the second floor of the keep, pacing down dim corridors. Gaston began to have an inkling of an idea as to where she was taking them, but held his tongue. He would not interfere with her plan, and an excellent one at that. He was glad he had not underestimated her cleverness.

As he suspected, she led them into the southwest turret and they carefully ascended the spiral stairs. Gaston was directly behind her in case she should lose her footing as they made their way to the tower room. Charles' room.

Thankfully, Charles wasn't there. Remington led the men into the room, a sinister assortment of implements and potions cluttered about the place as well as several books. The overall impression was chaotic, as if a mad sorcerer kept shop in the room. Remington pointed to the pentagram that decorated the near wall.

"You see? He worships Satan here," she announced.

The priest's mouth was open as he stared at the pentagram, eyed the potions and kicked at a bucket filled with something dark and slimy. He picked up a bowl and blew at it, only to be covered by a cloud of whitish dust. Coughing, he set the bowl down and eyed Remington.

In a cage hanging from the ceiling was a fat, nasty toad. The priest eyed it warily and the frog burped loudly at him.

"A toad," he announced distastefully.

"He kept it to house his soul," Remington said, hoping fervently that the man would believe that this was the room of a Satanist. Not the laboratory of a curious teenage boy.

"You are sure, my lady?" he asked.

She nodded unsteadily. "I told you I was married to Satan. I meant it."

The priest's gaze lingered on her a moment before he focused on a table holding several books. Gingerly, he retrieved one of the books and held it up to the light, examining it.

"Human skin," Remington blurted. "That book is covered in human skin."

The book clattered to the floor. "I have seen enough," the priest announced, sweeping to the door. He looked pointedly at Remington. "My lady, I will testify before the papal counsel that I myself observed your husband's house of devil worship. Have no fear that they will listen to me."

"Thank you," Remington breathed. "I simply want to be free of an evil, evil man."

"No doubt," the priest gave the room one final, disgusted look. "After seeing this disgrace, I have no misgivings that the baron should be burned at the stake. In fact, I might recommend just that."

"But there is more to it than just your word," Gaston entered the conversation. "What else is involved with the annulment?"

De Tormo was decidedly uncomfortable with Satan's den behind him; he kept inching away from the door. "Indeed, de Russe. You must obtain eight testimonies from notable and trustworthy people, who, for you, will not be difficult." He glanced at Remington. "But the lady must obtain testimonies from people who know of her husband's indiscretions which, I fear, may not be so easy."

Remington gazed back a bit fearfully. "But...but he kept his devotion secretive. How can I obtain eight testimonies if no one knew of his lust?"

"As I said, it may not be so easy," the priest glanced to the tower room again, shaking his head. "Yet, mayhap with my own witness, the church will relax the lady's restrictions. But you realize, of course, that not only must the lady's marriage be annulled, but Sir Gaston's marriage to his deceased wife must be annulled as well."

Gaston nodded faintly; he knew that, but he was not concerned. The only matter that concerned him was Guy Stoneley. "I am aware of that, priest. The church shall have their eight depositions from the most powerful men in Henry's court."

The priest snorted. "No doubt one from Henry himself."

Gaston lifted an eyebrow in response.

Without another word, the priest descended the stairs, leaving Gaston and Remington standing in the doorway to the tower room. When they heard the door slam below, they looked at each other.

Gaston smiled warmly at her. "My compliments, Lady Remington. A most brilliant move on your part."

She flushed. "I hoped he would believe it."

He took her in his arms. "Apparently he did," he said softly. "Is that book really bound in human skin?"

She nodded. "It really is. But it is also over one hundred years old, from Egypt. 'Tis a book of ancient recipes."

He laughed softly, rocking her tenderly in his arms.

She clung to him. "It is almost too good to believe, Gaston. Will he truly help us?"

"It would seem so, and without my having to blackmail him," Gaston replied.

"Is that what you were going to do? Force him into helping us?" she asked softly.

"'Twas my intention," he admitted. "I was going to pay several serving women to say that the priest slept with them if he refused to assist us with the annulment. As much as I loathe devious means to gain my ends, I would have done it. Anything for you."

"You said when you first entered the solar that you had a proposition for him," she said. "What was it?"

"That he help us attain our annulment and in exchange, I would not ruin his secular life," he replied. "As it stands, I may not need to resort to bribery at all. You, my brilliant little tart, seemed to have spared the priest and I a most uncomfortable situation."

She lowered her lashes shyly. "It wasn't much."

"Ha." He took her hand and preceded her down the stairs. "You are incredibly astute, my lady. Our son will be the most intelligent, brilliant being on the face of the earth."

She was rosy with the compliments as he led her to the second floor landing and opened the door.

"I must find Charles and tell him what I have done," she said. "I would not want something to slip out inadvertently before we leave."

"Agreed," he said. "Inform your sisters, too."

"I will," she nodded. "I shall do it now, before I retire."

They walked hand in hand down the corridor until they reached the main stairs, listening to the sounds of revelry floating up from the grand hall. There, he released her hand, but his gaze was soft on her face.

"And by the way," he said, a bit of reproval in his tone. "You told your sister of your condition, did not you?"

She looked a bit stunned, trying to play off her surprise but not succeeding. "What... why do you say that?"

He tapped her under the chin. "Because I know. What did you tell her?"

There was no use in denying it. However, she put her hands on her hips and turned it around. "And do you know what else?" she said sternly. "It seems that we were not the only ones who couldn't keep our hands off each other. Jasmine is pregnant, too."

He did not look surprised. "Antonius will marry her."

"And so is Skye."

He raised his eyebrows slightly. "Ah. Well, Nicolas might be another matter. He may have to be convinced."

"He does not know. Skye is afraid to tell him."

He nodded faintly, turning for the stairs and taking her elbow. "Mayhap I should speak with him."

"Aye, mayhap you should," she insisted, relieved he wasn't angry with her for spilling their "news". Even if he was, he had not admonished her.

The hall was still in full swing, Gaston's knights loud and boisterous with their games and songs. He kissed her hand and left her at the door, entering the room while Remington frantically beckoned her sisters to join her.

It was to be Remington's last day at Mt. Holyoak before traveling to London. Gaston had told the priest they would leave in two days to allow him time to make preparations for his trainees, and further to allow Remington to take care of any final details.

Oleg followed her through the castle, listening to her rattle off instructions. She most likely would not be returned by September, when the sheep would be shorn, and she made sure that Oleg understood to proceed without her. Grain stores needed replenishing and the fact that the providence had had a good season promised to fill the stores to capacity. No one would go hungry in Boroughbridge, or the neighboring towns of Helperby and Brafferton. With winter on the approach, food was of a primary concern.

She and Gaston had exchanged heated words this morning. Unsure of how long they would be in London, Remington wanted him to convince Antonius and Nicolas to marry her sisters before she left. To think of her sisters unwed and pregnant left her feeling hollow with pity, and she felt it Gaston's duty, as their liege, to convince the knights to do the right thing. Gaston replied, patiently, that he could not force his men into matrimony before they were ready.

Angrily, Remington had turned her back on him and left to go about her duties. Even as she went over the kitchen stock with Oleg, she was still angry with him. Aye, she knew she was being somewhat unreasonable, but she couldn't fathom the knight's reluctance to do the right thing. But the most maddening thing was when Gaston had told her frankly the whole situation between her sisters and their prospective husbands was none of her business.

None of her business! The words still riled her, even as Oleg went over the inventory of stored vegetables. Remington ordered a vegetable soup for the nooning meal from his tally and left him to sort out the rest of the kitchen supplies. Eudora was packing for her and she wanted to check up on the woman.

She passed into the grand hall and came face to face with Dane and another young page, laden down with stock for the kitchens. Her first reaction was to hug him, and she could see the light in his eyes as well, but just as quickly she averted her gaze and walked past him. Dane, with a sad face, passed into the kitchens behind the other boy.

Her anger at Gaston and her sadness for her son brought tears to her eyes as she made her way down the corridor. She was leaving on the morrow and not even allowed to say good-bye to her son. Her sisters were pregnant and unwed, and she was faced with an uncertain future. When did her life become so miserable?

As soon as she reached the narrow stairs, Gaston and Antonius entered the castle and nearly ran her over. She looked up to snap at them, but then noticed that they were in full battle armor.

"What's wrong?" she demanded warily, forgetting she was mad at him.

"Brimley is under siege!" he said. "It would seem that Lord Botmore heard of Brimley's meeting with me and decided to pay him a visit.

Brimley told Botmore that he was planning to support the crown and Botmore went wild. His troops were already inside the keep and from what I understand have managed to fairly wreak havoc. I must go and do what I can."

"Botmore!" she hissed. "He destroyed Crayke?"

"I do not know. But I intend to find out and make restitution to Brimley."

The day that had started out bad had just gotten worse. She sank down on the steps and shook her head. "Gaston, Derek was betrothed to Catherine Brimley, Lord Brimley's youngest daughter. Botmore was so proud of the alliance. I cannot understand why he would do this."

Gaston jerked his head at Antonius, who discreetly vacated. He gazed down on Remington's puzzled, sad face.

"Nor I, angel," he said softly. "Except to say that Botmore is seeking revenge on me and he knows it would be foolish to attack Mt. Holyoak with all of the troops I have here. Suffice it to say he intends to cause me a great deal of trouble."

She gazed up at him, her anger completely gone. How could she be angry at that beautiful, masculine face? "So you go to fight again?"

He smiled wryly, sitting heavily on the stair next to her. With all of his armor, he nearly squashed her into the wall. "I am afraid so. But I am leaving Arik behind, to guard you."

"Arik?" she was surprised. "Why would you leave your second in command behind to baby sit?"

He looked at her, his gaze tender as it lingered on her face. "Nothing is more important than you," he said softly. "I would stay behind if I could, but I must lead my troops. Besides, if this is a ruse, then I want Arik in charge of the fortress."

"But I thought you said Lord Botmore would not attack Mt. Holyoak?" she said, concerned.

"He would not do it while I was within the walls because he knows it would be futile. But he may try while I am off on some dandy pretense. I am not at all sure that this is not some sort of ploy to lure me away from my keep."

Her face went white. "My God, Gaston, could Botmore be luring you into an ambush?"

"Nay, I do not believe so," he assured her. "The messenger who brought the news was one of Brimley's men. But Botmore could have planned it this way to remove me from Mt. Holyoak while an army of Yorkists await at a distance to regain my seat."

Not only was she depressed, she was now completely frightened at that thought. Slowly, she wound her arms around his massive left arm and lay her cheek on his cold, hard armor. As she was thinking of something encouraging to say, tears suddenly found their way from her eyes and onto his armor.

"Why do you cry, angel? I did not mean to frighten you," he said tenderly.

She batted her eyes, trying to chase away her tears. "It's not that. It's just...why does everything have to be so bloody complex? Why can't everyone just leave us alone? I do not want to be involved in all of this intrigue and hatred; I do not want you to be involved in it."

He kissed the top of her head. "This has been my whole life, angel. I am used to it."

Her head came up, her eyes glittering like the rarest of jewels. She traced shaking fingers across his sensuous lips. "After we're married... promise me we will remove ourselves from all of this. I want us to live peacefully, Gaston."

"We will, love," he kissed her fingers, wanting to reassure her. "Do not worry so."

From down the hall they heard rapidly running footsteps. Small and quick, it could either be a child or a woman and they both turned as the footsteps came upon them. Dane suddenly appeared, his eyes wide and his face streaked with tears.

"Dane!" Remington knew she wasn't supposed to speak with him, but she couldn't help herself when she saw her son.

"You can't fight!" Dane blurted to Gaston, all but ignoring his mother.

"What's wrong, Dane?" Gaston was genuinely concerned. Dane's eyes were wide with fright and his little face pale. "I... I had a dream. I saw armor, your armor, and I saw an arrow through your heart. You were dead. We buried you in your armor."

Remington went to pieces. Her hands flew to her mouth and she moaned softly as Gaston got a grip on her. He never gave any stock in prophetic dreams, but he knew Remington did. She said that her son had predicted many things through his young dreams.

"'Twas only a dream, Dane," he said evenly, feeling Remington shaking violently. "If a dream comes true, it is only coincidence. Mayhap dreams are the only things in life we can change; we can choose to believe them or we can choose not to."

Dane wiped at his eyes, looking a bit embarrassed. "I fell asleep in the kitchen because I did not sleep very well last night. I dreamt you were killed. You can't go."

Gaston smiled and put his hand on the boy's head. "Are you a gloom-and-doom prophet, lad? Did you actually see my face?"

"Nay, I did not see your face. But it was your armor, the armor you wear right now." Dane insisted, glancing at his mother for the first time. "And I dreamed last night that my mother had a big stomach, like Aunt Jasmine did a couple of years ago. What does that mean?"

Remington's eyes widened at her son a split second before she turned to Gaston, grabbing him by his armor. "You cannot go!"

She was verging on panic; he could see it in her eyes. He gathered her gently against him and waved Dane off. "I appreciate your concern, lad. I am sure you have assigned duties, do you not?"

Dane nodded weakly, not wanting to disobey his liege. He turned hesitantly, his steps down the hall much slower upon returning.

"Come on," Gaston stood up with Remington in his arms, sweeping her up the stairs.

Eudora was finishing packing when Gaston brought her into the bedchamber, shaking and weeping. The old woman's eyes widened.

"What's happened to her?" she asked urgently.

Gaston lay her down on the bed. "She's simply overwrought. Fetch her a wine brew, Eudora, to calm her nerves."

The old woman fled as Remington struggled to a sitting position on the bed. Gaston removed his gauntlets and helm before sitting heavily on the mattress. Remington was still sobbing weakly and he took her hands between his own.

"Remi, get hold of yourself. You cannot put any stock in a young boy's dreams."

"But you heard him," she insisted loudly. "He dreamt of our child, Gaston, and I have not told him anything. Something awful is going to happen to you."

"Nonsense," he shushed her gently. "The heat and your condition has you overwrought. Remi, hordes of England's finest knights have been unable to kill me. What makes you think a minor skirmish will do me in?"

"Dane's dreams do not lie." Her crying had lessened, but she was shaking terribly.

As much as he wanted to stay and comfort her, he had a battle to fight. He couldn't give in to her son's telltale dreams, no matter if she believed them or not. There was always a logical explanation. *Black and white.* There was nothing unexplainable.

"I want you to rest until I return, angel," he said softly. "I shan't be long."

He had said that before, when he left to assist Templehurst, and he had been true to his word. But Dane's dream rang in Remington's ears and she couldn't shake the feeling.

"Promise me you shall take great care?" she whispered, knowing it futile to beg him to stay. "I will promise you that, madam," he said, pulling his gauntlets back on. "I will take great, great care with myself so that I may return to the woman I love."

She watched the gloves go on. She would have to believe in him, and she would have to believe that whatever fate brought them together would return him safely to her. There was nothing she could do or say to make him remain behind and she resigned herself to the fact.

He gathered his helm and kissed her sweetly on the lips. Thinking her to taste most delightful, he kissed her again and grinned broadly as his second kiss had brought a smile to her lips.

"That's better, love," he whispered.

"Gaston?" she called out softly as he moved for the door.

He paused, plopping his helm on. "What would you name our son?" she asked. She had to ask; what if he did not return and she had not asked him? She shivered involuntarily.

"I... I do not know," he looked thoughtful. "I have not thought on it. What would you name him?"

She shrugged and he smiled, latching his helm. "Think on it, then. I will expect several prospects upon my return."

She nodded, giving him a wan smile. He quit the room and she heard his footsteps fading down the hall until they vanished. Exhausted and distraught, she fell back on the bed and drifted into a deep, dreamless sleep.

On the second day since Gaston's departure, Remington was ready to climb the walls. Word had come back to Arik that Gaston and his army had engaged Botmore at Crayke and the baron was proving to be a handful. Worried and sickened, Remington tried to occupy herself with various projects, anything to keep from worrying.

Arik proved to be a delightful companion. When he wasn't out training the troops, he was with her constantly and she enjoyed his quick wit and conversation. He would play games with her and let her win, she was sure, but he acted the complete gentleman always.

Father de Tormo kept to himself much of the time, spending his hours in the solar chronicling his visit to Mt. Holyoak and his subsequent discoveries. Remington was glad he was able to keep himself occupied, for she had her own problems to deal with. She did not want to even think of London until Gaston returned to her safely.

Nicolas and Rory had another go-around right after Gaston left. Rory sabotaged the taper beside his bed with a concoction of Charles' doing so that when he lit the end, it exploded with a loud bang and sent wax sailing all over the room. Nicolas was furious and, frankly, frightened as hell and wandered the castle bellowing for Rory. He found her in Skye's room.

Rory was wise as well as mischievous. She planted herself snuggly in her sister's room so that the enraged knight could do nothing but smile sweetly at his love and glare at her sister in the same breath. Rory laughed at him silently when Skye's back was turned and he mouthed violent threats.

The heat of August was sticky and again the ladies turned their attention to the relief of the lake, as they had on so many occasions. Taking Arik and Nicolas with them, they packed food and retreated to the coolness and the shade that the little glen had to offer.

Rory, Skye and Jasmine plunged into the water, taking Mary with them. Nicolas stood at the edge of the water, watching them with a smile on his face. He hated water and refused to go in, even when Skye splashed him until he was soaking.

Arik and Remington watched from under the shade of the huge oak tree. The heat was draining on her and she simply wished to sit and rest, content to watch the others play for the moment. Arik chewed on a green apple.

"Your sisters are part fish," he commented.

She smiled faintly. "Sometimes I wonder," she gazed at his blond head, his angular Nordic face. "Will they return soon?"

Arik chewed thoughtfully. "Mayhap. If the skirmish was small, as it was at Templehurst."

She did not feel comforted. "Gaston is a magnificent warrior, is he not? He is invincible."

Arik turned to look at her over his shoulder; he could read her fear like a book. "He shall return, Remington. Have no doubt of it. He loves you far too much not to."

She flushed slightly and lowered her gaze. "You have known him a long time, have not you?"

"Since we were seven," Arik replied, still looking at her. "I have never known him to show soft emotion. No love, no tenderness, little kindness or compassion. I am constantly amazed at the depth of emotion I read in his eyes when he looks at you. You, madam, have done the one thing throngs of knights and soldiers have failed to do for thirteen years; you have brought the Dark One to his knees."

Her head came up in mild alarm. "'Twas never my intention, Arik. I would never intentionally weaken him."

"I did not mean to imply that you had. I simply meant that you have managed to achieve a far greater feat than any war ever has. You have tamed Edward's Dark Knight."

She looked at him. "I do not want to tame him. I only want to love him."

He chuckled softly. "Do not be offended by my words, Remington. I meant them as a compliment."

She wasn't offended, but she was puzzled. She shook her head at him. "Stop talking like that. You embarrass me."

He tossed the apple core and sat up. "Why is that? I merely seek to commend you. And tell you how glad I am that Gaston found you."

She grinned shyly and threw a piece of bark at him. Hit in the head, he brushed at his hair while she continued to pelt him. With a good-natured scowl, he moved out of her firing range.

"Aren't you hot in that armor?" she asked.

He shrugged. "I do not notice it. It is a part of me."

"It looks terribly uncomfortable," she remarked. "Why do not you remove it and go swimming? Unless, of course, you are afraid of the water like your fellow knight."

Arik made a wry face. "We have been through this once before, I believe. I do not swim."

She giggled, but as she relaxed, she suddenly realized how very tired she was. Swimming suddenly lost its appeal and the thick humidity seemed more cloying than ever. Strange that all of a sudden she should feel so terrible. She shifted uncomfortably, aware that she suddenly had to relieve herself badly.

"Arik, I think I shall return to the keep," she said. "I am tired."

He looked concerned. "Are you feeling poorly?"

"Just tired," she repeated, not sure if Gaston had disclosed their secret to his second. Unless he mentioned it, she was not going to offer any information.

"I shall escort you," he stood up, pulling her gently to her feet.

"No need, Arik, truly," she insisted. "I can walk through the trees and up the road all by myself. Truly."

He saw her jesting with him and shook his head. "Not a chance, my lady. Were you to trip and fall or should some other accident befall you, Gaston would skin me alive."

She merely shook her head. He followed her from the tree as she passed by the lake, calling to her sisters as she went. The more she

walked, the more fatigued she became until Arik was practically pulling her up the slope that led to Mt. Holyoak. He insisted strongly on
carrying her, but she waved him off. In fact, she nearly had to beat him
away and was glad when they passed under the razor-sharp teeth of the
portcullis.

He saw her safely inside the castle before returning to the group
on the lake.

Remington had fallen asleep, a weary sleep that was heavy. She failed
to hear the warning horns on the top of the wall, or the shouts of the
soldiers as they assembled hastily and rushed out of the castle. She did
not know anything was amiss until Eudora woke her in a panic.

Disoriented, she blinked the sleep from her eyes and noticed the
sun was nearly set. The old woman's fear ignited a panic of her own,
and Eudora could barely speak through her crying. She had to slap the
old woman to her senses to understand what she was trying to tell her.

She understood two words. Attack and death?

Death! Remington bolted from the room, rushing past her empty
sister's bedchambers and taking the stairs far too quickly. Fear and
apprehension gripped her like a vise as she hit the lower floor corridor
that led to the bailey. Her mind was a fog of incoherent thought; she
could neither form nor speak a rational idea. All she knew was that
something terrible had happened, and she had to find out what it was.
Who it was who had died?

The inner bailey was a hive of agitated activity. There were soldiers
on horseback racing across the drawbridge and still more soldiers mobilizing into ground troops. Remington searched for a familiar face, any
face among the mail and steel of the troops, and was seized with terror to see Skye and Jasmine being helped toward her by Sir Roald and
another knight. She leapt from the stairs to confront them.

"What happened?" she demanded severely.

Skye was hysterical and Jasmine was close to swooning. Before
Remington could ask again, Sir Roald answered her.

"An ambush at the lake, my lady," he replied, his lips white with emotion. "Sir Arik was killed! And your sister, Rory...."

His voice trailed away and Remington knew without being told that her sister was dead. Dear God, she knew. Her head began to swim as she spun away from him, searching frantically for her sister and Arik among the sea of men.

They were on litters not 10 feet from her; she had been so busy skimming the crowd that she had failed to look to the ground. With a stifled cry, she pushed forward through the knights and men until she reached the bodies. Dizzy with anguish, she nearly pitched forward onto Arik's still from, but strong hands steadied her from behind.

Arik had three arrows protruding out of him, one in the neck, one in the chest, and one in his thigh. Remington stood over him, not believing what she was seeing. His handsome face was peaceful in death. Her vision began to blur; she had just been speaking with him. How could he be dead? *How?*

Tears fell on his armor as she knelt beside him, taking his cold hand into her own. Gaston's friend, her friend! He was dead. Grief crept up on her like an unwelcome tide, but she fought it.

She had to remain strong, at least for the moment. Her shock was still too great to allow the grief to overtake her, and when her eyes settled on Rory's body not three feet away, rivers of tears fell on Arik's armor.

She was frozen for a moment, unable to do anything but crouch beside Arik and hold his lifeless hand as she stared at her dead sister. Around her, the bailey had quieted somewhat, attention moved to her as she dealt with the deaths. Respectfully, the soldiers backed off and allowed her a moment of semi-privacy.

Woodenly, she stood and staggered to a spot between the two bodies. Rory, her fire-colored hair spread gloriously, looked as if she was sleeping. She could see a huge red stain in the middle of her torso, but a discreet soldier had long removed the arrow. 'Twas one thing to see a knight with arrows piercing his body; 'twas another to see a horrible projectile jutting from a young lady's delicate chest.

Remington was far beyond shock and grief. She was in the realm of disbelief, denial. Haltingly, she took Arik's hand into her right hand

and Rory's limp hand into her left. The sun set, the world grew chill, and she continued to sit on her bottom in the middle of the inner bailey as if nothing else in the world existed. No tears, no shrieking; just utter, complete denial. When Roald brought out a cloak and placed it about her shoulders, she did not even notice.

The night progressed and still, Remington sat. She couldn't seem to force herself to move. Once she did, they would take the bodies and she would never see her sister or Arik again. She just couldn't let go, not yet. The grief, the shock, and the agony manifested itself in the hollow of her gut, aching with a dull pain she had never known. If she were to start crying again, she knew she would never stop.

Father de Tormo joined her in her silent vigil, performing last rites over Rory, and then Arik. His words were soft and monotonous and Remington was too dazed to feel a rush of anger at his words. Since when did God care about her family and loved ones? Did he care about them only in death? In life, he had never shown much interest. Were his concerns for their souls real or merely for show?

The bodies were stiffening. Rory's soft hand had formed a claw of death, but Remington continued to hold it. Arik's hand felt like stone.

Nicolas came out after the priest had left, watching her as guilt tore him apart. He had been there, aye; he had seen the arrows strike down Rory, and then Arik as he tried to save her. He had seen the soldiers strike and then retreat into the woods, and he had not pursued. He was far too concerned with returning the living to the keep to pursue the men and discover their identity.

The decision saved the lives of himself, Jasmine and Skye, but the cost was his personal pain.

He should have given chase, but in the same breath he knew his first priority was the remaining ladies, and his beloved Skye. He only hoped Gaston would understand his choice, and he furthermore prayed his brother did not take a dagger to him for allowing harm to befall his intended.

In spite of everything, Nicolas did not hate Rory. He had grown very fond of her in an irritated sort of way, and her death cut him to the bone. He knew Patrick was madly in love with the fiery redhead and he could only imagine the grief his brother would be feeling. The thought made Nicolas even more miserable; he had not only failed Gaston, but his brother as well. In general, he was hopelessly inadequate as a knight and anguish flooded him.

Before him he could see a far greater problem. Remington, stricken with grief, sat on the cold ground between two dead bodies. It was up to him to return her to the castle so the bodies could be prepared for burial on the morrow.

He wandered up behind her silently, greatly disturbed to see that she wasn't crying or carrying on. She simply sat, like a rock, cold, emotionless.

"My lady," he began softly. "May I help you inside? The night grows chill."

"Nay," she answered in a flat, firm tone.

He gazed down on her a moment. "Lady Remington, this night air is not good for your health. You are still recovering from your wound."

Remington snapped out of her daze. "Go away!" She roared at Nicolas, "Go away! I will hear no more talk of the night and the cold when my sister's only future is to be buried in the cold, cold earth. Leave me alone!"

He was stunned; he had never heard her raise her voice in the least, and especially not in anger. Knowing it was her grief talking did not make him feel any better.

"I cannot," he said gently. "You must come inside and allow the bodies to be taken away for burial."

"No!" She bellowed, turning to look at him with venomous eyes that startled him. "You shall not take them away, not until I say. Go away, Nicolas de Russe, before I kill you myself."

He felt a tremendous sense of despair. "My lady...."

"You hated her, did you not?" Remington seethed, grabbing both of Rory's hands into her own. "You are glad to be rid of her."

His composure vanished. "That's not true. We were fond of each other. I was the only knight she considered worthy of her pranks."

"Get out of my sight!" she screamed. Suddenly, the dam burst and the tears, the agony poured out. She threw herself atop her sister's stiff corpse and began to cry hysterically.

Nicolas dashed back the tears as fast as they came, but it wasn't fast enough. They streamed down his face, coating his stubbled skin, and dripped off his nose.

He couldn't let her weep so uncontrollably; she was already close to fainting from the way she was breathing and he swooped down on her, gathering her up in his arms. He expected her to fight and claw and beat at him for all she was worth, but instead, she collapsed against him and held him tightly.

"Why, Nicolas, why? Why did this happen?" she moaned desperately.

He couldn't speak for a moment; his voice would have cracked like a child's. "I do not know. But Gaston will find out and he will avenge your sister and Arik. I swear it, my lady."

She wept pitifully into the crook of his neck as he carried her into the castle. In their wake, soldiers scurried from the shadows to tend to the bodies, torches burning brightly in the night air.

The burial detail was ready at dawn. The humidity was already stifling as the two plain coffins were loaded on carts and moved into the outer bailey en route to the Stoneley cemetery at the base of the hill.

Two funerals in one week was about all Remington could take, but she forced her emotions down. Skye clutched Nicolas as they stood in the inner bailey waiting for the procession to organize, but Jasmine had been too overcome to attend the funeral. As the sun rose higher and the day grew brighter, Remington stood on the steps of the castle with her arm around her son, waiting patiently for the detail to move out.

She went completely against Gaston's instructions. Dane had slept with her last night and even now she continued to hold him and cradle him as if he were her son again and not Gaston's pledge. She needed him, and he needed her, and if Gaston said one negative word, she would kick him in the teeth. Her emotions were running terribly high, but she banked them outwardly. She knew she had to put on a strong front for her family. She would let her emotions run wild when, and only when, Gaston returned.

Charles, on her other side, was truly distraught. He and Rory had been particularly close and he was having a very difficult time accepting her death. Remington clutched his hand, wishing they would hurry up and start the procession so that they could get on with it. The lingering, the waiting, was painful.

Father de Tormo loitered by the door to the keep, sweating buckets in the humidity. Remington had asked him to conduct the mass since he had given Arik and Rory last rites the night before. He, too, wished the procession would hurry so that he could sooner return to the coolness of the castle.

Just when the delay seemed excessive, Nicolas broke from Skye and made his way to the outer wall. Sir Roald was there, pointing into the distance and conversing with the young knight. Quickly, Nicolas descended the wall and returned to the family.

"Gaston is sighted, my lady," he said with great relief. "His army is less than an hour away."

Gaston! Just the sound of his name flooded her with contentment and longing. Her defenses threatened to crumble, knowing that his strength would soon be here to support her, but she fought it.

"We will wait for them," she whispered.

With the heat of the day increasing, they did exactly that. Remington stood with Dane and Charles, waiting eagerly as the first signs of the approaching army came into view. She could see nothing of the road from where she stood, but she could tell from the activity on the wall that the troops drew near. When a hastily formed honor guard took position on either side of the portcullis, she knew Gaston was at hand.

She glimpsed the top of his head from where she stood before the inner wall obstructed her view. Nicolas had placed Skye in her care to deliver the news to Gaston, and Remington clutched her limp sister to her breast as the incoming army filled the outer bailey. Hundreds upon hundreds of soldiers milled about and the wagons bearing Rory and Arik were nearly swallowed up by the swarming mass.

But she could still see the wagons through the open inner gates, if little else. And she saw very clearly when Gaston approached Arik's casket.

Her heart lurched to her throat at the sight of him and hot tears stung her eyes. She was so desperate to hold him, to console him as he would console her, that she began to shake. Skye glanced up and saw her sister's expression before turning her gaze to the outer bailey.

"Oh...Remi, there he is," she whispered gently. "Go to him, Remi. He needs you."

She should have stayed where she was, but her heart controlled her legs. Without realizing it, she was walking across the inner bailey and straight for Gaston.

There was a sea of soldiers between her and Gaston, but it did not deter her in the least. She wove around them, moved in between, dodged destriers and wagons. Her eyes, as well as her heart, were focused on the massive knight several feet away. Roald was standing with him.

He did not even see her coming. One minute he was alone, dealing with consuming grief and anger, and the next moment a soft body was caving into him. He knew before he even looked that it was Remington.

His arms went around her, but he dare not show his grief in front of his men. His focus went to Remington and the loss of her sister.

"Angel," he murmured; he would have liked to have done and said much, much more. "Are you all right? You are unharmed?"

She was pressed against his armor tightly, her eyes closed. "I left before the ambush," her face came up, her eyes as bright as stars and he dashed away an errant tear with the tip of his glove. "Arik and Rory are dead."

Her grief, his own, ate at him. He was still reeling with the shock; the reality had yet to sink in. "I know, love, I know."

She put her hand to her mouth to stop the sobs from coming, sobs building in her throat. Her eyes fell on Arik's casket. "He had become my friend, too. I 'm so sorry for you, Gaston. I know how close you were to him."

He couldn't dwell on that, not right now. Later, in private, he would give into his grief, but not here in the midst of his men. He turned to Roald. "Are they ready to go? We should bury them before it grows too hot. Moreover, I am uncomfortable with anyone straying from the compound now. I want to get this funeral over with and close the gates."

"They're ready, my lord," Roald said sharply, his formal demeanor wavering a bit. "We buried Arik with his sword and helm. Even though it is his father's sword, we thought he would want to be buried with it."

Pain flashed in Gaston's eyes a brief second. "Aye, he would. The sword meant a great deal to him."

The bailey was still chaotic as the incoming troops disbanded and then were put on stand-by. With the ambush, the alert was heightened and even the novice troops were given assignments.

Suddenly, there was a great commotion as Patrick leapt up onto the cart carrying Rory's casket. Nicolas and Antonius were right behind him, yelling at him to cease. Gaston let go of Remington and bolted onto the wagon, restraining his cousin as he struggled to open the coffin that contained Rory's body.

Patrick was possessed; he slugged at Gaston, trying to shirk him, but Gaston was firm. Nicolas and Antonius jumped onto the bed of the wagon and grabbed hold of Patrick as Gaston spoke calmly and firmly to the young man. His eyes were wild with grief and disbelief as his friend, his brother and his cousin grappled with him.

Remington stood with her hand to her mouth, shocked at what she was witnessing. She could see Patrick's horror, his madness, and it tore at her. He was insane with grief.

"I just want to hold her," he begged Gaston. "Just for a moment. I just want to hold her."

Gaston had one hand on his arm and the other on his head, as if to comfort him forcibly. "Nay, lad, you cannot. We must bury her."

Patrick began to plead with Gaston and Remington's heart was breaking for him. Slowly, she approached the wagon as the men struggled to contain Patrick.

"Let him see her, Gaston," she said softly.

They all stopped somewhat, gazing down on her. She looked at Patrick, a gentle expression on her lovely features. "Let him hold her one last time. He never got to say good-bye."

Gaston's gaze lingered on her a brief moment before he released his cousin. Nicolas and Antonius let go, allowing Patrick to dislodge the lid of the casket. Gaston gazed at Rory's still body a moment, dressed in the emerald green dress Remington had worn the first time he ever saw her.

Rory looked sweet and peaceful and he slid down from the wagon bed and took Remington into his arms. To hell with appearance, if his men were foolish enough not to realize he was in love with her, they would know it now.

Nicolas was fighting off tears as Patrick lifted Rory from the casket and spoke to her as if she could answer him. Remington sobbed softly, turning away at the sight of her sister cradled in the knight's arms. She did not realize that the entire outer bailey had come to a halt, everyone watching as Patrick said his good-byes to Rory. Deep, tangible sadness filled the air.

Even Gaston was struggling with his feelings; he couldn't watch. He held Remington as she fought to regain control of her emotions, stroking her head and feeling his own anguish like a knife. Now and again he would glance at Arik's coffin, feeling the loss as deeply as if the man were a brother.

The funeral was brief. As soon as Father de Tormo finished the benediction, Gaston ordered the caskets buried and a full retreat into Mt. Holyoak. He vowed this would be the last funeral Remington would attend for some time to come; she looked so pale and fragile that it frightened him.

Once inside the keep with the bridge raised and the portcullis down, he felt a bit better. After settling Remington, he established himself in the solar to interrogate Nicolas about the attack.

"Did you see who it was?" he asked his cousin.

Nicolas had not changed his clothing or taken off his armor since the attack had happened the day before. He had not slept, either, and he was ashen with fatigue.

"It was Botmore, I am sure," he said quietly. "I recognized the colors; they were the same colors that Botmore's son was wearing when Arik killed him."

Gaston, too, was gray with exhaustion. He raked his fingers through his hair. "Brimley's siege was intense when we arrived, although none of my spies could pick out Lord Botmore. I had a feeling he was planning something for Mt. Holyoak, though I knew not what. The man's troops were there but, apparently, he was not to be found."

Nicolas nodded, draining the last of his ale. He had been living on ale since yesterday. "They struck quickly and then retreated," his eyes reluctantly found Gaston. "They were aiming for me, you know. Rory just happened to be in the way. She stood between me and the forest where they were hiding."

Gaston suspected as much; they were aiming for the knights, not the women. He closed his eyes and turned away, focusing on the thin window carved into the wall.

"Do we retaliate?"

The question hung there while Gaston remained riveted to the small window, seeing beyond the walls as his mind wandered. "As much as I would like to, I cannot. I have far more pressing business to attend to in London. Botmore will have to wait."

"But what if he keeps up these ambushes? Why not wipe the man out now? It should not take more than a week." Nicolas wanted revenge, for his brother and for Arik.

Gaston shook his head wearily. "Were Arik alive, I would send him to lay siege and go to London confident that Botmore would be no more. Patrick is next in the chain of command and he is not himself these days; I would not trust him with this assignment because it is too close to his heart," he stood up, having his answers and eager to get some sleep. "Botmore will have to wait, Nicolas. But have no doubt that Arik and Rory will be avenged."

Nicolas continued to sit, exhausted to the bone and frazzled of nerve. "Bastard," he muttered. "Was Brimley's siege a ruse, then?"

"Probably," Gaston nodded. "But one good thing came out of this; Brimley has pledged his loyalty to Henry."

Nicolas raised his eyebrows wearily. The cost of loyalty was too high, in his opinion. Gaston unlatched the solar door.

"Get some sleep, Nicolas, as I intend to do," he said. "We shall discuss this further when we have had time to recover."

Nicolas looked up at Gaston, realizing for the first time how badly his cousin must be feeling the loss of Arik. Until this point, Nicolas had only been concerned with Patrick and Rory. Looking at Gaston, he could see the dull pain.

"I am sorry about Arik," he said quietly. "He felt no pain...death was almost instantaneous."

Gaston abruptly lowered his gaze. "He was a fine knight and I shall sorely miss him."

It was as close as Nicolas as ever heard Gaston come to an emotional display.

CHAPTER NINETEEN

Two days after the burial of Rory and Arik, Gaston ordered the wagons readied for the trip to London. The priest had been cooperative regarding the delay, showing a small amount of consideration for Remington's loss. Her two extra days were spent with Jasmine and Skye, and Gaston made himself discreetly distant as the sisters came to grips with their grief.

But the fact remained that she was expected in London and they could delay no longer. While she spent her remaining hours with her sisters, Gaston made all necessary preparations including all of Remington's packing. Eudora packed everything but the bed and he found himself filling an entire wagon with her belongings. He could have been more firm and demand she lighten the load, but he did not have the heart. With everything that had happened and everything that she was preparing to face, he would not cause her additional grief.

Gaston found that keeping exceptionally busy helped him deal with the loss of Arik. Every time he entered the bailey or strode into the dim depths of the knight's quarters, he expected to be greeted by the familiar face and it cut him deeply that Arik was never to return. Patrick, fortunately, had come around quickly and had admirably stepped into the post vacated by the second in command. Keeping busy helped him, too.

He had missed Remington terribly these past two days, but he felt strongly that she needed the company of her sisters. They had slept together at night, not making love but merely holding each other. When dawn would break, they would eat together silently and Gaston would go about his duties. She was sad and distant, but her soft body and caressing hands told him how glad she was that he was with her.

With all of his concerns, he still had a keep to run and training grounds to oversee. Dane and Trenton were becoming used to their role in the scheme of Mt. Holyoak and the boys were becoming inseparable.

Dane still slept with Arik's sword, feeling very badly at the deaths of his aunt and mentor. But he was a brave boy, wise beyond his years, and he found the inner strength to carry on when others around him were preparing to give up. Gaston knew, one day, he would have an excellent knight in Dane Stoneley.

On the third morning after the funeral, Remington awoke in Gaston's arms and knew this would be the day she left for London. He had not so much as said a word, but in her heart she knew still.

She was sad to leave her sisters and son after what had happened, but she was eager to face what she must. She was eager to gain her annulment so that she and Gaston could return to Mt. Holyoak and await the birth of their child. She did so want the child to be born at her home, not the cold, impersonal rooms of Windsor.

She raised herself, gazing at Gaston's closed eyes. Delicately, she began to trace his sensual face, delighting in his masculine beauty. It was the first time in days she felt like focusing on something other than herself and her grief.

"If you keep that up, you are going to put me back to sleep," he mumbled.

She smiled as he opened his eyes. "I do not believe that you sleep at all. You are awake when I drift off at night, and then you are awake when I rise in the morning."

He sighed wearily, scratching his scalp. "I sleep as a soldier sleeps; aware of every sound and every movement. I do not think I have slept deeply since I was a child."

She flopped back down, snuggling next to him in the morning chill. "I sleep like the dead," she felt his hands caressing her, relishing the last few moments of peace before the day began. "When do we leave for London this day?"

He stirred slightly. "When will you be ready?"

"As soon as I bathe and dress, and gather the few things that Eudora did not pack," she replied. Then she was quiet a moment.

"Might I say good-bye to Dane?"

"Of course, Remi. I'd not be so cruel as to not allow you to bid farewell to your son."

"I simply did not want to break protocol," she sat up with a bit of irritation, the coverlet clutched to her breast. "God only knows I would not want to disrupt your military formalities."

"And you were correct to ask permission," he saw her annoyance and his lips twitched. "Being most gracious, I granted your request."

She pursed her lips wryly and he smiled, reaching out to stroke her beautiful hair. "I am sorry we have to leave for London so soon after the funeral. Are you up to this?"

"Do I have a choice?" she shrugged. "I can face this. As long as we are together, I can face anything."

He sat up beside her, kissing her head quickly as he vaulted from the bed. "That's my girl," he found his breeches and pulled them over his massive legs. Remington's delicious view of his taut buttocks was abruptly cut short as he pulled the trousers to his waist and secured them.

Clad only in his breeches, he moved to the door and summoned a serving wench to bring food and a bath. Remington sighed contentedly, watching his half-nude body parade about. There were few more pleasurable sights in this world.

The tub was brought in by three hearty soldiers and quickly filled. Gaston stood silent watch as the task was completed, his massive arms folded across his chest. Remington simply pulled the covers over her head until the duty was complete and the soldiers vacated the room.

"'Tis safe to reveal yourself," he told her, reaching for his shirt tossed carelessly over a chair. "I have duties to attend to this morn, but I shall return shortly."

She bound out of the bed, her sweetly curved body catching the early morning light as she rounded the bed. He eyed her as he tucked his shirt in, thinking her to be most perfect. He fought off the urge to grab her as she passed close to him en route to the tub, but he allowed himself the weakness of a distended groan.

His boots went on as she sunk into the tub and he paused, putting his hands on his hips and scrutinizing her closely.

"Madam, if I had any less control, I would join you in your bath," he said.

She grinned and submerged herself completely, coming up like Venus rising. She wiped water from her eyes, eyes that glittered at him. "Coward."

His control slipping, he backed away from the tub and strapped on his sword. "Aye, I confess. I am."

She giggled, splashing water at him and laughing with delight when he scowled threateningly. It was the first time he had seen her laugh in days and he was relieved.

"Any more of that and I take you over my knee," he said sternly, but they both knew he wasn't serious.

Gaston moved to the door, passing a lingering glance at Remington. "I shall send Eudora to you."

"Thank you, my lord Coward," she said flippantly. "My lord Coward Dark Knight."

He shook his head at her disregard for his title. "Saucy wench."

Since Gaston had already made all of the necessary preparations for their trip to London, only a few scattered duties remained. He took Patrick with him as he went on his rounds.

"And make sure the men move on to hand-to-hand combat by early next week," Gaston told him as they moved upon the inner wall. Down below were nearly a thousand recruits, listening to Antonius lecturing them on the great art of sword-to-shield warfare. "They've completed their shield work and 'tis time to move on. I have left a schedule to be followed precisely in the solar. With my absence, you are their trainer now."

"I will not fail, my lord," Patrick replied.

Gaston slanted his cousin a glance, but his face was emotionless. Since Rory's murder, Patrick had been the consummate warrior. He breathed, ate and slept his profession and had kept a distance from Remington and her sisters. Gaston knew he was hurting, but he was at a loss as to what to say to him. He had never been very good with expressing personal emotion.

"I will expect weekly updates sent to my manse in London," he continued after a moment. "I do not know how long I will be in London and wish to be kept abreast of the progress at home."

"Aye," Patrick nodded as they paused on the wall, gazing down at the troops. "How long has it been since you have returned to Braidwood?"

Gaston inhaled thoughtfully. "Not since the last we were there together," he replied. "Shall I give your father a message?"

Patrick's father was Gaston's father's first cousin; their mothers had been sisters. Sir Martin de Russe was a large, loud man who had given up fighting a long time ago. He preferred to stay in London at the de Russe manse, enjoying his wine collection and the ladies.

"Nay," Patrick shook his head. "No message. And for God's sake, do not tell him I have command of Mt. Holyoak. He shall insist on coming out of retirement and riding up here to assist me. The last thing I need is my father hanging over my shoulder."

Gaston's mouth twisted wryly. "He was the very best when he was young, Patrick. My father and your father were invincible."

"That was a long time ago. I heard rumor once that the enemy would turn and run at the sight of my father simply because they were afraid to be captured by the most obnoxious man in England," he snickered softly, looking at his cousin. "At least Uncle Brant's reputation was based on his skills and not his mouth."

Gaston returned the grin. "Brant de Russe was a terror. I oft admired him for his restraint with Martin. My father must have had the patience of Job not to run his cousin through at times."

"Do you remember your father, Gaston? I remember very little of him; I must have been five or six when he died," Patrick asked, pondering his childhood memories.

Gaston shrugged. "I remember mostly images, feelings. I remember he was the biggest, most powerful man I had ever seen and I wanted desperately to be like him. It's my mother I remember best. God, the woman loved me."

"Adeliza de Russe," Patrick murmured in thought. "I do not remember her at all, although my father said she was the most beautiful woman he had ever seen. Even more beautiful than my mother."

"Your mother was a saint," Gaston said flatly. He was growing depressed on the subject of his father and mother. He remembered his conversation with Arik, trying to explain why he had never allowed himself friends during his life, trying to explain how his parent's death had affected him. It never occurred to him that he was afraid to allow friendship into his life because he was a man of deep, deep emotion. All he knew was that friendship, and love, had hurt him terribly. 'Twas mayhap the reason he was so deeply involved with Remington; he had let his guard down for her and it would kill him to lose her.

"Patrick, I would ask one more thing of you before I leave. Watch out for Dane and Trenton, if you would. Both of them are likely to feel a bit lost for a while, in lieu of recent events."

Patrick nodded seriously. "I shall keep my eye on them. Truthfully, Dane seems very strong and Trenton most eager. I think they'll do fine."

"Arik thought so," Gaston suddenly felt a stab of pain through his heart at the mention of his friend. The conversation ended, he silently dismissed himself from his cousin and took the ladder from the wall.

Patrick hung over the top of the wall. "Are you taking Nicolas with you?"

"Aye," Gaston nodded. "I am also taking four other knights, although I have yet to choose. The rest will remain with you."

Satisfied, Patrick watched his cousin as he went to brief his knight corps on his plans. With the recruits occupied, Gaston had called the meeting in the troop house.

Patrick knew Gaston was shaken with Arik's death. Hell, he himself had difficultly believing what had happened. Which was why he occupied himself constantly; if he had a moment to think, grief ate at him like a cancer. But Gaston, as always, was dealing with the fact admirably.

Patrick squared his shoulders; he was in charge of Mt. Holyoak now and pleased with the opportunity. He would not fail his liege or his king, but he prayed secretly that Botmore would be stupid enough to try something while Gaston was away. He wanted a chance at the man; just one chance would be all he would need.

For Rory.

Gaston took no longer than necessary to explain his departure to his knights. Seasoned men that he trusted implicitly, he selected four knights to accompany him and sent the rest on their way. Issuing instructions to the four, they began immediate preparations for their trip to London.

The day was progressing and he made his way back to Remington, taking extra time to study his fortress and trying to remember anything he might have forgotten to deal with. As he was making his way to the inner bailey, a sentry shout on the outer wall halted him.

Incoming riders. Gaston quickly mounted the outer wall, standing beside Roald as the man scanned the horizon.

"They're flying yellow and gray standards, my lord," he lowered his spyglass. "Not Botmore."

"Yellow and gray," Gaston repeated. "I am expecting no one and am not familiar with those colors. I wonder who it is?"

One of the men on the wall was an old soldier of Stoneley's, an aged warrior who had served Guy and his father. He cleared his throat loudly.

"If I may, my lord de Russe," his old voice cracked, well aware that the men-at-arms were forbidden to speak to Gaston.

"'Tis Lord Ripley, of Ripley Castle. His keep is west of Scotton Woods."

Gaston looked at the old man. "Enlighten me. Where is Scotton Woods?"

"North and west of Knaresborough," the soldier replied. Seeing that he had not been reprimanded for speaking out of turn, he added: "He and Lord Stoneley held little love for each other, but Lord Ripley and Lord Botmore are allies. Ripley Castle is a massive keep, nearly as large as Mt. Holyoak. 'Tis even larger than Crayke."

Gaston raised a faint eyebrow, watching the small dots in the distance grow larger. He digested the information from the old soldier. "Lower the drawbridge, but keep the portcullis down. I want two companies of archers on the outer wall aimed at the incoming party."

Roald nodded sharply and began issuing quick orders. Gaston leapt to the ladder and took two rungs before pausing a moment.

"You there, soldier," he said to the old man. "What is your name?"

The old man almost choked on his own tongue. "Martin, my lord. Martin Sals."

Gaston almost smiled at the name; had not he just been speaking of a "Martin"? Instead, he looked at Roald. "Reward him for his information, Roald. Anything he desires."

He descended the ladder, leaving the old man astonished.

He moved quickly to the troop house and proceeded to don several pieces of armor, cursing himself because he had left the majority of his armor in his bedchamber. Sending one of his squires off at a run to retrieve the pieces, he managed to cover himself quite completely with the help of his remaining squire and a tunic of mail. The mail tunics were nearly obsolete in lieu of full plate armor, but it was all he had at the moment.

Patrick and Antonius met him at the portcullis as the approaching army reached the base of the hill. Four men broke off from the main body and began a slow ascent to the drawbridge.

"Who are they?" Antonius asked, in full battle armor.

Gaston crossed his thick arms, watching the approach with narrowed eyes. "I was told they are flying Lord Ripley's colors."

"Did you send a missive to him for a meet?" Patrick asked.

"Aye, I did, but he has not responded as of yet," Gaston eyed the four riders. "Apparently, this is his response."

The four horsemen came to a halt at the end of the dirt path, just shy of the drawbridge. The destriers snorted and danced, tossing their heads about as the humans astride them scrutinized the occupants of Mt. Holyoak through the closed portcullis.

"My lord de Russe?" one of the men addressed Gaston.

Something inside Gaston's head recognized the voice, but he could not place it. "Who asks?"

The knight flipped up his visor. "Sir Hubert Doyle, my lord. I saw you in Ripon a few weeks ago."

Gaston felt a bit more comfortable, but he was still properly leery. "Who are you serving, Doyle?"

"Sir Alex Ripley, my lord," Hubert replied, indicating the man next to him.

Gaston watched as the man raised his visor, meeting Gaston with curious eyes. He was older, his eyebrows graying. "My lord de Russe," he said formally. "I have come in answer to your writ. It would seem we have much to discuss."

Gaston uncrossed his arms and approached the portcullis. "You have caught me at an unfortunate time, my lord. I am due in London as we speak," he waved his hand and the portcullis went up; he saw no danger at all. The four horsemen were not even armed with swords. "Have your men set camp at the base of the hill. I will give you what time I can."

Hubert, Sir Alex and another man dismounted while the fourth man turned and descended the hill. The hooves of the destriers made hollow sounds as they clopped across the drawbridge.

"We were told of Sir Arik's untimely accident," Hubert said as he reached Gaston. "Boroughbridge can speak of nothing else. And I understand one of the ladies was killed as well."

Gaston nodded slowly. "An ambush by Lord Botmore."

Sir Alex cleared his throat, eyeing Hubert. "Ever since Derek was killed, Keith can speak of nothing but revenge. He thought to convince Brimley to band with him on an assault against Mt. Holyoak because Catherine Brimley was betrothed to Derek, but Brimley refused."

"I know," Gaston said flatly. "I helped Lord Brimley fight off Botmore's anger and the baron informed me as much."

Sir Alex looked decidedly uncomfortable. "He has come to me as well, my lord. He is trying to band the whole of Yorkshire against you."

Gaston fixed Sir Alex with an open gaze and crossed his arms again. "And?"

"And I refused him, naturally," Ripley replied. "He seems more driven to destroy you personally than to rebel against Henry's rule."

Squires from Ripley's army returned with the fourth knight and took the horses from the warriors. Ordering the bridge raised just high enough that no one could ride in or out, Gaston motioned the men inside.

Remington was waiting for them in the solar. Gaston was mildly surprised to see her until he saw that she had set out refreshments for he and his guests. As always, the perfect chatelaine, and his heart warmed.

"Lady Stoneley," Lord Ripley greeted her warmly. "May I say that you are blossoming outside of your husband's presence."

She swept her lashes against her cheek coyly. "'Tis a pleasure to see you again, my lord. I was unaware of your visit to us this day."

"I sent no word ahead," Ripley replied, his eyes full of Remington. There was a good reason he had not sent word ahead, but she did not need to know that.

Remington smiled and respectfully backed her way out of the room, her eyes lingering on Gaston overlong. He gave her a faint smile and closed the door behind her.

Ripley poured himself a huge goblet of wine as if he were in his own home, not a mere guest. "Thank God for Guy's imprisonment," he mumbled, his eyes lingering on the door again as if to see Remington. "She was... so unfortunate."

Gaston detected a trace of longing, or wistfulness, 'twhich he could not be sure and jealousy coursed up his spine at the man's manners toward Remington.

"We are not here to speak of Lady Remington," he said shortly. "We are here to speak of my presence in Yorkshire and the state of your loyalty to the crown. But before we begin, tell me why you did not send a missive ahead notifying me of your arrival?"

Ripley downed the wine. "Because of Botmore. Had he intercepted the missive, it could have meant trouble for me. He would most likely have lain in wait for my delegation. The man is mad, I tell you. Derek was his everything for living."

"Do you know why I killed Derek?" Gaston asked after a moment.

Ripley shook his head, pouring more wine. "I do not." Gaston glanced at Patrick. "Because he abducted Lady Remington and two of her sisters. When I caught up to him, he threatened to kill Lady Remington if I did not let him continue home unmolested. One of my men took him out and, therefore, saved the lady's life and possibly the lives of her sisters."

Ripley nodded slowly, thoughtfully. "He harbored a softness for Lady Remington. So did his father, after he was widowed. They were allies with Stoneley because of her, you know. They knew what went on around here and they both imagined she would welcome a lover."

Gaston couldn't help himself from asking. "She never did?"

Ripley shook his head faintly, observing his cup. "Guy would not have cared, of course, but she did not want anything to do with anyone. I. . . I feel sorry for her. She's the most beautiful woman in these parts and she's condemned to a living hell with Stoneley. I pray every night that Stoneley dies in prison, the bastard. He was a terrible ally and an even worse husband."

Gaston's careful facade was nearly gone. He wasn't so much jealous anymore as he simply wanted to run to Remington and hold her. He wondered if she knew just how public her "secrets" were. Hearing it reflected in someone else's words shook him.

Ripley looked up at Gaston from where the man stood, emotionlessly, contemplating the bank of tapers against the wall. "Forgive me, my lord. I am off the subject already. Please continue with your agenda."

"Indeed," Gaston looked at the man. "You will forgive me, then, if I seem rushed. As I said, I am due in London."

"Henry could never do long without you, my lord," Hubert said praisingly, thrilled to be in the presence of the Dark Knight again. "'Tis unlikely he would leave you alone for long, especially this far north."

Gaston looked at the man. "Actually, I am taking Lady Stoneley to London, but that is a long story. And you, Doyle; you are now sworn to Lord Ripley? What happened to the tournament circuit?"

Hubert shrugged. "I prefer real fighting to the slap and tickle of the tournament. Moreover, Lord Ripley made me his captain when he heard I had fought with you for Edward. I have charge of a fortress nearly as large as yours."

Gaston nodded faintly, moving around Patrick and toward the oaken desk. Reaching the table, he lowered himself slowly into the chair. When he raised his head, his face was unreadable. "Pleasantries out of the way, it would seem we have several things to discuss."

Lord Ripley stayed well past the nooning meal and Remington knew they would not be leaving for London that day. De Tormo was obviously agitated, going so far as to barge in on Gaston's meeting and demand to know the schedule for departure. Antonius had nearly taken the priest's head off.

It was late afternoon, close to sundown when Gaston's conference finally broke. Lord Ripley and his men would be staying for the evening meal and Gaston felt quite confidently that he had a strong ally in the man. An excellent judge of character, he gave into his instincts where Ripley was concerned. If the man was indeed lying, then he was the best actor in the world.

The sun was setting and the air was heavy as he retreated to the second floor in search of Remington. He had a tremendous desire to hold her, to feel her, to love her. His conversation with Ripley had been enlightening and heart wrenching at the same time.

He was aware of her voice, soft and melodious, as he approached her open bedchamber door. Curious as to whom she was talking with, he entered the room to find Trenton and Dane lying on her bed. Both boys were resting their hands on her lap and her soft hands gently caressed their hair.

His initial reaction was anger, for he had explicitly told her to stay away from her son. But that emotion was dashed by a warm, compassionate tenderness as he saw his own son cradled in her lap; his handsome face listening to her intently. Trenton had known little maternal love and the sight melted Gaston; only Remington could break through to the bitter, confused boy with her gentleness and caring.

"But was Osiris a great warrior?" Trenton asked.

"Osiris was indeed a great warrior, but he was more king than soldier. He was the wisest king Egypt ever had, and his wife loved him dearly, which is why she went to great lengths to preserve his body for the afterlife," Remington said softly.

"But why did he marry his sister?" Dane mumbled, his eyes closed and nearly asleep.

"Because brothers and sisters sometimes married in ancient times," Remington replied. "After Osiris' brother, Seth, killed him and dismembered his body, Isis went to great lengths to find the pieces and restore them with her magic. Posthumously, she conceived a son and her son, Horus, went on to defeat his evil Uncle Seth and thereby avenge his father's death."

"You can't conceive a babe from a dead man," Trenton scoffed.

"How do you know?" Dane's eyes rolled open, fighting sleep. "You do not even know how a babe is conceived."

"I do so!" Trenton snapped. "A man sleeps in the same bed with a woman and begets a babe."

"Uh-uh." Dane twisted in his mother's lap to better see Trenton. "There's more to it than that. He has to touch her, too. *Then* she gets a babe."

"Could you get a babe from Arik now that he is dead?" Trenton wondered aloud, looking up at Remington.

Horrified with the turn the conversation had taken, Remington opened her mouth to reply when, suddenly, Gaston lowered himself onto the mattress beside her.

"I do not think so," he said seriously. "I do not think she would want to try."

Remington felt guilty that she had been caught with the boys, but she smiled at Gaston anyway. "Good eve, my lord."

To her surprise, he smiled back. "Good eve, my lady." He then proceeded to peck her on the cheek.

The boys saw the whole exchange, but neither one said a word. In fact, they acted as if it were the most natural thing on earth as they gazed up from their vantage point on Remington's lap.

"More glory tales, I see," he looked down at the two faces. "Who were we discussing? Osiris and Seth?"

"Aye," Trenton nodded." One brother killed the other."

"So I have been told," Gaston replied. "But his wife loved him so much that she did everything she could to help him. That, I believe, is the point of the story."

"But how did he cut him up?" Dane asked. "With a sword? Or a saw? Did he chop him into lots of pieces or just cut off his arms and legs?"

Remington made a distasteful face at her son's question and looked to Gaston to answer it. The corners of his mouth twitched. "Dane, you have an unhealthy preoccupation with gore. Is it not sufficient to know that he was cut into pieces? Must you know how *many* pieces?"

"Aye," Dane insisted. "How many pieces means how much he hated him. Did he hate him a little or a lot?"

Remington and Gaston looked at each other, shaking their heads. Trenton looked thoughtful.

"If my father slept in the same bed with you, would you conceive?"

Remington's eyes widened at the question, but she kept her mouth shut. She would let Gaston deal with his son.

"That depends on a great many things, Trenton," he said steadily. "Did your mother never speak to you on the ways of men and women?"

Trenton shook his head. "Not... not really. What ways?"

Remington slanted Gaston a glance and looked away, aware that she was suddenly fighting off giggles. She liked to see him put on the spot.

Gaston scratched his chin. "We shall get into that later, but not now. The evening meal is approaching and I believe you two have duties to attend to."

"Aye, my lord," both boys suddenly leapt from Remington's lap as if they suddenly remembered they were pages and no longer young masters. With a quick bow to Remington and their lord, they dashed from the room.

Gaston turned to Remington, his gaze warm. "I should scold you, you know."

She smiled, snuggling up against him saucily. "But you won't. Not when I tell you it is Dane's birthday today, and I was treating him to a story."

He raised his eyebrows. "Hmpf. Of course I cannot become angry now. He is eight years old today?"

"Aye," she nodded, her gaze softening. "I can hardly believe my tiny little boy is eight years old. They grow up far too quickly."

"Aye," he agreed, his gaze roving to her belly. He placed a huge, warm hand on her stomach. "As will this child. Have you decided on a selection of names?"

She placed her hand over his. "There will be no selection, for I have already decided on his name."

He raised his brows reprovingly. "And?"

Her incredible eyes met his and she smiled gently, disarming him. "Erik. His name will be Erik."

He felt sadness shoot though him like a bolt, his grief inadvertently swallowing him up. Her compassion, her thoughtfulness filled him and he enveloped her in his arms, burying his great head in her bosom as if to hide from the world.

"Of course," he whispered against her flesh. "How considerate of you, my lady. I am ever grateful to you."

She felt his pain as he held her and she sought to comfort him as one would comfort a small, lost child. She held him against her fiercely.

"And if it is a girl, which it will not be, but if it is, I would like to name her after your mother," she said. "What was your mother's name?"

He looked at her, rather softly. "Adeliza."

"Adeliza," she repeated with satisfaction. "'Tis a lovely name. I like it very much."

They lay content together as the sun set and the smells of supper drifted on the warm evening air. Remington's stomach growled and Gaston snickered.

"I believe our child is talking," he said, sitting up.

"Not yet, at any rate," she said as he rose from the bed. Extending his hand, he pulled her to stand.

"I would change before supping with Lord Ripley and his son," she said, moving for the wardrobe.

Gaston eyed her a moment. "Ripley seems terribly fond of you."

She jerked her head to look at him, just as quickly looking away. "Why do you say that?"

He was instantly suspicious. "Remi, did you have an affair with him?"

She looked shocked and angered. "How can you ask me that?" she flared. "I have never slept with any man other than my husband, and you. How dare you insinuate that I dispensed favors as a common whore!"

He put his hands up. "I am sorry, truly, but his gaze upon you is most….tender. I did not mean to offend you, angel. Forgive me."

Her jaw ticked, still perturbed. "'Twas a terrible question, Gaston. You more than anyone should know just how foolish a question it was."

He knew it, knowing he had spoken before he'd had a chance to think about what he was asking. But her evasiveness had prompted him.

"I am sorry," he repeated. "Do you know him well, then?"

She cleared her throat, again looking uncomfortable. She fingered through a couple of surcoats before slowing her movements. When she spoke, she did not look at him. "You are correct in your observations, Gaston. Lord Ripley was very fond of me, as he told me repeatedly. He hated Guy for marrying me as much as anything else, and felt tremendously guilty for not being able to protect me from my husband," she turned to look at him, ashamed. "He offered to take me away once, far away. He said he would leave his wife and children and all that he had if I would run away with him."

Gaston began to understand the man's gaze, his words, far better now. He was jealous, true, but he was also appreciative in a sense. It would appear that whether or not Remington realized it, she had many admirers who were aware of her plight, men who were willing to help her. First Brimley had shown deep concern, and then Derek claimed to be saving her from her captivity, and now Ripley.

She was unaware of how she had affected the men. True, she knew of their feelings, but they mattered not to her. She would force herself to stay in a loveless, hellish marriage simply because she had no desire to escape one man into the arms of another. Moreover, it would have meant leaving people who depended on her. She had said once that she had no use for men in general, until she met him.

Suddenly, he felt extremely fortunate.

"I like Ripley," he said quietly, moving to her. "He seems to be an honorable man."

Her eyes widened. She had expected him to rage at the very least. "You do? He is a kind man, Gaston. I like him, but I could not go with him and leave my sisters. And it would not have been fair to him; I could have never loved him."

"But you love me," he smiled gently, stroking her cheek.

She returned his smile. "I would do anything for you."

He frowned slightly, though still smiling. "That, madam, is my line."

She giggled as he kissed her, tenderly. "Dress for dinner now. I shall see you in the hall."

Her gaze lingered on the door even after he was gone.

CHAPTER TWENTY

T he party to London was up and moving before daybreak.
Remington, still half-asleep, sat atop her palfrey as the column
departed Mt. Holyoak. The morning was heavy with moisture, though
bright, and the day promised to be sultry. Wrapped in a durable silk
cloak, she was alternately chilled from the temperature and sweating
from the humidity.

She was surrounded by knights and soldiers but she was so sleepy
that it took her nearly an hour before she realized Gaston was not riding near her. He was at the head of the column, riding alone aboard
Taran.

As she perked up, she passed glances at the knights who rode
around her, but she could see nothing through their lowered visors.
Four men-at-arms flanked her, holding aloft a great canopy to keep the
dew and sun off her. The men were very silent, and very imposing. She
felt very alone.

De Tormo rode to the rear of Gaston's soldiers, so she did not even
have anyone to talk to. Around her, the day was coming alive and she
soon found that she had no desire to talk to anyone at the moment; it
would have spoiled her view of the morning.

The Vale of York was a wonderful, beauteous dell. Green and fragrant, they passed through fields of sheep that belonged to Mt. Holyoak
and rode through a stretch of land Remington had not seen in years.
Off to the east was Halsey Manor, the manse in which she had been
born, and she found herself missing it terribly. Just a glimpse would
have made her happy, but the army continued on and carried her to the
west of York on their trek south.

The morning progressed and the day warmed, and she removed
her cloak with the help of one of the silent knights. She did not even
realize it was Nicolas until he responded to her thanks.

"Nicolas," she said softly. "Why did you not tell me 'twas you?"

He flipped up his visor, eyeing Gaston. "Because Gaston does not like to hear talking within the ranks. He says it is a distraction."

She looked at Gaston, too, riding far ahead of them. "Why does he ride alone?"

Nicolas shrugged. "Because he chooses to. He has always ridden alone, with the exception of Arik. Only Arik was allowed to ride with him on occasion."

Remington's heart tugged at the mention of the fallen comrade. "Where will we stop for the night?"

"Gaston would like to make it well south of Leeds," Nicolas lowered his visor.

She knew Leeds to be a half-day's ride from Mt. Holyoak and knew they were in for a long, long ride. Too bad, too; her bottom was already sore simply because she did very little riding.

The ride was long and by the time Gaston called a halt mid-afternoon, Remington swore she had become part of the horse. Her legs were so stiff she could barely move until Nicolas helped her from the animal. Gaston, long since dismounted, marched back through the column and Remington watched in awe, as men parted for him like the Red Sea. He did not say a word; he did not have to.

De Tormo, coming up from the rear of the procession, reached Remington the exact same time as Gaston did. The two men eyed each other.

"Return to your people, de Tormo," Gaston said. "I will see to the lady's comfort."

De Tormo lowered his voice. "My lord, I cannot allow you to be seen with the lady unescorted. Within the walls of Mt. Holyoak is one thing, but in the presence of the church and outsiders, it is quite another."

A small blue vein in Gaston's temple throbbed. "I have not yet placed her in the wardship of the church."

De Tormo was not being obstinate, a remarkable event. He seemed truly concerned for proper appearances. "'Tis not your duty to, my lord. As an emissary of the church, I have already placed her in sanctuary until this matter can be ironed out. 'Tis well within my rights, my lord, since you truly have no power over the lady."

"She is my vassal."

"She is your enemy's wife and, therefore, entitled to the protection of the church," the priest answered. "As soon as we reach London, I will place her in Saint Catherine's Convent until the annulment can be obtained. Until then, I am her guardian."

Remington was shocked and upset. She did not want to be kept from Gaston. Her head lowered and she bit her lip, trying hard not to weep.

"As lord of Mt. Holyoak, I am sworn to protect the lady," Gaston said, although he knew his claim was weak. He never suspected that de Tormo would immerse himself in their plans. Eventually, he knew that he would have to obey whatever the church dictated until the annulment was complete, but he had hoped that their journey to London would afford them their last bit of privacy together.

"And you shall," de Tormo responded. "But I am her guardian and anything that concerns her welfare and protection must be cleared with me. You understand this, do you not?"

Gaston could see that the priest was not trying to be cruel, merely proper. His manner was calm but firm. Gaston glanced at Remington's head and saw that her lashes were spiky with tears and he felt his composure slipping. "De Tormo, might I have a private word with you?"

The priest agreed and Gaston pulled him to the edge of the road, away from Remington and open ears. "I will come to the point, de Tormo. I will not leave the lady alone, ward of the church or not. You cannot mean to separate us."

"I must, de Russe. You know that," the priest held his ground. "Surely I cannot allow...whatever it was that was going on at Mt. Holyoak to continue in my presence. I would be allowing a sin."

Gaston let out a sharp sigh, grinding his jaw. "She carries my child, priest. You cannot and will not separate us, and if you tell anyone of our secret, I shall slit your throat from your chin to your belly. We....we are in love. That is why I intend to marry the woman. Because I love her."

De Tormo blinked, looking uncertain for the first time. He wasn't intimidated by the threat, but he was impacted by the words of the greatest knight since Gallahad. De Russe's reputation was beyond legendary;

it was mythical. But the man before him was laying himself wide open, as vulnerable as any mortal man.

He sighed heavily, his determination faltering. "Good Lord, de Russe. You are not going to make this easy, are you?" He paused long enough to scratch his fat chin thoughtfully. "Then I will allow you time together, within reason. But you shall be escorted. By me."

Gaston scowled. "By God's Bloody Rood. You intend to babysit us?"

"Not you; *her*," the priest corrected. "She is my ward and I must."

Gaston looked long and hard at him for a moment. Then, he rolled his eyes and hissed, *"God!"*

There was nothing more either of them could say. De Tormo glanced over at Remington, who now stood composed and waiting. He felt his firm stance slipping.

"Oh, hell," he muttered. "Take her and feed her. But warn her of her future so she is not surprised."

Gaston almost thanked the priest but refrained. He went to Remington and took her gently by the arm.

"Where are we going?" she asked.

"To eat," he replied, catching a bag of food his squire tossed to him.

"What about Nicolas? Won't he eat with us?" She turned to look for the knight. "And what of the priest? Where is he going?"

"Quit prattling, Remi," he admonished softly.

He took her into a bank of trees, sheltering her from the sun. She made herself comfortable on a stump and he took a moment to admire her as he drew forth the provisions. She was dressed in a silk surcoat the color of her eyes. The bodice was snug, lacing between her breasts and revealing a white blouse that peeked out beyond the neckline and extended slightly beyond the short sleeves. The neckline, however, was revealing enough and his mouth fairly watered at the white skin exposed.

He handed her a wedge of cheese. "How are you enjoying the ride?"

She took a healthy bite. "I would like it more if I could ride with you. May I?"

He cleared his throat as he rummaged through the bag. "Nay, angel, I prefer you to remain where you are."

She pouted. "You do not want to ride with me."

He looked at her. "'Tis not that. It's just...."

"It's the priest," she accused loudly. "He wants to keep us apart, does not he?"

He shook his head firmly. "Calm down, Remi. He shall not keep us apart. In fact, he promised to be quite lenient. Do not fault de Tormo for what he must do."

Her eyebrows went up in outrage. "What he must *do*? Gaston, I do not want to spend months in a convent, away from you and the rest of the world."

"Would you rather spend it with Guy?" he shot back softly, instantly sorry he had snapped at her. "Remi, if we want the church's cooperation in this annulment, then we must do as they say. Please, love; it won't be for long. You must be brave."

She plopped back down on the stump, her pretty face molded in a pout. She tore into the cheese angrily, eating with fury. He ate his own cheese and bread, fighting off a smile at her frown.

"Remi, we have not seen nor spoken to each other all day," he said, a twinkle in his eye. "Are you going to spend our short time together moping?"

She shoved the cheese in her mouth, her eyes angry at him. "I want to ride with you. I do not want to spend eternity in a convent, and I deplore this heat."

"Then you are going to pout."

"I am," she shook her fist at him. "I am sick of this already."

He let his smile break forth. "If I let you ride with me, will you stop sulking?"

Her stance softened. "Mayhap. What about the convent?"

He grinned, whipping her into his arms. "Angel, I can do nothing about the convent, nor the heat. Anything else you care to take offense with?"

She was melting in his arms, as she always did. He was grinning so openly at her that she could not stop the small smirk that played on her lips. "Give me but a moment and I shall think of something."

He chuckled low and kissed her tenderly, a kiss that suddenly ignited a passionate response and it was no time before their tongues were tussling erotically. From the trees, they heard a polite cough.

"The men are assembling, Gaston," Nicolas said.

Gaston glanced at his cousin. "Nicolas, tether her palfrey. The lady will ride with me."

Surprised, Nicolas bowed and strode away. Remington smiled, stroking Gaston's face.

"He told me you always ride alone," she said softly. "Except for Arik, sometimes."

Gaston lost some of his mirth then. He kissed her again and let her go, handing her a hunk of sweet bread before wadding up the food sack.

Remington ate the bread slowly, watching his distant movements. It only reaffirmed her ideas that he was terribly torn by Arik's death. But Gaston was a man of few words, and other than his declarations of love, she had never heard him voice any other emotion. Anger, hatred, sorrow; he kept them well concealed.

It was sticky in the trees, even with the canopy cover. She could hear the voices of the men on the road as they came to order and she knew the time for departure was close. Gaston turned to her, adjusting his helm.

"Any necessary business before we leave, madam? I shall not stop again until after sundown."

She nodded, shoving the last of the bread in her mouth and gathering her skirts. After relieving herself in the bramble, she rejoined Gaston.

He was gazing down at her, his expression returning to the stone-cold facade she had first encountered the very first time she had met him. It was the frontage of the Dark Knight, the perfect warrior, and the man who intimidated the hell out of her. It was almost as if there were two different personalities in one man.

"Ready?" he asked.

She nodded her head and he took her elbow gently, leading her back to the road.

"De Tormo has appointed himself your guardian until we reach London," Gaston said quietly. "Do not be alarmed if he seems solicitous. After we reach London, our visits together are likely to be closely watched and I want you to prepare yourself for the reality that the church might not allow me to see you at all at some point."

She looked stricken. "But...why? Why would they keep us apart?"

He kept his voice down. "Because you are another man's wife, Remi. The church must do what is morally right until this can be resolved. I told you this would not be easy, love, but we will have to do what they dictate until the proceedings are over."

She frowned, greatly distressed at the prospect of being separated from Gaston. "Why did not you tell me this before we left for London? You never mentioned any of this."

He shrugged. "I saw no harm in keeping certain facts from you. After all, you were suffering tremendously and I did not want to add to your distress. But know it now, Remi, and prepare," he paused by Taran and faced her. "You must be strong, as I know you are. No complaints, no tantrums. Just be a good girl and do as you are told, and we shall overcome. Very well?"

She made a face. "I shall try. I do not like any of this, but I shall try."

He smiled and lowered his visor with a clang. Just as he was preparing to lift her aboard Taran, de Tormo came bustling up.

"What are you doing?" he demanded of Gaston.

Gaston turned to the priest, nearly half of his own great height. The imposing helm was closed, rendering Gaston most fearsome, but de Tormo wasn't deterred. He wanted an answer to his question.

"The lady is fatigued and asked to ride with me," Gaston replied, knowing even as he said it, de Tormo would refuse the request. And he would have to obey.

"She may ride with me in the carriage if she is tired," de Tormo replied. He held out his hand to Remington. "Come, my lady. We shall play a card game if you are well enough."

Remington had never been stubborn a day in her life. She had always done what was asked of her, no matter what it was. Refusal was only met with pain, she had learned, and therefore had learned never to balk at an order.

She looked at the priest, wanting so terribly to ride with Gaston that she almost slapped the hand away. But she could not; it was not her way. She would have liked to reason with the priest but she knew he would have his way in the end. She could think of nothing to say, and the man was waiting for her expectantly. She did not want to ride with him; she wanted to ride with Gaston.

Whether it was the heat, or her still-tender emotions, or her pregnancy, she did not know. But suddenly her instincts told her to play on the priests' sympathy, and play she did. She burst into a flood of pathetic tears.

Gaston put his hand on her back comfortingly as she sobbed, perhaps a bit exaggeratedly. De Tormo started to speak to her, but she cried louder and blotted out his words. Her pretty hands were on her face, shielding her expression from the men. De Tormo tried to speak to her again, but she wailed loudly and turned her back on him, sobbing her heart out. It was a fine display of hysterics, she thought, and hoped the priest would give up and leave her alone. She was getting a headache with all of her forced wailing.

Much to her pleasure, the priest did indeed give up. Exasperated, he waved at Gaston and made his way to the rear of the column. Only when he was well out of range did

Remington cease her tears. With a sly glance at the figure of the priest a distance away, she turned back to Gaston.

"I am ready," she said without so much as a catch in her voice.

He stared at her through his lowered visor. "Are you...what did you do?"

She smiled brightly, wiping at the moisture around her eyes. "I believe I just gained permission to ride with you. Are you going to lift me up or must I mount myself?"

He let out a hiss. "Remi, you little devil. I ought to take a switch to you."

She rubbed at her bum. "It is already sore. Lift me up, my love."

He did, and mounted behind her. Lifting her a bit so she was seated on his thigh armor instead of the saddle, he lifted his fist in a silent gesture to move out.

Remington snuggled back against him, unaware of how uncomfortable he was to have her riding in front of him. He liked to be totally focused on his surroundings, keeping his eyes and ears open for any dangers. Were he to be attacked at that very moment, both he and Remington would have been extremely vulnerable. He found he was actually nervous as they continued along the road.

"Where will you be staying in London?" she asked softly.

"My family has a manse along the Thames," he replied. "And do not talk while you are riding with me. I must not allow my attention to be diverted."

"Diverted from what?" she asked curiously.

He sighed sharply. "From any threats. Please, Remi, do as I ask. If you wanted to talk, then you should have ridden with the priest."

Offended, she stiffened. "Next time I will."

He smiled faintly behind his visor, hoping she would indeed ride to the rear tomorrow and not ask to ride with him again. He would rather slit his own throat than tell her he did not want her riding with him, but he was truly uncomfortable with her sweet body seated in front of him.

She did not say anything for the rest of the ride. The army stopped well after dark near the small town of Featherstone and Gaston ordered a perimeter established and sup to be prepared. Dismounting, he pulled Remington down after him and held her steady while she regained her footing. Still, she did not speak.

De Tormo came and escorted her away, and Gaston's gaze lingered on her a moment before he immersed himself in camp preparations. It wasn't until very late that he sought her out again.

She was swathed in her silk cloak by the fire, the flames playing off of her colorful hair. De Tormo and a few other papal servants had drifted off to sleep on the ground, while three other men played a game of dice several feet away.

Remington glanced up when she heard the noise of his approach, but looked away when she saw who it was.

"Did you eat?" he asked, his voice low like distant thunder.

"I did, my lord," she said stiffly.

He moved closer to the fire, removing his mail gloves. He had taken off the heavy armored gauntlets long ago because they were difficult to work in.

"Are you ready to sleep, then?" he asked, his voice softer.

She refused to look at him. "I will go to sleep when I am ready, my lord. On the bed my guardian prepared for me."

He glanced over by the carriage; de Tormo had fashioned her a very nice bed out of cushions and cloth. But she would not be sleeping there tonight; he had pitched a comfortable, private tent for the two of them and he was anxious to be alone with her.

He reached down and pulled her to her feet. "With me, madam."

She yanked free from his grasp. "I think not. You told me to be good and obey and...."

He clapped a hand over her mouth, his eyes intense. "You shall wake the priest if you do not keep your voice down."

He pulled her with him into a thicket of dense brush. Somewhere, Remington could hear water bubbling and knew a brook was close by. He continued to lead her further away from the camp until Remington could see a small fire flickering in the distance. The closer they came, she could see a neat tarp strung up among the bushes and the fire had a spit over it, roasting some sort of animal.

Her annoyance with him fled. Suddenly, she was very eager to be alone with him, to cuddle the night away.

"Did you make this little camp?" she asked softly.

"I did," he tossed his mail gloves to the ground and unlatched his breast plate. "I even caught the rabbit."

She grinned in spite of herself, feeling very pampered as she sat under the tarp. He had spread out furs and one of her satchels was serving as a pillow.

Remington sat and watched as he ate the entire rabbit, followed by a half a loaf of bread and a bladder of watered ale. She leaned up against his back, staring dreamily into the fire, feeling her fatigue but not willing to give in to it yet.

The conversation was light, and Gaston actually did most of the talking in between bites. He said nothing of the afternoon when he had dealt her a most grievous insult, and she had truthfully forgotten about the incident. Her lids grew heavy as he droned on, lulled by the rich quality of his voice. It wasn't long before she was dozing against his back.

He felt her relax against him and wiped the grease from his hands, turning slightly to pull her against his chest. She startled at the jostling, but he soothed her. "It's all right, angel. Go back to sleep."

She was so tired she could barely keep her eyes open. "But I do not want to. I want to hear more of your trip to Paris."

He lay back on the furs, pulling her cloak tightly about her as she snuggled into the curve of his torso. He was so warm it was like sleeping against a furnace. "I shall tell you more of Paris tomorrow night, I promise. Sleep now, love."

"What happens when de Tormo awakes and finds me missing?" she mumbled.

"He is a smart man and will surely suspect where you are," Gaston replied, holding her tightly.

"Won't he be angry?" she was nearly asleep.

"Nay," he shushed her, closing his own eyes. "Go to sleep."

She awoke before dawn. The sky above the trees was a pale gray, as the sun had yet to break the horizon. She was alone on the furs and stirred a bit, looking around to see where Gaston had gone. He wasn't far.

Stripped naked but for his breeches, he was washing his neck and torso with a rag and a bar of soap. Remington sat up slightly, her sleepy eyes focused appreciatively on his beauty. Lord, the man was so well formed that he was nearly too perfect to be mortal. As massive as he was, everything on his body was well-proportioned and flawless. She watched him shove his head into the basin of water and lather it with soap before finally rising to her feet.

"Here, my love, let me help you," she said softly.

He turned to look at her, upside-down. "Why are you awake? 'Tis not dawn yet."

She smiled, pushing her sleeves up. Batting his soapy hands away, she continued to lather his hair with gentle fingers. Without a word, she poured water from the basin on his head until the soap cleared.

He shook his head like a wet dog and grabbed a linen towel, wiping his face and drying his hair. Remington dried her hands on the towel as he stood straight, drying off his neck.

"I am sorry if I woke you," he said softly.

"You did not," she replied, admiring his physique. "I grew chilly without you beside me and woke up."

He smiled faintly, shaking his head again. "I slept like a dead man last night. I cannot remember when I last slept so well."

She took off her cloak; the weather was temperate in spite of the early hour. The humidity almost made it cloying. "I heard a stream bubbling last night. Where is it?"

He tilted his head off to his left. "Not merely a stream, but a small lake. 'Tis very pristine and calm."

A lake. Nature's bathtub. Remington went back to the tarp and rummaged into her satchel, bringing forth the cake of scented soap Gaston had bought her. With a faint grin, she turned to him. "I think I shall have a bath, too."

He watched her gather a few things. "'Tis chilly, Remi. And the lake is sure to be freezing."

She simply smiled; she knew she would not be alone in the water and wasn't worried about the chill.

He followed her through the bush, still only half-dressed. When she reached the edge of the lake, she drew in a breath at the sight; limestone cliffs edged the water nearly halfway around, and the shore was of sand and not dirt. It looked heavenly.

Her silk dress came off, as did her stockings, slippers and shift. Stepping clear of her garments and grabbing her soap, she plunged into the cool waters of the lake and began frolicking like a fish.

He stood on the shore, entranced as he watched her splash about. She could swim better than anyone he had ever seen, floating way out in the middle of the lake and lathering an upstretched leg at the same time. Her glorious hair was slicked back on her head, making her big eyes look even bigger. The erotic sensuality of the situation grabbed at him, flooded him, and the more she swam, the hotter he became.

Remington heard a splash from the shore and knew Gaston would soon be upon her. Hands were suddenly touching her legs from under the water and she giggled as Gaston surfaced an inch from her face.

"You already had your bath," she admonished softly.

"Aren't you cold?" he asked, his voice raspy.

She shook her head and smiled.

His eyes were smoky with passion. "Give me the soap."

Obediently, she handed it over and he worked it into a thick froth before massaging it into her hair. She closed her eyes briefly, his attention sending bolts of fire though her limbs.

"Hold on to me," his voice was a husky whisper. "You shall tire yourself treading water."

She latched onto him, aware that he wasn't moving in the least; he was standing on the bottom of the lake.

He washed her hair within an inch of its life. She submerged herself completely, rinsing her hair, until Gaston pulled her up to the surface. He brought the wet hair to his nose, inhaling the special scent and running the strands between his lips. Remington watched him, forgetting to breathe, only aware of the liquid fire filling her veins.

She kissed him fully, her hair still on his lips. The bar of soap floated away on the surface of the lake as he clutched her fiercely to him, kissing her fully and deeply as that of a man starving. He couldn't get enough of her.

Somehow amidst the kissing and suckling and tasting, they managed to move inshore. When the water level lowered to her waist, he scooped his huge hands under her armpits and lifted her high, meeting her breasts with his eager mouth.

Remington gasped with the raw sensuality of his touch, his actions. She brought her legs up, wrapping them around his chest as he held her body aloft. Her woman's center brushed against his sternum, the coarse hair taunting him into wild arousal. But he was not ready to leave the sweetness of her breasts as of yet; they had teased him mercilessly all day yesterday and he would taste his fill before moving on to more delightful areas.

Remington was melting like fat on the fire. Her entire body was liquid, molten, begging for him to relieve her. His strength was unbelievable; he simply held her aloft while his mouth moved relentlessly. She wasn't even supporting herself against him; her hands wound in his thick, dark tresses, encouraging him to ravish her.

Suddenly he lowered her against him, bringing his mouth to bear on her sweet, fragrant lips. Their kisses were feverish, demanding in the coolness of the lake, and Remington wrapped her legs tightly around his hips, feeling his huge arousal brushing against her buttocks, seeking.

He was kissing her so hard she nearly forgot her own name. His rock-hard shaft was driving her insane, for she could feel it bobbing and twitching against her as it sought her tender core. She wanted him in her, his solidity filling her, and she shifted her hips until his rod found the opening it was looking for.

She was so hot and wet that he slid into her easily, stretching wide her walls. They both groaned with the unbelievable pleasure of it and his hands moved to cup her buttocks.

"My God, Gaston," she breathed, arms winding around his neck. "Surely God is jealous of our bliss."

His breathing was ragged, heavy. "I thought you did not believe in God."

She plunged herself down on him and he growled. "Only God could create you, my love. There is no other explanation."

He growled again, latching onto her neck as he began to move of his own accord. His huge hands covered her buttocks completely, holding her to him as he slid in and out of her. The friction, the carnal pleasure, was beyond believing.

Remington held onto him for dear life, unable to move because he was holding her so tightly. She gave herself over to him, the power he aroused in her, and the liquid fire he sparked. The harder he pumped, the hotter the fire burned until it flared wildly and her muscles convulsed in an explosion of passion.

Gaston felt her walls throb, draw at him, demanding his own release. He tried to prolong his pleasure, but he could not refuse her demands. He spilled himself with a violent shudder, filling her with his life. Remington clutched him as if she were drowning, feeling every last throb with complete ecstasy.

The water cooled their overheated bodies as the sun peeked from the eastern horizon, turning the sky pinks and blues. They held each other as if time had no meaning, though in the back of Gaston's sated mind, he knew the priest would come looking for them both shortly. His men were already up.

"Remi," he whispered. "Finish your bath and get dressed. We must be moving on shortly."

She pulled her head out of the crook of his neck, her damp hair curling wildly and her face flushed. She smiled. "Finish it for me."

His huge hands washed her completely. From her head to her toes, she was clean, soft, and sweet smelling of roses and lavender and lily-of-the-valley. For a man of his incredible size, his hands were as gentle as a woman's and by the time Remington was bathed and dried on the shore, she was absolutely limp. Never had she felt so completely relaxed or satisfied.

He wrapped her up in her dress and carried her back to their camp, setting her down gently on the furs. Somewhat recovered, she donned a fresh surcoat from her satchel, a sturdy cotton the color of a ripe peach. It would wear better on the journey than the standard silks and satins and was far cooler. It was a simple dress with a rounded neckline and short sleeves, but the skirt was full and luxurious.

Gaston dressed silently, glancing at her every so often. She put a simple gold and topaz belt around her hips and pulled the front of her glorious hair back, securing it at the crown of her head. Wispy little tendrils framed her sweet face and he felt like a gushing, silly fool as he watched her. His heart was liquid, his limbs like mush. He was absolutely besotted with her.

They dressed silently, for in truth, there was no need for words. They were both speechless with their joy.

Behind them, off to the right, they heard the bushes moving harshly and a muttered curse now and again. Gaston turned, quite calmly, to greet whoever was approaching and was not surprised to see de Tormo propel himself through the brush. His fat face lit up with mild outrage.

"I thought to find you two together," he announced. "Truly, my lord, I thought I made myself most clear regarding the lady's reputation."

"You did," Gaston answered evenly. "As you can see, the lady is not ravished or compromised in any way."

The priest rolled his eyes in exasperation. "Please, de Russe. Do not try and fool me into believing that you spent the entire night at a proper distance, watching the lady sleep," he put up his hands to prevent any explanation. "I do not want to know what happened. Just… give the lady to me. She will ride with me in the carriage until we reach London."

"Agreed," Gaston turned to look at Remington. "Is that satisfactory?"

She remembered the words they had had yesterday, how he did not want to speak to her when they were riding together. A day playing games and chatting sounded pleasant, even if it were with the priest. Moreover, she would not spend the day irritated with Gaston because he did not want to talk to her.

"Aye, it is," she secured her satchel and rose, the peach color of the dress emphasizing her beauty magnificently. In fact, she presented such a beautiful picture that even de Tormo softened his huffing.

He held out his hand, taking her bag. "I have brought several games along. I hate to travel; it bores me. Do you play cards?"

She passed a glance at Gaston as the priest took her by the elbow to escort her from camp. "Aye, I do. But do you have any dice?"

De Tormo was shocked. "Dice? What does a lady know of dice?"

She smiled, amused. "My sister taught me. The sister you buried. Mayhap your prayers will admit her into heaven, in spite of her gambling vice."

Gaston frowned. "Rory taught you to gamble? Really, Remi, how uncouth."

She laughed softly. "I could probably win everything of value from you, my lord. She taught me well."

He raised a reproving brow. "No future wife of mine will gamble. Not even with a priest."

De Tormo shook his head. "I do not gamble, not even for fun. Besides, I am not very good at it."

Both Remington and Gaston looked at the priest in surprise and Remington even laughed. "So you have gambled? A man of God? I am shocked."

"Do not be," de Tormo mumbled. "I have not lived as piously as some. Come, now, milady. Allow the Dark One to see to his men and be free of your burden."

A huge, armored arm suddenly shot out, blocking both Remington and the priest. They looked up in surprise to see that Gaston's face was as cold as ice. The pleasant expression from not a moment before was vanished.

"Never, ever think that she is a burden to me." His voice was as low as thunder. "She is the reason I am willing to take on the church. I would walk through fire for her, and I would kill an army of thousands single-handedly if she were to ask it of me. Never believe that Henry holds true power over me; this lady that you touch is my reason for living, and 'tis only she who holds my true power."

De Tormo was perfectly calm; Gaston had not offended him. In fact, he was coming to like the Dark Knight a good deal for his devotion to Lady Remington. So many knights were immoral and corrupt, and he found it refreshing that the greatest knight in the realm was capable of deep feeling. He also knew that de Russe expected complete confidence with his declarations, and de Tormo would see that he got it. He would not betray the man.

"I know," the priest said simply.

Gaston's gaze lingered on him a moment longer before he lowered his arm and allowed them to pass. Remington's eyes were searching and their gazes locked a brief second before she turned away, paying closer attention to the path ahead of her. But he continued to watch her as the priest led her off in the direction of the road.

He had an army to assemble. Emitting a piercing whistle between his teeth, a scant few seconds later there were squires and soldiers pouring into his little encampment and the tarp and the furs were hastily gathered. His squires helped him with his sword and gauntlets. Readied, he met up with Nicolas and they began to structure the troops.

Remington actually enjoyed the ride. She and de Tormo spent the entire morning playing a card game from France, something called Hearts. She loved the game and beat the priest every hand. To put a little fun into it, she demanded that they play for little crabapples and the loser had to eat the apples. When the column stopped for the nooning meal, de Tormo had eaten several under-ripe crabapples and was literally green himself.

Nicholas met Remington as she exited the carriage and he looked stricken to see the ill priest. Remington laughed at them both, especially Nicolas. As young as he was, he was very emotional and God-fearing.

"Do not look so upset, Nicolas," she said with a smile. "Where is Gaston?"

"Busy at the moment," Nicolas replied. "He asked that I see to your meal."

She sighed, happy to be out of the carriage and light of heart. She took his armored elbow. "I would like to walk a bit, if I may. I shall eat standing up."

He fed her cheese and dried beef, and a grand hunk of bread with cinnamon and raisins baked into it. He ate sparingly, alternately looking over his shoulder for Gaston and watching the lady. Remington watched his face; he seemed so young, although he was only a year younger than she.

"Do you miss Skye?" she asked. "I know she shall miss you terribly."

He cleared his throat uncomfortably and a faint pink appeared around his ears. "I....aye, I shall miss her."

Remington smiled. "She thinks a great deal of you, you know. In fact, she's quite smitten."

Nicolas looked as if he were going to die from embarrassment. He had no idea how to respond and Remington was enjoying his discomfort. She wondered if her sister had told the knight he was going to be a father. In her opinion, the man had a right to know.

"And what, may I ask, are your intentions toward my sister?" she asked pleasantly.

His eyes widened and he looked at her. "Intentions? I...I do not know what you mean, my lady."

"What are your plans?" she clarified as if he were a simpleton. "When do you intend to wed her?"

Nicolas went from bright pink to sickly white. "Wed....wed her? We have not talked of marriage, my lady."

Remington's frivolity was fading. "Why not? Surely she has told you of her condition?"

Nicolas went from a quivering, embarrassed human to a suspicious, cold man. "What condition?"

Remington saw at that moment that Skye, nor Gaston for that matter, had bothered to inform the knight of the pregnancy. She was suddenly angry at their lack of consideration. "She's pregnant," she said flatly. "Did you not know that?"

Nicolas reeled; he stepped back from Remington as if he had just discovered she carried the plague. His eyes bugged and his face was void of all color as he stared back at her. Instead of the pleasure she expected, a spark of rage ignited behind his dark eyes.

"If she is, then it is not my child," he spat. We never...I mean, we never actually...Oh, bloody hell. I never actually slept with her."

Remington matched outrage with outrage of her own. "What do you mean by that? How dare you accuse my sister of...of being a trollop!"

Nicolas was livid. "I did not say that," he said. "And what business is our relationship to you, anyway? 'Tis between us."

"Oh!" Remington shrieked. Her open palm met with the skin of his cheek and his head snapped back. "My sister's welfare is my concern, Sir Nicolas de Russe, since obviously I am the only one who cares anything about her. And I will not forgive you for slandering her in such a manner. Of course the child is yours; she says it is yours and she should know."

"And I say I have never... we have never... I have never truly bedded her in the literal sense!" he exploded.

Remington froze, her face wide open with shock and dismay. Her fury was deeper, more powerful, and much less superficial. The tone of her voice dropped to something low and threatening. "How dare you speak of her as if she was a whore!"

"I did not say that." His voice lowered, too, but he was still raging. "I never said that."

"You did," Remington shot back with seething fury. "You said her child is not yours. You may not have called her a whore in words, but you intimated it."

"I...damnation!" He hissed, turning away from her. He had always had a difficult time controlling his passions. He was shocked and angered by the news, the ensuing conversation. He faced her again, slowly. "I never meant to call her a whore. I would never call her that, for it would be untrue. But I swear to you on my mother's grave that I never actually ...." He made hand gestures, trying to describe what he could not bring himself to say in front of a lady. When she continued to stare at him, hurt, he gave up his charades. "I never penetrated her.

I will admit we did everything but the act itself; she was afraid to go any further."

Remington's face was pale with emotion. They were both calming somewhat, but she was still shaken. "Nicolas, my husband took her virtue when she was eleven years old. Of course she is afraid to bed with a man. Did she not tell you any of this?"

"She did," he sagged, his shock settling in. "I never pressured her in any way. Honestly, Remington, I do not know how she could be pregnant if we have never *been* together."

"That is Lady Remington to you," Gaston came up behind them, his face like stone. One look at his expression told both Remington and Nicolas that he had seen their anger, their gestures, and was greatly displeased. "Away, Nicolas. I will deal with you in a moment."

Nicolas bowed away without another word. Gaston's gaze was hostile on his cousin and Remington could see that his anger was not focused on her, but on the knight.

"Do not be harsh with him, Gaston," she said softly. "He was shocked and upset. Our argument was harmless."

"You struck him," Gaston focused on her. "I would hardly call that harmless. What did he say to offend you?"

She shook her head, lowering her gaze. "Nothing, truly. I was meddling again and he took offense to me. I should not have struck him."

"Look at me," he commanded. Her head snapped up and his eyes focused on her intently. "What happened?"

She sighed and went through the entire conversation, waiting for Gaston's reprimand. When she finished, his expression was the same as it had been when she started.

"The lad is a fool," he muttered.

"I agree. Does not he know that she can become pregnant even though he did not actually bed her?"

"Apparently not," Gaston replied. "I cannot believe that he is so naive. But he is correct, madam, when he says this is none of your business."

She went from being remorseful to bristling. "My sister's welfare is my business, Gaston. I shall not apologize for loving her and wanting to look out for her."

"You said yourself you were meddling," he reminded her. "I do not blame Nicolas for becoming angry."

She crossed her arms stubbornly. "Someone had to tell him. Since Skye was obviously tongue-tied, I felt it my duty."

He raised his eyebrow at her. "Let your sister and my cousin handle their own relationship, Remi. They do not need your help."

She looked away from him, hurt and angry all over again. He eyed her, inadvertently reminded of their encounter before dawn and his limbs grew warm and tingling. But he chased the giddiness away, misplaced as it was.

"How are you enjoying the trip?" he asked, trying to shift the focus of the conversation.

She jutted her chin defiantly. "Do not change the subject. Are you going to speak with Nicolas or shall I?"

He took her chin between his fingers and turned her to look at him. "I will not tolerate this insolent behavior. You do not make demands, madam."

She wasn't very good at making demands or standing her ground. She looked into Gaston's eyes and was intimidated by the mere fact that he was a man. Even though she knew Gaston would slit his own throat rather than raise a hand to her, somewhere in the back of her mind she saw Guy bringing up a hand and striking her senseless.

Fear flickered in her eyes like a frightened animal and she yanked from his grasp, stumbling back a couple of steps. He caught a brief glimpse of the panic and was not overly puzzled by it. He had seen it before in her.

"I am sorry, Gaston," she whispered quickly. "I did not mean to sound rebellious."

His heart softened for her. He reached out and grasped her hand. "Do not be silly, Remi. You could never be remotely rebellious, and even if you were, I'd do nothing more than yell at you." He smiled gently, for he could see she was truly afraid. "You know me better than to imagine I would ever lash out at you. Correct?"

She blinked, calming and feeling a bit foolish for her behavior. "Aye, I know that," she swallowed, looking about for Nicolas. "I must apologize to Nicolas for intruding in his affairs. I truly meant no harm."

"He knows that, and so do I," Gaston caressed her hand with his thick glove. "But you have got to realize your sisters are grown women with minds of their own. They are no longer children who need your guidance."

She flashed him a regretful look. "'Tis difficult to think in those terms. I have been mothering them since I was ten."

"I am well aware of that," he said patiently, his eyes warm. "Speaking of which, did Nicolas feed you properly?"

"He did," she nodded. "Where were you?"

"I had a few things to attend to," he replied evasively, but she did not catch the tone. "We will stop tonight, but if we are on the road early tomorrow morn, we should reach London before noon. I have already sent a messenger ahead notifying Henry of our arrival."

She gazed up at him, looking like a fresh peach tart. He wanted to take a bite. "Good Lord, Gaston, I can hardly believe we will be seeing Henry himself. It seems as if a dream to meet the king of England."

"You never met Richard?" he asked.

She shook her head. "Not him, nor Edward, either. Guy was not privileged enough to be included in the courtly circle."

"You belong in the courtly circle," he said softly. "You are by far the most beautiful woman in the realm. The other wenches will be highly jealous of you."

She giggled. "Do not tease me."

"I never tease," he said. "I am completely sincere when I say that every woman at Windsor will be hateful of your beauty. And I will be beating off the men endlessly," he suddenly looked thoughtful. "By damn, the convent is looking more and more attractive."

She snickered again, flattered. Pleased to see her smiling, he held out his arm to her. "We have delayed overly. Allow me to escort you back to the den of gamblers so that we may be on our way."

"Den of gamblers? Who told you such lies?" she asked innocently as he led her across the sweet grass toward the road.

"De Tormo," he said flatly. "The man is ill with eating under-ripe apples. Really, Remi; how cruel."

She gave him a sinister grin, looking away coyly. He was completely captivated by the gesture, but shook his finger at her. "Leave the priest alone. No more playing for apples. We need de Tormo and I shall not have you killing him with foul food."

Her good humor restored, she bowed submissively. "I swear it, Oh Dark One. No more playing for apples."

He raised an eyebrow. "No more playing for anything. Do your needlework like a good little girl."

"But I like to play Hearts," she insisted. "Can I continue to play if we do not play for winnings? Please?"

He opened the carriage door. "Get in before I take my hand to your backside, you naughty wench."

She obeyed, pausing a moment. "You shall apologize to Nicolas for me, please? Tell him... tell him I overstepped myself and I am sorry. And explain the ways of breeding to him, for God's sake."

He nodded. "I will, madam, have no fear. It makes me wonder how many other wenc... oh, never mind."

She knew what he was going to say and raised her eyebrows threateningly. Without another word, she seated herself comfortably and he walked away, turning one more time to give her a subtle wink. Remington sighed dreamily.

Up at the front of the column, Gaston mounted Taran. "Did you see any further signs, Matts?"

The knight next to him shook his head. He was older and had served Gaston since the days of Edward. "Nay, my lord," he replied. "If there are bandits about, they have since vacated. They would be fools to attack a fully armed column of men."

"But there were several campfires," Gaston adjusted his reins. "Which would lead me to believe that there are a great number of renegades. Keep the men alert just the same. Nicolas."

Matts turned away, being replaced by Gaston's cousin. "Aye, Gaston?"

Gaston gave him a critical look before lowering his visor. "You will assign ten men-at-arms to surround the carriage carrying Lady Remington and the priest. I want you to ride back there with her until we have passed through this gauntlet of forest. Understood?"

"Aye, my lord," Nicolas almost breathed a sigh of relief; he was expecting to be reamed for raising his voice to Remington. In fact, he was still expecting some sort of punishment. "What's the matter?"

"Matts found signs of transients in the forest, probably bandits, or worse," Gaston replied, scanning the tree line. "I want the lady well protected should we fall under attack."

"Aye, my lord," Nicolas turned away, digging into his saddlebag to retrieve his dagger. He drew forth the sleek, bejeweled weapon and examined it with satisfaction. Before tucking it into his gauntlet, almost as an afterthought, he unsheathed the weapon to inspect the blade.

Thick, gooey honey dripped from the blade and oozed from the sheath. Nicolas did not move fast enough and honey dripped onto his gauntlet, seeping into the joints. He cursed loudly, holding the knife aloft and away from the rest of him while the honey dribbled to the dirt.

"Damnation. Ror…!" His head snapped up to Gaston, his eyes wide. "Christ, Gaston. I have just cursed a dead woman."

Gaston gazed back impassively, watching the honey drip from the blade. "'Twas your misfortune to allow her to get close to your possessions. If I were you, I would check everything rather carefully when we stop this night. Rory was quite thorough in her torment of you."

Nicolas stared at the dagger, the honey running from it. "I…I would take her over my knee again if she were still alive."

The corner of Gaston's mouth twitched. "The first time you punished her had no effect. What makes you think the second time would reform her?" He gathered his reins and Taran danced excitedly. "Go back to Remi's carriage, Nicolas. And tell her of her sisters' haunts from the grave; I think she will enjoy the joke."

Nicolas gave his cousin a wry look before turning as ordered, riding back along the column with the dirk held high and away.

The party passed quickly through the trees. Gaston was very uneasy with the sighting of the smoldering campfires and his sixth sense told him to be alert. Robbers and bandits were plentiful in the woods of well-traveled roads ready to prey on unsuspecting travelers, but they were not a stupid lot; they stayed away from armies or heavily armed parties.

Yet the deserted camp had been quite large, as large as the group he carried, and he was not so sure that the outlaws would not make some sort of attack.

The attack would be deadly for the bandits. Not only were they attacking the church, but also they would be taking the offensive against the Dark Knight. Even though he flew his black and silver standards, mayhap a gutsy outlaw would think it quite a test of his power to take on the Henry's Dark One.

Remington continued to play cards with de Tormo, winning more than she lost, unaware of the uneasiness about them. She kept gazing out of the window of the carriage, feeling the sultry moisture off the trees. The humidity was so thick that even the birds had ceased to sing, finding a cool spot to rest. De Tormo broke out a bladder of cool water and they slaked their thirst.

The column moved on, southward, toward even more unbearable humidity. Remington's hair was becoming a mass of kinky curls, wet strands sticking to her damp forehead. To the right of the carriage rode Nicolas, visor down and shield slung over his left knee. She knew it was a battle-ready position, but she never imagined they were truly in any danger. After all, who would be foolish enough to attack the Dark Knight?

They passed out of the dense forest and into the soft rolling hills of England. The further south they drew, the less forest mass they would see. Only sweetly sloping rises in the earth, and Remington watched, entranced, as they rode the crest of a hill. Gazing off across the country-side, she imagined she could see all the way to the sea.

There were farmers about, peasants traversing the road, jumping out of the path to make way for the Dark Knight and his party. The papal colors next to Gaston's standards made a rightfully impressive sight to all who gazed upon them.

They rode until after dark, when Gaston led them into a small village with a bright inn. Even in the carriage, Remington could smell roast beef and hear the sounds of merriment inside. She was smiling with excitement, trying not to hang her head from the carriage like an eager child. Loud people full of ale and food burst in and out of the inn, laughing and singing and chatting. Remington wanted to be one of them.

De Tormo eyed her, knowing her heart's wishes, and furthermore knowing the inn was no place for the young lady. But it was out of the elements and she could have a hot meal on a real table, not eat off her lap. Watching her face, he groaned inwardly; he knew her demand before she ever spoke a word.

"I want to go to the inn," she declared, watching curiously as a soldier and a busty wench came falling out of the door, screaming with drunken laughter. She looked at the priest. "I have never been to an inn."

De Tormo raised his eyebrows, eyeing the hostel. "I'd hardly call that a reputable establishment. It looks more like a den of iniquity to me."

Remington watched the soldier and the wench push themselves off the ground and stagger into the night. "They're simply having fun, de Tormo. It sounds like a lovely place."

The priest snorted and looked away, knowing that de Russe planned to take her to the tavern. But even as he thought of a pretty speech to refuse de Russe, his mind wandered to the soft bed within the inn that surely awaited him. Lord God, he would love to sleep on something other than the ground this night. He was, after all, not a hearty man and the thought of a feathered mattress 'neath his body soothed him like a sexual favor.

How could he deny the two of them what he so desperately sought? After all, if de Russe was paying....

A knight appeared at the carriage, a man Remington recognized but did not know his name. He focused soft brown eyes on her. "My lady, Sir Gaston is seeing to the settling of his men and will be with you shortly," he said. "He asks that you remain in the carriage until such time."

Remington nodded, glancing at de Tormo as the knight bowed away. "He must think I am going to forget myself and go bounding into the inn."

"I can see by the expression on your face that you indeed wish to," the priest replied.

She scowled at him, but it was a humorous frown. De Tormo cracked a smile and looked away.

Remington leaned back against the bench of the carriage, letting out a weary sigh. She was tired of riding and eager to sample the atmosphere of the tavern. More people came in and out of the business, and she watched them closely. Most were soldiers, and the women were whores, ready for another night of business.

She watched the women thoughtfully, wondering how a woman could sell her body. She could not imagine consenting to sex with a man she did not love, paid or not. But, then again, she had been sleeping with a man she did not love for the majority of her adult life. Mayhap she was a whore, too, in a sense. After all Guy had called her one.

She shook herself, away from the degrading memories. She would not think on them, although the closer they drew to London, the more terrified she became. To even be in the same city as her husband made her break out in a sweat.

Gaston suddenly appeared at the door of the carriage, his face wet with perspiration. His visor was up as he threw open the door to the carriage.

"Out, my lady, unless you wish to spend the night here," he said, his mood obviously light. "De Tormo, you will join us."

"Of course," the priest slanted him a wry look. "I am my lady's shadow."

Gaston raised an eyebrow at him but said nothing as Remington climbed out of the carriage. She turned to look at the inn, her face bright. "Are we truly going to eat at the inn tonight? I have never been to an inn."

He couldn't help but grin at her enthusiasm. "Aye, we will be sampling their fare."

"Are we sleeping there, too?" she asked eagerly.

"Remi, if you slept in the tavern, you would certainly never get any sleep," as if to prove his point, three loud soldiers and one woman came stumbling out of the door, singing at the top of their lungs. He shook his head in disgust. "You would do much better in camp."

She looked crestfallen and, to Gaston's surprise, so did de Tormo. He raised his eyebrows at both of them. "So the two of you would rather stay in a noisy, smelly establishment and not gain a moment's sleep rather than endure a bit of nature's canopy?"

Remington lowered her gaze guiltily. De Tormo fixed his eyes on Gaston. "I could sleep through the return of Christ, de Russe, so noise matters little to me. I am not ashamed to admit that I crave creature comforts, such as a soft bed and a roof over my head. Besides," he passed a glance at Remington, "I would suspect that you two would spend tonight as you did last night. What better way to be rid of me than to pay for my room at the inn?"

Gaston's eyes widened slightly. "You would be bribed?"

De Tormo held up a chastising finger. "Not bribe, de Russe. I prefer to call it a gift. After all, you expect my services in London, do you not? My assistance does not come without cost."

Gaston eyed the short man and Remington held her breath. De Tormo merely smiled a humorless smile. "I am not stupid, de Russe. All of the nonsense regarding Guy Stoneley's devil worship was just that, nonsense. Young Dane had the consideration to tell me that the tower room was his cousin's. I can see that you would go to great lengths to obtain this annulment, and do it any way you can within the legal confines of the church. Therefore, it would stand to reason that you need me, and you need me badly. Badly enough to lie," he looked at Remington; her face flushed, she was staring at the ground. His face softened somewhat. "I can see the feelings you hold for each other, and I am not so aloof that I did not hear the tales of Guy's cruelty. So, in the spirit of true love, I will do what I can for you against the papal counsel. But I expect to be compensated, and I furthermore expect my advice to be heeded. Do we understand one another?"

Gaston's smoky gray eyes glittered. "We do."

"Good," de Tormo turned for the inn. "I expect a meal fit for a king and the biggest bed in the house. See to it, de Russe."

Gaston watched the priest walk away, his head spinning with thought. De Tormo's manner had been assured, confident, and factual. There was not the least bit of evil in his tone, and his motives did not appear to be sinister. He would help them, but he wanted something out of it. Gaston's clue as to what that might entail came in the priests own words; *creature comforts.*

"Oh, Gaston," Remington breathed, breaking him out of his train of thought. "What have I done?"

He turned to her. "Nothing, angel. In fact, I like his courage. He is not afraid to say what he feels, nor obtain what he desires. I feel we shall have a staunch ally in de Tormo, for he will not give up," he took her arm, smiling encouragingly. "Cheer up, love. I have not made a deal with the devil."

CHAPTER TWENTY-ONE

The inn was loud and stank of old ale and bodies, but it was warm and lively and Remington was delighted. It was much larger inside that it appeared outwardly, and it seemed as if every possible inch was crammed with people.

Nicolas and the four knights had cleared a table for them to sit at, literally. Six soldiers from Earlingham had been enjoying a pleasant meal when the Dark One's knights had descended upon them and threw every man from the table.

De Tormo was already seated, enjoying a massive trencher full of meat. Gaston gripped Remington's elbow possessively as they crossed the great room, his eyes focused on their destination, yet acutely aware of the looks from the crowd. Not only were they looking at him, as the Dark Knight, but also at Remington. He could feel the lustful stares.

Remington was thrilled to be in a busy, crowded place. She loved to people-watch and seated herself eagerly beside the priest. Gaston sat heavily on her opposite side, followed by Nicolas and the other knights. No sooner were they seated, than serving wenches were rushing forward with food and ale.

The innkeeper, a fat man with sparse, wild hair, followed the serving women. "'Tis a pleasure serving, the Dark Knight once again," he looked at Gaston, who did little more than glance up from his food. "We were told of your arrival and I demanded another sheep upon the spit."

He laughed loudly and Remington couldn't help but smile at him. The other knights, as well as the priest, ignored him. Then the innkeeper focused on her.

"Ah, you must be the Dark One's wife," he moved around Gaston and took her hand. "Only Sir Gaston could warrant such a beauty. What a pleasure, my...."

Gaston's hand shot out, yanking Remington's soft hand out of the fat, greasy one. The innkeeper looked surprised and took a step back, suddenly terrified that he had overstepped himself. Gaston finished chewing before he turned to the man.

"You will not touch her," he said, his voice low. He studied the man a moment, coldly. "Father de Tormo requests your best room for the night. See to it."

The innkeeper stammered. "But...but, my lord, that room is taken by Baron Marchant's son. He is already asleep. But I have another room that...."

"Rouse him. Move him. I care not what you do with him. Father de Tormo wants his room."

"But, my lord, be reasonable," the fat man pleaded. "One room is a good as the next. As long as there is a soft bed and a soft wenc....oh, sorry, Father."

Gaston's eyes were like ice. "Where is the room?"

"To the top of the stairs, last door at the end of the hall," the innkeeper replied. "But the room right next to it is quite pleasant and...."

Gaston turned to Nicolas and Matts, jerking his head slightly in the direction of the stairs. Before the innkeeper could finish his sentence, the two knights were up and mounting the stairs. The proprietor, as well as Remington and de Tormo, watched with open mouths as the knights disappeared down the upper hallway. Not even a minute passed before they heard a woman scream and a great deal of scuffling.

Remington, her eyes wide, looked at Gaston, who was quite calmly finishing his meal. He acted as if nothing in the world were out of sorts, even though there was a good fight going on upstairs.

From a table across the room, four men jumped up and started to mount the flight of steps to the second level. Gaston eyed his remaining three knights with a silent command and the men were up, intercepting the soldiers before they could assist their lord.

The innkeeper was beside himself, watching a heady fight blossom. "Please, my lord. No fighting. I shall clear the young lord out myself if you will call off your men."

"Too late," Gaston drank deeply from his cup.

Remington put a soft hand on his arm. "Gaston, there is no need for fighting. Father de Tormo can take any room."

Upstairs, swords came together and Remington jumped. Gaston, for the first time, turned to look toward the source of the scuffle with a bored expression.

"Gaston?" she pleaded softly.

He glanced at her, seeing that her very first visit to an inn was close to being ruined. He, personally, did not care if his men tore the place down around his ears. It would have been the proprietor's fault for denying him his request. However, he did not want to upset Remington and purely on that basis, he submitted to her wishes.

Draining his cup, he stood up and the entire roomful of men and women cringed; he was by far the tallest, most massive man in the room and therefore a distinct object of fear. Moreover, there was not a soul in the place who did not know who he was. Should he join the melee, there would be several newly dead men.

"Halt," he roared.

The entire room came to a grinding, startled arrest. All eyes turned to him, including the soldiers fighting on the stairs. From back down the upstairs corridor, Nicolas appeared, his sword gripped in his hand. His eyes were questioning on his cousin.

Gaston put his huge hands on his hips, eyeing the combatants. Then he gazed up at Nicolas. "Where is the young lord?"

Nicolas jerked his head. "With Matts. Truly not a problem, my lord."

Gaston raised a slow eyebrow, refocusing on the lord's men. "You do not wish for me to enter this fight, do you? Then lay down your weapons and return to your drink, or I will make it so that you will never drink nor fight again."

After a brief, hesitant second, the four soldiers who had been fighting Gaston's three knights slowly sheathed their swords. Looking properly subdued and respectful, they stumbled back to their table as Gaston's men took the stairs to see if they could assist Nicolas and Matts.

Timidly, the room began to return to normal. Fights were not unusual with a roomful of soldiers and no one was overly ruffled.

Gaston sat back down, looking at Remington. "There. Happy now?"

She blinked at him, a bit overwhelmed by what she had seen. She had nearly forgotten the fear she held for him when she had first seen him, the abject terror of the man and his reputation. Obviously, she was not the only person who had a healthy respect for Gaston.

She turned her back to her meal, befuddled. He watched her closely, afraid her gay evening was already damaged beyond repair.

"What's the matter, angel? Are you angry?"

She shook her head. "Nay....I am not." What was she feeling, anyway? Confusion, surprise, and a new respect for Gaston? She wasn't sure. Light-hearted moments before, she felt somewhat subdued.

The innkeeper was still standing behind them. "Thank you, my lord. I shall always consider your intervention a great favor."

"Do not," Gaston said; the tone he had used with Remington vanished in favor of an icy one. "I did it so as not to upset my... wife. She does not like fighting."

De Tormo, in his trencher, lifted an eyebrow but said nothing. He was afraid if he did that Gaston would cut his head off.

The innkeeper was not put off by Gaston's insult and his jovial mood was returning. "A room for you and your wife, then? No charge."

Gaston looked at Remington, who looked at the priest. De Tormo felt their gazes but did not look up. Instead, he shrugged faintly.

"I accept," Gaston replied quietly, his eyes still on Remington. She deserved a bed to sleep on, not the cold ground. She deserved anything and everything his reputation could obtain.

De Tormo coughed loudly, quickly drinking from his tankard. As the innkeeper strode away, Gaston put his hand on Remington's knee under the table. "Eat up, angel. You have had a long day."

She forced herself to eat at first, but quickly realized she was famished. The beef was excellent, the vegetables tasty, and she stuffed herself silly. With her appetite returned, so did her mood.

She ate and watched, watched and ate, paying little attention to what she was doing so that ale dripped on her dress. Gaston smiled and wiped it away, relieved to see she was brightening again. Nicolas and Matts, as well as the other knights, returned to the table a short time later and resumed their meals with gusto.

De Tormo excused himself, retreating to his recently comman-deered room with pleasure. Traveling with the Dark Knight had its advantages, he thought. Of course, he should have been troubled that he was allowing such adultery to go on in his presence, but it was more than carnal lust. Much, much more, and he did not believe God would fault him overly. God had, after all, created man and woman to love one another.

He retreated up the stairs, forcing his disturbing thoughts down. He could not prevent de Russe from sleeping with Lady Stoneley, and he would not try. Adultery was such an ugly word.

Remington enjoyed her meal, talking in between bites, pointing at groups of soldiers and demanding to know their seat. She would make snide comments about the serving wenches, especially the ones who served their table. Gaston, amused, drank warmed cider and listened to her rattle on. He'd imbibed quite enough for the night and did not want to muddle his senses.

Nicolas found himself the object of attention from a particularly busty brunette wench, pretty enough, but Remington was shooting silent daggers at him every time he made necessary conversation with the girl. He would flush and stammer through his request or question, glad when the girl swished away. He did not want to rile Remington, especially in light of their conversation earlier that day.

But the woman seemed intent on luring him for the night. Feeling increasingly uncomfortable, he let Matts take over the conversation and kept his head buried in his trencher. He had no desire to take the woman to bed, curvaceous as she might be, and did not want to encour-age her. He had his own woman at home.

The wench was talking to Matts, laughing loudly with him and the other three knights. Gaston ignored her completely, focused on the room and on Remington, while Nicolas wished she would simply go away. Remington continued to eat, fuming, and watched the girl.

Finally, she'd had enough. Her sisters' jokes and mischievous ways had apparently sunk in more than she realized, because she discreetly began to pile a load of food on her spoon with the sole purpose of flick-ing it at the wench. Keeping her eyes on the woman, she turned the spoon and took aim.

The food when sailing, smacking the girl on the neck. She screeched, jumping back from the table and wiping the mess from her skin. Her accusing eyes flew to Remington.

She smiled sweetly, licking some of the goo from her finger. "I am terribly sorry, sweetheart. How clumsy of me."

The girl had better sense than to say anything at all, considering the woman sat next to the Dark One himself. Without a word, she scampered away and Remington smirked victoriously. Gaston slanted her a glance.

"Ah, the ghost of Rory strikes again," he said softly. "Really, Remi. I thought you to have better manners than that."

"I do, of course," she said crisply. "But I found that woman extremely offensive. I am sorry, Sir Matts, if I chased away your quarry."

The blond knight with the soft brown eyes smiled faintly. "You did me a favor, I am sure, my lady."

The evening went on and the occupants of the room proceeded to get disgustingly drunk, all with the exception of Gaston and his men. He refused to allow his men to drink so much that they were reeling of their senses, and they passed their time with pleasant conversation. Remington snuggled up against Gaston, listening to his knights recount stories of valor and she was properly enthralled.

Some of the soldiers in the room were singing loud, bawdy songs. One of them had a mandolin and played quite well; it would have been pleasing had the song not been so obscene. Gaston kept an ear cocked, making sure they did not get out of hand in Remington's presence.

Gaston made it a habit not to socialize with his soldiers; it had long been his routine. To socialize with his knights was a limited occurrence, and he made it clear from the onset that he was not their friend, but their liege. Yet tonight, sitting with Remington, he was actually far more relaxed and amiable than he had been in a long, long time. His men were surprised by his mood, yet they knew the lady had everything to do with it.

There was not one man at the table that had served less than five years with Gaston, and they were all acquainted with the man and his personality. They found it nothing short of astonishing that one small, lovely lady could exert such power over him. And she was not even aware of it. They furthermore realized Gaston was a truly likable fellow with a droll sense of humor, something none but his closest advisors had come to know. They were aware that Gaston and Arik had the very same sense of humor, explaining a good deal of the attachment between the two men.

The singing soldiers were growing louder, and Remington kept turning around, smiling at their disorderly behavior. She thought it was comical, while the knights thought it was distasteful.

A serving wench joined in the singing, an older, well-used woman with pretty red hair. Suddenly, one of the men grabbed her and she screamed good-naturedly, but he began to rip off her clothing and her squeals continued, louder. The soldier hauled her up and threw her roughly on the nearest table, much to the delight of his comrades, and proceeded to throw up her skirts. The wench laughed and taunted the soldier about his manhood.

Gaston heard the commotion and was up before Remington realized what was happening. The soldier saw him coming and backed away, and the woman did a mad scramble off the table. The entire group of revelers looked at Gaston as if he were the Grim Reaper.

Gaston stopped and planted his feet, eyeing the collection of drunks. He did not say a word, merely raised a menacing eyebrow, before turning around and retreating back to his table.

The party of drunken soldiers called a retreat for the night, and the wench disappeared into the kitchen.

"What was that all about?" Remington asked.

"I was displeased with their entertainment," he mumbled, passing a glance at Nicolas. "Well, my lady, have you had enough excitement for one evening?"

She nodded. "In truth, I am fatigued. All of this food and ale has made me sleepy."

"No doubt; you ate as much as I did. Shall I escort you, then?"

She rose stiffly, smiling shyly at the knights and bidding them a good eve. They watched Gaston take her upstairs, their eyes following her until the two of them disappeared from view.

Matts let out a slow hiss. "Jesus Christ, he's sotted. Have you ever seen any man so overwhelmed with a woman before?"

One of the other knights with a heavy Irish accent concurred. "He's far gone, lads. I pity Guy Stoneley."

"Why in the hell would you pity that bastard?" Nicolas demanded with a scowl. "He's got what's coming to him, after what he's done to the lady and her sisters. To Skye."

"And are you going to marry Lady Skye?" the Irish knight asked with a faint grin. "She's a pretty little thing, just like a fairy."

Nicolas sneered and looked away. "None of your damn business, Jacob."

"He's touchy, lads." Jacob nodded to the other knights. "He's as sotted as the Dark One, I'd wager."

Nicolas tried to look severe. "One more word and I shall cut your heart out."

The knights laughed softly at Nicolas' expense. As they were tossing more insults around the table, the busty brunette sauntered up with a fresh pitcher of ale. "Gentle knights?" she asked, indicating the pitcher.

Nicolas watched her fill his tankard. By damn, if he wasn't going to be forced into marrying Skye. He never actually slept with her; even though Gaston's explanations as to how conception could have taken place made sense, how could he be sure? He was too damn young for a wife.

He stood up rapidly, grabbing the serving wench by the arm so hard that she spilled ale on Matts. "With me, woman."

She almost dropped the pitcher as she set it down, rushing to keep pace with Nicolas as he took her from the hall and out into the night.

He led her into a thicket of trees not far from the inn. She was barely to a halt when he was ripping open her bodice, his mouth clamping down on her tender nipples. She moaned with pleasure, her experienced hands moving to his breeches.

On her back, Nicolas drove into her eager flesh like a rutting bull. *This is how you beget a child, Skye. Not with that silly petting and teasing you do. How in the hell can you be pregnant?*

Even as he thought it, he was sorry he was thinking badly of her. Sweet, beautiful Skye!

God, how he wished 'twere she who was under him now. As he found his release, Skye's name poured from his lips and he wished with all of his heart that he was back at Mt. Holyoak with her in his arms.

Gaston was up before dawn, as was usual with him. He ran into Nicolas as the men broke camp, his eyes hot on his cousin.

Nicolas was concerned. "What is it?"

Gaston opened his mouth, and then shut it as if afraid to speak his mind lest he rant out of control. When he finally did speak, it was measured. "I will not ask you why you took the serving wench last night, especially after the conversation we had yesterday. But I will say this; I will hear no more of your conquests, Nicolas. If you do indeed bed another woman, then make sure she is discreet. That bitch you bedded last night has announced to anyone who will listen that you took her, and took her hard."

Nicolas lowered his gaze, but he was irritated as well. "Who I bed is my business, cousin."

The veins on Gaston's temples flared dangerously, but he kept his outward calm. "Aye, it is. But I made a promise to Remington some time ago that I intend to keep; I promised that I would not allow my knights to hurt her sisters. I forbid you to abandon Skye now that she is pregnant with your child, Nicolas. Do you understand me? And I will not hear that you have bedded anymore wenches."

Nicolas refused to look at him. "You shall not force me into marriage, Gaston. I shall marry when I am damn good and ready."

Gaston came very close to cuffing his cousin. He forced himself to take a step back, out of range. "You will do what is right, or you will not serve me. Is that clear enough for you? I will not be shamed by my rutting, irresponsible cousin who had no idea he could get a woman pregnant by releasing his seed on her thigh."

Nicolas was drawn with rage. Gaston watched his cousin's reaction, calming somewhat. He took a step closer and lowered his voice. "I can only pray, for your sake, that Remington does not hear of your indiscretions. If she comes to me with tears in her eyes, I shall take it out on your hide."

He turned and strode away, calling Matts to him as he went. Nicolas kept his gaze averted, angered, and ashamed.

Why couldn't he admit he loved Skye and did indeed want her for his wife? Was it because he was too unsure of himself, afraid of tying himself to one woman? He simply did not know; but he knew that the more Gaston pressured him, the more he would not give in. Nicolas possessed the supreme de Russe trait; he was as stubborn as an old ox. And he did not like being told how to deal with his personal life.

Remington exited the inn shortly after sunrise, clad in a magnificent dress of aqua-colored satin. It flattered her to a fault. De Tormo was her escort, along with six papal guards, as they made their way back to the carriage.

Nicolas was standing back by the coach, his gaze guarded as she approached. He fully expected a slap in the face and was surprised when she greeted him with a radiant smile.

"Good morn, Nicolas," she said gaily. "It promises to be a hot one today."

"Good morning, my lady," he opened the carriage door, placing her personal satchel inside.

De Tormo climbed into the rig, but Remington stood next to Nicolas, observing her surroundings in the daylight. In truth, she was waiting for Gaston to greet her and she scanned the column eagerly.

"Did you sleep well?" Nicolas asked.

She nodded. "I sleep much better on a bed than on the ground. Rory was the one who loved sleeping under the stars, although we did not get many chances for it."

Nicolas' gaze lingered on her a moment longer before looking away. He was vastly relieved that she obviously had not heard of his tryst, but not because he feared Gaston's wrath. He just did not want the lady hating him.

As they stood together, Gaston rounded a group of soldiers and headed straight for them. Remington's eyes lit up at the sight of him, and his gaze devoured her in return.

"My lady looks bright and lovely this morn," he said with a soft smile on his lips.

She dipped her head coyly. "My thanks."

Gaston's smile faded as he glanced at his cousin, who took the hint and left them. Alone, he moved closer to her.

"Madam, if I had any less self-control, I would kiss you in full view of the church and my men."

She giggled. "Coward."

"Must you berate me so? 'Tis not cowardice, but rigid discipline I employ," he looked over at de Tormo, seated in the carriage. "What do you plan to do today to occupy your time?"

She shrugged, brushing a stray lock of hair from her face. "More cards, I suppose. When will we be arriving in London?"

"If we leave now, by early afternoon," he tapped her gently under the chin. "Let us depart, then. And no gambling with the priest."

"We do not gamble," she insisted as he took her elbow.

"Playing for money would be gambling. We played for apples."

He smirked faintly, helping her into the carriage. His gaze lingered on her tenderly as she seated herself, turning to snap orders at his men the moment the door was closed.

The humidity was already stifling as they traveled south. The outskirts of the megalopolis of London came into view, towns that ran into one another until the main body of the city was reached. Remington forgot about de Tormo as she absorbed the sights and sounds and smells around her.

She was entranced with her first visit to the heart of the Christian empire. She couldn't believe there were so many people, all of them moving about their business before the day got too hot. They would stare at her in the carriage just as she stared at them, the peasants wondering who the beautiful woman was in the papal coach.

The morning progressed and they drew closer to Windsor. The Thames ran a quarter mile to the south and Remington could see the activity on the great river. She wished her sisters could see the sights she was experiencing and would have enjoyed herself completely had not the lingering horror been cloying her mind.

Guy was coming closer. 'Twas of no matter that her sworn protector and lover was the most powerful knight in the realm. The fact remained that Guy was still legally her husband, and she was almost faint with terror every time she thought of seeing him again. Even though she knew Gaston would do everything in his power to prevent Remington from meeting with Guy, somehow she knew she would see him anyway.

Gaston reined Taran next to the coach. Remington perked up at the sight of him. "How far are we from Windsor?"

"Not far," he said. "But my messenger has returned and informed me that Henry is at the Tower of London. I shall leave you off at Windsor and then proceed on to the Tower."

She ran cold and her smile faded. He saw her reaction, knowing exactly why the color had drained from her face. Guy was at the Tower. But more than that, she was terrified that he was going to leave her in a strange castle, surrounded by strange people.

He reined Taran closer to her, his thick legs in armor brushing up against the carriage. "Do not worry, angel. I won't be long; just long enough to see Henry and inform him of the purpose of my visit."

Tears were welling in her big eyes and she tried to blink them away. "Do not leave me at Windsor. Please take me with you."

"I believe it would be better if I went to see Henry alone," he said gently. "I shall leave Nicolas with you to keep you company."

De Tormo had been listening to the conversation; it was hard not to. "De Russe, you would be wise not to take her to the Tower. The further she stays away from her husband, for now, the better. And if I were you, I would not even tell Henry where she is. Yet."

Gaston looked at the priest. "He will surely find out, considering she will be staying in his residence."

The priest shrugged. "If you were truly wise, my lord, you would not leave her at Windsor at all. You would keep her with you at all times or you would harbor her somewhere else for the time being."

"Why?"

"Think on it, if you were to leave her alone, even with a knightly escort, Henry could send his men to take her to her husband behind your back. He is not beyond that, you know. Not for the purpose of betraying you, but if I cannot convince the papal legate that she should be given sanctuary until this matter is resolved, Henry will have no choice. If he does not know where she is, then he cannot send anyone for her, now, can he?"

Gaston looked at Remington. "Agreed," he looked back at de Tormo. "St. Catherine's?"

De Tormo shifted his fat body in the seat. "I may have spoken hastily on that matter. Henry would find her at St. Catherine's. Surely you have a manse in London, or at least know men who do? Men who are willing to do you a favor?"

"I have my family's manse along the Thames, but you can observe the home from the Tower," Gaston replied. "'Tis too close."

"Nay," de Tormo shook his head. "Keep her there, and keep her out of sight."

Gaston glanced at Remington again, who wasn't looking quite as fearful as she had been. He was pleased that the priest was looking out for her welfare, and not merely following the rigid moral code of the church.

"I...I appreciate your foresight, de Tormo," he said after a moment. Thanks, as well as apologies, came difficult for him. "We thank you."

De Tormo looked at Remington as well, a saucy smile on his lips. "My loyalties are not to you, de Russe, but to the lady. I have a fondness for a woman who gambles for apples."

She smiled back. Gaston interrupted the warm moment. "This conversation never took place, then."

"Never. I have had no knowledge where the lady is," de Tormo agreed.

"I did not know you had a manse in London, Gaston," Remington said.

"It belonged to my father. My uncle, Nicolas' father, lives there," he suddenly groaned softly. "By God, I cannot believe I am leaving you in Uncle Martin's care. If the man does not drive you daft within a day, I shall be surprised."

"I'd rather be with your uncle than in a castle full of strangers," Remington said, eyeing him warily. "Why would your uncle drive me daft?"

He let out a sound somewhere in between a choke and a laugh. "He's, well, he's a flavorful man. A character. Full of...personality."

"He is an obnoxious boor," de Tormo put in casually, picking at his teeth.

"You have met my uncle?" Gaston asked curiously.

Remington giggled as the priest shook his head. "Nay, but I can piece your clues together well enough."

Gaston raised an eyebrow. "I have used the same words to describe you."

De Tormo looked at him and prepared a sharp retort, but snorted humorously instead. "Then your uncle must be a saint as well."

Gaston grinned and passed a wink at Remington before reining Taran away from the carriage and thundering to the head of the column once more.

Windsor Castle came into view not a half hour later.

Remington caught sight of the great tower flying its huge blue, gray and white standards and her heart lurched into her throat. It was a massive place of soaring towers and grim gray walls. She was awestruck at finally seeing the mighty fortress.

Gaston brought the party in from the north, passing through the Great Park to the mighty double portcullis opening of the King's Gate. His standard bearers, six of them, rode in front of him as they rode the length of the Great Park, plenty of time for him to be recognized by the sentries on the walls.

He flicked his eyes upward, glancing at his standards. They were unmistakable; a black shield with silver lining, and in the middle was a huge boar's head with exaggerated tusks that thrust upward to needle-sharp points. A crown encircled the neck of the beast, and its eyes were silver with a spot of blood red. 'Twas a most fearsome, impressive banner, and surely the most recognizable in England.

The bailey of Windsor was a vast, open thing. Gaston brought the party around to the front entrance and Remington's mouth hung open at the sheer size of the castle. Three stories in some parts, sometimes more, it spread forever, larger than anything she had ever seen. Three Mt. Holyoak's could fit into one Windsor.

There were several household troops assembled, waiting to greet the great Dark One. Gaston turned to Matts, ordering half of his army housed. The other half, plus Nicolas and

Matts, he would take to London.

He dismounted Taran, leaving his two squires to deal with the excited animal as he made his way back to the carriage.

Remington's eyes were wide. "I have never seen such a huge place," she declared before he could even speak.

"Too large," he replied, looking at de Tormo. "I am dropping off half of my men, to be housed here. I do not want to go riding into London looking as if I plan to lay siege to the Tower. A small guard and two knights will serve me better."

Remington wasn't listening to their conversation; she was watching the people. Men finely dressed with pointy shoes and strange, pointy beards pranced about with elaborately dressed ladies on their arms. She self-consciously looked down at her own dress, thinking the aqua satin with gold embroider to be quite plain.

"Remi?" he broke into her thoughts. "Would you like to get out and look about?"

She was moving for the door before she answered him. "Aye, I would. Gaston, why are those men wearing such gaudy clothing? Who are they?"

He helped her from the carriage. "Pansies. They are nothing but noble men who look more like women."

She looked strangely at one man, his privates bulging obscenely. She found it so appalling that she began to laugh and Gaston passed a glance at the same man, who looked down his nose at the two of them before going on his way. Gaston shook his head. "Idiot."

They were standing in front of a huge doorway, carved into a tower four stories tall. Remington tilted her head back, gazing to the top of the tower.

"'Tis called Earl Marshall's Tower," Gaston told her. "St. George's Hall is this structure to the right. 'Tis where most state business is conducted."

She was actually speechless a moment, absorbing the sights. Behind her was a huge, cylindrical tower as large as any castle she had ever seen. "What's that?"

"'Tis called The Keep."

She shook her head, overwhelmed. "This is so large. And there are more turrets and towers than I have ever seen."

He smiled, taking her arm. "And they all have names, like the Lieutenant's Tower, Chancellor's Tower, Winchester Tower. Anything that remotely resembles a tower is named for someone or something."

He led her around the northeast side of The Keep, letting her stretch her legs and gain a full look at the tower. She held his hand tightly and he felt as prideful as a peacock; every soldier or knight who caught a glimpse of her was interested, until they saw who it was who held her arm. Every fighting man in England knew the Dark Knight on sight.

They had wandered over by the King's Gate simply because she wanted to get a better look at the massive structure. People were coming and going and Remington was in heaven with all of the activity. She turned her beautiful face to him.

"Can we go into London while we are here?"

He squeezed he hand gently. "I do not know, angel. A good deal will depend on my meeting with Henry, and your immediate future. But we shall try."

She smiled sadly, latching onto his arm. Every time she thought on their separation, tears stung her eyes. Fighting them back, she turned her attention to another interesting sight when a voice shouted out at Gaston.

They both turned to see a man crossing the bailey toward them. Average of height, but well-built in spite of the armor that covered him, the helmetless man was smiling broadly at Gaston. When Remington turned questioningly to Gaston, she was surprised to see he was smiling, too.

"You bastard," the man shouted. "I had no idea you were coming. Have you just arrived?"

"Greetings, John," Gaston put out his hand and the man shook it warmly.

Remington was astonished; she had never seen Gaston shake hands with any man, and his manner was nothing short of friendly. Obviously, this man was well respected by Gaston.

The man was older, with streaks of gray woven into his well-kept brown hair. His face had been extremely handsome once, but was now lined with age and scars. In spite of that, Remington still thought he was very handsome.

"It has been too long, Gaston," the man chided gently. "I did not even see you before Henry sent you north. So how is Yorkshire? Controlled like the dogs they are?"

Gaston snorted, smiling. "Quite cooperative for the most part, actually," he was acutely aware of Remington clutching his arm. "John, this is Lady Remington. Remi, this is John de Vere, Earl of Oxford. He is Henry's premier military general and advisor."

Lord John's brown eyes studied her intently. "My lady, 'tis a pleasure."

Gaston could see that John had no idea how to react to Remington. He and the earl went back for years and knew each other very well. John knew of Mari-Elle, of Gaston's troubles, and was frankly puzzled to see the Dark One in the company of a beautiful young woman. Gaston was not the type. And, because he and John were well known to one another, Gaston knew he could take the man in to confidence.

"Lady Remington is my future wife, John," he said quietly. "Mari-Elle passed away a short time ago."

The earl's eyes widened a brief second before taking another I glance at Remington. Knowing how Gaston felt about Mari-Elle, he did not even express his condolences. "God's Blood, Gaston, she's too beautiful for you! How much are you paying her to marry you?"

Remington blushed prettily. "'Tis I who am paying him, my lord. There was no other way he would consent."

The earl laughed. "Surely, my lady, I can talk you out of this."

Remington leaned into Gaston affectionately. "I am afraid not, my lord."

De Vere shook his head with pleasurable disbelief. "You did well for yourself, Gaston. Mayhap now you can produce some worthy heirs for your heritage."

Gaston caressed her hand, his mood sobering. John was one of the men he wished to have sign his petition for the church, a man of supreme standing with the king and country. "But not before we annul two marriages, John. I neglected to tell you that Lady Remington is Sir Guy Stoneley's wife."

The earl lost his smile. "Stoneley? The bastard that surrendered at Stoke?"

"The same. Henry sent me north to Stoneley's seat, Mt. Holyoak, whereupon I met Lady Stoneley," he glanced at Remington. "Without going into any unnecessary details, Lady Stoneley and I plan to annul both of our marriages to wed. But I will need your help, John."

"My help? What can I do?"

"I need eight testimonies from important, honorable men in order to obtain my annulment from Mari-Elle. Will you do me the honor of testifying before the papal counsel on my behalf?"   "I shall be the first," John replied without hesitation. "Tell me when and where, and I shall be there."

Remington almost sighed with relief, somehow afraid that the man would refuse Gaston. But she could see that the earl would do anything for the Dark One.

Gaston smiled gratefully. "I shall, my lord. And I will be forever indebted to you."

The earl waved him off. "God's blood, Gaston. With everything you have done for me? Your declaration is ludicrous. If anyone is indebted, 'tis I, and I consider it a privilege to help you and Lady Remington any way I can."

"Truly, thank you, my lord," Remington said sincerely. "'Twill not be easy to do what we must, and I thank you for easing us one less worry."

"Who will be testifying for you, my lady?" de Vere asked.

Her lips twitched with a smile. "A good many Yorkists, my lord."

De Vere laughed. "A good many people who hate me and your... Gaston," he sobered, waving his hand in the direction of the castle. "Would you take the nooning meal with me?"

Gaston shook his head. "I cannot, although I would love to. Henry is expecting me in London."

"Of course," John nodded, looking hesitant. "Does Henry know of this?"

"Not yet," Gaston said as they began to walk back toward his men. "But he shall, which is why I must ride to London. The sooner I begin proceedings, the better."

"Agreed," de Vere said. "But you must sup with Anne and I before you leave. I will insist."

"You know we will," Gaston replied.

The remainder of the walk was silent, but comfortably so. De Tormo was waiting for them beside the carriage as they strolled up.

"My lord earl," the priest bowed to de Vere.

"The great de Tormo," John said, a bit sarcastically. "What are you doing as the Dark One's traveling companion? Trying to save his soul?"

De Tormo glanced at Gaston. "'Twould be the utmost challenge for the holiest of men, my lord. I am along as Lady Remington's escort."

"Ah," John turned to Gaston. "Well, I must be on my way. I will wait to hear from you, Gaston."

"You will," Gaston nodded, watching the earl walk away. Then he looked at de Tormo. "You know de Vere?"

"I do," the priest replied. "I used to be assigned to the priory in Oxford and heard Lady de Vere's daily confessions. A good, pious woman with a great imagination. The earl and I became acquainted."

Gaston did not reply, instead, latching his helm. Remington watched a woman go by in the most bejeweled dress she had ever seen, her eyes wide. "Did you see that dress? Why, she has more jewels on that dress than I even own."

"Not for long," Gaston mumbled, pulling her toward the carriage. "I plan to buy you barrels of jewels, my lady, enough to put that wench to shame."

She smiled at him. "I did not mean to insist you buy me more jewelry, Gaston. I was simply making an observation."

"I realize that," he opened the door. "But I will do it nonetheless. I want my future wife to be well dressed, as befitting her station."

De Tormo, climbing back into the carriage behind Remington, snorted. "Since when do you care for stations?"

Gaston, thinking de Tormo was bordering on blasphemy, cooled. "What does that mean?"

"Just that," he said. "I heard rumor that after Stoke, Henry tried to grant you the dukedom of Warminster, and you refused. If you cared for stations, you would now be the Duke of Warminster and not a simple knight. You would not even take an earldom."

Remington was deeply surprised. She turned her sea crystal eyes to Gaston in astonishment. "You turned down a dukedom?"

Bordering on embarrassment, Gaston lowered his gaze and fumbled with his gauntlets. "I am not an ambitious man, Remi. I prefer fighting to courtly intrigue, and as a duke, I would be expected to participate in such activities. I am content to lead my army and train Henry's troops," he paused a moment. "Besides, it was one more thing Mari-Elle could sink her claws into."

"But...Gaston. You turned down a dukedom?" she gasped softly.

He slammed down his visor so she could not see his face; a modest man, he was uncomfortable with her question. "Aye, I did, but if the title of duchess appeals to you, then I am sure I can arrange it."

She shook her head, extending her hand from the window of the carriage and touching his arm. "Nay, my love. I would live as a pauper, so long as it was with you."

He looked at her a moment through his visor, thinking that with all of the donations and bribing he might have to do, and such a thing was not out of the realm of possibility. But, by God, if Remington did not deserve a dukedom! In faith, he had not given his recent refusal a second thought until now. He wondered how receptive Henry would be to reconsidering.

He raised his visor and brought her hand to his lips. "Then you forgive me for my refusal?"

She laughed softly. "My lord, you are too humble to believe."

He kissed her hand again and re-secured his visor. "I am not. I am arrogant where it is properly placed, and prideful as a peacock when it comes to you," he turned in de Tormo's direction. "And so you have your facts straight, priest, 'twas two dukedoms I refused. I had no desire to live in Lancaster, either."

He marched away, leaving both Remington and de Tormo to deal with the revelation. The two of them were silent the entire twenty mile ride to London.

CHAPTER TWENTY-TWO

The Tower of London sat right on the river Thames. From where Remington sat, it looked almost as if it rose out of the water like a mythical legend. To think she was actually looking upon the structure, which housed her husband, made her feel faint. Had it not been for morbid fascination, she would have turned her attention elsewhere.

The Tower was still in the distance when the procession called a halt. Gaston appeared at the carriage, opening the door for her. Silently, she disembarked; noticing that Nicolas and several soldiers had unloaded her belongings from the wagon and were awaiting orders.

In front of her was a huge manor house, a giant vine of spider fern covering nearly one entire wall and completely obliterating one of the chimneys. She observed the house curiously, noticing two soldiers standing at the front door, conversing with a servant.

"This," Gaston followed her gaze, "is Braidwood, my family's home. I will take de Tormo's advice and keep you here until it is safe."

"How safe can I be with your obnoxious uncle?" she quipped softly, trying to ignore the pain that was tearing at her heart.

He smiled, taking her arm. "As safe as if I myself were guarding you. Uncle Martin was a great knight, once. He's just…"

He was cut off by a booming laugh, so great that Remington jumped where she stood. Nicolas, his arms laden with Remington's belongings, was suddenly scooped up from the ground by a bear of a man. As big as Nicolas was, it was no easy feat, but the man was absolutely huge. He slapped Nicolas on the side of the head, his voice loud and his actions rough. Remington's eyes widened.

"Oh, please…do not tell me that he is your uncle," she half-begged.

Gaston clutched her arm tighter. "Aye, that is my Uncle Martin. Do not worry love. He is only rough with the males in the family."

Martin de Russe moved around his son, allowing the burdened knight to pass into the manse. He was a massive man, almost as big as his nephew, and possessed the de Russe dark hair. As he drew closer, she could see that he was handsome indeed, but she felt herself shrinking back from him.

Fortunately for her, Martin was focused on Gaston. "Gaston! You stupid little whelp, let me kiss you!"

Gaston stood his ground, but he suddenly felt as if he were five years old again. The urge to run and hide was overwhelming. "Kiss me and I shall skin your hide, Uncle. A handshake will suffice."

"You take away an old man's joy, lad," Martin sniffed, but indeed shook Gaston's hand with a meaty fist. His gaze was very warm on his nephew. "Holy Mary, if you do not look more like your father. Brant would be in heaven to see you now," he suddenly focused on Remington. "And what have you brought me? My God, she's beautiful!"

Gaston pulled Remington against him protectively, fighting off a smirk at his uncle's manners. "My most prized possession. We will speak of it inside."

Martin nodded eagerly. "As you wish," he said. "Besides, I have a surprise for you."

Martin lumbered back inside with Gaston and Remington in tow. He led them into a comfortable reception room, richly appointed and smelling of fresh rushes. It was cool inside, away from the humidity of the river, and Remington sank gratefully into the embroidered chair indicated by Gaston.

Gaston removed his gauntlets and helm, shaking his wet hair and raking his finger back over his scalp. Martin, meanwhile, had bellowed for refreshments and now stood eagerly, eyeing Remington like a Christmas goose. But Gaston let him wait until he had removed some of his things and taken position beside Remington.

"Uncle Martin, this is Lady Remington Stoneley," he introduced them quietly. "My future wife."

Martin looked at Gaston sharply. "What are you talking about?"

"Mari-Elle is dead," Gaston replied. "I intend to marry Lady Remington and have brought her here to London while I obtain the necessary annulments."

Martin's jovial expression faded, being replaced by confusion. "Annulments? I do not understand, lad."

"What madness are you spouting, Gaston?"

The voice came from behind, from a doorway that led to another section of the manse. Gaston's head snapped to the sound of the voice, recognizing it, and there was a smile on his lips even as he turned. He knew that voice; it was very much a part of his fabric as a knight, and as a man.

An enormous blond man came through the doorway, his big blue eyes glimmering and a huge smile on his face. He was dressed in mail and pieces of armor, well used, and held an air of power about him. His very presence filled up the room.

"Matt," Gaston said with satisfaction, holding out a gloved hand. "What in the hell are you doing here?"

Matthew Wellesbourne took the outstretched hand and shook it firmly. In fact, he and Gaston seemed to stare at each other for a few moments, studying one another, reaffirming ties and unbreakable bonds. Gaston was as pleased as Remington had ever seen him.

"I was in London on business," Matthew said, still holding on to Gaston's hand. "I happened to see Uncle Martin earlier today and we dined together. In fact, I was just preparing to leave when your messenger arrived announcing your approach. I thought I would stay around until you got here."

Gaston squeezed the man's hand and let it go. "I am glad you did," he said. "You are looking fat and happy. How is your new daughter?"

Matthew grinned; he had an easy smile on his handsome face. "Already ruling the house," he said. "My father swears she looks just like my mother, but I think she looks like Alixandrea. She has her mother's face, I swear it."

"At least she does not have yours."

"My feelings exactly."

As Matthew chuckled and Gaston grinned, Gaston turned   to Remington and extended a hand. As he pulled her up from the seat, he introduced her.

"Matt," he said, his voice unusually soft. "I would like you to meet Lady Remington Stoneley. Remi, this is Matthew Wellesbourne."

Remington had heard the name. Everyone in England knew that Matthew Wellesbourne turned tides against King Richard at Bosworth and, along with Gaston, cost the man his crown and his life. Matthew was called The White Lord for his benevolent and fair character, something in sharp contrast to Gaston's reputation. In fact, many people already forgave Matthew for his treachery at Bosworth whereas Gaston was still looked upon as vile and feared. As Remington studied the enormous man with an oddly kind face, she tried not to feel any resentment towards him for that very reason.

"My lord," she said, dipping into a practiced curtsy. "It is an honor to meet you. Everyone knows of The White Lord of Wellesbourne."

Matthew couldn't help himself from looking the woman up and down; he was very puzzled by her very presence. To see Gaston with a woman, *any* woman, was something of a shock, and having heard discussion of annulment, he was doubly confused.

"The honor is mine, my lady, I assure you," he said pleasantly, looking between Gaston and Remington. "Did I hear you speak of an annulment?"

Gaston nodded and relayed the entire story, including a repeat of the details of Mari-Elle's death. When he was finished with his most complicated explanation, Matthew's expression was almost calm whereas Martin looked somewhat distressed. A serving wench came with some refreshments, leaving the room without the customary spank from the master. Martin was too preoccupied.

"Well," he finally sighed. "You have set yourself up for a hell of a fight, lad. You are the last person I would have expected this from."

Gaston held Remington's hand. "Trust me when I tell you that I am as surprised as you are. I have learned late in life that there are some things we simply have no control over, and to fall in love was the last thing on my mind. But it is done, and I intend to have what I want. But I will leave Remington here, in your safekeeping."

"Absolutely," Martin agreed emphatically. "'Twould not do to house her at Windsor or the Tower. It would only make her accessible to those sympathetic to Guy Stoneley."

"I agree," Matthew said softly. "Keep her well out of sight. Better still, will you let me take her back to Wellesbourne Castle? No one can get to her there."

Gaston shook his head. "As much as I appreciate the offer, Matt, I must decline," he said. Then he looked between his uncle and Matthew. "I am under no delusion that her stay here will be long. They will figure out where she is, eventually, and in that event, she will go to St. Catherine's convent. But for now, I want her close to me and under my protection."

"Under *my* protection," Martin corrected. "Have no fear, Gaston, that your ladylove will be safe with me. No one will get past me."

"I know," Gaston replied softly, gazing on Remington's dark head. "One more thing, uncle. She carries the next de Russe heir. That makes her protection all the more important."

Martin grinned, the first time in the entire conversation, while Matthew just shook his head and laughed.

"You are a lusty devil, lad," Martin said. "Just like your father. Why, I would say there were no less than six de Russe bastards roaming the country."

Gaston's friendly demeanor was gone in a flash, his irritation full-blown. "I only know of two, and I would appreciate it if you did not bring up my father's indiscretions in my presence."

Remington was shocked but held her expression. Gaston had brothers? Or sisters? She wanted to look at him, but dare not. He sounded angry.

Martin held up a soothing hand. "Do not get agitated, lad, and do not act so pious. You are nothing like your father in that respect, though your reputation is less than desirable in other areas."

Out of the corner of her eye, Remington saw Gaston stiffen. "And just what does that mean?"

"Just that," Martin snorted loudly, reaching for the plate of marzipan. "At least your father was not branded a traitor, though God knows you had your reasons. I would not have shown the self-restraint that you did if my wife had slept with my king."

Remington closed her eyes, feeling the words like a stab through the heart. Gaston's hand still held hers, though the pressure had increased. She squeezed his hand tightly, comfortingly. She felt as if she could cry rivers on his behalf. Head down, she didn't see the looks that passed between Gaston and Matthew at that moment. There was something of sorrow and grief there, of untold secrets that would be buried with great men who had made great and terrible choices. Matthew finally hung his head.

But Martin was oblivious to the silent words between Gaston and Matthew as he smacked his lips loudly, chewing the marzipan with relish. He glanced at Gaston, and then Remington, and back again.

"I say what I feel, Gaston," he said. "You of all people should know that. I do not blame you for betraying Richard. My God, he was an evil bastard, killing his nephews and flaunting his affair with Mari-Elle in your face. He knew you were loyal to the core for Edward and assumed you would be loyal to him as well, no matter what he did to you. You made a wise choice to serve Henry and Wellesbourne made the right choice to support you. Henry would respect you again and would treat you with dignity. Richard used you for a doormat."

Remington couldn't stand it any longer. She bolted out of the chair, rushing blindly from the room. The front door was cracked slightly; she threw it open and continued running, anywhere at all where Gaston and his hateful uncle couldn't hear her sobs.

She had barely rounded the corner of the manse when Gaston caught up to her. Without a word, he threw his arms around her and she clung to him desperately, sobbing her heart out. She was so terribly hurt for him.

"Shh, angel," he soothed her quietly. "It's all right. 'Tis old history."

"Oh, Gaston," she sobbed. "The shame you suffered. Everyone thought you were a traitor to your king, when in fact you did what you had to preserve your dignity. You would allow everyone to think badly of you rather than make public the truth."

He held her tightly, her feet dangling off the ground. She had no idea why he really betrayed Richard at Bosworth and he wasn't sure he would ever tell her. Perhaps it was something that he and Matthew needed to keep between themselves. It was, after all, their secret.

"Angel, my shame is no greater than the shame you suffered at the hands of your husband," he said quietly. "Do not let my uncle's words upset you so; I have recovered. I have found you, and you have helped me heal my wounds."

She gripped him, her hands in his hair, wishing she could absorb all of his pain. God, they had both suffered so much.

"I told you my uncle was a boor," he reminded her. "He is a wise, brave man, but he's still an oaf."

Her face darkened and she hiccupped. "I do not like him."

He gripped her arms gently. "In spite of everything, I do. All I ask is that you tolerate him, please. You do not have to like him."

"I do not," she repeated stubbornly. "How dare he speak of your father so carelessly. How dare he speak of you as if you had no feelings."

Gaston shrugged and put his arm around her shoulders, leading her back toward the house. "That is simply his way, Remi. Kind of like Rory."

Her mouth opened in outrage. "Rory had more sense than to run off at the mouth like that."

"Mayhap so, but at least Uncle Martin does not put saffron dye into bathtubs or honey into beds," he countered gently.

She had to agree with him. Silently, he led her back to the house. As they reached the door, Matthew was exiting.

"Where are you going?" Gaston asked, grasping him by the arm. "Please stay. I would like Remington to become acquainted with you."

Matthew smiled at Remington. "As I would like that very much also," he replied. But his smile faded and he glanced back towards the house. "But I fear I must be on my way home and it would seem you have much here in London to deal with. Moreover, if your uncle cannot control his mouth then I fear I may have to slug him, which I am sure you will not like, so it is best I remove myself. However, if you would like for me to stay to support you in your endeavor against the church, I will be happy to."

Gaston shook his head. "I am afraid it is something only I can do," he said. "But I swear I will send for you if I need you. When can we see you again?"

"As soon as you can make it to Wellesbourne," Matthew's smile was back. "I am anxious for you to see my daughter and Alix will drive me mad with questions about Lady Remington, so I would encourage you to come as quickly as possible."

"We will," Gaston's gaze was warm on the man. "It was good to see you, Matt."

Matthew reached out and took his hand again, snorting at the expression on Gaston's face. "What on earth is the matter with you?" he asked. "I have never seen you so... emotional."

Gaston gave him a half-grin. "I am not entirely sure," he said, dipping his head in Remington's direction, "but I am sure it has everything to do with her."

Matthew turned to Remington and grasped her by the arms. It took her a moment to realize that he was only holding her with his right hand because his left was missing. It was a startling realization because she had never heard that the White Lord was missing his hand. As she pondered that mystery, Matthew leaned forward and kissed her on the cheek.

"Whatever magic you have over him," he said as he pulled away, "I approve."

Remington smiled bashfully. "I look forward to meeting your Alix," she said. "I am sure we will have many happy conversations together."

Matthew smiled warmly at her. "I am sure you shall," he said, turning to Gaston. "Promise you will call me if you need me."

Gaston nodded. "I swear it."

With a final smile, and a hand to Gaston's shoulder, Matthew continued on to the livery behind Braidwood to collect his horse as Gaston took Remington back into the house. Martin had devoured nearly the entire plate of marzipan, turning expectantly when they reentered the reception room.

"Ah. Are you well, my lady?" he asked. "You ran out of here so quickly that I worried for your health."

She felt Gaston squeeze her faintly and managed a weak smile. "You will forgive me, my lord. Sometimes this child announces itself at the most inopportune times."

"Of course," Martin said. "Another de Russe heir. By the way, Gaston, how fares your son? I have not seen him in years."

"Trenton is well," Gaston was calm again, reaching for the goblet his uncle offered him. "He and Remington's son are fostering at Mt. Holyoak."

Martin raised his eyebrows at Remington. "So you have a son, as well? Then there is no doubt that this child you carry will also be male."

Nicolas entered the room, his helm removed and his dark hair kinky with perspiration. Martin smiled warmly at his son. "Nicolas, I am terribly pleased to see you. But where is Patrick?"

"At Mt. Holyoak, training Gaston's troops," he replied.

Martin nodded. "You will relay my greetings to him." He eyed his son a moment. "How have you been, Nicolas? I have not heard from you in a year."

"I have been well," Nicolas replied, picking over the remainder of the marzipan. "So has Patrick. Gaston has all but put us in charge of his new keep and we have been extremely busy."

Martin nodded with satisfaction, very proud of his two sons. His only regret was that he was too old to fight with them anymore, for he missed them terribly. Being in London, far away from his sons, he was often lonely.

Nicolas popped a piece of candy into his mouth, not looking at his father. "But I do have news for you. I am getting married, and come spring, you will be a grandfather."

Remington nearly fell out of her chair. Her eyes bulged and she looked at Gaston; he too, was astonished.

Martin leapt from his chair. "A grandfather?" he repeated, delighted. "Holy Mary, lad, you do not know how long I have waited to hear you say that! I could never get a decent betrothal for you, being my second son. Everyone wanted Patrick, but not you," he clapped his hands together, oblivious to the insult he had just dealt his son. "Who is this lucky lass?"

Nicolas was red around the ears. "Lady Remington's sister, Lady Skye Halsey."

Martin looked at Remington. "How thrilling! She must be a beauty, then, like her sister. How large is her dowry?"

Remington ran cold. Skye did not have a dowry; none of her sisters did. She opened her mouth to stammer out an answer when Gaston interrupted her. "One thousand gold marks. Nicolas will be well set-up."

Nicolas passed a shocked glance at Gaston, who met his gaze steadily. Remington reached up and grasped his hand, and they clung together tightly. It did not surprise her that Gaston would provide Skye's dowry, and she was tremendously grateful to him. He constantly amazed her with the new ways he demonstrated his love for her.

"Delightful! Nicolas, you will be a wealthy man." Martin was ecstatic. "I look forward to meeting my daughter, and my future grandson. You must bring them both here after the babe is born. Better yet, I shall travel to Mt. Holyoak."

"I shall bring them here," Nicolas mumbled firmly, then spoke louder to his father. "Skye would enjoy the trip."

Remington's emotions had exhausted her. From the depths of despair to the pinnacle of joy, she found she was fairly spent. As Martin and Nicolas and, occasionally, Gaston, prattled on. She could only sit in silence, holding Gaston's hand, listening to his deep voice now and again.

They were at the manse over an hour before Gaston decided it was time for him to seek Henry. The supper hour was drawing near and he knew the king would be at the Tower, preparing for his meal, free of meetings and audiences. He motioned to Nicolas to vacate the room and he pulled Remington to her feet.

"I shall be but a moment, uncle," he said.

He took Remington into a small room off of the main hall, a musty little closet. But it was private.

"I must go seek Henry, angel," he whispered, taking her head between his great hands. "He will most likely keep me all night; mayhap even for the next few days. But I will return as quickly as I can."

Her eyes were bright with unshed tears, but he could see her lip quivering. "I am frightened, Gaston. What if he...?"

He cut her off with a bruising kiss; the pain of their separation was cutting him much deeper than he could control. He released his kiss and she gasped, wrapping his arms around her supple body fiercely.

"Be brave," he repeated. "No matter what, we will overcome. I swear it on my oath as a knight."

She could only nod, too numb at the moment for tears. He smiled gently at her and kissed her again before leading her out into the foyer. Martin was waiting, holding Gaston's helm and gauntlets.

Gaston latched his helm and pulled on his gloves. "Take good care of her, uncle. I shall return when I am able."

Martin took Remington's elbow gently as if afraid she would try and follow Gaston out the door. "I shall treat her as if she were my own daughter. Better. I might even take her into London and treat her to a play."

Gaston eyed his uncle. "I would prefer that she not leave the manse, but I know how persuasive she can be," his gaze fell on Remington. "Behave yourself."

In spite of her breaking heart, she frowned at him. "Do you truly feel it necessary to say that?"

Martin guffawed. "All women must be told to behave. Control is not a God-given gift in a female as it is in a male."

Gaston smiled at Remington's outrage. "Nay, I do not feel it necessary, but I say it for my peace of mind. My uncle is a weak man when it comes to feminine wiles."

He threw open the door. Beyond, Remington could see de Tormo sitting in the carriage, waiting impatiently and she wondered why Gaston had not invited the priest in. But she was glad he had not; mayhap Gaston had an inkling as to what his uncle was going to say and it was best that de Tormo did not hear his darkest shame.

The cold steel from a gauntlet brushed her cheek and she looked up into Gaston's smoky eyes. He was smiling at her, and she forced herself to smile back.

"That's a good lass," he whispered. Without another word, he ducked through the doorway and marched out to his men.

Remington stood in the doorway long after the column of men had moved on. The sun set lower, and she still stood. Martin stood behind her, feeling a good deal of pity for her. Finally, he gently pulled her out of the doorjamb and closed the door.

"My cook has roasted a lamb for supper, my lady," he said pleasantly, leading her back into the solar. "Do you like lamb?"

In spite of her daze, she found the question silly and she laughed. "I am from Yorkshire, my lord. There is naught much else there but sheep."

"God's blood," he exclaimed. "Then we shall have no more mutton while you are staying with me. You must be sick of it."

"I assure you, I do indeed like it. It will remind me of home."

"Good, then," Martin replied with a snort. "I was having terrible visions of the next few months with nary a sheep in sight. I can only take so much fowl, and beef is expensive."

They smiled at each other, and Martin escorted her into the dining hall.

Gaston was welcomed to the Tower by an astonishing array of household troops. Having been notified earlier in the day of his arrival, they had been waiting since noon for him to appear. Just before sundown, he rode the narrow passageway from the Middle Tower and the Byward Tower, into the bailey.

Henry was in the royal apartments, demanding Gaston to him by way of his chamberlain, John Stewart. Leaving his men in the bailey, including his knights, Gaston took de Tormo with him.

Henry was still dressing for dinner when Gaston was announced. As soon as the king caught sight of his Dark Knight, he forgot all about the heavy pendant his servant was trying to hang about his neck. Tall, with a rounded stomach and reddish hair, Henry VII rose to his feet.

"Gaston!" he exclaimed. "How good to see you."

Gaston bowed a deep, practiced bow for his king; de Tormo was still in the hall. "My lord, 'tis good to see you again as well. I trust you have been well."

"Indeed," Henry looked over his most fearsome knight as one would inspect a prize bull. "My God, de Russe, have you gained even more mass? I do not remember you quite this large."

Gaston's lips twitched. "Nay, my lord, no more mass. I am as you see."

Inspection complete and excitement rapidly faded, Henry resumed his seat and his servants finished primping him. "I take it you brought Lady Stoneley here from Mt. Holyoak," he said.

"'Twas an excellent excuse for a visit to London, I must say. How is Yorkshire faring?"

"Cooperative for the most part," Gaston replied honestly. He would tell Henry what he wanted to hear before delving into the real reason why he was in London. "Except for a renegade baron, I have had little trouble."

"Renegade baron? Who?"

"Lord Botmore of Knaresborough. I had to kill his son and in retaliation, he struck down Arik."

"Helgeson?" Henry looked surprised. "I am sorry for you, then. He was a fine knight. And this Botmore; I have not heard of him. A lesser baron?"

"Aye," Gaston replied. "He fought with Richard, I am told. I do not remember him serving the king, nor his brother."

Henry seemed to ponder the statement another moment before moving on. He was an extremely intelligent king with more brains that brawn. He did not need to have any brawn when he had knights like Gaston to do his fighting for him.

"I am pleased, then, to hear that Yorkshire is stabilizing," he said after a moment. "I had my doubts, you know, even though I have Yorkist blood. England considers me Lancastrian."

"They consider you Welsh Tudor," Gaston said. "May I ask how Elizabeth and Arthur are?"

"Well and good," Henry put his arms up as fancy cuffs were secured to his tunic sleeves. "Arthur will make a fine, strong king one day. He is a brilliant boy."

Gaston watched as the king's many retainers finished dressing the man. Even though supper would be a small, informal occasion, Henry always insisted on dressing the part. He was, after all, the king.

"We are supping with Peter Courtenay tonight," Henry rose on his long, skinny legs as a crimson mantle was placed on his shoulders. "And my Uncle Jasper, of course. A small dinner party. I am sure I will have more questions of you, but for now, I am content. You obviously believe that Yorkshire is contained by your manner, and I will trust you on that matter."

Gaston knew he would have to broach the subject now, while they were still in private. He found he was actually nervous doing so, not because he feared his king, but because it had never been easy for him to verbalize. He cleared his throat quietly and removed his helm. "My lord, might I have a private word with you before we sup?"

"Of course," Henry waved at him. Servants and attendants scampered from his presence. "What is it, de Russe? You have reconsidered the dukedom?"

Gaston smiled ironically. "Nay, my lord, not at the moment. What I wish to speak of is far more serious."

"I see. How serious?"

Gaston took a deep breath, forming his thoughts. "I remember after Stoke, my lord, you told me that whatever I wished would be mine. Anything. You offered me two dukedoms and an earldom to compensate me for my loyalties, but I refused. Do you recall why I refused?"

"Because you have no ambition," Henry said flatly. "You angered me, Gaston. I wanted to reward you properly, yet you would not allow me."

Gaston fixed his king in the eye. "You may reward me properly now, my lord. I would have a request of you."

Henry's eyebrows rose. "Is this so? Tell me."

Gaston set his helm down on an ornate cherry wood table. The gauntlets slowly came off. "A woman, my lord. I want a woman."

Henry was astonished. "A woman? By God, de Russe! You want a *woman*? Be so kind as to inform me of this woman whom you would accept above a dukedom?"

"Guy Stoneley's wife."

Henry stared at Gaston as if he had not heard correctly. Or, mayhap, he was waiting for more of an explanation. None was forthcoming. After a moment, he settled himself into an overstuffed chair with a weary, long sigh.

Gaston watched his king closely; from his expression, he knew he was not pleased.

"Gaston...," he shook his head mournfully, resting his forehead on his hand and rubbing at the building pressure. "Not you. This cannot happen to you. Why would you want Stoneley's wife?"

"Because I love her," Gaston said truthfully. "Mari-Elle is dead, and I plan to marry the woman. What I would ask of you, my lord, is to grant me permission, and then help me seek the needed annulments. I need Stoneley's cooperation in this matter, as you know. As I need the church's and they will not give it freely."

Henry looked as if a rock had just struck him right between the eyes; he grimaced. "You love her? Dear God, Gaston, since when does love have to do with anything? I do not love my wife."

Gaston felt as if he was being reprimanded, but he would not lose control of the conversation. He meant to have what he wanted. "I did not go to Mt. Holyoak for any other reason than to serve you, my lord. Have I not served you with complete devotion? Have I not suffered personal costs for your loyalty?"

Henry shook his head sharply. "Yes, yes, of course you have. No one is disputing your loyalty, and certainly not me," he looked up at Gaston, scrutinizing the man closely. "Are you sure? Is this what you truly want? Because, I can assure you, it will be most difficult. The papal legate and I are not agreeing these days, and for me to petition the church for an annulment will only irritate them further."

"This is what I want," Gaston did not hesitate. "As badly as you wanted England, I want *this*. I want her, and I shall have her if I have to kill Guy Stoneley and every man who refuses me until I receive the answer I seek."

Henry was stunned and his appetite was waning. He did not want to deny Gaston the only request the man had ever made of him. And he could see, clearly, that Gaston meant what he said. He suddenly felt very tired.

"Lord God, de Russe, when you make a request, it is certainly a ripe one," he sagged in his chair, scratching at his scalp. "Because I value you so, and because you have been my devoted servant, I will do what I can. But it may not be enough; not even I can order the church to issue you an annulment."

Gaston let out a long sigh; he had not realized he had been holding his breath. "I would make one more. Donate the dukedom of Warminster to the church in exchange for their cooperation. Warminster is rich land and they will be most grateful for the grant."

"Donate Warminster," Henry echoed with disbelief. "Gaston, do you realize what you are asking? The church will rule an entire dukedom. By God, man, they already vie with me for power. To grant them a dukedom will be to give them a larger foothold in England. *My* England."

"And I will give them Clearwell and Mt. Holyoak as well," Gaston said steadily, his voice low. "I will give them everything I have if it will buy two annulments."

Henry stood up, pacing the floor with nervous steps. Gaston watched his king's stiff back, waiting for a refusal. Henry did not like the church, and donating the dukedom did not sit well. Henry scratched and paced for several long moments.

"I am in your debt, de Russe," he said after a moment. "Had it not been for you at Milburn Haven, we would have never made headway onto land. Had you not been at Bosworth, Richard might have very well routed me. And at Stoke, you were brilliant. You are the greatest military machine I have ever had the fortune to see, and you are worth more than your weight in gold. I feel as if I cannot deny you your request in good conscience," he looked at Gaston. "I consider you quite possibly my most valuable military asset and I would not alienate you for the anything. But tell me this; this woman is not a passing fancy, is she? Is she worth the trouble she will cause?"

Gaston's jaw ticked. "I would do anything for her, my lord. Anything! I want to make her my wife through legal means, but if that is not possible, it will not stop me. I will have her anyway it takes!"

Henry stared at Gaston a moment longer before shaking his head ironically. "I would meet this woman who has branded you, Gaston. I am having difficulty grasping all of this."

"She is in a safe place, my lord, until this situation is resolved," he replied steadily. "She does not go near Guy Stoneley."

Henry looked at him, a bit coldly. "I granted the man's request and I will not go back on my word."

"You are not going back on your word. If you cannot find her, the situation is out of your grasp."

"You brought her to London, did you not? With a papal escort?"

"She is in London."

Henry paced over to Gaston, eyeing him. "*Where* in London?"

"Before I tell you, I would have your word that she does not go to Guy Stoneley," Gaston said plainly. "If she does, then I will kill him. I will not allow her near him."

Henry could see the depths of passion within the smoky gray depths. He was preparing to order Gaston into submission, but he rolled his eyes wearily instead. "You are a demanding bastard. Stoneley has been asking for his wife daily."

"I am sure he is, my lord," Gaston said with more emotion than he had exhibited yet. "He wants to pry her for information to feed the

Yorkist resistance. He knows she has been living at Mount Holyoak, with me, and he wants her knowledge. Surely you know that."

"I know that," Henry snapped. "Gaston, do not force me in this."

"I am not trying to force anything, my lord," Gaston said. "But I forbid Stoneley to see her."

Henry looked at his Dark Knight, knowing the man meant what he said. There would be blood, and there would be chaos if Gaston de Russe ran amuck with anger and jealousy. "I do not like the fact that I will be breaking my word if I do not allow Stoneley to see his wife," he said lowly. "If you supervised their reunion, would you allow the man a glimpse of her? I would not be breaking my word, then, in allowing him to see his wife."

Gaston hated the idea with a passion, but he knew he must give a little in order to secure this bargain. "I will do that if you will grant me a favor in return; that you will begin annulment proceedings on my marriage to Mari-Elle."

"I will," Henry nodded. "In fact, we can begin them tonight. Peter Courtenay is the bishop of Exeter."

Gaston nodded, feeling strangely weakened by all of this arguing. "I have brought my own papal representative to assist me in these unfamiliar matters, my lord. Would it be acceptable for him to sup with us, as well?"

Henry nodded, having no taste for supper after this conversation. "By all means. By God, I am tired already. You have sapped my strength with all of your illogical demands."

Gaston smiled weakly. "You will not think them so illogical when you meet her, my lord."

Henry perked up just a bit. "Is that so? She is a beauty, then? Worthy of all this heartache?"

Gaston pictured Remington's face and his expression turned tender. "Worth dying for."

Henry moved to the door, feeling all of his thirty-odd years. "Let us hope it does not come to that."

John de Vere arrived at the Tower the following morning, Gaston was sure, to prevent the Dark One from doing anything rash. Or mayhap it was to show his support; for whatever the reason, Gaston had a long conversation with the earl and de Tormo that constituted his morning.

Peter Courtenay had been somewhat encouraging in the matter of annulling his marriage to Mari-Elle; he seemed to think that if the king himself gave testimony before the papal board, it would be the only petition required. Since the woman was dead, there was no reason not to grant an annulment. But in the matter of Remington's marriage to Guy, he was not as positive.

He had been somewhat shocked at Henry's request. Gaston was not surprised at the passion of Henry's argument to Peter; the king could persuade the devil himself to give up his throne if he were so inclined. Gaston was silent for the most part, answering questions that were asked of him until the bishop seemed clarified on all matters. He promised to seek audience with the apostolic delegate, James of Imola, within the next few days and report back to Henry.

Meanwhile, Gaston would have to gain Guy Stoneley's agreement, and he had no idea what to expect. Would he outright refuse? Would he agree with his blessings, rid of his wife? Would he bargain? Gaston suspected the latter.

Which was why he spent the morning conversing with de Vere and de Tormo. He had an inkling that Stoneley might possibly demand his release, and the return of Mt. Holyoak for his cooperation. Gaston did not know why he suspected the terms; he just did. As much as he had grown to love Mt. Holyoak, he would gladly return it to Stoneley. But the matter of his release was another matter. Only Henry could grant his freedom, but Gaston was inclined to believe the king would do just that if Gaston asked it of him.

Henry sent for Gaston just before the nooning meal. Leaving de Vere and de Tormo in the Queen's council chambers, where they had been speaking, Gaston retreated to the king's private solar as requested.

Henry was fatigued as the heat and the humidity of London plagued him, explaining his short mood. When Gaston arrived, he ignored any greeting.

"Stoneley is demanding his wife again, Gaston. I think it would be best if you send de Tormo to explain the situation, since the priest has already formed a rapport with him."

Gaston nodded slowly. "Agreed."

"But," Henry pointed a thin finger at him. "I want Lady Stoneley brought here this afternoon to see her husband. Mayhap if he sees her, he shall cease his endless requests and we can get on with the matters at hand. The man is a pest."

Gaston's jaw ticked and Henry rose swiftly from his carved chair. "None of that, de Russe. I understand your feelings and I am not unsympathetic, considering what I was told about Stoneley by de Tormo. But sometimes we must do distasteful things in order to achieve a greater end. Besides, there is no reason for you to be uneasy; you will supervise the visit and, therefore, no harm will come to the lady. Do you comprehend me?"

"Aye, my lord," Gaston's voice was a low, distant thunder.

Henry slanted Gaston a long look to see if he could detect any sort of subversion or disobedience on the part of the Dark Knight; under normal circumstances, such a thing would be considered unheard of, but men in love were known to do strange, unpredictable things.

"And then the two of you will join me for supper," he added, quieter. "Elizabeth is due here from Windsor this afternoon and I should like us to dine together."

"My thanks, my lord," Gaston replied. "We would be honored."

The king scratched at his scalp a moment. "Be off, then. Send de Tormo to me."

Gaston bowed and turned on his heel swiftly, marching for the door. Only when he entered the dark, cool corridor did he mutter a sharp curse.

De Tormo remembered well his meeting with Guy Stoneley before he went to Mt. Holyoak. The man had made him incredibly uncomfortable, but it was nothing he could explain in words. It was merely a feeling. When the Tower guard opened the heavy oaken door and de Tormo's gaze fell on the sight of Guy Stoneley again, he suddenly knew why the man made him uncomfortable.

The man was pure evil.

Sir Guy Stoneley was standing at the opposite side of the small chamber, clad in leather trousers and boots. Naked from the waist up, he was an exquisite example of a well-formed man. He was average in size, in his mid-thirties, and he took great pride in keeping himself in top physical form, even in prison.

De Tormo watched the muscles on his back flex as he moved in the faint sunlight; he swore he could see every muscle in the man's back. Not large or bulky, but merely defined.

As he approached, he found himself watching the man's back so that when Guy finally turned around, the priest was almost startled. Those eyes stared back at him again, and de Tormo felt the evil like a tangible wave.

Positive all of those stories he had heard about the man had affected his judgment, de Tormo chased away the disturbing thoughts and inclined his head as a greeting.

"Father," Guy greeted, turning to face him fully. "How good to see you again. Do you bring my wife?"

De Tormo studied the face; chiseled to a fault, sharp of angle, considerably handsome. Blond hair that was perfectly groomed and the eyes; like blue ice. They were of such a pale blue that they were almost white.

"I see that you are well, my lord," de Tormo answered steadily. "How have they been treating you?"

Guy shrugged, pacing toward de Tormo as if he were stalking prey. "As well as can be expected. Where is my wife?"

De Tormo felt himself falter just a bit; why did this man intimidate him so? De Russe did not intimidate him as badly as this man did, and Stoneley wasn't near Gaston's size nor strength.

He made up his mind in that brief second that he must come to the point of this visit; the more stalling employed, the harder it would be to deliver the message. Clearing his throat, he indicated the table.

"May we sit, my lord? There is a great deal to discuss."

Guy hesitated a brief second before complying. His slim, developed body seated itself comfortably across the small oak table from the priest, the piercing eyes intent. "Remington did not come, did she?"

"She is in London, "de Tormo's palms began to sweat. He attributed it to the heat. "But there have been certain developments that we must discuss, my lord, before you are permitted to see her."

"What developments?"

Dear God, where to begin? The speech he had rehearsed on his way to the cell was suddenly forgotten and he struggled to form words at first. "Your wife will be brought to you later this afternoon, but you must be made aware of the circumstances. Firstly, she will not be joining you in captivity. She does not want to."

A muscle twitched on Guy's face. "I see. I was led to believe that she would not be given any choice in the matter."

"Normally, no, but these circumstances are abnormal to say the least. She will be visiting you briefly, and then placed in the wardship of the church," de Tormo made sure he met the ice-blue eyes. "It would seem, my lord, that Lady Remington will be seeking an annulment to your marriage. She cites several reasons, among them being cruelty. She is seeking an end to your marriage and she has the support of the crown."

Stoneley kept his cool. The only outward sign of his internal explosion was a faintly ticking cheek, but it was several moments before he could speak. "Henry is supporting her? How chivalrous. But the church will not allow an annulment, will they, de Tormo?"

The priest felt a chill skate down his spine at the tone. It was deadly, more a statement than a question. "It is possible. My lord, your wife wants an annulment so that she may marry another man."

Guy shot out of his chair and spun away from the priest, trying to control himself before he tore the priest's arms from their sockets. He began to shake, his mind working wildly. Remington wanted an annulment... she had crown support...she wanted to marry someone else. "Who is it that she would marry?"

De Tormo swallowed hard, his voice suddenly leaving him. "Gaston de Russe."

Guy froze. Then, slowly, he turned to face the priest. "The Dark Knight? The man who betrayed our king, who overtook my keep?" he took a disbelieving step toward de Tormo, his face glazed with astonishment. "She would marry the Dark One?"

De Tormo could only nod. Guy's eyes were burning holes into him and he was more uncomfortable than ever. He kept waiting for a fist to catch him in the jaw.

"A reward," Stoneley hissed. "A reward for his services. My keep, my wife. Henry would lock me up and throw away the key while de Russe takes over my life."

"Nay, my lord, 'tis not like that," de Tormo said quickly. "Lady Remington and Sir Gaston have fallen in love with one another and they wish to be married."

"Love!" Guy snapped, slapping his hand on the table. "Remington does not know the first thing about love! She is a naive, disobedient bitch and only I know how to deal with her." He was suddenly around the table, grabbing hold of de Tormo's robes. "I will not allow this, priest. I will never agree to an annulment, and I will write the goddamn pope if I have to, to keep my wife! She is mine and will remain so!"

De Tormo was shaken but he held his ground. "You do not even want her."

"She's mine," Stoneley repeated, his voice hissing and his face twitching. "By the law of the land and the law of the church, she is my goddamn wife and I shall keep her until I die."

De Tormo wrenched himself free of the grasp and stumbled from the chair, his eyes wide at the madman. "De Russe will have her no matter what you say. If you wish to preserve your life, then I advise you to agree to whatever he suggests."

Stoneley was preparing to physically assault the priest again but halted himself unsteadily. Instead, his eyes took on a strange, nervous light, a look of madness that ran through de Tormo like an icy wind.

"I love my wife terribly, priest. Surely the church will not allow an annulment on that basis. Surely they will protect the sanctity of a marriage, which the usurper king threatens to destroy. Surely they will not allow the king to punish his prisoner in this manner, by taking away his own wife and giving him to another as the spoils of war."

De Tormo did not realize he was quivering with emotion and fright. Stoneley was unbalanced, and incredibly clever. "I cannot say what the church will do, my lord. I merely came here today as a messenger, not a judge and jury."

Stoneley's sculpted body was glistening with sweat. He stood straight, a flash of sanity returning to his eyes. "I realize that. But I will need your help in this, de Tormo. I will need advice to...."

De Tormo shook his head, backing away to the door. "I cannot give it in good conscience. From what I have seen, Lady Remington would be much better off with de Russe. You, my lord, are a lunatic."

Fortunately for de Tormo that he was near the door. Guy flew over the table with such speed and grace that the priest had no time to react at all before he was being slammed into the wall.

"I shall not let her go," Guy seethed quietly. "She is my wife, and I shall not let her go."

The door jerked open and there were suddenly soldiers pulling Guy off de Tormo. The priest scrambled through the door, watching Stoneley shirk his accosters.

He had to find Gaston.

De Tormo was pale by the time he reached Gaston's rooms. Gaston was concerned.

"What happened?" he demanded.

De Tormo reached a shaky hand for the wine decanter. Gaston saw the man's hands and poured the drink himself.

"He's mad," the priest finally said.

Gaston tried to remain calm. He folded his arms slowly and waited until de Tormo had imbibed several fortifying gulps. "That, priest, has already been established. I take it that he did not receive the news well."

De Tormo snorted and sank into the nearest chair. "Hardly. He believes that Henry is behind this annulment, planning to reward you with Remington and Mt. Holyoak as the spoils of war. He cannot comprehend that love has anything to do with this."

Gaston took a slow, deep breath, forming his thoughts. "'Tis probably what it seems to him."

De Tormo looked at him pointedly. "He shall not cooperate with you in the least, Gaston. He does not want to let Remington go."

Gaston knew that. Now that his suspicions were confirmed, he could better formulate a plan of action. "Then I will go and see him. Mayhap he will listen to... reason."

The priest waved him away. "You'd better not. Knowing you, Stoneley will not live to see the sun set and you would be charged with his murder. The church would never grant you an annulment in that case."

"I shall remain completely in control," Gaston insisted, but even he did not believe it. To actually face the man who had caused Remington so much pain would drive him over the brink.

De Tormo shook his head again. "Do not see him alone. Take de Vere with you, if for no other reason, as a witness. Stoneley is clever enough that he would beat himself senseless after your visit and then say that you did it," he lowered his gaze. "He...he unsettles me, Gaston. He is not only utterly evil; he is as smart as the devil, too. I received the impression that he would do anything in his power to keep this annulment from going through."

Gaston's gaze was hard. "'Twill not be enough. I will triumph in the end, no matter what he says or does."

De Tormo stared at him a moment longer, the wine settling his nerves. "I concur with your requests that Remington stay away from him, although the point is mute now. He spoke of her most unfavorably and, coming to know the lady as I have, even I was offended," he sat back in the chair, wearily. "If my meeting with him is any indication, then you must maintain iron control when you supervise his meeting with her. I have a feeling he will try and provoke you, anything to use against you."

Gaston wasn't looking at the priest. Be seemed to be staring at the floor, his boots, his leather vest. He slowly fumbled with the fold of his vest before removing a long, narrow dagger. It was a wicked looking thing. De Tormo watched with curiosity as he fingered it smoothly, all the while seeming to think on other things.

Suddenly, the dagger went sailing. In a fine, straight line as true as time, it landed with deadly accuracy into a large wall tapestry. De Tormo's head snapped with surprise, overwhelmed with the speed and force in which the blade was tossed. It took him a moment to see that the dagger had pierced the figure of a man, pinning the tapestry to the wall.

Upon closer scrutiny, the razor-sharp point of the dagger penetrated the head of the man, dead center, in the eye.

With a slow sigh, de Tormo faced Gaston again. "Well done. Take your aggressions out on the furnishings, but not on Stoneley. Not yet, anyway. 'Tis far too early in the game to create more problems than you already have."

Gaston did not answer him for, in truth, he did not trust himself to speak. Anger and hatred toward Stoneley was growing by the minute.

"I promised Henry I would collect Remington," he murmured, moving for the door but not bothering to retrieve his blade. "We are supping with he and Elizabeth this eve, alone. Mayhap you can use the time to recover from your meeting with Stoneley."

De Tormo lifted an ironic eyebrow. "I fear I might have to go to Westminster and have myself exorcised. I feel as if I have tangled with the devil."

Gaston paused abruptly at the door. "You are wrong on that account. By tonight, Guy Stoneley will have met the devil face to face. They do not call me the Dark One for frivolous reasons."

CHAPTER TWENTY-THREE

Gaston was determined to see Stoneley. He was nearly blinded with rage with the results of de Tormo's meeting with the man and he fought a losing battle to control himself.

He crossed the compound of the Tower, passing by the White Tower where Stoneley was held and fighting the urge to race to the third floor, tear the door from its hinges, and then proceed to gut Guy Stoneley with his bare hands. He almost veered for the entrance to the Tower, but he forced himself away.

De Tormo had been quite correct in one thing; he would have to bring another man with him when he met with Stoneley if for no other reason, than to prevent him from committing murder.

John de Vere had not yet left the Tower and was more than happy to accompany Gaston. De Vere could see the banked rage in the Dark Knight's eyes and spent the entire walk from the Queen's council chambers to the White Tower trying to calm Gaston's fury. A wise man with a keen intellect, he was able to force some reason down Gaston's throat so by the time they approached Stoneley's cell door, Gaston could think somewhat rationally again.

Outside of the door, Gaston paused to collect himself further. De Vere had helped him a great deal with his wisdom, but now he felt himself start to slip again. The fact that he was actually to face Guy Stoneley was overwhelming him.

"Come to grips, Gaston," de Vere said quietly. "You will gain your ends, eventually, but not if you kill the man first. Control yourself, as I have seen you do in battle so many times. There is no one greater at remaining calm than you."

Gaston let out a hiss. "Except when it comes to Remington. I am tremendously unstable when it comes to her and I do not like being unstable. I feel as if I have no control over anything I say or do, as if my words and actions are coming directly from my heart."

De Vere watched him for a moment, the disturbing body language of a man his size. "A suggestion, if I may, Gaston. Detach yourself. Handle this problem as if it were Patrick or Nicolas, and not you. Pretend, if you have to, that you have come here to plead on Patrick's behalf. You are far too close to the situation and it is tearing you up. For your own sanity, you must detach yourself."

Gaston was staring off, listening but not looking at the earl. John wondered if he had even heard what he had said. Then, finally, the smoky gray eyes focused on him.

"Wisely spoken. I suppose I can do no more than try."

"Good," de Vere said quietly. "Now; shall we meet the man?"

Gaston paused a moment longer before nodding his head to the sentry and the door was swung wide.

A surge of adrenalin hit Gaston the minute he passed through the threshold and he knew it was not a good sign. But he fought it, controlled it, and his eyes came to rest on the half-naked man at the far end of the room. The man he had learned to hate above all else, his enemy, and his worst nightmare.

Guy Stoneley turned around when the door opened, his ice-blue eyes focusing intently on the two knights entering his room. When Gaston's eyes met with his, there was nearly a visible arc of electricity. Each man felt as if he had been slapped and tension filled the room.

Gaston studied Guy closely, for it had been a long time since they had last met. The man was pure of muscle, sculpted if not a bit thin. Gaston was almost physically impacted by the mental visions of the man using his muscle, his strength against Remington and her sisters. He could suddenly picture the man raping his wife and her sisters, breaking Rory's arm, impregnating a crying Jasmine. Every evil thing had been told of the man suddenly came pouring down on him.

"De Russe," Stoneley said, still on the far side of the room. "I did not think it would take long for you to come and see me, and I was right."

Gaston's hands began to twitch as he paced leisurely into the room. Behind him, he heard the door close. All he could think of was racing to the man and throwing him from the window by which he stood. Black, swirling hatred consumed him.

"You were indeed," he managed to force out. The bastard who had beat and humiliated the woman he loved was no more than a stone's throw away and he was nearly wild with the idea. By God, how long had he dreamed of meeting Stoneley and cutting his heart out?

Stoneley smiled thinly, a humorless smile. He walked closer, unaware or uncaring of the mortal conflict he was creating inside Gaston.

He'd had time to think since de Tormo had left him. Aye, at first he was outraged at what had been suggested, not because he cared for Remington, but because Henry wanted to take everything away from him. But as he pondered the proposal, he became increasingly aware of the lengths Henry would go to provide de Russe his wish and he realized that he was at a great advantage. The church would not grant an annulment without his consent, and Henry would most likely do anything to gain it.

Anything.

For the first time in over a year, Guy felt hope. Hope that he would return to his beloved Mt. Holyoak, home to his family, such as they were. He could live without Remington, so long as he had another whore to take her place. But he would not let on, at least not so soon. He wanted Henry and Gaston to stew about it to the point where they were willing to grant him anything he asked.

The game was afoot.

"So you have come to plead with me to consent to an annulment?" he jumped straight to the point; no meaningless conversation, no pleasantries.

A muscle on Gaston's cheek twitched dangerously. Behind him, de Vere eyed him warily. "I have."

Oh, Guy was pleased to hear it. *God, how he loved to be in control!* He sat slowly in a chair, eyeing Gaston carefully. He was a big man, as big as Guy had ever seen, but the Dark One did not intimidate him; on the contrary.

"Then do."

Gaston almost flinched, but he steadied himself. "I would ask your agreement in gaining an annulment to your marriage to Lady Remington."

Guy sat and waited a moment, expecting more. He raised his eyebrows expectantly. "Is that all? No begging, no pleading? De Tormo said you were in love; you do not act like it."

Gaston cursed de Tormo under his breath. How dare the man give Stoneley ammunition like that? Suddenly angered for another reason, he was also instantly irritated at Guy's smug attitude.

"How would you have me act? I have stated my business. What is it that you would have me say that would elaborate on what you already know?"

Guy crossed his legs in a decidedly feminine gesture and Gaston was enraged to see a smile playing on his lips. *Please, God, give me strength not to kill him!*

"You have bedded her, have you not?"

Gaston did not hesitate. "Aye."

Guy snorted. "You have broken two commandments of the church. Not only did you covet my wife, but you committed adultery, too. The church will not be happy to hear that."

Gaston did not reply; he continued to watch Stoneley like a hawk, his huge body tensed. Guy's gaze was smirking, taunting.

"What about her sisters? I trust they told you everything."

Gaston released a soft sigh. "Aye, they told me all about your cruelty and debauchery but, fortunately, I am not as deviant as you. Let us come to the point, Stoneley. I will obtain this annulment any way I can, including and most likely murdering you. But barring any severe action, what do you want for your cooperation?"

Guy's smile faded somewhat. *By God, if the man wasn't like ice,* Gaston thought. He could see why the man had unnerved de Tormo so. "Want? Nothing, really, except my wife to stay here with me in the Tower. I merely want my wife."

He drew out the word wife, purposely rubbing salt into Gaston's wound, reminding him that what he so desperately sought belonged to another.

Gaston couldn't take much more; he leaned forward on the table that separated them and allowed his fists to pound heavily against the table. The thump reverberated against the stone walls.

"There is not a chance in hell that Remington will be brought to you to stay, my lord, and the sooner you understand that, the better for us all. You will now name your price to me and I will do everything in my power to grant it."

"I have no price," Guy's smile was gone, his eyes like glittering ice, cold and harsh and potentially deadly.

"Aye, you do," Gaston said, his voice a thundering rumble. "Name it."

"There is nothing to name."

"There is. What will gain your cooperation?"

Stoneley gazed at him a moment longer. "I do not want to relinquish my wife, de Russe. Can you not understand?"

"The choice is not yours to make. Your only decision in all of this is what you will gain for your collaboration. You can come away with a great deal, or you can lose your life. *That*, my lord, is your only option."

Guy lowered his gaze, pondering the statement confidently. He was very good at playing these games. "The church will not like it that you have threatened me, de Russe. And they shall hear of this, have no doubt. You shall never gain my wife that way."

Gaston straightened, his temples throbbing threateningly. De Vere moved a bit closer to him, just in case.

"Think on this conversation, Stoneley," he said after a moment. "I shall return to seek your answer. And you will have an answer for me."

Gaston was moving for the door; he'd had about all he could take and was surprised he had managed to keep himself in check so well. He was almost free when Stoneley called out to him.

"If Remington herself were to ask me for an annulment, I might possibly reconsider my position," he said quietly. Like the quietness of the wolf before it strikes. "I understand she is in London. Will you bring her to me so that she may ask me herself, so that I may hear from her own lips that this is what she desires and that she is not being used as a pawn in Henry's game?"

Gaston's hand was on the door, his knuckles white with restraint. "As fortune would have it, she will be visiting you this afternoon, pursuant to Henry's order and your innumerable requests. You will see her then and she will tell you herself."

Guy's face actually lightened. "Ah. Then the Tudor did not go back on his word, after all. I am pleased. 'Twill be good to see my sweet, tasty wife again."

De Vere put his hand on Gaston firmly, opening the door himself. He was not about to allow Gaston to reply in any manner, considering they had just danced in the fire for several minutes without getting burned. Both men knew that Stoneley was trying to provoke the Dark One.

Guy laughed as the door was closing. "Take her hard, de Russe. She likes it that way."

De Vere heard the comment and pushed Gaston from the door, following him closely. Gaston did not protest the manhandling; in fact, he welcomed it. He needed the additional control, for he had exhausted his. It had taken every last ounce of strength to walk through the door without tearing it off its hinges. His fury, unfocused, was a lethal explosion waiting to happen.

"Walk, Gaston, just walk," John pushed him again, moving him down the corridor and away from Stoneley. "You did very well. I am pleased with you."

Gaston did not reply until they were out in the hot afternoon, the bright blue sky overhead. "When this is all over, I am going to kill him. I vow this, John."

"I know," de Vere replied softly. "You can feel his evil when you walk into the room; it grabs at you like a vise. How is it that such a lovely woman is married to such a vile man?"

Gaston shook his head faintly. "Betrothals are strange things. See how mismatched Mari-Elle and I were."

De Vere nodded. "I suppose I should convey my sympathies to you on her passing, but it seems to me as if it were more of a blessing."

"More than you know," Gaston replied, his anger fading and being replaced by an empty fatigue. He felt an overwhelming desire to hold Remington.

They paused at the entrance to the Queen's house and Gaston faced the earl. "I would thank you for accompanying me. The situation is most undesirable and I apologize for making you uncomfortable."

De Vere slapped him on the shoulder. "What are friends for, Gaston?"

He slipped into the door, leaving Gaston speechless a moment. Arik had been his only friend, had not he? Gaston had always made very sure that he had no other friends. Yet, mayhap, he had unknowingly made far more friends that he cared to admit. After all, friendship was painful and cloying and... by God, why couldn't he admit it? Of course he had more than one friend. He had a whole damn country full of them.

The revelation was startling, yet he felt a tremendous sense of comfort in it. Had he indeed been so blind? Apparently so.

He caught sight of Nicolas across the compound, by the armory. He watched his young cousin a moment, being reminded of Mt. Holyoak for some reason. And Mt. Holyoak reminded him of Remington.

He would go and see his very best friend this moment.

In spite of her anxieties, Remington's stay with Uncle Martin had not been bad. In fact, when she got past the loud voice and overbearing manner, she found Martin de Russe to be a very charming man.

They sat up into the wee hours the first night of her stay, playing chess until she finally called checkmate. Martin had moaned and raved, but as a true gentleman, he conceded her victory and gave her a big, wet kiss on the cheek that set her to grinning. She had never been around such an affectionate man and had to admit she found it comforting.

Her father had been a mildly caring man with his girls, but the fact remained that he was not demonstrative in the least. He had wanted sons, and when Kerry Halsey presented him with four daughters, he was not pleased. He was never actually hostile toward the girls, yet he did not lavish attention on them. Remington saw in Uncle Martin what she had wanted from her father all along; approval, affection, friendship. Martin gave these things willingly.

The next day dawned hot and bright and she broke her fast with Uncle Martin in the lovely garden of his manse. The roses were in full bloom, as were a myriad of other flowers. The pungent smell of gardenias wafted on the air as they enjoyed bread with melted cheese and beef.

From that point on, the day had gone very well and she had settled in quickly. She found it amusing that Uncle Martin only employed female servants, except for the ancient little man who tended his garden. He said he did not like the scent of males, but Remington knew it was because he did not want to compete with anyone for the women's attention. And they lavished him with care as if he were the only man on earth.

And they lavished attention on Remington, too. When she had finally gone to bed after beating Uncle Martin at the game, a hefty serving woman with a Scandinavian accent had been there with warmed, scented water and a strange oil. Like any good, strapping mother, she proceeded to give Remington a sponge bath and then poured the oil on her back.

Flat on her stomach on the mattress, the strong woman gave Remington the most wonderful massage she had ever experienced. The last thing she remembered was the woman's strong hands kneading her tired muscles, and then she had awoken to a bright day in a fresh bed. It had been heavenly.

Uncle Martin had taken great pleasure showing her his garden as the morning progressed. The humidity seemed to bring out the most in the scents, and the air was heavy with fragrance. By midmorning, a serving wench brought out a snack of cool water with lemon and honey and sweet little tarts with fruit. Having just eaten a large breakfast not two hours before, Remington begged off, but Martin ate the entire plate.

Lunch came and went and Remington's thoughts wandered to Gaston. From the battlements on the manse, she could see the Tower quite plainly, looming over the Thames. She knew him to be within the walls, as was Guy, and she was anxious and unnerved. She tried not to imagine what might be happening, but it was difficult to not allow her imagination to run wild.

Uncle Martin stood on the battlements with her after the nooning meal, pointing out various spots of interest and commenting on the traffic along the river. Noble barges floated by slowly, decorated with all sorts of fine adornments and Remington was greatly interested in them. Merchant vessels docked on the opposite side of the river, unloading wares from exotic ports.

Remington watched and listened to Gaston's uncle as he kept a running conversation about the various boats and mercantile houses on the opposite side of the river. Truly, she was fascinated and Uncle Martin was a very interesting man.

With the heat of the afternoon cloying and intense, they retreated to the cool innards of the manse. Remington found that she was terribly tired these days, content to sleep and eat and naught much else, as she had been when she had been pregnant with Dane early on. She sank gratefully into a hide-covered chair while Uncle Martin started into the subject of Gaston's father, Brant. Over the course of the next few hours, she would discover Brant de Russe to be a remarkable, exciting man.

However, due to the heat and Uncle Martin's low, soothing voice, she fell into a deep sleep in the comfortable chair without meaning to. Martin continued his stories for a good ten minutes before he realized what had happened. Quietly, he vacated the room and proceeded to find every servant in the house to personally warn them to remain silent while Lady Remington slept.

Satisfied she would sleep unimpeded, he moved to his own chamber and promptly passed out into a dreamless sleep of his own.

CHAPTER TWENTY-FOUR

The first thing she was aware of was a deep, rumbling voice. It was a rich voice, sensual and comforting, and it took her a moment to realize she was listening to Gaston. He wasn't speaking to her, however; he was saying something to his uncle.

She twitched and opened her eyes, sighing deeply. Gaston was standing in front of her, still speaking to one of his men, but gazed down on her when she stirred.

"So you are awake," he said gently. "Did my uncle put you to sleep with all of his talking?"

She sat up, smiling sleepily at him. "Actually, he did. But it wasn't because I lacked interest in the subject; I am just increasingly tired these days."

He took her hand in his glove. "No doubt," he jerked his head at the soldier standing at the door and the man vacated. He looked down at her again. "Are you awake enough that we might carry on an intelligent conversation? We must discuss a few things."

She nodded, rubbing the sleep from her eyes and he deposited his huge body on a very sturdy stool just in front of her. He still held her hand, his eyes on her warmly.

"I am glad you are back," she said. "I expected not to see you for weeks the way you were talking. Did your meetings go well?"

The warmth in his face faded. "About as I expected," he replied softly, holding both of her hands now. "Henry was receptive to me, as I knew he would be. I was able to speak to the bishop of Exeter and he assured me that it should be no problem to annul my marriage to Mari-Elle and he promised that he would see to it as quickly as he could. That portion of my talks went most favorably; however, the problems lies where we knew it would. With Guy."

At the mention of his name, Remington's face went white and Gaston squeezed her hands sympathetically. "Did you see him?"

He nodded. "He was not cooperative in the least, angel. In fact, he seemed to take delight in the entire situation. I fear he will make a nightmare out of all of this."

She lowered her gaze, her stomach quivering nervously and making her ill. Gaston could see her fear and cursed silently that he was not yet finished with his news.

"Henry demanded that Guy be allowed to see you, under my supervision of course, and I had to comply. You knew that this might happen, Remi, and I am sorry that I could not prevent it," his voice was soft. "But it might be more beneficial that we realize. Guy said that if you were to ask him for an annulment personally, that he might consider it. You do not have to do it if you do not want to, though. You can sit and stare at the wall the entire time if it pleases you."

He could feel her hands shaking. "If there is a chance he will consider granting our request, then I will ask him. But I truthfully do not know why he would listen to me; he never has before."

Gaston knew Stoneley's request was probably a ploy to see his wife and nothing more, but if there were a chance that he honestly would reconsider his position, then they would have to take it.

"I am sorry, angel," he whispered again. He felt as if he were failing her somehow, unable to protect her from the turmoil.

She nodded shakily, acknowledging his apology. She opened her mouth to speak, but words would not come. Finally, she threw her arms around his neck and squeezed him so tightly that she would have choked him had it not been for his armor. He held her tightly, wishing he could absorb all of her fear and pain.

"I am so scared, Gaston," she whispered after a moment. "I have not seen him in over a year and I feel as if I am about to relive my worst nightmare."

"There is nothing to be frightened of," he assured her. "I will be there the entire time, love. There is naught he can do or say to you to harm you."

She pulled back, wiping daintily at her nose and blinking back tears. "I know that, but I am still scared. I hate him so."

"So do I," he answered. "But you will only have to see him this one time if I have anything to say about it. Try not to let him upset you so. I do not like to see you so upset."

She nodded again, attempting to compose herself. Gaston rose from the stool and pulled her gently to her feet. He sought to brighten the mood a bit. "Henry has invited us to sup with he and Elizabeth tonight. Why do not you go and change into a pretty surcoat."

Her mouth fell open in horror, forgetting all about Guy for the moment. "The king wants to sup with us? Lord, Gaston, I do not own a surcoat worthy of the king's table."

"Of course you do," he insisted, giving her a gentle tug toward the stairs. "Where are your things? I will decide what you are to wear."

An hour later, looking absolutely ravishing in a scarlet brocade surcoat and a lovely necklace with rough garnets, Remington left Braidwood for the Tower. Gaston had commandeered a litter for her, which she thought was silly, but he insisted. She giggled as he settled her on it, complaining that she felt like Cleopatra. He eyed her sternly, but there was a smile playing on his lips. He was glad she was laughing, knowing the tears and anxiety would descend upon her quickly enough once they reached the Tower.

The Tower fascinated her as they passed through the entrance and through the narrow corridor between the Byward and Middle Tower. There were household troops everywhere, lining their path as they rode into the open courtyard.

In the middle of the courtyard stood the White Tower, looming above her. Her smiles faded and terror seized her; she knew Guy was watching her now. She could not see him, but she could feel him. Feel his evil. He was here, and she was quickly going back on her promise not to be afraid anymore. She was horrified.

Gaston reached the litter and gently lifted her off, seeing that the color had gone out of her cheeks and knowing why. He sought to ease her. "Would you like to tour the Tower first? There are several points of interest."

She nodded numbly, knowing a tour would only delay the inevitable, yet it might afford her the opportunity to regain some of her shattered composure.

With Nicolas and his other knights in tow, Gaston took her all over the structure, not really taking her into any buildings but pointing out specific towers and relaying stories. He was careful not to point out the Bloody Tower, or mention anything about the nephews Richard had murdered. He tried to make her more at ease in the unfamiliar place before he led her into the depths of the lion's den.

As he had hoped, she regained some of her color and poise by the time he was finished showing her about. She asked small questions, seeming to take some interest in her surroundings when he knew the only thing she was truly focused on was the massive Tower in the center of the compound.

John de Vere joined their small party when the tour was nearly complete. Much to Remington's surprise, he kissed her pleasantly on the cheek in greeting and proceeded to tell her how lovely she looked.

Remington eyed him as he conversed with Gaston, wondering if all men were as friendly as she had come to see since being introduced into Gaston's world. Before she had met him, all men were cold, unfeeling bastards and she had hated them. But since she had met the Dark One, she had come to meet a great many men who were nothing but kind and courteous. Was it possible, then, that they were the norm, and that her father and Guy were the exception to the rule? She wondered.

Gaston turned to her after a few moments of conversation. "Well, angel, shall we get this over with?"

She was much more comfortable than she had been earlier and squared her shoulders. "Aye, let's do. I am eager to get on with it."

He smiled gently at her and took her arm, leading her across the compound. Remington noticed that not only were Gaston's knights following him, but the earl as well. "Are they coming, too? Must I have so many protectors?"

Gaston gazed up at the tall, white structure. "I am your only protector. They are my protectors." She looked puzzled and he smiled. "As I will be watching you, they will be watching me to make sure I do not get out of hand."

She grinned back, timidly, not seeing his humor but smiling anyway. Truly, she was more than concerned with the prospect of Gaston losing his control. "Gaston, you promised me that you would not commit murder. Would you break your promise to me?"

"Of course not," he said. "But we sometimes do things in the heat of anger that we only have regrets for later on. I have no intention of deliberately breaking my promise to you, but...."

They entered into the dark structure of the White Tower and were met by two sentries. Taking the stairs to the third floor, Remington's palms began to sweat and her heart began thumping in her ears. Aye, she was terrified, but with all of the men accompanying her, she also felt a strange sense of bravery. She knew Guy couldn't touch her, and even entertained the thought of telling him what she really thought of him. Everything she had wanted to say to him but did not dare risk it.

They paused in front of a massive oak door and her heart surged into her throat. She swallowed hard, meeting Gaston's eyes. He smiled as he removed his helm and motioned for the sentry to open the door.

The door to hell!

The knights and the earl preceded them both into the room. Gaston followed, leading Remington by the hand. Her eyes darted about nervously, searching for the figure of her husband when she came to rest on him several yards away.

All of her reasoning, her mental courage, fled.

Guy was looking directly at her, a thin smile on his lips and she jerked back from Gaston, stumbling back toward the door. Gaston quickly snatched her before she could bolt from the room, but he did not pull her forward. She was as far into the room as she wished to go at the moment, and he would not push. Her eyes were wide and senseless, like a frightened deer.

Guy took a few small steps, still smiling at her. "My God, Remington. I did not believe it possible that you could have grown any more beautiful, but you have. You are exquisite, darling."

She shrank even more, a flush mottling her cheeks. She had completely lost the power of speech and Guy drew even closer. "What? No words of thanks, nor greeting? It has been over a year since we last saw one another. Are you not happy to see your husband?"

Her cheeks flushed a deeper red and she found her tongue. "I hate you, you bastard! God damn you to hell for the horror you have put me through for nine years, and may he further damn you for the pain you have caused my family! I hate you and I want nothing to do with you ever again!"

Old habits are hard to break. Guy had never heard that tone from Remington, because he forbade her to raise her voice. Instinctively, he stiffened and moved toward her, which was his grave mistake.

Gaston lashed out a huge, gloved fist and caught Guy in the side of his head, sending him crashing to the floor. Before the earl or Nicolas could reach him, he was looming over Stoneley like the angel of death.

"You were going to strike her, weren't you?" he snarled. "You whore-skin, I shall kill you if you make another provocative move toward her."

John and Nicolas pulled Gaston back, steering him back toward Remington, who reached out and pulled him to her. She clung to him, terrified he was going to kill Guy right before her eyes. But she truly did not know why she should prevent him from murdering a most vile creature.

Guy was slow to come around, for Gaston had dealt him a brutal blow. He shook his head several times before weakly pushing himself onto his knees, the world spinning and his ears ringing. His cheek throbbed terribly, and he was sure the bone was broken.

"The church will have something to say about your treatment of a prisoner," he finally gasped, putting his hand to his head and rising to unsteady feet. Not a man in the room moved to help him.

Gaston's face was drawn with rage as he watched Guy move for the nearest chair. De Vere, seeing that the meeting was already going rather poorly, took charge.

"My lady, sit down if you would, please," he eyed Gaston. "Sit down before you fall down, Gaston. Next to Remington."

Woodenly, Remington sat several feet away from Guy and pulled Gaston down onto a taller stool as the earl pushed him. She was not so worried for herself anymore, but increasing concerned for Gaston's stability. It was absolutely amazing to see him not in complete control of his emotions; she had never seen him in a rage and was, frankly, frightened.

Guy was lucid again, watching his wife with narrowed eyes. He stared at her for several moments. "You should control your trained dog better than that, Remi. You will most certainly not gain what you want if you do not! Now, darling, let us return to the subject. How have you been? How is my son?"

She fought to keep her breathing normal as she spoke. "Dane is well. He is fostering now."

A ripple of rage brushed Guy's face. "Fostering? Where? And by whose order?"

"Sir Gaston's," she replied. "He is eight years old now and it was time to begin his training."

"Where is he?" Stoneley repeated.

"At Mt. Holyoak with a dozen other pages under Sir Gaston's ward," she replied; it was becoming easier as she went.

Guy did not answer for a moment. The swelling on his face was already darkening. "How are your sisters?"

Remington lowered her gaze. "Rory is dead, but Jasmine and Skye are well."

"What happened to Rory?" Guy asked, puzzled more than concerned.

"An accident," Remington replied vaguely.

The group sat in silence for several minutes while Guy studied his wife from across the room. He could feel Gaston's glare on him but refused to look at the man. "So, darling, I understand you have a request of me. I would hear it now."

Her eyes flew up to meet the hated ice blue orbs. Next to her, Gaston shifted his massive weight on the stool but she did not look at him. If there were a chance Guy would listen to her, then she would have to take it. She prayed swiftly to whatever god was listening for much-needed courage.

"I wish to annul our marriage," she said after a moment. "I would ask for your cooperation in the matter."

He studied her. "Say 'please'."

Her rapid breathing returned, knowing he had the upper hand in this game as he always had. Lord, did he plan to humiliate her in front of everyone? What was going on in his sinister mind?

"Please, Guy," she stammered. "Surely you have tired of me by now."

He snorted a chuckle. "Tire of your sweet body? I should say not. I understand you have been giving the Dark One samples of your delicacies. He knows what I mean when I say sweet."

Remington flushed a dull, deep red and looked at the ground. The more uncomfortable she became, the more Guy liked it. His mood perked.

"I see it is true, then. Did you enjoy bedding with another man, darling? Did you find yourself comparing him to me? I like comparisons, in truth, but your sisters could not compete with you, only Skye, mayhap, because she was so tiny. 'Twas like taking a virgin every time with her."

Remington let out a sickened choke and Gaston shot to his feet again, only to be corralled by de Vere and Matts.

"You are a sick man, Stoneley," Gaston growled, his huge body rigid. "And we are not here to speak of conquests, but of an annulment. She has asked you politely and you will do her the courtesy of answering."

Guy looked smug. Overly so. Gaston refused to sit back down, but he took Remington's hand in his and held it tightly. Guy seemed not to care or take notice.

"An annulment," he mulled over the word as if thinking on it. "Well, 'tis true, I have no real use for a woman who cannot bear me any more sons. I do not understand your need for a barren wife, de Russe, but that is your privilege. Yet, in good faith, I cannot condone an annulment. I believe in the sanctity of marriage."

"If you did, then you would not have bedded her sisters!" Gaston shot back in a low voice. "Your actions refute your words."

Guy shrugged. "They were mine to do with as I pleased, and since when do you have the right to act so pious? You bedded another man's wife."

Remington was shaking with fury and terror. "He did not. *I* bedded him!"

Gaston hated hearing such personal details coming from her mouth, but he knew Guy was driving her to it. He turned the focus of the conversation back to the subject at hand.

"I told you that I would return to hear your price for an agreement," he said. "I would hear your terms now."

Guy stood from the chair. "I told you, de Russe, I have no terms. There will be no annulment."

Remington was quickly becoming a quivering wreck. She leapt from the chair, tearing her hand from Gaston's. With quick strides, she crossed the room and stood face-to-face with her husband.

Ignoring her disgust at standing so close, she focused a hard gaze on him.

"You are a greedy, immoral man. I know you too well, Guy, and you do indeed have a price. What is it so that we may be on with this? The longer I stand here, the more I hate you."

He raised an eyebrow, and then a hand. Gaston lurched forward, but strong hands reached out to steady him when they realized Guy was running a gentle finger down Remington's cheek. "How can you say that, darling, when we have a son together?"

"That is all we have together," Remington hissed. "There is no affection, no respect; only fear and intimidation and pain. I have always hated you, since the day I met you. I will be free of you if I have to kill you myself!"

The hand that had so gently stroked her cheek came to rest on her arm, gripping it firmly. She felt the vise tightening and fought the urge to yank away; if she showed any sort of fear or pain, Gaston would rip Guy's head from his shoulders.

"Do not say that, Remi. I want you to stay here, with me. I have always been fond of you."

"You have always been fond of beating and humiliating me," she said frankly, her emotions surging from fear one moment to confidence the next. "Let me go, Guy. I shall do anything you ask, if you will only agree to an annulment."

He looked at her, his mind working madly. He could see how badly she wanted this, and he could see that the stakes in this game were even higher than he had originally thought. Being a wise man, he knew how to play what he was dealt.

"I want to speak with you alone, then," he said quietly. "Tell your companions to leave us alone for one hour, and I shall sincerely consider your request. We have much to speak of in private, wife."

"Like hell." Gaston broke free of the hands restraining him, marching toward them with deadly strides when Remington suddenly held out her hand to stop him.

"It's all right, Gaston," she assured him quickly. "There is no harm in talking to him for an hour."

Gaston did not stop and she moved quickly to intercept him. Grabbing hold of him with all her strength, she turned him around and pulled him with her until they were nearly to the door. Her soft, white hands wound themselves in his dark hair and pulled his head down to her level.

"Take the men and wait for me in the hall," she whispered. "You may stand right by the door if you wish and listen to every word, but if there is the possibility that he is sincere, then we must do as he says. Please."

"I shall not leave you alone with him," Gaston growled.

"And you will not be. You will be right outside the door should I need you," she hissed urgently. "Please, Gaston, just do as he asks. Please?"

He sighed heavily. "I do not like this, Remi."

Her lips were against his ear and she kissed him tenderly. "Nor do I, my love, but I am willing to do as he asks. Please go along with me."

He looked at her a moment before straightening and turning to the knights against the wall. He struggled to spit out the words. "We will wait in the hall for the lady," he rumbled, turning with a deadly glare to Stoneley. "One hour. If you so much as spit in her direction, your death will not be painless."

Guy did not say a word as Gaston and the other men filed out. When the door shut softly, his eyes fell on his wife.

"Thank God they are gone," he said. "Now we may speak the truth. How is it that you have become Henry's pawn, Remington?"

"I am not his pawn." She was still on the other side of the room, a good distance away. "And I have been speaking the truth the entire time. I hate you and I want out of this marriage."

His jaw ticked and she involuntarily flinched, waiting for the pain that was sure to follow. Surprisingly, he did not come toward her with murder on his mind. Instead, he turned toward the narrow window, feeling the heat wafting on the stale breeze.

"As you say, Remi," he said lightly. "But I warn you, if you intend to go through with this, it will cost you. Dearly."

"It can cost me nothing more than you have already taken," she said flatly. "You have stripped me of everything in life, Guy. What more could you possibly want from me?"

He smiled humorlessly, still staring out the window. "Do you wish to know my terms?"

"I do." She was shocked and wary that he did, indeed, have terms. He had insisted to Gaston that there were no terms to be met.

He looked at her, then. "Kiss me."

She blanched. "What?"

"I said kiss me."

She backed away, shaking her head but he held up a finger of warning. "Kiss me or there will be no more discussions."

She froze, bile rising in her throat. Dear God, did this man have no mercy? Forcing her feet to move, she shuffled unsteadily to where he was standing. Expectantly, she stood in front of him and prayed fervently that she would not vomit on him.

"Kiss me, Remington," he repeated.

It suddenly occurred to her that he wished for *her* to do the kissing. As if she were servicing him. Like a whore. She stood on her toes and pecked him lightly on the lips, backing away so fast she nearly tripped. He frowned.

"That was not a kiss," he said. "When I said kiss me, I meant it. Let me feel your tongue."

She let out a whimper and closed her eyes, hanging her head. "Guy, why must you...?"

"Kiss me!" he snapped. "Do it or I will speak with you no further."

She had to get it over with; arguing with him would be to no avail and she was desperate enough to do almost anything to gain her means. Thrusting herself forward, she latched onto his lips and pried his mouth open with her tongue, only to be met by his eager response. Frightened and sickened, she pulled away as quickly as it started and staggered away from him, truly fearful that she would become ill.

Guy smiled. "You see? That was not so bad."

She wiped at her mouth with the back of her hand, ashamed and disgusted. "Get on with it, Guy. What are your terms?"

He was smiling smugly at her. He wandered away from the window and seated himself comfortably in a chair. His gaze was lingering, while hers was hateful. The tension in the room was building as far as she was concerned, but he seemed very much at ease. Her impatience was growing.

"Go and sit," he ordered.

Haltingly, she looked for the nearest chair and planted herself rigidly, waiting.

Guy continued to stare at her, entirely too confident.

"You will sit there for the remainder of the hour," he said finally, his voice quiet. "You will not say a word, and you will return to me tomorrow when I have decided just what precisely my terms are. And I will have terms have no doubt. And you will not tell de Russe what has transpired during this hour. Is that clear?"

Stunned, she nodded. She knew him well enough to know there was nothing more to say; she had heard the tone before, and she was scared to death of it.

When Gaston opened the door an hour later, she bolted from the room as if her hair was on fire.

CHAPTER TWENTY-FIVE

Gaston carried her from the third floor of the White Tower, all the way to his quarters near the Martin Tower. She was so upset that she was having difficulty walking and fury seized him as he held her tightly in his arms. He was terrified to know what Stoneley had said to her, and furthermore terrified that he would no longer be able to maintain his slimly held control. If Stoneley had threatened or harmed her, then he would truly kill him this day.

She pushed herself from his arms when they reached the small, but comfortable room he had occupied the previous night. As she sat, he poured her a strong drink and bade her drink the entire glass.

It was strong and she choked it down. As the warmth of it seeped into her veins, she felt herself calming. She calmed even more when Gaston pulled her out of the chair, took it himself, and then seated her on his lap.

His strength filled her. Free of Guy's piercing stare, she was able to rationalize herself somewhat. Gaston waited for her to speak first.

"Bloody hell," she mumbled, laying her head on his massive shoulder as he sat back in the chair.

"What did he say, angel?" he asked gently.

She thought a moment. Guy had told her to keep silent, but she would be damned if she was going to keep secrets from Gaston. Besides, there had been nothing much said.

"He told me not to tell you anything," she began.

Gaston was torn between forcing the truth out of her and leaving her alone. She did not give him the chance to make a decision.

"But I did not promise him anything, so I would not be breaking my word," she continued, snuggling against him and relishing the feel of his body. "But promise me that you will not become irate, no matter what. I cannot take any more strong emotion this day, Gaston. I will surely swoon."

"I promise you, angel, I shall remain calm," he assured her, but he wondered if he meant it. "What did he say?"

She sighed. "I get the impression that he believes I have been brainwashed by Henry somehow; he asked me why I was allowing myself to be the king's pawn. Then…," she paused, still disgusted by what had happened. "Then he told me to kiss him. I had to, Gaston, or else he said he would not speak to me anymore. After that, he had me sit in a chair for the rest of the hour. He told me to return to him on the morrow and he would relay his terms for his cooperation. He promised he would have terms, and he furthermore promised that it would cost me dearly. I wonder what he could mean? I have nothing of value."

Gaston fought down his rage, concentrating on stroking her lovingly.

"He's a clever bastard," he muttered. "He was told he would only be able to see you one time, and now he has managed to stretch it into two visits. Do not be surprised if he does not have his terms readied by tomorrow. He might drag this out as long as he can."

"But why?" she sat up and looked at him. "What can he possibly gain by my repeated visits?"

He smiled ironically. "He knows that you have my ear, angel. And I, in turn, hold Henry's ear. He is not a fool, and I fully believe he realizes what his possibilities are."

She sank back against him, silent and thoughtful. "I want this to be over with so badly when, in fact, it has only begun."

He lifted an eyebrow in agreement, continuing to caress her gently as the heat of the afternoon seeped into the walls.

"At least he promised me that he would have terms," she said after a moment. "That, I think, is something."

He let out a long sigh. "I am curious as to what those terms are. I fear for what he will demand."

"Mt. Holyoak?" she asked.

"I care not about the keep; as much as I have grown fond of it, I will not hesitate to return it. However, it will leave me one less bribe for the church. I am afraid I shall have to rely on Henry for donations to our cause."

"He will do this for you," she murmured.

"Fortunately, Henry would do most anything for me," Gaston replied, thinking about Warminster and suddenly wishing he had accepted the dukedom. If it was his, then he could donate it to the church and Henry would have virtually no say in the matter. He regretted that he had asked Henry to donate it on his behalf.

"Will I like living at Clearwell?"

She broke into his thoughts and he shifted her in his arms. "It is rugged terrain, not the sweetly rolling hills of Yorkshire," he replied, thinking of the home he had not seen in a long time. "But I find it peaceful and lovely. The Welsh border is not far."

"If the church takes Clearwell, then we can live with Uncle Martin, can't we?"

"I thought you did not like him."

She grinned. "I have changed my mind. I like him a great deal, although he talks too much."

He smiled, too. "He does everything in excess; drinks, eats, wenc... everything indeed."

She laughed softly and sat up, rising from his lap. Her silk dress was becoming damp in the heat and she did not wish to muss it before supper. In fact, she wanted to strip down to her skin and take a soothing nap, far from the horrors of the day. She wanted to forget about Guy for a short while.

"Gaston, help me from this dress," she motioned the stays. "I shall stain it in this heat."

He obediently released her from the garment, throwing it over the chair when she stepped from it. She sat on the bed and kicked off her slippers, unrolling her stockings and shaking them out. Clad only in her thin shift, she lay heavily on his cool linen coverlet.

He raised an eyebrow at her. "You intend to sleep, do you?"

"I do," she sighed, hugging the pillow. "I am exhausted. This child of yours makes me weak."

He snickered, his gaze licking over her luscious form underneath the nearly transparent shift. He put his hands on his hips.

"I have a better idea."

She smiled, her eyes closed and pretending to ignore him. She heard his armor coming off, hitting the floor with resounding clangs. When she finally heard his boots hit the ground and the rustle of his clothing, she pulled the coverlet over her protectively.

"Leave me alone, Gaston. I have no desire to satisfy your lusty urges."

He ripped the coverlet off her so hard that he tore it completely free of the bed. She giggled as he plopped into bed beside her, and then squealed loudly when the feather mattress nearly swallowed her whole because of his weight. He pulled her against him, smiling into her hair.

"I did not believe we would be together so soon," he purred. "But I see that the opportunity has presented itself. No de Tormo, no Uncle Martin, no king to interfere."

She was facing away from him, her giggles turning into moans of pleasure as he ran his hands under the shift and latched onto her rounded breasts. His breathing was hot and heavy on her neck.

"God, Remi, you are so sweet," he whispered.

She smiled, her eyes still closed as his huge hands massaged her sensually. "I missed you last night. 'Twas the first night we have spent apart in many weeks."

"I do not think I slept but an hour or two," he confessed, teasing her nipples into taut buds. "I found myself on the battlements before the sun rose, gazing across the river at Braidwood."

She was rapidly losing her control with his attentions. His hot hands were working her into a frenzy. With a grunt of pleasure and frustration, she sat up quickly and tore off the shift. In a flash, she was supine again, her back to his taut chest. He buried his face in her neck as his hands roamed freely.

He wanted to go slow with her, gentle, but his passion overwhelmed him and grasped her knees and pulled her into a fetal position. Knees almost into her chest, he thrust into her from behind and she cried out, clutching at the bedclothes as he drove in his long, hard length. Withdrawing, he lurched into her again deeply.

Remington pulled the sheets into her mouth to keep from screaming with passion. In the small quarters, she was positive someone would hear her.

He held her tightly as he thrust into her, again and again, building the heavenly friction. She whimpered over and over, her mouth stuffed with sheets, feeling his hot breath rapid on the back of her head.

She felt herself approaching the familiar, exquisite release and she silently urged him onward, her entire body aching with want of pleasure. One arm unwound itself from her and he reached between her legs, closing in on her wet heat and feeling the junction where their bodies were joining in passion. It was too much; he released himself with a violent eruption and she joined him as his fingers found her taut nub.

He had manipulated her into a stupor. When their convulsions died down, Remington was limp. Eyes closed, she could only lie there and feel his body still within her, hearing his soft laughter.

They lay together, sweating in the humidity of the afternoon, dozing occasionally. Truth was, neither one had slept well the night before and they were tired. Now that things were as they should be, as they were together once again, the comfort was overwhelming.

They fell asleep in the huge bed, the lazy afternoon waning away in a haze of heat and thickness. Just before sunset, Gaston awoke and found himself staring at the back of Remington's head, studying the curls in her hair leisurely and his mind wandering to silly, unimportant things. It was in moments such as this that he felt they had all of the time in the world.

A loud rap echoed on the heavy oak door and Gaston's head shot up, looking at the panel as if he could see through it. "Who comes?"

"Me!" de Tormo called out sharply. "Let me in."

Remington woke, rolling onto her back and she and Gaston passed wry glances. He was the first one to climb from the bed, reaching for his trews. "Hold a moment, priest."

Remington tossed her legs over the side of the bed, slowly moving for her shift and grunting softly with the effort. He smiled at her. "You move like an old woman."

"I feel like an old woman," she agreed, pulling the shift over her head. "In fact, I am old. I am almost twenty-seven years old."

He snorted. "And I am thirty-seven. What does that make me? Ancient?"

She looked sharply at him. "Are you really that old? Good lord, Gaston, did you know Socrates personally?"

He laughed deeply. "Really, Remi; how heartless you are."

She grinned, pulling on the surcoat. He pulled his shirt on and helped her with the stays. Outside in the hall, de Tormo knocked again.

"Open the door, de Russe."

"I am coming," Gaston mumbled, jerking on a boot. The other boot slipped on as Remington straightened her hair and tried to look unruffled. Gaston waited until she was seated by the window before he obliged the priest's request.

De Tormo breezed in, smelling so foul that Remington could smell him from where she sat. The man obviously did not believe in bathing.

Even Gaston wrinkled his nose. "What is it, priest?"

"I knew I would find her here," he said shortly. "Gaston, I come with news."

"What news?"

De Tormo looked at Remington. "Peter Courtenay has ordered that Lady Remington be placed in the custody of the church," he watched her face go pale. "It would seem that after the lady's meeting with her husband, Guy summoned Courtenay personally and convinced the man that she was being forced into requesting an annulment against her will. He managed to persuade the bishop into believing the lady is somehow in danger and Courtenay has placed all further annulment proceedings on hold until the matter is clarified."

Gaston's face was beyond grim. He was stunned. He gazed at Remington, who could only stare back helplessly.

"Oh, Gaston...," she breathed.

But de Tormo wasn't finished. He threw up his hand to prevent any further conversation.

"There's more, Gaston," he said. "Remington is to be taken away to a place of the church's choosing and you will not be allowed access to her. In fact, they will not tell you where she will be sequestered. They seem to think that time and separation might clear the lady's mind."

Gaston was already moving for Remington. He pulled her up into his arms, holding her closely against him. De Tormo watched slow tears trickle down Remington's cheeks, her face half-buried in his chest.

"There is nothing we can do?" Gaston asked tightly.

De Tormo shook his head slowly. "Not at the moment. To refuse to cooperate would surely bring the archbishop's wrath, not to mention they would probably order the lady to stay with her husband."

Gaston was silent a moment, stroking Remington's hair. "How long of a separation?"

"They are speaking in terms of months, at least," de Tormo replied, greatly saddened that he had been unable to argue successfully against separation. "I tried. God knows I did. And I shall still try, but at this moment, Courtenay is sending his personal guard to escort Remington to Saint Catherine's. From there, she will be spirited away until this can be settled."

Gaston was shocked and angered, but he held his temper and his tongue. He knew there was nothing to say, at least not to de Tormo, and he could do nothing more than comply with the orders. If he were to defy them, then the situation would look very much as if he were forcing Remington in all of this. He had to cooperate and he knew it.

But there was still Henry. If he had to get down on his knees to the king and to every bloody bishop in England, he would. This challenge would not go entirely unanswered.

"Remington's possessions are at Braidwood," he said hoarsely, feeling her soft sobs against him.

"I know," de Tormo replied. "She will not be taken away until after supper, since you are dining with Henry. There will be time to collect them."

Gaston looked drawn. De Tormo walked up slowly on the two of them, wishing he could say something encouraging. He couldn't think of anything as far as the church was concerned, but he did bring a few tidbits that might lighten the darkness.

"You have my support on this, as you know," he said quietly. "Courtenay is truly not trying to be cruel, Gaston, but he is acting on higher orders. Archbishop Thomas Bourchier of Canterbury has commanded him to act in this manner. I have a meeting with the papal legate, John of Imola, in two days and I hope to sway him on your behalf. Meanwhile, the lady must go and Guy Stoneley is demanding to see you on the morrow."

Gaston's jaw ticked threateningly. "So that he might gloat, no doubt. Is de Vere still here?"

De Tormo smiled thinly. "He says he's not leaving and he has every right to stay, considering he is the constable of the Tower of London. In fact, he has sent for Lord Stanley, Earl of Derby, and his brother Sir William to keep him...er, you...company. Edward Courtenay is on his way here and de Vere has also sent word to Matthew Wellesbourne." His smile turned somewhat genuine. "It would seem that he is calling the premier fighting men to your support, Gaston. If you cannot win the lady by legal means, mayhap every powerful warrior in England can intimidate the hell out of the church and you can take her by force. In any case, I would venture to say that you did not realize you had so many powerful friends to rally behind you, did you?"

Remington, gaining control of her shock, wiped at her eyes. "Who are these men, Gaston?"

Friends. They were his friends. "Men who fought for Henry against Richard, the best warriors in England. They are friends of mine."

De Tormo smiled at Remington. "Men who are eager to heed the call and rally behind Gaston. This battle is not over by a far sight, my lady, so do not lose hope," he glanced up at Gaston again and chuckled. "You will also be pleased to know that Henry's Uncle Jasper, the Duke of Bedford, gave Bourchier an earful on your behalf. So did Lady Margaret."

"Beaufort?" Gaston looked surprised, though his eyes were still glazed with grief. "I had no idea Henry's mother was in London."

"Indeed," de Tormo nodded.

It was amazing what had transpired in the languid afternoon while he and Remington had slept the hours away. He could scarce believe it, all of it.

De Tormo moved for the door, knowing the two would want to spend their final time alone. "It would seem, de Russe, that you do not need my help overly. You have every influential person in England to spring to your defense. Still, I will do what I agreed to do."

"Thank you," Remington had pulled herself away from Gaston and went over to the priest, in spite of his putrid stench. "For everything you have done and continue to do, de Tormo. We will be forever grateful."

De Tormo flushed slightly around the neck. "My pleasure, my lady. But I must confess, I am seriously considering using your tale of devil worship to gain headway against my superiors. It may be our secret weapon."

She smiled. "You would lie to help us?"

"I would do what is right, and if that entails a fib, so be it," he left the room, closing the door softly.

Remington turned to Gaston; he looked more upset than she did. After hearing of all of the people that were uniting on Gaston's behalf, she did not feel quite as hopeless for their cause. But the thought of separation was tearing at her like a knife.

But it upset her terribly to see how pale and taut his face was. She knew the tremendous troubles he had on his mind, and her hysterics would only weaken him further. Forcing herself to sport a brave front, she went to him and they enveloped each other.

"I will write my sisters and tell them where I am," she said. "You may find out where I am through them. Any messages I must send you, I will do it through Jasmine and Skye."

"I do not know if you will be able to reveal your whereabouts to them, angel," he said. "But they will let you send short missives to your family. You are clever in your thinking in that respect."

She was silent a moment. "Guy hasn't changed. He has always been a liar, but I hoped he was sincere when he said he would deliver his terms tomorrow."

Gaston sighed deeply. "He still may, considering he wishes to see me tomorrow," he kissed the top of her head. "I am sorry, angel. It seems things are not working out as easily as we had hoped."

"But they *will* work out," she said confidently. "Yet...the one thing that concerns me is the fact that de Tormo said they were considering keeping me isolated for months. They will discover my condition before too long."

"True enough. Mayhap that will only serve to hasten the proceedings."

"But we shall be apart. What if we are still apart by the time your son is born?"

"I will not allow it. If I have to tear down all of England to find you, I will. I will be by your side when you bring my child into the world."

"Erik," she sighed.

"Or Adeliza." He smiled for the first time. "It could very well be a girl."

She looked up at him, running her hands over his face, memorizing it. "Will you be disappointed?"

"By God, Remi, of course not," he exclaimed. "Male or female, it makes no difference to me. Only that if it is a girl, I will have to provide a sizable dowry and drain my coffers. Girls are expensive."

"And boys are not?" she said with mild outrage. "Boys require swords and shields and war implements and...."

He kissed her firmly to shut her up. "It could be twins, you know. One of each."

She rolled her eyes. "Say not so. I had a difficult enough time giving birth to one child, much less two."

His smile vanished. "Dane was a difficult birth? How difficult?"

She could sense his fear; as if he needed something new added to his substantial problems. "I did not mean it like that. It was a normal birth, my love, but to every woman, birth is difficult. The only true problem was Guy, because afterward, he...."

"I know," he said quickly; he did not want to hear the brutal details again. It made him sick. He stroked her cheek. "I have two sons, Remi. I would cherish a daughter. And I would take a third son. "

She smiled, warmed that he referred to Dane as his son. The horror of her impending departure shoved into the recesses of her mind, she hugged him fiercely. Were she to dwell on it any longer than a moment or two, her hysteria would overtake her and she did not want to burden him further.

"We had better return to Braidwood to secure some your belongings," he said finally. "And I am sure Uncle Martin will want to bid you farewell. I'm told he has grown quite fond of you."

She sat on the chair to pull on her hose and slippers, securing the silk garters as he watched. "I wonder what I should pack, considering I have no idea where they will be taking me."

"Warm clothes, love," he murmured, his gaze lingering on her a moment before retrieving his armor. Remington watched, impressed, as he donned all of it unaided and quite efficiently.

"Clothes that stretch," she stood up, trying to keep the mood light. "You should have seen me when I was pregnant with Dane. I was as round as a pumpkin." She put her arms out in front of her in a plump circle.

He smiled weakly, latching the top portion of his cuirass breastplate. "I look forward to it, madam."

She tried to maintain her smile, but the tone of his voice set her heart to lurching. Her vow to remain brave was slipping rapidly, like water through her fingers. Her chest tightened painfully and she had to look away, else she knew the tears would start. *We must comply with the church's demands.*

She pretended to look out the window, but her attention was turned to him as he secured the last of his armor. He concentrated on his task until, sans helm, he was in full protection. Only then did he face her, his eyes riveted to her elegant back.

"Let us depart," he said, his voice husky. "We must return in time to sup with Henry and Elizabeth, and he eats precisely at eight o'clock."

With a deep breath for strength, she turned abruptly and marched to the door. Gaston was close behind her, opening the door so that she might pass into the corridor.

Without another word, he took her tender hand into his massive glove and they proceeded to the courtyard of the Tower.

⚬❧⚬

Uncle Martin was not pleased. In fact, he ranted and raged as Remington tried to pack, accusing Gaston of lacking backbone where the church was concerned. Remington did not say a word as Gaston's uncle berated him in front of her, pretending to be interested in her task. But she wanted to slug Martin in the mouth.

Gaston remained cool. He eyed Remington from time to time, knowing how his uncle's words must be upsetting her, but she had yet to give any sign that she was even paying attention to them. Even though he wanted to remain with her while she packed two large traveling bags, his more pressing concern was to remove his uncle from her earshot.

Pleading thirst, Gaston retreated to the solar downstairs with Martin in tow. The older man had yet to run out of fuel on the subject at hand, but Gaston had had enough.

"Cease," he hissed, holding his hand up sharply. "I have heard enough of your prattle, Uncle. I must do as I must, and I apologize if it does not meet with your approval."

Martin closed his mouth, but only for a moment. "Leave her here with me, Gaston. Tell the bloody church that she has run away, that you do not know where she is. If they send her away, you shall never find her. There are abbeys and convents all over this bloody country."

Gaston's jaw ticked as he studied his goblet of wine. "Henry will not allow that to happen. I shall find out where they have taken her, have no fear."

Martin sat heavily in a chair, his huge, fattened body settling. "She shall be alone, Gaston. Without protection. Why not send Nicolas with her? Surely they will allow her one escort?"

"I doubt it. Nicolas is my cousin. Her escorts will be Courtenay's men, I suspect. He seems to have taken a sincere interest in our plight. I will trust his men."

"You give your trust too easily," his uncle snorted softly.

"You would trust the life of the woman you love and your child's life to unknowns? Pah!"

Gaston's head came up sharply. "I have no choice. If I send any of my men, it will appear as if I am trying to maintain my control over her. Do not you see? Guy has suggested that Remington is being forced to seek an annulment against her will; if I insist on sending one of my knights with her, it will only reinforce Guy's accusation. I must separate myself from her as ordered, Uncle."

Martin saw the logic, but hated it all the more. However, as Gaston spoke, a seed of an idea planted itself in Martin's mind and took root. The more Gaston spoke, the more the seed was nurtured.

"You have Henry's support, for all the good it is doing you," Martin mumbled after a moment. "The man is king. You would hope he would have more influence over the church than he is exhibiting."

"You know that Henry's relations with the church are strained at the moment for various reasons," Gaston reminded him. "He is trying to eradicate ecclesiastical sanctuary for all priests who have committed crimes against man, as well as trying to lessen the church's governing influence in England. My problems, such as they are, could not have come at a worse time."

Martin snorted. "And you had the audacity to suggest donating Warminster to the church. Really, Gaston."

Gaston shrugged. "I may as well accept the dukedom and donate it myself. I suspect Stoneley will ask for Mt. Holyoak back as one of his terms, which only leaves me with Clearwell for leverage."

"Clearwell is a fine fortress, Gaston. Do not give so little stock in it. The church could turn it into an abbey or something; they'll find use for her and her wealth."

Gaston's heart sank; if he lost everything to obtain two annulments, what on earth could he offer Remington? He was old, nearly too old to regain his fortune. He knew that Henry would not allow him to be a pauper, but he was a proud man. If the king were going to give him money and lands, then he would be obligated to work for them, which would rule out any thoughts of living peacefully away from the politics and strife of London.

The men were silent; Gaston was lost to his depressing thoughts and Martin was concentrating on his earlier idea. He was too single-minded to think and talk at the same time.

Gaston was glad his uncle had shut up. His mind turned to Remington, packing upstairs, and he felt the pangs of separation already. God help him, he couldn't stand to have her out of his sight for five minutes much less months. How on earth was he going to survive?

"I must help Remi," he set down his goblet.

Martin watched his nephew leave the room, hearing his heavy boots mount the stairs. Aye, Gaston was virtually helpless. But Martin, being a retired warrior, was not included in this incapacitated state. He could indeed do something. This was the perfect opportunity for him to prove to Gaston and the world that he was not a useless old man waiting for death. He would prove his worth - again.

Gaston stood in the door way just as Remington was pulling on a pair of slippers. She had changed surcoats, out of the scarlet brocade and into a surcoat of pale yellow silk that brought out her beauty like nothing else. It was snug and fit her form incredibly, and she smiled at him as he entered the room.

"I...I did not want to wear the scarlet," she said softly. "I like the yellow much better. Do you recognize it?"

He nodded faintly, fingering a springy curl. "You wore it the night I fell in love with you. Aside from the green that you buried Rory in, 'tis the surcoat I remember best. It does you justice, madam. Henry will be most envious."

She blushed. "I do not care what the king thinks. I only care what you think."

He sat down on the bed next to her, raising his eyebrows. "You *know* what I think."

She met his gaze, warm and tender, and a stab of anguish shot through her. She was trying so desperately to be brave, but it was becoming more difficult with each passing moment.

She stood up, moving to secure her bags. She couldn't look at him anymore. He watched her graceful back, the way the dress flared at the hips, memorizing every line of her. His smile faded and his entire body began to ache with agony. How could he let her go?

Remington was thinking the same thoughts. How could he allow the church to separate them? Anger, borne from grief, bubbled forth against her nature.

"I do not want to go, Gaston," she murmured. "Why must I?"

"Because we must cooperate, Remi; you know that."

She pulled at the bag sharply, her emotions unveiling themselves. "I do not want to!" She suddenly snapped. "Why are you letting them do this to us?"

"You know why."

She spun around, her face filled with sorrow and fury. "No, I do not. I do not understand why you are not fighting them tooth and nail on this, Gaston. Why are you being so bloody cooperative?"

"Calm down, angel. 'Twill do no good to get upset now."

"I shall get upset if I want to!" she raged. "'Tis I who will be isolated in some God-forsaken convent for an indeterminate amount of time - not you. Separated from you, from my family, from my son. Why aren't you at Canterbury right now convincing the archbishop what an evil bastard Guy is, and how he would do or say anything to keep us apart? *Why?*"

He stood up, reaching for her, but she shrank away. She did not want to be comforted at this moment. He sighed heavily when she yanked herself from his grip, his gaze sad.

"You are distraught, angel. Sit down and calm yourself and we shall converse rationally."

"No. I do not want to sit!" she snapped, feeling the tears beginning. "Tell me why you are not fighting for me!"

He put his hands on his hips, his face tired. He suddenly looked as if he had aged ten years in the past day. "I cannot fight, Remi. To fight would only confirm what Guy has said of me. I must do what the church says; I cannot make them bend to my wishes, no matter how badly it pains me. And if this separation does not kill me, I will be surprised."

Her eyes welled, but she fought off the cascades that threatened. "If you were to fight, it would only confirm to the church that your feelings for me are sincere." Her hands suddenly flew to her mouth and her voice turned into a shriek. "I do not want to be separated from you, not even for a moment! I cannot bear the thought of spending months and months away from you Gaston, I shall go mad!"

He was upon her in a half-second, enveloping her in his massive arms and shielding her from the world. She sobbed harshly, painfully, her agony blooming. 'Twas no matter that she had vowed to remain brave; she couldn't help herself anymore.

He held her, gripping her with the anguish he felt. Was she right? Should he be proving himself difficult, fighting like a tiger? Should he be substantiating rumors of his reputation, that there is more to the Dark Knight than merely a seasoned warrior? Mayhap if they believed he was truly in league with the devil, then they would give him what he asked for simply to avoid Lucifer's wrath?

Yet he chased those thoughts away rapidly. He was doing what he believed best, no matter how painful. Fighting the church would only make them angry with him; cooperating would put him in their good graces.

And then his mind clouded with thoughts of Guy Stoneley. Aye, he would see the man on the morrow and be done with these foolish games. He would have his agreement and his terms.

And then he would kill him.

CHAPTER TWENTY-SIX

Henry was seated in the dining hall in the Queen's House, well into his third goblet of wine. His wife and his mother had yet to arrive, as Gaston was similarly late. But he was not angered; it was, after all, a small sup and he was in no hurry.

Christopher Urswick, Dean of York, entered the hall clad in his traditional broadcloth robes, as indicative of his ecclesiastical station. He and Henry had been together since well before Henry had been crowned king of England, and the two men shared a close bond. Among other duties, Christopher had been chaplain of Henry's troops.

A slight man with a balding head in spite of his young years, Christopher seated himself next to his king and turned down the offer of wine, opting for flavored water instead.

"I shall be damn glad to leave this place," Henry murmured. "I prefer my Windsor to the Tower."

Christopher smiled faintly. "I rather like it here. There is much history."

"You like it because I keep my prisoners here and you feel important counseling their souls," the king eyed the dean a long moment as a servant lit the hearth. "What do you think of all of this with de Russe?"

Urswick pondered the tabletop a moment. "I have yet to speak with him, but I understand he is deeply in love with Lady Stoneley. And I think Sir Guy Stoneley is... evil. He makes me uncomfortable."

"De Tormo said the same thing. Tell me, then; is this man the incarnate of the devil that he should make men of God fearful of him?"

Christopher shrugged. "I only know what I feel; I cannot vouch for de Tormo. Were it up to me, I would grant Lady Stoneley her annulment without question. De Tormo told me the stories of her husband's bloodlust. Shocking."

"Indeed," Henry took another drink of wine. "Courtenay was hard-pressed to carry out Bourchier's orders, but he had no choice in the matter. Especially since John of Imola is involved. He must do everything according to the law of the church."

"Of course he must," Christopher agreed, shifting in his chair. "I pity de Russe. I understand his wife was most unfaithful to him with Richard, and now the poor man has fallen in love with a woman who is married to Satan's apprentice. Were it me...,"

"Go on."

Urswick paused. "Were it me, I would do what I had to in order to marry the woman I love. All I have spoken with agree on that account."

Henry was silent a moment. "Are you thinking that de Russe might do something drastic; something disobedient? Speak out, man."

Urswick shook his head, drinking from his glass. "I am thinking nothing of the sort. I am merely sympathizing."

"They will be here tonight. De Russe and his lady."

"I know. I am looking forward to meeting her, and speaking with de Russe."

Henry motioned to a servant for more wine. "Tread lightly, Chris. Gaston is completely different on the subject of his lady. He is not the controlled man we have grown to know. Furthermore, I doubt he will be in a talkative mood with the lady's impending departure tonight."

Christopher nodded in regret. "I saw the papal guard downstairs. I take it she is leaving after supper, then?"

Henry was quiet as he drank his wine, pondering the design on his golden goblet. "I will try to make it as painless as possible for them both. Courtenay's knights are waiting for my signal on this matter; I plan to send Gaston out of the room on some hasty errand and will have the lady escorted out while he is away. When he returns, I will inform him that the lady is en route to St. Catherine's. De Vere will be here to support me, of course. If anyone can prevent de Russe from rushing after her, he can."

"I suppose a quick extraction is as painless as any alternative," Urswick agreed.

Henry's brown eyes were intent on his dean. "I do not like doing this, Chris. With everything Gaston has done to advance my cause, I do not like deceiving him in this manner. I can only hope to make it up to him when I convince the apostolic delegate to grant an annulment with or without Stoneley's consent."

"Will you donate Warminster?" Urswick asked.

"Nay," Henry said flatly. "Warminster is Gaston's when and if he wants it. It goes to no one else."

Behind them, the door to the dining hall opened, ushering forth a fair young woman in blue silk. Elizabeth, queen of England, entered the room and curtsied for her husband. He was pleased to see that she had left her ladies behind, as he requested. Lord only knew how Elizabeth liked to be surrounded by her women to remind her that she was the king's wife.

"My lord," she said.

Henry glanced at his wife. "Good eve, Elizabeth."

Silently, she moved to her husband's left hand and took a seat. Henry and Christopher continued to speak quietly all but ignoring young Elizabeth until another, older woman entered the hall.

Lady Margaret Beaufort eyed her son, furthermore gazing disdainfully at the dean. "Henry, are all of those guards downstairs for Lady Stoneley?"

"They are," he replied.

Margaret snorted lady-like and took her seat on her son's right hand, demanding wine in a crystal goblet. She refused to drink from a metal cup because she swore she could taste the element. "Ridiculous. An entire company of men for one small lady."

Henry and Christopher passed glances; an entire company of men would be required should de Russe lose his control. "Do not worry overly, mother. The men are there purely to protect the lady, not to wrest her from these walls."

"I understand she is lovely," Elizabeth said, directing her statement at Lady Beaufort.

"We shall soon see," Margaret replied, her manner as imperious as the rest of her. "I am curious to meet this woman who would capture the heart of the most powerful fighting man in England's history."

"You would compare de Russe to the likes of Lancelot, Gallahad, St. George, or Christopher de Lohr, Richard's champion on the crusades?"

Henry raised an eyebrow. "Or William de Wolfe? Surely there was no greater warrior than de Wolfe. He controlled Scotland's borders for many years for Henry III."

Margaret shook her head; she was not about to engage in a fighting man's conversation. "Aye, they had stout reputations and lived long lives. But mark my words; Gaston de Russe is more powerful than even they."

"He shall be flattered to hear you say that, Mother," Henry smiled.

Margaret was not a woman to be toyed with. She gave her son an icy stare and looked away. "If you mention this conversation, I shall strip the hide from your back."

There was a knock at the door and a steward opened it. Gaston and Remington entered the hall.

All eyes went to Remington, who felt the weight of the stares. She had been quite calm upon entering, but suddenly felt apprehensive, as if she would not meet with their approval somehow. As if they would think all of the fuss was ridiculous.

She looked ravishing in the yellow satin, the front of her hair pulled back and secured with a golden clasp. Gaston, holding her elbow tightly, was dressed in "common clothing", as he had called it. The black breeches and fine leather boots belonged to him, but the black silk tunic with the gold embroider was Uncle Martin's. Gaston hated to dress in fancy clothing and did not even own a fine tunic. Remington had felt as if she were arguing with her son as she tried to get Gaston to dress finely for dinner; he wanted to wear his armor.

Henry actually rose to his feet, followed by Urswick. "Introduce us, Gaston."

Gaston smiled faintly and Remington dipped into a low curtsy. "My lord, this is Lady Remington Stoneley," he said with a touch of pride.

Henry studied her openly. "Look at me."

She did, meeting his eyes for a brief second before lowering her gaze. She was humbled and nervous to be in the presence of the king.

But Henry continued to observe her even as he regained his seat. Urswick seemed tongue-tied.

"We approve," the king said after a moment, his voice low. "Gaston, she's marvelous. No wonder you are willing to defy God."

Gaston continued to hold onto her, meeting Lady Margaret's gaze. "My lady, a pleasure to see you again," he said gallantly.

Lady Margaret rose from her seat, walking around the table to stand in front of Remington. Good Lord, Remington knew who the woman was and was even more intimidated by her than the king. Dressed in expensive silk and gobs of jewelry, she looked every inch the mother of a king. Remington struggled to keep her nerves from gaining an upper hand.

Lady Margaret put her hand to Remington's chin, tilting her face up. Their eyes met a moment, brown ones to sea-crystal green.

"How old are you?" Lady Margaret asked.

"Twenty six years, my lady," Remington replied.

The older woman nodded faintly, scrutinizing every detail of Remington's face. Finally, she turned to Elizabeth. "What do you think, my queen?"

Elizabeth was a petty, childish girl who was jealous of virtually every beautiful woman she met. It was obvious that Remington was to be of no exception.

"She's old," she sniffed.

Remington felt the insult but did not react. Lady Margaret was moving to regain her seat and Gaston directed her to a chair opposite Henry. He seated himself next to her.

Well-dressed servants brought out the trenchers; pheasant in sauce, boiled summer vegetables and bread with butter was abundant. The diners dug in.

"Mother was comparing you to the likes of Christopher de Lohr and William de Wolfe before you arrived, Gaston," Henry said, ignoring his mother's earlier threat. "I had no idea she thought so highly of you."

Gaston's head came up from his food; he looked at an angered Lady Beaufort. "Nor did I. I am honored, my lady, that you would group me with such legendary men."

Lady Margaret did not reply; she would not dignify her son's disobedient remarks. Instead, she focused on Remington.

"How do you find London, Lady Remington?"

Remington was having a difficult enough time eating in the presence of the king; was she expected to eat and talk, too? She swallowed a large bite and almost choked. "I have had no time to see the sights, my lady, but from what I have seen, it is an exciting city."

Elizabeth was thoroughly riled with the presence of lovely Lady Remington. She'd had no idea how beautiful the woman was and was distinctly upset. Not having her ladies about her to reinforce her vainness was unbalancing.

"It is," she said coolly. "A pity you will not be here long enough to become familiar with it."

Remington looked at the queen; younger than herself, she was a plain, blond girl of high breeding. Too high; she appeared fragile and pale.

"I do intend to tour London, someday, highness," she replied softly. "And may I congratulate you on the birth of your son." "Thank you," she said stiffly.

Gaston knew Remington was going to confront this sort of reaction from Elizabeth and he was pleased she was handling it well. But, truthfully, there was nothing else she could do.

In fact, she had been remarkable since de Tormo had delivered the shattering news. Gaston was terribly proud of her.

"Gaston, I do not think I have ever seen you in a tunic and hose," Christopher found his voice. "I thought you were, in fact, born with your armor on. This is a remarkable event."

Gaston looked somewhat sheepish. "You may thank the lady for that. She refused to eat with me if I wore my armor to the king's table, so I was forced into complying."

Henry and Christopher chortled. "No armor or weapons of any kind? Even underneath the tunic?"

Gaston looked down at himself; the tunic was stretched taut across his magnificent chest, and his leg muscles were bulging through the breeches. "I have no idea where I would put it."

Remington even smiled, looking him over with glittering eyes. "My lord looks every inch the nobleman."

Gaston raised a disapproving eyebrow, but there was a smile on his lips. "Never again, my lady. This is the last time you will see me dressed as a dandy."

"You look wonderful," Remington repeated, daring to bring Lady Margaret into the conversation. "Would you not agree, Lady Beaufort?"

Margaret looked up from her pheasant, passing a well-practiced eye over Gaston. "I have always thought so."

Gaston dipped his head at the compliment, feeling just the slightest bit uncomfortable at the tone used. It bordered on seductive.

"I understand that your half-brother is preparing to take his vows, Gaston, Henry said. "Courtenay told me that Richard de Russe is finally preparing to be ordained. A remarkable event, I would say. I did not believe the man serious to take the vow of chastity. A good deal like your father, I am told."

Gaston met Henry's gaze steadily. "I have not kept in touch with Richard, my lord. I prefer to ignore my illegitimate relations."

"But Richard is deacon at Newby Prior, a prestigious post," Urswick put in. "Surely you consider the man worthy of the de Russe name, bastard or no."

Gaston shrugged, his only answer. Henry knew better than to press Gaston on the subject of his bastard brothers and turned his eye once again to Remington.

"I understand you have several sisters, Lady Remington," he said. "Are they married?"

"Not yet, my lord," she replied, aware that Elizabeth was watching her. "But soon. My youngest sister is marrying Gaston's cousin, Nicolas."

"Convenient," Elizabeth remarked. When everyone looked at her, she made haste to clarify her comment. "She will remain close to you."

Remington merely nodded; she sensed tremendous hostility from the queen and was not about to enter into any sort of verbal battle. Puzzled at the reception, she lowered her head to her trencher.

The evening passed, the conversation mostly between Gaston and the king. Remington kept silent for the most part, still in awe of her dinner mates and furthermore fearful to antagonize the queen. The woman kept glaring at her.

Lady Beaufort, however, kept her eyes on Remington in a sort of appraising manner, as one would inspect a side of beef. Remington met the woman's eyes a few times, smiling weakly and quickly returning to her food. Nauseous as she was, it was the only thing she could put her attention to that wasn't staring back at her.

Gaston kept his hand on her knee underneath the table. Every so often he would squeeze it gently, just to let her know he had not forgotten about her. She appreciated his support and wished she could tell him so.

When dinner was cleared and dessert was brought, an elderly man entered the dining hall and, without a greeting, kicked Christopher Urswick out of his chair next to Henry and resumed it himself. Muttering and tugging at his tunic, he demanded his share of the pastries first.

Obviously, everyone at the table knew who he was, except Remington. She stared at him curiously as he grunted and bickered about anything and everything. Then, his eyes came up and he focused on her.

"Lady Stoneley, I presume?"

Remington blinked, almost as if she had been physically jarred by his words. "Aye, my lord."

His eyes narrowed, as he looked her over. "Stand up, girl."

Hesitantly, she stood. The old man let his eyes wander over her a brief moment before turning to Gaston. "She's marvelous. What in the hell does she want with the likes of you?"

Gaston smiled faintly. "She is with me out of pity, most likely, my lord. She is a gracious woman with a good heart."

"And a figure to match," the old man snorted, gazing at her once again. "She's the best piece of female flesh I have seen in many years, Gaston. No wonder you stole her from that Yorkist bastard."

Remington sat down quickly, feeling distinctly uncomfortable. She still had yet to discover who this crass man was, but Gaston turned to her.

"Remi, this is the Duke of Bedford. Henry's Uncle Jasper."

As if a light suddenly blazed, Remington understood. This small, boorish old man was Henry's powerful uncle. Militarily, she understood he was brilliant and had been by his nephew's side for years as Henry fought for the throne.

She found it difficult to believe the man was Uncle Jasper. The man had been of such value to Henry that he had been named the new Duke of Bedford after Henry was crowned. Somehow, she had imagined the duke more....refined. But then again, she had made the same superficial observation of Martin and had been completely wrong.

Gaston served Remington a custard tart himself, smiling gently at her until Uncle Jasper roped him into a discussion. She ate politely, eyes downcast, listening to Jasper rattle on. The ladies of the table seemed to have been forgotten.

The evening wore on and Remington was growing exceedingly bored, even in the company of greats. Lady Margaret and Elizabeth had yet to say one word, even to each other, so Remington pressed herself close to Gaston's side and sat quietly. His hand, back on her knee, caressed her through her surcoat.

Unfortunately, when the men's conversation lulled, Jasper's attention turned to her once again.

"I hear your husband beat you," he said bluntly. "What kind of bastard is he? I understand he is as black as Satan."

She looked at him, stunned, and struggled to recover. "He...he is an evil man, my lord. Which is why I am endeavoring to obtain an annulment."

"But what if Gaston had not come along? What then?"

She swallowed, feeling Gaston's hand squeeze her gently. "Then I suppose I would still be at Mt. Holyoak with my family, praying that Guy Stoneley rots in his cell."

Jasper wiped his nose, picked at it, still scrutinizing her. "He's a smart man; proved it at Stoke. I know this, for I was in the battle," he sat back in his chair, his manner somewhat less crude. "I pity you, sweetheart. I sincerely hope the church sees its way clear to grant you what you seek. If they do not, let me know and I shall kill Stoneley myself and say it was an accident. You shall have your annulment then."

Henry smiled faintly, but Remington looked shocked. She had no idea whether or not he was jesting until Gaston stepped into the conversation.

"We shall keep that in mind, my lord," he said.

Remington was terribly thankful for Gaston's intervention, but she was entertaining a more embarrassing thought; did the whole court know of her beatings? How much did they know? Was her life, unfortunately, now for public display? She realized that Gaston had to reveal all of the reasons why she desired an annulment, and she had further realized that the facts and gossip had spread.

But she wasn't surprised, truly. She had not expected less, but it did not prevent her from feeling somewhat ashamed.

The dessert dishes were cleared and the servants set out bowls of water for cleansing. The men were still conversing about something unimportant, tax tariffs from what Remington could gather when she decided to pay attention, when a soldier entered the room and saluted sharply before his king.

"Speak," Henry commanded lazily.

"My lord, Sir Richard Guildford has arrived to the Tower," the sergeant said crisply. "He is being shown to the Brick Tower."

"I sent for him," Henry mumbled to Jasper, then looked at Gaston. "Gaston, would you be so kind as to greet Guildford and bring him to me."

Gaston rose without question, but Remington suddenly looked frightened. Her huge eyes gazed up at him and he patted her cheek gently. "You are in good company, my lady. I shall return shortly."

"Good company, indeed," Jasper sniffed. "Get out of here, Gaston, before I am driven to return the insult."

The corner of Gaston's lips twitched and he gave Remington one final wink before quitting the room behind the sergeant.

Remington couldn't help it; she watched wistfully until the door closed, acutely aware that nearly the entire royal family was watching her. Feeling horribly alone and anxious, she forced herself to turn around and smile.

They did not smile back.

CHAPTER TWENTY-SEVEN

"I am sorry, my lady, but there seemed to be no easy way to do this," Henry said softly.

Remington blinked in confusion. "I do not understand, Your Grace."

Henry stood up. On the opposite side of the room from where Gaston had just left, there was another door. The king opened it.

Two large knights and four soldiers filed in quietly and Henry beckoned the two knights to follow him. Remington watched with growing apprehension as they made a path directly to her.

"This is Lady Remington Stoneley," Henry said quietly to the armored men. "Her items have already been loaded into the wagon and she is ready to leave. If you will be so kind as to escort her to St. Catherine's."

The impact of the situation slammed into Remington and her eyes widened. She sought the king's eyes.

"I cannot say good-bye to Gaston?" she whispered.

Henry took her arm gently and pulled her to stand. "My lady, Gaston means more to me than you could possibly know and believe me when I tell you that I do not relish provoking his anger. But I believe it best to whisk you away while he is calm and controlled, not wait until painful farewells crack him, I am afraid. Truthfully, he will have the utmost difficulty letting you go; even though he knows he must. This way, it is less painful for you both."

She was stunned. "You tricked him into leaving?"

"I did. But I had to."

Her mouth opened in shock, but she quickly closed it. Her whole body started to shake and she struggled to maintain her composure. Should she scream for Gaston? Should she balk, fight, fall into fits? Dear God, she did not want to go without saying good-bye to him!

Lady Margaret was up, moving to her side and taking her other arm. "Henry, let her go. I shall walk with her to the courtyard."

Remington was trying so desperately not to cry as Lady Margaret's warm hand clutched her. She was so shaken she could barely speak, but she felt compelled to. She knew Gaston's rage would be great when he returned and she did not want him to do something he would regret.

"Very well, my lord, if you think this best," she said hoarsely. "But be sure and tell Gaston that I went willingly, with no struggle. Make sure he understands that."

"She needs a cloak," Lady Margaret mumbled, looking at her son, the knights. "Where is her cloak? The night grows damp."

"On her mount, my lady," one of the knights replied. "She is prepared to face the evening air."

"Where is Courtenay?" Henry asked the same knight.

"At St. Catherine's, my lord," the man's voice was deep and husky. "He awaits the lady there."

Henry nodded. "Good. Waste no time, then. Take her to the convent and make haste; I fear when de Russe returns, he shall not be pleased and I want the lady far away."

The knights bowed as Lady Margaret led Remington toward the open door. When the panel closed softly behind them, Henry turned back to the table with a weary sigh.

"Easier than I thought," he muttered, moving back to his chair. "I hated to do that, you know. I took no pleasure in deceiving de Russe."

Jasper drank from his cup. "I hope you can explain that to him before he tears your throat out."

"Your support, as always, is appreciated," Henry took his goblet and drained it, aware his wife was looking at him. "Do you wish to say something?"

Elizabeth shook her head. In spite of the fact that she was extremely envious of Lady Remington, she thought what her husband had done was cruel. But she did not voice her opinion. "I would ask your permission to retire, my lord."

Henry barely nodded and Elizabeth rose, silently leaving the room. Henry did not give her a second thought as he returned to the conversation, mentally planning his speech for Gaston when the man walked back through the door. Guildford wasn't at the Tower; he was in Dorchester.

Henry suspected by the time Gaston reached the Brick Tower and realized there was no Guildford, that he would suspect something was afoot. He kept glancing at the door, waiting for Gaston to tear it off its hinges.

Elizabeth wasn't heading for her chambers as she had told her husband; she was walking the path to the Brick Tower that she had suspected Gaston had taken. Passing by a bank of narrow windows that opened out onto the courtyard, she could see her mother-in-law loading Lady Remington onto a small brown palfrey while the two knights stood by the animal, making sure the lady was comfortable and properly set. She knew they would be leaving soon, and she knew she must hurry and find the Dark Knight.

It wasn't that she had a particularly good heart; Elizabeth was shallow and petty, and she never did anything for purely unselfish reasons. She was afraid of the Dark Knight; everyone was, even her husband, but he would not admit it. She thought that, mayhap, informing de Russe of her husband's devious deception might somehow put her in his good graces. She would do a favor for him, and he, in return, might someday reciprocate.

The path from the Queen's House to the Brick Tower was a long one. The corridors were quiet and dimly lit, a household soldier occasionally seen. This portion of the Tower was always quiet and, Elizabeth thought, haunted. Her fine silk slippers scuffed the stone floor faintly as she rounded a sharp corner and proceeded down the straight hall to her destination.

She was preparing to mount the stairs to the Tower when she nearly ran headlong into Gaston, who was descending. She let out a small cry and he reached out to steady her, so that she would not tumble to the floor.

"Forgive me, my lady," he said quickly. "I was...."

She shook her head sharply. "There is no time, my lord. Courtenay's men are taking your lady away as we speak."

Gaston did not look overly surprised, but his expression cooled dramatically. "Where?"

"In the courtyard," Elizabeth said. "They were mounting her on a palfrey as I passed by, not five minutes ago."

Gaston did not wait to thank her. He was running off, with more speed than one would have suspected for a man his considerable size. Elizabeth watched until he disappeared from view, positive she could feel the ground beneath her shake with every step he took.

Feeling somewhat satisfied, and a tiny bit vengeful, she took the long route back to her rooms.

Gaston ran until his chest ached and his head swam. The courtyard was vacant and he ran the narrow corridor to the main entrance, only to be met with empty roads and no sign of the escort. He stopped, breathing heavily, knowing that the escort had probably left at a gallop, at orders to put as much distance as possible between Lady Remington and Gaston de Russe.

There was no way he could outrun horses. They were long gone, and anguish swelled within him until he let out a loud grunt of pure frustration. Weaving with exertion and agony, he stumbled his way back down the entryway and into the courtyard. Several household soldiers watched him curiously, wondering what the matter was, but none daring to be bold enough to ask.

Well and good for the soldiers that they did not ask. Gaston's pain was seeping through his pores, gushing from his heart and he paced circles in the middle of the compound until his breathing slowed and he was able to maintain some sort of control. Had Henry confronted him at that moment, he would have ripped his heart out. He could not believe that a man he had sworn his loyalty to had tricked him.

He would have expected this from Richard. But not from Henry.

Nicolas stood several feet away from him. Gaston had no idea how long his cousin had been standing there and he did not care. He was torn with indecision and grief.

"I wish I could help you," Nicolas said quietly. "Tell me what I can do, Gaston. Anything at all and I shall do it."

Gaston snorted into his hands, still pacing like a caged animal. Then, he choked out a loud burst of laughter. "Anything at all," he repeated, muttering as if he were talking to himself. "Kill Stoneley! Kill Henry! Kill the whole goddamn church!"

Nicolas watched him pace, his eyes glittering with concern. He'd never seen Gaston come close to losing his control, ever, and he was scared.

"Do you want me to follow Remington and see where they take her?" he asked steadily.

Gaston did not say anything. He continued to pace and twitch, running his fingers through his hair in a nervous gesture. At some point, de Tormo joined Nicolas, and the two men watched the Dark Knight walk off his pent-up fury.

Gaston's mind was a black jumble of rage. He still was not entirely capable of forming a coherent thought, but he caught sight of de Tormo's robes from the corner of his eye.

"Did you know about this treachery, priest?"

De Tormo looked confused. "What do you mean, de Russe?"

Gaston stopped and looked at him. "The ploy to separate me from Remington so that Courtenay's men could take her away. Well?"

De Tormo gazed into Gaston's stormy orbs. With everything the two of them had been through, with all of the threats and emotions, he had never once feared the Dark Knight. But at this very moment, looking deep into the man's soul, he was afraid of him. All he could read was death.

"No, Gaston," he said quietly. "I knew of no such betrayal."

Gaston's ashen face was as tight as the head of a drum. He had stopped his pacing, but his whole body was still twitching. "Can Remington get an annulment without Guy's consent?"

"I doubt it," de Tormo replied. "The circumstances would have to be extreme, to say the least."

One second Gaston was several feet away. Within the blink of an eye, he was standing in front of the priest, glaring down at him. "You do not call beatings, rapes and the like extreme? What of the devil worship?"

De Tormo took a step back; he had to. Gaston was scaring the hell out of him. He fought to keep his fear down and mull over the possibilities of what Gaston was suggesting. "It is extreme, I shall grant you. Mayhap... mayhap if the lady's sisters and family testified to Guy's cruelty, and if we could possibly secure witnesses that had first-hand knowledge of his brutality, the testimonies would weigh heavily enough that the church would advance the annulment without Guy's agreement," he met Gaston's gaze seriously. "That is the only possibility I can think of, de Russe."

Gaston pictured Jasmine and Skye trembling before the papal council, confessing their darkest shame to a group of indifferent men. He could see Dane, struggling to be brave as he told them of the nightly beatings, the screaming, and the fear. And he could see Remington, begging to be released from her hell.

Instead of comfort, as de Tormo had meant to give, Gaston went in the other direction. The past several minutes of struggle to calm were erased in a split second and he was suddenly whirling, making a break for the White Tower. Nicolas and de Tormo watched in horror, knowing exactly where he was going.

"Get de Vere!" Nicolas snapped to the priest, taking off on a dead run after his cousin.

Nicolas did not know how he was going to prevent Gaston from killing Guy. He was twice his size and strength. But he followed close behind, hearing his cousin's heavy footfalls as he mounted the stairs on his way to the third floor cell of Guy Stoneley.

Nicolas called to Gaston, trying to plead with him as they raced up the stairs. But his cousin wasn't responding; he did not expect him to.

Gaston reached Stoneley's room ahead of Nicolas and ordered the sentry to open the door. The panel was barely released before Gaston was plowing into the room.

Guy was on the other side of the room, by the windows. He turned disinterestedly to Gaston, apparently unconcerned with his visit. From his vantage point, he could see nothing of the workings of the courtyard and had no idea of what had transpired.

"Get out, de Russe," he said. "I have no desire to speak with you tonight."

Gaston did not even reply. Suddenly, he was hurling himself across the room, grabbing Guy by the throat and tossing him over the wide, oaken table. Guy flew like a rag doll; his body went skidding across the floor and slammed into the stone wall. Before he could react in any way, Gaston leapt over the table and hit Guy so severely that the man instantly lost four teeth. Blood splashed onto the floor.

"Your agreement," Gaston seethed, his hand still clenching Guy's throat. "Your agreement or I kill you."

Guy was struggling with the darkness that threatened to claim him. Stars danced before his eyes and his mouth was an agonizing, throbbing mass. "Go to hell!"

Gaston hit him again, in the torso this time, and Guy exhaled loudly from the force. He folded in on himself, but Gaston still held him around the neck.

"I will say it once more," Gaston said through clenched teeth. "Your agreement or your life!"

Guy couldn't breathe; he couldn't walk, or stand, or think either. Horrible rasping noises flushed forth from his chest as he fought to take in air. He tried to form a word, any word, but was thwarted each time. Finally, he managed to spit out four words. "To hell with you!"

They were not the words Gaston was looking for. He slammed Guy again, tossing him against the wall and then pouncing on him.

"Gaston, no!" Nicolas was over his indecision as to whether or not to intervene; any more pummeling and Stoneley would be dead. He jumped on Gaston, using all of his young strength to pull his cousin back. "No! You shall kill him!"

Gaston was possessed. He let go of Guy long enough to hit Nicolas so hard that the knight staggered backward and tripped over a chair, breaking the chair. He landed heavily, his head swimming and his jaw feeling as though it had been crushed. But he struggled to his feet, knowing he was the only one at the moment who could slow his cousin's rage. Shaking off the stars that skipped before his eyes, he thrust himself forward once again.

Gaston had Guy by the hair when Nicolas pounced on him. Guy was only semi-conscious and fell back to the floor in a heap as Gaston turned his rage, full-blown, on his cousin.

Nicolas held his own, but he never really had a chance. Gaston's huge fists pummeled him and Nicolas found himself doing nothing more than defending himself. There was no way to win and he knew it, so he tried to protect his head as he staggered and tripped and fell away from the wrath of his cousin. Nicolas fell heavily over a small table, landing with a heavy thud. Breathing hard, Gaston swung from his incapacitated cousin and took long strides across the floor to where Guy was beginning to raise himself on shaky arms. He snatched the man by his shirt collar, swinging him into the nearest chair as if he weighed no more than a small child.

Bloodied and swollen, Guy's eyes rolled open to find Gaston's flushed face inches from him. Blue veins were bulging on Gaston's temples.

"Let us try this once more," he growled breathlessly. "I will have your consent for an annulment or I will finish what I have started."

Guy hacked up blood and mucus and spit out a tooth, all on Gaston's arm. Gaston did not flinch; he was waiting for an answer. And Guy was taking his leisure time in responding.

"Answer me, Stoneley. My patience is gone."

"And so is Remington, else you would not be here," Guy said, muffled with his missing teeth and swollen mouth. "You may beat me, de Russe, torture me, and eventually kill me, but always remember that I am her legal husband. I am. 'Tis I who legally hold what you so desperately want, and no amount of blood and pain can change that."

A muscle in Gaston's cheek twitched involuntarily as smoky gray eyes met with ice blue. "Your agreement."

Guy met his eyes, his breathing slowing and the pain beginning to increase. Several feet away, Nicolas rose to his feet like an old man, hunched over with the pain in his torso where Gaston had punched him. He wiped at his mouth, watching and waiting.

"If you kill me, you shall be deemed a murderer and you will never gain an annulment," Guy said softly.

"I am willing to take the risk."

"What of Remington? If you are charged with murder, what will happen to her? You profess your love for her, yet you are not thinking of her in this matter. You are only thinking of yourself."

Gaston's muscle twitched again. "Your agreement, Stoneley."

Suddenly, Henry and John de Vere were in the doorway, followed by several of Gaston's men. Christopher Urswick and Uncle Jasper followed closely.

"Gaston!" Henry bellowed. "Let him up!"

Gaston did not react for a moment; he was still hunched over Stoneley in the chair, his arms braced on the arms, trapping his prey.

"Damnation, Gaston, I said let him up!" Henry moved forward, grabbing Gaston's arm.

De Vere put both arms around Gaston and pulled him back, but not without a great deal of effort. It was like trying to move a wall.

Henry gazed down at Stoneley and shook his head regretfully. "Gaston..."

"I did it, my lord," Nicolas suddenly interjected, moving forward so that all could see his wounds. "I fought Stoneley and Gaston separated us. I did it... because of what he's done. I was protecting my cousin."

"And you are protecting him now," Henry said plainly, grabbing one of Gaston's bloodied hands. The knuckles were raw and torn. "Your loyalty is commendable, young de Russe. But I well know what happened here tonight, and I furthermore expected Gaston to deal me more of the same when he finished with Stoneley."

Gaston, still in de Vere's grip, kept his gaze averted. Henry studied his most powerful knight remorsefully. "I thought it would be better this way, Gaston. I honestly did not enjoy deceiving you. I merely thought a quick removal, minus the painful good-byes would be better for you both. If the tooth is aching, is it not better to extract it rapidly and be done with it?"

Gaston did not answer, although he felt somewhat better. He had never truly believed Henry had betrayed him, but he wondered. It seemed as if his whole world was unbalanced, and he was not sure of anything anymore, except his feelings for Remington.

Henry passed a glance at Stoneley, grossly swollen. "I suspect you have me to thank for your life this night. I can see that the Dark One was quite efficient."

"That may be, my lord, but he still did not gain what he set out to obtain," Stoneley replied, looking at Gaston's profile.

Henry's face hardened. "Then I can see I must do the bargaining. Well, out with it, then. What are your terms for an annulment agreement, Stoneley? And do not waste my time with haggling. Spit it out."

Guy looked up at Henry, seeing the other important men in the room. Men he had fought against, despised. But to actually be negotiating with Henry brought a whole new meaning to the game and he felt most powerful, in spite of his aching body. He shifted in his seat.

"Look at me, de Russe, when I speak, for I shall not repeat my words," he said icily.

Gaston stiffened a bit. Reluctantly, he turned to face Guy, his face like stone. All of the rage, the fury, the hatred, was expertly banked and Stoneley's twisted mouth smiled.

"Excellent," he glanced up at Henry. "I will list my terms in order. First, I would be released from the Tower."

"Done," Henry did not miss a beat. "And?"

"The return of my keep. My lands and wealth, as well."

Henry glanced at Gaston. Seeing no reaction, he nodded his head. "Agreed. Is that all?"

"No," Guy said flatly. If the king were responding so agreeably, then he would push him to the limit. "Since I will be losing my wife, I wish another in return. Her sister, Jasmine."

Gaston's eggshell composure cracked. "Impossible. She is married and with child."

Guy raised an eyebrow. "Is that so? My wife neglected to tell me that. Oh, well. With Rory dead, I suppose that leaves little Skye."

"Out of the question," Gaston's jaw ticked. "She is also married and with child."

Guy raised both eyebrows. "Truly? Now that is remarkable. I wonder if it is also true."

"It is," Nicolas stepped in beside his cousin, his youthful face taut. "I married Skye."

Guy looked between Nicolas and Gaston as if seeing right through their half-truths. Then he looked at Henry. "I would have my son returned to me. When Remington marries de Russe, my son stays with me."

Another crack appeared in Gaston's facade. "The boy is fostering."

"At Mt. Holyoak, I am told," Guy, said coolly. "He will stay there and remain with me."

Dane. Remington's most prized possession, her beloved son, and the boy Gaston himself had come to love. Gaston could not make that decision; neither could Henry. "Gaston?" the king pushed.

Gaston's eyes flicked to his king helplessly. "I cannot agree, my lord. That will be for Lady Remington to decide, but I can tell you without a doubt that she will refuse it."

"All or nothing, de Russe," Stoneley said with a confident growl. "All of my terms or no agreement."

"Is that everything?" Henry demanded roughly.

Guy looked thoughtful a moment. "Aye."

Henry looked to Gaston, who was staring at Guy as if the man had just declared he was Christ in the flesh. "Well, Gaston?" Henry prodded gently. "You have his terms. They are not entirely disagreeable."

Gaston stared a moment longer. "Nicolas, send word to Mt. Holyoak. All troops and weaponry is to be dispatched to Clearwell. The keep is to be vacated without delay."

Nicolas blanched. "What of... what of Jasmine and Skye?"

"To Clearwell," Gaston still wasn't looking at him. "Dane and Charles will remain at Mt. Holyoak."

Nicolas' jaw swung open. "Christ, Gaston. You are going to leave them? What about...?"

Gaston's eyes riveted to his cousin, boring a hole clean through to his brain. Nicolas met the gaze, feeling its impact as if he had been physically hit. Without another word, he quit the room.

Gaston turned back to Guy. "De Tormo will write up the agreement this night."

"Shouldn't you discuss my terms with Remi?" Guy asked, his mood lightening. "She will not want to leave Dane, you know. She could end up hating you for leaving her son behind in your haste to gain her."

Gaston knew that only too well, but he had no other choice at the moment. Hoping to throw Stoneley off the track, he said: "We will have more children, Stoneley. One son will not matter in future years, not when she will bear me ten."

Even Henry thought the remark was rather callous but he did not reply. He had done his work and moved for the door, making sure de Vere and Uncle Jasper had hold of Gaston.

"When can I expect my freedom, my lord?" Guy asked pleasantly.

Henry paused coldly. "After the priest writes up the consent, and after the annulment proceedings have been completed, and no sooner. You are still an enemy of the crown, Stoneley. I do not take those charges lightly."

Guy lowered his head respectfully, watching the great group of men file from his room.

When the door closed and he was alone, he smiled. Remington would never leave Dane behind and he knew it. De Russe had no right to agree to that particular term, but he had taken the liberty anyway. Guy snickered into the darkness; he had his freedom promised and his keep returned. And mayhap, after all, he would still retain his wife. There was no reason to gain an annulment if she was not going to marry anyone else. Especially if she ended up hating the reason for all of these troubles - Gaston de Russe.

Remington did not sleep at all that night. The convent was cold, her pallet made of straw, and her stomach hurt with all of the emotions she was feeling.

She wondered where Gaston was and how he was handling her removal. He had always seemed remarkably calm, with the exception of when she'd met with Guy. It was the only time she had ever seen him rage, but she wondered if he had not torn the Tower apart when he realized what had happened.

The nuns had been kindly to her, older women with wrinkled faces exposed underneath their wimple. One had seen that she was made comfortable, bringing her bread and wine before leaving her utterly alone in her tiny cell. She felt as if she were in prison.

The next day after her sleepless night dawned sticky and hot. As soon as Remington rose, her stomach announced itself loud and clear and she knew it was because of the child. Nibbling on bread calmed it somewhat, and she was able to sponge herself with cool water and don a soft linen surcoat. Her hair gathered back at the nape of her neck, she continued to nibble bread and gaze from the narrow window, wondering what would happen to her now. She had never felt so alone in her life, and memories of Mt. Holyoak and her family seemed years past.

St. Catherine's Convent was a huge place. Young, noble girls were schooled and finished here, and the place was full of novice nuns. She could see them down below occasionally, dressed in rough woolen garments and wooden clogs, even in the oppressive heat.

She spent the entire morning pondering her future, losing track of time. Before she realized it, the sun was over her head and there was a soft knock at the door.

A novice nun entered the room. Remington turned to the girl, looking at her curiously.

"My lady? The nooning meal is being served below, and your knights said that you could enjoy it outside of your room," she said softly. "I would escort you there."

Remington stood up. "I'd like that. This room is a might small."

The girl smiled, a beautiful smile. In fact, she was very pretty in spite of the fact that her hair was hidden and she was dressed in shapeless brown wool. Remington guessed that she was close to her own age. "And this room will become quite hot as the day progresses," the girl assured her. "Which is why you have been allowed the coolness of the common room."

Their walk down the corridor was silent. Remington glanced about her curiously, having never been inside a convent before. It was barren of anything other than necessary furnishings, but it was absolutely spotless. Somewhere in the distance, she could hear children laughing as they descended the stairs.

The common room was a cavernous hall with simple wooden tables and benches, reserved for travelers and others seeking refuge. There were few people in the room, but the young nun dashed away from her as one of Courtenay's knights approached.

It was a knight who had brought her in the previous night, as tall as a tree and broad. His armor banged loudly and his faceplate was up, revealing his handsome face.

"My lady," he greeted pleasantly. "I thought you would appreciate a change of scenery. Your meal is over here."

She followed him silently to a small wooden table. A variety of fruits, cheese and hard bread awaited her, but she drank two large goblets of water before she even looked at the food. Meanwhile, the knight had moved far, far away, watching her from the shadows.

She ate slowly, her confusion and depression reflected in her movements. The food was fresh, but she thought it tasteless. She missed Gaston so terribly that her whole existence was tasteless at the moment. And she missed her son, her sisters.

The novice nun came to her, making sure she had enough to eat and drink. Remington almost asked the girl her name, but she lost her nerve. The girl moved away again, leaving her alone. Depression overwhelming her, she stopped eating and dropped her hands to her lap. She sat and stared at the table.

"You must eat more to keep up your strength," came a voice.

She did not raise her head; instead, she peered sideways toward the source of the voice.

A figure dressed in coarse, dirty garments sat a few feet away. It was a large figure, with filthy hands that picked at a chuck of bread. Remington looked away, ignoring the man.

"I demand you eat what is put in front of you," the man said again, and Remington looked up sharply. There was suddenly something strangely familiar about the voice.

Martin de Russe pulled the hood of his cloak back slightly, winking boldly at Remington. Her eyes widened and her mouth opened, but she recovered her shock quickly, glancing about to make sure no one was looking their way. The knight, over her shoulder but several yards away, was of no immediate threat.

"Uncle Martin," she whispered sharply. "What are you doing here?"

"Watching out for you, lovely," he whispered back, pulling the hood down over him once again.

"Did Gaston send you?" she asked, her eyes flicking about nervously.

Martin snorted, shoveling bread into his mouth. "Good God, no. He does not even know I am here. He was adamant about not sending anyone to protect you, but I thought he was being ridiculous. I am here of my own accord."

"How did you find me?"

"Waiting outside of the Tower entrance, lovely. When your party passed, I followed you. 'Twas not difficult."

She eyed him with disbelief and amusement. "Well, what are you doing dressed as a peasant?"

"A disguise," he told her as if she were a simpleton. "I can stay close to you this way," he suddenly let out a series of horrible, gravelly coughs and snorts. "And I am desperately ill until they see it fit to move you, Remi. Then, suddenly, I will be gone that very day."

"To follow me," Remington supplied with a smile.

He smiled back, eyeing the knight in the corridor. "Exactly. These buffoons in their fancy armor cannot protect you properly."

She snickered, her appetite suddenly returning and she popped a grape in her mouth. "I do love you, Uncle Martin."

He stopped a moment, the gentlest of expressions washing his face. "You do? Well, of course, I love you too, else I would not be here."

"Have you heard anything of Gaston?" she asked, more grapes in her mouth. "I am terribly worried about him."

"Nothing," Martin drank from his cup. "I have been here in this convent since you left the Tower. See here; here comes your watchdog."

Surely, Courtenay's knight marched up on her table, eyeing Martin threateningly. "Is he bothering you, my lady?"

"Not at all," she said steadily. "In fact, I find him rather interesting. He deals in...rags."

The knight put himself between Remington and Martin. "Be gone with you, filth. Leave the lady alone."

"It's all right, truly," Remington, insisted, rising and putting her hand on the knight's armored arm. "He's not bothering me. By the way, I do not know your name, my lord."

He looked at her through cool green eyes. "Sir Steven de Norville, my lady. I serve Peter de Courtenay."

She smiled, hoping to distract him from Martin. "You have been most kind, sir. Have you eaten?"

He glanced at the nuns hovering in the alcove by the kitchens. "Indeed. But the sisters are most uncomfortable with any contact you and I have. Which is why I must linger so far away, in the halls, to protect you," he lingered a glance on Martin. "Keep to yourself, fool, or I shall remove you."

Giving Remington a polite bow, he strode away and Remington regained her seat. "Whew."

"No more talk, Remi. The nuns will surely kick me out of their sanctuary if I continue to molest you."

She obeyed, finishing her meal in silence. When the young nun came to return her to her room, she went willingly. Somehow, things did not look so bleak anymore.

Remington slept the afternoon away. It was hot and sticky and she had not slept well the night before. It was a deep, dreamless sleep until a knock on the door woke her.

The young nun was back, her pretty face flushed with the heat. "Your presence is requested, my lady."

Remington sat up groggily, rubbing her eyes. "Who?"

"I do not know, my lady. Would you come with me, please?"

She nodded, taking a moment to brush at her hair and splash cool water on her face. Still tired, she followed the nun.

The sun was setting and the torches in the hall were being lit as they traveled down the stairs and into the common room. From there, the nun led Remington down another narrow corridor and paused before an open door. The young woman indicated for Remington to enter.

Courtenay's knights were standing on either side of the door. Steven de Norville looked at her, his eyes unreadable, and she was understandably puzzled.

Suddenly hesitant, Remington slowly entered the archway. But her hesitance was fleeting when she saw Gaston and Father de Tormo inside the room.

She let out a whoop and flew into Gaston's arms. He swept her against him, holding her so very tightly. She was so happy she was shaking and laughing and crying all at the same time, and he clutched her fiercely. The very faint smell of her perfume, the fragrance he had purchased for her, filled him like a heady drug. His throat was so constricted with emotion that he couldn't speak for a moment.

Behind them, someone cleared his throat. "My lord de Russe," Sir Steven said quietly. "I am supposed to be present for any and all meetings."

Gaston pulled his face out of Remington's hair. "Wait out in the hall," he said to the priest, ignoring the knight.

De Tormo rose from his seat and moved to the door. "Grant them a minute, de Norville, and then we shall rejoin them."

Gaston waited until the door closed, and then he kissed her feverishly. She responded, whimpering weakly as their lips met and their tongues intertwined. After the hellish night Gaston had spent, he needed to feel her more than he needed to breathe.

"Are you all right, angel?" he finally managed to speak. "Have you been treated well?"

She nodded eagerly. "Verily. All have been kind to me. My God, Gaston, what is happening?"

He sat in the nearest chair and drew her onto his lap, holding her a moment as he collected his thoughts. He had not slept a wink last night. His eyes roved over her beautiful face as he spoke.

"Guy has given me his terms, Remi. All terms were agreed to and de Tormo drew up the contract. Guy signed it about an hour ago, and now we need your signature on a similar contract."

Her face lit up, her smile as bright as the sun. "He agreed? Oh, Gaston." She threw her arms around his neck and squeezed him tightly. But then, as if the horrors of the imagined terms occurred to her, her grip slacked and she pulled back to look him in the eye. "What were the terms?"

He touched her cheek gently. "His freedom, which Henry granted. And the return of Mt. Holyoak."

Her heart sank; she knew how much Gaston had grown to love the keep. "I am so sorry, my love."

He shook his head. "I am not. I have something far more valuable that an old building. I have you."

She smiled. "So you do. Is that all he asked for? I cannot believe his terms were so simple. He told me that the annulment would cost me dearly, and...."

"That was not all, angel," Gaston interrupted her. "At first, he wanted to marry one of your sisters to replace you, but Nicolas and I insisted both Jasmine and Skye were already married and with children. Mind that you do not refute our facts."

Her eyes widened. "How clever of you. My God, did he really want to marry Jasmine or Skye in my stead? How awful."

He nodded faintly, dreading what was coming next. His grip on her tightened. "And Dane...he demands that Dane be left in his care."

She blinked, gazing at him as if she had not understood a word he'd said. He felt her stiffen, slowly, like water rising. It started at her feet and rippled up to the top of her head.

"He shall not keep my son."

"I had to agree to it, for now," he said evenly. "But what happens after we gain our annulment is another matter."

She stared at him. "You agreed? You agreed? What gives you the right to agree to a term like that? He's my son, for God's sake. I shall not let that man have him!"

"Most likely, he will never get the chance," Gaston said. "Henry intends to keep Guy imprisoned until all proceedings are complete. By the time that takes place, I will have Dane spirited off. But for now, I must leave him there."

She pulled herself off his lap, her face gone taut. "And my sisters?"

"Going to join their husbands at Clearwell."

"Charles?"

"He shall stay, unless he wishes to accompany my army," Gaston replied.

"He shall want to go," she said shortly. "Which will leave Dane, alone, at Mt. Holyoak. I shall not agree to this, Gaston. I will not leave my son at the mercy of his father."

He sighed heavily. "I realize how you feel about this, Remi. I feel the same way, but I saw no other alternative."

She had moved to the other side of the room. When she faced him, her expression was hard. "I will not agree to that term."

"Then there will be no annulment."

Her jaw ticked and tears stung her eyes, fixed on Gaston's smoky gray orbs. "Then I will seek sanctuary for my son and myself within the church. I will do that before I agree to that term, Gaston. I mean it."

"Do not be so stubborn. I told you that Dane will never even see his father, not if all works as it should."

"Nothing has worked as it should!" She exploded. "Nothing! You promised me I would never have to see Guy, yet I have. You told me that Henry would fight for you, but I have yet to see the evidence. Nothing is working as you have said, Gaston, and I cannot believe you anymore."

He looked at her as if he had been struck. All of the calm was gone from his expression, all of the patience. He was deeply hurt. "I have never deliberately lied to you. I have always tried to prepare you for what might come."

Her anger, her desperation, was gaining speed. Her eyes darkened, bright with tears. "How could you trade my son away?" she hissed.

"I did not trade him away, Remi," he said quietly. "I agreed to the term, but only to gain the signed consent. Guy only did it to drive a wedge between us. He knew how you would react."

She turned away from him, tears spilling over. "Does my contract bear that term? Must I agree to it, too?"

"Aye."

"And if I sign it and we go back on the term and bring Dane to Clearwell, can the church come and take my son away?" her voice was a shaking whisper. "Can they return him to Guy?"

"He will not be with us at Clearwell," Gaston said softly. "When I take Dane from Mt. Holyoak, I will take him to another house to foster. He will never be with us at Clearwell."

"How can you do that?" She turned to look at him deliberately. "If Guy is legal guardian, with all say in his future, you will have no decision in his future whatsoever."

He swallowed hard; she saw it. Then, he stood, removing his helm and scratching at his scalp. Apparently he had no answer, and it angered and scared her all the more.

"You are asking me to relinquish all rights to my son," she hissed in desperation. "You are asking me to give him over to a man who is a beastly monster. There is no telling what he would do to Dane without me and my sisters there to take his aggressions out on. Gaston, I would rather remain married to Guy than see that happen. I will not give up my son. Not even for you."

He looked at her. His face was expressionless except for the naked, raw pain in his eyes. It seemed to reach out and grab her, matching the pain in her heart.

"I cannot believe you said that."

"And I cannot believe you would disregard my son's welfare simply to obtain your wants. Do your own desires mean so much to you that you would cast aside an eight year old boy who worships the ground you walk on?"

"I love him, too, Remi. You are not being fair," he said quietly. "Obviously, I do not intend to honor that particular term. I did not realize it would create such a conflict between us."

"Oh? And just how do you intend to hide my son from the church and his legal guardian? Keep him hidden in the vault for years until the matter is forgotten? Or send him far away so that I will never see him again?" Her insides were eating themselves out, her emotions raging. "You are asking me to sign a binding contract, one that can literally be enforced. Do you not think that Guy would make our lives miserable for years using his leverage with Dane? We will never be rid of him."

"I am not concerned with it," he repeated. "If I was, I would not have agreed."

"You had no right to agree," she said coldly. "I will not allow it. I will not surrender my son."

His heart was breaking in a million pieces. "Those were his terms, Remington. All or nothing."

"Then I choose nothing," she whispered. "Gaston, I love you more than life itself. I suppose if it were to come down to it, I love you more than my son. But I will not give up the very reason that has kept me living until I met you. You ask too much."

His face was ashen. "You do not mean that."

"I do. Every word. There will be no annulment," she whispered. "Since you are keeping Mt. Holyoak, I will not seek sanctuary with Dane. He can stay and foster with you. But I will seek it for myself. I will not go back to Guy, and I will not marry a man who would knowingly give away my son."

He sank into the nearest chair with a thud. His eyes were wide with disbelief. "Remi, you can't mean any of this. Think about what you are saying."

"I have," she couldn't look at him; her pain threatened to tear her apart.

"You would hate me for loving you so much that I was willing to do anything?" he asked hoarsely. "You are not being fair, love, in any of this. I would not knowingly give Dane up, but I do not see where we have any choice. I still do not believe we are giving him up. He will be sent away to foster somewhere, out of Stoneley's reach."

"By whose authority?" She swung around to him, tears wetting her cheeks. "When I sign that contract, I sign away my rights. I cannot order my son away to foster; only Guy can do that. And I swear to you, he will not. He shall keep my son with him, if only to torture me and he knows it."

Gaston gazed back at her, hearing her words over and over, *I cannot believe you anymore; No annulment; I will not give up my son, not even for you.*

"What would you have me do, Remi?" he asked softly. "Return to Guy and tell him that you will not agree to his last term?"

She couldn't think anymore; her mind was fogging over with despair and confusion. Her stomach was starting to lurch again and she felt faint.

"Go away, Gaston," she whispered. "I cannot think anymore. Just... go away."

The pain, the anguish of yesterday was nothing compared to the pain and anguish he felt at this moment. "I love you, Remi. More than anything, I love you."

Hot tears spilled down her cheeks as she faced the wall. "Go away and do not come back. I do not want to see you anymore."

He stood up, his body rigid. "Do not say that. Do not even suggest it."

"Get out!" she suddenly shrieked. "Go back to Mt. Holyoak and stay there. I do not want to see you ever again."

He was pale and shaking. "If I leave, Remi, you most certainly will never see me again. Think about what you are asking."

She put her hands on the stone wall, leaning her forehead against it. Her soft sobs filled the room. "I... will not... give up my son. I... hate you for... suggesting it."

"You would give me up instead?"

She did not answer, continuing to sob. Without another word, Gaston quit the room.

CHAPTER TWENTY-EIGHT

February 1487
Somerset, England

Winter this far south was not such a terrible thing. Remington stood by the hearth, folding freshly washed laundry, feeling the warmth of the fire against her flesh.

And there was laundry aplenty, as there usually was on laundry day. She continued to fold rough woolen underwear; just like the kind she had been wearing all these months to remind mortals of their vanity. But with her itching belly, woolen underwear was torture. There were days when she wore no underwear at all simply because she couldn't bear it.

Next to her, Martha was folding briskly. "Keep up the pace, Remington. There is much more to do."

Remington smiled at her friend, younger than she and a ward of the church. Her family had perished some years ago, leaving young Martha an heiress. Edward had placed her in the care of Prioress Mary Margaret of Wells Abbey, and the nuns of the abbey had raised her from birth.

"Faster, Remi," Martha urged, pushing a stray lock of pretty brown hair from her face.

"I cannot move so fast these days," Remington remarked, tossing a folded garment on the pile.

Martha nodded sympathetically. "How much longer do you have to go? Seven weeks? You shall never make it."

"I hope I do," Remington patted her hugely swollen stomach. "I should not like to give birth to a seven-month baby."

Martha's blue eyes roved over Remington. She knew little about her friend, only that she was escaping a bad marriage. Prioress Mary

Margaret knew the whole story, of course, but she was the only one. No one else seemed to know much about the beautiful pregnant woman.

Missives came for her all of the time, but she never read them. She sent them back, unopened, and continued with her new life. She had traded in all of her beautiful dresses for those of coarse linen or wool, all of her jewelry for headbands and aprons. Once, a man dressed in armor from head to toe came to see her, but the prioress sent him away. Someone said he was Matthew Wellesbourne, the White Lord, but no one had asked Remington about it. She would not tell them, anyway.

Missives came from the north of England all the time. She never read any of them, but she had sent one north. Only one missive in reply to dozens she must have received. Indeed, lovely Lady Remington was a mystery.

Wells Abbey was a small establishment, gleaning the Somerset countryside and schooling the young peasant children. It was a peaceful existence, devoted to knowledge and charity. It was a life completely different from the one Remington had left, and she consumed it eagerly. Anything to forget Gaston!

But it was difficult to forget him every time she felt the child move, which was constantly. Every time she closed her eyes, she saw his face. There wasn't a night that went by that she did not dream of his hands on her body, his mouth against hers. And there wasn't a night that passed that she did not cry softly for the want of him.

But she had to separate herself from him. Every day, she repeated their last conversation in her mind and she was torn between great remorse and great anger. How could he have agreed to surrender Dane? How could she have been so cruel as to tell him she could not believe him anymore? Why had she been so brutal to him, saying things she did not mean, telling him to leave her be? It all came down to one thing; that he had traded her son like a commodity to gain an annulment. She would not do it, and she knew Guy would not reconsider his term. She knew exactly what he had meant when he had said her request would cost her dearly. It had cost her her soul.

She had taken her anger out on Gaston. He had walked out and she had not seen him since. All of the missives she had returned unopened simply because she was afraid to read what had transpired as a result of her rage. She did not want to read of Gaston's hate for her in writing. She knew Guy was laughing at the both of them, and she was deeply sorry for Gaston. He was a proud man and had suffered through so much humiliation in his life, and she was grieved that she had contributed much to his humiliation.

The church had been more than happy to grant her sanctuary. Father de Tormo had selected Wells Abbey because the prioress was his cousin. But she had severed all contact with de Tormo after she had arrived at Wells, simply because she knew he would tell Gaston. And she did not want him to know anything.

She had no idea what had happened to Uncle Martin. After her fight with Gaston, he had disappeared and she had not seen him again. She hoped he was all right, but the fact was that he probably hated her, too, for being so stubborn and cruel. So did Henry, and everyone else who had supported Gaston. It made Gaston look like a fool, of course, to rally such support for no reason and she was miserably embarrassed for them both.

In the six months she had been at Wells, she had tried to forget about him. The one missive she had sent to Mt. Holyoak had been addressed to her son, to let him know what had happened. She wondered if he had let Gaston read it.

Tears tightened her throat every time she thought of Gaston finding another woman to love. With Mari-Elle dead and his annulment to her most likely complete, there was no reason for him not to marry again. The thought of him lying with another woman made her insane with grief and pain. But it would serve as just punishment to her if he had remarried.

God, she was so confused.

"Remington?" came a sharp voice.

Remington's head came up. Sister Josepha was standing a few feet away, her cracked face inquisitive. "My goodness, child, your mind doth leave you."

Remington smiled weakly. "'Tis the child, sister. It saps my brain, I think."

The old woman laughed. "I will have to take your word for it," she said. "You have a visitor, Remington. In the small solar."

Remington stiffened. "A visitor? Who?"

"Father de Tormo."

She shook her head, turning her nervous hands back to her laundry. "Send him away, sister. I have nothing to say to him."

Sister Josepha cleared her throat. "He says he is not leaving until he speaks with you. It is most urgent, he says."

A bolt of fear suddenly shot through her. What if something had happened to Gaston? She would have never known. She refused all missives, and there was one sent not three weeks ago that she sent back, unopened. She had not even looked at the seal. What if...?

Suddenly, she had to know. Panic flowed through her veins as she raced past Sister Josepha and into the narrow corridor that linked with the small visitor's solar.

Father de Tormo was shocked when she barreled in through the doorway, her face flushed and looking more beautiful than he had ever seen her. Her enormous belly protruded under the folds of her surcoat and he found himself staring at the newest part of her.

"My God! Remington!" he exclaimed. "So you are alive."

"Is Gaston all right?" she fired at him.

He blinked at the nearly shouted question. "Yes, of course. He..."

She threw up her hands. "No more. I do not want to hear about him. As long as he is well, I have quenched my fear. Be on your way, Father. I have chores to do."

She moved swiftly for the door, but he reached out and grabbed her. She started to protest, but he sat her heavily on a chair and gripped her arms. "Not so fast, lady. I have come a very long way to see you and you are going to listen. No one has been able to communicate with you for six months."

She twisted against him. She did not want to hear anything. She wanted to live in complete ignorance, far away from Gaston and the troubles of her world.

"You cannot hide here, you know," he said as if he were reading her mind. "You must deal with your problems, Remi. They will not go away!"

She stopped her struggles, refusing to look at him. "I am...I am not hiding."

"Then what do you call it?" de Tormo refuted gently. "I sent you here because I thought it would clear your head, but instead, you have become a hermit. This is not what I intended."

She could feel the tears starting and she fought against them. "I am happy here, father. I like it. I never want to leave."

"Not even to marry Gaston?"

Her head snapped up sharply and she suddenly realized she was talking to someone who had recently seen Gaston. But she couldn't get past the confusion, the agony of her grief. "No."

"You do not love him anymore?"

The tears started; she couldn't help it. "More than life, Father. More than anything. But I cannot abandon my son for the love of a man."

De Tormo sighed. "You are still angry about that?"

"Why shouldn't I be?" she demanded. "He was willing to...."

"He was only doing what he thought was best, what he thought you would want," when she started to protest, he put up his hand. "He assumed you had faith in him that all would work out in the end. He thought you trusted him."

"I do!" she snapped, and then hung her head miserably. "I did. Oh, I do. My God, Father, I am so confused I do not know anything anymore."

De Tormo sat down opposite her. "And you hope to clear your mind wearing woolen drawers and working dawn until dusk? Has it helped?"

She shook her head, wiping at the silent tears. "No."

"Do you want to return to London?"

"No!" she exclaimed, standing up. Her movements were agitated. "I... I am trying to forget about Gaston, and I cannot do that in London."

"Trying to forget about him? Why in the bloody hell would you want to do that?"

She stopped pacing, only stood there hanging her head. "You said you still love him," de Tormo reminded her.

"But he surely does not love me, not after all of the heartache and trouble I have caused him," she said quietly. "It's better this way, Father. I am away from Guy, and away from Gaston. No more trouble."

"Gaston is devastated, Remington," de Tormo said softly.

Her head came up, her eyes red-rimmed. "Did he send you here?"

"No," the priest confessed. "I came of my own accord. He's a prideful, stubborn man. He shall not come begging."

She stiffened. "And I shall not grovel at his feet. Why are you here, then?"

"To try and talk some sense into you," de Tormo said. "He's not the same man, Remi. He's bitter and distant and... so cold. He never smiles anymore. When you left, you took his heart with you."

She thought on that a moment, rubbing at her belly when the babe kicked firmly. "Does he hate me?"

De Tormo shook his head. "Never."

"What about Guy? The annulments?"

"His annulment with Mari-Elle was complete in October," de Tormo answered. "Guy remains in the Tower, still recovering from his wounds."

She looked at him curiously. "Wounds? What wounds?"

"The wounds Gaston dealt him the night you were taken from the Tower," de Tormo explained. "Did not Gaston tell you? He nearly killed Guy wringing forth the man's terms for consent."

She shook her head, surprised. "Nay, he never told me. He beat him up?"

"Pounded him within an inch of his life," de Tormo replied. "He thrashed Nicolas when the young knight tried to stop him. It was an ugly scene."

Remington dropped her head. Gaston had not told her any of that, only that Guy had agreed to consent. What was it he had said? That Guy would have done anything to drive a wedge between them, and that he knew Dane would be the wedge? Her mind began to swirl, realizing that Guy had probably thrown the terms regarding Dane in at the last minute. Gaston had physically hurt him, and Guy would retaliate by hurting Gaston far deeper. Dear God...Guy knew her so well that he knew how she would react to such a suggestion. Gaston, so desperate and unbalanced because of her removal, had agreed.

She began to shake. She had played right into Guy's hands...again.

"My dear God," she whispered, sinking against the wall. "What is it that I have done?"

De Tormo frowned. "What? I do not understand."

She let out a loud gasp, her hands to her head. "I have been so foolish, Father. I have ruined everything."

De Tormo stood up. "My God, Remington, I hope this means you are finally coming to your senses."

She looked at him, her hand over her mouth with the horror of what had happened. "How could I....oh, Father, I shouldn't have said what I did. I have always regretted it, but I did not want to admit it. I should have trusted him!"

De Tormo sighed heavily, saying a silent prayer of thanks. "If you two aren't the most stubborn people I have ever had the misfortune to come across."

"Oh, God, he hates me," Remington moaned. "He would have come himself if he did not."

"He tried sending you missives, but you did not respond," de Tormo told her. "You sent them back unopened. He even sent Wellesbourne because he thought mayhap your anger would not be so great on a middleman, but you sent Wellesbourne away, too. I tell you, Remington, he's simply not the same man since you left."

She stared at him, her face glazed with misery and hope. "Where is he, Father?"

De Tormo blinked. "Warminster. Gaston is now the Duke of Warminster."

"*What?*" she burst.

"He's abandon Mt. Holyoak, because it reminded him of you," the priest said quietly. "He refuses to return to Clearwell at all. Henry pushed the dukedom down his throat, thinking it would ease the pain of his loss of you, and Gaston had no choice but to accept."

"He's a duke?" she repeated in disbelief.

"A powerful one."

She shook her head slowly. "No one deserves it more than he for everything he has been through in his life. Do you know where my sisters and son are?"

"Nicolas married Skye. I performed the ceremony, in fact. As I also performed the mass for Antonius and Jasmine," de Tormo said. "They are all in Warminster, with the exception of Patrick. He's turned Clearwell into a larger training ground than even Mt. Holyoak and resides there. Gaston divides his time between Clearwell, London, and Deverill Castle."

"Deverill Castle?"

"His fortress in Warminster," the priest said.

"What about Mt. Holyoak? Is it vacant?" she asked, feeling greatly fatigued all of a sudden.

"For the most part," de Tormo replied. "It is still Gaston's and he keeps about one hundred and fifty men there, a skeleton guard for the region."

"What of Lord Botmore? Is he still raiding the area?"

"With Gaston gone, there is no need to," the priest answered. "Besides, Lord Brimley seems to be acting as Henry's liaison in the region. Henry himself traveled to Yorkshire to meet with the baron, knowing how Gaston felt about returning to Mt. Holyoak."

She was silent, feeling the babe kicking and rubbing at her belly. De Tormo watched her, thinking she looked ravishing pregnant. He'd never truly seen a beautiful pregnant woman up until now. He knew Gaston's stubborn, bitter heart would melt if he could only see her.

"Gaston's child is large," he commented. "You still have some time to go yet, do you not?"

"Six or seven weeks," she answered absently, turning her gaze to de Tormo. "I cannot travel, father."

"I know," he said softly. She would go to him if she could.

"Shall... shall I take a message to Gaston?"

She lowered her head again, folding her hands over her belly. "Tell him... tell him if he sends a missive, I will not return it unopened."

Wells was not far from Warminster. In fact, the distance could be traveled in a little over half a day. There were thousands of times when Gaston wanted to jump on a horse and ride hard to the abbey, break the doors down and shake some sense into Remington. There was not a minute that passed that he was not thinking of her, wondering how she was faring, wondering if she had stopped hating him.

She was the reason he had accepted Warminster. He could be close to her in Warminster, much closer than Clearwell or Mt. Holyoak. Even if she did not want to see him, he could still be close to her. But having missive after missive returned unopened nearly killed him. Not a drinking man, he had drunk himself into a stupor every time a missive had returned untouched.

He relived their last conversation nightly. She did not trust him anymore. She did not want to see him anymore. His stomach hurt so terribly that he had taken to drinking cow's milk in the morning to sooth it.

With Henry's new recruits divided between Clearwell and Deverill Castle, he was amply occupied with his duties. In a desperate attempt to divert his attention from his agony, he had taken to training the men personally. Having amassed at least fifteen more pounds on his already massive frame, he was more muscular and tighter than ever before and looked forward to the grueling regime he had set forth for the men. It helped him to forget, even if his men thought they were training under the devil himself.

When de Tormo had arrived from Wells late one night with news of Remington, Gaston had turned into an emotional bundle and downed two big bottles of wine as the priest told him of Remington, of their conversation. Nicolas and Antonius had sat in on the first few minutes of the meeting for emotional support, but left at the priest's insistence. Without Arik's wisdom, Gaston often felt a bit lost when he was feeling particularly emotional. Arik always managed to calm him down somehow. Matthew was the head of reason, too, but he had a new family and his focus needed to be with them even though he had spent an inordinate amount of time with Gaston lately. At this moment, however, Gaston was without him and quickly growing unsteady.

He had stopped drinking when de Tormo told him that Remington promised to read any missive he should decide to send. It had been enough for him to toss the bottles in the hearth and draw forth vellum. But he had been too drunk to write, and de Tormo took over the duties. They had wasted an entire piece of valuable vellum because Gaston couldn't decide what exactly he wished to say. Everything sounded too emotional, or too detached, or just plain silly.

He just couldn't seem to tell her what he was feeling on a piece of parchment. He had to go and see her, beg her forgiveness, to see her once more. All of his pride and bitterness was forgotten, replaced by a soaring hope.

De Tormo couldn't have been more pleased. He was glad he had taken the chance to go and see Remington, pleased that Gaston was surmounting his considerable pride in the matter. He only hoped the brandy would not make him forget everything he had vowed come morning.

He never got the chance to make good on his vows the next day. Henry had trouble in southern Yorkshire at a major stronghold known as Spofforth. Gaston mobilized eight hundred men and sent a missive to Clearwell for four hundred more. Even as both armies moved northward, his mind was with Remington, aching with every fiber in his body to see her. He wondered if she would take the delayed response as a negative reaction. Dear God, he hoped not.

He did so want to see her himself, personally. Since it was an impossibility, he sent de Tormo back to Wells Abbey to tell Remington that he would come when time allowed to see her himself. The priest was only too happy to comply.

As Gaston and his mighty army went northward to Spofforth, de Tormo mounted his small mare and took six soldiers with him for his mission of peace back to the abbey.

Gaston returned to Deverill Castle almost three weeks later. His new keep outside of Warminster welcomed him with open gates and an honor guard, as befitting the duke. The small skirmish had been overwhelmingly successful in Henry's favor, an insignificant battle with two minor barons. Spofforth had held magnificently, and to Gaston went the victory.

As his army entered the huge bailey in the dark of night, Gaston's thoughts were already on Remington. A thousand torches lit the night sky as he dismounted Taran, leaving Antonius and Nicolas in charge of dismantling the army. He knew de Tormo was inside, waiting for him with Remington's reaction, and he had to speak with him. Were the reaction favorable, he would leave for Wells Abbey this night.

The great double doors to the castle were open and the first sight to greet him was Jasmine and Skye, wrapped against the chill of the castle. Their pretty faces were pale and drawn.

"Where is de Tormo?" he demanded, foregoing any greeting.

"Not here," Jasmine said, extending her hand. There was a rolled, sealed piece of vellum. "This came this morning, Gaston."

Gaston stared at it a moment before snatching it away, breaking the seal. There were only three words:

Come immediately. De Tormo

Gaston couldn't help it; his stomach lurched and he crushed the parchment in his fist.

"What is it?" Jasmine demanded. "One of the priest's men brought it. What does it say?"

He was shaking; sweat was beading on his upper lip. "I have to go."

Skye was starting to cry and Jasmine dashed forward, grasping Gaston's arm. "For God's sake, Gaston, what is it? Has something happened to Remington?"

His voice was quivering when he spoke. "I do not know. I have to go."

Taran had already been taken away when he reached the bailey. Panic ruled his brain; he took the nearest mount and set out for Wells Abbey. Nicolas and Antonius saw him ride off, too far away to yell to him. Puzzlement was rampant, but they stuck to their orders and continued to dismantle the troops. Wherever he was going, he did not need them, else he would have summoned their assistance.

Gaston rode like the devil. His mount was a warmblood, not too winded, and took his commands easily. Armor and all, he weighed over four hundred pounds, but the horse handled him well.

The moon above was full and bright, like a great silver plate in the sky. The landscape around him, softly rolling hills that would be green and fragrant in another month or so, passed by him an eerie gray color. It served to fit his mood, mindless and bleak. Looking at the countryside, his terror suddenly took on a shape.

He was afraid to anticipate the reason for de Tormo's urgent missive. Were he to imagine the possibilities, he would transform into a quivering lump of flesh, unable to function. He had to retain his sanity just long enough to discover the reason for the missive. Only afterward would he determine his reaction.

When he reached Wells Abbey an hour before dawn, his horse collapsed underneath him and died.

Loaded with armor and weapons, the war machine known as the Duke of Warminster marched into Wells Abbey. He paused in the dimly lit foyer, raising his faceplate as a gaggle of nuns hovered nearby.

"Where is de Tormo?" he demanded. "Better yet, where is Lady Remington?"

One nun, an older lady with a creased face, approached him and bowed respectfully. "I am Sister Josepha. Who are thou that wouldst invade our sanctuary?"

Above his anxiety, he realized he must look like the devil himself to these women. He tried to calm his brusque manner.

"I am the Duke of Warminster, Gaston de Russe," he said calmly. "Would you please tell Father de Tormo that I am here? He sent me a missive to come right away."

The nuns in the corner began to whisper to each other urgently, two of them rushing off in a flurry. Gaston heard two words, *Dark One*.

Sister Josepha maintained her calm demeanor. "He is expecting thou. I shall send someone to fetch him."

She called to a young girl hovering nearby to fetch the father and beckoned Gaston to the visitor's solar. Being so close to Remington, Gaston's skin was prickling even as the old nun poured him a drink into a crude wooden cup. He had not been this close to her in months, and his excitement made his skin hurt. He did not want the offered beverage, but took it anyway.

"Where is Lady Remington?" he asked again. "I would see her as well."

The old woman cast an appraising eye at him. "Thou art the husband?"

He blinked and shook his head. "Nay."

She nodded. "Ah. The lover. The Dark Knight."

He almost choked on the sour wine. "I intend to be her husband, one day." He did not know what else to say.

The old nun nodded faintly and Gaston began to feel uncomfortable as well as anxious. What had Remington told these women of the cloister?

"She did not tell me, my lord," the nun finally said, a twinkle in her dull eyes. "Prioress Mary Margaret confided in me one day, and we prayed for thou both. It would seem that Remington doth not put great stock in God. We felt it our duty."

Gaston set the cup down with a gentle thud. "Thank you, sister. Your concern is appreciated."

"There are apparently a great many people concerned for you both," Sister Josepha said. "Our prayers have been powerful indeed."

"And how is that?" Gaston asked.

She smiled, a cracked ancient smile. "Thou has come, has thou not? Thou are not so dark, as the name implies. God speaks and thou listens."

Gaston nodded faintly, not knowing what else to say. His mind was increasingly preoccupied with Remington and de Tormo. He hesitated to ask the old nun where Remington was; she had avoided his question twice.

They heard rapid footfalls coming down the corridor. Gaston smelled de Tormo before he saw him.

"Gaston! Thank God," he exclaimed quietly. "You are finally here!"

Gaston forgot all about the old nun standing behind him. "What's wrong?"

De Tormo glanced at the woman behind Gaston; Sister Josepha moved for the door discreetly, but she did not leave entirely.

"It's Remington, Gaston," he said quietly. "She entered into labor two days ago and...."

Gaston suddenly grabbed his head in agony. "Dear God, she is dead!"

"Nay, Gaston, she is not," de Tormo assured him quickly. "But she... she is not well, not at all."

"Take me to her," Gaston was begging and de Tormo was struggling to keep the man calm. He put up his hands soothingly.

"Get hold of yourself, my lord, for there is much to tell," he instructed firmly. It would not do to have Gaston lose control early on. "Listen to me completely, if you would. Remington went into labor two days ago and delivered your children this morning. But she lost a great deal of blood in the births, Gaston. Too much blood, and she continues to lose a great deal of blood. A physic from Glastonbury is with her, and I must be completely honest with you when I say that her outlook is grim. The physic believes she will eventually bleed to death."

Gaston was literally white. His helm came off shakily, his face so white that his lips were gray. The smoky gray eyes were wide.

"Children?"

"Two girls. She named them Adeliza and Arica."

Gaston let out a ragged sigh, dragging his hands over his face. He could barely speak. "How are they?"

"Adeliza, the eldest, is well. But the physic says that something is wrong with Arica. He does not expect her to live. I have already given her last rites, and the prioress continues to pray over the babe," de Tormo was trying to be gentle, but there was simply no easy way to deliver such devastating news. "They are three weeks early, you know."

Gaston was looking at the floor. When his head came up, his cheeks were streaked with tears. "Take me to her," he rasped.

De Tormo was shocked at the emotional display from the feared, almighty Dark One. But his heart was breaking for the man, for Remington, and for the children. He was simply thankful for the fact that Gaston had come when he did.

He took Gaston down to the end of the corridor, followed closely by Sister Josepha. At the end of the hall was a narrow staircase. Remington's door was the first door to the right at the top of the stairs.

There were three or four nuns in the room, each busying them-selves with something or another. Gaston paid them no attention; his eyes were instantly riveted to the ashen figure on the bed and his tears flowed even faster.

She was buried under a mound of covers, her damp hair plastered to her pasty face. Her breathing was shallow and every so often she would twitch. The head of the bed was lowered dramatically, so much so that her feet were nearly sticking up in the air. She looked as if death were her shadow, waiting for the fleeting moment to step in and whisk her away.

He was oblivious of everyone else in the room; efficiently, mechani-cally, he began to unlatch his armor. Huge, heavy pieces fell on the floor as de Tormo and the elderly nuns struggled to cart them away. Gaston had eyes only for Remington; when he was completely free of his protective gear, he rolled up the sleeves on his heavy linen shirt and moved to the edge of the bed.

The physic was on the other side of the bed. "You are her husband, my lord?"

Gaston was so choked he could barely speak. He wiped at his tears with the back of his hand. "Aye."

The physic nodded faintly. "She has lost a good deal of blood, my lord. She continues to bleed and I have been unable to stop it. I have packed her, sewn her, but there has been no relief."

Gaston sniffed loudly, taking Remington's hand and holding it to his lips. His eyes never left her. "How much longer can she…will she…?"

"If she continues this way, she will not survive to the nooning meal," the physic said bluntly. "The next few hours will tell."

Tears fell from Gaston's eyes onto Remington's hand. He could only nod for the moment. "And my daughter?" he whispered.

"Her fate is consigned to God, my lord," the physic said softly. "She is too tiny to survive, I am afraid. The other female is healthy enough."

The physic moved away from the bed. Gaston sat on the floor next to Remington's head, holding her hand and crying silently. He had never cried in his life and had no idea how to stop his tears so he did not try; he let them flow.

The nuns vacated the room for the moment, leaving de Tormo standing at the doorway. Blinking back his own tears, he closed the door quietly.

The day dawned and still Gaston sat by Remington, stroking her hair. He spoke softly to her, speaking of anything he could think of, praying fervently that she would hear him in her stupor.

They had been so foolish to allow a misunderstanding to go so far. The time they had wasted bewildered him; she had told him to go away, and he had been stupid enough to listen. Why, by God's Bloody Rood, had he listened to her? He shouldn't have! He should have returned later when she was calm to finish their conversation. Instead, he had returned to the Tower and ceased all further annulment proceeding, purely out of anger.

He gazed at her dark head, more tears falling. How could he have been angry with her? God, he loved her so much. He refused to believe she was dying.

Shortly after dawn the physic and two nuns returned to the room.

"We must check her progress, my lord," the physic said. "You... may want to retreat for a few moments."

Gaston, gray and looking ill, rose stiffly to his full height. De Tormo stood in the doorjamb. "Why do not you visit your children, Gaston?"

Gaston turned woodenly toward the priest, his smoky gray orbs dull with pain and fatigue. "Arica is still alive?"

"She is," de Tormo reached out and took his arm. "Come and see your beautiful daughters."

Gaston passed a lingering glance on Remington and de Tormo pulled harder. "Come on. She is in good hands."

He allowed the priest to lead him from the room and the door shut softly behind them. De Tormo took Gaston into the very next room where several nuns were making themselves useful. His gaze was drawn to the make shift altar several feet away where two nuns rested on their knees, one holding a swathed bundle. He knew they held Arica.

"I would hold her," Gaston whispered, pointing feebly in the general direction of the altar.

They went over to the robed woman holding the swaddled bundle and de Tormo touched her on the shoulder.

"The father has arrived," he said quietly. "He would hold his child now."

The woman rose, assisted by de Tormo, and faced Gaston with a creased face and sharp eyes, eyes that looked into his very soul.

"My lord de Russe," she greeted. Her voice was sweet, like honey. Without hesitation, she held out the wrapped infant.

Gaston had never held an infant before; he had never even held Trenton. He extended his hands hesitantly and the nun saw his newness. Gently, she instructed him to crook his left arm, and she deposited Arica neatly in the fold.

He gazed down at his daughter, so very tiny that she could not have weighed any more than three of four pounds. Tears that had stopped not an hour ago suddenly came freely again, raining from his cheeks to the swaddling below.

"She has a great will to live, my lord," the prioress said softly. "We did not expect her to survive thus far, but she has. She is an eager eater."

Gaston couldn't speak; he was too choked with emotion. He could only gaze down on her tiny, perfectly beautiful face, feeling more pain and pride than he ever thought possible. Sobs were on the surface, but he swallowed them away.

"She... she is dark," he managed to whisper.

"So is her sister," de Tormo commented. "Both girls are as dark as their father. Poor lasses."

As if on cue, a lusty wail penetrated the air and Gaston turned to see Adeliza, laid out on the bed as a nun changed her swaddling. She was as red as a beet, waving her angry fists and screaming like a banshee. Through his tears, he smiled. "She has strong lungs."

De Tormo and the prioress glanced in the direction of the babe, too. "She's as healthy as an ox, my lord," the nun said. "She seemed to have taken all of the nutrients from this one. We did not even know there was another child until Remington's contractions continued even after she birthed the first babe," she peered affectionately at the tiny bundle in her father's arms. "This little lass was backwards. The physic had to pull her out by her feet."

Gaston shuddered at the thought of Remington going through such a painful, laborious birth. He cursed himself continuously for not being there for her and his tears threatened to overwhelm him. But he choked them back, swallowing hard, fighting to keep a rein on his surging emotions.

Mayhap God was punishing him for his sins by taking what was most precious to him. God had proven already that he was not particularly fond of Gaston by providing him a cheating wife and a lifetime of pain and humiliation. If Gaston thought praying might make the difference, he would have gladly dropped to his knees. But he knew from experience that God did not listen to his prayers.

If God could take away, only He could give back. He turned back to the prioress.

"You were praying for my daughter. I wish for you to continue," he whispered, gazing down at the little face. "And Remington ... you will pray harder for her."

"Sister Baptista has been praying for Remington since before dawn," the prioress indicated the other kneeling woman. "I call her my miracle worker. Her prayers are stronger than mine, I believe. God always listens to her."

Gaston nodded, wiping at his eyes with the back of his right hand. The babe jostled slightly, issuing forth a weak screech and frightening Gaston out of his skin.

"What's wrong? What have I done?" he demanded.

"Nothing, my lord," the prioress smiled. "'Tis good for her to cry and strengthen her lungs. Do not be alarmed."

He gazed down at his mewling daughter, his eyes wide with apprehension. De Tormo and the prioress exchanged amused glances, a bit of brightness amidst the worry and suffering.

In spite of what the prioress said, Gaston was scared to death to hear her cry. He started to talk to her, to soothe her, and no more than four words came out of his mouth and the babe stopped fussing. One baleful eye opened, looking at him, and he was astonished.

"She is *looking* at me," he exclaimed softly.

"Of course she is. She knows her father," the nun said confidently. "Speak to her, my lord. Let her hear you."

He obeyed, saying anything that came to mind. Arica continued to look at her father for quite a while before yawning a tiny yawn and closing her eye, fading off to sleep. Tears forgotten for the moment, Gaston was enchanted.

He dared to wander over to the bed where Adeliza lay, sleeping in the center of a mound of pillows. He spoke to both girls, telling them how much they looked like their beautiful mother, wondering aloud if their eyes would be sea-crystal green or his ugly brown, as he put it. The nuns tending Adeliza smiled encouragingly at him, telling him of his new daughter, and they were rewarded with a weak smile.

The physic entered the room, eyeing Gaston. Gaston caught the man from the corner of his eye and swung around rapidly.

"You may go back and sit with your wife if you wish," he said quietly.

The brief reprieve of anxiety and fear Gaston had enjoyed for the past few minutes suddenly returned full-bore, slamming him like a ton of bricks.

"How is she?" he asked hoarsely.

The physic looked tired. "The bleeding is lessening somewhat, a good sign. But she has still lost a tremendous amount of blood, my lord. She is very weak."

Gaston still clutched Arica. He felt sick to his stomach, and his head swam. Managing a weak nod, he moved past the psychic and back into Remington's room.

She was in the same position, only she had turned her face toward him. In the dim light, the contrast of her dark hair against her white skin was striking. Even her lips were white. Fighting off tears yet again, Gaston sank to the floor beside her head.

He stared at her a long, long time, holding Arica and watching Remington's ghostly face. He stopped fighting the tears after a while and simply let them fall. He'd never cried so much in his entire life.

"My God, Remi," he whispered. "Has it come to this? Will you die before I have a chance to tell you how much I love you and how sorry I am for what happened?"

Arica stirred at the sound of his voice and he rocked her gently. "I have brought Arica. She's beautiful, like her mother," he paused, his throat tight as he touched Remington's clammy face with his right hand. "Oh, please, Remi. Wake up, angel. I need you; the babes need you. Please do not leave us."

A sob bubbled out. And then another. Before he realized it, he dropped his chin to his chest and sobbed like a child. He simply couldn't help himself. He couldn't bear to face life without her.

He cried until there were no tears left. His face was swollen and pale, his eyes red and puffy. Remington twitched once in her stupor and his heart jumped, but it was an involuntary movement. He heard her sigh raggedly and he leaned forward and kissed her sweet lips.

The day progressed and dread began to fill him. The physic had told him that she would not survive the day if she did not begin to show signs of improvement, and his fear mounted. Grief threatened to overwhelm him, and he wrestled heavily with it.

Toward noon, he stood up, still clutching featherweight Arica. He gazed down at his tiny daughter, then stared hard at her. It took him a moment to realize that sometime that morning, she had passed away in his arms and he had not even noticed.

"Oh, God, no....," he breathed, touching the little face, looking for any sort of movement. There was none. Grief swept him. "Oh, God, no!"

His shout was heard throughout the entire abbey. De Tormo and the prioress threw open the door to Remington's room, but he barked them away savagely. They barely had time to back off when he was kicking the door closed, shaking the entire structure like an earthquake. He clutched the baby to his chest tightly, finding that he did indeed have more tears to spare, and wept loudly for his daughter.

"Gaston?" came a weak voice. "Gaston?"

Startled, he looked up to see Remington focusing on him. Her eyes were huge pools in her white face, and he could see they were full of concern. "Gaston, do not cry. Come here, my love."

It was far too much for him to take; he came apart. He fell to his knees, crawling the length of the room until he reached her bed. His sobs were deep and unbridled as he buried his face on Remington's chest, still holding the babe and feeling Remington's feeble hand on his head.

Remington was so weak she could barely move. She had heard his sobs at a distance until gradually, she had come around. It did not matter that she was on her deathbed and could barely move; what mattered was that Gaston was crying and she had to comfort him. She shushed him softly.

"Do not cry, my love," she whispered thickly.

"Oh, Remi," he sobbed. "Do not die, too."

"I won't, I promise," she breathed. "You came just in time."

He choked on an ironic guffaw, raising his head to look at her. "I was so foolish, angel. I let our argument go on and...."

She stilled him with a weak hand. "No more. 'Twas my fault and I am sorry. I never stopped loving you, Gaston. I said...hateful things. Forgive me."

He kissed her eagerly, shakily, still sobbing. "I love you, Remi. You had every right to be angry with me. Please...oh, God, please ...." He trailed off again, unable to continue.

She touched his head as it rested on her chest. She had not been so dazed that she had not seen the bundle in his arms. And she understood his words. *Do not die, too.* Her heart was twisting with grief.

"Arica?" she whispered.

He struggled to gain control of himself, lifting his head off her, still clutching the babe fiercely. "She... wasn't alone, Remi. I held her the entire time. She was here, with us."

Remington was too weak to cry, but the anguish gnawed at her with excruciating force. She closed her eyes, reaching out a feeble hand to touch the swaddling. "Give her to me."

He laid the babe next to her and Remington put her frail arms about the bundle, holding it close to her bosom. A lone tear trickled from the sea-crystal eyes. Gaston stood over the two of them, wiping at his face with the back of his hand, wishing he could make the grief and sorrow go away. He had never felt so utterly helpless!

"She was too small," Remington finally whispered. "Too small."

"I know," he smoothed her forehead with his trencher-sized hand.

She stared at the still babe a long while before turning her head to him, her eyes unnaturally bright against her pale face. "Are you all right? De Tormo said you went to war again."

He was back on his knees, wrapping his arms about the two of them. "I am fine. I thought of you every minute, every day. Ever since we fought, I have thought of nothing but you."

"You are a duke now," she whispered. "I am so proud of you, Gaston."

"It means nothing," he whispered back, pressing his face to her shoulder. "You mean everything. You and our children."

"How is Adeliza?" she asked.

"Fine," he replied, a bit of hope in his voice. "She's a loud little magpie. Screams like a banshee."

Remington smiled weakly. "I know. I heard her."

He did not want to talk anymore for the moment. He only wanted to hold the two of them, feeling Remington's life in his arms. He could do nothing more for Arica, and he felt the loss to his bones.

Suddenly, they both heard a weak cry. At the same time, they turned to the swaddled bundle in Remington's arms, only to see the tiny little mouth open again and cry like a kitten.

"Dear God...." Gaston breathed.

"She's not dead, Gaston!" Remington declared with as much excitement as she could muster. Weak, shaking hands began unwrapping the swaddling. "Look. She's moving!"

He was dumbfounded, watching as Remington unbound the child, revealing stick-thin arms and legs, wriggling about.

"She wasn't breathing, Remi, I swear it," he said helplessly. "She did not move when I touched her."

Remington stared at the tiny baby flailing about on the bed beside her. "Thank God! Look at her; she's moving!"

He couldn't believe what he was seeing. He would have sworn on his mother's grave that the babe was dead. But the tiny, skinny body before him was not dead in the least.

"I thought you did not believe in God," he leaned forward on her, reaching out a finger and touching the babe. His finger was bigger than one tiny arm.

"I do when I look at her, when I look at you," she whispered, fatigue and weakness overtaking her. "Wrap her up, please. I cannot."

Concern surged through him. "What's wrong, Remi? Are you feeling worse?"

"Just... tired," she breathed.

He wrapped the babe up as best he could, knowing it was nothing like the experienced swaddling of the nuns. He picked the infant up, clutching her to his chest and saying a silent prayer of thanks. Mayhap God would hear him, just this once.

De Tormo and the prioress were hovering near the door when Gaston opened it. Their faces were glazed with concern and apprehension.

Gaston smiled weakly, handing the babe over to the prioress. "She is unhappy. Mayhap she is hungry."

The woman accepted the child, confused but focused on the infant. "Is... is everything all right? You cried out and...."

Gaston put up a hand to stop her words. "Everything is fine. I think Remington could use some nourishment, too."

De Tormo watched the nun walk away, turning back to Gaston. "She's not dead? We thought that when you yelled, she had passed away."

Gaston was feeling his great fatigue and sagged against the doorjamb. But there was a faint smile on his face. "Nay, priest, she is not dead. In fact, we have had a most wonderful conversation."

De Tormo was amazed. He peered around Gaston, into the dim room where Remington still lay with her feet pointed skyward. He thought she was asleep until she raised a weak hand to him in acknowledgement.

"God be praised," de Tormo whispered, crossing himself. "Sister Baptista has come through once again."

Gaston pushed himself off the jamb. "I would be alone with her now, but I want to baptize both girls before dusk."

De Tormo nodded. "I already baptized Arica after she was born, but Adeliza has not yet been christened."

"She will be before the sun sets," Gaston said, his voice scratchy from all of the crying he had done. As de Tormo walked away, Gaston suddenly reached out and stopped him. "You know, I truly hated you when we first met, priest. How is it that you have become such a part of Remington and I?"

De Tormo cracked a smile. "I am not such an arrogant, pushy little bastard after all, am I?"

Gaston grinned, hearing his own words reflected. "You have your moments. I will be forever grateful for bringing me to my senses. I owe you a great deal."

De Tormo actually looked humble. "I am a romantic at heart, I suppose," he eyed Gaston warily. "But since you have declared your thanks, mayhap you will not be angry when I tell you that I took the liberty of giving Arica a middle name when I christened her."

"You did? What?"

"Why, Christine, of course. Arica Christine de Russe," de Tormo snorted. "We must honor the man who made her life possible, mustn't we?"

Gaston returned the snicker. "Then I suppose we should throw Henry's name in there somewhere, as well."

De Tormo sobered seriously. "What of the annulment now? Yours is complete - what about hers?"

Gaston sighed heavily. "I shall send word to Henry tomorrow. We begin proceedings all over again."

De Tormo glanced at Remington. "What about...?"

Gaston shook his head. "Not to worry. Dane will not be part of the terms, I can guarantee you that."

The men went their separate ways, de Tormo to the chapel, and Gaston back into the bedchamber with Remington.

Outside, the day was bright and green and heavenly, unusual for mid-March.

CHAPTER TWENTY-NINE

July, 1487

"I can't stand this squalling," Nicolas put his hands to his ears to block out the wailing babies.

"Then go away," Skye snapped.

Remington laughed at the young father. "It is your son doing most of the yelling, Nicolas. Notice that the girls are quiet."

Nicolas scowled. "Naturally, my son is the loudest and strongest. Isn't he, sweetling?"

Skye thrust her chin up and looked away; they had been quarreling since the morning about something nonsensical. Remington and Jasmine smiled at each other as they tended their respective broods in the large nursery. Gaston had had the massive bedchamber redone to accommodate the babies and their nurses, although the nurses were rarely alone with the children. As was uncommon in noble houses, the mothers wished to do most of the work.

Remington sat with Adeliza in her lap while Arica slept soundly in her crib. Mary went back and forth between her new sister and her two new cousins, trying to be helpful by retrieving a toy or making faces at the babies. Her own new sister, Sophia, responded readily to her, as did Adeliza and Arica, but grumpy little Robert wanted nothing to do with her. He screamed every time she came near him.

"When is Gaston due to return from London?" Jasmine asked as Nicolas tried to make his son smile.

"Soon, hopefully," Remington replied while a colicky Adeliza suckled her finger. "The annulment board must take time for the testimonies presented, and then I will have to go to London to testify. But I wish he would hurry; I have been here three weeks and have only seen him two of those days."

"But he was with you while you convalesced at Wells," Jasmine said. "He was with you for nearly two months. How can you complain over a few short weeks?"

Remington dropped her head and Jasmine bit her tongue; she knew what had happened, about the fight, the separation. It nearly killed Remington when Gaston brought her back to Deverill Castle with two new babies, only to abruptly leave her again.

"I am sorry, Remi," she said softly. "I did not mean to sound callous."

Remington shook her head. "You are right, of course," she raised her head again, brightly. "He sent Trenton and Dane to foster in Oxford with de Vere. Did I tell you that?"

"Oxford isn't far," Skye put in. "You can still see them on occasion."

Remington shrugged. "Neither boy has seen their new sisters yet. I was hoping Gaston would bring the boys home around Easter, but he did not want to leave me."

"I do not blame him," Nicolas said, triumphant that his son had smiled at him. "I would not have left you either after you nearly bled to death. How could he...."

Skye slugged Nicolas in the gut and he grunted loudly. "Shut your mouth. Have you no tact?"

Remington smiled weakly at the interplay. "It's all right, Skye. It does not upset me to talk about it."

"Well, it upsets me to hear it," Skye insisted. "When I think that you could have... oh, my. I am starting to sound like my husband."

Old Eudora bustled in, a snack for Mary on a tray. Remington watched the old woman; the fear out of her eyes, walking with hardly a limp. With the addition of Mary and the babes, Eudora was in heaven. She had a new sense of purpose, raising this new crop of children, just as she had practically raised Remington and her sisters. She paused a moment in her hustle to coo at Robert on his mother's lap, and to plant a kiss on Sophia's sleeping face.

Remington stood up, setting Adeliza down to nap. In the next crib slept Arica, as big as her sister easily. They both had their father's smoky gray eyes, but their dark hair had a distinct hint of auburn to it, like Remington's. And they were so identical that even Remington had difficulty telling them apart at times. To listen to Gaston speak about the twins, one would think he had fathered the Virgin Mary. She had never seen him so proud.

God, she missed him so. She left the nursery and wandered the wide, cool hall to the main stairs. Downstairs, a massive common room opened wide before her, Gaston's boar head banner hanging above the hearth. It was a receiving room mostly; the standard fully intended to intimidate all who entered the castle, reminding them of who was lord and master, Henry's Dark One, the mighty Duke of Warminster.

She passed by the cavernous dining hall, flying the same colors, as well as Henry's rose standard. The room could house hundreds. She had grown very fond of Deverill Castle, but she still had difficulty believing how very large it was. Even with her sisters, their children, and their husbands, she felt as if they were all rattling about the enormous structure. The entire village of Warminster could probably live most comfortably within the old walls.

Oleg met her as he bustled about his duties. As steward to the new duke, he had his hands full with Deverill Castle and Remington could see how much he was enjoying his new duties. He had actually put on a bit of weight with his new life, away from a master who beat him to serve a man who respected his abilities.

"Busy, I see?" she remarked with a smile.

He nodded vigorously. "Much, much to do. Cook says that three barrels of grain went bad with the rot and we must take immediate stock of all of our stores. It could be a blight."

"Goodness, I hope not."

Oleg shook his head again, mumbling rapidly about something or another and Remington fought off an amused smile at his state. As he brushed past her, she reached out her hand.

"Oleg, about Gaston," she said. "Do you remember the conversation we had before he came to Mt. Holyoak? Do you remember how apprehensive you were?"

He paused, looked puzzled, and then nodded. "Unfounded, my lady."

She smiled broadly. "I am glad you have come to realize it. And, by the way, he does not have a tail nor does he sprout wings come nightfall."

Oleg returned her smile, looking somewhat sheepish. "He's not an incubus, then? Thank God. I was wondering how I was going to explain to God why I had willingly worked for the devil."

Remington snickered as he scuffled away. She moved on toward the carved front doors of the castle, so heavy they individually weighed as much as the war horses. They were polished to a high sheen by the servants, servants Gaston had brought from Mt. Holyoak. In fact, except for the skeleton guard he kept there, the castle was empty of every last servant. They had all been quite happy to come south to serve the new duke.

She smiled to herself, feeling the warm wind caress her face. Beyond the walls of the structure was the village of Warminster. South of that on the horizon, she could see the green line indicating the edge of Warminster Forest, a dense, huge growth that covered most of Gaston's providence, spilling into Essex. Warminster wasn't as populated as some providences, but it was lush and rich. She liked it a great deal.

There were times when she missed Yorkshire, the sheep, and the people she had grown up with. But she would not have traded what she had now to return to what she left, not ever. Her new life with Gaston, wife or no, was far more precious than faded memories.

She did miss Dane terribly, however, but she knew Gaston had done what he felt was best for him. Sending he and Trenton to foster with the earl of Oxford had been a brilliant maneuver, a place where Guy could not have physically retrieved Dane if he tried. The earl's keep was too fortified, and Dane was surrounded by soldiers who knew who he was and would protect him.

She gloated at Guy's expense; he could spend his entire life trying to regain his son to no avail. Dane was safe. She was safe. Annulment or no annulment, she was home to stay.

There was a good deal of activity on the walls and she shielded her eyes from the bright sun to see what was going on. Deverill Castle had a massive outer wall that was nearly eight feet thick. The bailey had been a massive, oblong-shaped yard that he had divided and even now men were working on an inner, protective wall. Portions of the castle were actually built into the wall, but the rise upon which the castle sat afforded it a great deal of protection.

But it had not been enough protection for Gaston; he had fallen in love with the design of Mt. Holyoak and set teams of men to shearing off the sides of the rise and tunneling out a deep moat, making the fortress extremely inaccessible to invading armies.

A small party of riders entered through the outer gates and Remington recognized Father de Tormo. Happily, she moved out to greet him.

"Father!" she called.

De Tormo brushed the dust on his brown woolen robes, the familiar stench greeting Remington's nostrils as she closed in on him. He actually smiled. "My lady! How wonderful you look. Why, when I last saw you, you were as round as a cow after birthing the babes. All of the weight has left you."

She looked down at herself, wearing a lightweight linen surcoat that emphasized her newly small waist, yet her breasts were plump with milk and enticingly large.

"Most of it," she said, thinking his comment to be undiplomatic, but letting it slide. "Where's Gaston?"

"Still in London." De Tormo took her arm and together they walked for the castle. "He sent me to relay his messages to you."

"Does the church still believe I am at Wells Abbey?" she asked.

He nodded. "Still. Mary Margaret is a party to our lie; Henry's men visited the abbey two weeks ago and she told them that you were still recovering after your most difficult birth, in isolation. They left and reported back to Henry and Courtenay."

"But what of the men you brought with you?" she gazed over her shoulder, seeing four soldiers with Canterbury's tunics.

"Won't they tell that they have seen me?"

"They do not know you on sight," de Tormo took her into the castle. "Do not worry overly. I shall make up some excuse should the question arise. For all they know, I am here to deliver a message to Gaston's cousin."

She took him into the solar, ordering wine and food. When the serving girl left, she turned to him.

"What's going on? Why is he still in London?"

"The annulment proceedings are taking longer than he thought," he replied. "Henry sent for the men you listed to testify on your behalf;

Lord Brimley and his sons, Lord Ripley, Sir Alfred Tarrington from Crigglestone Castle. Ripley even went so far as to declare he would kill Stoneley on sight if he ever saw him again; the man was most convincing."

"And what of the men presiding over the council? Are they men of good standing?"

De Tormo raised an eyebrow. "You mean the Board of Inquisition? Only the most powerful men in the country, next to Henry, of course. John Morton, bishop of Ely and his brother Robert, the bishop of Worcester; Christopher Urswick, dean of York; Richard Fox, bishop of Exeter; the papal legate John of Imola, and the archbishop himself, Thomas Bourchier. Believe me, Remi, 'tis a mighty papal council."

She swallowed, feeling rather apprehensive. "Are they receptive? Can you tell?"

De Tormo shrugged. "'Tis difficult to say. But you have a most convincing argument, and they have yet to put me on the stand. I shall persuade them without a doubt that your marriage to Guy must be dissolved."

She let out a long sigh and sat heavily, chewing her lip thoughtfully. "Who testified on Gaston's behalf?"

The serving wench brought in a huge tray of cheese and bread and de Tormo dug in with gusto. "No one, yet. But the men gathered behind him are the likes of which even I have never seen, Remington."

She felt a small surge of hope. "Truly?"

De Tormo nodded, chewing noisily on a piece of cheese. "Statements on his behalf will not begin until after yours are finished." He eyed her a moment. "Guy has demanded to speak, too. You should be aware of that."

She stiffened slightly. "All the better. Then they can see for themselves how evil and insane he is."

De Tormo shrugged; pleased she was looking at it from that angle. As far as he was concerned, his main worry was that Guy would present himself as the victim in all of this. The man was cunning enough to make such an attempt, but he did not voice his thoughts. She had enough to worry over.

"Gaston should be returning in a few days to take you back to London," the priest said. "Mayhap you should think on packing."

"I have already packed," she said. "In fact, Jasmine made me two new surcoats to take. I am ready to go, father. I just wish...he'd hurry."

De Tormo smiled. "And do you know who else wishes he would hurry? Martin. He is dying to see you. Gaston did not want him coming with me to Deverill Castle, afraid he would never leave."

She smiled. "I miss Uncle Martin. He came to me at St. Catherine's, but I only saw him once. He said he was planning to trail me so that I would always be protected, but he did not."

"Because Gaston recognized him in the common room when we came to see you," de Tormo replied, licking his fingers. "He chased his uncle out and told him he would lock him in the Tower if he was insistent on disobeying Gaston's wishes."

She understood, a faint smile on her lips. She would have loved to have heard the argument between Gaston and Uncle Martin, both men grimly determined to do their own will. She was surprised she had not heard the shouting that surely must have taken place.

"Will I be staying at Braidwood?"

"Most likely not," de Tormo answered. "I fear St. Catherine's shall again be your home. By the way, Remi, no one but Henry and a select few know of the babes. Not even Guy knows. Gaston thought it best not to tell anyone, lest you be viewed as...well, a concubine."

"You mean a whore?" she smiled ironically. "I do not care, Father, truly I do not. But I will keep silent."

He lifted his eyebrows sympathetically; she and Gaston loved each other so that it was unfair to brand her as a kept woman. It simply wasn't the case. "Speaking of which, how are the little ones?"

Her face brightened. "Fat and happy. They are looking more like Gaston every day. And Adeliza is already cutting a tooth."

"Is that so?" de Tormo smiled. "Well, I must be sure not to stick my finger in her mouth lest I get bitten. Gaston misses them dreadfully, you know. They are all he speaks of."

She smiled sadly as the priest stood up, wiping his hands on his robe. She suddenly caught a heady whiff of body odor and fought the urge to pinch her nose, rising along with him.

"Now that we have eaten, I find myself exceedingly fatigued," he said. "I think I shall sleep until sup."

She nodded. "Aye, a nap and a bath will do you wonders."

"A bath?" he eyed her and snorted. "Water is my enemy. It dries the skin and reveals parts of our bodies that are better left unseen... well, to those of us who are celibate, baths are a danger."

She raised her eyebrows timidly, thinking his philosophy most disgusting but trying not to show it. "Then you never bathe?"

"Never," he insisted. "A gateway to sin for men and women of the cloister."

Oh, lord, she groaned inwardly. "Well, then, take your nap and I shall see you at supper. I have a few things to attend to now."

She preceded the priest from the solar, calling to Oleg. The old man appeared out of the woodwork, greeting de Tormo and taking him away to his rooms.

Remington watched them go, still smelling de Tormo, and giggling with distaste as she thought of his hygiene habits. The man must have been a pig in a previous life.

⚜

The clerical quarters of Westminster were lavish, gaudy surroundings. Gaston stood by the long, narrow windows, gazing out over the gardens absently. Henry sat near the center of the room in a silk chair, 20-foot ceilings soaring above his head.

The whole room smelled heavily of incense; Gaston wasn't sure of what type. But it was heady and old-smelling and, in fact, intimidating. Gaston was sure the scent was psychologically placed. It reminded one that they were in the most omnipotent house of worship in the civilized world, outside of St. Peter's Cathedral.

"Do you know why we have been summoned?" Gaston finally turned from the window.

Henry lounged comfortably, appearing almost bored. "I do not. I suppose they must have come to some snappish conclusion and intend to deliver it to us personally."

Gaston stomach's plunged. His palms were sweaty. "They'll not permit the annulment. The law of the church will outweigh all of the compelling testimony given. God above all, including the laws of mercy and love."

Henry shushed him, knowing there were ears everywhere. Gaston knew it, too, but he did not care. "Have faith, Gaston. You cannot know what conclusion they have come to."

Gaston turned back to the window, his jaw ticking with agitation. After a moment, he shook his head. "I have known all along what their answer would be, but I had hoped…aye, I have prayed that they would reconsider given the extreme circumstances."

Henry contemplated the rings on his hand. "Have faith, Gaston."

Christopher Urswick stood in the shadows, listening. Gaston was right, he knew. The church had gathered them together to deliver what de Russe suspected. An annulment was impossible with both spouses still living, and a divorce was completely out of the question. This had been a futile endeavor from the inception, but Henry had gone along because of what Gaston meant to him and he felt he had to put forth the effort.

Urswick pitied the Dark Knight, and the lady. To love each other so terribly, but to be forever denied matrimony was tragic at best.

On the far end of the room, a huge carved oak door swung open with a groan. Three men spilled forth, all dressed in lavish garments, all various ages. The tall young man that stopped just inside the door passed an eye at Gaston; he met Peter Courtenay's eyes steadily. Courtenay lowered his gaze hesitantly and took up station against the wall, silent and out of the way.

Archbishop Thomas Bourchier sat with a grunt behind his elaborate cherry wood desk, dark with stain and time. His aged face was thin and pale, belying the man's power. He almost appeared docile and dense. Behind him, a young, dark-haired man stood stoically. John of Imola was the apostolic delegate, a man with a direct line to Pope Innocent. He was very young for a man in his position, but he was extremely bright and wise, which he had more than proven during the weeks of testimony.

Bourchier gazed at Gaston standing over by the thin windows. Somewhere in the cathedral, the monk's choir was rehearsing the sweet strains of haunting music floated faintly on the air. Gaston merely gazed back unemotionally.

Bourchier cleared his throat. "Thank you for coming."

"Get on with it, Thomas," Henry said, almost unkindly.

Bourchier's eyes flicked to the monarch as Christopher came out of the shadows to stand behind his king. Gaston remained by the windows.

"Very well," the archbishop said with a matched tone. "As you know, divorce is forbidden by the church. Annulments are granted only in extreme cases with the provision of severe circumstances. The papal board has heard the testimony on behalf of Lady Remington Stoneley and I must be honest when I say that the collective board feels that the basis of the annulment request is weak. Unless Lady Stoneley herself can provide more substantial evidence, your request will be rejected."

Gaston moved away from the wall. "You are telling me, in essence, that the testimony of five reputable barons, all stating to the effect that Guy Stoneley was an evil, cruel barbarian, is insufficient? My God, what kind of evidence is it that you require? Irreversible damage to Lady Stoneley, or her family?"

"Gaston," Henry admonished quietly, turning back to the archbishop. "I suspected that this would be the church's reaction from the beginning, and I am not surprised. If sworn testimony will not bring Lady Stoneley her annulment, then you may name your price. I am willing to pay what you ask on Gaston's behalf."

Bourchier's eyes widened briefly. "An annulment cannot be bought, my lord."

"Ha," Henry snorted softly. "Anything can be bought within the church, Thomas, and you cannot pretend otherwise. What is it that you will demand? Well?"

John of Imola stepped forward, his almost-babyish face concerned. "Annulments are not to be bought and sold as a commodity. You are speaking of dissolving what God has created."

"God did not create this marriage," Gaston rumbled. "This is the devil's doing, and he continues to delight in the torment of an innocent woman and her sisters."

"That is your opinion, my lord," the legate responded pointedly. "You see what you will, considering you are in love with the woman. Even as it stands, you are breaking the tenth commandment with your lust for her, and I suspect you have already broken the fourth."

Gaston did not flinch, but the vein in his temple throbbed faintly. "We are not here to speak of what I have or have not done. We are speaking of Lady Stoneley."

"Will she be able to enlighten us further on this matter?" Bourchier asked, drawing Gaston's hostile attention away from the legate. "Or will it be a waste of time for all concerned?"

Gaston looked at the archbishop, feeling a lie coming forth, demanding to be released. A lie Remington started, a lie that de Tormo threatened to use when all else failed. Gaston could see that Remington's annulment was slipping through his fingers, and he prayed that God would forgive him for lying to a man of the cloth, and furthermore not punish him by having his story backfire in his face.

"It will not be a waste of time, for she will testify to a distasteful fact that not even the barons knew of," he said quietly. "Guy Stoneley worships the devil. I have seen his sanctuary for myself; a pentagram decorates the wall, and skin-bound books line the shelves. His worship of Satan explains his deviant actions and bloodlust towards his family."

Bourchier and John looked at each other, then back to Gaston. "Do you have proof of this?"

"Father de Tormo saw the sanctuary himself. He will testify to that fact."

Peter Courtenay moved from his spot along the wall. "Are you sure, Gaston?"

"Aye," Gaston nodded, having difficulty looking his friend in the eye. "Pentagrams, potions and other strange medicaments. He is a student of Satan."

Everyone was looking at Gaston. "Why did you not bring this up before?" Henry wanted to know.

"Because I was trying to spare at least some of Lady Remington's dignity," he replied, somewhat honestly. "My God, her life is already displayed for scrutiny by the church, her reputation, every horribly thing her husband has ever inflicted on her. The beatings, the rapes, impregnating her sister... I thought to spare at least some of her feelings. I care not for myself, of course; there is nothing about me and my personal life that all of you do not already know, but this woman has been laid open to strangers."

"My lord, if what you say is true, then it changes things considerably," Bourchier said seriously. "If he is a disciple of Lucifer, then we cannot allow the lady to be exposed to the dark forces. John and I must return to the board with this information."

Gaston felt a surge of hope, and a bit of guilt. "I shall return to Wells Abbey and return the lady to London for her testimony. Father de Tormo, too."

Bourchier stood up, nodding. "By all means. I would hear more of this shocking revelation."

Gaston watched the men a moment. "You realize that Stoneley will deny this."

"Of course he will," Bourchier said strongly. "To admit to it would mean instant death. However, if it is determined that he does indeed worship Satan, I will recommend that he be burned at the stake."

Gaston wasn't sorry to hear that. He watched the three holy men exit the room, the soft hum of conversation following them. When the room was deserted, Henry rose from his silk chair.

"Bravo, Gaston," he said softly. "A brilliant story. But can you truly prove it?"

"Without a doubt," Gaston looked at his king. "And it was not a story. I really did witness the tower room with evil paraphernalia." *Aye, paraphernalia of a curious young boy!*

Henry shook his head. "Disgusting. I pity Lady Stoneley more than ever, and I wonder if I should not send a priest to bless the entire White Tower. Stoneley has probably cursed it."

Gaston's lips flickered with a smile as he followed his monarch and the dean of York from the room.

⚜

Nearly a week later, Gaston made an appearance. Riding alone in front of fifty men-at-arms and six knights, Remington caught sight of him from their bedchamber window.

With a shriek of delight, she raced to her polished silver mirror and took quick stock of her looks, her hair and surcoat. She was so excited that she was making happy little grunts as she smoothed everything, combed and finally perfumed. He was finally here.

She made a mad dash for the door to the chamber, only to stop abruptly. Hand on the latch, her gaze wandered back to the massive oak bed against the wall. A thought crossed her mind and she smiled wickedly. Her hand left the latch, and the door remained closed.

Gaston rode into the newly created outer bailey, fairly broiling in his armor in the early July weather. Nicolas and Antonius were there to greet him, but he ignored their salutations as he dismounted.

"Where's Remi?"

"I do not know," Nicolas replied, weaving out of the way as Taran tried to take a bite out of his arm. "She was up in the nursery last I saw her."

Gaston stripped off his gauntlets absently, searching the compound for the familiar figure. He was disappointed and surprised that she had not come out to greet him.

Antonius was attempting to relay something of importance to Gaston, but he wasn't listening. Instead, he strolled across the outer bailey, through the opening of his nearly completed inner wall, and on to the castle.

De Tormo almost crashed into him at the door leading into the castle. The fat man reeled back, his hand over his chest.

"Good Lord, Gaston. You nearly killed me."

Gaston raised an eyebrow. "With all of that blubber to soften the blow, I doubt it. Where's Remi?"

"I have no idea. What happened after I left you in London?"

"Later," Gaston rumbled, moving past the priest.

His disappointment was turning into anger as he made his way up the massive stone staircase to the second floor landing. He took a step toward their bedchamber when a noise from the other direction caught his attention, a baby crying.

Gaston pushed open the nursery door, fully expecting to see Remington seated with one of the twins. The only adult face that greeted him was Skye, and she hopped up from her seat in surprise.

"Gaston," she gasped. "I did not know you were...."

"Where's Remi?" he interrupted.

"I... I do not know, in your rooms, mayhap," Skye stammered. Gaston still made her nervous, even though she knew in her heart that he was completely harmless to the female sex.

In a chorus, Adeliza and Arica suddenly began to wail. Having heard two words from Gaston's lips was all it took to wake them. Indeed, they knew their father.

His anger abated and he went to their cribs, cooing like all new fathers. Skye watched him, amazed at the speed with which his expression went from hard to soft. He picked Arica up; the baby's face a mirror of his own as they smiled at each other.

He held the baby around her torso; the only thing visible was her head and arms, and her legs. She kicked her legs vigorously in response to his smiles and whispered words, drooling all over his wrists.

"God help them, they are looking more like me," he bemoaned lightly.

Skye smiled, picking up Adeliza so she would not scream herself ill. "Remington was saying that this morning. They have your eyes."

He turned to Adeliza, bending over to nibble on her fingers. "Poor little things. Not to have their mother's magnificent color."

Adeliza grinned. "But they have her smile already; broad and magnificent," he announced with satisfaction, looking back at Arica. "Oh, lord, Skye. I swear that I cannot tell them apart. How horrible of me; I am their father, after all. Shouldn't I be able to distinguish my daughters from each other?"

Skye shrugged. "They are as two peas in a pod. But there is a trick Remington uses; look at Arica when she smiles. See? She has a tiny dimple in her left cheek."

He looked closely. "Ah. She does indeed."

He kissed the babe once more before laying her back down. Briefly turning his attention to Adeliza, his mind began to return to the whereabouts of the girls' errant mother.

"I must find Remi," he said, moving for the door. Arica began to scream again and he shrugged helplessly at Skye, who waved him on.

Once again, he set out for their bedchamber at the end of the corridor. If Remington was not there, then he would tear apart the whole bloody castle until he found her.

His anger had returned by the time he reached the door. Slamming it open, he stomped into the spacious bedchamber.

"Remi!" he bellowed.

He received no answer, but he caught movement out of the corner of his eye. Turning sharply, he was met with a figure dressed entirely in white. White, fine silk that was absolutely transparent, provocative and enticing, covering all but not concealing. His anger melted into liquid fire.

"Greetings, my lord," Remington said seductively.

He was actually speechless for a moment. He found himself drawing in a long, appreciative breath. "You... you did not meet me in the bailey."

She smiled, making his heart thump madly in his ribs. "I thought I would greet you here. Properly."

He watched her, frozen, as she approached. Her hair was unbound, cascades of curls flowing to her waist. He'd never seen her so beautiful.

Remington stopped before him, her face upturned and gazing at him with such a seductive expression that he felt his knees go weak. By God, he had missed her.

"I am pleased," he managed to choke out. "You look incredible, Remi. When I last left, you were...."

"I know," she interrupted softly. "As fat as a cow."

He shook his head, reaching a hand up to remove his helm. "Nay, love, you were not fat. You looked every bit a new mother."

She raised an eyebrow at him. "Well put."

He smiled, his gaze raking over her. "We were speaking of something else not a moment ago. Ah, yes; you were preparing to welcome me home."

She returned his smile, standing on her toes and snaking her arms behind his neck. "So we were."

He pulled her to him, all hard armor and mail, but they both knew the gear would come off momentarily. "Make me a warm welcome, then."

She lifted her mouth for a kiss and he instantly responded, but she stopped just short of meeting his lips. She lingered a moment, feeling his body quivering with anticipation, and they both smiled at her "torture".

"Welcome home, my lord."

Their mouths met with a furious clash of passion, lips fusing intensely. Her fingers entangled themselves in his inky hair, feeling the sweat and strength of the strands. He was gripping the back of her head with his gauntleted hands and they both laughed when he tried to remove them, entangled, in the silken web.

"I should not have done that," he said, unwinding a curl from his index finger.

She smiled, reaching out to unlatch his breastplate. In less than a minute, his armor was off and they were both going to work on his clothing, their desire doubling by the second. By the time he removed his breeches, Remington had already removed her filmy robe and was lying on the bed, completely naked, demanding he hurry.

Her eyes raked him hungrily, drinking in his beautiful body. "Gaston, is it possible you have grown larger since we were last together? I do not remember you being quite so... muscular."

He ripped the breeches free of his feet. "Fifteen more pounds of beef, angel. All I did was work myself ill during the time we spent apart. It kept my mind off you."

She had not the chance to respond. Suddenly he was on her, their naked skin touching for the first time in months. They had not made love since she had been three months pregnant with the twins, and Gaston's breath was shaky as his hands roved her newly luscious body. He couldn't touch her fast enough, tenderly enough; he couldn't get enough.

Her breasts, so round and plump and engorged, drew his mouth and she moaned softly with the sensitivity. He kneaded her breasts, somewhat surprised when milk dripped forth.

"I am sorry... did I hurt you?" he whispered, concerned.

She smiled, running her finger to catch the drops, and then plunging her finger into his mouth. "What does it taste like?"

He'd never seen a more provocative action; a painful jolt of pure lust shot thought his body. All of his resolve to go slow fled like a puff of smoke.

"Sweet," he said huskily. "Like you."

She cried out softly as he suckled her hungrily, low groans of pleasure rumbling from his throat. He kneaded and suckled, finally trailing down her slightly rounded stomach to her satin thighs. His actions were almost rough, firm, and she encouraged him lustily.

"Oh, damn," he suddenly muttered.

"What?"

His mouth came up from her fleshy mound, his eyes glazed with passion. "I...brought something for us to use."

"Brought what?"

He looked hesitant, almost at a loss for words. His fingers probed her fleshy lips, stroking her, before he answered. "You almost died with the twins and...Remi, I would rather have no more children. I do not want to lose you, angel, not even for the sake of heirs. We have two sons and two daughters. Our family is complete, I think."

She looked at him curiously. "No more children? You would not want a son from me?"

He touched her face, his hand shaking. "Oh, angel, a son would be the greatest gift. But I will give it up if it means losing you. Do you understand what I am saying?"

She did; sort of. "But just how do you intend to prevent me from conceiving again? Gaston, I conceived the twins within a few weeks. We happen to be potent together, my love."

"There is a woman in London who makes pessaries," he said softly. "She guarantees that it will prevent pregnancy. I paid a good deal of money for them."

"A pessary?" she repeated. "I have heard of them. What are they made out of?"

He was stroking her thighs, running his hand over her belly. "Coltsfoot. Bayberry. And other things; I did not ask."

"Where are they?" she asked.

"In my saddlebags," he laid his great head on her torso.

She raked her fingers through his hair. "You are not leaving to go and get them," she grabbed hold of the hair, yanking him up sharply to look at her. "Take me. *Now.*"

He looked hesitant for a brief moment, but she smiled and wrapped her legs about him. He wanted to protest; to bid her wait until he could dress and retrieve the pessary, but the words would not come. He wanted her so badly that he couldn't wait, either.

Bracing his arms on either side of her body, he arched into her. She cried out softly and he thrust again, shuddering. She was so terribly tight that he swore he was elongating as her walls clutched him, drawing him inward. He thrust again, and again, before he was finally seated to the hilt. Beneath him, Remington was moaning softly with pure pleasure.

They rocked together, pelvis' meeting with force. Remington's legs gripped him tightly, her nails biting into his massive arms. She clung to him, moving with him, feeling their heat take flight like a racing fire.

It wasn't long before they were cresting together, the waves of pleasure rolling over them like ripples on the surface of a lake. The ripples faded, the pleasure blanketing them in a warm glow. Gaston held Remington tightly, his face buried in her hair.

"I wasted my money buying those damn pessaries," he mumbled.

She smiled, snuggling against his huge body. "Nay, you did not. What is this one time out of the rest to come? By the way, how do I use them?"

"You put them inside you - thusly," he took his index finger and shoved it upward, and then he grinned at her. "In fact, I may do it for you."

"You may have to," she made a face of displeasure. "I do not think I want to stick my finger – thusly." She made the same motion and they both laughed.

They settled into comfortable positions, he holding her tightly, and she pressed up against him as if she were a physical part of his body. It had been so long since they had been together as this, and each one savored it.

The afternoon passed, closing in on dusk. Remington dozed lightly in his arms, never so content as she was at that very moment. Gaston stroked her back absently, staring off into the room, not thinking on anything in particular. He was simply enjoying the feel of her, the smell of her. He was enjoying *her*.

"What happened in London?" she asked.

He thought she was asleep. Shifting her slightly, he gazed down into the sea-crystal eyes. "Let's eat supper first, and then we will discuss it later with de Tormo."

She sat up. "Why do not you want to tell me now? What happened?"

He sighed. "Remi, we have just spent a wonderful afternoon together. Do you really want to spoil it with talk of the papal council?"

"Am I getting my annulment?"

"Not at the moment."

"Did they deny me already, before I have a chance to speak?"

"No, they did not deny you. In fact, you and de Tormo and I will have to speak on the future testimonies," he ran a finger up her soft arm. "I told the archbishop and the legate that Guy worships the devil. They were most outraged, of course, and I believe if we can convince them that Guy is the devil's disciple, then you shall have your annulment."

"Truly?" her face lit up with hope.

He smiled faintly and touched her cheek. "Truly."

She suddenly bound out of bed, hunting for her clothes. "Well, get up. We must eat and meet with de Tormo. And when do we leave for London?"

He snickered, rolling to his side and propping himself up on an elbow as she paraded about, collecting garments. His flaccid manhood began pulsing with life again at the sight of her nude body, nubile and round.

"'Tis a shame you must cover that magnificent body," he said, eyeing her as she walked past him.

She gave him a coy look, laying her shift and dress across a chair. "I do not think de Tormo would appreciate my showing up to supper in the nude," she put her hands on her hips. "Do you know that he does not believe in bathing? He told me so. He says it is a danger for men of the cloth to expose parts of the body that should remain covered."

"I believe it. He reeks something fierce."

"Well, I think it is disgusting," she pulled the shift over her head. "Gaston...do you think that ordained men are subject to the same urges as normal men? I mean, do they feel lust and desire as you do?"

"Of course," he replied, watching her dress with pleasure. "I'd wager that de Tormo's handprints are all over his manroot."

She gasped and he laughed. "Oh, Remi, do not look so shocked. He's a mortal man, no matter how hard he tries to pretend otherwise."

She frowned, the mental picture of an aroused de Tormo disgusting. "How unpleasant."

Gaston sat up, throwing his massive legs over the side of the bed and scratching his scalp. "I have got to find Antonius and have him cut my hair. It is getting far too long."

She pulled her surcoat over her head, a clingy bit of pale green satin that molded to her breasts and torso and hung gracefully off her hips. "It looks fine."

He ran his hand up the back of his head. "Too long," he repeated, moving for his thin leather breeches that were almost like hose.

She looked closely at his head as she fastened a silver link belt around her hips. The front was long as it usually was, almost hanging to his mouth. The back was shorn, nearly to the top of his skull and she shook her head. "If Antonius cuts your hair any closer to your scalp, you shall be bald."

He grunted as he pulled on his breeches, giving her a vague shrug. She sat on the bed, pulling on cream-colored hose and he groaned softly, turning away so he would not have to watch as she ran her hands up her legs. She grinned knowingly, pulling on soft leather slippers.

"There, you coward, I am dressed," she said. "You can turn around now."

"How many times must I tell you that I am not cowardly," he insisted, pulling on his boots and moving to don his armor. "I am simply exceedingly wise in my judgment. Were I to watch you any longer, all of your efforts at dressing would be lain to waste. The surcoat would come off."

She held her grin, kneeling before him to help him with his leg armor. The stuff was heavy; Gaston would position it and she would latch it. She found it little wonder that he had two squires to assist him.

"Off your knees, love," he pulled her to her feet. "I have a few things to attend to outside, and then we will sup. I trust our meal will be fit for a returned duke?"

She put her arms out exaggeratedly, bowing worshipfully. "By your command, Oh Great Duke. The great Dark Duke of Warminster."

"Dark Duke, am I?" he muttered, swatting her playfully on the exposed rear. "Mind your manners, wench."

She yelped weakly and grabbed her behind, but she was smiling. Gaston grinned at her as he pulled on his gauntlets, and then indicated the door. "After you, madam."

She thrust up her chin. "I like a man who knows his place. A proper distance behind a woman."

He smirked, moving to open the door for her. "That will change after we are married. For now, I plan to lull you into a false sense of security into believing I am a true gentleman."

"I believe no such thing," she insisted.

He shook his head, watching her luscious backside as she sashayed through the open door.

Supper that night was nearly like the first few days when Gaston had arrived at Mt. Holyoak, except for the obvious vacancies of Arik, Rory and Patrick. Remington had ordered mutton, reminiscent of Yorkshire, and had it prepared several different ways. Gaston was digging into his third helping of herbed mutton, listening to Skye and Jasmine argue with Nicolas over something silly, smiling every so often when Remington would jump in and deliver a scathing blow to his cousin.

De Tormo sat on the opposite side of Antonius, far gone into his food and ale. The priest was not as pious as he liked to believe; in addition to turning a blind eye to Gaston and Remington's adultery, he was also guilty of gluttony. Not only that, but after the conversation Gaston had had with Remington that afternoon, he swore he saw the priest give one of the serving wenches a second glance.

It was strange, he reflected, how his life had changed within the past year. For a man who was alone most of his life, he suddenly found himself surrounded by his family and wondering why he had ever chosen to be a loner. There was so much more to be gained by allowing himself to feel, to love, to laugh. A pity Arik wasn't alive so he could tell him just that. Arik had spent the better part of twenty-four years trying to tell him so.

"Remi, did Gaston tell you he is to have a birthday soon?" Nicolas said, snapping Gaston out of his train of thought.

Remington turned accusing eyes to Gaston. "He did not. When, Gaston?"

"The twentieth day of June," Gaston mumbled into his cup.

"In two days?" she gasped. "How dare you not tell me? There is no time to plan a fitting celebration."

"How old do you think he is going to be?" Nicolas asked his wife mischievously.

Skye looked at Gaston openly. "Oh...twenty-seven? Twenty-eight?"

Nicolas snorted loudly. "He's older than that. Try again."

Gaston met Skye's gaze and she blushed terribly. "I do not know, Nicolas. I am a horrible guesser. Do you know, Remi?"

Remington smiled. "I do indeed. Gaston remembers the fall of the Roman Empire."

Antonius and Nicolas roared loudly at Gaston's expense. "How old?" Jasmine demanded.

"Thirty-eight," Gaston told her, smiling faintly while his knights whooped. "I shall be thirty years and eight."

Jasmine nodded, her eyebrows raised in surprise; she did not think he was that old. "What about you, Remi. Are we celebrating your birthday?" Skye asked.

Remington looked surprised, hoping Gaston did not hear what Skye had said. But he turned to her. "Pray, when is your birthday, madam?"

Remington shot Skye a deadly look. "Uh... soon."

He gathered her hand in his own, still smiling. "When?"

She rolled her eyes, knowing there was no way out of his question. "The day after yours. The twenty-first day of June."

He raised his eyebrows in feigned outrage. "And you thought not to tell me? How dare you."

"Honestly, I had not thought about it," she said truthfully. "With so much going on, I'd almost forgotten."

"She shall be twenty-seven," Skye announced, turning to her husband. "She does not look it, does she?"

Gaston kissed her hand. "She's ageless. And what is it you would like for your birthday gift?"

She shrugged. "I have everything I could possibly want. Except...."

Her voice trailed off and he knew what she was going to say, *except an annulment and a proper marriage.*

He squeezed her hand. "I know. How would you like to see Dane?"

Her face brightened. "Oh, Gaston, I'd love it! When can we go?"

"When we leave for London," he was pleased to see that she was so happy. "We shall travel due north to Oxford Castle. It shouldn't take any more than a day."

Her cheeks were flushed with excitement. "I have not seen Dane in so long. I am sure he's grown a mile," her smile faded a bit. "Do you think... could we bring the girls?"

"I do not think it would be a good idea," he said gently.

"They are too small to travel, angel. Moreover, I would not want them to go to London and I would not trust anyone to return them to Deverill but me, and I cannot take the additional time."

She nodded in reluctant agreement, understanding his reasoning. But then it occurred to her that she would be separated from her girls for the duration in London, and that thought did not sit well with her at all. "We cannot take Adeliza and Arica to London? We must leave them behind?"

He nodded. "Sorry, love. No one knows of them but Henry and a few others, and it would not be a good thing to have them there."

Her light mood was spoiled and she could feel tears stinging her eyes. She tried to drown her sorrow in a large gulp of wine, but it did not help. She took a couple of bites from her tart, but her mood did not improve. Instead, it sank lower. Hastily, she excused herself from the table.

He knew she was upset and followed her from the great hall. He caught up with her in the corridor outside and silently put his arm around her waist as they continued to walk down the hall.

The night was warm and he took her to the battlements looking north, facing Warminster and the Vale of White Horse. There were few soldiers on that portion of the wall and he stroked her hair as she gazed out over the moonlit land.

"I am sorry you cannot take the babes," he said softly.

She shrugged. "I will miss them. How long do you think we will be in London?"

"As long as it takes," he leaned on the ledge next to her, resting on his elbows as she was. They looked at each other a moment until she looked away sadly. He continued to look at her.

"I told de Tormo we would meet after sup. We should go and find him."

"No need," de Tormo came out of the shadows, strolling across the battlement. "I thought we could talk out here, enjoying the evening."

The priest rested against the ledge, gazing up at the moon. Remington caught a whiff of his odor and edged closer to Gaston, who put his arm around her.

"You know of the basics, de Tormo, so I will not repeat them," Gaston said, to the point. "Little has changed since you left London, except for a particular meeting Henry and I had with Bourchier and the papal legate. Apparently, the council was leaning toward a rejection of the plea and I felt I had to resort to desperate measures. I told them that Stoneley worshipped the devil, and they are now eager to hear testimony from the both of you supporting my allegation."

De Tormo nodded calmly. "I am prepared. Did you go into any specifics?"

"No. I was vague, mentioning the pentagram and the skin-covered books but naught else."

The priest nodded again. "I see. As I will only be able to testify to those as well," he looked at Remington. "It would seem the details would have to come from you, Remi, as his wife."

Gaston stiffened and Remington put out a hand to calm him. De Tormo had inadvertently referred to her as Guy's wife, which she was, but Gaston did not like to hear the term used in that context. He did not like to be reminded of it.

"What details?" she asked.

"Details of the room, I suppose," de Tormo eyed Gaston with a silent apology for his slip. "Do you have any knowledge of devil worship?"

"No," she insisted, slighted.

He put up his hand supplicatingly. "I did not mean to insinuate anything, as you know. I simply meant to know if you had ever read anything, or heard anything."

She shook her head. "Nothing."

The priest thought a moment. "I could tell you several things, but I have a better idea," he looked at the two of them. "It will make your testimony far more compelling if your sisters were to testify to support your statements. Mayhap we should gather them together and prepare one story. One story that we will all memorize until we know it better than we know our own name."

Remington looked to Gaston for his approval; he looked intrigued. "A simple story that will stand up under cross-examination?"

"Absolutely," de Tormo said firmly. "Nothing terribly detailed, but enough to lead the council to their own conclusions."

Remington was torn between hope and reluctance. "Must my sisters be pulled into this?"

De Tormo looked to Gaston. "We must do what is necessary, angel," Gaston said quietly. "And we must trust the priest in this matter. He knows far more than we."

She nodded faintly. "If you say so."

Gaston enfolded her in both arms, fixing his gaze on the de Tormo. "Gather the flock then, priest. We shall meet you in the solar in an hour."

Remington watched de Tormo walk down the battlement. "Guy will deny everything, Gaston. 'Twill be our word against his."

"And he has already proven himself to be difficult and noncommittal, and the council is aware of his characteristics. Our story will work. It must, else there will be no annulment."

She shuddered involuntarily. "And if it does work? What will happen to Guy, a proven devil-worshiper?"

"He will be executed, most likely."

She thought a moment. "And what of Dane? Surely it will get around that his father was executed for devil-worship. It will reflect badly on him."

"It will be forgotten," Gaston assured her quietly. "Believe me, it will pass in time and people will see him for his great skill and forget about his long-dead father."

She sighed. "I worry for him."

"Do not," Gaston turned her around to face him, a smile on his lips. "You worry overly for your children, angel. From what de Vere has told me, Dane will be promoted from page to squire come his birthday in August. John says Dane is the best page he has, next to Trenton, of course."

"He is?" she asked, her mood lightening. "I am so glad to hear that."

He put his arm around her shoulders and led her toward the narrow stairs leading to the courtyard. "John also says he had grown considerably. The other pages look to him as their leader."

She bristled with pride. "Truly? But what of Trenton?"

Gaston shrugged, helping her take the top stair. "He acts at Dane's side. Trenton was never much of a leader, really. More of a follower."

She gathered her surcoat, taking the stairs carefully. He was directly behind her, taking her hand as they strolled back across the bailey. Above them, the moon was bright and somewhere in the still night air, a night bird sang sweetly.

CHAPTER THIRTY

Gaston and Remington slept past dawn the next morning, unusual for both of them. The babes were taken care of by a wet nurse throughout the night, giving the exhausted parents time alone.

A stray beam of sunlight pierced thought the gap in the heavy curtains, hitting Gaston right in the eye. He twitched, rolled away from it, but by that time he sleepily realized Remington was out of his arms and he rolled back over to correct the situation. The bright light was annoying and warm on his eye once again.

He muttered a curse and burrowed down into the covers, burying his face in the back of Remington's neck. Unfortunately, all of his fidgeting awoke her and she sighed heavily.

"Gaston, stop moving," she mumbled into her pillow.

He grumbled something into her hair, pulling her tighter. She lazily opened her eyes, noticing how radiant the room was and wondering what time it was. She reached behind her and touched him.

"Wake up, Gaston. It's late."

He did not say anything for a moment. Then, he blew out a heavy breath and raised his head, squinting in the brightness. "Too damn brilliant. My eyes hurt."

She sighed contentedly and he pecked her on the cheek, propping himself up on an elbow. "It is going to be warm today," he murmured, seeing the deep blue sky beyond the windows. Then he looked down to Remington's dark head. "When will you be ready to leave? If we depart before noon, we should reach Oxford just after nightfall."

"I can pack within an hour or two," she said, rolling on her back to look up at him. "How long can we visit Dane and Trenton?"

"Not long," he brushed away a wild strand of her hair. "Just for the day, angel. The sooner we get to London, the better."

She nodded reluctantly, feeling the warm breeze already wafting through the windows. "I am not looking forward to the interrogation, Gaston."

He played with the same strand of hair. "I know. But you and your sisters are excellent students. You know your story, and you will stick to it. As long as you do not waiver, we will have your annulment by next month."

"I hope so," she murmured. "But I am still afraid."

"Of what?" he tossed back the coverlet, revealing a body as large and tanned as hers was petite and white. "You worry overly, Remi."

She watched him sit up, the rippling muscles in his broad back. Vaguely, she shrugged. "There is much to worry over."

"Not for long," he said, pulling on his breeches with a grunt. "We will be over and done with this madness before the end of summer, hopefully. And then we will be married."

He dressed efficiently, quickly, as soldiers do. She sat up in bed to watch him finish with his boots, tugging at his tunic and strapping on his sword. He was not wearing any armor at all, an extremely rare state for him.

"What do you do now?" she asked.

"I have an entire keep I have not seen in over a month," he said. "I intend to make my rounds before our departure, just to make sure Antonius and Nicolas have not run Deverill into the ground. And since they are accompanying us to London, I want to make sure the keep is in excellent hands before we leave."

She hugged her knees, smiling. "Uncle Martin will be surprised to see Skye and Robert, won't he? I wish I could stay with him until this is over."

"No," he said flatly. "Uncle Martin is in love with you. You will never be alone with him again."

Her eyes widened. "Do not jest with me like that. 'Tis a terrible accusation, teasing or not."

"'Twas no jest, I assure you," he paused a moment when he saw her outraged expression, hands on his hips. "Remi, why do you think he trailed you to St. Catherine's, intent on following you to your end destination? I nearly had to wrestle him from the convent, and with the mood I was in following our argument, I nearly tore his head off. I would not be surprised if he refuses to speak with me for the rest of his life."

She looked at him with uncertainty, feeling vastly uncomfortable at the new knowledge. "You must be mistaken, Gaston. On both accounts."

He gazed at her a moment before bending down and depositing a sweet kiss on her lips. "Mayhap on the latter, I am. I would hope so. But as far as my original allegation, I most certainly am not. Even Nicolas agrees with me."

He moved for the door. "Rise and pack, love. And tell your sisters to pack hurriedly," he stopped and pointed a finger at her as he opened the door. "And limit the trunks we must carry. One per lady, please."

She raised an eyebrow. "Impossible, my lord. Have pity."

"No," he said firmly. "We are not a merchant caravan. One trunk for each of you."

He winked at her and shut the door.

Remington sat a moment, a faint smile playing on her lips. Without another wasted minute, she bound from the bed and called for a bath.

Nearly two hours later, bathed, hair washed and drying, Remington scurried down the hall to Skye and Jasmine's rooms to make sure they were almost complete with their packing. She knew Gaston would return shortly and she wanted to be able to leave as soon as possible. The sooner they left, the sooner she would see Dane.

She supervised the men-at-arms who had come to take the trunks down to the waiting wagon. As promised, each lady had only packed one large trunk, but that did not prevent them from packing several smaller bags and satchels to carry a myriad of other necessities.

Jasmine and Skye were thrilled to be going to London. Dressed in the finest surcoats they owned, they chattered like magpies while the soldiers took their baggage. Remington, dressed in cream satin and gold, shushed them in between relaying orders to the soldiers; *that bag on top, do not turn this one on end, and whatever you do, do not let that one fall.*

Gaston lumbered up the stairs, eyeing his soldiers as they descended, laden down like porters. The first person his gaze fell on was Remington.

"I told you one trunk," he said with a cocked eyebrow.

"Aye, you did," she met him evenly. "And we only packed one trunk a piece. But you said nothing of traveling bags, Gaston. Not one word."

Jasmine and Skye cowered behind Remington as Gaston drug a hand wearily over his face. "By God, madam, you know exactly what I meant," he jabbed a finger at her. "If all of the bags do not fit within the confines of the wagon, that is your misfortune. Those that do not fit will be left behind, for I will not consign another wagon. Do you understand?"

She smiled, taking hold of his arm and softening his harsh stance. "Perfectly, my love. Not to worry."

He tried to remain stern, but she won out and he cracked a smile. He patted her hand as they walked toward their chambers. "I would take a bath before we leave. I fear I am smelling as badly as de Tormo."

"Not *that* bad," she slanted him a glance. "But I think a bath is a fine idea."

Shortly, the huge copper tub was brought and filled with steaming water. Gaston complained that it was too hot for a hot bath, but Remington insisted and ordered him into the water. Careful as to not muss her fresh dress, she donned a heavy apron and washed him from his head to his feet. Gaston was scrubbed, rinsed, and rubbed until his body was weak with pleasure from the attention. Had they not been on such a tight time frame, he would have ripped Remington's clothes off and bedded her that moment. As it was, he was sorely distended and she laughed at his discomfort.

"Hmpf. You laugh, madam," he grumbled, standing up in the tub as water rushed off him.

She giggled, helping him dry off with a heavy linen towel. He dried his hair vigorously, watching her as she selected his clothes. Something she was holding caught his attention.

"What is that?"

She turned to him, holding up a lightweight linen tunic of an off-white color. "A new tunic I made for you. Do you like it?"

He blinked. Did he like it? He always wore black. Always. This was... white. "It's... nice, Remi."

She lowered the tunic, eyeing him with a slight smirk. She knew exactly what he was thinking. "I am tired of seeing you in black, Gaston. Black, black, black! There are other colors, you know."

He shrugged, throwing the towel down and moving to his breeches. "I have never thought so. I have never worn anything other than black, even as a lad. Why do you think they call me the Dark Knight?"

"Because you are blood brothers with Lucifer?" she teased, holding the tunic out to him. "Please try it on. I want to see how it fits you."

He took it from her, hesitantly. He turned to the polished glass mirror, holding the tunic up in front of him. "It looks as if it will fit well enough. What did you use for a model?"

"Your horse," she quipped, motioning impatiently. "Put it on."

He pulled it over his head, straightening it just as Remington had. She ran her hands all over his chest, tugging at the shoulders, pulling at the hem. A slow smile spread across her face as she observed her handiwork. "Put your sword on. I want to see how it looks belted."

He strapped on his sword, the studded black leather belt and the matching scabbard. The entire time, he watched himself in the mirror, thinking he looked terribly strange in the light color. It was peculiar, as if he were looking at another person. He wasn't at all pleased until he looked at Remington's expression.

She was smiling the most wonderful smile. "Oh, Gaston, you look magnificent. I have never seen you handsomer."

Her expression, her obvious delight, made him take a second look. "Truly?"

"Yes!" She rushed to their chamber door and before he could stop her, she was calling eagerly to her sisters. He started to protest weakly, but almost instantly Skye and Jasmine were rushing in, exclaiming favorably at his new tunic.

Gaston was embarrassed as they fawned over him, laughing and touching and tugging at the material. He managed a thin smile at Remington, who laughed at his humiliation and patted him sweetly on the cheek. He eyed her sisters, thinking their praises to be well rehearsed.

When they were gone, she turned to him, still smiling.

"Now, you see? You look wonderful in white. I think I shall make you several more of the same."

He shrugged; resistance was futile. If she thought he looked handsome in white, then he would humor her. He leaned over and pecked her cheek. "I will wear white. But I will not wear pink, or blue, or green, or yellow, or any other pastel color. I do not care if you make the tunic with your own hands or not; I shall burn it before I wear it."

She giggled as he pulled on his boots. "Agreed, my love."

He took her hand and led her from the room. "Now I am going to ruin this lovely tunic by putting my armor on."

"I expected as much. But thank you for wearing it anyway."

They paused in the corridor and he kissed her sweetly. "And I thank you for thinking enough of me to make it. I shall always cherish it."

They gazed lovingly at each other a moment, warm silence between them. A door opened down the hall, the door to the nursery, and they both turned to see Eudora exiting into the corridor with a bucket in hand. Remington sighed.

"I suppose we had better go and say our good-byes to Arica and Adeliza," she already felt her throat constricting with emotion.

He put his arm around her shoulders, pulling her down the hall. "They'll hardly miss us, I assure you. As long as they are fed and warm and dry, they'll never notice our absence."

"What a terrible thing to say!" she exclaimed, and he laughed.

"A mere jest, angel. Please do not dissolve into hysterics."

She slapped at him playfully, between outrage and giggles. "Gaston, you are most inconsiderate and cold. Would you prefer that I not miss them at all?"

"Of course not," he squeezed her gently, letting her pass first through the nursery door.

It wasn't Remington who cried as she told her babes good-bye. It was Gaston. But his tears were short lived. As he cradled Arica in his massive arms, Nicolas came bolting in through the nursery door.

"Gaston," he said urgently. "A small army approaches."

Gaston carefully set Arica back in her crib before turning to his excited cousin. "Colors?"

"Yours," Nicolas smiled with delight. "Patrick approaches."

"Patrick?" Remington repeated happily, Gaston was already moving for the door. "Did he send word ahead of his arrival that I was unaware of?"

"Nay," Nicolas shook his head.

Remington hastily lowered Adeliza into her crib. "Can I come, Gaston? Please?"

He shrugged. "You are chatelaine, are you not? 'Tis your duty to greet guests to Deverill."

Remington preceded the men from the room, but not before she sent several serving wenches scurrying with orders. Gaston observed with approval the manner in which she dictated command, firmly, calmly, and pleasantly. She was obeyed because she treated the servants like people, not like animals, and was always rewarded with swift action and loyalty.

It constantly amazed him that a woman who was treated like an animal for nearly half her life was so patient and kind. As if all she had ever been dealt in her life was the same.

She smiled up at him as they made their way to the bailey, and he smiled back, still engrossed in his thoughts. This was the same woman who had reared back from him like a crazed creature, who had bore secrets too horrible to believe.

It was incredible how she had blossomed, how they both had blossomed in each other's company. She craved affection, touching, as did he. Away from Guy and Mari-Elle, they had both been allowed to taste the true meaning of love.

His soft feelings faded as he thought of what was coming. All testimonies had been given on Remington's behalf, and still the church was staunch in their stance. Resorting to lies seemed to be the only way to obtain what was so desperately wanted for the both of them, as much as Gaston loathed doing it. Skye, Jasmine, and Remington herself were the secret weapons in this fight. If they could convince the papal council of Guy's evilness, then there was no way the annulment could not be granted.

But what if it wasn't? A persistent little voice pushed, taunted, and irritated him. What then? Gaston thought seriously a moment. *What then?*

...If Guy were not proven a devil worshiper, he would remain a prisoner of the crown for the rest of his life. He had not given his consent for the annulment, in spite of nearly being beaten to death; therefore, there were no provisions to be made for him. The papal hearings were moving ahead on the basis of Gaston and Henry's insistence that Guy was an unfit husband and an immoral, cruel barbarian. Guy continued to cry foul, insisting that Remington was a reward for Gaston's service to his king, and that she was furthermore being forced against her will. She was a victim of Henry's power game.

Guy was still insisting that he loved her.

Gaston's blood began to boil again, as it did every time he thought of Guy's pathetic pleas. He wondered seriously why the man was so eager to hold onto her. Mayhap he truly did believe he loved her, as much as the vile man could love anything at all.

Thank God that Dane was safe at Oxford. He could not be used as a pawn anymore by his father, considering no one but Gaston, Henry and John de Vere knew where the boy was. When Guy asked, he was simply told Dane was fostering. Period. Certainly the church did not like the idea that a father was not being allowed knowledge of his son's whereabouts, but Henry was firm with them. The problems were between the father and the mother, and the boy was not to be involved in any way. When the circumstances allowed, his whereabouts would become common knowledge.

They entered into the nearly completed inner bailey, the sky overhead a brilliant blue. Gaston could see that the outer gates were beginning to swing open for his cousin, and he could see his threatening black and silver banners flying in the distance. Removing himself from his train of thought, he clasped Remington's hand and moved forward to greet his cousin.

Patrick rode ahead of the column of forty men, astride a great brown destrier. Remington noticed he was riding alone, like Gaston. He came to a halt, cuffing his horse when it tossed its head irritably.

"Greetings, my lord," Patrick dismounted, raising his faceplate.

Gaston nodded faintly. "To what do I owe the honor of your visit?"

Patrick took a few steps closer. "Merely progress reports on your men at Clearwell," his blue-green eyes drifted to Remington. "Greetings, my lady. You look well."

She smiled, although she thought she could detect a bit of coldness in Patrick's voice. Not at all like the gentle Patrick she had come to know. "Thank you. How have you been?"

"Well," he turned away from her and back to Gaston. "You look as if you are mobilizing, I am at your disposal."

"We are preparing to leave for London," Gaston detected the indifference to Remington, as well, and was puzzled. "I do not know how long we will be there, but I would welcome your support."

"London?" Patrick's eyebrows drew together. "What goes on there?"

Gaston raised his eyebrows in a helpless gesture. "What does not go on there? We are still in the midst of seeking an annulment for Remington and we are taking Jasmine and Skye with us for testimony."

Patrick's eyes drifted to her again. "I heard of the twins. I suppose I should congratulate you both."

The tone was icy. Remington was shocked and she took a step back from him, lowering her gaze. Gaston stiffened.

"No need," he said steadily. "You are tired, cousin. Retreat to the castle and I shall seek you later."

Patrick removed a gauntlet. "I shall sleep in the knight's quarters, Gaston. No need to house me in the castle."

Gaston's eyes narrowed at his cousin. This man in front of him was not the Patrick he knew. He went beyond the pleasantries, the overtures. "What's the matter with you? Since when are you so distant and cold?"

Patrick fixed him in the eye. "I do not know what you mean. Surely this is what you expect of me, cousin. Seeing as I am only fit to train your men at Clearwell, and not reside in the duke's residence."

Gaston was surprised. "What in the hell are you talking about? You are training my men because you are the best man for the task, Patrick. How could you possibly think it was because I did not want you with me?"

Patrick refused to look at him, fussing with the other gauntlet. "I shall not delve into the subject with you here in the open. We shall discuss it later, if you like."

"We shall discuss it now. Explain your words to me, Patrick. And explain your callous tone to Remington."

"You mean your whore?" Patrick wasn't fast enough to duck the blow that caught him in the jaw, a blow so hard that his helm was half-ripped from his head. He landed on the ground heavily, spitting out teeth and blood.

Nicolas and Antonius rushed forward, but not to stop Gaston. They were there to protect Remington.

Gaston loomed over his cousin, bending over the man as he struggled to push himself up. "You will apologize now or I will deal you a far more serious blow."

Patrick sat up, his hand to his mouth. When he looked up, there were tears in his eyes and Gaston was torn between great remorse and his still-peaked anger. He knew they were not tears of pain. Puzzlement won out.

"Patrick?" he whispered questioningly, almost demandingly.

Patrick rubbed his jaw, wiping at the blood and saliva coursing over his chin. "I'm sorry....I did not mean it." His voice was barely a whisper.

Gaston reached down and picked him up, putting his arm around his shoulders in an extremely rare gesture of affection. "Why, Patrick? What's wrong with you?"

Patrick's whole face was leaking some sort of fluid, tears, spittle, blood, and mucus. He wiped at everything. "Lost, I guess. Banished to Clearwell, I was feeling lost and rejected. I came here today because I did not want to stay there anymore and I was hoping you would allow me to remain with you," he glanced over at Remington, seeing the tears in her eyes. "I am so sorry, Remi. I did not mean it. I have not seen you since Rory died and....I look into your eyes now and I see her. I was feeling the pain all over again and I guess I lashed out. Forgive me."

She went to him and kissed his swollen jaw, blood and spit and all. Patrick let out a sob as she patted his cheek sweetly, hugging him. "Everyone has a lady but me. I am sorry, Remi. I...I have spent the better part of a year feeling sorry for myself and hating the world."

He sounded like a little boy lost. Remington took firm hold of his arm and pulled him with her, into the castle.

Gaston accompanied them. Inside, he bellowed for hot water and linens and sent a servant scurrying for Rastus. As Gaston followed closely, Remington took Patrick into the small solar and set him down. She tried to remove his helm, but it was so badly bent from Gaston's blow that Gaston had to literally tear it free from the breastplate.

A bearded, haggled Patrick faced them and they were shocked at his appearance. He had let his gorgeous curly black hair grow untamed, giving him a wild appearance. His face was black-bearded, unkempt. Remington slanted a concerned glance at Gaston as she ordered Patrick to open his mouth so she could see the extent of the damage.

Gaston watched his cousin respond painfully to Remington's request, distressed to see his state. He had not seen Patrick in over six months and was shocked at the transformation.

He had sent Patrick to Clearwell to get away from the memories of Rory. He did not imagine that Patrick would sink further and further into despair, letting his mind run wild with crazy thoughts. After nearly a year, Patrick was still grieving for the wild redhead that had made Nicolas' life so miserable.

For the first time in his life, Gaston regretted a decision he had made. He should have not sent Patrick to be alone at Clearwell. Had he but known....

"You are missing two teeth," Remington said, peering into Patrick's mouth. "On the bottom. And I can see pieces of a third tooth still in the socket."

She winced as he spit more blood on her clean floors, knowing from experience how much a blow to the face hurt. Patrick could barely move his jaw.

A serving wench came in bearing hot water, linens and witch hazel, and a bottle of alcohol. Remington moved to pick up the linen, but Gaston was shoving the bottle of wine at Patrick.

"Take a drink. Do not swallow, but swirl it around in your mouth and spit it into the basin. The second drink you may swallow."

Remington cringed as Patrick did as he was told. She could only imagine the stinging pain, but he did not flinch. Instead, he swirled the liquor for several long seconds before evacuating it into the wooden basin. She noticed his face was pale when he took two long, healthy swallows from the decanter.

Gaston gazed into Patrick's mouth a moment, then ran his fingers along his jaw. "I broke your jaw, I am afraid. And Rastus will have to remove the pieces of that broken tooth, or the tissue will not heal properly," he stood back, eyeing his cousin firmly, yet with regret. "I am sorry, Patrick. For everything. It would seem that my oversight has caused you a great deal of pain."

"Oversight?" Patrick repeated.

Gaston nodded. "I sent you to Clearwell to help you heal your grief. I should have realized...nay, I should have known that you would have been better off in the company of your family."

Patrick put his hand to his jaw gingerly. "You did as you thought best, Gaston. I suppose I knew that all along, but it was easier to focus my grief on my anger towards you for sending me away. It made it easier to deal with my loss if I hated you for causing it."

Gaston's guarded expression faded and he sat opposite his cousin. "It was my fault. If I had not ordered Derek Botmore killed, then his father would not have seen fit to retaliate. If...."

"If I had not gotten myself abducted, then you would not have had to kill Derek," Remington put her hand on Gaston's shoulder. "Then neither Arik nor Rory would have been killed. 'Tis an endless cycle; we are all to blame, yet no one is to blame."

Patrick looked at her a moment. "And if we had not even come to Mt. Holyoak in the first place....."

He let his words trail off and they all laughed softly. Gaston sobered first. "If we had not come to Mt. Holyoak, I would not have two beautiful daughters. And I would not have a dukedom."

Remington looked down at him, waiting for him to state the obvious. When he did not, she elbowed him in the bicep with her pointy elbow and he winced, rubbing the spot. "Oh, yes. And I would not have come to know such irritation and chaos. Is that right, angel?"

She scowled at him, balling her fist threateningly and he laughed, kissing her hand and drawing her onto his lap. "And I would not have you. Satisfied?"

Patrick watched the two of them, more in love with each other than they had been when he had last seen them. He tried not to envy their happiness overly.

Rastus entered the solar, a small man whom Remington had become well acquainted with when he had tended her shoulder. He smiled at her, a twinkle in his faded blue eyes, before moving to Patrick.

"Sir Patrick, back again, I see?" he opened Patrick's mouth deftly, running a trained eye over the teeth. "Brace yourself, lad. This might hurt."

Remington did not want to watch. Leaving Gaston alone with his cousin, she swept from the room, intent on seeing her daughters one last time.

The road to Oxford was awash with spring flowers, the grass a luminescent green that promised the sweetness of life and earth. The day was brilliant, not too warm, and Remington was blissfully happy as she soaked in the surroundings. By nightfall they would be at Oxford Castle, and she would see her beloved son. She could hardly wait.

She rode in the carriage with Jasmine, Skye and Father de Tormo. Nicolas and Antonius rode on either side of the rig, sweating furiously underneath the plate armor. Patrick and Gaston rode at the head of the column, together, and high above their heads extending for the entire length of the hundred-man army furled the colors of the Duke of Warminster.

Remington relaxed against the cushions, trying not to notice the stench from the priest next to her. Across the cab, Jasmine was helping Skye work on a robe for little Robert, for the younger sister simply wasn't an accomplished seamstress. Skye couldn't sew to save her life, and her needlework and tapestries looked as if they were nightmares one would have after eating rotten food.

Jasmine was trying terribly to be patient, but Skye was irritable and accused her sister of being bossy. They would squabble and fight, and then ignore each other for a minute or so before resuming their work. Remington watched and smiled, and couldn't help thinking that if Rory were here, she would be boxing their ears for fighting so much. Not to make them stop, no simply because if there was a fight, Rory liked to be in it.

Of course, they were also irritable because they missed their children. They both had to be pried from the babes and practically carried to the awaiting rig, a move that did not sit well with either of them. But their misery was blotted by the excitement of traveling to London, and the more time passed, the better their moods.

Remington craned her neck to peer from the open window, catching a glimpse of Gaston and Patrick riding together way out in front. She was surprised to see that Gaston had allowed his cousin to ride with him, knowing how well he liked to ride alone, but she also knew that Gaston felt very bad for what had happened. It was his way of making it up to his cousin.

After Rastus had tended Patrick's jaw, the knight had shaved and bathed and cleaned himself up. Looking more handsome than Remington remembered, except for his swollen jaw, he had come to see his newest cousins and nephew before departing for London. He had been terrified to hold the girls, but for some reason, he was unafraid of little Robert.

Remington watched him with the babe and couldn't help wondering if he were feeling a stab in his heart, a stab for the children he and Rory would never have. But Patrick was quiet and calm, as he usually was, and she could detect no discernable emotion. Even as he handed Robert back to his mother, he had been smiling warmly.

This was the Patrick she remembered, the man who melted her tomboy sister's heart.

Patrick had come home.

The day passed on and the caravan continued north, through the gently rolling lands as they closed in on Oxford. Once, she caught sight of a Fallow deer near the edge of the woods, a doe grazing on buttercups. Skye and Jasmine had crowed their delight, but Antonius and Nicolas kept threatening to kill it for supper. The two women took to throwing apricot seeds at their husbands, making loud pinging noises off the armor.

De Tormo had been unusually quiet during the journey. In truth, he had been unusually quiet since Gaston's return to Deverill. As Jasmine and Skye bombed the knights, Remington turned to the priest.

"Are you feeling well, father?"

He shifted in his seat. "The heat bothers me."

"Me, too."

They sat in silence a moment before de Tormo twisted a bit, reaching behind him. Remington watched as he pulled forth a roll of vellum and handed it to her.

"What's this?" she asked, examining the scroll with de Tormo's own seal.

"Just keep it," de Tormo said, his expression unusually soft.

"Why?" she looked at him, his flushed face.

"Keep it safe," he repeated. "'Tis only to be used in the case of a dire emergency."

"Dire emergency? Father, what are you talking about?"

"Just that," he patted her hand, pushing it toward Remington's satchel on the floor. "You shall know when that happens. Then you may open the scroll."

She was greatly puzzled, but put the vellum away as requested. "What is it? A black spell to make the church bow to our wishes?"

He smiled. "If it were only possible."

He looked away, gazing from the window, but she continued to watch him. He seemed very pensive and distant and Remington was beginning to feel depressed. "What are you thinking? We do not have a chance with this annulment, do we?"

His fat face turned to her, flushed; yet she noticed the pale ring around his lips. And his lips were a very strange color, almost blue. "I truly do not know, Remi. I wish I did."

"But with your testimony, surely they will be convinced," she persisted. "If anyone can convince them, you can."

He shrugged. "I can but try, my lady. And I will, believe me."

She stared at him a long moment, reading in his eyes everything he could not say. "But it would take a miracle."

He met her gaze and nodded once, faintly. Patting her hand, he turned back to the window.

Gaston did not stop for supper. The column continued on into the night and Remington took to lighting a small oil lamp for some illumination, breaking out the bread and cheese and wine they had brought along. Nicolas rode next to the carriage, flipping up his faceplate and opening his mouth like a fish as his wife fed him bits of food.

De Tormo did not eat. He complained that he was too tired and laid his head back against the carriage, closing his eyes to gain some rest. Remington was worried about him and sent Nicolas to fetch Gaston for her.

Gaston returned to the rig, reining Taran on Remington's side. The horse, even with his armored face and heavy chain bit, nibbled at Remington's arm with his silk lips and she scratched him affectionately.

"How is the ride?" he inquired, watching her "ruin" his warhorse. How many times had he told her the animal was a war machine, and not a pet?

"Fine," she lowered her voice, her eyes locking onto his. "I fear Father de Tormo is ill, Gaston. He does not look well."

Gaston leaned forward a bit so that he could see inside the cab. He raised his faceplate after a moment, as if to get a better look. "What's wrong with him?"

She glanced over her shoulder at de Tormo. "He seems extremely fatigued and his color is bad."

"So? 'Tis the heat, Remi. With all of the weight he carries, it is no wonder that...."

"And his appetite is gone," she cut him off insistently. "Moreover, he gave me a scroll this day and bade me to keep it, only to be opened in case of a dire emergency. He told me that I would know exactly when that occasion would arise."

Gaston gave de Tormo one last glance before sitting straight. "He would not tell you what the parchment contained?"

"Nay. He only told me to keep it."

Gaston thought a moment, his gaze raking over the darkened surroundings. "We shall be at Oxford within the hour. I am sure a good night's sleep will do him good."

"But what do you think it is?" she leaned forward out of the window, trying to keep her voice down.

He shook his head and lowered his visor. "I do not know. But do as he requests; hold on to it."

Oxford Castle, seated on a crest above the river, was not as large as Remington would have thought. It was grand, of course, but not nearly as big as Deverill or Mt. Holyoak. Still, the massive outer gates were most impressive as Gaston's party rode in under a full salute.

There were soldiers everywhere. The nearly full moon offered a good deal of light as the bailey swarmed with activity, but still torches added additional brightness as Remington and her sisters disembarked the carriage. De Tormo, roused from a heavy sleep, nearly fell to the ground as he stepped from the rig.

John de Vere greeted Remington warmly, a kiss to her cheek as if she were an old friend. Remington was delighted to see him; she had come to like him a great deal. An older woman fell into place beside him and he put his arm around her shoulders.

"Lady Remington, this is my wife, Anne," he introduced the two.

Remington curtsied deeply. To her surprise, the woman reached out and took her hand gently. "My lady, I have heard much about you. I see now that John did not exaggerate your beauty." She blushed furiously. "Thank you, Lady de Vere. I am flattered."

The woman's eyes were warm on her. Anne de Vere was in her late thirties, a very handsome woman. Remington liked her.

"Allow me to introduce my sisters," Remington indicated her two siblings standing next to her. "This is Lady Jasmine Flavio, and Lady Skye de Russe."

Lady de Vere greeted them pleasantly, but returned her attention back to Remington. "We have a late meal prepared in the morning room for you and your family. If you would follow me, please."

Remington nodded, searching over her shoulder for Gaston. He was several feet away, taking to the earl, and caught her glance. With a faint smile and a nod, he encouraged her to go along.

She felt a little lost that he was not to accompany her into a house full of strangers, but did as she was told. Gathering her sisters and taking de Tormo by the arm, she followed the countess into the elegant castle.

The "morning room" was simply a glorified name for a large solar. Richly appointed, as was the rest of the castle, Remington took a small plate of food and studied the artwork as Lady Anne and Father de Tormo kept up a running conversation. Jasmine and Skye ate like pigs, eating as if they had not eaten all day.

Rich custard pies covered a damask-covered table, breads of cinnamon and currants, almond-and-sugar pastes molded and colored into a variety of shapes. Jellied raisin puddings were decorated with lovely flowers and a half of a pig sat dead in the middle, smelling deliciously. It was an impressive spread, which did not go to waste on the two younger sisters.

Remington delicately nibbled on a marzipan pastry as she intently observed a particularly fine painting, a lovely scene of flowers painted on bone-white linen. The watercolors were striking.

"Do you like it?" Anne came up behind her, smiling.

Remington nodded. "It's lovely. Did you paint it, my lady?"

"My daughter did," the smile faded from Anne's face as gazed at the painting. "Alicia painted it the year before she died."

Remington was saddened. "She had a tremendous talent, indeed. I am sorry to hear of your loss."

Anne gazed at the painting a moment longer before tearing her eyes away, smiling brightly at Remington. "'Twas God's will, my lady. She died in childbirth, although she was no more than a child herself. I lost my darling at seventeen."

Remington was doubly saddened, glancing over her shoulder at her remaining sisters. "We suffered a similar loss last year. Our sixteen year old sister was killed in an ambush."

Anne put her hand on Remington's arm. "Then we both know what it is like to lose one so vibrant and sweet," gently pulling Remington with her, the two of them walked back toward the food-laden table. "I understand you recently bore twin daughters. How very wonderful."

Remington smiled. "I miss them already."

Anne smiled sympathetically. "Well, I have an idea as to how to ease your ache."

She tinkled a little silver bell on the table and instantly there were servants whisking through the open door, laden with trays of more food for the table. Remington glanced disinterestedly at them and almost turned away until she caught sight of a smaller servant bringing up the rear.

A very familiar figure!

Dane Stoneley caught sight of his mother the very same instant that she recognized him. They both froze, unsure of what to say or how to act. Gaston had always been all too clear about protocol. Remington's eyes were huge on her son; he had filled out, grown up, and was nearly as tall as Skye. She felt hot tears filling her eyes, but she refused to give in to them, at least not until she greeted her son properly.

Anne gave her a nudge. "Well? Do you recognize your fine young man?"

She could only manage a nod, her throat too tight to speak. She couldn't take her eyes off him.

Anne could see her dilemma and motioned to Dane. "Put the food down, Dane. And then you will retreat to my solar."

Dane snapped out of his trance, doing as he was told. He set the tray down carefully and bolted from the room. Remington stood, dazed.

"My solar is across the hall," Anne said softly. "I shall tell Gaston where you are when he arrives."

Remington looked at the woman, a million words of thanks rushing to her lips, but all she could squeeze out were two. "Thank you."

Dane was waiting stiffly in the solar. Remington shut the door softly behind her, turning to face the son she had not seen in nearly a year.

"Hello, sweetheart."

"Hello, mother."

She smiled. He did, too. She was shocked to see that his missing front teeth had grown in, as had several more new permanent teeth. He almost did not look like the same boy and she felt herself crumbling.

"I have missed you terribly."

"You have?" he swallowed. "Mother, I….are you and Sir Gaston married yet?"

"Not yet," she said softly, emotions tightening her throat. "But soon, hopefully. We are traveling to London right now to finish the proceedings."

Dane's sea-crystal eyes stared at her a moment. "What if the church says no? Then what?"

She lowered her gaze and perched herself on the edge of a heavy silk chair. "Then we continue to love each other and raise your new sisters at Deverill. And we will continue to love you and Trenton very much. Nothing will change."

Dane thought a moment, lowered his eyes and staring at the floor. "I have heard some of the squires call you a whore. The knights do not, because they respect Sir Gaston, but sometimes...sometimes I have heard them talking about Sir Gaston and then they shut up when I enter the room. Do you suppose they think he is wrong to annul your marriage to my father?"

Remington felt sick to her stomach. She knew Dane would be subjected to this kind of talk and wasn't surprised at his question. "It does not matter what they think. We know what is right, do not we? We know that Sir Gaston loves us far more than your father ever did, no matter if he is my legal husband or not," she studied her son's face a moment, his boyish features transforming into young manhood. "I am sorry if you are ashamed of me, Dane. I never meant to humiliate you."

His eyes met hers, shocked. "I am not ashamed of you! And Trenton beat up the last squire who said bad things about you. Everyone is afraid of Trenton."

"They are?" she asked, puzzled. "Why?"

"Because he's so big," Dane insisted. "He's as big as you are."

Remington looked at him doubtfully. "He's not a bully, is he?"

"Nay," Dane shook his head. "Not at all. But he does not like it when people say bad things about you or Sir Gaston. It makes him mad."

Remington gazed at her son, thinking how very much he had grown in the past year. He was nearly nine years old, and Trenton was almost ten. It was hard to believe how much had changed.

"How do you like it here?" she asked, feeling a little better now that the most ugly subjects had been dealt with.

Dane's face lit up and he proceeded to tell her all about his six months at Oxford. Remington listened intently, laughing and genuinely enjoying his tales. Time flew past as she listened to her son, so very glad to see him again that she was content to listen to him all night. In the middle of one particularly comical story, there was a soft rap on the door.

Dane, as he was so trained, opened it.

Gaston entered the room, a young man at his side. It took Remington a moment to realize she was looking at Trenton.

She stood up, her eyes wide. Trenton was, indeed, as tall as she was. Probably taller, and he outweighed her, too.

"Trenton!" she gasped.

Gaston grinned, looking down at his son. "My reaction precisely. Greetings, Dane."

Dane bowed a polished gesture. "My lord de Russe. Congratulations on your dukedom, my lord."

Gaston's eyebrows rose faintly as he let go of Trenton's shoulder and moved to Remington. "My, so formal. You have learned your lessons well."

Remington couldn't take her eyes off Trenton. He was growing into the exact image of his father, and he smiled weakly at her.

"Good health to you, my lady."

She went over to him, her mouth open, inspected him. Then she looked at Dane. "You were correct, Dane. He is as large as I am, larger, in fact. Forgive me for doubting you."

Dane grinned and Gaston put his hands on his hips. "By God, Dane, you have all of your teeth in. And look how fat you are. I must speak to de Vere; he is feeding you far too much. Both of you."

Remington laughed at the expense of the boys. "It's not just the food, but the exercise, too. We have been putting in hard hours on the training field since we are to be promoted to squires at the end of the summer," Dane said proudly.

"So I am told. I am also told that Sir Steven de Norville has demanded you both squire for him," Gaston said with approval. "A fine knight, indeed."

"De Norville?" Remington recognized the name. "Did not he serve Courtenay?"

"He did until de Vere bought his services from the bishop," Gaston replied, his gaze still warm on the boys. "The man is a splendid warrior and de Vere was willing to do anything to gain his loyalties. De Norville's own squire is due to be knighted next month and he is in need of a new one. Two new ones."

Remington smiled proudly. "How wonderful. Imagine that I have two sons who are squires."

Trenton looked to his father, surprised that Remington called him "her" son and looking for a reaction. Gaston merely smiled faintly. "And they will be the finest, will they not? As befitting the sons of the Duke of Warminster."

If there was ever any doubt that Remington and Gaston had not completely accepted the boys as their own, as if each respective boy was not loved any less because they were not of the same blood, those fears were dashed. Blood or not, Dane and Trenton were brothers.

After living for nearly a year with boys whose parents were glad to be rid of them, young men who were abused and cast aside and forgotten, Dane and Trenton knew how very lucky they were to be loved as much as they obviously were.

Dane thought the sun rose and set on Gaston. The man was his hero, his father, and his friend.

And Trenton loved Remington as if he had never had another mother.

No one got very much sleep that night. The four of them retreated to the chamber provided by Lady de Vere and spent most of the night talking. Both boys proudly showed off their blossoming muscles for their parents, Trenton's being far larger, like his father's, but Gaston praised both boys for their physical development. They spoke of their new sisters, their new cousins and life in general at Oxford.

No one brought up London, or the papal council, or the proceedings. It was as if it did not matter anymore; Gaston and Remington were married in their hearts and in their minds, even if the church did not recognize it. Nothing could change their love and devotion to one another.

Toward dawn, Remington fell asleep on the big bed even as Gaston and the boys continued to talk. Dane seemed to do most of the talking for Trenton, who would chime in every now and again in his already-deep voice. Gaston could see so much of himself in his son that it was frightening.

When dawn finally broke, Gaston knew the boys had assigned duties and reluctantly bid them a farewell. He promised that Remington would seek them out to say her own good-byes before they departed.

Just as he snuggled in beside her and closed his eyes, Remington woke and demanded to break her fast with her sons.

With a weary groan, Gaston rolled out of bed.

Jasmine and Antonius, Skye and Nicolas, Remington and Gaston, and the earl and his wife broke their fast in Lady Anne's small solar. Dane and Trenton joined them a short while later, feeling peculiar sharing a meal with the earl when they should be serving him.

Father de Tormo did not show up for the meal and the earl sent a servant to fetch him. Not ten minutes later, the servant was back.

De Vere was conversing with Gaston when the manservant bent over and whispered in his ear. Shocked, the earl turned to Gaston.

"Gaston," he said hesitantly. "I have just been told that your priest was found dead in his bed. Mayhap we should see for ourselves."

Gaston bolted out of the chair, on the heels of the earl. Remington, ashen at the earl's words, watched with horror as the men disappeared from the room. After several long, shocked moments, she turned wide-eyes to her sisters.

"My God," she rasped. "What will we do now that he's dead? He was our counsel, our chief witness, our....friend!"

Jasmine touched her arm. "All's not lost, Remi. You still have us."

Skye nodded eagerly. "We shall convince the papal council. Jasmine can cry and carry on a good act, and I shall....I shall faint for good measure."

Remington was too shocked to respond to Skye's attempt at humor and encouragement. De Tormo was dead. She remembered yesterday, how terrible he had looked, and she knew something had been wrong with the man. She had even told Gaston her fears. The priest simply had not looked well at all.

And de Tormo....he had not eaten well, and mostly slept the entire trip. He certainly wasn't acting himself, and when he had given her the scroll....

The scroll.

He had *known* something; mayhap he'd had a premonition of his own death, for he told her the scroll was to be opened only in case of a dire emergency.

His death was a dire emergency.

Remington bolted from the room, her sisters and brother's-in-law in heated pursuit. They followed her up the narrow staircase and down the dimly lit corridor until, one by one, they disappeared into the bower.

Remington dove into the wardrobe and tore out her traveling satchel. With shaking hands, she tossed it on the bed and dug into it. Triumphantly, she jerked forth the vellum.

"Here!" she gasped.

Nicolas and Antonius looked at her as if she had gone insane, but Jasmine and Skye were as eager as she was.

"Open it!" Jasmine demanded.

Remington did not hesitate; she broke the seal and rolled open the parchment.

She read the contents carefully, the color draining from her face. Her wide eyes opened wider and she re-read the message.

The group in the room waited with anticipation, waiting with increasing impatience for her to announce her finding. Finally, Skye could wait no longer.

"Remi?" she encouraged her sister to tell all.

Remington tore her eyes away from the vellum; focusing astonished eyes on her loved ones.

"He knew," she breathed. "He knew he was going to die and he.... my God, I have got to find Gaston."

She wandered past them, the parchment clasped tightly in her hands. As she made her way down the hall toward de Tormo's room in the southern wing, her little entourage followed.

"She's mad," Antonius muttered.

Jasmine shushed him loudly. "She's not. De Tormo must have left her a most powerful message."

Nicolas left his wife to walk beside Remington, glancing at her with concern. She was preoccupied and dazed. When they reached the priests room, he helped her through the door by shoving several servants out of the way.

Gaston and de Vere were huddled by the window, a serious conversation between them. One look at Gaston's face and Remington could see that he was having the exact same concerns she had been having not ten minutes earlier. She forgot about protocol, knowing she shouldn't be calling to him across a room full of people, but not caring at the moment. He had to know.

"Gaston!"

His head snapped to her, his eyes full of concern. Before he could break from de Vere, she was rushing to him, the vellum held in an outstretched hand.

"The parchment de Tormo gave me yesterday," she stammered, unsure as to where to begin. "You must....for God's sake, read it."

Puzzled, he took the missive from her and read the contents. His reading slowed as he reached the bottom and he, too, turned amazed eyes to her.

"By God," he breathed.

She nodded shakily. "He knew he was going to die. Gaston, if we present this to the council, they'll surely grant the annulment."

Gaston glanced at the missive again and John interrupted. "What is it?"

Gaston cleared his throat, roving over the message again as if he were still trying to convince himself they were real. He held out his arm to Remington, and she pressed herself against him.

"It says...," he glanced up, eyeing the servants and various employees of the earl. De Vere, sensing his hesitation, ordered the room cleared.

Not a minute later, the room was devoid of the household staff. Jasmine and Skye crowded closer to hear Gaston.

"It says that de Tormo heard Guy's confession, in which he admitted his servitude of Satan. De Tormo states that Guy confessed to killing infants and drinking their blood, transforming into an incubus during the full of the moon and seducing virgins, only to return to eat the offspring their union produced, and furthermore trying to prepare his wife to be a receptacle to house a demon soul," his eyes moved from the missive to Remington. "He also confessed to be the concubine of Hecate."

"Who is that?" Nicolas demanded, horrified by what he was hearing.

"The Greek goddess of pernicious sorcery," de Vere answered softly. "She is as vile and as evil as Lucifer himself and is the queen of the dead. Continue, Gaston."

A muscle in Gaston's jaw twitched. "It goes on to say that Guy also confessed to such crimes as sodomizing goats, changing the course of the weather by burning snakes, and having sex with his wife's sisters in hopes of planting a demon seed; he hoped to bring Satan back to earth in the flesh. De Tormo furthermore states that he is a personal witness to the sanctuary in which these dark spells were cast."

The room was eerily silent. Remington watched Gaston's face intently, seeing the emotions that were usually so well controlled. Gaston lowered the missive and turned his eyes to the body of the priest, stiffening on the bed.

"He signed it as his dying declaration, swearing that Satan was taking his life because he knew too much of Guy's dark workings. He says the only way to be rid of such evil is to desecrate Guy's body and erase all written record of his name."

Jasmine and Skye were terrified. "Remi...," Jasmine whispered. "What of the story Father de Tormo had us memorize? Is what he says really true?"

Remington was shaking. "No, it is not. He lied, Jassy. He is probably burning in the fires of hell right now for this falsehood, but he did it for Gaston and I. As a dying declaration, it will weigh more heavily that any testimony any living person can give. The church will take it almost as the word of God."

Everyone in the room turned to look at the cooling corpse, thinking of the most unselfish sacrifice from a most arrogant and annoying man.

"Why would Guy confess these things? Was he looking for absolution?" De Vere asked thoughtfully. "If the church believes he was confessing to repent, the missive could mean nothing."

Gaston shook his head. "De Tormo says that Guy was not confessing in the literal sense, but more to brag of his accomplishments. The priest claims that Stoneley was very proud of his dark alliance and told de Tormo these things simply because he was well aware of the priest's inability to discuss confessions. He knew de Tormo would not, and could not, tell anyone."

De Vere nodded, clarified, and moved away thoughtfully. Gaston clutched the missive in one hand and Remington in the other. He tore his gaze away from de Tormo, turning to his knights.

"Mobilize the men. We leave in an hour."

Exactly an hour later, everyone was ready to leave but Remington. Gaston searched everywhere for her, but was unsuccessful in locating her.

He wasn't truly concerned, merely annoyed. Nicolas and the earl were looking for her, too, when Gaston finally met up with de Vere near the keep's chapel.

"I found her," de Vere announced. "She's in the chapel."

"In the chapel?" Gaston repeated. "What on earth is she doing in there? Remi does not believe in God."

John smiled and jerked his thumb toward the stained-glass structure. "Go and see for yourself."

Puzzled, Gaston did as he was told.

Remington was sitting in the front pew. On either side of her sat Dane and Trenton. Gaston entered quietly, skirting the outside aisle as he approached, hearing the soft rumble of Remington's voice. Gradually, her murmured words became clearer.

".....he was considered the wisest man in the world. The Queen of Sheba, hearing of Solomon's wisdom, traveled to Israel by camel caravan to test the king's intelligence. With her, she brought all sorts of valuable goods; spices, gold, precious stones as gifts for the king," her arm was casually draped around Trenton, gazing at Dane as she spoke. Gaston slowed his pace, listening. "She tested Solomon with many, many difficult questions, but he answered every one of them perfectly. Impressed, she praised the god of Abraham for creating such a brilliant man and she fell madly in love with him. Solomon had many wives, but he courted the queen on his magic carpet that was carried by desert winds, bringing her costly gifts. The only problem, however, was the fact that the queen worshipped the sun instead of the one true god. Solomon would not marry her unless they worshipped the same deity."

"I would not marry her, anyway," Dane sniffed. "What a bold wench to attempt to test a man's intelligence."

Trenton nodded in agreement. "Queen or no, I'd take my hand to her backside, the saucy female."

Remington scowled at the boys. "Since when do you address women in those terms? I do not think I like it."

"Not all women. Only women who do not know their place in the world," Dane insisted.

Remington raised an eyebrow at her son. "Dane, I fear you have been listening to arrogant knights and their loud talk. Men respect a woman who knows her mind and is a valuable asset."

Dane wrinkled his nose. "Wenches are no good."

Trenton tittered and Remington was about to lay into both of them when Gaston came to the rescue.

"She's right, you know. 'Tis a good thing to have an intelligent, beautiful woman by your side and you'd better watch your next move, or I suspect your mother will plant her hand in a place few have touched."

Remington tittered now as Dane and Trenton looked uncertain. Gaston sat down next to Dane, smiling at the three of them. "The column is ready when you are, my lady."

She gave Trenton a squeeze and lowered her arm. "I am ready, I suppose. I just wanted to see the boys one last time."

Gaston glanced at the two young men. "And so you have. More glory tales?"

"Solomon and Sheba," Trenton told him.

"Pushy wench," Dane muttered and his mother pinched him, much to Trenton's amusement. "Ow!"

Gaston laughed softly at Dane's discomfort. "Enough abuse, Remi. We must be on our way."

The boys stood up and kissed her dutifully, telling their father a warm good-bye. When they vacated the chapel through a small side door, Gaston pulled Remington to her feet and assisted her from the pew.

"What were you doing in here, anyway?" he asked softly, curling her hand into the crook of his elbow.

She watched the ground as they walked down the center aisle. "Praying. Dane and Trenton found me."

"Praying?" he looked at her curiously. "You do not believe in God, Remi. Just whom were you praying to?"

"God," she insisted. "I thought... mayhap he would listen to me and forgive de Tormo for his lies on our behalf. I had to try, Gaston."

He patted her hand and she stopped at the wide oaken doors that led into the chapel, her gaze raking over the still hall. The polished oak altar thirty feet away caught her attention, as did the polished pewter candle banks. A huge ivory cross hung on the wall overlooking the altar, and lavish silk curtains graced the walls.

"I would be married in a church, Gaston," she whispered, turning her gaze to him. "Guy and I were married in the dining hall of Mt. Holyoak. When you and I are married, I want it to be in a church."

He kissed her hand. "Westminster. I promise."

She smiled shyly, allowing him to lead her out into the bright sunlight.

CHAPTER THIRTY-ONE

Gaston and Remington hung back with the troops while Nicolas and Patrick greeted their father. Martin hugged Jasmine happily, and refused to let go of Skye. While Patrick talked, Nicolas pried his wife away and whisked her and her sister into the manse.

As Gaston had said, Martin ignored him completely. He did not even come out to the carriage to greet Remington, and she was saddened, but there were more important matters weighing on her mind.

Nicolas, Antonius and Patrick rejoined the caravan, leaving Jasmine and Skye in Uncle Martin's care until they were so required by the papal council. Patrick wanted to know why his father was so upset with Gaston, but his cousin waved him off and ordered the troops to straighten ranks and prepare for the move-out.

De Tormo's body was sent ahead to Westminster as Gaston's column set forward once again, en route to the Tower. Henry was there, awaiting Gaston's arrival, and Gaston was extremely eager to show the king de Tormo's missive.

Remington felt the familiar pangs of fear as they crossed the Thames and the Tower drew close. Guy was there, looking down at her, she just *knew* it. He could sense her, as she could sense his evil. When the party passed down the narrow entryway and into the courtyard, she shivered involuntarily. He was *here*.

Henry met them in the courtyard. He greeted Gaston pleasantly, turning his attention to Remington as Nicolas helped her from the carriage. Dressed in ecru-colored satin with gold embroider, she looked radiant.

"My lady, what a pleasure it is to see you again," Henry received her.

Remington curtsied low. "Thank you, Your Grace."

The king's gaze lingered on her a brief moment longer before turning to Gaston. One look into Henry's brown eyes and Gaston could see that something was terribly wrong. He wished Remington wasn't with him; if the news was bad, he wanted to hear it alone. Only after he'd had time to calm himself would he deliver the information to Remington.

"There are refreshments in my solar," Henry said, walking toward the Queen's House.

Gaston took Remington's arm, instructing Nicolas and Patrick to settle the men and take station in the knights' quarters until he sent for them.

The solar was cool and smelled of fresh rushes. Remington accepted a cup of wine from a servant and stood stiffly beside Gaston, nervous in the king's presence. After what happened the last time she saw him, she was uncomfortable.

Henry sat heavily, stretching his long legs. Gaston stood like stone, waiting expectantly for the revelation to spill forth from the monarch's lips. The two men looked at each other, silent words filling the speechless void until Henry finally spoke.

"Guy spoke to the papal council while you were gone, Gaston," he said quietly. There was no need for formalities, or empty conversations leading into the real reason for Gaston's visit. They were long since past any overtures.

Gaston's face slackened in shock. "But I thought they were going to wait until the rest of Lady Remington's testimony was heard."

Henry put up a silencing hand. "They were indeed, but Guy begged and pleaded until he obtained permission to speak. In fact, he wanted to speak without you present because he claims you intimidate him," the king snorted ironically. "I cannot imagine why."

Gaston was not interested in the king's attempt at humor. "And?"

Henry examined his jewel-encrusted chalice. His slight attempt to lighten the mood had failed and he was not particularly eager to continue the conversation without a company of men to protect him, but Gaston was waiting. And so was the lady.

Henry met Gaston's eye. "Guy spent four hours in front of the council. Gaston, I have never in my life seen such a display of pitiful hysterics. He cried and moaned, relaying to the council that fact that he was a helpless victim in my greater scheme to control England. His keep, and his wife, were being used as a reward to my most powerful warrior. He claimed that he and Remington shared a great love for one another, and the only reason she had requested an annulment was because you had bewitched her weak mind."

Gaston had suspected that Guy would come across as a casualty in Henry's war and was not surprised. But he had a suspicion that Henry was not finished with his tale and he pulled Remington against him before replying. "And what happened?"

Henry looked to his cup again. "No annulment will be granted based on God's law of the absolution of marriage. I was berated before the entire council for attempting to apply my law over God's, for trying to dissolve a marriage for the purpose of bestowing a reward to my faithful. Furthermore, they are pressuring me to release Stoneley so he can return to Mt. Holyoak and live peaceably with his wife."

Gaston's jaw dropped. Next to him, Remington nearly collapsed with shock but he held her firm. He could feel he soft sobs beginning.

Henry could see the shock, the pain, and he was greatly remorseful that he had been unable to sway the council. Instead, he had taken a browbeating. "Gaston, I am sorry. I tried, I truly did."

Gaston swallowed hard, trying to comfort Remington and striving to gain command of his reeling mind. After a moment of struggle, he turned to his king. "It's not over, my lord. Not at all."

"It is," Henry said gently. "There is nothing more to...."

"Aye, there is," Gaston said forcefully, speaking to Henry yet still clutching Remington to him. "Father de Tormo died yesterday, Henry. But before his death, he swore out a dying declaration that announces to the world that Guy Stoneley is a proven devil worshipper. Stoneley confessed these acts to the priest in a confession and de Tormo wrote them down. Additionally, Remington and her sisters are prepared to verify the confession with their own first-hand knowledge."

Henry looked astonished. "Where is this parchment?"

"In the carriage," Gaston replied, his throat tight with emotion. "I would deliver it to Bourchier personally. Now."

"Absolutely. My God, Gaston, they will have no choice but to reopen the case and grant the annulment if de Tormo can prove Guy is Satan's student."

Gaston knew that. So did Remington. So what if it was a lie.
Anything for you.

Bourchier read the missive. John of Imola read the missive. The arch-bishop summoned John Morton, bishop of Ely, Robert Morton, bishop of Worcester, Christopher Urswick and Peter Courtenay. They all read it, pondered it, and discussed it. The discussion and arguments that ensued went on into the night.

Gaston, Henry and Uncle Jasper waited in the lavishly appointed visitor's solar of Westminster. Gaston sat motionlessly, staring from the window at the three-quarter moon, listening to the nightbirds sing. He wondered how Remington was faring, having left her at the Tower in the care of his knights. He hoped she wasn't too frantic.

De Tormo had told Remington to open the missive only in the case of a catastrophic emergency. Death was considered an emergency, Gaston reasoned, and it furthermore seemed to him that de Tormo knew how the delegation was going to rule. Was it possible that de Tormo killed himself in order to make his testimony absolutely irrefu-table? Gaston knew it wasn't possible, but he wondered just the same. There was nothing more potent that a dying declaration.

He had to shake his head at the haughty priest he was so intent on hating when they first met. It still amazed him that the man had turned out to be his mightiest weapon in the fight for Remington.

"Are you worried?" Henry asked him quietly, sitting a few feet away.

Gaston turned from the window. "Worried? No. I think concerned is a more apt term, my lord."

"Concerned nothing," Jasper snorted, scratching at his scalp. "Once they read what a decrepit bastard Stoneley is, there should be no doubt. They will not allow Remington to remain in such a marriage, for the sake of her soul."

Henry raised a weary eyebrow. "My God, I hope not. I would like to be over with this, Gaston. I have aged unnaturally since the day you informed me of your love for this woman."

Gaston half-grinned. "I have, too."

The meeting lasted into the night. Rapidly approaching midnight, Gaston and his two companions were startled when the chamber door opened with a groan and Courtenay came forth, bearing a tallow candle. Gaston was on his feet.

"They want to speak with Stoneley, Gaston," Peter said quietly. "I have sent my personal guard to escort him here for more interrogation."

Gaston did not realize he was shaking with anticipation, emotion, every possible feeling he could experience. "How goes the opinion, Peter?"

Much to his shock, the bishop actually gave him a small smile. "Well for you. The need to speak with Stoneley is merely a formality."

Gaston could hardly grasp what he was hearing. After so much disappointment and anguish, he almost did not understand what he was being told. "Then.....Remington does not need to testify? Or her sisters?"

Peter shook his head. "The council has enough faith in de Tormo that they will take him for his word. Besides, he signed his name in his own blood, which is as good as swearing on the name of the all mighty. Better, in fact. De Tormo will be well-rewarded in heaven for his loyalty."

Gaston felt a sickening feeling in the pit of his stomach on de Tormo's behalf. As Remington said, the man was most likely roasting in the sulfur lake for his lie. Only a select few mortals would know of his great sacrifice.

He turned away from the bishop, relief flooding him like nothing he had ever tasted. De Tormo had been right all along, about everything. He knew how the council would react to his signed revelation, sparing Remington and her sisters the horror of testifying.

By God, the man *knew*.

Months of testimony on Remington's behalf had failed to convince the council to provide an annulment. Brimley, Ingilsby, Sir Alfred Tarrington all had been unable to convince the church that Guy Stoneley was nothing short of a demon himself. Gaston's testimony had been inadmissible because he was in love with the woman. Henry couldn't vouch for Remington and was therefore useless, except to bully the church on Gaston's behalf.

All of the worry and agony was now finally coming to a conclusion and Gaston could scarce believe it; if all went well, by next month, Remington would be the duchess of Warminster.

He shuddered with joy at the thought of calling her his wife. He would use the term liberally, freely, with every other breath. He had waited too long not to.

So miracles were possible, after all. Mayhap if he thanked God this night, the Lord would finally hear him. And he would pray for de Tormo's soul in the process.

"What about me? Is there still to be testimony on my behalf?" he asked in a raspy voice.

"Why?" Peter shrugged. "They know you and your reputation, Gaston. There is nothing anyone could say that could convince them that you would be any less than a grand husband for her."

Gaston slanted him a glance. "What of the business of my betraying Richard? Surely that scars my character."

"I told them what happened," Henry said from his chair. When Gaston turned surprised eyes to his king, Henry nodded affirmatively. "They know of Richard's liaison with your wife, how he humiliated you. And they know that you disapproved of the murder of his nephews. They understand that you could not serve such an immoral man."

Gaston was surprised. "And when did your testimony come about?"

"Right before Guy's," Henry rose wearily, weaving a bit. "My spies told me that Guy was going to present a piteous, wretched case and I wanted to balance it with statements on your behalf. Do not look so angry, Gaston. I did what was necessary, and you know it."

Gaston wasn't angry, simply off-guard. He cleared his throat in a nervous gesture, combing his fingers through his dark hair. "Then I thank you, my lord."

Henry looked at his Dark Knight, the most powerful warrior he commanded. But even Gaston was humbled by the church and the laws of God, as was the king. The fact that the annulment was near approval was an absolute miracle, and they all had de Tormo to thank for it.

But Gaston did not ever truly clarify if the charges were true; Henry would not ask. He did not want to know, being a party to a lie of cataclysmic repercussions. He did not want God to blame him for knowing too much.

Silence settled in the room as the conversation lulled. While Henry went to pour himself his third goblet of wine, Peter moved to Gaston hesitantly.

"I hope you can forgive me for what has happened, Gaston," he said softly. "We were friends once, you and I. Whatever happened with Lady Remington's annulment was with the church alone and beyond my scope."

My friend, Gaston thought. "We're still friends, Peter. Your help has been invaluable."

Peter's fair face relaxed and his smile blossomed. "I have tried, truly," he lowered his voice. "I'd grant you the damn annulment if it were in my power, church or no. Especially after Guy's testimony yesterday."

Gaston raised an eyebrow. "How so?"

Peter shook his head in disgust. "The man's entire statement was a farce. I have never seen so much blatant dribbling, pleading and carrying-on. It was embarrassing to say the least, but John and Thomas listened to every word. They believed him, even if the rest of us did not."

"What's this I hear that Henry is being pressured into releasing him?"

"True enough. The papal council feels Stoneley had been unfairly singled out and punished. To release him would be to make restitution."

Gaston snorted. "Restitution, is it? They feel he's been treated wrongly because of what he possesses. Have they forgotten that the man is a prisoner of the crown?"

Peter shrugged. "He is married to Remington and you want her, and they know Henry will stop at nothing to grant you your desire. Prisoner or not."

Gaston let out a repugnant sigh. What a mixed-up, chaotic mess he was involved in.

Peter moved to Henry and Gaston moved away from the group, standing in front of a narrow window and feeling the cool evening on his face. Remington, a few miles away at the Tower, filled his mind even as the wind caressed him, and he found himself imagining the gentle fingers of the breeze were hers somehow. If he closed his eyes, he could literally feel her.

Guy had no idea there was anything amiss until his door opened and one lone papal guard entered. The older man was dressed in the crimson colors, fully armored, and he paused stiffly just inside the door.

"My lord," he said formally. "You have been summoned. Please collect yourself and accompany me."

"Accompany you where?"

"To Westminster. The papal council demands your presence, my lord."

Guy continued to sit at the small writing table, a quill in his hand as he composed a letter to his son. He still did not know where Dane was; no one would tell him anything, not even the church. He hoped that somehow his letter would find its way to Dane, wherever he was.

Not because he cared for the boy; but he wanted the church to think he did. Then, mayhap, someone would take pity on him and tell him where his son was.

Anything to use against Remington.

He had already succeeded in stopping the annulment proceedings, claiming victimization. That bastard de Russe had not bested him, after all. He kept his wife, and from what he had heard, the Dark One had abandoned Mt. Holyoak. And he had almost secured his release, a mere technicality as far as he was concerned.

God, he was clever.

"More questions? Why is that?"

"I do not know, my lord. Please come with me."

Guy rose slowly, a shadow of concern crossing him. "Is there a problem, sergeant?"

"I do not know, my lord," the man repeated.

Guy frowned, moving to don his shirt. Even in the coolest days, he avoided tunics unless absolutely necessary. He hated to cover up his beauty. "Would you be so kind as to tell me if I am to be released this night? Is that why I am being summoned?"

"I have not been so informed, my lord," the soldier said. "All I know is that the papal council wishes to speak with you. Most likely Henry and the Duke of Warminster, as well, considering they are at Westminster."

Guy felt a bolt of shock move through him. "The duke is here? Did he bring his... lady?"

The guard nodded. He had not heard of the details regarding the board's proceedings, only that there was something very potent going on if Henry and Gaston de Russe were involved. He had no idea where Stoneley fit into this, and that was his undoing. The guard was a fairly dim man who did what was ordered of him and did not move far beyond his limited world.

"The duke arrived this afternoon with his household, including his wife, I believe," he replied. "She is housed in Martin Tower."

Guy was seized with another shocking bolt, only this jolt was one of excitement. Remington was not far from this very room, and he was suddenly extremely excited to know that.

His sharp mind was working quickly. Remington was here... de Russe was at Westminster, miles away. A plan took root, began to nurture and take shape.

Guy glanced at the soldier one more time before moving to his great wardrobe and pretending to rummage through. The rapid movements of his hands disguised his shaking; he was literally shaking. His plan was blossoming, consuming his mind, until he knew there was no possible alternative.

He was confident he was to be released. So, what if he were to release himself a bit ahead of schedule? And Remington was to remain his wife, was she not? He would take her with him.

Home.

Home to Mt. Holyoak.

So far away in Yorkshire, surrounded by his fellow loyal barons, not even Henry could return him to London. And, mayhap, the church would go so far as to demand the king leave him in peace. After all, the church was on his side after his performance yesterday. Who would *blame* him for taking what was his and fleeing London as fast as he could?

Even if he was, technically, escaping jail.

Guy pushed those thoughts aside. Once escaped home, mayhap Henry would eventually forget about him and focus on his many other troubles instead. And de Russe would find another whore, and leave Remington alone.

Aye, it would work out... eventually.

But first, he had to get out of the White Tower. And there was only one possible out, as he saw it.

Certainly he could wait for the king to release him. But why should he? He had been in this damnable hell long enough.

"You there," he motioned to the sergeant. "Come here and give me a hand with this."

The soldier was either too dim to ask what he needed assistance with, or he simply did not care. He walked over to the wardrobe expectantly.

Guy stood slightly aback of him, one hand shrouded in the clothes that were slung over the wardrobe door. "Can you jar that boot free? It seems to be stuck in the drawer."

The soldier bent down, yanking at the leather boot. It took Guy less than a second to wrap the belt around the soldier's neck, tightening the noose so tightly that the mail hauberk cut into the skin.

In a strangled heap of mail and blood, the soldier slipped to the floor.

Guy smiled. Death always made him smile. Even if the soldier was bigger than he was, the armor fit well enough.

It wasn't difficult to slip past the guards at his door. He kept his eyes averted and his helm on, telling the guards that Stoneley was ill and that he was summoning a physic. If the Tower guards happened to look into the room, they would see a man in bed, covered to his head with a blanket. Guy knew his guards well enough to know that they would not bother to enter the room and check the prisoner personally.

Taking the papal guard on his word, they continued to stand vigilant watch at the door, expecting a physic shortly.

Free! Free! Guy's mind sang with the glee of it, the simplicity of it. He could not believe he had not thought of this strategy earlier, but in truth, the opportunity had not presented itself. What he had done moments ago was done in the spur of the moment.

He knew his way out of the White Tower easily, and he moved directly for the Martin Tower. His heart was pounding in his ears as he moved across the dark courtyard, moving freely as he had not moved in over two years. It was almost too good to believe!

His mind was reeling with plans, possibilities, and escape routes. Over his shoulder, he could see the small papal escort waiting patiently by the Tower entrance, but they apparently had not seen him. With the three-quarter moon, it was dark enough in the shadows that they could not make out the color of his crimson tunic from that distance away.

As soon as he rounded the White Tower, he was out of their line of sight and he relaxed. Several hundred yards in front of him loomed the Martin Tower, and he lowered his head as he scurried down the walk. Behind him, the Salt Tower provided him ample shadow coverage.

There were sentries posted at intervals and he passed them with no problem. His excitement, his confidence, soared.

Sweet Remington would soon be within his grasp. But as he approached the Martin Tower, he slowed. As soon as he entered her bower, she would know it was he. And he had no doubt that she would give him away to her guards, who would most likely be de Russe's men. And they would kill him.

His pace slowed more dramatically. Mayhap he could send someone else in to retrieve her, to deliver her straight into his hands far away from de Russe's dogs.

Wise man that he was, Stoneley thought quickly on his feet. At the entrance to the Martin Tower was one of Henry's household soldiers. He approached the man.

"The papal delegation wishes to speak with Lady Stoneley," he stated firmly. "You will summon her and bring her so that I may escort her to the hearings."

The guard looked him up and down. "An' what's wrong with your legs, pansy? You can mount stairs as well as I can."

Guy's first reaction was to strike, but he clenched his fist instead. He gave a helpless shrug. "I have got the gout, man. It'll take me all night to take those stairs. Be a good chum, will you?"

The household soldier grumbled and cursed, but he complied. Guy smiled smugly, pleased at his cleverness and glancing overhead. The moon was beautiful this night.

Remington was asleep when Patrick roused her. Stumbling from the great bed, she donned her ecru-satin surcoat and pulled her hair back into a golden net. Still half-asleep, she splashed cold water on her face and pinched some color into her cheeks, gradually becoming increasingly anxious as she groomed. Why did not Gaston come personally for her? She prayed that nothing was terribly wrong, realizing she had done more praying recently than she had done in her entire life.

Running her finger in a small vial of mint balm and rubbing it over her teeth to freshen her breath, she was ready and threw open the bower door even as she struggled to shove her shoe on.

"I am ready, Patrick," she said hurriedly.

Patrick steadied her as she adjusted the hasty shoe. "You shall need a cloak, Remi. 'Tis cool outside."

With a sharp exhale, she dashed back into the room and retrieved a cloak of crushed golden silk, a gift from Gaston after the twins were born. The lining was of white rabbit, almost too hot on the cool night, but it matched the dress so, therefore, she took it anyway.

"Let's go!" she said eagerly.

Patrick escorted her to the base of the Martin Tower, where the household guard was back at his post. The soldier pointed to the papal guard several feet away.

"He's come for the lady."

Remington swung the cloak over her shoulders, gazing at the guard in the distance. It never occurred to her that it was odd that the man had not come for her personally, or that he had not met her at the base of the stairs. All she knew was that the man was to take her to Gaston.

But Patrick demanded to accompany her. She tried to protest, but he insisted. With a resigned shrug, she and Patrick made their way to the papal escort.

Guy saw her coming; his heart pounding so loudly that he was sure the entire keep could hear it. But who was the fool with her? Damnation. He would have to dispose of the knight, and do it quickly. Remington would recognize him in a heartbeat and he could not allow his perfect scheme to be foiled this early in the game.

Panicked for the moment, he turned away from Remington and Patrick and motioned for them to follow. They did, nearly catching up to him as they rounded the corner on the green by the Chapel of St. Peter and Vincula.

But Guy kept a pace ahead of them, working a small dagger out of his waistband. Passing the chopping block, adjacent to the Beauchamp Tower, Guy clasped the dagger close to his arm and worked his belt loose. His sword went clattering to the soft ground.

"Good Christ," he said in an exaggerated lower-bred London accent. "'Ow in the 'ell did 'at 'appen?"

Remington came to an abrupt halt, watching Patrick bend down to pick up the sword. One moment Patrick was grasping the weapon; the next moment, the papal guard was on top of him.

And in the next moment, Patrick collapsed on the ground with a dagger protruding from his neck.

Remington did not quite grasp what she was seeing. It was the farthest thing from her mind. A second or two after Patrick landed in a heap, a scream rose to Remington's lips and her eyes flew to the papal guard, now moving toward her with lightning speed.

Sea-crystal eyes locked with icy-blue. Guy Stoneley was staring back at her.

"Guy!" she shrieked.

It would not do to have a shrieking, screaming captive. Instinctively, Guy brought up a mailed fist and crowned Remington on the side of the head, just like old times. She dropped like a stone.

He left her, a mound of silk and satin, and dragged Patrick across the moist dirt to deposit him in a small doorway. With any luck, he would not be found until morning and by then, he and Remington would be on their way to Mt. Holyoak. With little exertion, he swung Remington into his arms and carried her out into the main courtyard.

The small papal escort looked concerned as he approached, but Guy kept his face lowered and waved them off. "Part the way, men," he declared.

The three guards looked at him strangely as he commandeered the nearest destrier. "Now where do you think you are going with that horse?"

Guy threw Remington up over the animal and she grunted softly, beginning to come around. Guy slapped her on the rear. "She's ill, man. Can you not see that? I have got to find a physic."

The guards looked at each other hesitantly, but Guy was forceful. He mounted behind Remington and gathered the reins. "I shall send the horse back, I promise. You have Bourchier's word. God bless you for allowing me to seek care for this woman."

Guy was too fast, too slick. He was spearing the horse toward the main entrance before anyone could stop him.

With a shout that sounded suspiciously like a triumphant bellow, he tore through the narrow entrance as if the demons of hell were on his heel.

CHAPTER THIRTY-TWO

It was just before dawn. Gaston was ashen by the time he reached the Tower; so pale he was nearly green. Not a word was spoken between he and Henry, or Nicolas or Antonius. Uncle Jasper seemed to be doing most of the talking, and it was minimal at that.

It had taken the papal escort three hours to realize they had been duped. A search of Guy Stoneley's rooms turned up a dead comrade in the prisoner's bed. By the time they returned to Westminster with news of the prisoner's disappearance, it was an hour before sunrise.

Gaston realized within the first few sentences what had happened. Stunned beyond believing, he knew what had taken place and his only thought at that moment was to reach

Remington. No one had so much as mentioned her, but he knew instinctively that she would be missing.

He did not know how he knew. But he knew.

Gaston did not stop until he reached their bedchamber in the Martin Tower. Even then, he only stood in the door like a stone statue, staring at the bed as if he could will Remington to appear.

"Dear God," he breathed. "She's gone!"

Nicolas came up behind him, surveying the room. "Where's Patrick?"

Gaston felt sick. Every emotion he could possible feel was crowding his mind, torturing him. "Send the household troops to search the grounds. Mayhap he's been...."

"No!" Nicolas stumbled back, horrified. "Do not even suggest it! There is no way Guy Stoneley could best Patrick in a fight!"

Gaston could not react to Nicolas' grief. He was filled with quite enough of his own. "He must have found out she was here," he mumbled, feeling as if he were going mad. He did not even realize Henry was standing beside him. "How is it possible that he found out she was here? How did he *know*?"

"'Twould not be difficult for a soldier to mention it," Henry said quietly. "There are a thousand different ways he could have discovered her arrival."

Gaston was dazed. He shook his head with disbelief. "Why was only one guard sent to escort Stoneley? Why did not the whole damn company attend him? Why did not the household troops insist on more than one man in Stoneley's room?"

Henry shook his head; he did not have the answers. "Security was lax, Gaston. Stoneley has never given us any problems; he's never been belligerent or combative in the least and, therefore, not considered a real threat. 'Tis the only explanation I can offer you for the presence of merely one guard."

Gaston's eyes were wide with shock, his face taut. He was having difficulty thinking, for the possibilities literally overwhelmed him. "So Stoneley killed the papal guard sent to escort him back to Westminster, then donned his uniform and spirited Remington from the compound. But how did he get past Patrick? Damnation, I do not understand any of this."

Henry put his hand on Gaston in an ineffectual attempt to calm him. "We shall interrogate the guards who were on duty. Someone had to see something."

Gaston's eyes were locked onto the bed, the indenture Remington had made in the feather mattress. Woodenly, he wandered to the wardrobe, as if it would lend a clue. He simply couldn't believe what all of the facts were leading him to believe.

Guy had escaped and took Remington with him.

His huge hands gripped the open doors of the wardrobe as he gazed inside. Be seemed to stand there for an excessive amount of time when suddenly a loud popping noise filled the room, crumbling and snapping.

The wardrobe doors came off in Gaston's hands.

Henry stared, astonished, as Gaston tossed the doors aside as if they did not weigh a couple of hundred pounds apiece. It was then, and only then, that every man present realized the extent of Gaston's anguish.

"Where would he take her?" Henry asked, still shocked. "To Mt. Holyoak?"

Gaston nodded absently, reaching into the wardrobe and drawing forth a small glass vial. Reverently, he pulled the stopper and inhaled the contents. All watched him curiously as he gently replaced the stopper and shoved the vial into his waistband.

The scent reminded him of Ripon and the first time he had ever made love to Remington. He would; nay, had to, keep it with him. It would keep him steady when the pain was more than he could bear.

"I ride north," his voice was tight, his manner hard. "Nicolas, find your brother, or what's left of him, and return to Deverill. Antonius, you will ride to Oxford and notify de Vere of what has happened. Tell him to keep close watch on Dane."

"Are you going to Mt. Holyoak?" Henry demanded again. "Are you so sure he will take her there?"

"There is nowhere else he could go. I will find him, and I will kill him."

Henry watched the Duke of Warminster transform himself into battle mode. Hard. Cold. Calculating. The perfect killing machine. He pitied Guy Stoneley.

"I shall notify Bourchier of what has transpired, Gaston," Henry said quietly. "Have no doubt that they will support you in your endeavor."

Gaston did not reply.

"We shall search for Patrick," Antonius took charge; Nicolas was having difficulty controlling himself. "And I shall interrogate the household guards personally. If I discover anything valuable, I shall try to send you word."

Gaston was busy with his gauntlets, tightening the interior strap of one. He listened, but said nothing. This was the Gaston who was preparing for the battle of his life, and they all knew it.

"Is it not possible that Lady Remington is with Lady Beaufort?" Jasper interjected at the last moment, trying to find reason in this chaos. "She is still at the Tower, you know. It is possible that Margaret sought the lady's company. Mayhap Patrick is with her, as well."

Gaston paused a brief moment. "Send someone to check. I will only wait that long."

Jasper snapped to the nearest soldier, who dashed away in a jingle of armor. Until the man returned, it became the mission of every man in the room to keep Gaston calm.

No one wanted to meet their end as the wardrobe doors had.

Gaston remained calm, but he also remained as a block of stone, cold and unmoving. In truth, he was afraid to speak or move for fear it would release the dam building inside him. He was afraid to explore the feelings growing within his heart, afraid that he would be unable to deal with them.

So he remained still and aloof, waiting without hope for the soldier to return from Lady Beaufort's room. He knew that Guy had taken Remington.

He did not have a doubt.

He also knew that Guy would take her back to Mt. Holyoak. It was his home and there was no reason to believe he would take her anywhere else.

Gaston would then ride to Mt. Holyoak to retrieve Remington, but logic told him that it would be useless to bring his army. With as well fortified as Mt. Holyoak was, he could lay siege for months and never see progress. He doubted that he could even catch up to them with the head start they had.

Nay; the intelligent thing to do would be to go alone and wait for an opportunity to take back what was his. And kill Guy in the process.

He couldn't even think on what the man might have done to her already. He refused to imagine the beatings, or mayhap he had even raped her by now. Gaston angrily shoved those hideous thoughts aside, for there was nothing he could do at the moment.

Forcing himself to remain calm in the wake of such a catastrophe was the hardest thing he had ever had to do in his life.

They waited for nearly an hour. Gaston had remained immobile the entire time, standing by the wardrobe, waiting. But he was near to bursting with impatience, merely reining himself because of Henry's presence. But he could not hold out much longer. He had to get to Remington.

Mercifully, the same soldier that had gone in search of Lady Beaufort reappeared in the company of another soldier. The men appeared breathless and wide-eyed.

Henry snapped at them. "Speak."

The soldier bowed crisply, almost as an afterthought. "My lord, Lady Beaufort has returned to Windsor, but her serving woman told me that Lady Remington had not been to visit her," he indicated the soldier standing next to him. "Malsgrave was on duty last night, standing watch by the Middle Tower. He saw... well, go on, man."

The second soldier, a young man, paled in the presence of the mighty men. "A p-p-papal guard rode through the main entrance last night with a woman slung across his saddle."

Gaston suddenly came to life. "Could you see much of his face? What did he look like?"

The soldier shook his head. "Nay, my lord, I could not see his face for the helm. But the woman...well," he brought up his hand. In his fist was a golden hair net, delicate and torn. "This came off her hair as they rode by. That is why we took so long in returning to you; we went to find it. I remember seeing something fall, but....."

Gaston snatched the hair net, examining it closely. His heart crashed into his heel, the evidence in his hand confirming everything he had pieced together. He began to sweat with apprehension and horror, completely sickened.

Henry stood beside him, eyeing the hair adornment. "Well, Gaston?"

He could barely speak. He swallowed hard. "It's hers. Stoneley has her."

Henry nodded faintly, placing his hand on Gaston's arm. "Go after her, man. Waste no time about it."

Gaston did not have to be told twice. He stormed from the room, his mind ahead to the most potent battle of his life. His mind was still reeling with the rapid falling of events, of the turn of tides. The very thing he had promised Remington would never happen again had, in fact, happened.

Remington did not believe in God. He wasn't sure he did, either. But he had prayed for Arica and she had lived, and he had thanked God profusely for Remington's own life being spared in childbirth. Mayhap God was becoming used to hearing his prayers.

He prayed again.

Even as Gaston rode a hasty trail north to Mt. Holyoak, Antonius left his wife and sister-in-law at Braidwood with Martin. With Guy on the loose, he wanted the women far away from Mt. Holyoak and well protected. By the time he left the Tower, Nicolas was still searching for his brother and Gaston had not yet ridden from the keep.

He reached Oxford by mid-day, reining his great roan destrier to a halt in the middle of Oxford Castle's massive bailey. Coincidentally, Dane and Trenton were out in the bailey with several other young pages going through their routines with a combat sticks and saw him ride in.

Antonius dismounted his steed, casting a long look at Dane, several feet away. He wasn't even sure Dane should be told of what was happening and hoped the boy had enough discipline not to break rank and rush to him, demanding to know why he had come to Oxford. Antonius wasn't sure he could lie effectively.

De Vere came to greet him. Steven de Norville stood next to the earl, his handsome face creased with concern to see Antonius' weary appearance.

"Sir Antonius," de Vere acknowledged him.

Antonius bowed to the earl, indeed weary from his long ride, but his message was of vital importance. "My lord, I bear a most urgent message from the duke."

De Vere drew in a long, slow breath. "I am required in London? I take it the proceedings are not going well, them."

Antonius shook his head, glancing over his shoulder at Dane. "Could we discuss this inside, my lord?"

The earl retreated into the castle without another word, leading Antonius into Lady Anne's small solar. It was cool and dim, away from the bright June day.

"What is it?" the earl demanded quietly. "What's happened?"

Antonius took a weary breath. "Grand trouble, my lord. 'Tis difficult to know where to start. Guy Stoneley has escaped the Tower and taken Lady Remington with him. Gaston is positive he travels to Mt. Holyoak, but all the same, he wants you to be aware that Stoneley is on the loose and he fears for Dane's safety. He asked that you take special precautions with the boy, at least until Stoneley can be located."

De Vere stared at him a moment, shocked. "Stoneley escaped? How in the hell did that happen? Good Christ, no one escapes the Tower!"

"As near as we can determine, he attacked a lone papal guard and stole the man's uniform," Antonius said quietly. "With the disguise, he was able to abduct his wife. Patrick, Gaston's cousin, was guarding her at the time and he cannot be located. That is as much as we know."

De Vere looked horrified and disgusted. "My God. Gaston must be frantic!"

Antonius could only nod, knowing Gaston was far beyond frantic. He was consumed. "Gaston is riding for Mt. Holyoak as we speak."

"Alone?" de Vere demanded.

"Aye, my lord. He insisted on going alone."

De Vere turned away and crossed himself, the possibilities cutting him. With everything Gaston had done for him, and for Henry, he was helpless to assist his friend.

Except to keep Dane safe.

"Where do you go now?" he asked the knight.

"To Deverill," Antonius replied. "He asked that I wait for him there. My wife and Lady Skye remain in London under the protection of Martin de Russe for the time being."

De Vere nodded, still stunned with the turn of events. He glanced at Antonius questioningly. "I am curious, however misplaced. Did the papal board agree to annulment?"

"On the basis of Father de Tormo's sworn statement, they were seriously considering the plea. But beyond that, I do not know."

There was nothing more to say. Antonius had delivered his message and was obviously exhausted. De Vere turned to de Norville, lingering near the hearth, and insisted the man show the knight food and bed.

The earl of Oxford sat heavily in the nearest chair, shaking his head in disbelief. Gaston had known so little happiness in his life, and now he was being subjected to even more heartache. Was nothing simple about the man?

As much as he wished to help his friend, there was nothing he could do. His fate, as well as Lady Remington's, was consigned to God.

After the men had retreated from the bailey, Dane had feigned an ill stomach and retreated to the interior of the castle. They believed he was ill, of course, for he had never once been ill or injured since he had arrived. So his master let him go and told him to rest a bit. They had enough faith in him to know that he was not a weakling boy, attempting to be free of his vigorous lessons.

Something inside him told him that the situation was terribly amiss. Antonius could not be at Oxford for a good reason, and the way he had looked at Dane made his skin crawl.

Something had happened to his mother. Instinct told him that he must find out exactly what that was.

Dane was cunning and silent as he trailed the earl and Antonius. When they disappeared into Lady Anne's solar, Dane had simply slipped into the servant's corridor that flanked the room and lodged himself against the wall by the hidden door. From his position, he could hear almost all of what was said.

And what he heard terrified him.

His father had escaped and his mother was with him. Dane's eyes stung with hot tears of fear, knowing what his father was capable of. And his mother, so sweet and loving, was terribly incapable of defending herself. He felt somewhat heartened to know that Gaston had gone after them, but his father hated Sir Gaston and would try to kill him, too.

Not only would Sir Gaston be fighting to save his mother, but also he would be fighting for his own life against a man who had never known the taste of compassion, a man with a lump of coal where his heart should have been.

A body suddenly bumped into him from behind in the dark corridor, and Dane startled sharply until he looked into familiar smoky-gray eyes.

"It's me," Trenton hissed. "What's happened?"

"What are you doing here?" Dane countered harshly.

"I faked a fainting spell in the heat so I could come inside, too," Trenton informed him. "What are they saying?"

Dane looked sick. "My father escaped from prison and took my mother captive. Antonius says that they are heading for Mt. Holyoak, and that Sir Gaston is going after them."

Trenton's eyes bugged. "Will your father kill Lady Remington?"

Dane shook his head miserably. "I do not know. Trenton, I have got to help her."

Trenton frowned. "You can't. There's nothing you can do."

Dane shot to his feet, his entire body tense. He shook his fist at his brother. "I can, too! I can go to Mt. Holyoak and protect my mother while Gaston takes care of my father."

"You are mad. We can't leave," Trenton insisted.

"Not we; me. And I am too going. I have to!" Dane shot back. "I must protect her, Trenton! She cannot defend herself, and Gaston may have difficulty gaining entrance to the keep," he sat back down, less agitated and far more serious. "Do not you see? I can tell my father that I have returned home to see him and he will let me in. He won't imagine that I have come to protect my mother from him; if I pretend hard enough, mayhap he shall believe I am truly glad to see him and he won't suspect how... how much I hate him."

Trenton watched Dane with big eyes. "You would kill him?"

Dane shrugged, averting his gaze. "I won't let him hurt my mother."

Trenton eyed him for several long moments, trying to determine his intentions. He knew how badly Dane resented his father, and how much he feared him. "You are going to kill him, aren't you?"

Dane did not answer the question. "I have got to leave now."

Both boys stood up. "I am coming with you," Trenton said firmly.

Dane shook his head firmly. "Nay, Trenton. You will stay here. I must do this, not you."

"But my father is riding north to rescue your mother, is he not? My father might need me, just as your mother needs you," Trenton was already walking away from him. "I am going and you cannot stop me."

Dane caught up to him angrily. "Well....just do not get in my way, agreed?" he demanded, just to show Trenton that he was still in charge. "And you do what I say."

Trenton snorted. "I always do what you say."

"Aye, you do. Do not forget I am smarter than you are."

"And I am bigger."

Foiled, Dane tried to maintain his superior stance. "I am always right, Trenton. You would not get anywhere without me."

Trenton, a head taller than Dane and thirty pounds heavier, put his hands on his hips in a gesture reminiscent of his father.

"Then tell me, Oh Keeper of the Brain. How are we to get to Mt. Holyoak? Walk?"

Dane smiled smugly. "Hardly. Come on."

It was only at supper that eve that the earl realized he had not seen Dane since the morning. Trenton, for that matter, but he wasn't overly concerned. Only when de Norville returned from a search of the keep saying that the boys were naught to be found did he begin to worry.

Good Christ, Gaston would have his hide if Stoneley succeeded in not only capturing Remington, but young Dane as well.

Guy and Remington rode the rest of the night and all day, without stopping. Remington thought she fainted, twice, but she couldn't be sure. Mayhap she had only fallen asleep, because she was so damn tired she could hardly think. Yet one thought occupied her horror-glazed mind continuously; she was in Guy's clutches.

He held her tightly, not a word spoken between them. Remington was literally sick; she knew he was going to kill her, without a doubt. The only question was when.

Toward sunset that day, Guy finally reined the frothing steed to a halt. He did not bother to help Remington from the horse; he merely tossed her onto the ground and dismounted. While she struggled to stand, he led the horse to a small stream to water it.

Remington wildly considered running, but she had no idea where she was or where she would go. Moreover, Guy would simply catch her and use it as an excuse to beat her silly.

She gazed at his taut back as he watered the animal, wrestling with her disbelief. She still could hardly grasp the very fact that he had captured her right from under Gaston's nose. It was enough to bring horrified tears to her eyes, tears she quickly dashed away. She would not let him see her fear.

"By now your lover should be on his way," Guy commented, gazing off across the rolling fields. "Lord, it's been a long time since I have seen these sights. I never knew I would miss the smell of grass or the stench of an opossum."

Remington did not say anything; she was too terrified to reply. Guy looked up from the horse, his ice-blue eyes focusing on her. "You look quite delicious, Remi. De Russe spares no expense on you, does he?"

She did not know what to say, keeping her head down and her eyes averted.

Guy let go of the reins and stalked toward her. Remington could feel him coming closer and her breathing quickened, all of the terror in her heart rushing to her veins and causing her to shake violently. She heard his footfalls on the grass like crashing boulders, deafening to her ears. When his hand reached out to touch her face, she nearly fainted with fright.

He felt her sway and grabbed her by the hair. "No, you do not. You will not shy from me. It has been far too long since I have seen you or tasted you, Remi. You shall not back away."

Sharp little pants came to her lips, cries of fear, but she bit them back. With every breath, it was more and more difficult.

Guy's grip on her hair softened and he began stroking her hair, touching her shoulder. His expression was almost loving.

"Tell me, sweet. Was de Russe as good a lover as I? Was he as tender, or as fulfilling? You can be honest."

She knew her honestly would most likely bring severe injury. "No, Guy, he wasn't," her lips were quivering, her eyes filling with tears.

"Tell me the truth," Guy purred, his hands gently touching her shoulders. "I want to know."

"I told you," she whispered, his touch bringing bile to her throat.

Guy massaged her shoulders, smelled her hair. Remington wished she would die.

"You look even better than I remembered," Guy whispered against her ear. "Your body is fuller and more luscious. I think I would like to taste you, sweet."

She did cringe from him then. "No, Guy. You...'tis my woman's time."

He was upon her in a minute. "What does that matter to me? Spread your cloak. I will have you now."

The tears came. She took a step back, attempting to refuse, but he grabbed her wrists roughly, even as he tore her cloak from her shoulders and threw it on the ground. Remington began to struggle, fighting him with every ounce of strength she possessed, until he hit her and knocked her cold.

When she came to, it was upon her damp cloak with Guy standing several feet away, eating something she could not see. His back was to her and he didn't seem particularly interested in her. Having no idea how long she had been unconscious, or what had transpired during that time, she realized she didn't want to know any of it. All of this, this hell she was forced to endure, was more horrific than anything she could have imagined. Closing her eyes, she feigned unconsciousness for the rest of the night.

CHAPTER THIRTY-THREE

Taran was built for stamina, thankfully, but even he needed rest. Gaston could have ridden all the way to Mt. Holyoak, were it not for his horse.

It was after nightfall when he stopped outside of the small town of Rothersthorpe to water and rest his horse. Just south of Northampton, he guessed that Guy and Remington were all the way to Leicester by now, possibly even nearing Sheffield. He had tried so hard to keep from focusing on the horrors of the situation that he was mentally exhausted.

He sat by the small stream in the light of the moon, listening to his horse slurp fresh water.

Why did this have to happen? Was it God's punishment for betraying Richard, an evil man at that, but nonetheless Gaston had betrayed him. Was it punishment for the men he had killed, the battles he had won, the women he had widowed or the orphans he had made?

All of his life he had been a loner, the consummate warrior, pure knightly perfection. He had no flaws. But he had one weakness - Remington Stoneley. Dear God, how he loved her.

Suddenly, his head came up. He had left a skeleton crew at Mt. Holyoak, men faithful to him. Guy did not know this; at least, he hoped he did not. He could imagine Guy riding through the gates of Mt. Holyoak and Remington sounding the alarm, only to have Guy swarmed with his soldiers and dismembered.

He wondered if Remington would see through her fear long enough to remember that it was Gaston's men who staffed Mt. Holyoak, for he could only imagine how terrified she was. It was enough to make him boil with anger all over again.

The urge to reach Mt. Holyoak pushed at him as never before.

"If you were going to steal a horse, why did not you steal a fast one?" Trenton demanded, shifting his bottom on the animal's boney rear.

"At least I got us a horse. You would have us walking," Dane shot back, steering the nag along the road. "And this horse could go faster, only you complain every time we move faster than a walk."

"That's because he trots too hard," Trenton said. "His backbone digs into my arse and it hurts."

Dane pursed his lips irritably. "Get down and run beside him, then. I am sick of listening to you complain."

Trenton bailed off the animal and Dane gored the old nag into a trot. As ordered, Trenton ran alongside easily.

"We shall make time now," Dane insisted. "We're closing in on Northamptonshire."

"In two or three hours," Trenton puffed. "We have a long way to go yet."

"Then run faster," Dane yelled back, spurring the horse into a canter and leaving his friend in the dust.

Trenton staggered to a halt, knowing he couldn't keep pace with a running horse. But Dane did not stop and Trenton had visions of being left behind to fend for himself. The boney rump of the animal suddenly looked very appealing.

"Hey – wait!" he yelled.

Trenton ran almost as fast as the horse, making up for lost ground.

As night fell, Guy declared his want for a hot meal. In the next town of Stanford-on-Avon, Gutter's Inn, a rousing establishment near the banks of the river Avon, seemed to beckon the loudest to Guy, and he drew the destrier alongside a hitching post.

This time, he helped Remington from the animal and proceeded to secure the beast.

"Have you any money?" he asked.

She shook her head, gaze averted. The blow he had landed her this afternoon had left a sharp bruise on her cheek and she was deeply ashamed. He raised an eyebrow.

"Then we shall have to go about getting some," he said, glancing about. His gaze drifted back to her. "You are a whore. Do what you do and get me some money."

Her eyes snapped up to him to see if he was sickly jesting. From his expression, she could see that he was entirely serious.

"Oh, Guy... no. You cannot be sincere."

His jaw twitched and she flinched, waiting for the blow to come. But Guy showed a remarkable amount of restraint and controlled himself; it would be difficult enough to find a customer with the bruise she was already sporting.

"Come on," he jerked her by the arm and led her into the warm establishment.

The interior was cloying and stank of ale and bodies, the loud roar of knights and men filling the common room. Wenches abound, doling out food and drink. In the corner, two minstrels sang and played a lute, trying desperately to be heard above the commotion.

Guy gripped her tightly as he guided her inside, his ice-blue eyes alert for a well-dressed traveler or knight. It did not bother him in the least that he was to offer his wife's services; he was simply interested in eating.

The inn was jammed with men. Guy took Remington well into the room and pushed her into an empty chair, next to the garderobe.

"Wait here," he growled. "If you so much as move an inch, I shall kill you."

He was serious and she knew it.

Guy moved into the room, searching for the correct customer. Remington was so horrified that she couldn't watch; she kept her head down, staring at her hands. She felt completely helpless and sickened; Gaston surely would not want her returned after he learned what Guy had done to her. Had she a dagger, she would have turned it on herself.

She knew she should at least try to escape him, but she had nowhere to go. She did not even know what town they were in, for she had not asked. And, surely, what citizen would not return an errant wife to her irate husband? She couldn't be sure that anyone would help her, even if she did manage to escape.

She sat there for a long time, unaware of the conversation her husband was having with a large, well-dressed knight. The knight had not been interested at first until he glanced over and saw Remington's lowered head. After a moment of hesitation, he paid Stoneley several coins and retreated up the stairs.

Guy moved back to Remington.

"Get up," he hissed. "A knight has paid a good deal for your services and you will not disappoint him. Do you hear me? If he tells me that your wares were substandard, I shall take it out on your hide."

Remington fought off the tears of shame, or horror, nodding once. Guy grabbed her by the arm, his fingers digging into her soft flesh, and escorted her to the base of the stairs. "The second door to your right. Get."

He shoved her and she almost stumbled on the bottom step. Catching herself, she slowly mounted the stairs, the rumble of the common room fading as she proceeded down the hall.

She was shaking so badly that she could barely knock on the designated door. Out of the corner of her eye, she caught sight of a window at the end of the hall. God, how easy it would be to throw herself from the window and be done with all of this pain and humiliation. She wished she had the courage, but she did not.

Her fisted hand froze an inch in front of the door, the tears she had fought so valiantly against taking hold. But she wiped them away, knowing she had no choice and praying to the God she did not believe in that Gaston would understand.

The open window was looking more and more appealing.

She never got a chance to make her decision. The door in front of her flew open and a large body was suddenly in front of her. Before she could move, a hand reached out and snatched her into the room.

Gasping with shock and surprise, Remington heard the door bolt behind her and she swung around to face the knight, volumes of panic welling within her. A handsome blond man gazed back at her with concern, and he was oddly familiar.

Remington's panic banked somewhat, but she was still filled with trepidation. The knight remained where he stood, highly cognizant of her fear.

"You do not remember me, do you?" he asked gently.

Remington did not realize that her hands were up in front of her protectively. Slowly, the hands came down. "You…you do look familiar. Do I know you?"

"We have met," he said softly. "I am Sir Hubert Doyle, my lady. We have met on two occasions."

Her eyes widened. "Sir Hubert of Ripley? And we met in Ripon, as well. I remember."

He smiled, a gentle smile. "Good. Then, my lady, would you mind telling me what is going on? Who is this man selling your…services?"

Her knees went to liquid and he caught her before she fell, lowering her carefully into the nearest chair. Between great gulps of wine, she told him everything.

Hubert was shocked. He stared at her in open astonishment, running his fingers through his hair in a gesture that reminded her of Gaston. His soft gray eyes were filled with pity and, she thought, anger.

Leaving her to finish her third goblet of wine in peace, he rose on his long legs and paced the room soundlessly. Every so often he would break from his train of thought, looking over at her quivering head.

"Did he do that to your face?" he asked.

Her fingers flitted to her bruised cheek. "Aye."

"Has he harmed you in any other way?"

She looked up at him, opening her mouth to speak, but sobs bubbled forth instead. Hubert went to her, timidly patting her shoulder. "I am sorry, I shouldn't have asked."

She continued to cry. "You paid….a good deal of money for me. Do you intend…?"

He cut her off. "Absolutely not. The moment I saw you, I recognized you. I paid what your husband was asking simply to prevent another man from taking advantage of Sir Gaston's…woman. My God, this is confusing, isn't it?"

A choked laugh sputtered forth among the tears. "Aye, it is."

He crouched beside her, smiling faintly. She met his gaze, wiping at her eyes and he patted her hand. "I am taking you out of here, away from him."

Her eyes widened. "You are? How? Where will we go?"

He was already standing, gathering his necessary things. Remington watched apprehensively as he strapped on his sword and stashed two daggers in unobtrusive places. He was a big man, quick and agile, with a handsome face and gentle manner.

Suddenly, he moved to the door and unbolted it. Remington jumped, startled, as he bellowed for a servant. When a girl came running, he shoved five gold pieces into her palm.

"Find Lord Stoneley downstairs," he commanded. "Tell him I am retaining the lady's services for the night. And furthermore tell him not to disturb us until morning. Is that clear?"

The wench nodded and Hubert gave her a coin for her trouble. When she dashed off, he slammed the door and bolted it again.

"There," he said softly. "That ought to take care of that bast... your husband. Now, to get us both out of here unnoticed."

She nodded shakily, rising to unsteady feet. He looked at her a moment. "When did you last eat?"

She thought a moment. "Yesterday, in London, I suppose."

He moved to a table by the hearth and collected a few bits of food. Into her hands he deposited an apple and a large chunk of bread. "You can eat this on the way," he told her with an encouraging wink.

Grateful, she took a healthy bite of the bread as Hubert secured a huge black cloak about his shoulders. She watched him a moment, dazed at her turn of luck. In fact, the past two days had left her reeling and unbalanced so that she hardly knew her own name anymore.

"Sir Hubert," she said softly. "How is it that you happen to be at this inn?"

"I was returning from Daventry on business for Lord Ingilsby," he replied, donning his helm. Then he smiled. "It would seem that God was listening to your prayers this day, my lady. I almost did not stop at this place, but all of the other inns were full."

God had been listening to her, indeed. She smiled timidly. "You know, I have never really believed in God. I only believed in the devil because I was married to him."

Hubert's own smile faded somewhat. "From what I have seen this night, I certainly believe that. But have no fear, my lady. I will protect you with my life."

Remington sighed with relief. It was almost enough to start her weeping again. *Thank you, God.*

She finished the bread and started on the apple. Just as Hubert was moving for the door, there came a sharp rap and he unbolted it swiftly.

The serving wench was standing in the archway, eyeing Remington as she spoke. "The lord says that he shall give you until midnight and no longer," she said. "He says they need to be on their way."

Hubert nodded sharply and shut the door, turning to Remington. "It would seem that my coinage did not buy as much time as I would like, but it still gives us nearly four hours. Enough to make it into Yorkshire, at any rate."

"You are taking me to Yorkshire? Why not back to London?" she demanded.

"Think on it, my lady," he said gently. "Gaston is most likely on his way to Yorkshire already. I shall take you to Ripley Castle for safe keeping and send word to Gaston."

"He shall be traveling to Mt. Holyoak," she murmured, her eyes distant. "But so is Guy. What happens if...?"

"If Guy intercepts the message? He won't, I swear it," Hubert was pulling her to stand. "I shall send one of my most trusted men to seek out Sir Gaston, wherever he might be. In fact, I'd wager to say that your husband will not be welcome at Mt. Holyoak as it is. The fortress is staffed with Sir Gaston's men."

She'd forgotten that very real fact. Her eyes widened, feeling more energy than she had in a day. "Then....Guy has nowhere to go."

"Most likely not, unless he plans to engage one hundred of Gaston's troops," Hubert moved her to the door. "However, Guy has several sympathizers in the area he could easily house with, including Botmore."

Remington's mouth went agape with the possibilities. "And if Gaston occupies Mt. Holyoak again, the raids could start anew." She tilted her head at Hubert. "My God, this is confusing, isn't it?"

He laughed softly, a dazzling smile of white teeth and she joined his snickers. To laugh, to smile, improved her mood immensely. "'Tis good to see you smile," he said approvingly. "And, please... call me Hugh. No one calls me Hubert except my mother, and she only uses my full name when she's angry with me."

She nodded in agreement, mayhap a bit shyly. Hubert's eyes lingered on her for a brief moment before he moved to the door again. Silently, he opened the panel and glanced down both sides of the hall. Unfortunately, there was only one way down, and that route led to the common room where Guy Stoneley was enjoying his meal.

And there was the window.

Hubert held his hand out for Remington, who slipped her soft hand into his mailed one. Silently, they slipped from the room and closed the door.

He led her to the window at the end of the hall. Below, a twelve-foot plunge beckoned and he was reluctant to drop the lady from that distance. But he had no choice.

"I shall go first," he said quietly, placing his big body in the sill.

Remington watched with anticipation as he hung by his hands from the window. Sir Hubert was a tall man, not nearly as tall as Gaston, but large nonetheless. Even so, the twelve-foot chasm was a long way for him to fall.

When his fingers let go of the sill, she gasped softly and hung her head from the window just in time to see him land heavily. Hubert stumbled to his knees but rose, unharmed. Hurriedly, he turned to Remington and held out his arms.

"Jump," he hissed. "I shall catch you."

With only the slightest hesitation, Remington swung her legs over the side of the sill. Horrified that Guy would mount the top of the stairs at any moment and see her dangling, she scooted herself off the wooden ledge without further delay.

All Hubert saw was a billowing mass of gold and cream satin falling. The very next thing, she was cradled in his arms with surprising ease, her arms gripping his neck. Her crashing weight had barely been mentionable and he was vaguely pleased that he had not tripped over his own feet and broke both their necks. He'd never caught a woman in his arms before. With Remington still in his arms, he rushed to the livery behind the inn.

There was a young boy on duty. Hubert put Remington down just outside the door, out of the boy's view. Remington could hear the knight conversing easily with the lad, the sounds of a horse being led out of its stall. Hubert continued to talk the entire time his destrier was saddled and she heard him pay the boy for his trouble.

He rounded the corner of the stable with a great brown destrier in tow. Reins in one hand and Remington in the other, they moved into the shadows of the trees before mounting.

Hubert was silent now as he lifted Remington onto his saddle, mounting behind her lithely. Gathering his thick reins, he clucked softly to the horse and spurred him into the sheltering safety of the forest.

Remington leaned against him as he took her through dense foliage, crossing over a creek and through more trees. They were paralleling the main road north; actually taking a short cut that would chop two miles off their trek. She would find out later that Hubert grew up in Leicester and, therefore, knew the surrounding area very well.

She prayed to the God she did not believe in, yet the God she was coming to know very well. She prayed that Guy was still content with his ale and food, that he would not bother to check on her until the allotted time was concluded. She prayed beyond hope that he would do what she wanted him to do, just this once.

Even so, she had no doubt that Hubert could competently protect her even if Guy discovered their absence and caught up to them. Her greatest fear, however, was that Guy would accuse the knight of stealing his wife, and rally the township into a lynch mob. He was not beyond any sort of lie or deception, as he had proven when he testified before the papal delegation.

Guy could not be anticipated, and that frightened her.

Her mind would run wild if she let it. Banking her fears, her exhaustion-fed imaginings, she convinced herself calmly that she was safe now, thanks to Sir Hubert.

Thank you, God.

At exactly midnight, Guy mounted the stairs to the second floor of the inn. Expecting to find a verily pleased knight and one exhausted woman, he rapped softly at the door. When he received no answer, he knocked louder. He continued to knock until, irritated, he called out to the knight to awaken and open the door.

Still no answer, he rattled the latch himself and was surprised to find it open. Cautiously, he pushed the door open but did not enter the room. He stood back in the jamb, his ice-blue eyes inspecting every shadow and crevice of the dimly lit room.

It was empty.

Anger settled in his chest and his eyes narrowed. Strolling slowly into the room, he glanced about for any signs of his wife and the knight. There was a half-empty wine flask on the table and an empty cup, and the remainders of a meal.

The bed had been sat on, but was not mussed beyond that. He wandered off to the small bed, his eyes grazing the dirty coverlets. It did not take a brilliant man to deduce that the bed had not been used for the illicit encounter.

So where were they? Guy turned a complete circle, scanning the room. The window was closed, and everything was fairly in order. But there was no knight, and no Remington.

They had vanished.

Impossible, he told himself calmly. He had been seated in the common room the entire evening and they had not escaped him, of that he was sure.

So where were they?

Guy went back downstairs. It was late and there were several soldiers snoring on the dirty floor, the smell of ale and urine heavy in his nostrils. The innkeeper was wiping at a stack of wooden trenchers when he approached.

"There was a well-dressed knight who sought board from you this night. A tall man, young. He occupied the second room upstairs, on the right. Did he, perchance, leave?"

The innkeeper glanced at him. "Ye mean the man with the polished armor? The new gloves?" When Guy nodded, the proprietor shook his head. "I 'aven't seen 'im. Why do ye ask?"

A muscle in Guy's cheek twitched, not particularly eager to answer the question. "Would his horse be stabled in the livery out back?"

"Aye, it would," the innkeeper said. "A fine animal, my son says."

Guy did not say another word. Be pushed past the owner, through the kitchens, and out into the yard. The night had grown cool as he made his way back to the dilapidated structure.

A young lad was asleep on a cot of straw. Guy kicked him on the foot and the youth let out a yelp, rubbing his heel. The boy looked up into a very angry, very frightening face.

"What the... what is it, m'lord?" he swallowed.

"Did anyone leave this night?"

The boy nodded slowly. "A few."

"Did a knight leave? And did he have a woman with him?" The boy thought a moment. "Aye, a knight left three or four hours ago. But 'e did not 'ave a woman with 'im."

Guy's nostrils flared and the lad instinctively moved away, rising unsteadily. The man with the pale blue eyes scared him.

"Was the man tall and fair? Well-dressed?" Guy asked patiently.

"Aye, m' lord," the boy nodded. "And 'e 'ad a very fine animal."

"But no woman?"

"No," the boy shook his head.

Guy thought a moment. "You did not catch his name, mayhap?"

The young man shook his head hard. "'e did not give me 'is name. But he paid me a coin for saddling 'is destrier. Said he 'ad to be on 'is way."

Guy drew in a deep, calming breath. He had no doubt that the knight had stolen Remington from him, as one man steals a loaf of bread.

No wonder the knight had paid him so well. His intentions had been to steal Remington from the first and mayhap he thought he was compensating Guy for his loss.

Damnation. He spun away from the boy, anger and frustration expanding in his disbelieving mind. To come so close to escaping home with his wife, only to be foiled by a lustful knight who decided he wanted Remington for his own.

It was his fault, of course, and he cursed himself as he marched back into the tavern. He shouldn't have sold her services to a young knight; he should have sold her to an older knight who would have been too tired after the deed to do anything more with her. Young and vital, the salacious knight took Remington as his chattel.

Guy passed through the tavern. His horse was still tethered to the hitch post and he untied the animal hastily. Guy wasn't angry that the man had taken Remington herself, merely angry because a tremendous bargaining tool had been stolen away from him.

Bargaining tool? Of course. No doubt de Russe was on his way from London already to rescue Remington from her husband's evil clutches. And no doubt Henry was ranting for justice, demanding his escaped prisoner be returned. And no doubt the church was on Guy's side, demanding Henry to leave the man alone, to allow him to live peacefully at his native fortress. Remington could provide the bargaining chip to control all three.

Firstly, de Russe would do anything Guy dictated if Remington were threatened. Secondly, Henry would do whatever de Russe demanded of him. Thirdly, the church would be pleased to see a husband and wife back together again.

Damn. Guy gathered the reins roughly, slugging the horse when it protested the treatment. He would track down the lecherous knight and gut him cleanly for taking what did not belong to him.

Hubert stopped just after dawn to allow Remington rest. Pale and drawn, he helped her sit on a rotted tree stump while he started a small fire. The night had been cool and the morning damp and cloudy, and he thought she could use a bit of warmth.

As Hubert built the fire from dried twigs and dead leaves, Remington slid off the stump and sat upon the ground, using the tree to lean against. She was so damnably tired that she needed help to simply sit erect. She wasn't particularly cold in her crushed silk cloak, but the small fire felt wonderful on her cold feet and before she realized it, she was asleep.

Hubert had not noticed that she was sleeping until he turned to say something to her and saw that she was propped against the stump, snoring very lady-like. Her eyes were dark circled, indicative of the harrowing past few days.

Poor little waif, he thought, sincerely wishing he could send word to Gaston on her whereabouts this very instant. He had seen the way the Dark Knight had treated her, how obviously attached he was to the petite woman. And he had no doubt that Gaston was fully prepared to tear apart Yorkshire in search of his lady-love, who happened to be another man's wife.

Hubert shook his head, moving to sit beside her. He pitied the woman, lovely and fragile, married to the devil's twin. Compounded with the fact that the Duke of Warminster was in love with her, it all compiled to make an entirely perplexing situation. It wasn't any of his business, of course, but somehow he found himself mixed up in it all.

He gazed down at her pale, beautiful face, thinking of the first time he ever saw her. In Ripon, at the tournament, three other lovely young women had surrounded her, but he'd had eyes only for her. It amazed him to this day that he had not noticed Gaston and his men sitting beside her, for the men were certainly not invisible. But he had only had eyes for her. She was still the most beautiful woman he'd ever seen.

Hubert turned away from her, chasing the ridiculous thoughts from his head. He had one duty and one duty only; to take her safely to Ripley and send word to Gaston. Another six or so hours would have them on Ingilsby's doorstep.

Remington slept for an hour, as long as Hubert dared to let her rest. As the sun crept higher in the sky and the morn warmed, he rose and doused the fire before rousing her.

"My lady," he said softly. "Lady."

She stirred a bit and her eyes fluttered open. Seeing a mailed glove in her face, she startled violently as if positive the hand was placed to harm her. Hubert dropped to his knees and grabbed her by the arms before she could bolt.

"Calm, my lady, calm," he urged firmly. 'Tis me; Hugh. You are safe, but we must continue on."

She blinked at him, the great sea-crystal eyes coming into focus. In his grip, she visibly relaxed.

"Oh...good lord, I thought...." She swallowed hard, brushing the hair from her eyes. "I am sorry, Hugh. You startled me."

He smiled faintly, his gray eyes twinkling. "I was waiting for a fist to catch me in the face."

She grinned, embarrassed, as she struggled to stand. He pulled her to her feet, helping her brush the dead grass and leaves from her cloak.

Remington smoothed at her hair, still tired but feeling the least bit refreshed. Her mind was clearing, too, now that she had put some space between she and Guy. "Where are we, Hugh?"

"Just shy of Wakefield, my lady," he replied, moving to untie the destrier from its post. "We should be at Ripley in six hours."

She shook out her dress and made her way over to him where he was readying the horse. "How long was I asleep?" she asked, suddenly showing apprehension. "Could my husband have...?"

"You were only asleep about an hour," he replied, quelling her fears. "And even if Lord Stoneley were right on our heels, I doubt he could have found us in this bank of trees."

She looked back to their small camp. "What of the smoke from the fire? Surely that would alert him?"

"It was such a small fire that the smoke dissipated before it reached the canopy," Hubert held his hands out to her. "He would smell the smoke but nothing more."

He lifted her onto the beast and mounted behind her. Shifting her bottom to gain comfort against his heavily armored thighs, he waited until she stilled before spurring his destrier onward.

The day was beautiful and warm, the humidity lacking. Remington shunned her cloak, enjoying the warmth and fresh air and allowing the brilliance to lift her spirits. With each hoof-fall, she felt safer, more at ease. Hubert rode silently, listening to her hum a lullaby his mother had sung to him when he was young.

"You have a son, do you not?" he asked.

She nodded. "He's fostering at Oxford. And I have twin daughters, as well."

"Oh? I was not aware of any daughters when I visited Mt. Holyoak, but your son was pointed out to me."

She giggled. "That's because the girls were not born yet. They are three months old."

He looked surprised. "You do not look as if you have recently birthed children. In fact, you look...." He stopped himself, mortified that he was about to compliment the Dark One's woman as if she were an unattached, available female. 'Twas the natural male instinct in him to compliment and flatter, and her femininity brought out every ounce of his maleness. "You look quite pleasant, my lady."

She giggled louder, amused at his embarrassment. "It is very well if you tell me I look pleasant, Hugh. Every woman likes to be showered with tribute."

He was glad she wasn't looking at him; he was blushing like a fool. As fair as he was, his cheeks were glowing red. "I did not mean to sound... well, bold."

She shook her head, pulling her mass of curls over one shoulder and off her neck to cool it. "You did not. You were very polite."

He went silent, still humiliated with his near-slip. Sensing his embarrassment, she sought to ease him. "Are you married now, Hugh?"

He looked off across the green hills. "Nay, my lady. Not yet."

"Are you betrothed, then?"

"Nay," he replied. "Much to my mother's concern. She should like grandchildren before too long."

"Where does your mother reside?" she asked, fanning her face.

"At Ripley," he said. "Lord Ingilsby was kind enough to provide for her. She does a good deal of sewing and other services for Lady Ingilsby."

Remington fell silent, thinking of plain Lady Ingilsby. She couldn't help but remember when Alex Ingilsby had pleaded with her to run away with him, declaring his affection for her. It had been so hard for him to admit his feelings, as he was shy and somewhat reserved, and she had been as kind as she could when she declined his offer. He was such a tremendously nice man.

"Lord Ingilsby traveled to London to testify on my behalf for the annulment hearing, you know," she said softly. "I was told he was a most powerful witness."

"He was," Hubert concurred. "I accompanied him and he was most passionate, which I found surprising. He is usually a quiet man."

Remington did not say anymore, afraid of where the conversation would lead. She was married to one man and the lover of another. If Hubert discovered that still another man had declared his want for her, she would appear as nothing more than a whore. She did not want him to think less of Gaston because he loved a whore.

Yet he already knew she had bore Gaston twins, and that she had been committing adultery with him for a year. Still, his manner and words indicated nothing but the highest respect for the man. If he did not greatly regard Gaston, then he would not be risking his life to save his lover from her legal husband.

It never occurred to her that he would think less of her for the life she had chosen. She was simply worried that he would perceive Gaston differently. And with the humiliation the man had suffered through the hands of his wife and former king, she would not allow that to happen.

They rode quietly for a short while. As they passed Wakefield and drew closer to Leeds, activity on the road increased. Remington eyed the peasants and travelers on the road suspiciously, as if she expected every one of them to seek out her husband and tell him exactly where she was. But other than a glance or two, no one seemed to show any interest in her or the knight at all.

They skirted Leeds and Hubert spurred his destrier into a jogging trot. The great bouncy gait made Remington burp very unladylike and she was embarrassed, hoping he would either slow or speed up the pace. Much more of the jostling and she was sure she would bounce right off.

Hubert took them off the main route and onto a smaller, less traveled road. Whereas the main course dipped and curved into the towns it serviced, the less-worn road plowed straight and true north. Ripley wasn't far off.

The afternoon faded. Remington felt boneless, weary and weak as she lay against Hubert's broad chest. His armor was hard and cold, but it comforted her. It reminded her of Gaston.

Her heart leapt into her throat at the thought of him. She knew he was pursuing her, but her heart ached when she realized he knew nothing of her fate. The panic and the pain he was surely feeling brought tears to her eyes. How she wished she could comfort him, convince him she was sound and whole.

Her arms pained to hold him, and her lips quivered to kiss him. God, how she hurt for him.

Tears came but she dashed them away discreetly, hoping Hubert would not sense her sadness. She had no right to be sad; after all, he had saved her from certain humiliation and death. She tried to steady herself, to think ahead to Ripley, and to Gaston.

Hubert heard her sniffling, sympathy for her situation squeezing at him. He patted her arm gently.

"No need for tears, my lady. We shall soon be safe at Ripley."

She nodded, drying at her eyes. "I know that. Forgive me for being foolish, Hugh," she turned to look at him, forcing her face to brighten. "I have thought of a way to repay you for your sacrifice. I swear to you that I will name my next male child Hubert, if indeed I have another child."

He smiled weakly. "No need, my lady. A simple thanks will be quite sufficient."

Her smiled faded, sincerity filling her eyes. "Thank you," she whispered.

He nodded vaguely, tearing his eyes away from her consuming gaze. It was not difficult to see why Sir Gaston was so deeply in love with her.

They were riding through a light bank of trees and Remington heard the rushing of water not far off. Thinking it to be a delightful place to stop, if just for a moment, she turned to Hubert.

But her words died in her throat. Suddenly, Hubert was hit from behind so forcefully that both he and Remington went pitching off his destrier.

Dazed, Remington struggled to her knees only to hear a piercing hoot that made her hair stand on end. Panicked, she fought to gain her footing just as she heard a sword unsheathe behind her.

Hubert was on his feet, disoriented and shaken, but otherwise unharmed. He started to yell at Remington, but was cut off as two men charged him from the trees, barbarians from the way they were dressed. As the two rushed him, another man closed in on Remington.

She saw him coming, big and hairy and unkempt. With a scream, she bolted for the destrier, hoping to find a weapon strapped to the saddle.

The horse, however, saw her charging for him and began to snort and dance, preparing to fight. Fortunately, Remington looked up from her panic and saw the animal's agitated state. Thinking quickly, she continued to dash and wave her arms, working the horse into a frenzy. Praying she was fast enough, she veered sharply from the animal just as he started to charge.

The horse did not care who he injured. The big, hairy accoster was confronted by a very angry warhorse that proceeded to bite his arm nearly in half. Screaming and howling, the man stumbled back the way he came.

But the reprieve was short lived. There was another man ready to take his place, barreling toward Remington like a runaway wagon. Over to her left, Hubert had dispatched one man and was struggling with the other. He was quick and efficient, and the unintelligent bandits were no match for him. Two dead men lay at his feet as Remington rushed toward him for protection.

The man rushing toward Remington had a weapon in his hand, a thick broadsword, tarnished and dirty. Just as Remington ducked behind Hubert, the man was upon the knight and the sound of metal against metal clanged loudly in the still summer air.

Remington stood back, panting loudly with fright as Hubert engaged the tall, youngish man. Her hands clutched at her throat in fear, cringing every time the alloy swords came together.

The fight was ferocious and bitter. Hubert fought extremely well against the man, who seemed as if he intended to chop his quarry to death. His strokes were jerky, harsh, and unskilled, but there was a great deal of power behind them.

Suddenly there were hands grabbing her from behind and she let out a whoop of shock and terror. Someone had her around the waist, pulling her up off the ground and breaking for the nearest thicket.

Remington screamed and fought, trying to kick and punch, battling for her very life. It proved to be difficult, however, for her molester held her quite easily and provided her with no opportunity to land a good blow. Her balled fists were meeting with air.

Another man came up beside her, grabbing her by the hair and the man who fisted her hair so savagely leaned closed to her, telling her in no uncertain terms what he planned to do with her. Horrified and sickened, Remington began to bellow at the top of her lungs, far less screaming and far more blatant anger.

The men who held her merely laughed. The one who carried her tightened his grip as the other one ran his dirty hands up her bodice, fondling her tender breasts. Remington lashed out, aiming for his groin, but being rewarded with a sharp crack to her skull.

Stars danced before her eyes and night was beginning to fall, but she fought it. She had to. She refused to die at the hands of rapists.

She stopped yelling for Hubert, knowing in her heart he must have met with the cold blade of his opponent. Her heart ached for the brave man, and for herself as well. *Why, God, did you save me from Guy, only to meet my end out here in the wilderness? Gaston will never find me now.*

The man with his hand on her breast suddenly grunted. His eyes bugged, and blood dribbled from his mouth. Remington's eyes widened as he fell away from her, dripping blood on her ecru-colored dress. She glanced up to see Hubert descending, his sword arcing a blinding streak.

She cried out as his sword came down inches from her shoulder and she felt the hands that held her open. She did not hesitate; she was free and she leapt clear of the fight, tripping over the man who had so recently touched her breasts. As she struggled over his body in her hysteria, one glance at the corpse showed a rugged dirk protruding from his back.

She fled, although she knew not where she was going. Only that she had to run, to escape the ambush. She was positive there were more bandits rushing forward to capture her, to rape and ravish her. She had to reach safety, wherever it may be.

Panic clouded her mind as she ran, skirts hiked up to her knees. Just as she reached the perimeters of the trees, a shout came from behind her. Someone was calling her name.

"Remington!"

She was panicked, as a hunted animal. There was no earthly way she was going to stop; surely it was a trick. Heart pounding, she ran even faster for the shelter of the trees.

"*Remingtooooonnnn!*"

A shadow of sensibility filtered into her hysteric mind. The roar sounded sincere, somehow... almost gentle, if that were possible. And the tone was thoroughly pleading. Although she did not want to, she stumbled to an unsteady halt and turned to the source of the shout.

Hubert was walking toward her, covered with gore. She couldn't see his face through the lowered visor until he lifted it with shaking fingers. His gray eyes were wide with excitement and fear.

"All is well, honey," he said gently. "They are all dead."

She couldn't reply for the moment, still panic-stricken. He closed in on her, sheathing his sword wearily.

"Let me see your head," he said, his voice a husky whisper.

She had not realized that her head was aching terribly. Suddenly, the pain hit her full bore and she whimpered, her panic fading. Her whole body began to shake.

"Oh, my God," her face crumpled, racking sobs spilling forth.

He grabbed her head with his great mailed gloves, inspecting the split scalp directly above her right ear.

"All is well, my lady," he whispered again. "You are safe. I killed them all."

She heard him, still terrified out of her mind.

Satisfied the wound to her head wasn't severe, Hubert tried to lead her away but she couldn't seem to walk. In fact, they both seemed to be shaking a great deal, almost too hard to function. But Hubert was desperate to remove her from the area, away from the memories of horror. Sweeping her into his arms, he carried her back to his horse.

Remington continued to cry even as he mounted behind her and spurred the charger onto the road. Behind them, four dead men littered the quiet countryside, bright red blood staining the sweet green grass.

Even after Remington's sobs died and she fell into an exhausted sleep, Hubert remained deeply shaken. His good deed had almost turned deadly for both of them, and he would have never forgiven himself if tragedy had befallen the lady. He could still hear her shouts and her tears, and the memory cut him to the bone.

How fortunate he had not been overwhelmingly outnumbered. It made him ill to think of what might have happened if there had been but a few more outlaws, all intent on killing him and stealing his ward. Although bandits were quite common to the roads of England, he was still unnerved by the incident.

The urge to reach Ripley was greater than before. Spurring his steed into a canter, his grip on Remington tightened.

CHAPTER THIRTY-FOUR

Sweet, sweet Yorkshire! After passing through the sheep town of Leeds, Guy was gleeful to finally be entering the providence of his birth. Even if he was at least a day from home, he was still drawing close and that fact boosted him considerably.

He'd had the rest of the night and the most of the next day to think of the knight who captured his wife. Having no idea who the man was or where he went, there was truly no way to follow him. Moreover, the closer Guy drew to Yorkshire, the more eager he was to reach abandoned Mt. Holyoak.

Guy spent half the night determining how he would gain the necessary men simply to defend the place. He was sure his loyalist allies would provide him with ample manpower until such time as he could raise his own army, but the fact that de Russe was no doubt close on his heels worried him. With the size of Gaston's army, Mt. Holyoak could possibly fall under siege. With no army of her own to defend herself, it would simply be a matter of time before she was breached.

He forgot more and more about Remington and focused on his keep and immediate future. After all, de Russe would assume that Guy would take Remington to Mt. Holyoak. Guy was still bound for his fortress, but now without the considerable addition of his wife.

Guy without Remington would not be worth the air he breathed. Unless, of course, he lied and told de Russe that Remington was indeed with him, but forbade any contact between his wife and the Dark Knight. That would keep de Russe guessing, desperate for a glimpse of his beloved and making it easier to keep the powerful duke at bay.

Or.... Guy could steer clear of Mt. Holyoak and retreat to one of his many allies in Yorkshire. That would throw de Russe off and keep him guessing all the more. Mayhap after enough guessing, he would eventually give up and return to London. That in turn would leave Guy free to move about, free to occupy his keep, and free to search out his wife. Eventually. But Remington was not the greater priority at the moment.

An insane, evil man with insane, evil thought patterns. Guy had no true rhyme or reason for doing what he was doing, other than in the end, he simply wanted to be free to live out his life at Mt. Holyoak. All the rest was purely because he liked torturing de Russe and Remington. And because he was an escaped criminal, the two were also the key to keeping Henry managed.

Once, during the first months of his captivity, he had entertained the thought of a rebellion against Henry. Carefully worded missives were sent between he and his allies that indicated such an uprising would be substantial, but from what Guy had seen and heard during his incarceration, it would not have been successful. There were too many powerful people supporting Henry.

Guy had had enough of war, to be truthful. A selfish man, his attention had turned from rebellion to merely regaining his keep. He wondered if talk of rebellion still filled the Yorkshire circles, but he did not care anymore. He simply wanted to return home.

Dane had no meaning in his life. Neither did his young cousin, Charles. And he had long forgotten about his wife's sisters. He had a new future ahead of him, and he faced it with eager anticipation.

It took him nearly the entire day to reach Wakefield, just south of Leeds. Another five or six hours would have him at Mt. Holyoak, depending on how well his horse withstood the vigorous pace. So far, the animal had done very well and Guy was confident he could reach his keep before the next morn.

He had long since dumped the papal tunic and pieces of too large plate armor. Lightened, he drove the destrier onward.

Just north of Leeds he stopped to water and rest the animal. Under normal circumstances, he would not have cared if the horse had fallen and died under him, but he had to rely on this particular steed if he was going to make it to his destination. Aye, he would ride to Mt. Holyoak first, just to see his beloved fortress for himself. But after that, he was torn between riding for Knaresborough Castle or Summerbridge Castle. Both housed valuable opposition allies, men he had been in contact with since his imprisonment.

Certainly Keith Botmore was closer, but Douglass Archibald of Summerbridge was more of an ally. Botmore was only interested in Remington, Guy thought, but an ally nonetheless. Trying to decide between the two seemed to occupy him for the moment.

Guy was preparing to mount again when there was a commotion of riders on the road. Out in the dead of night, he knew they were either robbers or cutthroats. As he scrambled into the saddle, one of the men shouted at him to hold.

He was outnumbered and his horse was exhausted as it was. Anymore hard running on the animal's part and he would find himself walking the rest of the way. Confident he could talk his way out of any situation, he did as he was bade.

The riders swarmed around him, swallowing him up. Guy remained impassive, controlling the fear that sweated him. One of the knights rode alongside and scrutinized him.

"Identify yourself."

"A poor knight, riding north in search of a fortune," Guy lied humbly.

Another knight rode alongside, studying him intently. Guy tried to avert his gaze, yet his natural reaction was to meet the open stare. After a moment, the knight spoke.

"Remove your helm."

Guy's first thought was that he had run into a horde of Gaston's men. Knowing it would be useless to refuse, he did as he was commanded.

"Stoneley," one of the men gasped.

There was no use in pretending otherwise. Eyes hard, Guy lifted his gaze to silently challenge all men present. "Who do you serve? De Russe?"

One of the knights shook his head. "Nay, my lord. We're Lord Lowrie's men."

"Of Harewood House?" Stoneley felt his whole body run hot and cold with relief. He knew Baron Lowrie well. "What are you doing so far from home?"

"'Tis the old feud, my lord," the knight replied. "The skirmish between Harewood and Bramham has been going on for as long as anyone can remember. Earlier this eve, one of Bramham's men slipped into Harewood and stole off with Lowrie's youngest daughter. Thirteen, she is. We have already burned half of Bramham, but she's not there. Lowrie's frantic."

The man had five daughters. How could he worry so over one? But Guy nodded, greatly relieved that he was not the subject of the search. He was very eager to be on his way.

"Ye have not seen anyone, have ye, my lord?" the other knight asked hopefully.

"Not a thing," Guy replied honestly. "Well, good men, I must be on my way."

"Say, we heard ye were locked up in the White Tower after Stoke," the same knight mentioned. "I see the Tudor released ye?"

Guy gazed at the man a moment, seeing the possibilities of useful information. "So it would seem. How goes all in Yorkshire during my absence?"

"The same," the other knight replied. "Botmore, Brimley, Ingilsby, and Tarrington; all the same. Except for Botmore, of course. He hasn't been the same since the Dark Knight killed his son."

"Killed Derek?" Guy repeated, surprised. "How did that happen?"

"We heard Derek was raiding Mt. Holyoak," the knight replied confidently. "Sir Gaston de Russe killed him for trespassing."

Guy lifted an eyebrow in thought. "Is that so? Fortunate that he has vacated the keep, which I have returned to claim."

"He has not vacated it entirely," the knight shook his head. "He keeps about a hundred men stationed there. Brimley oversees the fortress while the Dark Knight is in London," he peered closely at Guy. "Did the Tudor not tell you this when he released you?"

Guy did not know what to say for the moment. But he rebounded instantly. "Of course he did. I plan to stay at... Knaresborough until de Russe evacuates his men from my keep," he gathered his reins hastily, eager to be gone. "Allow me passage, good men." They parted for him, watching as the weary brown destrier pounded down the road once more. He was well out of range when the first knight turned to the second.

"I never thought I'd see him again," he mumbled.

"The man stenches of the devil," the second said. "Lowrie told tale of what he did to his wife. Say, I heard she left with the Dark One as his concubine. I heard the sisters were all killed."

The first knight shrugged. "Who knows? Mayhap they are all rumors and lies. Mayhap he isn't as bad as everyone says."

⚜

Gaston did not stop again. Taran was frothing and sweaty, but he was used to difficult conditions and hearty. Gaston kept a slower pace, but he did not let up. His searing sense of urgency had gained in strength and power, pushing him onward with no hope of relief until he reached Mt. Holyoak. Then, and only then, would he rest and plan.

He passed through Wakefield, heading into North Yorkshire. Skirting Leeds, he headed northeast and passed the cities of Boston Spa and Collingham. After Collingham, it was nearly a straight ride to Boroughbridge.

And then Mt. Holyoak.

He closed his eyes, if but to rest them a brief moment, but Remington immediately thrust herself into his weary mind. The familiar weakening, the familiar longing, saturated his limbs with liquid warmth. And pain.

He most definitely felt pain.

He saw the sea-crystal eyes twinkling back at him, her magnificent lips curved into a sweet smile. Her face, so sweet and beautiful, broke his concentration. The more he gazed at her beloved face, the more helpless and desperate he became.

His eyes flew open, forcing himself to breathe deeply, to refocus. He'd never felt so impotent and powerless in his whole life.

Be brave, angel. I am coming.

⚜

Ripley Castle loomed into view in the wee hours of the morning. Barely after midnight, Hubert reined his destrier into the large, if not cluttered, bailey. There were several soldiers on hand to greet him, all of them reaching up hands for the lady.

"Back away, you buzzards," Hubert bellowed, keeping a firm hand on Remington. "Where's the lord?"

"Inside, Hugh," a calm-looking knight stood by his right leg, eyeing Remington. "She looks familiar. Who is she?"

Remington gazed at the knight. "She can speak for *herself,* I am Lady Remington Stoneley."

"Stoneley?" the knight repeated with surprise, looking at Hubert, "Good lord, Hugh, what goes on?"

Hubert handed Remington down to the knight and dismounted, but he quickly took her back into his protective grasp. "Quite a story. Ingilsby is going to want to hear this."

Hubert and the other knight led Remington inside, away from the curious stares of the men-at-arms. Ripley Castle was a smaller keep, quiet for the night. The corridors were dimly lit as they made their way into a great room, illuminated golden by the dying fire in the hearth. Two huge dogs lying by the hearth barely gave the three humans a glance.

Hubert sat Remington down and sent the other knight for wine and food. When the man returned, Hubert gave it all to Remington.

"Aren't you going to eat, too?" she asked softly. "We have been riding a long time and after the attack, you must...."

He shook his head, biting off her words. "Nay, my lady, you go ahead and eat your fill. I am not much hungry."

"An attack? What attack?" the other knight demanded.

Remington looked up at the man as she ate in an appraising sort of way. Young, with wide brown eyes and an impish face, his cropped brown hair was standing straight up. Hubert, on her other side, removed his helm and set it loudly on the scrubbed table.

"On the road," he mumbled wearily. "We were set upon by bandits. I shall tell you the all of it when Ingilsby arrives."

The young knight looked at Remington curiously, obviously eager to hear their tale.

Alex Ingilsby entered the common hall, his eyes widening dramatically when he laid eyes on Remington. She smiled weakly and he sputtered.

"Remi," he gasped. "What on earth are you...Hugh, did you bring her here? What is going on?"

"An unbelievable tale, I assure you," Hubert indicated a chair for his liege to sit.

Alex hesitated a moment before seating himself next to Remington, his astonished eyes studying her. "Are you all right, Remi? What....?"

She nodded, patting the baron's hand. "I am fine. Allow Hugh to tell his tale, my lord. I would do it, but I sorely lack the strength at the moment."

Alex's gaze lingered on her a moment longer before turning to Hubert expectantly. Without delay, the knight relayed the entire story, from Guy's escape until their arrival at Ripley. When he was finished, Lord Ingilsby looked nothing short of stunned.

"Stoneley? Escaped?" he repeated, turning to Remington. "And what he did to you... my God, Hugh, I think I am going to be ill. Fetch me a chalice, please."

Hubert filled a goblet full of wine and placed it in his lord's hand. After a healthy gulp, Alex took a deep breath. "God directed Hugh to that inn, I know it. He was looking out for you, Remi. I will have a mass said at day break for thanks of your rescue."

Remington turned warm eyes to Hubert, tired and still coated with black splotches of blood. "Sir Hubert was my true savior. He was magnificent, my lord. I am sure Gaston will reward him tremendously."

"As will I," Alex glanced at his captain. "Good lord, Hugh, you looked whipped. Why not take a meal and go to bed?"

"Not until my lady does," he said firmly. "She has had a rougher time than I, let me assure you."

Remington ignored him, putting her hand beseechingly on Alex's arm. "We must send word to Gaston right away, my lord. He must be told where I am."

"Absolutely," Ingilsby agreed. "Adam, see to it."

The second knight nodded sharply and Hubert put in, "My lord, I would have Adam deliver the message personally."

Ingilsby nodded again. "Agreed. Not knowing where exactly the duke might be, it would help to send a messenger who would know him on sight." As Adam strode from the hall, Alex stopped him.

"Nothing written, Adam. If Stoneley or his allies were to intercept the message, we'd have them all over us like a horde of locusts. Dress well, lad, and return to me before you depart."

When the second knight quit the hall, Alex turned to Remington again. "Do you have any idea where Gaston would go?"

She thought a moment. "Mt. Holyoak, to be sure. But he and Brimley have become allies. Or he might even come here, since you are loyal to him as well."

"True enough," Alex was lost in thought a moment longer before gently grasping Remington's hand. "Come now, my lady. I suspect you would like to rest now after your most harrowing experience."

She nodded, passing a final glance at Hubert before allowing the baron to lead her upstairs.

Hubert's gaze lingered on the stairs a moment, even after she disappeared. He was actually a bit remorseful that their adventure together was over, because he had so enjoyed getting to know lovely Lady Remington. He thought the Dark One to be a very lucky man indeed.

Except for being nearly deserted, Mt. Holyoak looked better than Guy had ever remembered. Seeing his fortress for the first time in two years actually brought tears to his eyes, tears of joy but also tears of sadness. He could not occupy his keep for the moment, and that distinctly upset him. Yet, he reminded himself, the situation was only temporary.

He could see sentries up on the walls, patrolling the keep vigilantly. Guy lingered in the shrubbery, smelling the beech wood and pine and reluctantly agreeing that there was no possible way he could rid his keep of the soldiers that occupied it. There were several dozen, mayhap even one hundred. As much as he wanted it back, one man against one hundred was deadly odds.

He sighed heavily, reluctant to leave his beloved keep. But he knew the sooner he reached Knaresborough, the faster he would regain what was his. No doubt Botmore would pledge manpower to regain the fortress, and Guy was positive he could convince Archibald to contribute forces as well. With as little as two hundred and fifty men, he was positive he could take back his keep. He had, after all, built the thing. He had made it impenetrable, but he was confident that he could think of some way to regain it.

Keith Botmore had been stunned to see his old friend ride into his keep. Surprise turned to glee as the two greeted each other, speaking of the glory of the Yorkists all the way into the grand hall. Even as food and drink were brought forth, Botmore kept up a running conversation about Richard and Edward, and how someday soon another Yorkist would sit upon the throne. Buckingham and his weak rebellion had failed, as had the uprising that reached as far north as Trent. But someday soon, Botmore swore, the Tudor would fall.

The subject of Remington inevitably came up, to which Guy explained the events in Stanford-on-Avon, in his own way; Remington had tried to kill him and ran off when her attempt was unsuccessful, he said, and was obviously insane. Which explained why she was trying to seek an annulment and why she had willingly gone with the Dark One. Somehow, de Russe had poisoned her weak mind. Botmore clucked with sympathy, promising that they would send a search for her.

But Guy wasn't interested in searching for his wife yet. He was far more interested in regaining his keep. Changing the subject back to the Yorkist resistance, Keith followed admirably.

Guy listened less enthusiastically with each passing moment, sorry he had not seen fit to broach a subject other than this. He did not care about putting another Yorkist on the throne. He wanted his damn fortress back.

"Tell me what you know of the occupation of my keep," Guy interrupted a rich speech, bored.

Keith looked thoughtful. "De Russe keeps a skeleton guard there, but nothing more. The wealth and employment of Boroughbridge depends on the keep, and I suppose keeping it running is the only good thing that bastard has ever done. How do you plan to get it back? Petition Henry?"

Guy shook his head. "Hardly. The crown would not award an escaped prisoner his lands returned."

"But you are only an escaped prisoner until the church declares you freed."

"The church cannot declare me free. Only the Tudor can do that, with a great deal of pressure from Bourchier. I have no doubt that in time my pardon will come, but I do not want to wait that long to regain what is mine. I need your help in this matter, Keith."

"Help? How can I help you?"

"Men," Guy leaned forward on the table, his ice-blue eyes glittering. "I want your army."

Keith looked at him for a moment. "I have nearly five hundred men. As skilled as they are, I have been told that de Russe left behind a block of his elite guard. They're the very best. Moreover, how in the hell do you plan to lay siege to a fortress that is designed as yours is? I'd lose all of my men in the first wave."

Guy would not be dissuaded. "I can find a way. 'Tis my fortress, is it not? If anyone can breach it, I can."

Botmore shook his head reluctantly. "I shall support you, of course. But I would hear this plan before I commit my men."

His lack of confidence angered Guy, but he hid it well. 'Twould not do for him to strike his host. Instead, he forced himself to smile.

"After a good rest, I shall be more than happy to discuss it with you."

The two men rose, strolling leisurely for the second floor of the castle. Old, dried rushes crunched underneath Guy's boots and he thought the place, in general, looked worn, unusual for the usually organized and well-kept Botmore.

As if Keith could read his mind, he spoke in a low voice. "It's been nearly a year since Derek was killed by de Russe. We're having a mass said tomorrow for his soul. You shall join us, won't you?"

"Of course," Guy replied, although he had no interest in attending a church service. But he would do it to gain what he sought. "And allow me to convey my sorrow on your loss, Keith. Derek was a fine knight."

The pain was still fresh in Botmore's face. "He was all that I had, you know. His mother died some time ago and...well, the priest says I should marry again and produce another heir. But I can't seem to find the will."

Guy paused at the bottom of the stairs. "We have a good deal in common, you and I. De Russe took everything from me, too. My keep. My wife. My son. Everything."

Botmore's face went rigid. "Aye, he did. Derek was killed trying to rescue your wife from de Russe's clutches," he averted his gaze, clenching his hands into hard fists. "Damnation, Guy, I wish I'd never sent Derek on that mercy mission. I curse myself every night for relaying those orders to him. I should have....oh, hell!"

Guy smiled thinly. "No need to relive your horror, my friend. What's done is done. What remains now is to make de Russe pay for his sins. And we will start by regaining my keep."

Keith looked at him a long moment. "I shall ride with you."

Guy's smile turned real. "Of course you will."

CHAPTER THIRTY-FIVE

Gaston skirted the edges of the trees that lay at the bottom of Mt. Holyoak's rise. The very same trees and shrubs where Remington had once collected flowers the summer before, the very first time he had actually had a chance to speak with her. When he met Dane. When he realized that he felt something for her.

In early summer they were awash with gardenias, wild roses, jasmine, dogwood and other delightful blooms. The smell was heady in his nostrils as he paused at the very border of the trees, his eyes scanning the walls of the great fortress that two men so dearly claimed.

He drank in the sight of the stone edifice, feeling the warm memories and possessiveness filled him like a bottomless well; it ran much deeper than he realized. True, he was extremely fond of the fortress, but gazing at it again brought him to the realization that he was home. His and Remi's.

His eyes scanned the battlements and he could see sentries walking their posts. *His* sentries. Although he knew it was not possible, somehow he had wildly imagined that Guy would return and kill all of his men, replacing them with rebels. He could see now that that was not the scenario.

Spurring Taran on, he galloped up the steep narrow road that led to the drawbridge of his mighty keep.

The men stationed on bridge-duty saw him storm up. Shocked, the cries that the duke had returned bounced among the soldiers until every one of them had turned up to greet their liege. By the time the bridge was lowered and the sharp-teethed portcullis raised, Gaston's men were assembled with waiting arms.

He rode in, balanced atop his excited warhorse. Roald and Charles were the very first to rush forward and greet him.

"My lord," Roald called, smiling. "What brings you back to Yorkshire?"

Gaston bailed off Taran, sidestepping all pleasantries. "Did Guy Stoneley return here?"

Both Roald and Charles looked shocked. "Returned?" Charles gasped. "Is he free?"

Gaston's answer was before him; they had no such knowledge of Stoneley's return and Gaston felt as if he had been hit in the stomach. No Guy, and no Remington.

His breath exhaled painfully, laboriously. "He escaped and took Remington with him. I was expecting...nay, I was hoping he would come here."

Charles went white and closed his eyes. "God help her. Oh, dear God, help her."

Roald looked concerned, glancing at his young friend before turning his attention back to Gaston. "We have heard no word of his escape, nor of his presence anywhere in the area. He took Lady Remington, did you say?"

Gaston nodded, suddenly very weary and sickened. He had no idea where else to look, or where to go. But he knew without a doubt he would spend the rest of his life looking for her. He would never, ever rest.

Roald could read the fatigue and the defeat in his liege, an expression he had never seen before on Gaston's face.

"You are exhausted, my lord," he said quietly. "Mayhap a bit of food and rest and we can help you search. In fact, Charles can send messages to the likes of Brimley and Ingilsby and ask for their help. Can't you, Charles?"

Charles was nearly overcome by the news, but he managed to nod. "I...I can go to the solar and compose the necessary letters."

"Good lad," he gave the boy a shove in the direction of the castle. "On your way, then. The duke will rest while you write the directives."

Gaston couldn't speak for the moment, too overwrought. He felt Roald give him a slight nudge and he followed, into the familiar interior with the familiar musty smell. Inside, Roald directed him to go to the master chamber and promised he would have food sent up to him.

Not realizing that his knight had just ordered him about, Gaston did as he was told.

The bed that greeted him was the same bed he and Remington had shared, the same bed where the twins were conceived. He simply stood and stared at it, the pain welling within him almost more than he could bear. Tears filled his weary eyes and dripped down his stubbled cheeks and he did not care; he felt as if he could cry rivers.

Armor and all, he fell forward onto the mattress, his entire body aching with fatigue and anguish. My god, if she wasn't here, then where could she be?

Where could she be?

Roald came up not a quarter hour later, bearing food for the duke. The meal was set quietly on the table by the hearth and Roald closed the door softly, listening to Gaston's snores rattle the furniture.

The rest did him wonders. When he awoke several hours later, it was with a clear mind and a determined heart. He bathed and shaved, donning clean clothes. An off-white tunic that Remington had made for him embraced his torso, resting next to his heart. Somehow he felt closer to her as he wore it, to be clad in something that she had made with her own hands. It eased his ache and intensified it at the same time.

Charles and Roald met him in the solar. Charles presented the two missives destined for Castle Crayke and Ripley Castle and Gaston nodded his approval.

"You will write one more missive for me, Charles," he said.

"I would like you to send word to my cousin Nicolas and instruct him to bring four hundred of my men here to Mt. Holyoak. If I am going to reside here for the present, then I would be well supported. And instruct him to bring at least fifteen knights as well."

Charles, eager to do the duke's bidding, sat and drew out a length of parchment.

Unfortunately, it was late and the sun had set, rendering any searching out of the question for the time being. Even so, Gaston and Roald sat in the solar discussing the possibilities as Charles wrote a careful missive to Sir Nicolas, instructing him to bring the duke's army to Yorkshire.

Near dawn, a rider was sighted. In fact, two riders on one horse and the
sentries on the wall sounded the alert loudly. Gaston and Roald, still in
the solar, left Charles sleeping at the desk and made their way to the
outer bailey.

As they reached the bailey, the portcullis was already going up. The
closer Gaston drew to the opening, the more curious he became. His
soldiers seemed most eager to tell him that two young women were
approaching and his curiosity was piqued.

Gaston stood just to the inside of the portcullis as a dirty, ratty-
looking nag plodded over the drawbridge. There were indeed two figures slouched over the horse, two small figures, and he nearly turned
away from the riders to leave them in the hands of his soldiers when
something made him stop.

A familiar face with sea-crystal eyes was looking back at him.

"Sir Gaston!" Dane gasped.

Gaston was stunned. "Dane!" Another head came up behind Dane,
even more familiar because it was Gaston's mirror image.

"Trenton!"

"Hello, Father."

Gaston rushed forward, taking both boys off the ancient animal.
They clung to each other for several long moments until Gaston pulled
back to look each boy severely in the eye.

"By God's Bloody Rood, what in the hell are you two doing here?"
he demanded.

"Where's mother? Did you find her?" Dane countered swiftly,
urgently.

Gaston felt as if he had been slapped. Now he knew why they were
there and he felt his pain and anguish start anew. "Nay, Dane, I have
not found her yet. Did the earl tell you what happened?"

The two young men looked at each other guiltily. "Nay, he did
not. We overheard Antonius tell him that my father had abducted my
mother," Dane replied.

Gaston raised an eyebrow. "Then I would assume that the earl does
not know you are here?"

Dane shook his head firmly. "Nay, he does not. But I had to come to protect my mother. Why have not you found her yet?"

Gaston's heart was being squeezed as he gazed back at the young face. "Because I do not know where your father has taken her. But have no doubt that I will find them both, and I will kill...."

He stopped himself but Dane finished the sentence for him. "You will kill my father, isn't that right? I should like to help you."

A flicker of regret crossed Gaston's face and he put a hand on each boy's shoulder, leading them forth into the outer bailey. "No matter what your father has done, and no matter what your differences, 'tis not right that you should want to kill him, Dane. He is still your father, the man from whose loins you sprang."

"I hate him," Dane said simply. "Why is it acceptable for you to kill him and not me?"

Gaston thought a moment. How could he answer the question? He could give the boy a myriad of empty reasons, moral ones, but somehow none of them applied in this situation. How could he tell Dane it wasn't right that he should want to kill his father?

"Because I am not his son," he said lamely, knowing it was no reason at all. "No matter what has happened, a son should not kill his father. I know that my explanation does not make sense now, but someday it will. You will not like to grow old knowing that you killed your father in your youth. It will sit heavy on your soul."

Dane did not understand, but he did not press. He had confidence that Gaston would regain his mother.

"I know you do not believe in my dreams as my mother does, but... well, I remember having a dream about my father trying to kill my mother just after you came to Mt. Holyoak," Dane said quietly. "It was right before I dreamt about your death, but it turned out Sir Arik died instead. Whenever my dreams come true, I do not dream about them anymore. But I still dream about my father and mother sometimes."

Gaston led the boys into the inner bailey. He paused a moment, facing Dane's solemn face. "What happens in your dream?"

Dane hung his head. "I am not exactly sure. My mother is afraid, and she's screaming. And I see blood. I can see swords, mayhap two or three," he looked to Gaston again, puzzled. "I am not exactly sure what it means. It's never very clear."

Gaston put his hand back on the lad's shoulder, pondering the statement. He did not believe in dreams, but he knew Remington did. And Dane's dream of death did come true, although it wasn't Gaston's death he foresaw. Ah, well, he attributed it all to a young man's imagination.

He squeezed Trenton's shoulder gently. "And you, young master? May I ask why you are here on this foolhardy mission?"

"Because you might need help," Trenton said simply.

Gaston raised an eyebrow at the quick, simple answer. He could only imagine the panic de Vere was feeling at the moment, having misplaced the Duke of Warminster's two sons.

Hand on each boy, the three of them took the stairs into the castle. Cool, damp musty air met with their nostrils and Dane seemed particularly content. Gaston took them into the grand dining hall and sat them down, ordering hot food and ale. As the boys ate, he stood over them with hands on his hips. The more he thought of them riding all the way north by themselves, the more angry and frightened he became.

"I ought to take you both over my knee," he said. "The earl must be having fits with you two missing."

"We had to come," Dane insisted, mouth full of mutton. "You are going to fight my father, and someone had to protect my mother while you were occupied. And Trenton wanted to assist you in your fight, and...."

Gaston put up a silencing hand. "Enough, Dane. Finish your food and then you may finish your words," he shook his head, propping a massive boot atop the bench next to Trenton and leaning on his knee. "I suppose I should commend you for your bravery. 'Twas an astounding bit of luck that you reached me unscathed."

"We hid in the trees and stole food from peasants," Trenton said, rather proudly. "We even stole a rabbit on a spit from a traveling merchant. He fell asleep and Dane snagged his dinner."

The boys giggled as Gaston frowned, although his expression bordered on amusement. He shook his head. "Thieves. My God, your mother will have fits."

Dane shook his head. "Aunt Rory was worse. She used to steal from the men-at-arms. Once, she stole a pair of little silver balls in a silk pouch. We never did figure out what the balls were for, but they rolled rather nicely."

Gaston's eyes widened and he cleared his throat, choking off a guffaw. He'd seen such balls, although he'd never personally used them on a woman. Tale had it that they were from the continent, far beyond the Teutonic countries, even beyond India.

He took his leg off the bench, watching the boys drain their cups. He found his gaze drawn to Dane.

"Tell me, Dane. Did your father have any close friends in Yorkshire? I mean particularly close?"

Dane thought. "Douglass Archibald of Spofforth was a friend of my father's. And Lord Botmore. Lord Brimley and his sons used to visit sometimes, as did Lord Tarrington. But that was all."

Gaston knew of those men and planned to contact them. He pondered his options as his sons finished the last of their food and drink, wondering where in the hell to begin this most monumental search. Truth was, he wanted to search every castle and manor house personally, but he knew the impossibility of such a feat, which was why he wanted Nicolas and a good portion of his knights to assist him. With enough manpower, he could cover all of North Yorkshire and his chances of finding Remington would be positive.

The stab of pain sliced at him again, the familiar cut he was coming to associate with her disappearance. With each cut, he felt his determination double, triple. He would find her and he would kill Stoneley, and he would furthermore kill whoever assisted Guy in his dastardly deed. His fury was beyond anything he had ever felt before. More hatred than he thought possible.

The Dark One's wrath would know no mercy.

He ordered an older serving woman to see to Dane and Trenton's comfort as he wandered back to the solar. Charles had awoken from his slumber and was finishing the final touches on the missive to Nicolas. Gaston read the missive with satisfaction; Charles was a well-learned young man and Gaston suspected he would make a better scholar than knight, no matter how badly he wanted to fight. As frail and thin as he was, Gaston made a mental note to discourage the further pursuit of warrior arts.

The sun rose and riders were prepared to deliver the three missives. Gaston himself saw to the readying of the messengers, lecturing each man on the importance of what he was to carry. Charles sealed the missives in sheepskin pouches to protect them, carrying them out into the dusty bailey, smelling of manure and urine and dirt in the rising temperature. Already late June, the heat of the summer was beginning to announce itself loudly.

A sentry on the wall let out a call of an approaching rider. Gaston instinctively stiffened, thinking Stoneley was indeed closing in on Mt. Holyoak and he was wildly gleeful with the surprise that awaited the man. But the soldiers on the wall indicated only one rider, and his heart sank a little. If it were indeed Stoneley, then he was sans Remington.

And he would only be without her if she were de....he broke out in a cold sweat.

The rider was bearing Ingilsby yellow and gray. Gaston called for the portcullis to raise and greeted the rider just inside the entry.

The knight, young with wide brown eyes, saluted sharply.

"My lord," he greeted loudly. "Thank God I have found you. Lord Ingilsby suspected that you might be at Mt. Holyoak, but we were not entirely sure. With Stoneley running loose, we...."

Gaston grabbed the reins of the destrier, his eyes wide and his massive body rigid. "What do you know of Stoneley's escape?"

"We know that he abducted his wife and brought her north," the knight replied. "He sold her to Ripley's captain at a tavern in Stanford-on-Avon and...."

Gaston cut him off by grabbing him sharply, yanking him completely off the destrier. The young knight struggled to his feet, still in the iron grip of the Duke of Warminster. When he turned surprised eyes to the duke, he was met with a glare of such anger that it frightened him.

"Cease with your prattling tale," Gaston hissed, mere threads away from snapping the knight's arm in half. "Where in the hell is Remington?"

The knight winced as Gaston twisted his arm even tighter, but a faint glaze of a smile managed to twist his lips. "That is what I am trying to tell you, my lord," he said quietly. "She's at Ripley, safe and whole."

Gaston's mouth went agape and every last bit of color drained from his face. He stared at the knight as if he did not comprehend him, or at least he thought mayhap he heard only what he wished to hear. But the knight was smiling, whipping him back to his senses as he realized that, indeed, he had heard correctly.

"She's at *Ripley?*" he echoed, his voice a whisper.

The knight nodded. "Aye, my lord. Sir Hubert Doyle saved her from her husband."

Gaston blinked, slammed with the news. He let go of the knight's arm and put a hand against the entry wall to steady himself; he could feel himself weaving with shock. "She's all right?"

"Not a scratch, my lord," the knight replied.

Gaston gazed at the knight a moment longer and closed his gawking mouth, licking his lips that were dry. He could hardly believe what he had just heard, but believe he did. Excitement and relief exploded in his chest, coming forth as a loud exhale of pure disbelief.

When he turned to Roald, he was aware that his whole body was shaking with pure assuagement. "My destrier," he ordered hoarsely.

Roald was already moving, bellowing for the duke's mount and ordering an escort readied to accompany him. Gaston turned away from the knight, his mind consumed with Remington, but he retained enough of his manners to stop before he rudely departed.

He faced the young knight. "Thank you for delivering the message, my lord. Might I have your name?"

"Sir Adam Nelson, my lord," the man said. "And it was my pleasure. Lord Ingilsby and Sir Hugh surmised just how frantic you would be. As soon as Lady Remington arrived, I was sent on my way."

Gaston looked pale and shaken. He was elated beyond believing; in fact, he still had difficulty grasping the situation. "Not a scratch, you say?"

Adam shook his head, smiling broadly. "Nary a mark. She is tired, of course, but that is all."

Gaston nodded slowly, his eyes becoming distant. But not before he extended his gratitude one more time. "Thank you."

Within a quarter hour, he was mounted and riding for Ripley.

The plan was simple. Lay siege to Mt. Holyoak, distract the army inside, and slip in through the secret entrance Guy had built into the wall by the kitchens. It was an entrance seldom used by the peasants because of the sheer fifty-foot drop to one side of the two-foot-wide path. When Guy had it built, it had originally been constructed as an escape route should the drawbridge ever be compromised. He never dreamed he would use it to breach his own fortress.

Problem was, that only one man at a time could enter through it. This would lay them open to snipers by the greater forces inside, when and if the breach was discovered. It was Guy's hope that he could lead enough men through the opening to effectively quell de Russe's men and reach the greater goal of opening the portcullis and drawbridge.

Keith Botmore was more than eager to mount two hundred men for the reclamation of Mt. Holyoak. After Guy convinced the man that they both had suffered so terribly at the hand of de Russe, and after they had drunk a good deal of wine and discussed Derek's entire life, Keith was over-anxious to go to war against the Duke of Warminster.

He was a foolish man, rash to seek revenge before stopping to think of what he was doing. He knew full well of de Russe's reputation, of his strength in aiding Henry. He knew de Russe led an army of a thousand and he furthermore knew the man wielded mayhap the greatest military power in all of England. But he was still eager to overrun Mt. Holyoak and regain it for his ally, escaped prisoner though he might be. He simply saw that he was exacting revenge for his son; Guy saw it for what it was, and that was regaining what was morally his.

Guy was using Botmore for what the man could do for him; as long as Botmore agreed to Guy's demands, Guy was his very best friend. But any refusal on Botmore's part, and Guy would turn on him like a viper.

In armor that had once belonged to Derek, Guy sat astride a powerful gray destrier next to Keith as the lord's army was assembled. He felt a distinct pull of power, the days of old when he led his own army against the Tudor. In a sense, he was doing it again, only this time the adversary was far more powerful.

He would rid de Russe from his keep once and for all.

Guy and Keith led Botmore's army from the confines of Knaresborough, edging the town of the same name on their trek northeast to the Vale of York. The peasants turned out en masse to witness the army mobilizing, wondering if the War of the Roses had not yet ended, in fact, and they were due for another series of battles. The fact that their liege was moving to overtake another Yorkist keep never occurred to them.

The army moved along the vacated road, not a town nor an obstacle between them and their destination. They veered northeast just south of Boroughbridge, trampling the early summer grass in the fertile vale. The closer they drew, the more Guy's adrenalin began to flow.

Mt. Holyoak would soon be in his grasp. He predicted no more than twelve hours before the fortress fell and her gates opened wide for the invading army. The design was rudimentary; Botmore would create a diversion and lay siege to the bridge of the keep, drawing the attention of the army inside. Meanwhile, Guy and 75 men would build ladders to straddle the moat. When the makeshift bridges were complete, they would lay them across the deep moat and crawl across to the small footpath that bordered the wall. From there, they would breach the small wall gate and file in.

Simple enough, but Guy knew they were likely to lose a great many men against de Russe's skeleton force. Moreover, he wondered if de Russe wasn't already there; spies had returned stating that activity was normal, which meant additional men led by the duke had not arrived. If, in fact, de Russe was bringing a massive army to rescue Remington, he could quite possibly have come alone, the idea of which intrigued Guy. Why would he come alone to rescue his whore? Why would not he bring all of bloody England to assist him?

He still could and Guy knew it, which was why the quick recapture of Mt. Holyoak was imperative. Guy wanted to be in complete control when de Russe arrived.

The very top of his revered keep came into view shortly after noon. Men moved into battle-heightened positions, shields raised and swords drawn, as they continued to march. The knights, only six of them, slung their shields over their left knee for quick access. Guy felt the familiar surge of battle flush through his limbs, the excitement that finally, he would regain his home. Even as they drew nearer to the keep and they could see the drawbridge hastily rising, he felt the thrill of the fight like a potent aphrodisiac. It excited him like none other.

There was no pretense, no words exchanged. Botmore led the majority of his army up the narrow road to Mt. Holyoak and let loose a barrage of Welsh archers, flame arrows to the drawbridge. Most fell, a few stuck, and the burning began.

Down in the surrounding trees, Guy was whipping his smaller army into a frenzy cutting down trees and stripping saplings. He could smell the smoke from the bridge and he could hear faint shouting and he smiled; battle always made him smile.

Finally the time was upon him and his redemption was at hand; the redemption of his *pride*. Turning back to his sweating soldiers, he whooped words of encouragement.

CHAPTER THIRTY-SIX

It was late afternoon when Gaston and his small escort rode into
the cramped bailey of Ripley Castle. The sun was hot, the air
dusty around him, but he wasn't aware of anything other than the fact
Remington was within these old walls. He was completely focused as Sir
Adam led him to the stairs of the castle. Gaston's gaze was locked to the
structure, as if he could look through the stone and find Remington
inside.

Minutes seemed like hours, long and drawn out as their separation
drew to a close. The closer he came, the more time expanded as if to
torture him just a bit more. It was enough to drive him insane as he
approached the entrance to the castle, his desperate eyes seeking what
his heart so desperately sought.

He did not have to look any further. As soon as his boot hit the bottom step of the structure, a flash of scarlet silk came bolting out of the
open front door. He barely had time to look up as Remington hurled
herself at him, hitting him so hard that he grunted and stumbled off
the step.

"Gaston!"

His arms went around her reflexively, shocked at first, but transforming into wild delight. Her hair was in his face, in his mouth, caught
in the joints of his neck armor and the wonderful fragrance of soap and
wildflowers assaulted his senses. Her warmth in his hands was the most
comforting sensation he had ever known.   He had never been so
damn thankful for anything in his whole life.

"Remi!" he gasped, squeezing her fiercely. "Oh, God, are you all
right?"

She nodded vigorously, still clinging to him, refusing to loosen her
hold. Gaston clutched her to his armored chest, relief running rampant

in his limbs and rendering him as weak as a kitten. Yet in the same breath, he had never felt so strong nor whole.

He simply held her, no words between them. Their embrace said everything that needed saying. His pain faded more and more with each successive breath.

He lost track of time, holding her protectively, thanking God over and over for her safety. The feelings wreaking havoc in his soul were indescribable.

Somewhere, someone cleared his throat and Gaston was aware that there were others standing about, observing the touching scene. Reluctantly, he set Remington to stand, pulling strands of her hair free from his armor. Much to his surprise, she was smiling at him, tears of joy in the sea-crystal depths. As emotional as she was, he had expected days of hysterics at their reunion and was pleased to see that she was controlling herself. It made it far easier on him to deal with his own emotions if she were rational.

He smiled back, ignoring the group crowding around them. "Are you sure you are all right, angel? He did not...?"

She shook her head, stopping his line of questions. "I am fine, my love. Truly."

His great hands were touching her face, her hair, relieved beyond words. As long as she appeared fine and untouched, he would not press. But when they were alone, he would know every gory detail. There were a million questions he wanted to ask her, but they would all have to wait. The only thing that mattered was that she was safe.

Alex Ingilsby stood several feet behind her, smiling openly at Gaston. When their eyes met, the baron shrugged. "She's been rooted to the windows for the past six hours, waiting for you. When I heard her running down the stairs, I knew of your arrival. Call it intuition."

Gaston grinned, patting Remington affectionately. "I am forever in your debt, my lord. I cannot adequately express my gratitude for what you have done for Remi and myself. Had it not been for you...."

Ingilsby shook his head. "I had nothing to do with this, my lord. 'Twas Hugh's doing, all of it, and it is he you should thank."

Hubert stood at the door of the castle, his handsome face expressionless. He had watched the entire scene unfold and had experienced a distinct stab of... something, he wasn't sure. Jealousy? Envy? Sorrow? Something he could not quite isolate, but it depressed him nonetheless. When the duke's gaze found him, he tried his best not to let his confusion show.

Gaston took the steps, keeping Remington clutched to his side. He walked past Ingilsby, focusing on the captain. He had fully intended to thank the man but mere thanks seemed grossly insufficient. He struggled for a brief moment.

"To thank you appears quite deficient. I should offer you my life, my wealth at the very least," Remington hugged him tightly and he glanced down at her dark head, returning soft eyes back to Hubert. "I am grateful, Hugh. Never consider any request too great to ask of me. I shall do everything within my power to repay you for your loyalty."

Hubert nodded faintly, humbled with the adoration of the Dark One. "I have always been loyal to you, my lord, since the days of Edward. When we met at the tourney last year, I was surprised you remembered the green young upstart, newly knighted, serving his king," he looked at Remington, positively glowing in Gaston's arms. "What I did, any man would have done. It was nothing out of the ordinary."

"Not true," Remington insisted, turning to Gaston. "Guy tried to sell my services as a whore and it was only by luck that Hugh was the prospective client. He helped me escape and fought off ten robbers during our journey here. He is far too modest, Gaston. He's a hero."

Gaston looked at the knight with astonished eyes. "Is this true?"

Hubert swallowed, flushing slightly at Remington's praise. "There were only five robbers, my lord, unskilled and wild. 'Twas not a difficult match, but I worried greatly for the lady's safety."

But Remington was not finished with her honors; Hubert was being far too modest in her opinion. "Two of them grabbed me and tried to molest me, but Hugh killed them both, even after he had already killed two attackers. He was magnificent, Gaston, truly. He is far too humble."

Gaston's arm tightened on Remington, listening to her relay the horrors of her journey. "And in Stanford-on-Avon, he bought me when Guy tried to sell me as a whore," she continued, looking to Hubert. "Hugh recognized me and paid Guy a good deal, explaining that he wanted me for several hours. It bought us time to escape."

Gaston looked to Hubert again, his face taut with emotion. "There are no words to express my thanks, Hugh. I am forever in your debt."

Hubert bowed awkwardly, not knowing what else to do. He was uncomfortable and flattered at the same time. "Simply upholding the code of chivalry, my lord."

It was far beyond that and they both knew it, but Gaston kept silent. He had never been very good at expressing himself, and left it at that.

Even as Ingilsby led them inside, Remington continued to relate their adventure to Gaston. He held her close, listening intently to every word. Alex took them to the grand dining hall where a sumptuous spread had been lain out in honor of the duke's arrival. But in faith, Gaston had no appetite, and more so after hearing the traumatic tale Remington was relating to him. Yet as a courtesy to his host, he sat and accepted a full goblet of premium wine, still listening to Remington talk.

And as she talked, he watched her face with loving eyes, still stunned at the rapid turn of fortune. She was returned to him, where she belonged, and he was deeply grateful to the knight who risked his life to help her.

Eager to be alone with her, he spent a nominal amount of time in the dining hall before excusing them both into a small solar near the entrance to the castle. Remington held his hand tightly, even as they entered the room and he closed the door behind him. When he turned to her, it was to kiss her forehead reverently.

"God, I still cannot believe I have you back," he whispered. "I thought...I did not know when I would see you again, angel."

She smiled bravely. "I would have found a way to escape him."

He held her at arm's length, studying her. Really studying her. Remington gazed at him openly and watched his face darken.

"You have a bruise on your face," he said softly. "Did he do that?"

Her hand flew to her face unconsciously. "Aye."

A muscle in Gaston's cheek twitched. "I want to hear everything, Remi. Not the pretty story you gave me in the dining hall. I want to hear every little detail of what happened. How did Guy abduct you?"

Her happy mood faded and she sank into the nearest chair. "He wore a papal guard's tunic. He sent a soldier up to my rooms to tell me that the papal council wanted to speak with me, and when Patrick brought me down he was waiting for me. Only I did not know it was him until...." Her eyes filled with tears and she wiped quickly at them. "Until he killed Patrick. I do not know how we got out of the Tower, because he knocked me unconscious. I did not come to until we were nearly out of London."

Gaston's smoky eyes went to black with rage. "He killed Patrick? You saw this?"

She nodded, sniffling. "Guy dropped something and when Patrick bent over to pick it up, he stabbed him."

Gaston clenched his teeth, absorbing the information. He could see how upset she was becoming and put his hand on her shoulder. "It's all right, angel. Go on with your story."

She told him everything, including the beatings that seemed endless. She watched his face after she told him, seeing the veins on his neck pump furiously. By the time she was finished, Gaston held no particular expression although he was sweating profusely. She watched him with eager eyes.

He stood there a long while after she finished and she was slowly dying inside, wishing he would scold her or rage or react somehow. Anything but silence. It was enough to kill her.

"Are you angry with me?" she asked in a small voice.

He moved away from her chair. "Of course not, angel. Why would I be?"

She did not believe him. She rose from her chair, tears of anguish spilling over. "Then why do not you look at me?" she demanded loudly. "Why do not you hold me and tell me how much you love me? Why do not you...?"

He spun around to her, grabbing her into his iron embrace and pulling her hard against him. She sobbed loudly, sobs full of humiliation and terror. He stroked her hair.

"I am sorry, I am sorry," he whispered over and over. "'Tis not what you are thinking, Remi. I am simply overwrought with the news, 'tis all, and am trying to compose myself lest I tear this room apart with my bare hands."

She continued to sob, the horror she had suppressed surfacing and demanding release. He held her tightly, his heart smashing like fragile glass. Hot tears stung his eyes, too. "If anyone should be angry, it should be you," he said softly. "I failed to prevent this from happening."

"How could you have foiled him?" she sniffled loudly. "There was no way you could have known what he was going to do. Who would have expected that Guy Stoneley would be the first man to escape from the White Tower?"

Gaston was guilt-ridden with impotence, nonetheless. "I should have put more knights on guard, or mayhap more soldiers. Mayhap I should have had my men guarding Stoneley. Oh, hell, I should have done something more."

She raised her face to look at him, regaining her control and wiping at her wet face. "You are being ridiculous, Gaston. There was nothing more you could have done to protect me. What happened was a mischance."

He gazed down into her sweet face, tenderly kissing away her tears. "No more mischances, Remi. You shall never be out of my sight again, for as long as you live."

She raised an eyebrow at him humorously. "You plan to take me into battle with you?"

"Absolutely," he responded without missing a beat. "I shall make you my quartermaster. I shall not go into another campaign without you."

She smiled, dashing away the last of her tears. He smiled faintly at her, pleased to see her humor returning. But as he saw the sweetness that was Remington resurface from her shattered shell, the more black hatred filled him and the more he wanted to find Guy and destroy him. How dare the man lay a hand on her, or try to sell her as a common whore. Gaston felt violated almost as much as Remington did.

"What now?" she asked softly.

He touched her cheek. "You will return to London. And I will find Guy."

She somehow knew this. "Do you know where he has gone?"

"Nay. But he had enough supporters in Yorkshire that I am sure he is in the area, somewhere. I shall find him."

She was silent, thankful for the fact that Gaston was going to kill Guy. She wanted the man dead, if for no other reason than she would no longer be living in fear, fear that somehow he would find her again someday and do far worse than beat her.

Gaston eyed her lowered head, a thousand thoughts flooding his mind. He loathed the fact that he would be breaking his vow and sending her back to London without him, but it was necessary. He did not want her anywhere in Yorkshire where Guy could get his hands on her again. He wanted her far away, safe with her sisters at Braidwood until he came for her. And after that, he promised himself, he would truly never again be separated from her.

He reached out a thick arm and pulled her to him, embracing her tenderly as each was lost in their own thoughts. She caved into him, her supple body against his hard one. She could feel his gloved hands slowly rubbing her back, telling her wordlessly how very much he loved her.

"Do you want to hear something funny?" he said, his cheek against the top of her head. "Dane and Trenton rode north from Oxford to help me. You can imagine my surprise when two young boys arrived at Mt. Holyoak astride an old nag that was one step before death."

"They came alone?" she looked up at him, shocked. "All by themselves, all the way from Oxford?"

He nodded, smiling. "It would seem that Dane was hell-bent on protecting you from Guy, while Trenton was going to act as my second."

Her brow furrowed. "Why do you smile? 'Twas foolish for them to come, Gaston! I hope you blistered their backsides!"

"I smile because they are far braver than I was at that age and I am proud of the fact. And no, I did not blister their backsides, but I made it quite clear their mission was foolhardy and that they were wrong in their actions. My purpose was to discourage them, Remi, not beat them senseless. Properly worded reprimands oft work better than welts across the buttocks."

She lowered her gaze, feeling ashamed that he was so sensible and patient. "Are they still at Mt. Holyoak?"

"Aye, I left them there with Roald," he answered. "They can ride back with you when you return to London."

She met his gaze, running a tender finger along his scratchy stubble. "You shall not be escorting me?"

He kissed her finger when it traced his lips. "As much as I am torn, I cannot. I must stay here and find Guy. Nicolas and Matts are riding from Deverill as we speak, bringing reinforcements for the guard at Mt. Holyoak. They'll escort you back to London."

She watched her finger as it ran over his cheeks, his square jaw. She was quiet a moment. "What of my annulment? Did the papal council give you an answer before... all of this happened?"

He shook his head. "Unfortunately not. The papal guard uniform Guy was wearing was stolen from the soldier that had been sent to retrieve him. The council wanted to speak with Guy one last time after reading de Tormo's missive, presumably to hear what the man had to say in his defense. But Guy killed the soldier and escaped before that could happen."

She rolled her eyes wearily, so very tired of all of the legalities and arguing. She almost did not care anymore; annulment or no annulment, she and Gaston were forever destined to be together. "Oh, Gaston, when will it be over? I do not know how much more of this I can take."

"I know, angel. But Courtenay seemed to think the council was quite convinced an annulment should be granted, based on de Tormo's testimony. I think after this latest escapade with Guy, they will finally see the truth of the matter. I tend to believe that we will have your annulment upon your return to London."

She made a wry face. "A lot of good it will do me. We shall not be married right away, considering you shall be chasing through Yorkshire after Guy," she threw her arms around his neck and he lifted her high so that their faces were level. "Return with me, Gaston. We shall have our annulment and we shall be married the very same day. Then you can return to Yorkshire and do what needs to be done. Please?"

He nuzzled her cheek. "I cannot, love. I have got to take care of Guy before he does any more damage. I must make him pay for what he has done to you."

"There will be all the time in the world for that after we're married," she closed her eyes at his touch, her arms tingling wildly. "Please return with me first."

He was forgetting his rage, losing himself in the smell of her. "I cannot, Remi."

His lips were grazing her jaw line, her neck, suckling gently on her sweet skin. Her horror, her tears faded into the recesses of her mind as Gaston reminded her of life's sweetest pleasure. Her grip around his neck tightened.

"I shall make you come with me," she whispered. "I shall force you."

"Force me?" he mumbled, nibbling on her shoulder. "And just how do you plan to do that?"

She answered him by reaching around to her back, undoing the stays on her borrowed dress. Scarlet silk cascaded like a waterfall to the floor, landing in a pile around his feet. The boned corset underneath grazed his armor and he laughed low in his throat.

"You laugh, my lord?" she said huskily. "Is something, perchance, humorous about my undressing before you?"

"God no," he whispered into the white flesh of her upper arm. "But you are resorting to trickery to gain your ends and I find that mayhap I shall enjoy submitting to your 'force'."

She grabbed his great head, forcing him to look at her. He was shocked to see her eyes brimming with tears and he froze his onslaught, horrified that he had been so inconsiderate of her feelings. "Oh Remi, I am sorry," he said softly. "I thought....I shouldn't have pushed, but you removed your surcoat and. . . I should have been mindful of your...."

She put her fingers against his lips, silencing him. "This is what I want, Gaston. I want you to touch me, my love, and make me forget about... make me forget about everything."

Her words were a plea from the soul and he was seized with passion and fury all over again. His lips slanted over hers, tongues searching and tasting, relishing each other in worship. He kissed her long and hard, his great hands roving her sweet body. To think of Guy taking her brutally brought rage beyond rage, but his passion for her won out.

Armor off, he took her on the baron's oaken desk. Remington wrapped her body around him, weeping with joy and relief as he entered her with sweet force. He never stopped kissing her the entire time, thrusting his long length into her quivering body, becoming a physical part of her. She was already ingrained into his mind like a scorching burn, never to be removed and somehow he imagined that their bodies were melting into each other and wishing that permanently, they would be of one form.

She came rapidly, in a blinding shudder of glory. He answered with a hoarse cry, whispering her name as his convulsions died a lingering, magnificent death. Still, he continued to kiss her, to be a part of her. Surely there was nothing sweeter on the earth.

"Damn," he muttered, still suckling on her lower lip.

"What?" she still clung to him, still feeling his semi-arousal twitching within her body.

He shook his head, grinning. "Those damn pessaries are doing absolutely no good at all. I do not know why I bought the things."

She laughed and he kissed her teeth because they were so beautiful. "I have probably conceived triplets this day, knowing how fruitful you and I seem to be together."

"God, I hope not," he mumbled. "I have enough trouble telling my daughters apart. Besides, I do not want any more children."

She raised an eyebrow at him. "Want or not, we take what we are given. And considering we have made love the last few times without your pessaries, it may be possible that I have...."

"Enough," he kissed her again, loudly, and withdrew himself. She moaned softly, her gaze hot on his semi-limp member as he moved for his breeches. She sat up as he dressed and managed to clutch her surcoat to her but not much more. She was fixed on his marvelous body as he moved in the light.

It was as if her entire abduction was a fleeting, unpleasant memory. No longer did she feel the fear or the terror, only a distinct displeasure. Her horror was vanished and she knew it was but for Gaston's comfort and presence. Only he had the power to make her feel safe, like nothing else in the world.

He slapped a latch on his chest plate where it met the back armor and glanced up at her, noticing she was still nude but for the surcoat held against her chest. And she was watching him with the most amazing eyes. He smiled. "What is it?"

She shook her head slowly, her eyes raking all over his form. "Nothing, my love. Nothing."

He looked puzzled a brief moment as he finished with the rest of his armor. "Get dressed then. We have things to do."

She obeyed and he helped her with the stays of the surcoat. When she was finished and her slippers were donned, Gaston held out his arm to escort her from the room. She grasped his elbow with a smile.

"I hope we were not too loud," she glanced at the desk behind them and then gasped when she saw a small wet spot on the surface. Quickly, she wiped her hand across it until it disappeared and he laughed softly.

"You worry overly, Remi," he said. "The stain would have dried."

Her cheeks were flushed with embarrassment as he led her from the room, positive her host and his household had been witness to their joyous reunion.

Rather than ride in the dark back to Mt. Holyoak, Gaston graciously accepted Lord Ingilsby's offer to stay at Ripley for the night. That evening they had a group of entertainers as the evening's diversion and Lady Anne seemed to think a great deal of their skill.

Both Gaston and Remington were exceedingly tired but they remained in the grand dining hall after the meal had been cleared to enjoy the entertainment. There were jugglers, acrobats that walked on their hands and feet bent over backward, and a woman with a duck that, she said, divined the future. Remington watched it all with interest, completely enjoying the feel of Gaston's hand on her knee as he conversed with Alex.

She was relaxed and happy for the first time in many a day and she enjoyed the lightness and worry-free state. Considering their future together was still rather unclear, she was determined to enjoy the present. As far as she knew, Gaston was still intent on sending her to London without him and her heart sank when she thought of being separated from him. Again. Would it never end?

The woman with the duck came to the head table and stopped directly in front of Remington.

"Tell yer future, milady?" she asked pleasantly.

Remington glanced at Gaston, who shrugged with a smile. The woman with the duck bade Remington to extend her hand, which she did, and the duck nibbled on the soft flesh of her hand. Remington giggled at the tickling until the woman commanded the duck to stop, and it did. Rubbing her coarse hand over the nipped flesh a couple of times and mumbling some sort of prayer, she peered closely at the skin.

It took a moment for her to speak. "I see a great many things, milady. Ye have left children that are dear to ye, have ye not?" when Remington nodded, the woman dipped her head again.

"I see... girls. Beautiful girls that look like their father. And I see another son in the not-too-distant future."

Remington glanced at Gaston, who did not look entirely amused by the prediction. She grinned at him, anyway, as the woman continued. "I see a great deal of happiness, but not after..." she rubbed at Remington's hand again and again, as one would rub at fogged glass. Remington watched the woman closely as her eyes widened and she dropped Remington's hand to the table. "That's all, milady. I see naught else."

She turned away rapidly and Remington was confused. "Wait." she called after the woman. "Wait a moment."

The woman did halt, but reluctantly. Slowly, she turned to face her again. "Milady?"

Remington could see something in the woman's eyes, a flicker of fear. Deeply curious, she rose from her seat and extended her hand again. "You saw more. What did you see?"

"Nothing, milady," the woman insisted, her eyes lowered to the duck.

"She asked you what else you saw," Gaston's voice was as low as thunder. "You will do her the courtesy of answering."

The woman looked at Gaston as if God himself had just spoken to her. Hesitantly, she went back to the table but refused to meet Remington's eyes. Again, she rubbed her skin and looked hard at the tiny red welts. Remington observed the woman intently as she struggled with her prediction.

"I see....a great deal of pain," she whispered quickly. "I see a goodly amount of anguish. Possibly even death."

Remington tried not to react to the prophecy but she couldn't help herself from pressing. "For me? Or for my family?"

The woman nervously glanced at Gaston, whose expression was neutral. "Yer family, I suppose."

Remington swallowed and took her hand away. After a moment, she forced herself to smile as she took her seat. "What would a prediction be without death and destruction? If you told me my life would be perfect, I'd think you to be a liar."

The woman gazed back at her with uncertainly. With a quick curtsy, she fled the table. Gaston leaned close to Remington.

"Do not tell me you believe that blather," he said softly.

She maintained her flippant attitude. "Of course not. But it is fun to hear. Especially when she tells me there is another son in my future."

He snorted into his cup, refusing to respond. Her smile turned genuine at his reluctance and she leaned against his arm. "No son? Are you truly that dead-set against any more children?"

He eyed her. "We have been through this. I do not wish to discuss it now."

She laughed softly and stroked his stubbled cheek as the minstrels began to play a lively tune. "You are a terrible coward, Gaston."

"Why is that?" he drank from his chalice.

"You are afraid of your children," she said simply. "You have already told me that you are afraid you will not be able to handle Dane and Trenton when they grow older, and I know for a fact that Adeliza and Arica scare you to death because they'll grow into young women with minds of their own, and they've already got you whipped into submission."

"Whipped into submission?" he looked at her. "I beg to differ, madam. I am their father, not their servant."

Her eyes were smoky as she gazed back at his incredible face.

"They could ask you for the world and you would not deny them, and that scares you. You are a weak-willed soul when it comes to your children because you love them so. Isn't that right?"

He gazed back into her eyes, his limbs filled with the liquid warmth of his feelings for her. "Astute, my lady. As always."

She kissed him gently, feeling the heat of the contact bolt through her body. "More children, Gaston, a whole castle-full. The Dark Duke must have a great legacy."

He shook his head slowly; she was intent on disobeying his wishes in the matter. She started to laugh at him again when Hubert appeared on her other side.

"A dance, my lady?" he asked, entirely aware of Gaston's intense gaze on him.

Remington did not even ask Gaston's permission. She was up and on the floor with Hubert, and he swung her into the downbeat of the tune with great flourish. Gaston watched her, laughing and giddy, as the knight twirled her about the floor. He could have easily been jealous, but he wasn't thinking along those lines; he was simply thankful to see her enjoying herself.

This woman who cringed with terror the first time he tried to dance with her.

But the woman dancing before him was not the same woman. She was confident, delightfully charming and poised. And the fact that she was the most beautiful woman in the room had all eyes upon her. Gaston sat back in his chair, his face creased with satisfaction.

"I have known Remington since she was sixteen years old," Alex said softly from his other side. "I can only remember seeing her this happy one time; right before she wed Guy. It was almost the last time I ever remember seeing her smile."

Gaston watched Remington spin before him in Hubert's arms, a great whoosh of scarlet. "After what's happened, I thought it would take her a good deal of time to recover herself. I am glad to see I was wrong."

Alex watched Remington, too, remembering how desperately in love with her he had been. If he thought about it, he probably still was. But she was, as always, unattainable, especially now. But that knowledge did not stop him from admiring her flawless beauty.

"I shall loan her more clothes until she can retrieve her own, my lord," Anne leaned around her husband and was speaking to Gaston. "Surely she cannot make do with only one surcoat."

"Thank you for your consideration, my lady," he replied.

Anne gazed at the duke a moment, certainly the most handsome man she had ever laid eyes on. When he looked at her with his smoky gray eyes, piercing and jewel-like, it was enough to make her heart flutter like a young maiden's. "What are your plans come the morrow, my lord?"

"We return to Mt. Holyoak and await the arrival of my knights who will escort her back to London," he said, watching Remington as she danced by once again. "I shall remain in Yorkshire a while longer."

Alex knew why although he wasn't sure Anne did, and was thankful when she did not press the duke. When she turned back to one of her ladies, Alex leaned close to Gaston.

"Should you require my help, my lord, do not hesitate to ask," he said quietly. "I should like to see Stoneley dead as much as you."

Gaston nodded in thanks. "If you hear of his whereabouts, I can be reached at Mt. Holyoak. I shall remain in Yorkshire until I find him."

Alex scratched his chin thoughtfully. "He was particularly allied with Keith Botmore and Douglass Archibald. 'Tis possible he's made contact with them."

"My contacting Botmore is out of the question, and I have yet to meet Archibald."

"I shall send missives to them and find out what they know," Alex said. "However, they know I have allied with you and may not respond."

"True. I shall contact Brimley and Tarrington and see what they have heard. Hopefully, someone has caught wind of Guy's whereabouts." Remington waltzed by again, this time with a different knight and Gaston raised an eyebrow. "Who is that?"

Alex turned to look, grinning at what he saw. "That is Sir Drake Connaught. That man is, shall I say, a rogue. He's got at least a half dozen bastards about these parts and I'd release him from his oath to me if he were not an outstanding knight. Anne can't stand him."

Gaston watched the knight intolerantly as he cradled Remington in his arms. She was smiling brightly at him, chatting amiably. He shifted in his seat. "I shall give him thirty seconds. If he's not released her by then, I shall step in."

Alex chuckled, drinking of his French wine. "Have no fear, my lord. He's already been rejected by Remington."

"He has?" Gaston looked at the baron.

Alex eyed Drake, tall and dark and striking. "She was most unkind with her rejection, as I recall. Something about a self-absorbed, supercilious bastard." When Gaston smiled humorously, Alex looked thoughtful. "And if I remember correctly, he went for every one of the Halsey sisters, trying for yet another conquest. Jasmine cowered from him, Skye would not even acknowledge him, and Rory gave him a black eye. I always liked Rory a great deal."

Gaston laughed softly. "So did I. When she wasn't playing tricks on my knights."

Alex let out a loud guffaw. "She put some sort of tree sap on Drake's saddle that turned into mortar when he sat on it. We couldn't get him off the saddle; he sat outside in the rain for six hours while the knights tried to pry him free. They finally resorted to removing him and the saddle together and then wrestling him from the armor," he laughed again at the memory. "I thought Anne was going to burst a vein with all of her laughing."

Gaston laughed too, eyeing the knight once again as he held Remington. He wasn't so worried anymore.

The dancing and merriment went on into the night. Alex's knights, seeing that the duke had not prevented Hugh or Drake from dancing with his ladylove, all vied for their turns and Remington found herself dancing the evening away with several dashing young men. Sir Adam was the next brave man, daring to take her to waltz on a slow ballad. As Gaston watched with a critically protective eye, Remington became the undisputed belle of the ball, surrounded by virile young men eager to chat with the beautiful woman. She laughed and joked with them, displaying her delightfully dimpled smile for their enjoyment. Gaston merely sat back, wine in hand, conversing leisurely with Alex. His pride went beyond words.

It was a strange experience for him. He had avoided social situations with Mari-Elle at all costs because they usually ended with his wife finding a young man to bed and he slipping out to attend military duties. Never had he attended a social occasion where his better half was the center of attention. He could have very easily been jealous, but he found instead that he was as prideful as a stud stallion. Arrogant because the woman being drooled over loved him with all of her heart, and because he loved her desperately in return. She turned to look at him several times and they smiled at each other warmly.

Most of the diners had retired for the night with the exception of Alex, Gaston, Remington, and several knights. The music was still playing softly but there was no dancing. Instead, Remington was surrounded by six or seven knights on one side of the room while Gaston and Alex were still seated at the head table on the other side of the hall. The hour was late and the night still.

Gaston could hear Remington's sweet voice from where he sat as she demanded Sir Drake tell her more of his Irish home. Being half Irish herself, 'twas natural that she wanted to hear of her mother's homeland. Having long since finished their final goblets of wine, Alex and Gaston broke out a chess set while Remington and the knights continued their party. They played chess and shared a pitcher of warm cider between them, listening to Remington's occasional laughter and the low hum of male voices.

Under normal circumstances, Gaston would have put an end to her evening long ago. But the past few days had been so traumatic for Remington that he was not opposed to allowing her a bit of laughter and gaiety. She seemed to have forgotten all about her brush with the devil for the moment and he was thankful.

While he and Alex were in the middle of a particularly critical move, Drake turned to the musicians and demanded they play an Irish jig. Complying, the four minstrels lapsed into a wild Celt melody and Remington found herself swung across the floor in Drake's arms. She squealed with laughter and they cavorted across the floor, but in faith she was terribly tired and begged him to cease. He simply laughed at her, twirling her nearly senseless until a large, imposing figure appeared in their path.

Drake stopped and Remington, still moving with the momentum, pitched forward into Gaston's arms.

Gaston was staring straight at the knight. "She asked you to stop quite nicely. Since you do not seem apt to obey her wishes, I will motivate your self-control."

Remington, flushed and gasping with excitement, took Gaston's hands into her own. "Truly, Gaston, he was not being cruel. It was all in fun."

Drake was decidedly afraid of the Dark One. He bowed crisply. "I meant no offense, my lord. As the lady said, 'twas all in fun, I was simply showing her a true Irish jig."

Remington nodded vehemently to back his statement. "Honestly, Gaston. Please do not be angry."

His cold facade faltered slightly, realizing he had overreacted. But when he had heard her pleading with the knight to stop, memories of Guy flooded back on him and he could hear her pleading with her husband to stop his brutal onslaught. It was a peculiar flashback and he found himself on his feet before he realized it, moving to halt the knight. Now, looking at her earnest face, he felt a bit foolish.

"I am not," he said. "But it is late and I think it is time we called a halt to the festivities."

She nodded. "I am fatigued," she turned to Drake and curtsied prettily. "My thanks, Drake. I enjoyed discussing our mutual Irish heritage."

"As did I, my lady," Drake smiled and moved to take her hand, but realized who was standing behind her and quickly put the outstretched hand behind his back. "Good eve, my lord."

Gaston eyed the knight as he moved away rapidly. Remington followed him as well and waved sweetly to her companions as they dispersed themselves. She looked up to Gaston to find him gazing at her with a cocked brow. She smiled and clutched his arm.

"Why do you look at me like that?"

His gaze rested on her a moment longer before he chuckled, patting her hand. "Because I am the luckiest man who has ever lived," he led her over to the table where Alex still sat. "Bid good night to Alex."

She extended a warm good sleep to Lord Ingilsby as Gaston put his arm about her waist possessively and led her from the grand hall. A servant was waiting at the mouth of the hall with a brightly lit torch, waiting to show them to their room. Talk was soft between them, smiles warm as they followed the servant through the foyer and toward the main stairs. At one point, Remington lamented her fatigue and Gaston swept her into his arms to a screech of delighted giggles. She squirmed her way out of his grasp only to find herself heaved over his shoulder as they hit the stairs. Both of them laughing, he mounted the stairs behind the smirking servant with Remington slung over his broad shoulder. She pounded on his back and he slapped her playfully on the behind.

When they reached the first landing where the stairs split in two directions, the front door swung open and several soldiers spilled forth. Gaston glanced disinterested until he saw they completely bypassed Alex in the dining hall and headed straight for him.

"My lord!" one of the soldiers called out to him.

Gaston put Remington down gently. "What is it?"

"We have received a messenger from Mt. Holyoak, my lord. She's under siege!"

Gaston did not react but Remington's hand flew to her mouth. "By whom?" he asked.

"Botmore," the soldier said. "The messenger is outside with Sir Hugh. He shall be...."

At that moment, Hubert and a disheveled soldier marched into the hall. All attention riveted to the warrior in Mt. Holyoak's colors, especially Gaston. "Who attacks my keep?" he demanded of the soldier.

The soldier was one of Gaston's elite guards, seasoned and intelligent. He was bloodied and dirty, but saluted his liege sharply. "Botmore, my lord. And we were told that Stoneley rides with him."

Remington couldn't help herself; she shrieked and closed her eyes, feeling the ground sway beneath her. Gaston did not look at her, but he put out a hand to comfort her. "You know for sure that Stoneley is with him?"

"His own men identified him, my lord," the soldier said firmly. "Sir Roald ordered me to ride forth to find you, and then I was to take a message to Lord Brimley and seek reinforcements, with your approval."

Remington was shaking heavily with shock and fright. "Gaston, Dane and Trenton are inside the keep. Guy mustn't...."

He looked to her, then, seeing the terror in her eyes. He gathered her against him as he took the steps down to Hubert and his soldier. "You will continue on to Brimley and seek his support," his eyes flicked up to see Alex moving into the foyer and their gazes locked. "I shall solicit Lord Ingilsby's assistance."

"No need to request, my lord," Alex said. "Consider my force your very own to do with as you please. I can have all three hundred mounted within the hour."

"Thank you," Gaston's gaze fell back on his soldier. "You may tell Brimley that I rode forth with Ingilsby."

"Aye, my lord," the soldier saluted again, assuming he was dismissed until Gaston stopped him.

"What was the status of Mt. Holyoak when you left?"

"We received word from a perimeter patrol that an army was approaching from the southwest, armed to the hilt, and Sir Roald put the fortress on alert," the soldier said. "Sir Roald sent one of Stoneley's men back with the patrol to see if the man could determine who was approaching. Word came back that it was Botmore, riding with Stoneley at his side. At that point, two messengers were sent to seek you. Unfortunately, we ran into an advance party and there was a brief skirmish. I managed to get away, but my colleague was dispatched."

"Then the army was just upon the keep when you left," Gaston clarified.

"Aye, my lord. The battle was just engaging."

Which was four hours ago. Quite a bit could happen within four hours, but he was positive the keep had not been breached within that amount of time. Yet the one seed of knowledge that blossomed in his mind was the fact that Stoneley had built the keep and, therefore, would know all of her weaknesses. If there were a fault to be exploited, then Guy would know it. He began to feel distinctly uneasy with that thought.

Dismissing the soldier, he turned to Remington. "You shall stay here and keep Lady Anne entertained."

She blinked, dashing her tears away as they fell. "My sons are within the walls. What will happen if Guy...?"

"He won't," Gaston insisted firmly, grasping her by the shoulders. "You know the keep, too, Remi. Are there any tunnels or passages I should know about? Any secret caves?"

She shook her head. "There is no way in or out except the drawbridge," she paused thoughtfully. "Except... except there is a seldom used servants entrance in the wall next to the kitchens. A postern gate. But the servants rarely use it because it is so dangerous."

"I know of the door, I have seen it," Gaston nodded. He'd made note of it on his security sweeps of the kitchen storage areas. "As I recall, it was blocked off by heavy barrels of wheat and had not been used in some time."

She was trying to compose herself, her eyes focused on him as he thought. After a moment of pondering the unlikely possibility that Guy could capitalize on the entrance, he gathered her quaking form against him tightly.

"Do not worry, angel. At least we know where Guy is now and I can do what I should have done a year ago."

"Off to war again. I hate it when you go off to fight," she sniffed.

"I know," he smiled gently and kissed her nose. "I get the same speech from you every time. Have I ever gone back on my word and not returned to you whole? You worry overly."

She threw her arms around his neck and he pulled her off the floor, embracing her sweet body reverently. Actually, he was relieved that Stoneley was attacking Mt. Holyoak. Gaston would be in his glory in the middle of a battle, striking Stoneley down as he would any other enemy soldier. Then it would not matter if the church intended on granting Remington's annulment petition or not; Guy would be dead and there would be nothing to prevent Gaston and Remington from marrying.

The thought brought a smile to his lips and she caught it. "Why are you smiling?"

He kissed her, smiling broadly now. "Because I am happy."

She looked shocked. "Happy. How can you say that? Guy is attacking Mt. Holyoak, our sons are inside, and you are *happy*?"

He laughed and lowered her to the ground. "Aye, I am. Don't you see, Remi? Guy has lured me into a situation where I am more at home than anywhere else. I shall find Guy, strike him down in a fair fight, and we shall be rid of him. I should thank him for making it so easy for me to dispose of him."

She looked at him dubiously. "You are mad. The smell of battle is making you insane."

"Mayhap," he kissed her loudly. "But I am always right. I shall make short work of Lord Stoneley and we shall bury him next to Mari-Elle so that they may rot in hell together."

She shook her head, still upset but growing more relaxed with his easy manner. If he wasn't truly concerned about the battle, then why should she be? He was the authority on warfare, was he not?

"You are sure there is nothing to be concerned over?" she asked insistently.

He shook his head. "Roald is a fine warrior and will hold the keep strongly. With Ingilsby and Brimley attacking from Botmore's rear, he will be fighting on two fronts and it should be a decisive victory. Even so, Nicolas and Antonius are riding north at this very minute with five hundred more troops. Guy and Botmore do not stand a chance in hell, Remi."

She still looked doubtful, but the tears were gone. Frowning, she crossed her arms and eyed him. "I want the battle done by the second morning. And do not linger any longer than you must; I want you to bring me home when the fight is concluded."

He raised an eyebrow. "Aye, general. Any other orders?"

"Yes. I do not want you to bury Guy. I want you to burn his corpse and spread his ashes to the wind. I want nothing left of his evil."

His expression softened hearing the frightened woman speak. He touched her cheek gently. "Anything for you, angel. Anything at all."

A smile creased her lips and he smiled in return. He knew the men were beginning to mobilize in the bailey; Alex and his soldiers had long since vacated the foyer and he and Remington had been alone for quite some time. He took Remington's arm, intent on settling her for the night before retreating to the bailey to join Ingilsby.

"Gaston, I have decided something," she said decisively as he led her up the stairs.

"What's that, love?"

"That I am going to take a switch to both Dane and Trenton for getting themselves into such a predicament." They topped the flight of stairs and headed down the corridor. "I know you said that a reprimand oft works better than a welted backside, but in this case, I'd feel better if I spanked them myself."

"Is that so?" he raised an eyebrow at her as they approached the door to their room. "If you feel it necessary, then I will hold them for you myself."

"You do not need to. I shall do it."

He opened the door, fighting off a grin. "Remi, Dane can outrun a horse and Trenton is bigger than you are. Now, do you truly think they'll not protest whilst you take a switch to them?"

"Of course they will," she insisted. "They'd not dare run from me."

He laughed low in his throat as she kicked off her slippers, laughing again when he thought of Remington chasing the boys up and down the corridors of Mt. Holyoak with a willow branch in her hand. "On behalf of the offenders, my lady, I beg you to reconsider. 'Tis only their first offense, after all, and they were only thinking of you."

"And it will be their last offense if they remember the sting of the switch."

He shook his head, still chuckling. "Pray show mercy, madam. I believe I can vouch that the punishment de Vere plans for them will be quite sufficient to deter any future infractions. They are, after all, his pledges and we must leave the discipline to the earl."

She looked at him, uncertainly, and released the last few stays of her surcoat. The scarlet silk coursed to the floor and she threw the garment on a chair. Clad in the corset and shift, she shrugged. "If you say so."

"I do," he wanted to help her undress but he knew he would never make it downstairs if he were to lay the slightest hand on her. It was going to be hard enough to kiss her good-bye. "Now undo that torturous contraption you wear and get into bed. It has been a particularly fatiguing day."

She agreed silently, unfastening the corset that Anne had loaned her. It was the only way she could fit into the borrowed dress for Anne was considerably thinner and less busty. The corset minimized her magnificent assets just enough to make the dress fit. The corset landed next to the scarlet dress and Remington climbed into the feathered bed as Gaston pulled up the coverlets.

"Lay down, angel," he tucked the covers in about her as she sank into the bed and sighed with contentment. "That's a good girl. Now dream sweetly, love. I shall return as soon as I can."

Her eyelids were already heavy as she gazed up at him. "A pity you cannot join me." He gave her a half-smile. "Pity indeed." When he leaned over to kiss her, she brought her arms up and wrapped them around his neck. Losing his balance, he tumbled onto the bed and ended up in a most provocative position, his massive body completely covering her. Remington giggled, holding him tightly and suckling his lips as he tried to protest. But in a split second, he gave up the fight and fully delved into her delicious mouth. Moments later, he regretted his lack of control for he was dangerously close to bedding her again.

"Nay, angel, let go of me," he whispered against her chin. "I must go."

"I shall let you go after you have comforted me," she hissed back seductively.

He had to be firm or he was lost. Deliberately, he pulled away from her and vaulted off the bed as if she terrified him. They grinned at each other a moment and he adjusted his tunic where his arousal strained against the material.

"Go then, my love," she whispered, snuggling against the pillow. "I may be your wife soon, but I suspect war will always be your mistress."

His smile faded. "War is my vocation, my constant companion, but never my mistress," he moved for the door, drinking in her face one last time. "When I return, you shall be a widow. I swear it on my oath as a knight."

Her smile faded, too. "I know. In my wildest dreams I never dared to hope, Gaston."

His face was cold, unreadable, as indicative of the Dark One. The warm expression from not a moment before was vanished. "This is vengeance, Remi. Guy will pay for everything he's ever done to you and to your sisters and I promise you it will be excruciating. He shall suffer as you have, as you all have. This I do for you, love."

Tears sprang to her eyes. "I know."

He saw the tears and felt her years of pain coming to a conclusion. The thickness of the emotions was palpable, tearing at his heart, and he felt the familiar rage building once again.

"Anything for you," he whispered, and shut the door.

Remington lay awake for a long, long time.

Three hours before dawn, Alex and Gaston left Ripley at the head of a column of three hundred men. Alex's eight knights rode behind their liege and the duke, and Alex actually rode beside Gaston. Gaston allowed this because of his obvious debt to the man, even though he was decidedly uncomfortable not riding alone as usual. Alex, thankfully, kept his mouth shut and they rode in silence.

It was strange for Gaston not riding with his own men. He almost felt like an outsider, although Alex had readily placed him in charge of the men. Still, it was strange not seeing familiar faces, being able to anticipate these soldiers like he could read his own. But he was extremely grateful for the support and made note to tell Henry of Alex's unselfish assistance. There could quite possibly be an earldom in it for Ingilsby, incorporating even more lands into his baronetcy. With Botmore's defeat imminent, Alex could rule the surrounding towns of Knaresborough, Harrogate and Ripon. It would be a most impressive earldom, in Gaston's opinion, and he fully intended to press Henry.

The night was bright under the half-moon as the army made its way to Mt. Holyoak. Spies had been sent out an hour back and Gaston eagerly await their report, although he suspected Mt. Holyoak was holding quite nicely against Botmore and Stoneley. Truthfully, he wasn't worried; Mt. Holyoak was so well designed that he doubted God himself could lay a successful siege. Gaston was an expert on siege patterns and knew that even for him, a struggle to breach the fortress would be frustrating.

He wasn't worried about the approaching battle. In fact, he looked forward to it. Once and for all, he would destroy Guy and crush Botmore and Yorkshire would return to a peaceful shire. He might even consider residing in Mt. Holyoak again, considering how much he and Remington loved the place. Deverill, as the seat of his dukedom, was still not home to him. And neither was Clearwell. Only at Mt. Holyoak did he truly feel he belonged.

They were an hour away from Mt. Holyoak and the sun was beginning to rise. Gaston caught sight of the spies cresting the road in the distance, confident in their report that Mt. Holyoak was still as solid as the gates of heaven. Which was why he was shocked to the core to hear a very different tale.

Mt. Holyoak was breached and her bridge was down. Systematic execution of Gaston's elite guard had taken place and headless bodies littered the grounds.

Mt. Holyoak, Dane and Trenton, were in the hands of a madman.

CHAPTER THIRTY-SEVEN

There was no easy way to go about the attack. The only possible answer was a full frontal assault, hoping to catch Botmore and Stoneley off guard before they raised the bridge. Not expecting assistance so soon, Gaston was sure they would not be prepared for an onslaught. In this case, he was pleased to be correct.

Ingilsby's army pounded up the road to Mt. Holyoak with grim determination, the earth quaking under their feet. Botmore's army was in the process of burning the bodies of Gaston's soldiers in great pyres when the army came upon them. Startled, they began to scramble for the road that led to the keep, but by that time it was already too late and Ingilsby's army engaged them where they stood. Inside the keep, the alarm was sounded and chaos broke loose.

Gaston and Taran charged the bridge, followed closely by Hubert, Adam, and Alex.

"Jam the wench," Gaston hollered above the roar of the ensuing battle. "Jam it so they cannot raise the bridge."

Alex promptly wedged his sword into the wheel, jamming it solid when the soldiers on the wall tried to activate the pulley. Adam, on the other side, dismounted his horse and grabbed a fallen spear. Shoving it through the chain, it broke off and rendered removal completely impossible.

With the bridge properly waylaid, Gaston roared into the outer bailey with a vengeance. *His* outer bailey.

Guy was inside the castle when the alarm sounded. Startled, he barely had time to make it to the nearest window when he saw his men scrambling to ward off invaders. There was a good deal of shouting and panic and then, suddenly, there were enemy knights pouring into the outer bailey. *His* outer bailey.

Rushing into the hall, he was met by Keith.

"What's happened?" he demanded.

"De Russe," Keith gasped. "He's come."

Guy looked awestruck. "But....Christ! How could he have come so soon? My God, we secured the castle not three hours ago. How could he have come?"

Keith shook his head. "Who knows, Guy? All that matters is that he is here with Ingilsby's army. They carry more men, and they're fresh."

Guy growled in frustration and pushed past Keith. "'Tis of no matter!" he snarled. "Where are the boys?"

The flush in Keith's cheeks drained. "In the tower room. Why? What are you planning?"

Guy paused recklessly at the top of the stairs. "De Russe's defeat, what do you think?"

Keith followed him warily to Charles' tower room, which had become a prison for the three young men. When Guy threw open the door, three sets of wide eyes greeted him.

He smiled thinly at his son. "I am returned. It would seem we have a problem."

Dane and Trenton were stone-faced, but Charles was quaking.

"What problem?" Charles asked.

Guy's eyes riveted to his young cousin. "Shut up, woman. I wasn't speaking to you."

Charles flushed, looking at the ground, but Dane remained calm. "What problem, my lord?"

Guy stepped into the room, followed by Botmore. His steps were leisurely, amazing for a man who was under attack. "It would seem de Russe is here. Will you tell me, then, if your companion is his son? I heard rumor he had a son, and this lad looks conspicuously like the duke. I want an answer, Dane."

Dane clamped his mouth shut. Already they were in trouble. Their first mistake had been coming to Mt. Holyoak in the first place. Secondly, when the siege started and Sir Roald told them to retreat to the tower, they did the opposite and plunged into the battle, help-ing the soldiers in their warfare. They stood atop the parapet when the enemy army shot flame arrows into the drawbridge and partially burned it, and they furthermore watched in horror as ladders were laid out across the moat and men began to cross. When the bridge was burned enough for men to pass through, they went down into the outer bailey to help in the fight.

The break in the bridge was manageable. But, suddenly from inside Mt. Holyoak, enemy soldiers began pouring out of the castle and they were trapped. Dane suspected that the soldiers came in through the blocked-off kitchen gate and he was ashamed he had not thought of the possibility sooner. But by that time, it was too late. There were rival soldiers everywhere, and he and Charles and Trenton found themselves in the heat of the fight.

It occurred to Dane that very few people knew of the kitchen gate. Horror rose in his throat as he realized his father must have spear-headed this attack to gain Mt. Holyoak back, and at nearly the same moment he realized his fear, his father strolled from the interior of the castle as if he were God himself.

Charles, Dane and Trenton were all that remained of Gaston's elite force. Dane had watched in horror as Roald lost his head. After that, they were sequestered in the tower.

Until now.

Dane stared back at his father, into the hated eyes. "I am not going to tell you anything."

Guy did not react for a moment. Then, he charged at Charles and grabbed the young man around the neck. Charles shrieked and Dane and Trenton yelled loudly as Guy carried Charles toward the narrow window. They watched in horror as Guy thrust his cousin into the windowsill and half-hung him from the opening, a gaping five-story drop below.

"Tell me or he dies!" Guy yelled.

Dane hurled himself at his father, pounding him with his fists and Guy kicked his son away brutally. Dane slammed to the floor, dazed, but scrambled to his feet for another try. Over his shoulder he could hear Trenton yelling at him to stop.

"Yes, yes, yes," Trenton was shouting. "Yes."

Dane charged his father again, but Guy reached out this time and grabbed him by the tunic. Holding his terrified cousin in one hand and his struggling son in the other, he focused on Trenton.

"What did you say?" he asked, almost calmly.

Trenton's handsome face was dark. "I said...yes. I am his son."

Guy let both young men go just as they were. Charles would have tumbled to his death had Dane not rushed to grab him. Guy crossed the floor to Trenton, eyeing him intently.

"I knew as much. What is your name?"

"Trenton," the youth replied with a steady voice.

"Trenton de Russe," Guy repeated, flashing Botmore a confident look. "You see, Keith? The battle is won already."

"What do you plan to do with the lad?" Botmore asked warily. "He's just a boy, Guy. Surely you are not thinking to...."

"Of course not; not yet, anyway," Guy crooked his finger at Trenton, indicating for him to stand. When the boy was on his feet, Guy silently motioned for Dane to take position next to Trenton.

With the boys side by side, Guy grabbed a length of leather and lashed their hands together, Trenton's right to Dane's left. Dane and Trenton passed glances at one another, wondering what was in store for them, yet neither one was truly frightened. Dane was too busy hating his father to be frightened, and Trenton was simply angry. Over near the window, Charles was exhibiting enough fear for all three of them.

"Come with me," he motioned the two young men, exiting the room with Botmore bringing up the rear.

Charles continued to hover by the window, his heart still in his throat from his fright. It was all he could do to stand, much less follow. Guy had not even bothered to close the tower door, knowing Charles was no threat.

Charles swallowed hard, regaining his wits about him and trying to steady his shaking. He truly had no idea what Guy was planning for Dane and Trenton, but he was terrified that whatever it was, the boys were in mortal danger. Far below in the double baileys he could hear shouting and sounds of combat engagement and he peered from the window to observe the clash.

He would have liked to help. Roald had been kind to him in recent months, training him with various weapons and schooling him on the knightly arts. The thought of his mentor killed before his eyes was almost more than he could bear, but with it brought an unfamiliar anger. An anger so deep that he realized it could only be the fire of revenge.

Dane and Trenton needed his help. Roald was dead. 'Twas time to stop cowering or he was truly the woman Guy accused him of being.

Squaring his narrow shoulders, Charles moved to his work area that housed all of his potions and experiments.

No threat indeed.

Guy took Dane and Trenton down into the foyer area, but he paused at the base of the stairs and turned to Keith.

"Do you know de Russe on sight?" he asked.

Keith shook his head. "I have never seen the man. I'm told he's a big bastard."

Guy glanced around him as if looking for something. Keith watched him curiously for a moment, but Guy focused on him and smiled. "He's in the outer bailey, I suspect. You will send him to me."

Keith's eyes widened. "He shall kill me if I approach him."

"Then send one of your men if you are a coward. If you mention his son's name, then I am sure he will do nothing rash."

Keith cleared his throat, glancing at the boys before doing as he was asked. Guy waited until he was gone before turning his attention to the young men in his control.

His smile was most sinister.

The battle in both baileys was raging. Keith exited the castle and promptly took to the inner way, scanning the boiling mass of men for the largest man he had ever seen. 'Twas not difficult to spot the Duke of Warminster, cutting down men with a broadsword as tall as the young boys held captive inside. It was the biggest sword Keith had ever seen and he was struck with fear as he watched the man fight.

This was the man he had wreaked havoc on ever since Derek's death, the man who had not retaliated. Keith had felt powerful running amuck over the Dark One until now. It was plain that the duke could have easily crushed him had he so desired. As it was, he still could crush him and Keith decided to stay where he was and not venture into the melee. From the looks of it, the Dark One was cutting down soldiers like blades of tall grass and Botmore had no desire to be mowed.

So he began to yell. Hollering de Russe's name, screaming at the top of his lungs. The closer the duke came, the more Botmore maneuvered himself closer until he was standing directly over Gaston as he fought his way into the inner bailey. He continued to yell his name, finally resorting to yelling Trenton's name. Within the second shout of his son's name, Gaston came to a halt and turned his head upward.

Keith felt a bolt of fear shoot through him as Gaston de Russe focused on him. Although he couldn't see his face, he knew his expression to be most intimidating.

"Guy wishes to see you," Keith yelled down. "Dismount your horse and release your weapons."

"Where is he?" Gaston bellowed.

"Inside," Keith responded. "Do as you are told. He holds your son captive."

Gaston did not hesitate. He dismounted Taran and dropped his sword to the ground. His shield went clattering and he marched in through the inner gate as if there was no war going on around him. Keith was astonished at the fearlessness demonstrated.

Hastily, Botmore descended the wall and met Gaston at the castle entrance, a safe distance between the two men. Even though Keith was armed, he had no doubt that the weapon was meaningless against the Dark One. Gazing at the most feared man in the realm made his knees quiver.

"Are my sons whole?" Gaston demanded.

Keith looked puzzled. "We have but one. Trenton."

"What of Dane?"

"Guy's son is whole, too."

"He is *my* son," Gaston repeated in a tone that would tolerate no contradiction. "Where is Stoneley?"

"In the grand foyer," Keith replied.

Gaston did not wait for any more talk or instruction. Purposely, he marched forward into the cool bowels of Mt. Holyoak.

The corridor leading to the foyer was dark and musty. Gaston's footfalls sounded like hammer blows as he stormed toward the designated area. Ahead at the end of the hall he could see the faint glow from the foyer torches and he focused on the light, trying to fight down his anger and apprehension. He could not predict that Guy had not harmed either boy; Guy had proven he was highly unpredictable and intelligent. There was absolutely no telling what he had done.

Gaston stomped to the threshold of the foyer, preparing to seek out Stoneley's form. Yet the very moment he stepped from the corridor, something heavy and massive slammed into his face and he was reeling, crashing to the floor with the force of the blow. He thought he heard yelling, Dane and Trenton's voices, but he could not be sure of anything. His ears were ringing and the world was spinning recklessly as he tried to regain his footing.

Another blow caught him on the back of the head, not so severe as the blow to the face, but even with his helm protecting him he was nearly knocked unconscious. The world dimmed and he saw stars threatening to swallow him up, but he fought against the rocking floor and rolled away from the source of the attack, trying desperately to regain his feet. He had to get to his feet and face his accoster, although he knew exactly who it was.

"Stay down, de Russe," Guy said behind him somewhere. "Stay down and I shall not strike you again."

His instincts told him to get to his feet, but his common sense told him to do as he was told. Dazed, he rolled onto his back and raised a shaking hand to his dented visor. It took quite of bit of effort to raise the visor, for it was badly misshapen from the heavy hit, but eventually he was able to work it up.

Stoneley stood several feet away, smiling at his handiwork. "Consider that revenge for the beating you dealt me last year, de Russe. Now we're even, although I doubt you lost any teeth."

Gaston was grunting with his pain and shock. He raised a mailed finger to his bloodied nose. "No teeth, but you broke my nose. And you probably fracture my skull with that blow from behind."

Guy laughed, a hollowed snort. "Good. And now, my lord, we come to the purpose of your visit. By what right do you invade my fortress?"

"It is my fortress," Gaston said, propping himself up on an elbow so he was not flat on his back. "And I came to kill you!"

"Is that so? And why is that? Because I tried to reclaim my wife? Because I managed to take back what was rightfully mine?"

In spite of the order to stay down, Gaston pushed himself into a sitting position. The world was still swaying sickeningly. "The fortress is rightfully mine by order of our king. And by what right do you execute all of my soldiers?"

"They are my enemy and are to be shown no mercy."

Gaston closed his eyes a moment, shaking off the ringing in his head. "Where are the boys?"

"Do not you even want to know where Remi is?" Guy asked, surprised he should ask for his son first.

"I know where she is," Gaston said. "I asked where my boys are."

Guy looked perplexed and faltered a moment. "You….you found Remi? Then I suppose she told you what happened."

"She told me you sold her to whore at an inn," Gaston replied, trying to control the furious quake in his voice. "Fortunately for her, you sold her to a knight who serves my ally. Not a very wise move, Stoneley."

"A small flaw in a brilliant scheme," Guy answered quietly.

"Actually, it matters not where she is for the moment. The point is, I will have her back. And you will deliver her."

Gaston grinned, a humorless gesture. "Are you truly stupid or do you simply act the part?"

Guy grinned in response. Slowly, he turned away from Gaston and wandered over to the wall. Gaston's eyes followed him hawk-like, wondering what he was up to. When Guy drew forth a dagger and examined it closely, Gaston waited for it to come hurling at him. But no blade was forthcoming and Guy leaned casually against the wall. Next to him was a rope, secured to an iron bracket. The rope supported the massive chandelier that hung twenty feet above the foyer, but Gaston wasn't paying any attention to that. Not until Guy pointed to the ceiling.

"And I say you will bring her to me, or your boys will meet a most unpleasant end," he toyed with the rope, running the tip of the dagger along the fibers.

Gaston's gaze jerked upward. Hanging from the chandelier were Dane and Trenton, their legs dangling fifteen feet above the hard stone floor. Although Gaston maintained his expression, inside he was absolutely ill. Without taking his eyes off the boys, he rose unsteadily to his feet.

"Damn, Stoneley, this goes beyond what even I thought you capable of," he muttered, moving to stand directly underneath the helpless young men. Two pairs of frightened young eyes met his gaze.

"What say you, de Russe?" Guy asked casually. "The boys or Remi. The choice is yours."

"You have given me no choice," Gaston's voice was as low as thunder. He took his eyes off Dane and Trenton long enough to turn to Guy. "Why in the hell do you want to make a trade? What good is Remington to you?"

"She is my guarantee that you will leave me in peace," he replied, glancing up at the two boys. "Actually, I was planning on using our young sons simply to chase you away from Mt. Holyoak. With Dane and Trenton as my captives, it would be guaranteed that you would leave me in peace. Henry, too, considering he will do what you ask. But 'twas your misfortune to inform me that you knew of Remington's whereabouts. Being a quick thinker, the game has changed."

"There is no game," Gaston rumbled, wishing he could make it to Stoneley before he slit the ropes. His hands were shaking with want to strangle the man. "You cannot have her."

"Then you would forfeit the lives of two young men? I find that particularly selfish."

"Nay, Stoneley. Selfish is using your own son as a pawn in a game with high stakes. Selfish is threatening to kill your own flesh and blood."

"Remington or the boys, de Russe. My patience wears thin."

Gaston was caught. He knew Dane and Trenton were terrified listening to the exchange and he so wanted to reassure them, but he dare not look at the terrified faces. His mind was racing with possibilities, forming solutions, trying to gain time and the advantage.

"Lower them to the ground and we shall talk," he said.

"No. There is nothing to talk about. Make your decision."

"Do you truly think I would bring Remington to you? Good God, man, you must be out of your mind. After everything you have done to her and her sisters? 'Tis insanity to make such a request."

"Then you will watch the boys die," Guy said plainly.

"You would kill your own son?" Gaston was trying desperately to stall, all the while taking slow steps toward him. He prayed that with enough talk and enough distraction, he could edge close enough and reach Guy before the rope was completely severed.

But Guy was not easily distracted. He saw that Gaston was moving closer to him and he put the blade to the rope, sawing hard a couple of times and releasing several strands of fibers. The rope shifted and the boys screamed in terror, and Gaston froze.

"Cease!" Gaston roared.

"Your decision."

Above him, the rope slipped again and the boys cried out. "No more, Stoneley, or I shall kill you where you stand!" Gaston bellowed, wondering wildly if he could catch the chandelier and save his sons.

"Tell me you decision."

Guy was fully prepared to cut the rope the rest of the way and Gaston put up his hands beseechingly. "Cease and I shall agree to your terms." He hated himself for uttering the words, but he felt he had no other choice at the moment.

Guy smiled genuinely. "Very good, de Russe. I am pleased that you are finally seeing the truth of the matter. 'Tis not right for a husband and wife to be separated, even if the wife did bear the bastard of another man. She never did tell me if she bore you a son, though. Another son to replace the one you are going to lose if you betray me."

Gaston was shaking with his injury and his anger. "There will be no betrayal, Stoneley. But I do not leave until the boys are lowered to the ground."

"You do not give me orders, de Russe!" Guy flashed in a display of irritation. "I give them, so listen to me well. You will call off your men and ride out of here. If you do not return with Remington by nightfall, I shall kill Dane. If you still have not arrived by midnight, I shall kill Trenton. Do you understand me?"

Gaston's face was emotionless. "If you kill the boys, I can guarantee you will never know peace. I shall lay siege to Mt. Holyoak and burn her to the ground, and you with it," he crossed his massive arms, although his stance still wasn't entirely steady. "I know your threat is false because you would not thwart your advantage in such a manner."

"Would not I?" Guy looked thoughtful. "I tend to disagree."

Gaston believed him, but he would not allow Guy to see just how unbalanced he was. Gaston uncrossed his arms and pulled his demolished helm from his head, tossing it to the floor. The back of his hauberk was stained red from the split on the back of his scalp, and the bridge of his nose was swollen and bloodied. Even his mouth was bloodied, having bit his lip on the second blow.

"I have a counter proposal, Stoneley," he said quietly. "I will take the boys and keep Remington and on my oath as a knight, I will promise to leave you in peace. I will convince Henry to leave you alone and you can live at Mt. Holyoak without harassment from the crown. You shall never see us again. Is that not satisfactory?"

To his surprise, Guy actually looked thoughtful. "I do not know if I can trust your word, de Russe. After all, if I agree to those terms, who's to say that you won't go back on your word and destroy me anyway?"

"I swear it on my mother's grave," Gaston said steadily. "What you seek most is peace, is it not? Give me what I want and you shall have it."

Guy gazed back at him, shaking his head slowly after a moment. "You cannot be trusted. You who betrayed Richard."

Gaston sighed heavily. "I wasn't the only one, Stoneley. You and I fought for the king and you know what dissention there was in his ranks. Good lord, there were more plots against him than could be counted. And my actions against Richard were well thought out and calculated; 'twas no spur of the moment decision."

Guy was leaning against the wall again, calmly, listening to Gaston. "I heard rumor that your wife slept with Richard. Is that why you betrayed him? For revenge?"

"My wife slept with anyone who caught her eye," Gaston said irritably. "Were I to seek revenge for her indiscretions, I'd be killing half of France. There was far more to it than that."

Guy nodded and Gaston was surprised at the civil tone the conversation had taken. "So you would take on another cheating woman? Remi has never been remotely faithful to me, you know. She has slept with Ingilsby, and Derek Botmore to name a few. She did not think I knew, but I did."

Gaston cocked an eyebrow. "And just how do you know that?"

"I could tell from the way they looked at her. A husband can tell these things," his voice was quiet. "That is why I punished her so often. She deserved it, the lying whore."

Gaston felt himself tensing again, the banked rage taking on fuel. "Then let me have her. You obviously do not want her."

"No, I do not want her, but I am stuck with her," Guy replied with disgust. "You shall never get the annulment, whether or not I agree."

Gaston wasn't going to delve into all of the details, the recent developments in Remington's favor. He merely shrugged. "I can try."

The conversation lagged and Guy straightened, again wielding the blade. "Since I cannot trust the word of a traitor, I 'm afraid I shall have to keep the boys here while you retrieve my wife. So sorry, de Russe."

Gaston's heart sank. All of the stalling and conversation had been for naught. His gaze drifted up to Dane and Trenton, suspended above the floor and he knew their arms were probably numb by now. He had to do something, and do it quickly. Trouble was, he was running out of ideas and options and he realized with horror that he was going to have to leave the boys and rethink his strategy. There was no possible way he was going to deliver Remington into Guy's waiting arms and she was going to fall into hysterics when he told her of the situation.

"I shall go," his voice was tight, no more than a whisper. He glanced up at his sons, his heart breaking that he was powerless to help them. "I shall return for you."

"Do not bring mother back here," Dane hollered, swinging his legs. "Do you hear me? Do not bring her back."

Gaston did not reply. He lowered his gaze and ignored his dented helm; it was useless anyway. Carefully controlled anger burst its reins and filled his body like a wildfire as he focused on Guy, standing smugly several feet away. He wanted to curse him, holler and rant at the very least, but it would only serve to Guy's advantage. Stoneley mustn't know how very badly he was affected.

Like a rat, he was trapped. Trapped and feeling desperate.

Gaston caught a flash of a shadow on the balcony above Stoneley. By the time he looked up, a loud explosion detonated a foot or so away from Guy, who whooped with shock and bolted from his strategic position. Gaston did not care what the explosion was or how it happened; Guy was hurtling towards him and he retained enough of his senses to reach out and grab the man's wrist, snatching the dagger from his grasp. In the same breath, he threw Guy to the floor brutally.

"Gaston! Your sword!" came a youthful voice. Gaston's head snapped up in time to see his sword sailing from the second floor like a bolt from heaven. His hand reached into the air and caught it by the hilt as if the sword had a mind of its own, knowing whose hand it belonged to. Steel and flesh fused and became one and suddenly, Gaston became whole. It was a magical moment.

Another explosion billowed into the air a foot away from Guy. Stoneley scrambled away from it as Gaston swung his sword in the man's direction. Guy's ears were ringing from the concussion of the blast as he lurched to his feet, coming face to face with the tip of Gaston's massive blade. Almost as fast as he faced it, he whirled away from it and made a mad dash toward the grand dining hall. Gaston saw something sail through the air and hit the doorway just as Guy stumbled through it, exploding loudly on contact. Gaston heard Guy grunt with fear, but he still kept running.

Gaston had no concept of what the explosions were or even where they were coming from, but they had saved Dane and Trenton's lives. His initial reaction was to run after Guy but above him the boys were yelling and he could not go anywhere without helping them.

"I shall get you down!" he yelled up to them.

Suddenly, Charles was on the stairs, descending them so quickly that he nearly tripped. "Go after him, my lord. I shall release Dane and Trenton."

Gaston, pale and bloodied, stared at the lad. "What did you do, Charles? What were those... blasts?"

Charles grinned, immensely pleased with himself. "A recipe from one of the Arabic treatises in the solar. I have been experimenting with it."

Gaston let out a hissing sigh of understanding and relief. "By God, lad! I thought the angels were on my side!"

"Nay, my lord. Just me," Charles moved eagerly for the trussed rope, fumbling with the ties.

Gaston was shaken and dazed, but he grabbed hold of the rope holding his son's aloft. "Stand back!"

He brought his blade down and severed the rope, clutching the cleaved end and lowering his sons to the ground. Charles rushed over to the chandelier as Dane and Trenton's feet touched the ground, cutting the bindings around their wrists. Gaston waited until the boys were set free before lowering the chandelier completely to the floor.

Gaston, Trenton and Dane came together in an emotional embrace. Gaston hugged them fiercely, incredibly grateful that they were safe. All three of them were shaking with terror and Gaston stepped back, getting a good look at both of them.

"Are you all right? Did he harm you?" he asked them both, demanding an answer.

Two heads shook negatively. "We're unharmed," Dane replied, but he was terribly shaken. "But he hit you with an iron stand. You are bleeding."

"I am all right," Gaston replied, although his nose hurt terribly and his head was aching. Yet, his sons were safe and that was all that mattered. Still clutching the boys, he turned to Charles.

"Your bravery is to be commended," he said to the young man. "Since you have demonstrated your great courage, I will ask that you escort my sons to the tower and stay there. Do not move for any reason, and do not open the door for anyone but Lord Ingilsby or myself. Do you understand?"

Charles nodded solemnly as if Gaston had just entrusted him with the royal jewels. "Aye, my lord."

Gaston literally handed him the two boys and moved to pick up his sword. Gripping the hilt firmly, he pointed to the stairs. "Go now. I have a man to kill."

"He's going for the servant's entrance in the kitchen," Dane said quickly. "He breached it."

Gaston's eyes trailed to the dining hall and the kitchens beyond; kitchens full of potentially lethal instruments. Considering the ambush he had walked into upon entering the foyer, he was extremely wary.

"I shall take care of him," he said confidently, tilting his head in the direction of the stairs. "Go now. To the tower and stay there."

The three boys were gone and Gaston made his way hastily through the dining hall, feeling his skin prickling with anxiety. Cautiously, he paused at the door leading into the kitchens and peered inside.

There was no movement and little light. Ducking low, out of the line of fire, he crept low into the kitchens, pausing every so often to listen carefully. In all of his armor he was hardly silent, but the room was dimly lit and that worked to his advantage; Stoneley may be able to hear him, but he couldn't see him. Gaston crept along the floor, finally rising at the next doorway and pressing himself against the wall. His breathing was rapid with excitement and the palm holding the sword was sweating.

The next room was void of motion. Off of this room was the storage area where the servant's entrance was located, and that was Gaston's destination. If Stoneley had escaped he was apt to follow, but he did not believe the man to take the coward's way out. Stoneley was too clever and sinister for that.

Gaston crept along the wall toward the storage room. At the doorway, he paused and tried to stop his harsh breathing. Stoneley was a worthy adversary and Gaston was uncomfortable in the confines of the kitchens. Out in the open was an ideal situation for him; he was far too large to fight effectively in close quarters such as this. But Stoneley knew that, which was why he had retreated into the kitchens as opposed to the bailey.

The storage room was silent. The breached door was open a man's width, the light from mid-afternoon casting a blinding stream into the storage room. Gaston paused at the threshold, too blinded by the bright light to be able to see very well. He almost stepped in at his full height, intent on studying the open door. But at the very last second, his sixth sense told him to crouch and he did. Not three feet above his head, a six-foot-long iron spit went sailing into the wall with a startling clang.

Gaston flinched and whirled in the direction from whence the spit had been launched. Guy stood several feet away, a sword gleaming in his hand.

Not a word was said. Gaston raised his sword offensively and rushed Guy, who brought his own sword up and fended off a blow hard enough to send him to his knees. But he was quick and skillful and was on his feet again, bringing his blade up to avoid another lethal blow. Gaston had him cornered, but he ducked another slice of the blade and danced through a doorway leading into a smaller kitchen room.

Gaston was almost as big as the room itself and it was extremely difficult for him to maneuver in. Guy took the offensive, whipping his sword through the air at Gaston, who put up his sword to avoid having his head cut off. He returned the blows, meeting with air as Stoneley, lighter and smaller and without all of the excess weighty armor, eluded the chops. Angered that he was not being successful in his attack, Gaston heightened his swordplay and gave Guy no time to raise his own sword in the offensive; Gaston's slices were fast and furious and powerful and he succeeded in completely demolishing the room as he pursued Stoneley.

Guy tripped into the larger of the kitchen rooms where both men had originally entered. Rolling to the floor, he was instantly on his feet again and bringing his blade up in answer to Gaston's furious blow. In the larger room, both men had ample space to work properly and sparks flew in the air as metal met metal with bone-shattering force.

The pain, the anguish behind Gaston's mighty blows told Guy that, indeed, the man was entirely serious in his quest to murder him. Up until that point, Guy was never truly concerned that the Dark One could managed to do him harm. Guy was too fast, too skilled, and too brilliant. De Russe would have no chance against him.

But fending off Gaston's blows told Guy that the Dark One was not only serious but that he fully intended to carry out his desires. For the first time, Guy began to feel a bud of blossoming fear.

Gaston had again managed to back Guy into a corner. Surprised that he had been directed into a compromising position, Guy tried to use strength to drive Gaston backward, but it was a foolish mistake; Gaston was by far stronger than Stoneley and brought his sword up in a fierce uppercut with the intention of puncturing Guy's belly. Guy, however, brought his sword down at the same time and barely managed to fend off the blow, yet in the process, Gaston had managed to disarm him. He watched for a split second as his weapon went hurtling across the room.

There was no chance to regain it; if he tried he would again be forced into a dead end and Guy would not risk it. Instead, he had to find another weapon or get the hell out of the kitchens. Gaston, seeing his prey was defenseless, charged the man, but Guy was quicker and managed to evade the tackle. Sword flashing, Gaston followed Guy in a wild course through the kitchens, the pantry, and back out into the dining hall. Guy was fast, but Gaston encompassed a greater distance with his long strides, keeping the gap between the two men close.

Guy mounted the stairs with Gaston hot on his heels as he followed him to the second floor. However, Gaston lost ground on the stairs simply because it was extremely difficult to take them quickly in his bulky armor, but once he reached the landing he made up for lost time.

His determination was feeding off his quest for vengeance. He was focused on the one task ahead of him; to catch Guy and to kill him. When Guy raced into the family's corridor, Gaston followed closely and began to formulate a plan to trip him. He would have liked to sail his sword along the floor for Guy to stumble over, thereby allowing Gaston to catch up to him, but he did not want to part with his sword and risk the possibility of Guy retrieving it.

Unfortunately, Guy was widening the distance between them simply because he was running without hundreds of pounds of armor. Gaston's pace had not slacked, merely the fact that Guy's had increased. Gaston began to reconsider throwing his sword yet extremely reluctant to hand Guy a potential advantage. But it was increasingly evident if he did not do something quickly, Guy would lose him shortly. And he meant to have Guy at any cost.

Guy breezed past the rooms that had housed Jasmine, Rory and Skye. Rooms he had raped them in, rooms where Jasmine had borne his bastard. Rooms full of shame and pain and horror. The rooms were silent now, having once been filled with screams and pleas from frightened young women.

Guy did not give them a second glance; he was too busy putting space between him and the Dark One. De Russe's footsteps were falling behind him and Guy began to feel a seed of hope that he could somehow lose him, at least long enough to gain a weapon. Triumph began to rear its head in Guy's mind as he rounded the corner and headed down another corridor; he knew he was gaining the edge until he saw Rory standing in front of him.

Guy stumbled to a halt, astonished beyond belief. Gaston rounded the corner and saw Guy standing there, victory within his grasp until he too saw Rory standing several feet in front of Guy. Gaston came to a halt and nearly tripped over a rug in his amazement.

Rory just stood there, gazing at Guy serenely. It was an expression Gaston had never seen before on her face, and he furthermore wondered if he was hallucinating. Guy was frozen to the spot in front of him; Gaston should have taken the opportunity to kill him right there, but he couldn't seem to overcome his shock at seeing a ghost.

"Rory!" Guy bellowed.

The apparition did not respond to him, simply continuing to gaze as if she were looking right through him. Dressed in the emerald green surcoat she had been buried in, Gaston took a good hard look. Never had he seen her look lovelier, her red hair flowing and soft, her pretty face bordering on a smile. In spite of his shock, he found himself smiling at the surprise of it all.

"You said she was dead!" Guy boomed.

"She is," Gaston replied with amazing calm.

Guy clenched his fists, terrified out of his mind. "Good God!"

Rory had effectively blocked his path down the corridor. Rather than rush a specter, Guy turned abruptly to his left and chose another route. The route to the tower.

Gaston let him go for a moment, knowing there was nowhere to go inside the tower. Instead, he continued to gaze at Rory and was not surprised when the vision focused on him. His smile grew wider and he swore he saw her smile broaden, too. It was as if she were lending Gaston assistance by sending Guy into the twisting confines of the tower. As if she had known that Guy was gaining headway on Gaston and most likely would have evaded him down the length of the long corridor.

Gaston took a step toward her, his initial shock turning into fascination. She continued to smile at him and he could see every detail on her face, Remington's eyes, Jasmine's nose. There was no light, no aura. Had he reached out to touch her, he would have sworn he would have grasped flesh.

"Rory?" he said timidly.

She did not answer him but continued to look at him gently. He heard sounds in the tower and briefly turned to look, but his attention riveted back to the apparition in front of him. As helpless as she had been all these years against Guy Stoneley, she had contributed heavily to the final battle to do away with his evil once and for all.

"Thank you," Gaston whispered.

He ducked inside the tower. Guy was two stories above him rushing for the room in which Charles, Dane and Trenton were held. Gaston eyed the man a moment before mounting the stairs, knowing there was nowhere for Guy to go once he reached the top. His pace slowed dramatically as he climbed.

Guy saw Gaston below him as he reached the door to the tower. Laying into the latch heavily, he was shocked to find it bolted from the inside. Angered and panicked, he rattled it loudly.

"Who's in here?" he yelled. "Open the damn door."

There was no response forthcoming. Again, he rattled the latch so heavily that he cut his palms on the iron handle. He kicked at the door, all the while hearing Gaston's footsteps drawing closer and closer. Anxiety cut at him; unless he was planning to jump or unless he found a weapon, quickly, he was as good a dead. De Russe was closing in on him.

He began to kick at the door as if he could force it open. He punched at it, driving his fists against the oak as he did when he beat his wife. The Dark One was on the landing below him and Guy could feel the weight of his stare, knowing that when he turned to face him that he would only read death in his eyes.

But he couldn't help himself from peering over his shoulder. De Russe was approaching him with the look of the Grim Reaper, his massive sword gleaming in the weak light. Panic shot through Guy and he pounded on the door one last time, as if that would make any difference. As if somehow fate would step in and open it.

But the door remained closed. Guy, hysterical with anxiety, knew he was breathing his last. As a final show of bravery, or mayhap cowardice, he turned to face the Dark One.

Smoky orbs met with ice blue. Gaston paused six steps down from Guy, staring at his quarry with open contempt. There was something he wanted to say before he gutted the man.

"What I do now, I do on behalf of Remi and Rory, Jasmine and Skye. Women you tortured for nine long years. When I drive my blade into your gut, it will be small compensation for those years you stole from them, but it's the least I can do. Their comfort will have to come from the fact that you will burn in the sulfur pits for all eternity," he was calm and controlled as he raised his blade. "But most of all, I do this for Remington."

Guy was ashen as he listened to the speech. His mouth worked as he formed a reply when the tower door flew open.

"My lord! Your weapon!" Charles cried.

Guy whirled around and caught the dull blade. Glee and hope flooded him and he crowed with the thrill of a second chance. In a flash, he spun around to Gaston and held high the blade.

"Pretty speech, de Russe!" he exclaimed. "Now let us see who indeed is going to burn in the sulfur pits of hell."

Gaston was stunned at Charles' action, betrayal at the deepest level. Horrified, he wondered if Charles had not killed Dane and Trenton and if all along he was allied with Guy. But he couldn't linger on that thought now, not with an imminent attack on his hands.

Guy's sword came up and Gaston moved into a defensive position, at a distinct disadvantage on the stairs as he was. But he would have to compensate somehow. All that mattered now was that Guy bore a weapon and he did not relish a sword battle in the steep confines of the tower.

He waited for the down parry. And waited. Guy still held the sword aloft, but there was a strange look to his eye. The triumphant smile on his face was slowly turning into a grimace of horror and Gaston eyed him with deep curiosity. Why did he not strike?

Guy was listing dangerously to the right, sword still aloft, face still glazed with a grimacing expression. He continued to lean, to fall, and Gaston watched as Guy toppled over the top landing and disappeared into empty space. Shocked, Gaston peered over the side of the stairs and watched incredulously as Guy fell five stories to his death below. Guy perished in a loud thud of bone against stone, instead of the soft hiss of steel through flesh.

Gaston was stunned. He continued to peer down into the dark depths of the tower as if he were unable to comprehend what had happened. Guy was dead, but he had not killed him. Somehow, he had fallen to his death. Astonished, Gaston turned his gaze to Charles, still standing in the open tower door.

Only Charles was not alone. Dane and Trenton were squinting into the bowels of the tower as well.

"What in the hell happened?" Gaston managed to choke.

The three boys looked at him and Charles smiled. From his side, he raised his arm and clutched within his fist was a small, bloodied blade that looked suspiciously like a child's sword. It took Gaston a moment to realize it was Arik's sword.

"I killed him," Charles said. "With this."

Gaston was literally white with shock and disbelief. "You...you *killed* him?"

Charles nodded. "Dane wanted to, but I insisted that he let me do it," he said, afraid that his hero was not pleased. "I did not think it right that he kill his father, and this is not Trenton's fight. It was only logical that I do it."

Gaston gazed back down into the dark depths one last time, the clarity of the situation dawning on him. "You knew he would turn to you when you opened the door, thwarting any striking him from behind. So you tossed him the sword to distract him and when he turned to attack me...."

"Charles jammed Arik's sword right into his back," Dane finished for his father. "It was my plan."

Gaston couldn't decide if he felt more like vomiting or fainting. He opted for neither and smiled weakly at his son. "A brilliant strategy, Dane. I'd expect no less. But where did you find Arik's sword?"

"I gave it to Charles when I left for Oxford," Dane replied. "He kept it in the tower and practiced with it when Roald and the other knights went to bed."

Gaston sank back against the tower wall, wiping at his sweaty, bloody head. He was completely dazed, but not senseless. The boys watched him eagerly as he composed himself as best he was able and then mounted the rest of the stairs towards them. They were expecting praise, or a spanking, but instead Gaston did the unexpected.

He pulled them all into a giant bear hug and wept.

EPILOGUE

"By the power vested in me by God and his Holiness, Pope Innocent IX, I have the pleasure of pronouncing you man and wife. My lord, you may kiss your bride."

Gaston tore his eyes off Archbishop Bourchier and focused on the radiant vision before him. Lady Remington de Russe smiled back, tears already coursing over her cheeks as he took her in his arms and kissed her far more passionately than he should have in front of the church. Remington sobbed through the kiss and Gaston chuckled as he released her to a chorus of applause. Westminster Abbey had never been quite so gay.

Bourchier was the first man to congratulate the happy couple, unusual that the clergy should include themselves in the well wishers. Henry and Elizabeth could barely wait for Gaston and Remington to descend from the dais before pushing forward with hearty best wishes. Everyone seemed completely intent on congratulating them all at once so Gaston merely stood in one spot while his friends kissed his new wife and shook his hand happily. Matthew Wellesbourne went so far as to coordinate the admiring throng, making sure no one person occupied the duke's time for too long before ushering them along their way to make room for the next well-wisher.

The guests knew full well that there was to be a lavish reception following the wedding at the Tower, yet none could wait that long to convey their wishes. After all, Gaston and Remington had waited terribly long for this day and the excitement was tangible.

Dane and Trenton stood next to their parents like proper young men, dressed in their finest. Guests would file by and slip the boys coins as congratulatory gifts, which they would stuff happily into their tunics. It wasn't long before they were quite rich and looking eagerly for more wealth. Gaston saw what was happening above all the commotion and shot them both reproving looks, to which they smiled innocently. Unwilling to dampen their day, Gaston allowed his sons to become wealthy off the tribute from the guests.

Jasmine and Skye remained seated in the pews as the throng rushed forward to congratulate the newlyweds, bouncing Sophia and Robert on their respective knees and attempting to keep Mary entertained. Beside them, Patrick had hold of Arica while Eudora contained Adeliza. Patrick was still recovering from the knife wound dealt to him by Guy and had therefore lacked the strength to stand with Gaston at the altar. However, keeping Arica quiet had proved quite a task and he wondered if standing beside Gaston would have been less strenuous. Between Arica and Adeliza, there had been an abundance of baby chatter during the service and he was embarrassed that he had not been able to control them better.

When the horde had died down, Wellesbourne and de Vere cleared a path for Gaston and Remington down the center aisle. The couple went to their daughters, who babbled and screeched with delight when their father reached for them.

"Ah, my little magpie," Gaston said happily as he took Arica from Patrick. "By God, if you two aren't the noisiest little birds I have ever heard." He held out his other arm for Adeliza. Clutching both babies, he turned to his wife and smiled. "Now that I have all of my women, shall we retreat to the reception?"

"They're not going to the reception," Remington informed him. "Eudora is taking them back to the Tower."

"Not going?" his face fell. "Why can't they go?"

"Because they need to go to sleep, Gaston, it's already past their bedtime," she insisted, waving over Eudora. "Patrick is going back to the Tower, too. See how tired he is?"

Gaston's gaze lingered on his cousin. After Guy had stabbed him, the man had lain bleeding in a doorway for nearly a day before someone happened upon him. It was by pure luck alone that he had survived, although he was still terribly weak. But he had made a remarkable recovery, for which Nicolas, Martin and Gaston had been extremely grateful.

Gaston never did tell him about Rory's specter. Neither had he told Remington. Mayhap someday, when the time was right, he would divulge the turning point in his struggle against Guy. Even if Rory wasn't with them anymore, she'd been instrumental in the most major event of his life. As had Arik; dead or not, his spirit had been within the sword that had slain Guy. Gaston knew that without a doubt.

As if on cue, Martin de Russe came alongside Remington and kissed her loudly on the cheek. Any hard feelings from a year back were dissolved due to the fact that Martin loved Gaston and Remington far too much to hold a grudge. Hurt that Gaston did not think him capable of protecting Remington in her time of need, Martin's pride had been restored when Gaston had asked him to protect Skye and Jasmine after Guy's escape. The small gesture had meant a great deal to the once-powerful knight.

"Lady de Russe!" he boomed. "Surely the most beautiful woman to bear the de Russe name, except for Skye, of course."

Remington beamed at him, radiant in her pale yellow surcoat and pearl tiara. "Thank you, Uncle Martin."

He hugged her closely and pinched Arica's cheek. "Beautiful babes, like their mother. Now, I must go and make sure the reception is properly prepared."

Martin kissed Skye and bound off, thrilled to be of use once again and acting as if he were someone of import. Gaston chuckled. "He acts as if he is in charge."

"He thinks he is," Nicolas said from behind Gaston. "You should have heard him and Henry arguing over the types of ale to serve. He acts as if he is paying for your wedding celebration instead of our king."

Gaston shook his head at his aggressive uncle, reluctantly handing Arica and Adeliza over to Eudora and Patrick when his wife nudged him to do so.

Around them, the crowd was filing from the church to waiting carriages and horses outside. Lord Brimley passed Remington, kissing her hand sweetly and barely able to speak for the lump in his throat. Clive and Walter were behind their father, smiling broadly at her. They moved to kiss her hand but Gaston raised a threatening eyebrow and they settled for a kind word instead. Lord Tarrington extended his congratulations as well, as did Ingilsby. In fact, Ingilsby seemed particularly emotional and Remington was driven to tears again by the man's demeanor. He had truly been her friend through the bad years and she valued him greatly.

Ingilsby's knights filed past as well, respectfully conveying their best wishes. When Hubert came upon Remington and offered his congratulations, she threw her arms around his neck and hugged him tightly. Hubert did not know if he should respond or not with the Dark One gazing at him, but he overcame his fear and hugged her back. Blushing, he went on his way.

Matthew had been absent during Remington's kidnapping and the subsequent fight for Mt. Holyoak because Gaston had been too swept up with the events to send for him. He eventually received word of what was happening from Henry himself and had made his way from Wellesbourne Castle to be by Gaston's side. He hadn't left the man since everything had happened and had been forced to leave his newly pregnant wife at home, even for the event of Gaston's wedding. Even now, he stuck close by Gaston as at the man escorted his new wife out of the cathedral. Best of friends, the two of them shared a bond closer than brothers. Thick or thin, they were always there for one another.

Gaston took his wife's arm as they made their way out into the bright July sun. He gazed down at Remington, thinking her to be well worth the trouble of the past year. In fact, they had met exactly one year ago this month and when Gaston took possession of Mt. Holyoak, he never dreamt it would change the course of his life forever.

He had gained a wife, two daughters and a son. He had lost friends to death, but he had gained a whole new perspective on life. He discovered he had friends who were willing to do anything for him, priests who were willing to make the ultimate sacrifice, and even a woman who returned from the dead to help him in his most valiant struggle. The one event he regretted was de Tormo's offering; with Guy's death, the sworn confession from the priest had been unnecessary. Gaston had paid the church five thousand gold coins for de Tormo's soul, hoping it would lessen his time in purgatory. Lying to the church surely entitled the priest to the seventh level of hell and Gaston was determined that he not spend an over amount of time there.

And there had been other sacrifices, too. Botmore had been wiped out as punishment for assisting Guy. Douglass Archibald, although indirectly involved with Botmore and his weak resistance, had been stripped of his lands. Gaston would have rather made allies of them than enemies, but his vengeance for Remington had extended into political boundaries and he had shown all of Yorkshire his considerable wrath. Lord Ingilsby, or more rightly, the Earl of Hampsthwaite, ruled the lands of the now-disposed Yorkists.

Taran was waiting for the couple, decorated in polished armor and banners of black and silver. He snorted at Remington happily, dragging his big tongue across her hand. Gaston lifted her up into the saddle and she smiled at him.

"Are you sure you want me to ride with you?" she teased. "We tried this once before, as I recall, and I ended up angry with you."

"I am sure, wife," he mounted behind her, cradling her against his armor. "Do you know I have never liked the word 'wife?"

"And now?" she asked.

He squeezed her gently. "I like it a great deal. In fact, there has yet to be a more beautiful word invented."

"Aye, there already has been. Husband."

I want for you to be my husband. The wish that had come true.

Remington knew little of Guy's death not three weeks before and was not overly curious. She had not asked the circumstances, and Gaston had not offered. All that mattered was that they were finally wed and she never believed she could ever be so happy.

"I have a surprise for you," he said as they fell into the wedding procession. "We are going on a trip."

"A trip? Where?" she was instantly excited.

He smiled at her enthusiasm. "Venice."

"Italy?" she exclaimed. "You are taking me to *Italy?*"

"Absolutely. Are you pleased?"

"Oh, Gaston!" She turned in the saddle, kissing him happily. "I am so excited. I can hardly wait."

He returned her kisses. "You won't have to wait long. We leave tomorrow on the *Majestic,* one of Henry's private vessels. Have you ever been to sea?"

"I sailed to Ireland with my mother, twice," she replied. "Unfortunately, I was seasick most of the way."

"Hmm," Gaston said thoughtfully. "Mayhap we should simply sail the channel and go the rest of the way by caravan. I would hate for you to be ill during our journey."

She sat back against him, a coy smile playing on her lips. "I am afraid I shall most likely be ill whichever way we travel."

"Oh? Why is that?"

Her coy smile grew. "I have a surprise for you, too."

He did not answer for a moment. When he spoke, it was with the greatest hesitation. "And what is that?"

She turned to look at him. "By the look on your face, I believe you already know the answer."

Venice was lovely. The following spring during the month of March, Cortland Henry Hubert de Russe was born without incident.

AUTHOR'S ADDITIONAL NOTE:

∽

What a ride! Gaston's story was written back in the day when the author believed the longer, the better. War and Peace Revisited! But those dreams were quickly cooled by an agent who told her marketable books are no longer than four hundred pages. Gaston's tale, double-spaced, is about twelve hundred. That would make a regular paperback at about 800+. That agent also instructed the author to cut the book in half to make it marketable, which she refused to do. She knew that someday there would be the opportunity to present it in whole, so she waited... waited... and its time has finally come. It's a very long book, but indeed, an epic for the ages.

It also survived numerous obstacles that could have easily destroyed it – created on a HP 286 (which crashed), only surviving in hard copy form (and surviving 7 house moves in a box!), finally being scanned – 1 page at a time, but the original manuscript was so degraded that it had to be re-typed. Finally, after all that, it made it to publication. No book I've ever written has deserved it more. Gaston is, if nothing else, a fighter.

Divorce is still frowned upon by the Catholic Church, and back in Gaston and Remi's day, men were only allowed to instigate divorces and only then in cases of adultery, devil worship (seriously!), or something very unsavory. Women were property, so they had no rights when instigating a divorce.

Gaston only appears in his story and in The White Lord of Wellesbourne, but there are at least two additional novels that have his relatives – one is entitled "Lord of War: Black Angel", which stars his great-great grand-father, and the other is "The Dark Son", which stars one of his younger boys. These books are slated for 2013 and 2015 release.

Gaston and Remington went on to have seven children total - three girls and four boys – so it's quite possible that, in the future, there will indeed be more novels involving Gaston's progeny.

You never can tell!

CPSIA information can be obtained at www.ICGtesting.com
Printed in the USA
LVOW10s1412250614

391678LV00010B/232/P